DAGGER OF DECEPTION

STARSIDE SAGA BOOK EIGHT

ERIC KENT EDSTROM

UNDERMOUNTAIN**BOOKS**

To J

1
____

THE BLACK DAWN

A strange bird chattered outside Dunne Yples's window. Its repetitive *chak-chak-choo-chak* came in sets of five, after which it would go quiet. Just as Yples's mind settled and sleep came, the bird would start again. It had to be just outside his window. Whatever it was, it deserved a fiery death. Had it been a proper nightskirl he might have been lulled by it. But here, in the humid southern islands called the Shudderlins, all manner of foul creatures kept night hours.

It was an evil place, no doubt. Truly evil. Here on the southernmost island, called Ittiti, demayncor wizards struck blood bargains with demayne in return for dark favors.

Yples would earn redemption here. He would turn their evil against them. Just as the Hargothe had sought to do. But unlike that decrepit seer, Yples would not be corrupted by power-lust. His motive was pure: to atone.

Chak-chak-choo-chak!

His bamboo bed squeaked and wobbled as he sat up. The servant boy had left a cloth and bowl of water by the bed. Yples dunked the fabric and swiped it across his brow and cheeks. A slight breeze disturbed the stillness of his room, oozing though the open window slats. The island's moist heat poured in, making the air a broth in which Yples slowly braised.

He stuffed a corner of the damp towel under the rim of his *vaz'on*. The bolt penetrations through his scalp had healed long ago, but they always itched. The heat made it worse. He no longer cursed the relic that severed him from the mercus. He knew that his madness was tied up with the mercus. His ravings against Kila Sigh were vague to him now, unreal, a faint echo. *Dem-Kisk!* He had little memory of battling her on Garden Island.

She would be the doom of them all, probably. Still, he rather liked her, despite her designation as Highest of Kil. Anyone could see she had not sought that position, nor did she seek to glorify Kil. In fact, she'd been saddled with the responsibility as unwillingly as he had been with this *vaz'on*.

The door to his chamber swung open and a young man strode in. He held a little bamboo flute to his lips. *Chak-chak-choo-chak!*

"You? What is this all about?"

The man said nothing. Another man came in, holding a folded garment over one arm. He laid it on the bed and motioned for Yples to put it on.

So. The time had finally come. He'd been here for several weeks, following a rather thrilling escape from Starside. His minder, Dunne Ergin, had thought they were merely going for a brisk walk. Ergin had not expected Yples to take him to a vergent pass within the city. Nobody knew of that pass, not even the shadline Zirhine, whose map of the passes had been so instructive in Yples's understanding of the geography of Ennith.

It took two ten-days of hiking, taking a circuitous route through several vergent passes to finally bring Yples to Ittiti. Ergin hadn't possessed the power to compel Yples to return to Starside, and Sigh herself had conveniently warded the *vaz'on* so none could use its gems. The demayncors had taken Ergin in payment. A pity, for the man had been mild and amiable. But he was also a fool, and these times were not kind to fools.

The fresh robes were clean and white and smelled of lavender and vetiver. Comforting.

The flute man kept up his bird-like chirping, which Yples now understood had been intended to keep him from sleep. The rite about to be performed relied on its participants to be in Lumne-dazed states of mind. The exhaustion of sleep deprivation would certainly make Yples more susceptible to whatever came next.

The demayncors had been rather vague on that point, but he was not concerned. They thought to use him, but they would discover that he could not be used. The *vaz'on* protected him just as much as it protected them from his mad power.

The Ittitians were tall folk, with round eyes and thin lips. He had never seen one of them smile, nor heard one curse. They were solemn and deliberate. The flute man led the way, still keeping up his chattering noise. Up to this point, Yples had only seen the interior of his room, having been hooded before being admitted to the pyramidal temple on the side of the mountain. He noted the black, porous basalt walls of the corridor, stone formed from the mountain's bloody magma emissions. The walls were covered here and there with elaborate tapestries that depicted jungle creatures. Birds and strange cats with spots. He wondered if those cats could speak using demaynic powers as did Kila Sigh's.

His guides led him up countless stairwells. Huffing with the exertion, and sweat making his robes cling to his stomach, he was about to ask for a moment to catch his breath when they came out into open air beneath a sliver of moon. They stood upon a square plaza high over the town. The impenetrable canopy of the surrounding forest gave off a rising mist that lit up in the moonlight. Braziers of purple flame stood at the corners of the little square. Oriented now, he realized this was the very top of the demayncors' pyramid. It had seemed to come to a point when viewed from far below. He saw now that this was due to a framework of iron beams converging overhead, leaving the four sides open to the outdoors. A globe of ruddy light hung from the peak. It throbbed with a sinister pulse.

In the center of the square stood an altar cut from the same porous stone, but topped with a sheet of pounded gold. Inlaid into the floor was a huge brass circle, encompassing all but the corners of the square. The demayncors stood on the outside of it. They motioned for Yples to go into the circle and lie upon the altar.

Yples knew little of demayncy, but every housemother knew that demayne were summoned inside protective circles. Balking at their command, he said, "The demayne is to gift me powers, not receive me as a gift."

"The demayne will not harm you," said the High Demayncor. None of the men had given him their names, but he knew this man was important by his gold vestments, skull headpiece, and gold mask. It was ghastly with its bulging eyes and grimacing maw. Yples could not look directly at it. The High Demayncor continued in his resonant baritone: "It desires you to *take* the powers for which you ask. But it must lay hands upon you. This is a risk you must accept, or the rite cannot proceed."

"Did the Hargothe do as you ask?"

"He did."

Yples had prayed upon this problem. Atonement by definition required discomfort. Otherwise it was mere pantomime, without meaning. Sacrificing comfort and certainty was a small price to pay for his own crimes. In the end he wished only death for himself, to be released into Til's care, having earned his place at the glorious table of righteousness. He stretched out on the altar, groaning as his old limbs and spine pressed upon the warm gold.

The demayncors began to chant. The flute man chirped in time to their words. Yples's scholarly curiosity distracted him from his fear. He did not recognize the language of the chants at all. It wasn't Elnisian. In fact, the tongue lacked any consonants at all. Perhaps it was nonsense. The folk who lived in the town below believed in tree and stone spirits. They sang to them in ecstatic ceremonies that had no real words.

A shimmering blue haze appeared over him, forming a dome that sealed upon the brass ring encircling the altar. An unseen drummer added booming emphasis to some of the chants, and a high pitched chime rang out from another performer. From the entry stairway came a strained cry. "Unhand me, foul devil!"

Yples knew that voice. It was poor Dunne Ergin. He'd thought the man already dead. The Donse Master stumbled through the blue haze and into the circle. His robe was soiled and tattered, his face gaunt and unshaven. "So! It's demayncy is it?" the man howled. "Fiends!"

He caught sight of Yples. "And they will sacrifice you too, Dunne Yples? Ah me, old friend, haven't you suffered enough?"

The poor stupid man. Did he truly not see that Yples wanted this? Did he think that they'd simply stumbled through that last vergent pass by chance? Such stupidity was beyond pity, and Yples's lips twisted upon the bile of contempt. The idiot deserved no better than he was about to receive.

The chanting built in volume and pace, the drums thundering, chimes clashing. Dark, sweet smoke drifted past Yples's nose, and the blue haze of the dome turned purple to match the dancing brazier fires. At a signal from the High Demayncor, all chanting ceased, though the flute and drums persisted.

Boom-thwack-ack-BOOM!

Chak-chik-chik-choo!

"Rise, Lord!" the High Demayncor bellowed. "Rise and receive our gift."

Yples trembled, suddenly gripped by doubt. What was he doing? The horrific nature of this rite had sounded academic when he'd read about it. Yes, there were to be some theatrics, but he'd never imagined the effect they would have upon his mind. Nor had he foreseen the stark fear on the face of the man to be sacrificed. Yples's contempt soured into dread as Ergin gibbered and whined, his eyes fixed on some unseen terror in the middle distance.

Screaming, Ergin dashed to escape the dome, struck his face against the purple light and stumbled back. Blood gushed from his nose. His hands clamped over it. His wail rose to a higher pitch. Then it stilled as his head tore free of his body. More than his head; a large section of his upper body went too. The accompanying crunch of bone and wet squish of flesh and fluid sounded like what it was: an enormous bite.

What remained of Ergin, still standing upon noodle-jointed legs, was a bowl of guts. This remainder fell forward, splashing gore across the circle.

A satisfied gurgle came from the air, followed by a guttural rumble.

Tendrils pulled from the purple haze of the dome to coalesce into a man-shape. He was hooded, with drooping sleeves of light. From within the depths of the hood came an icy wind. Fear tickled over Yples's legs and body like the dance of innumerable spiders.

The figure floated close to him, bent to inspect him more closely.

Yples tasted blood, discovered he was biting his own lip to keep his mouth closed, to keep a scream locked in. He hugged his arms over his chest, knees pulled up. The desire to spring from the altar and flee shot through him, but he found he could not move. A force like the mercusine—but clearly not *of* the mercus, else he would have felt it—held him to the altar as surely as the claw of a dragon. His skin rebelled from the oiliness of the invisible touch.

"At last!" said the newly summoned demayne. The words did not come from the hood, but from all around. Whatever this spectre was, it was not the entity's true form. It likely had no true form a human mind could understand. "With the *cold eye* I see the path," it said. "It leads to annihilation!"

With that final word, the empty sleeves sprouted insectile stingers where hands should have been. These drove down, taking Yples in the throat and groin. They pierced deeply, throbbing. If they drank from him or pumped venom into him, he could not tell. The pain was the smallest part of the sensation that overwhelmed his meager human mind.

He saw Kila Sigh. Far below him, standing upon muddy ash. Such a slight figure, drenched from rain, covered in filth. This slip of a girl had engendered in him such hatred, such frenzied need to kill. *Dem-Kisk!* How often had he warned them? But she was a mere lass. A lonely soul burdened far beyond her strength.

His throat was destroyed by the stinger, but his lips formed the words he wished to say. "Forgive me."

The evil he surrendered to now was so much greater than he'd anticipated. There was no way he could subvert it, no way to yoke it to Til's service. The Hargothe had been no more a fool than he was. It was too late now. Yples would become a sword in evil's hand.

His parting thought was an unanswered question. *Can you forgive me?*

The blackness claimed him, alchemizing his mind into something new. A blend of man and demayne. He retained all he knew, but gained an eternity of learning in that scalding second. The illuminated form of the qiznithan lord thrust its essence into his body until the apparition folded in on itself and vanished. The gaping stinger wounds in Yples's mortal body sealed shut.

The gems of the *vaz'on* burst forth beams of blue and red and purple and green, then each shattered like a glass struck by a hammer. The bolts did not unscrew from Yples's skull, but simply melted and oozed from their penetrations. The band of gold encircling his head turned liquid and dripped upon the altar. His flesh did not suffer so much as a blister from the heat.

The entity who had been Dunne Yples sat up. The demayncors threw themselves onto the stone tiles outside the dome. They knew there would be no mercy. A qiznithan lord would not comprehend the notion of mercy. Their only protection was the circle.

The Yples entity breathed in the moist air of the island, delighting in the revolting decay he smelled upon it. This place was perfect. So many had been murdered here in demaynic rites that the Revulsion congealed in a thick layer, like the foul curd atop a pot of spoiled milk. This black power flowed into him now, filling all the space the mercus had once illuminated.

His revulynic bolts formed just as any mercus feat might be formed, but this power was of negation, of obliteration, of annihilation. He blasted the circle apart, stepped across and screamed with delighted rage. He sent a black beam of light-devouring power at the cowering demayncors. Their flesh liquified upon his command. It flowed toward him, blackening as it swirled around his feet. He soaked it in. He took strength from it.

He consumed the High Demayncor last, but not before ripping off the man's mask and hurling it way. Bending, Yples tenderly cupped the quivering cheeks, forcing the man to behold what he'd brought into the world.

"Wh—what are you?" the pathetic mortal asked.

"I am Annihilation."

The High Demayncor's screams never truly ceased, though none in the mortal world could hear them. Within Yples they went on and on, as they would go until the ultimate moment. And then all things would cease and there would be the final silence.

It was the black dawn of the Evernight.

Yples flexed his body, reveled in the mortal tissue as it throbbed and stretched. He listened to the Revulsion squirming and oozing through his mind and guts. There were no men remaining upon the pyramid, and those in the town below were of no use to him. He knew where to go, where the Revulsion strained and yearned for more hosts. It ran through this world in fat veins and concentrated in a few wondrous pools.

Dymensing, he came to just such a place deep within a mountain cavern. All was blackness, but he did not need light. For what he sought shed its own violet illumination, making a constellation of eldritch spots all around him. He bent and plucked a thick-stemmed mushroom, felt the Revulsion pulsating within it.

"Come, holy mimak. There are those who must taste of your flesh and be transformed."

2

TEACH HER MADNESS

The raven wheeled above the Citadel, black as the clouded sky. None saw her, but her presence stiffened necks and shoulders across Starside, interrupting everyone's Winternight revelries for a chilled moment.

Her heavy soul pressed upon mortal minds, made them spill their whisky or stumble amidst a dance.

She was a harbinger. Not evil in herself, but acting upon mortal hearts like the tea of the box myrtle, forcing the body to purge an evil already within it.

A dream of black annihilation took hold of one mortal girl, the silent and blind sleeper called Pennie. There were no Winternight joys for her, lost as she was in Lumne's dream.

She found herself standing upon a pleasant meadow of daisy and foxglove, while butterflies flitted in sun-glanced and lazy routes around her head. But this loveliness was ruined as dissonant harp strokes drew her eyes to a rift opening in the air.

From within this crease stepped a girl in her own image, save that her eyes were black and her skin shot through with veins of sickly brown. This newly born Pennie crushed the flowers beneath her feet, turning them to dust. The butterflies near her wilted and curled in on themselves, their remains parting into ash before they reached the ground.

"I can see you," the blackborn vision said to Pennie. "And I see with the *cold eye.*"

Another voice arose, this one from behind the true Pennie. "Flee, child! You must warn them."

"Roya Reth?" Pennie cried, backpedaling from the horror before her. "I can't find my way back!"

"Hurry! You must warn them!"

The blackborn's face stretched and smoothed. The curls of her hair lifted in smoke and streamed away. Her limbs stretched, hands reaching, fingers elongating and narrowing to blade points.

Pennie turned to run, but the blackborn was there. It was everywhere. No longer a mirror image, but instead a hole in the air, expanding, hungry.

In the last gleam of meadow light, Pennie shrieked. Her throat tore open, her heart surged and exploded, her eyes burned in their sockets. Every sinew popped and snapped as all that she was came out in her voice.

She formed a single word, but consonants and vowels could not contain the pure terror of her warning. Everyone heard the scream, but only one of them caught the word of her warning: *"Evernight!"*

THE HUNDREDS OF GOVERNMENT OFFICIALS, scribes, maids, and visiting dignitaries celebrating Winternight in the Citadel suddenly gasped for air and grasped their breasts to contain the wild flailing of their panic-stricken hearts. Had that sound—that scream—been their imaginations? Or had it come from the raw throat of terror nearby?

Mistress Wiley, head of Morning Chambermaids—who were duty-bound to sleep on Winternight in order to be of service at dawn—crabbed-walked her fingers over her nightstand to find a flashtaper. She managed to tear one and light a candle. The blooming flame burnished her roommate's sagging face. "Did you have a nightmare, Miss Frily?" Wiley asked the young woman. "Your scream shot me out of my hair!"

Frily leaned up on one arm, the other clamped across her chest. "Twasn't *me*. I thought it you."

The loud whispers of frightened maids cut under the door as more of the Morning Chambermaids stirred. Wiley cursed under her breath and padded to the door. "All of you back to bed," she said in the high, scolding tone of a housemother. There'd be no pointless whispering from her ranks. What was it with these woolheaded girls and their gossipy minds? "Someone had a nightmare and it has nothing to do with any of you."

The locked door at the end of the hall bashed open. A chorus of squawks filled the corridor as two fell guardsmen pounded past. Miss Wiley wrapped her arms around herself as best she could. For Til's love! She wore only her nightgown and robe! Her hair wasn't even bunned!

But the men took no notice of her scandalous state as they clomped past. "Is something amiss?" Wiley called after them.

True to their nature, the fell guardsmen ignored her. Once they were gone, Wiley shooed the other women out of the hall. "Back into your rooms. No gossiping, mind. You know nothing, so you have no business saying anything. Else you'll make nosg faces of shadows. And then you'll be droopy of eye and dull in spirit for your morning duties. This is Her Enlightened Majesty's Citadel! Have pride in your position here, or I'll free up your future and you can find work downslope."

The misses answered with a soft "Yes, Mistress Wiley," and

doors closed. Fortunately none had seen how her heart raced, nor the gooseflesh that still covered her body.

GARRET SIBIN, Minister of Her Enlightened's Treasury, patted the woman curled next to him in bed. He tried crooning soothing nonsense to her, but she wouldn't stop wailing. Someone might come to see what was amiss. That would never do, since she wasn't his wife. In fact, he didn't know whose wife she was. They had slipped away from the festivities just a quarter of an hour ago. "My dear, please do have a sip of this trezz. You're wearing out your own nerves."

"B—b—but that scream! And she sounded so afraid!"

Garret lifted the cup to her lips and tilted it such that she had to swallow or be doused. She swallowed, and coughed, but the fiery liquid turned her sobs into chokes, which at least were quieter.

"It was merely the prank of an over-drunk lass. Mayhap she saw a shadow and thought it a boggle or bingle or somesuch storybook nonsense. I always say, 'Teach a girl to read and you teach her madness.' Here, come into my arms. That's it. You merely need a distraction. I know just the thing . . . lend me your lips."

ADMINISTRATOR MARLOW CALLED to the fell guardsman outside his office. The tall man, armored and capped with a plumed helm, appeared at once. His stoney gray eyes sucked in Marlow's gaze, making him feel like a freshly robed acolyte confronted by an elder Donse Master.

"Did you hear that scream?" Marlow asked.

"I did, Administrator."

Marlow waited for more. But the fell guardsman did not deign to speculate. Nor would any others be dispatched to Marlow with explanations. If he wanted to know what had happened, he'd have to order the man to go find out. He did so. The man vanished, the sound of his boots fading as he double-timed down the tiled corridor.

Marlow made a face as he sipped his tea. It was cold and had been so for hours. He'd fallen asleep at his work again, papers clumped in one hand. His vast desk was layered with dispatches, supply reports, census tables, and ledgers from the Minister of Granaries and Stockyards. To think he had actually *wanted* this position at one point. Power, it turned out, was burdened with tedious responsibility. He could not remember a Winternight when he'd not been red-faced and dancing with a jolly lass or two.

The scream still occupied his hearing, a resounding memory his mind simply would not release. It had been so ragged, so full of terror. Childhood stories of the screamclown rose unbidden, and he couldn't help but recall a drawing of the fabled stealer of infant souls he'd once seen. Elongated pale face, like melting candle wax. Bugging eyes. Mouth gaping and black as it shrieked to frighten the spirit from a newborn babe's heart. A housemother's tale, but he shivered nonetheless.

Rubbing his elbows he called upon his mercus and ignited the logs in the fireplace and added heat to his tea. Such feats were easier for him now. He'd learned so much from Kila Sigh. If only he'd known these tricks before she'd awakened to her powers. Had he been better prepared to guide her, he could have saved her and Starside—and himself—loads of suffering.

He was, ostensibly, a leader. Second in power only to Her Enlightened Majesty, Ell LiMinluit. But in truth, being the

Administrator of Government meant he was dragged by the nose from crisis to crisis.

He'd diverted a bit of coin and trade to his own private interests, of course. That was only sensible. There was still a chance the world would survive Kila Sigh and Dem-Kisk and Kil reborn. Not a very good chance, but Marlow liked to have contingencies in place.

The tea soothed his shivering and a bit of tuneless humming covered the resonances of that horrid scream enough for him to get back to work.

His eyes fell on the unbroken seal of a letter received just at dusk, the red wax debossed with a helmed raven. This was word from General LiMillar who had taken five thousand of Her Enlightened's men to the Sablefort far to the northwest. Marlow broke the seal and scanned the dispatch. Her Enlightened's army had arrived at the old fortress on the southern edge of the Sackwood a ten-day ago. Repairs had commenced. Teams of soldiers were clearing the surrounding forest which had encroached during decades of neglect. LiMillar concluded with a query about when the army from Tordain might be expected. And who would be in command of the combined force?

Marlow blew out his cheeks and tossed the dispatch onto the pile. Tordain would be sending no army to the Sablefort. With the Autarch dead, they were too distracted to care about the nosg threat. Jallisea was sending no men, nor was Sorgan. Marlow had not heard from Flyssn, which meant they were reserving all their forces for defense of Lockt. Marlow couldn't blame them.

From far away came the toll of the hour. No point in going to bed now. He sipped his tea, noticed his hand shaking still.

An echo of the scream came again to his mind. Shivering, he went to his door. Where was that guardsman? Surely he'd discovered the source of the scream by now.

3

ILL NEWS

The Privileged Suites at the Citadel occupied an enormous stone manor house. It was detached from the main fortress and secluded behind a stand of pines and well upslope from the administrative buildings. Each of the house's huge apartment suites offered magnificent views of both the Citadel and the city of Starside.

It was here that visiting dignitaries and their retinues set up house for their often lengthy stays in Starside. Her Enlightened Majesty's hospitality was legendary, and schemes abounded in the seats of power across Ennith to be chosen as an ambassador. Even now the smells of Winternight roasts, bread, and sweet-bake filled the halls, food of unmatched quality anywhere save Tordain.

At the end of a fourth story corridor, two fell guardsmen stood watch at a set of white-painted double doors. True to their training, they did not blink or flinch or smile when voices were raised within the chambers beyond. Nor did they try to discern the subject of the argument. Such were common in there, drifting though like winter squalls. The guards' purpose was simple. Protect Highest Sigh and her ward, a young girl called Saiya.

Even when the scream tore through the air, sounding like it had come from just behind the door, neither man jolted. The senior guard merely broke his stance and opened the door. "Is all well, Highest Sigh?"

"What was that?" came the reply, followed by the appearance of a girl of seventeen, shoeless and dressed in loose black trousers, snug white ruffled blouse, and shoulder length blond hair framing her face. On her right pinky flashed a garnet ring. Her dagger was sheathed, rather foolishly, on her right thigh.

To the fell guardsman, Kila Sigh looked like a wealthy merchant's daughter, not like the most powerful merculyn in the world. Certainly not like the Highest of a Way. He noted the cat that peeped its face into view, hugging the wall, white feet primly together. Another appeared a moment later, this one orange and sized a third larger. It seemed much more agitated, for its fur was up.

"I heard a scream, Highest," he said. "Is all well?"

"It didn't come from in here," she said, brows bunching in vexation. "We looked in every room."

Henley Mast came around the corner, dressed in more traditional attire for Winternight celebrations. Loose shirt, properly laced to the throat, knee pants and hose, with fine buckled shoes. His ginger hair flamed in the mercus lights of the suite's foyer. "Nothing here, though I swore it came from Saiya's room. But she was with us in the study."

"It's Winternight," Highest Sigh said. "Probably some drunk servant girl out among the pines with her lover. Sound bounces around this place most freakish sometimes."

The final resident of the suite ambled into the foyer, a girl of nine or ten, or so she appeared. The fell guardsman had held this post since the trio had moved in, three ten-days prior. The child had been a babe in arms then. Only his training, and pride as a fell guardsman, kept his mind calm at the sight of her. Mercus feats were usual in the Citadel, but fast-growing children were not. Rumors abounded about the child, but he knew the truth. The Fell Guard could be trusted with any information and none would repeat it even under the most horrific torture.

But even an experienced fell guardsman like Brother Eyvin couldn't help but have his pulse increase at the sight of her. He was looking at Kil reborn, the Despised God, Lord of hate, greed, pestilence, and deceit.

Her Enlightened Majesty had told Brother Commander Docit that the child would be raised to be just, righteous, and good. And that no threat to her would be tolerated. That was all Brother Eyvin or any of the Brotherhood of the Fell Guard needed to hear. Her Enlightened was their master in all things and they were bloodsworn to protect her and those she acknowledged as vital to the realm.

"I shall leave you to your Winternight observance," he said and backed from the suite. He resumed his post and returned his mind to the equanimity of duty.

HENLEY MAST TURNED AWAY from the door, skin still thrilling from the scream. "I swear, those men's hearts are made of solid ice."

"Nax says he was nervous," Kila said.

Was that man nervous? Henley sent to Huff, who had returned to his favorite dozing spot near the fireplace. Henley had placed a large pillow there to serve as a bed, but both cats had rejected it, favoring instead to snuggle together atop a crinkly pile of discarded letters next to Kila's chair.

Who? Huff answered sleepily.

Never mind.

Kila resumed her seat and pulled Saiya onto her lap. The child was sleepy, which was unusual. The Winternight Ball here at the Citadel had worn her out with all the racing around with other children, stuffing her face with sweetbake, and the general overwhelm of jollity. Henley also suspected that Kila had allowed the girl a bit too much wassail.

Kila kissed her head. "It's time for bed, Saiya."

Saiya yawned, but forced herself to stand rigidly upright. "No. It's *past* time for bed. It's *so* far past time that using the time as a reason to send me to bed now is silly."

Kila grinned. "I have the authority to decide when it's time for bed. And I'll use whatever reason I want."

Standing there with her mouth turned down and her eyes glimmering, the child didn't look like a god. Not in the way Henley would have expected. No glowing flesh, no swirls of mercusine power surrounding her. At one month old she should still be a squalling babe. But Saiya looked like a girl of nine. That was what made her so obviously godblooded. Otherwise she was just a child. An extraordinarily bright-minded, precocious child with an enormous unawakened mercus potential.

Kila pressed her lips to the girl's cheek and blew, making a rude noise that sent the girl into shrieking giggles. "You have never won this argument," Kila said. "You need to sleep, so you are going to bed."

"But I'm not sleepy."

"Sleepy has nothing to do with it."

"But it's Winternight. Everyone's supposed to stay up all night and dance and eat and drink."

"It's past middlenight. So you did stay up all night. It's morning now." She steered Saiya down the hall to the girl's bedroom.

"But it's dark out."

The argument continued, voices muffling as the door to the bedchamber closed behind them. Henley slouched into a cushioned armchair and lifted a tumbler of apple-cinnon whisky to his lips. Winternight's traditional indulgence heated his belly. But it soured there, and the false cheer he'd been putting on all evening finally collapsed.

The scream had shaken him. It was as if the Citadel itself had tired of the building tension in the air and finally gave voice to the frustration festering in every heart in Starside. Not even Winternight festivities could ease the discord in the city.

Rationing, enlistments for Her Enlightened's Army, and an influx of refugees from Tordain had set every citizen on edge. The growing encampment of the so-called Way of Kila in the old Blasted Quarter just made things worse. Not to mention the damage Kila had done to the city when she had battled the Hargothe here. Half the city hated her, the other half feared her too much to voice their hate.

And then there was Saiya.

Kila seemed determined not to think about the girl's very near future. If Saiya continued to grow at this rate, she'd have the maturity of a woman of eighteen in a month. And twenty-seven the following month. But being a god, she would not age into dotage by next Winternight. No, by then she would be something other than a mere woman. Exactly *what* she would become was unknowable.

Kila had cut the child from Yiothizandra's womb, adopted her, and named her Saiya Sigh. It almost rhymed with Kila's name, which was fitting. They certainly bore a remarkable resemblance to each other. Which made no rational sense, since they were not blood kin.

Saiya was the offspring of the Hargothe and Yiothizandra. Shivering at the mere thought of those two coupling, Henley sipped more of his drink and let out a quiet grunt of morose amusement.

"What's funny?" Kila asked, returning from Saiya's room. She slipped into his lap.

"I was just remembering that the Hargothe was Radiant Peline's brother. That means Saiya is Quinn's cousin. And Marlow's niece."

"Shush. I don't want you talking about that. Saiya thinks I'm her mother, and that's how we're going to keep it."

He didn't like it, but he wasn't going to argue about it now. He kissed her, which she welcomed for a moment before pulling away and wrinkling her nose. "You taste like whisky. How can you drink that stuff?" She took the tumbler from him and sipped it. "Yuck."

"You just don't understand tradition. Tradition is tradition. It doesn't matter if it's good." It certainly didn't taste good tonight. "You know, stories about Saiya have spread all over Starside. Has to be coming from the servants. They might not know she's Kil reborn, but they know she's—"

"Don't say it!"

"—unnatural. Don't give me that look. That's not *my* word. But it's the gossip-word on every servant's lips."

Kila tossed back the rest of his whisky. Swallowing and grimacing, she said, "Let them talk. But if anyone uses that word in my hearing, they'll wish they were working in a Cheapsgate brothel."

A sharp rap came at the outer door of their shared quarters. A heavy footfall resounded in the foyer, belt rings of the fell guardsman jingling softly. "Highest Sigh, a Spinster of Pol is here to see you. She claims it is urgent."

Henley rubbed Kila's back and offered a sympathetic smile.

She pouted and sighed. "I just wanted one night without an interruption. If this is another complaint about those Way of

Kila fools, I'm going to go down there and dymense them halfway to the Shudderlins."

"Halfway would dump them in open ocean."

"Yes. I know that."

The Spinster padded in, white gown flowing around slim legs. She wore a silk ribbon of blue to hold her medallion, the only indication of her observance of Winternight. Spin Fria was young, smooth-faced and serious. She gripped the medallion at her breast and dipped one knee. "Highest Sigh, I bear ill news. Coin Inlina, Medallion of the Way of Pol, died just prior to middlenight. She dictated this letter to me in her final hour. I was instructed to deliver it into your hands immediately after her death." The woman extended a thin roll. The imprint of the Coin's seal stood proudly on the black wax. Black seals were indeed dire, reserved for death notices, news of lost ships, broken armies, and severed relationships. Kila snatched the letter.

Henley urged her from his lap. Receiving such a communication required a modicum of formality. Besides, he was never comfortable displaying their intimacy in front of others.

The Spinster swiveled her head, as if looking for someone— or something. Henley realized the woman was curious. She had never been in Kila's presence before and she was looking for the cats.

Nax and Huff were curled on the letter stack, sleeping in total contentment. The Spinster finally spotted them. Her lips parted on a quick inhalation, but she mastered her fascination and made her face expressionless. "I shall leave you now. Good Winternight to you . . . all." She made another little half curtsy and left.

Kila ignored her entirely, brow furrowed as she scanned the letter. Her lips moved as she re-read one particular line. She threw up her hands and rattled the letter as if she wanted to shake the ink out of it. "Kil's eyes, that woman! Even dead, ol' Inlina burns my biscuits." She shoved the letter into Henley's hands and took his empty tumbler to the crystal decanter on the sideboard.

The letter was in a flowing hand, the paper very fine.

To Kila Sigh, *Highest of Kil. The proof of Saiya's godblood is plain to see. She grows too swiftly, and her uncanny speech betrays an unnatural deviousness of mind. She is argumentative, defiant, and distractible. Yet you continue to deny what she is. Even the dragnithans Klayne Itopolo and Eckso Ezeel admit she is Kil reborn. Kil's nature is set, and no amount of care and nurture will divert him from it. Death, war, pestilence, and greed are his cherished ideals. Do not let the child's sex fool you into complacency. I have noted your maternal protectiveness. It is a* severe *error. Thus far you have ignored my demands to put the child to the blade and save this world from destruction. So I say to you this one last time, end this godling! I've heard reports of what you did in Stallid. You cut the child from Yiothizandra's belly with your shadline blade. Fate Breaker may be the only weapon that can cut the girl's flesh. Use it!*

"There's nothing new here," Henley said, crumpling the letter. "But did you notice what she left out?"

Kila had refilled Henley's tumbler and was nursing it with sour lips. "No, what?"

He tossed the paper into the fire, where it flared for a moment and became smoke. "She didn't mention any spins of her medallion. Did you ever know the woman not to mention the results of her inquiries to Pol?"

"What do you think it means?" Kila asked, setting the whisky aside, barely touched.

"I don't know. But it's odd. Too bad that spinster left so quickly."

Kila slipped back into his lap and tucked her head into the crook of his neck. "I don't think it's bad. We don't get enough time alone."

He agreed whole-heartedly. And now that Saiya was in bed, he thought it wise to take advantage of the moment. He lifted her chin and marveled at her loveliness. But before their lips could touch, the fell guardsman announced another visitor. This was a page boy, swaying unsteadily, his livery in disarray. His cheeks were flushed from running—or possibly from Winternight indulgences of his own. He bowed low to Kila, averting his eyes. "Her Enlightened Majesty requires your immediate presence in her spire council study. It is a matter of grave urgency."

"It's Winternight," Kila said. "Tell her to come by here tomorrow. Late."

The page was not accustomed to people refusing Her Enlightened's summons, much less suggesting that the monarch come to them. He stammered and looked to Henley for help.

"It's probably about Coin Inlina," Henley said. "You should attend. I doubt it'll take long,"

"Then you go," she snapped. "The Coin's dead. What needs to be discussed?"

The page's faced drained of color. Henley again eased Kila from his lap and stood. Arguing with her now would be pointless. "Fine, I'll go. If it's truly urgent I'll let you know. Keep the fire going." He tried to kiss her, but she turned her head away.

Henley dismissed the boy and pulled on his over-jacket. One did not go into the presence of the monarch half-dressed. "I'm sure it'll only be a few minutes." Kila waved him away, sullen.

You coming? he sent to Huff.

That cat mewled softly in his sleep and snuggled closer to

Nax. Henley eyed the leather satchel containing the Motherlight. The relic was bound to him, and could provide enormous reserves of mercus, nearly enough to match Kila's power. But he was weary of toting it everywhere he went.

With the fell guardsmen posted at the door, and with Kila in the room, there was no chance of someone walking off with it. So he left it where it hung from a cloak tree and dymensed to the entry of Her Enlightened's council chamber.

4

A NEW TRADITION

He left me! Kila sent to Nax, flopping into Henley's vacant chair and hugging her knees. *That fool left me.*

You told him to go. Nax's tail tip flicked, but she didn't deign to open her eyes. That she had understood Kila's spoken conversation with Henley no longer surprised Kila. The cats had all developed the skill, though they refused to admit it.

Kila took up the whisky and drew in a mouthful. But she couldn't swallow it. The apple-cinnon flavor was too sweet. She spat it back into the tumbler and put it down.

I didn't think he'd actually go. He shouldn't have. Irritated, she sprang up and started pacing. This whole evening had been a trial. As much as she'd enjoyed spending it with Henley and Saiya, she'd been struggling with a vague unease all day. Something pulled at her, made her jittery with useless energy. And that horrid scream had set her nerves on edge. Whoever had done it ought to get a good ear-boxing.

She shook her arms and blew out her cheeks, trying to shed her restlessness. The Coin's letter certainly hadn't helped. Henley had been right about it. Nothing new. Old Inlina had been for killing Saiya since the first night that Kila had revealed the babe to Ell's council.

Kila huffed. Council of idiots.

Aren't you a member of that council? Nax asked. Her eyes slitted open just enough to send emerald sparkles toward Kila.

Kila flapped a hand at the cat. She was in no mood for Nax's unsolicited insights. Continuing to pace, she felt the restlessness surge. Henley's willingness to run off at Ell's untimely summons was the last snowflake on the roof. The whole notion of a pleasurable, festive night had collapsed on her head. Winternight should have been enjoyable. It had turned out to be a disaster.

What was it Henley had said about the nasty whisky? *Tradition is tradition. It doesn't matter if it's good.*

So be it. Kila had a Winternight tradition of her own. Maybe that's why her body had felt full so of energy all day. It was preparing for her usual Winternight rambles, but instead she'd been lounging around like these lazy cats.

Want to go running about? she sent.

In answer, Nax rolled onto her back and stretched until she was incredibly long. This disturbed Huff, who wakened enough to mirror the stretch until his head was hanging at a weird angle from the pile of letters.

I'm leaving. If Henley thinks Ell's business is more important than — Kila felt the incoherent pulses of Nax's dreams coming through the bond. Sniffing in disgust, she reached for her mercus, pushed away the faint fingers of Revulsion that sought her attention, and formed the bolts to dymense.

SHE EMERGED from the icy bath of dymension moments later. She now stood on the roof of the Yin Inn in Terriside, her old thieving grounds. The misty night air swirled around her, filling her senses with the smell of wet cobblestone, garbage, and animal dung. A dusting of soggy snow covered the street and rooftops.

Mercus lights glimmered on the oozing street, where foot traffic had mushed the snow into slushy trails. Heavy round snowflakes mixed with the mist, obscuring the lights of the Starside Wall. The Divide was lost in impenetrable night.

Kila slipped off her shoes, gasping as the slush squeezed between her toes. She wondered if it had always been so chill on Winternights past, when she and Wen had stalked these roofs. She decided it must be a colder winter than before. Else it meant her feet were grown soft from wearing shoes all the time. She considered using Flaumishtak's weather-cloak feat to ease the chill, but decided against it. She would warm herself by running.

Instinct led her to Lower Terriside, over rooftops she knew so well she didn't have to count strides to time her leaps. Or so she'd thought. Her first jump, over a rather wide alley, left her wobbling on a ledge, frantically windmilling her arms to keep herself upright. Breathless, she tipped forward to safety. They must have widened the lane there.

She continued her run. It was hard, but by Kil and his seven sisters, it felt good to fly along the roofway. She wondered why she'd waited so long to do this. The fresh cold air was just the tonic she needed.

Another jump cleared Festle Lane and put her atop the chandler's shop. She didn't have any copper plugs on her, so she dropped a gold skillet in the toll pail. "Happy Winternight, Boyd," she said, knowing the chandler's apprentice would never report finding a gold skillet in the bucket.

She was about to dash off again, but movement on the street below drew her attention. A dark figure walked directly beneath her perch, singing "Winternight Lark" and leaning like a ship on a tack. He'd imbibed more than his share of trezz this evening.

"Hold close to yer love, sir,
Tell her she's yer life;
Then stumble home at dawn, sir,
And make up with yer wife."

By the quality of his greatcoat, he belonged to a merchant family. She crouched and watched, feeling the thrill of the stalk rising. The mercus vision arose unbidden, as it was wont to do in such moments. She studied the contents of his purse, which hung heavily from his belt. Several gold, a couple silver, and a sprinkling of copper.

She shoved away the thought that she carried double his purse in her own. This wasn't about the coin, it was about the art of the take.

He moved out of shadow and into the full glare of a nearby mercus light. His hair seemed to glow, nearly white it was so fair. Kila balked, paralyzed by a rush of confusion.

Ragin? But no, this man was older and taller. But that hair. There was no mistaking it. Only the Keels had such white locks. Must be one of Ragin's brothers.

Remembering that the older Keel brothers had burned down Henley's greathouse and murdered his father, she reached for Cayne. The warm smoothness of the leather-wrapped hilt gave her encouragement. But rather than draw the blade, she released it. Wen had never wanted her to rob a mark while armed. The Watch would punish a thief for pickpocketing with a few days in a cell, but an armed thief would lose a hand.

She snickered silently. As if the Watch could do anything to her. She could ash them where they stood. Or simply dymense away.

Her thrilled moment extinguished at this thought. She sat heavily, not caring about the cold dampness that claimed her bottom. "What am I doing?" she said aloud. "It's colder than a Spinster's corset out here."

The Keel wandered off. She sat atop the roof and imagined that Wen was crouching beside her, eyes aflame with delight at the hunt. He would cough into the crook of his arm to stay quiet, and he'd make her wait, studying mark after mark until they found one rich enough and drunk enough to be worth the risk. And when she returned with his purse, they'd count it together and Wen would beam with pride.

"Ah me," she said softly, blowing out her cheeks and feeling her eyelashes crusting with a freezing dampness. Henley shouldn't have gone to Ell's summons. He should have stayed with her. They would be curled up before the fire, making a new tradition. A good one.

In her loneliness, she flashed on Quinn and wondered where her friend was. Off on some shadline foolishness, of course. With Fallo. The silly girl would follow that ugly rascal into the doom-fires.

Thoughts of Quinn recalled to Kila the sickness that had claimed Quinn at the Hackwatch. She had been slipped a heavy dose of tresh, a ferneater brew that put Quinn into a sort of will-shift. Her old friend Critt Sanglo and also been treshed. They'd both tried to murder Kila while under its sway. The man who'd treshed them had been a shadline. What was his name?

Varl Akton.

Kila turned to look east. Toward Cheapsgate.

Varl had worn a tattoo of a curved blade called a "gutter." The gutter mark was unique to a certain class of villain in Cheapsgate, Dox Viller's henchmen: Viller's Killers.

Even now Dox Viller was warm in his stronghold. Him and his hounds.

Shivering, Kila looked from the slums to the wealthy

merchants' neighborhoods of Terriside. Where the Keels lived. Ah, but the Keels were Henley's problem, not hers.

Dox Viller on the other hand . . .

Lips pinched and heart aching, Kila resolved to leave Starside a bit lighter in evil by Winternight's end.

5

STRAPPED THE BURDEN

Henley had expected to find others waiting in Ell's council chamber. But when the fell guardsman opened the door, he walked into a cold, dimly lit room. There was no fire in the hearth. The monarch of Starside faced an open window, staring out over the mist-shrouded city.

The fell guardsman announced him: "Henley Mast on behalf of Highest Sigh, Your Majesty."

Her Enlightened didn't turn to face him. The only light came from a shaded mercus lamp across the room. It cast its reluctant glow onto her tumble of black hair, which spilled down the back of her blue ball gown. "I'm not surprised Kila didn't come," she said. "Are you her official ambassador now?"

"Nothing as formal as that. You know Kila." He bowed, though she wasn't looking. He hadn't thought of himself as Kila's ambassador until that moment. Realizing his role, he thought it prudent to make an excuse for Kila's absence. "There was a scream near our suite. It frightened Saiya. Kila stayed to comfort her." Ambassadors were expected to offer small lies out of politeness.

"The scream is what I had hoped to discuss with her.

Everyone in the Citadel heard it. And everyone thought it came from very nearby. How is that possible?"

"You heard it?"

"I did. And I heard the word inside the scream. Did you?"

"No."

"Did Kila?"

He had the 'no' on his tongue but cut it off. "She didn't mention any words to me. What was it?"

"'Evernight.' It refers to Night's long sought dominance over Day. I also know the source of the scream." She turned to face him. Her face was ageless, lovely, and stern. And tired. "It was Kila's young friend from Garden Island. Pennie Montlieve. She has been in Lumne's twilight these past weeks, unwakeable and unresponsive to pinch or stroke. You were here in this room when she collapsed and spoke prophecy, no? I believe her mind has since wandered in some liminal realm that separates this world from the demaynic ones. We know she communed somehow with the dead seer Roya Reth to speak prophecy. 'Evernight' will be the last we hear from either of them, I'm afraid."

"But if she can scream with such force, surely there's hope she will wake. Maybe she can explain it to us."

"She's dead. Her warning consumed the last measure of her life."

"Kila will be gutted." He considered sending the ill news to her through their bond. But he wanted to be there to offer comforting arms when she found out. The thought drew his attention to the bond, and he noticed the change in it. Like his bond to Huff, his bond with Kila told him in which direction she lay. She was somewhere east, out in the city.

Huff, where did Kila run off to?

The cat replied with a sending so sleep-muddled, Henley couldn't help but yawn. *Nax says she went out to run the roofways.*

Where exactly?

I'm not waking Nax again. She's mean when her naps are disturbed.

Henley discovered the monarch watching him and realized he'd been staring into the middle distance and saying nothing. "Begging your pardon, majesty. Communicating through cats is never as simple as one would hope. I had thought to get Kila to come, but Nax is asleep."

"I'll leave it to you to tell her about Pennie. Please encourage Kila to be vigilant. Just because Yiothizandra has been imprisoned does not mean all danger is past. Kil's rebirth was a beginning, not an ending. I do not know what part Night will play, but they are not defeated in this world." Her gaze lost focus for a moment and her hand brushed across her chest, fingers pressing to her heart.

Despite a heavy reluctance, Henley decided to mention Coin Inlina's final letter. He was surprised when the monarch's lips parted in surprise at news of Inlina's death. "I was sure you knew," he said. "Why wouldn't Pol's Tower inform you?"

Her Enlightened clicked her tongue and flashed her brows, revealing far more of the woman's low opinion of the Way of Pol than Henley had ever suspected. "The Raven Throne and the Way of Pol have been uneasy allies in the best of times. It shouldn't surprise you that the Coin of Starside wanted a seat on my small council. She wanted to perform spins to guide my decisions." She made a sour face and plopped into her chair. With a small flick of her hand, she motioned for Henley to sit. He did so, stomach feeling squishy and giving him an unwelcome second tasting of his whisky. He knew that being brought into Her Enlightened's confidence was a rare privilege. But he also knew that access to her private thoughts wouldn't come without a price. She wanted something.

"Coin Inlina was a formidable woman," the monarch said.

"In a different time she would have been an excellent head of her Way. I suppose her letter encouraged Kila to slay the child?" At his nod, she continued: "That's because Inlina believed in spins of her medallion more than she believed in a shadline's sensitivity to the pushes and pulls of the force of destiny. Did you know that the Way of Pol once issued a charter declaring the Shadlines a cult of frauds? It states that the Way of Til created the Shadlines to weaken the public's regard for Pol. They claim to have performed many spins to prove it."

"Are you saying the spins are hoaxes? Because I've witnessed Coin Inlina tossing her medallion with eerie results, including one instance where the medallion didn't even bounce when it struck a stone floor. It was unnerving. *Something* was speaking through that spin."

"I'm not saying they are hoaxes. Not all of their spins, anyway. Coin Inlina truly believed in what she was doing, which was why she was so irritatingly blunt." She laughed softly and shook the question off. She looked at Henley and he felt it coming, the burden she had prepared for him.

"Saiya is a problem," she said. It was matter of fact. "Coin Inlina was right about that. But her solution was wrong. The force of destiny brought Kil into our world for a reason. It cannot be simply for us to kill her. The consequences of such an act would be more terrible than we could imagine. No. Kila is correct about one thing. Saiya must be raised to know right from wrong, compassion from indifference, generosity from greed. But Kila is wrong in one essential point."

"And what is that?" He wished he could be anywhere but here.

"That *she* is the one to teach Saiya these things. Kila, who was raised a thief, and who robbed my subjects of their coin, on my streets. Kila, who is nearly a child herself, and who refuses to even discuss Saiya's unnatural aging and what the consequences of that will be in a very short time."

The monarch was rehearsing his own thoughts back to him, which provided absolutely no comfort. Quite the opposite. "But Kila loves her," he said, as if this fact could counter the monarch's list of Kila's deficiencies as a parent. "And if you think I can convince her to turn Saiya over to you, then you have greatly overestimated my influence."

"Do you believe Saiya will obey Kila three ten-days from now, when they are the same age? How about a ten-day later, when Saiya will clearly be her senior by several years? You see, don't you, that we have at most a month to teach this young god to be other than what she has always been. And that's if we are lucky. When Saiya awakens to her powers there will be nothing we can do to stay her hand should she choose to lay waste to this world."

Her eyes were wide and pleading. She leaned toward him, hands out in supplication. Seeing Her Enlightened so desperate made his chest tighten around his heart.

The monarch's face went still and she leaned back into her chair. The regal calm returned so quickly he wondered if the previous lapse had been real. But her voice shook as she finally strapped the burden to his back. "I want you to loan me the Motherlight. And then I want you to leave Starside for a day or two. And before you ask, I am willing to be promise-bound to you that I will do absolutely nothing to harm Kila. Nor will I separate her from Saiya."

"What will you do?"

She didn't answer. Just stared at him. His mind raced over schemes she might have in mind. Perhaps she intended to use mind probes on Saiya to seed the lessons she didn't think Kila could teach. The Motherlight just might be powerful enough in her hands to let her contend with Saiya's godmind. Henley had dived into it himself, just to see what Kil's mind looked like. It had been like a fellstorm, impenetrable, wild, and supremely dangerous. Or perhaps the monarch planned to do something similar to Kila in order to make her a better mother. That seemed more likely, and that's all Henley had to know. "I will never betray Kila," he said.

The monarch didn't blink, or wince, or shake her head in irritation. She simply nodded and withdrew a rolled note from her sleeve. She had expected this answer. The letter was bound with a blue silk ribbon, the Raven-in-Flight mark emblazoned along its length. A lovely mercus ward curled around the paper as well. "Only Kila may open it," she warned.

Henley took it. "I'm sorry that I cannot do as you ask. It doesn't mean I don't share your fears. I've tried to get Kila to see the risks, believe me. But she has made one unassailable argument. Saiya is good already. She's willful, true. She's prone to breaking rules, but what child isn't? She has a loving nature, and I've not seen a glimmer of greed in her, much less hate or jealousy or the slightest violence."

But Her Enlightened Majesty had risen from her chair and was walking back to her favorite window. "I pray you are right, Henley Mast. You may leave me now. Give my letter to Kila."

6

THE BLACKSHINE SWARMLIGHT

Under the weighty gloom of the Haelshok mountains, a relentless wind scraped with icy claws over an encampment of the nosg army. The shelters of G'galas Oopax's remaining force huddled as close to the lee side of a great mountain as they dared. The further out of the wind they were, the greater their risk of annihilation from above. For a great curtain of ice overhung their position, fangs of a mountain well known to drop tons of frigid death without warning.

For the grand shaman of G'galas Oopax, Wurgu Zir-Fir, their situation beneath the overhang was a blatant taunt to Shish-Jek, the goddess of fortune, who had forsaken the nosg ages past. She would surely drop the whole thing on their heads. Had he his way, his army would be nowhere near this place. In fact, had he his way, he would disband the gr'hils and send every warrior nosg back to their drikks, to return to kin and productive labor. Yiothizandra's ill-considered war was over, the nosg broken by Kila Sigh, and the queen herself captured and imprisoned.

Had he his way, they would purge the whole debacle from their memories and pray to Shish-Jek for forgiveness.

But it wasn't up to him.

He lay in his low-ceilinged pavilion, a thick stretch of sauk-hide born up on rough timbers and carpeted with furs. It would protect him and his pleasure females from the wind, and would do well to hold in the warmth emanating from his dung-fired stove. But it would do nothing to save him from an instant crushing from above.

He pulled two of his females in close, enjoying the coarse-ness of their hairy limbs against his. They clung to him, whimpering obsequious praise.

A stone pot bubbled over the stove, sending out musky vapors of mimak and sauk meat, winter onion and sweat-salt. A few very wilted leeks had been thrown in, too. The stew would soon warm him and lift his mind farther into the realm of the swarmlight. And once within its power he would have to decide how he would confront Razk-Ka, Yiothizandra's Prime.

It was time to put an end to the madness of this winter encampment. For all anyone knew, Yiothizandra was dead. There was no reason to maintain the "army in being" as Razk-Ka incessantly repeated. No. It was time to admit defeat. This was not *aggalamas-alamas* as the fire queen had promised. Her war against Stallid had not been the first in a long series of conquests to reclaim the lands of men for nosg-kin. Her war had been for herself, and for her unnatural babe. And it was over.

One of his sentries coughed and rattled a bone chime outside the tent.

"What is it?" Zir-Fir called.

No answer. The front flap of the pavilion pulled back and a tall figure oozed through, leaving the flap gaping, chill wind cutting into the warmth.

Zir-Fir's curses died on his upthrusting tusks. It was a human.

He shoved his females away and reached for his skull staff, already drawing the swarmlight into the red gems in the eye-sockets. A man, here? Intolerable. How had his army allowed such a creature to pass?

He released rays of fire from his skull staff. They beamed into the intruder's body but didn't even singe his robes. The red light struggled, then retreated, pushed away by a consuming shadow emanating from the man. Zir-Fir added more of his rage to the effort, but this too was consumed.

"You will stop this," the man said softly. His voice was low, deep, and carried absolute authority. The females cowered away from him. Zir-Fir, too, could not resist the impulse to step back. The man smelled strange, like the fumes of the poisonous frog-capped mushrooms every young shaman learned to avoid.

"Who are you?" Zir-Fir demanded, thick tongue struggling to enunciate the Ennish speech of man.

"Call me Lord Yples. Where are the rest of your shamans at this hour?"

Defiance being Zir-Fir's first instinct when being questioned in his own tent, he clamped his lips together. But a cold finger slipped into his mind and he heard himself say: "Sleeping. Keeping warm."

"You will summon them to a sweat."

Zir-Fir fought against the command, knowing that the man used mercus tricks to slather his mind with obedient inclinations. Yet, even knowing this, he was unable to shake a sudden eagerness to comply. And that eagerness prompted a thrill of terror. Zir-Fir wanted nothing more than to run past the man and keep running through the frigid night. The man moved with oily grace around the pavilion, stopping to inspect each item of furniture, each weapon, each fur and pot. He finally paused over the brewing mimak stew. "This will do."

Zir-Fir's will broke in that instant and he called for his sentries to fetch all his shamans.

"Prepare a sweat fire," Yples commanded, "for you shall all be initiated this night."

"We cannot spare the timber for such a fire. I am Wurgu and even I am reduced to burning dung for heat."

"Burn timbers from the others' tents. Burn the hides. I care not if you must burn your females, but you will prepare a sweat fire."

"I will," Zir-Fir said, and called out for warriors to begin fetching timbers from the tents of lesser shamans.

The shamans of G'galas Oopax came to his summons, most weary, all shivering. They did not notice the visitor right away, for they were suddenly merry to discover a sweat in the offing. All except those whose tents were being sacrificed for the cause.

The nosg began to shed their hides and furs, until all were naked to their furry skin. The oldest sat closest to the open blaze that now occupied the center of the pavilion, where Zir-Fir's bed had recently been cleared away.

Already the heat was pulling beads of sweat from the early arrivals. Zir-Fir counted heads, and when the last straggler entered, smelling of milkwine, he secured the tent flap and warded it with swarmlight. None could enter now without him first releasing the magic.

"What occasions this sweat?" asked the eldest Shaman, Rin-Rew. He was a scrawny figure, bent under one hundred and ninety hard years of mountain life. His skull staff lay across his knees, sickly yellow eye-gems barely picking up life from the sweat fire.

Rather than answer, Zir-Fir deferred to the shadow at the back of the tent. Yples had not removed his robes, but his skin did not so much as glisten with sweat. Zir-Fir noted for the first time that the man wore no shoes. His feet were black with filth.

When the man stepped through the circle of shamans, the assemblage began to shout. Several called the swarmlight to their skull staves. This excitement was short lived, for the man produced from his pocket a thing all had heard of, but which none had seen. Not even aged Rin-Rew.

"I present to you shamans this gift," Yples said. "Know you what it is?"

Zir-Fir gaped, so shocked by the object he couldn't form a coherent thought, much less words to voice one. So it fell to old Rin-Rew. "That be *zchelik-sczynn*, may Shish-Jek hear me say it."

Yples smiled with his lips, but not his eyes. "Yes. It is as you say, though I know it as Blackshine mimak." The mushroom was large, phallic, and glossy black with phosphorescent violet splotches over the thick cap. Zir-Fir sucked in a shaky breath as awe and avarice enlivened his bones. Blackshine! Drawings of such a mimak had been passed from shaman to shaman, but those crude likenesses had not captured the frightening beauty of the actual fungus. Even so, there could be no mistaking this specimen for any other. Zir-Fir saw in the other shamans' eyes the same rising desire that flooded him now. The power of the Blackshine was thought to be a hundredfold greater than the most potent red-caps. As did all wurgus, Zir-Fir had cultivated his own secret mimak varieties, but all of them collected would not match the tiniest taste of true Blackshine.

"You shall all imbibe the sacred Blackshine this night," Yples announced.

And then he dropped the mushroom into Zir-Fir's stewpot. The shamans howled. Some with glee, others in horror. For the latter, destroying this one specimen was the ultimate sacrilege, a gob of spit in Shish-Jek's eye. For them it was to declare the great luck of merely beholding the Blackshine insufficient. But they numbered only two, so their concerns were ignored by those who eagerly awaited their sip of the concoction. And in each of those greedy hearts festered a secret belief that given enough power they could unseat Zir-Fir, whom all held in fearful contempt. It was known that he had inherited strong strains of red-caps and that was the only reason he had claimed the title of wurgu in the first place.

Even ancient Rin-Rew harbored the hope that he would treat Zir-Fir to the killing fires of the Blackshine swarmlight. And so it was that the sweat of the tent became a stew of ambition, hatred, envy, and hope. In each shaman's mind came a follow-on idea. If Zir-Fir could fall to their new power, then why not Razk-Ka too? He was Yiothizandra's Prime, but where was that wicked fire queen anyway? Captured, probably dead.

They all hated Razk-Ka, not only for leading them to defeat, but also for requiring them to stay in this frozen war camp for so long. *Yes,* each mused to himself, *once full of the Blackshine power, I will depose Zir-Fir, and Razk-Ka after him. And since I'm purging the nosg of those two, why not thin out a few more? There are too many wurgus and too many g'galasi as it is. Yes. It would be well to unite them under one supreme wurgu. Me!*

Rin-Rew thought this, or something very much like it, and so too did Sik-Pok, Cril-Swyb, Plof-Grum, Suli-Frip, Wi-Polk, and Grimno-Li. In the vile sweat Yples had so tainted with the Blackshine, they all thought the same. Each saw himself as supreme, bowing only to Shish-Jek, who had likely been waiting for just such a savior to unite the nosg under one firm claw before she would deign to favor them with her smile again.

Yples interrupted these thoughts by sneakily lifting the stewpot from the heat with magic feats. None of the shamans liked to see such strange powers at work, but their consternation was short-lived, for the pot lowered in front of Zir-Fir. A bone ladle was slanted into the steaming brew. Rin-Rew barked a complaint that he should be first, as he was oldest. "The sweat tent knows no rank but age."

Zir-Fir took up the ladle, saying only, "Then come take it from me."

Yples smiled darkly at this exchange. "All of you must drink of the broth and eat of the Blackshine meat. One mouthful is all you may take now. There will be more later."

Zir-Fir trembled as he lifted the spoon to his gnarled mouth. The bubbling broth scalded his lips and cooked the surface of his tongue. The flavor of the sauk meat did little to mask the acrid bitterness of the Blackshine. Zir-Fir mastered his gags and swallowed. The brew tore down his throat like molten iron, and he choked and moaned and wept. But he kept it down.

The pot floated to Rin-Rew, who lost his sour look as he took up the ladle. And so the pot passed from shaman to shaman. All struggled against the poisonous flavor and searing heat of it, but only two spilled their mouthful onto the floor. In their greed they bent and slurped from the carpet of furs as much as they could, clamping claws over their fasciculating lips to hold in by force what their reflex sought to expel. One of them failed, and he cried out in humiliation at his own rank weakness of stomach. But even worse was the knowledge that the others here would know the Blackshine power long before he'd had another turn at the pot. Weeping, he covered his head with a blanket and mumbled imprecations at the memory of his dead father, who also had been weak of stomach.

For Zir-Fir, these antics were a vague distraction. For his eyes were locked upon the sweat fire, seeking the onset of the Blackshine swarmlight. Even the strongest red-cap was usually slow to awaken, but he had already been opened by earlier doses of mimak tea. He expected the Blackshine to make itself known very soon.

Rin-Rew sat across from him, small black eyes also fixed on the flame. They both knew this was a race. Zir-Fir had been favored by several seconds, but every shaman fell to mimak at his own pace. Rin-Rew was notorious for slipping under very quickly. He was also known to have a weak swarmlight, even under the strongest strains. But this was Blackshine! Zir-Fir knew it could be enough to give even weak Rin-Rew enough fire to burn a hole through his head.

Zir-Fir implored the goddess who had abandoned his kind to hear him and grant him the glorious sight of the mimak. "Shish-Jek hear me! Quickly now." All the others had now slurped down their share. Yples had floated the pot back to the dung-fired stove.

And then it came over him, a blurring of air as the fire seemed to sweep toward him in a rush. Leaning away, mouth forming a tight circle, he let out a whoosh of air. Rin-Rew did likewise as his mind exploded into the realm of swarmlight. Zir-Fir sought to harness the power, fill his skull staff with it. He would melt Rin-Rew before the old bastard could attack.

But the Blackshine swarmlight was beyond the grip of his sight.

"The first of you to surrender will surely be lord of you all," Yples said. His voice came from all directions. Zir-Fir could no longer see the others, nor even the fire. The interior of the sauk-hide tent had been replaced by a swirl of color and repeating patterns. Jagged-edged shapes flew at him, revealing within their seams repetitions of their larger outlines. And these too rushed toward him, and in infinite cycles revealed still more seams that blossomed with patterns.

Yples voice boomed: "You will all succumb, no use fighting it. Surrender, friends. Surrender and be free. The hour of Annihilation draws near. Until then there will be only one truth for you. It is the only truth, the bedrock of life. Do you know what it is?"

Zir-Fir's skin began to burn. He screamed and flailed. His cries were not the only ones. Rin-Rew howled across from him, shrieked as if he'd fallen into the sweat-fire itself. And so too did the others.

"Do you know the truth?" Yples asked again.

The seams of the ever repeating vision went abruptly black, widening as they flew toward Zir-Fir, filling his vision. And he felt reoriented, finally. The vision was not flying toward him; Zir-Fir was falling into it. The chasm below was a lightless void, widening, and widening until there was no horizon. There was only the sucking void. And from within it reached black tendrils. *Yes!* they whispered. *Embrace us and be free.*

Zir-Fir suddenly knew the answer to Yples's question. His agonized howls cut off and calm settled over him like a shroud. The blackness curled into his sight, and he gently directed it toward his skull staff. The eye-gems dimmed from sapphire to black.

He spoke: "Suffering. The truth is suffering."

"You have done it," Yples said. "Rise, Zir-Fir, Blackshine shaman."

He obeyed, blinking to clear his vision. The tent had returned, as had the others. The fire still burned, but Zir-Fir no longer sweated in the heat. The others rose one by one as the truth was revealed to them. Gone was the intention to overthrow anyone. Gone was all ambition save one.

"Will you please annihilate me?" Zir-Fir asked, a low stirring in his gut the only emotion he could muster. Hope for his own end of suffering.

"Soon, my friend. Soon all of us will be released from suffering. The agony of existence will be relieved. This is truly your *aggalamas-alamas.*"

Zir-Fir believed the man. Nothing had ever felt so true before. The real redemption of the nosg would not be to reclaim the lands of men. That would merely exchange one suffering existence for another. No, the Blackshine had showed them that existence itself was the intolerable state of the nosg. The only ambition worth pursuing was the end of all existence. The Revulsion promised only that. The end of all suffering.

"What must I do to bring the glorious day?" he asked.

Yples again smiled without it reaching his eyes. "Your lesser shamans must imbibe the Blackshine. Each of your gr'hils must be opened. Even the warriors for whom the swarmlight is an unexplorable realm. All must succumb and be free. G'galas Oopax is the first, but you will bring the glory of the truth to the other g'galasi."

Zir-Fir thrust the butt of his staff into the ground and cried with unrestrained joy. And soon the others joined him, raising a cacophony that thrilled through the overhanging ice shelf far above. It released a fang of ice that exploded onto a cluster of tents not a hundred paces to the north, liquifying the nosg huddling within. Zir-Fir feared not, for if death came to him in such a manner, then it was surely the will of Shish-Jek.

But no more ice fell that night, and by morning all the shamans of the G'galas Oopax had been opened to the Blackshine. Lord Yples revealed to them that he possessed a large sack full of the precious mimak.

"You will come with me, Zir-Fir. You and two others. I have special work for you far to the south."

Yples opened a black square in the air and beckoned them to step through.

7

IN RETURN FOR HER MERCY

The stink of Cheapsgate was different on Winternight.

Instead of the stench of fish oil lanterns and burning trash, the air was redolent of woodsmoke. Instead of the usual dinner smells of boiled cabbage and sludge-fish stew, there arose the hearty odor of atlen skewers with onion.

Folk saved coin all year for this night of revelry, scrimping copper plugs and scavenging driftwood from the shore of Sourwater Inlet to make for one night of delectable—by Cheapsgate standards—eating. Instead of a moldy crust of bread, fish-cheese, and watered ale, even the poorest would enjoy a bite of pike-fish and a thimble of trezz.

Kila was thankful that she'd always had more than that, for she had been able to steal enough coin for good food. Once, she and Wen had appropriated an entire roast atlen chick, enough meat for a week. They'd eaten it all in one gut busting night and slept through the next day like old hounds in a patch of sun.

The smells of better quality food emanated from one particular area of Cheapsgate. Dox Viller's hive of murderers occupied a territory of three square acres in the center of the slums. Kila had steered wide of it for years, well aware of the unmarked boundary where foul hands might clamp over one's mouth and drag one down into an inescapable horror.

Dox's influence was known to reach into Terriside, and all the way to the Westbunk, where he had involuntary allies within the city Watch. Blackmail was his preferred weapon with such men, often alloyed with bribes of fleshly pleasure. Within his Cheapsgate compound, Dox was the absolute law.

Kila had no reason to fear the place now, as powerful as she was. But the old cautions were hard to put out of her body. The nervous bubbles in her stomach came on without regard to what she had become.

In the center of the compound was an open courtyard, a rare roofless space in the continuous run of interconnected rooftops of the slums. She dropped onto the ground, softening the fall with a bend of her knees. Her hand rested lightly on the hilt of her shadline blade. A few of Viller's Killers leaned against support beams of an overhanging awning made of crate lids, ship-builder's scraps, and oiled sailcloth. The hot miasma of debauchery spilled from three doorways, smokey, trezzy, and heavy with the sweaty odor of unwashed men.

"I'm Kila Sigh. I've come to see Dox," she said to the closest man. He wore the gutter tattoo on his right cheek. His receding hair, wispy and gray, lay upon a spotted scalp. He was clear-eyed, unlike his compatriots. He took down a whale oil lantern from its hook and held it forth to better see her. She was in her black jacket and trousers; the glossy ravens embroidered on her sleeves flamed in the ruddy glow.

The man swept his tongue across his upper lip and nodded. "He been 'spectin' ya fer sev'ral weeks."

Kila motioned him to lead the way. He shrugged a little and nodded at the others to fall in behind her. The route through the maze of trezz dens, brothel compartments, and smoke-filled lounges made her head feel full of clouds. Whatever was in the smoke, it made its victims glassy-eyed and dull. Several men and women of good dress watched her pass without the slightest recognition. These were Dox's thralls from Terriside, moneyed folk who came here for indulgences unavailable within the city proper.

Viller's men were posted throughout. There was food everywhere, all fresh, and cooked with great skill. Kila had heard of the fabled kitchens here. She had known folk who had joined up with Dox just for the food. Whether the price of their honor was worth it, only they could say.

Kila had been within these walls only once before, long ago. That had been upon a Winternight as well. Binni Keel had traded a lovely dress for Kila's street-urchin clothes so that she could flit around Cheapsgate without drawing notice. Unfortunately for Binni, Dox had believed that Kila had recently murdered one of his sons. It wasn't true, but Dox didn't need such justification for the sick pleasures he had planned. Thinking Binni was Kila, he had her abducted and tied to a chair in his bedroom. Then he'd released his infamous hounds to slowly tear her apart. Wen had saved Binni's life and returned her to her father's greathouse. But Dox hadn't suffered any repercussions. He was untouchable.

Tonight was all about repercussions.

For too long Kila and her loved ones had been misused by the world. If she'd learned one thing fighting the Hargothe and Yiothizandra, it was the folly of merely eluding one's enemies. If you awaken to find a spider on your pillow, you do not return to bed until you've found its curled up corpse. Why should it be different with even more dangerous enemies?

Kila's guide asked her to wait outside a sliding door covered with translucent paper. A soft orange glow lit up the panels, oddly homey and comforting in this den of villainy.

She decided to go along with the false politeness of her reception. The man was probably warning Dox that he was about to die, but there would be no escape. Would he call upon his men to attack her? Would he sic his dogs on her?

Let him try.

The door slid aside and the man beckoned her in. Dox Viller, self-proclaimed Lord of Cheapsgate, sat in a throne-like chair amidst a finely constructed and luxuriously appointed bedchamber. His immense body was covered by a silky gown of blue-green which lay open from neck to navel. A pale expanse of hairy chest and belly protruded into the room. Kila wanted to drive her dagger into that flesh, but what she saw propped next to the man prompted her to relax her grip on Cayne. She ceased clenching her jaw, too, as a shocked inhalation parted her lips.

Leaning next to Dox's huge wooden chair was a painting. It depicted two men in formal pose wearing what looked like ship captains' greatcoats.

Dox's throaty chuckle joined the low warning rumbles of two hounds sitting to his right. Their ears stood forward, bodies tense.

"You are Wenton Sigh's adopted girl, no?" Dox said cordially. "A pity about your brother. I remember him as a sharp lad. But that was a long time ago, back when your father and I ran schemes together."

The painting was of Dox—much thinner and younger— standing next to a man Kila had not seen in years. Her father. Hair swept back, firm jawed and sharp eyed. The likeness captured his presence, which had commanded every eye when he entered a room. Kila had adored him. He had made her feel loved. More than that, she'd felt *heard* when he listened.

"He was a friend to me, after a fashion," Dox said. "I was no friend to him. Ha ha."

"Wen told me you betrayed my father in some business

dealing or another," Kila said absently, still absorbed by the painting. "I don't know the specifics."

"That is well, for the specifics of my betrayal were even more underhanded than your brother knew. I am, after all, a *terrible* man." He threw his head back and roared with glee. The dogs jerked their heads toward him and let out antsy moans. Dox snapped his fingers and they fell silent. After his humor subsided, he furrowed his brow and patted his knee. "The last time I saw Wenton I told him I would be willing to look after you. In a way, you could say I'm your father."

As he again shook with laughter, Kila couldn't decide if he was mad or simply cursed with a terrible sense of humor.

His humor vanished with another finger snap. "Leave us, Jerrip. If Highest Sigh wishes to kill me, or you, there isn't ought we can do to stop her." He wiggled his fingertips at the man, shooing him out. He put on a mock frown. "Ah, but isn't it just the way of things that daughters eventually turn on their fathers."

"Yer not my father. Ya never looked after me. Tried to kill me once, that I know of."

He shrugged, lips pulling down like a bull mastiff. "I have hundreds of children. Maybe you're one of them, maybe not. Who knows where Wenton got you, but I wouldn't be surprised if he became enamored of one of my cast-off women. It would be just like him to love another man's bastard girl. Ah, I see I've offended you, daughter. It was not my intention."

"I'm not yer daughter. My mother was never in Cheapsgate."

"So certain, are you?"

She wasn't about to tell him her mother was the demigoddess Semūin. She owed Dox nothing, no explanations. It was clear now that he simply sought to put her on the back foot by insinuating he might be her father. He knew she had come to kill him. He would try anything to escape her wrath.

Striding toward the obese criminal, she noted an enormous ceramic flagon perched on the armrest of his chair. It gave off the sickly sweet stench of apple-cinnon whisky. The panting hounds' breath stank, hot and sour. She wondered how many men and women these two had killed. How many Dox had watched being devoured.

"The painting is my gift to you," Dox said. "Hire one of those womanish artists in Terriside to blot me out of it if you wish. Have him daub your likeness over mine. Try Farlthly on West Ridle. He's a mealy mouthed bastard, but he does good work. If you can keep him off his slymok smoke for a fortnight."

Talking, talking. The man couldn't stop talking, the confident smile never slipping from his purple lips. Kila realized he truly thought he could talk his way out of justice. He actually believed this painting could buy his life.

"One of your men, Varl Akton, tried to kill me by treshing my friends."

"I heard whispers of that. I assure you, daughter, I had nothing to do with that particular job. His contract came to him directly. I would never have sanctioned such a roundabout scheme. If he was to kill you, he should have done it with his own blade. Do you have any notion what it cost me to procure a shadline blade in the first place? I would never waste having a member of your cult in my employ merely to kill you. There'd be no gain in it for me." He let out an enormous laugh, then he made a falsely conciliatory face. "My apologies for the misbehavior of Varl Akton. Were he here, I'd give him to you to do with as you wished, sweetlight."

"Do not call me that! I'M NOT YER DAUGHTER!" Her power uncoiled like a furious serpent, lashing out with fangs of fire. The flame shot forth from her outstretched hands, engulfing the man in scintillating orange. Oily glee leapt into her mind. *Yes! Roast his skin with flame. Dissolve the bonds of his flesh and drift him away. Make him finer than dust, finer than ash. Slip him into annihilation!*

The Revulsion was an oozing flood that slopped over her mercusine, replacing her flames with a power that vanished the very air through which it passed.

From across Starside came a horrified cry, filling Kila's mind.

NO! Nax commanded.

Shocked into sudden wakefulness, Kila recoiled and tried to shake free of the hateful power. It clung to her like tar. The coldness of it surged in her, making her mind ice, her heart stillness. Dox would be undone totally, and then this room, this compound. Every soul who occupied its fetid rooms would—

NO! came Nax's declaration again. The cat's sending sliced through the Revulsion, a slender and imperious blade shaving the evil tar away from Kila's mind. A thousandth of a hairsbreadth gap opened. The ice in her mind heated just enough that her heart became sensible to what was human in her. The distinction between what the Revulsion thought right and what Kila knew to be right blurred into her awareness. Just enough that Kila paused, pulling back her Revulsion feat.

Fight it, Kila! Nax screamed in her mind.

Nax's voice was the only light she knew and she drove toward it, seeking the pure mercus. Finding the tattered edge of her mercusine, she pulled and strained until she could draw in a full measure of its light. With will alone she ripped way the sticky tendrils of Revulsion and was free of the last of it. With a mournful cry the vile fingers of blackness retreated, leaving Kila gasping between sobs of relief.

Suddenly emptied of both rage and terror, Kila fell to one knee. Her belly convulsed, bringing up her earlier sips of Winternight whisky and half of her dinner.

Dox trembled on his chair, somehow still alive. "Oh. Ha!" He had slipped down in his seat, face red, belly looking sunburned.

The hair of his torso was singed away. "It worked!" he cried. "All these years, I had dared not try it. Ha. Lovely. It worked!" He lifted an arm and shook one sleeve, letting a silver bracelet slide low upon his wrist. Kila heard the faint hum of its mercus charge. A mercus relic, warded to provide a negating shield around the wearer. But that should not have saved him from the Revulsion.

Dox stared down at a patch of ruin where a rug had once been. The missing section showed the progress of Kila's Revulsion feat. The destruction ended less than an inch from Dox's bare toes, which peeped from the hem of his silky robe. Nax's intervention had saved him.

It had saved Cheapsgate as well. Maybe all of Starside. For the Revulsion would not have stopped with Dox Viller. It would have urged Kila to erase the man's whole compound, and from there the rest of Cheapsgate. It did not know enemy from friend, for it despised all things equally.

Kila stood, noting two shaggy tails protruding from under the bed. Dox's hounds whimpered in their hiding spot, but neither dared to poke a snout into Kila's view.

Smoke wafted in the room, thick enough to make her cough. Her fire attack had charred Dox's chair. "No," she said, gutted to see the painting of her father destroyed, the canvas gone, the remains of the frame only two sticks of smoldering wood in a pile of ash.

Yet Dox lived. The unfairness of it rekindled her fury.

She drew Cayne.

Dox's eyes widened at the sight of it. His purple lips quivered up into a smile. Fear paled his flaccid cheeks, but his eyes sparkled with eager life. Terror seemed to embolden him. How many times had that impulse saved him, made him take action when lesser men cowered? Even now he thought he could survive. With genuine good humor he said: "I know Wenton's blade well. Do you have any idea how many times I tried to steal it from him? Such an interesting weapon. Had I known it was a shadline blade back then, I would have had him killed sooner."

Two strides took her to the man. He shrank back in his chair, hand fumbling in his robes. And yet he continued to laugh, delighted by his own fear.

She brought the tip of the blade to his flabby chest, let it hover there so that he could suffer another moment of torture, knowing that death approached.

Beneath the phlegmy rasp of his nervous chuckles, a harsh tone arose. Like the dissonant ring of two hateful little bells, faint but clear. But this ringing didn't fade. It sustained. She looked down at her blade, noticed how the black steel gleamed. Unreflecting yet somehow shiny. This contradiction was not new to Kila. Over the years she had grown accustomed to the weapon's peculiar nature. But this bell tone was new. Squinting at the razor edge, she was sure the sound came from the very apex of that sharpness. Dox's eyes were on the weapon, too, but not for the same reason. The hounds had fallen silent. The sounds of revelry elsewhere in the compound fell to nothing as the clashing chime drew Kila's entire focus.

She had come here to kill Dox. The mercus had failed; the Revulsion had been stopped; and now the blade was singing. Yes, the tones were changing as the competing pitches lifted and fell. The melody was not that of a song, but of a language. No consonants distinguished syllable from syllable, but Kila knew the blade was telling her something with this painful dissonance.

To kill Dox? Not to Kill Dox?

She pulled her eyes from the blade, saw Dox shivering, still slumping low in his throne. His lips had loss their purplish flush and were now pale, with sticky white residue at the corners. Jeweled rings hung heavily on every fat finger. He laughed nervously. Withdrawing a hand from his robes, he brought forth a slender dirk. He thrust it to parry Cayne away from him. The effort was effete and did little but move the tip of Kila's blade an inch before she forced it back. He jabbed out at her, but his reach was limited by his own grotesque mass. He slashed at her arm, but she evaded with no difficulty.

A new stench punctured the air. He'd soiled himself. This produced another laugh from him, choked off by a round of panting. Sweat boiled upon his forehead.

Fighting back a gag, Kila suddenly envisioned herself from where he sat. Dressed in fine black, damp from the roofway, holding out Cayne, and having just wielded a power that had vanished part of his rug without leaving so much as a frayed edge. She was a terrible, black-garbed apparition, bearing a black blade. A mythical hate-witch come upon a Winternight to devour souls.

"Ah me," she whispered, wincing at the clashing tones of her blade. She pressed the tip into his flesh and the song increased, the dissonance juddering in her skull.

Cayne did not wish to be used this way. She withdrew the blade and slid it back into the sheath. The horrid tones went silent.

Dox panted heavily, pressing a meaty hand to his chest. A trickle of blood oozed from the small puncture she'd made, mixed with the sweat that now dribbled down his paunch. More sweat ran in runnels down his cheeks. Seeing that Kila did not mean to stab him after all, he snapped his fingers. Both hounds burst from under the bed, fangs bared, throats rumbling with growled threats.

Kila raised a finger at them, arching an eyebrow. No mercus, just will. The beasts froze.

"Flee!" she snapped at them, for she did not wish them harm, no matter the cruelties to which they had been trained by their master. Something in her voice, perhaps in her very posture, overwhelmed their training. Their growls changed to yelps, and they did flee, tails tucked, nosing through a curtained passageway hidden behind the bed.

Kila turned again to face Dox. She had almost let him live. In return for her mercy, he had sicced his dogs on her.

"Yer a Kil-kissin' idiot," she said. In one motion, she drew Cayne, twirled it into an overhand grip, and drove the blade into Dox's chest. The blade let out dissonant squeals that drove into Kila's ears like spikes. But she didn't care what Cayne wanted or didn't want.

Dox's eyes squeezed shut. One heavy hand fought with hers, the other lashed out with his dirk. She caught his wrist and wrested the blade away, reversed it and drove it in next to Cayne.

"That's for my father," she said through bared teeth.

The shrieking tones grew, squealing like the rust-bound hinges of an ancient iron gate. The assault grew too much to bear and she yanked Cayne free of Dox's chest. The wound was bloodless, for Cayne had drunk deeply.

Dox let out a final gasp and slumped to one side, knocking his flagon of whisky to the floor. The sickly sweet smell of apple-cinnon burned Kila's nose. She stepped away from the body, sheathing Cayne. Her mind was roiling with unconnected thoughts. Of Father, of Wen, of Henley, and Nax, and Ell, and Quinn, and Parlo Odok, and Finta, and the Hargothe. The face of Ahl-Mish-Lah, the hateful nosg shaman who had once kept Kila prisoner, floated before her, laughing in approval.

As a girl in Cheapsgate, the idea of killing Dox would have been as fanciful as seeing a dragon. It would have made her a hero.

She didn't feel like a hero. Her mouth was stale, her head ached as if she'd indulged in too much wine. Her belly rebelled at the sight of Dox's bloated corpse, and at the ruin of the only likeness of her father she had ever seen.

Kila tested the mercus again, gently reaching for it without drawing it to form her next bolt. The Revulsion rose, but she easily pushed it aside, for her heart held only grief.

Viller was dead, but nothing had changed for the better. If anything, she had made things worse. She felt the ragged edges of dread flutter over her like the shadows of dragon wings.

8

—————

THE OPPOSITE OF LIFE

One thing about watch duty they had never mentioned when Devin joined the Iron Scholars: it's brutally boring.

He adjusted the ancient leather belt again. The damned thing pinched the bulge of fat around his waist. He'd pulled it nearly to his chest because the sword it supported was long and he was short. Kil-damned thing was sharp now at least. Nothing like an invasion of nosg to snap a scholar out of his daydreams. And now he was playing at being a soldier.

Soldier. What a trezz-lark that notion was. They called themselves Iron Scholars because the founder of the order, Richliu Dasn, had been an actual soldier before retiring here to study the stars. The Hackwatch had been long-abandoned when he moved in. But the armory still held swords and axes and hammers and armor. Any scholar wishing to join had to train in the martial arts. The Iron Scholars had been feared and respected once. These days they might be feared, but mostly because of wild rumors. Devin certainly hadn't seen any of his brothers eating human flesh. Yes, the Hackwatch was cold, damp, and haunted—of that he had no doubt—but it also had the elnisian Stardome, and that was all he cared about. And in truth, he didn't care much about that either.

He hiked the sword belt up again.

Devin had missed most of the nosg attack, fortunately. He'd slept right through it, up until someone started screaming about their severed arm just outside his room. He'd opened the door, seen the blood, puked up his lentil stew, then fainted like a hammer-struck hog.

Later he'd come out into the Hackwatch to find bodies everywhere, most of them nosg. The rest were Iron Scholars and those odd shadline folk who'd been holding their meeting in the Stardome.

Brother Gignon had announced the new watch schedule within hours. And a new training schedule the next dawn. Nobody was happy about either. These wall-walks hadn't felt the boots of a patrol guard in fifty years.

Devin kept a hand on the crumbling merlons to support himself, ill-fitting boots scuffing stone as he trudged along. A cold wet wind cut across the wall, burdened with fog. Watchfires burned at intervals along the wall, ruining his night vision. But orders were orders. Who was he to tell Brother Gignon anything?

In fact, *how* was he to tell him anything? They'd all sworn themselves to silence when they'd taken their oaths. He'd come here to study, not to pretend to be a warrior. The whole "Iron Scholar" moniker was pure folly. And yet here he was, stalking the battlements as if he knew what he was doing.

He paused by the next fire and nodded to Scholar Hill who fed logs into the blaze. Devin roasted his hands and backside for a minute before continuing on.

The compound inside the wall was lit for festival it seemed.

So many torches, lanterns, and braziers burned it took half the brotherhood to keep it all fueled. The rest slept. But despite their efforts the dreary gray stone buildings lay more in blackness than in orange light, and where the firelight didn't reach . . . Devin shivered and pulled his cloak more tightly around himself. Cursing his ill fortune at having been born a fifth son, he continued his patrol.

Thing was, his brother Reggil would have been better suited to this life as both warrior and scholar. Devin didn't much care about looking at the stars and reading portents in them. As far as he could tell, Brother Gignon didn't use the information for any purpose. In fact, if the stars truly told the future, then the Hackwatch should be bursting with scholars and furnished with gilded chamber pots. Instead it was a ruin. A haunted, Kil-cursed ruin.

Devin turned the corner at a decapitated watch tower and proceeded along the southern stretch. He hated this part because a hill topped with a flat stone rose above the height of the wall just inside the compound. It obstructed his view of the interior and so cut off the light of the timid torches.

"Fifty paces," he muttered, too anxious to be concerned about his vow of silence. There weren't many who kept strictly to the vows these days. Devin couldn't remember the last time he'd tossed back his morning dose of woodworm brew. It worked, he knew that much. Made any sort of lustful arousal impossible. Also made a man maggoty pale. Caused weird dreams, too. Devin dealt with his human needs the same way most of the scholars here did. By himself. He couldn't afford the other options available in Tearling, and he didn't go in for other men. They stank. The whole Hackwatch stank.

"Forty paces," he said.

The next watchfire was weak. Too weak. Brother Jirry must have fallen asleep again. Or he was drunk. Or both. Devin resolved to give him a good kick. The anger bolstered his nerve and he squared his shoulders a bit despite the clammy feeling of sinister eyes looking at his spine.

"Thirty more."

His boots didn't fit very well. They belonged to the brotherhood and were sized very large so that any man on watch duty might fit them. Devin's feet were no bigger than his sister's. He'd stuffed socks in the toes to take up some space, but the damn things were heavy.

The flat-topped cemetery stone loomed to his right now. Rumor had it the monarch of Starside had been murdered up there during the nosg attack. Another rumor said a beautiful woman had sneaked in after the attack and gone up to the rock and leapt off. Her body was never found.

Jirry said her ghost sometimes came onto the wall. But he said that only to scare the patrol walkers. Still . . . Devin picked up his pace. These heavy boots were about to haunt Jirry's ribs.

Panting from his effort and from more than a little fear, Devin strove toward the fire. He'd take care of Jirry. He'd kick him like the rabid dog he was. Kick him in the head, the way Devin's father had done to him.

The weak firelight caught plumes of frost coming from Devin's mouth. Strange. It was still winter upon the Kovi-Mest, but it hadn't been this cold just a few paces back.

The chill in the air carried the scent of a northern winter, sterile and bleak. Devin hadn't felt any such cold since coming south to this place. Tearling and the Hackwatch were mostly rainy and windy in winter. It rarely snowed. Now sizzling ice flakes snapped against his cheeks. The wall-walk was becoming slick.

"Ten paces." The fire looked much farther way than that. Odd.

Cemetery rock was behind him now. The interior of the

Hackwatch lay to his right. Or it should have. But there was no light down there now.

A shriek rose then cut off from below.

Devin ran the last five paces to the fire, discovered the timbers barely sustaining flame, though they should have towered over his head.

Kil take his vows. "Jirry! Where are you, you mangey cur?"

The last lick of flame retracted into the failing embers. Devin tucked his hands under his arms and stamped his feet. "Ji-Ji-Jirry? Why did you—?"

A heavy footfall sounded behind him. So! Jirry was playing tricks, was he?

"You daft rabbit!" Devin said, spinning and clenching his fists. Youngest of five brothers, he knew a thing or two about brawling. He would teach young Jirry not to play him again.

But it wasn't Jirry.

It was a man in thin white robes. Gray bearded and gaunt, with sunken eyes and small round scars on his temples. "Relax, son," he said in a kindly voice. But his tone carried the sound of breaking bones and the rasp of stone upon stone.

"Who are you?" Devin demanded, hand going to his hilt.

"I'm the opposite of life."

A faint buzz tickled the back of Devin's mind. A Donse Master had told him long ago that feeling was the mercusine. Devin had failed to grasp it, but he always felt when a merculyn was working one of their tricks. But this was different, for it grated and scraped in his consciousness, like a rusty portcullis being forced up in a succession of short, painful hefts.

The man's face went slack. His hands gripped Devin's head.

Nausea struck Devin's belly even as a desert chill claimed his throat. He clamped his mouth shut against both as he fumbled to draw his sword. But his numb fingers couldn't grip it. His arm lacked the strength to pull it free anyway. It was all he could do to remain standing, for his knees threatened to buckle.

A thin blade-like touch pressed between his lips, and no matter how he strained to squeeze them together, it penetrated. An unresistable strength pried his mouth open, the invisible blade expanding even as it drove down his rebelling gullet, defying the convulsions in his abdomen that sought to bring up his greasy dinner of ham, beans, and spinach.

He needed to be sick, but the urgent and absolute requirement to throw up was denied to him. Flashing over with cold sweat, he fell to his knees and clutched his belly. Still the cold blackness drove into him, down, down, filling his guts, his limbs, his chest, and finally chilling his head until he was nothing at all but suffering sickness.

The change happened instantly. Devin's thoughts turned cold, distant. His eyes blinked several times. He got to his feet. His small hand—small as his sister's—drew the blade. His lips moved, but it wasn't the old Devin who spoke: *"Rachizhach! Stilik noschk."*

Angry arcs of red plasma coursed up and down the rusty iron blade, strengthening and honing it. Devin's mind and body stood very still, not breathing. Breath would never be necessary again, just as beats of his useless heart would no longer be required. His revulynic bolts faded, leaving the blade silvery even in the blackness.

He sheathed the blade. "I am Devin."

"I am Lord Yples," the old man replied.

Together they continued on his patrol route, stopping by each fire to awaken the scholar posted there. Within half an hour there were two more revulyns among the scholars, and two dozen reviled, those who possessed no mercus but who could wield a weapon.

Devin descended from the wall and continued his search. Only five more of the hundred and seventy-nine Iron Scholars possessed the spark. These were too willful to turn, so they were killed.

One by one the watchfires burned out. And from within the walls and ground of the Hackwatch rose a black fog. It bulged through alleys, and into windows, and filled up every hollow, save one. The Stardome, the elnisian structure that had stood here a thousand years before the rest of the man-built obscenity that was the Hackwatch had been constructed.

The Stardome resisted. The mural of stars continued to move across the inside of the dome, showing constellations that could not be seen in the clouded sky. The Revulsion pressed hard against the outer walls, surged at the door, squeezed the Stardome from all sides.

The Stardome resisted. A crack streaked across the dome. But it held.

Devin chose five reviled, each armed with revulynic blades. These men strode with greater strength than their human selves ever had. They filled bottles with Revulsion fog to carry with them. They breathed deeply of it, like men charmed by slymok smoke.

Yples took Devin and his reviled guard deep into the bowels of the Hackwatch, descending beneath the cellars of man to the ancient elnisian halls. It pained Devin to penetrate so deeply into the Hated Folk's realm, but he sniffed from his bottle and endured the pain.

The Derslin Wheel nearly sent him running back. But he soldiered onward. For the mission Lord Yples assigned to him was necessary. Too long had the light of life disturbed the restful Evernight. The chaos and noise of this realm served nothing but the Great Lie. Devin would bring the cold eye of Truth to bear.

Yples worked his magic upon one of the columns at the center of the Derslin Wheel. A black tear appeared in the air. "Bring the child god to me."

Devin and his men stepped through.

9

NOTHING TO PROTECT

The fire had gone out. The cats had slipped into Saiya's bed to share her warmth. Henley sensed Kila was still in the city, too far away to reach through the bond. He put the monarch's note on the side table next to the official silver letter tray so that it wouldn't be mixed in with the dozens of others she received each day. The ones that ended up as bedding for the cats. Every merchant and Radiant in the city wrote to her, frequently. Each sought some favor, or teased some bit of gossip they hoped would intrigue her enough to visit them.

A far off bell tolled the hour, two bells morning. His eyes were gritty with exhaustion, head achy and feeling stuffed with wool. But his mind jittered between anxious notions. Seeking sleep would be pure folly. Perhaps Kila had the right of it. Fresh, cold air might help clear out the dust.

He looped his satchel over his shoulder, felt the heft of the Motherlight press into his side. He'd go find Kila, tell her about Pennie and his meeting with Her Enlightened.

He chose a destination he knew well in Terriside, a park opposite the plot where his family home had once stood. From there he'd have a better sense of where Kila was.

But when he arrived in Terriside, Kila's presence had moved west, back to the Citadel. She must have dymensed in the opposite direction at the same instant. He snorted a humorless laugh. It seemed they were always on opposite tacks these days.

The air was full of smoke from campfires across the street. The lot where his home had once stood was now an encampment of some sort. Not a usual occurrence in this wealthy district in upper Terriside. He wondered if it was a Winternight celebration, neighbors taking advantage of the newly opened space to get out of their overheated drawing rooms. Voices were raised in song near the center where a bonfire danced. The scene struck a high-pitched dissonance within him, like an ill-tuned nyckelharpa. The last time he'd been here a much greater fire had raged in that spot. Now the ruins of the old house had been carted away, probably by these same neighbors who didn't like it spoiling their view.

As the sole heir to the Mast estate, Henley still owned the charred foundations and the small park that surrounded it. His father's trezz import business was gone, as were all the ships, either sunk by the Keel family or sold by his creditors.

He hadn't intended to inspect the grounds, but he was pulled across the street by indignant fury. This was his property, the last piece of the Mast legacy remaining. He would not tolerate his neighbors making a public park of it for their Winternight frolics.

"Hey there!" he barked at the first face he saw. "This is private property."

His steps slowed as he saw the tents were not the cheerful pavilions of rich merchant families, but were instead the ragged sailcloth shelters of the destitute. A middle-aged man came toward him wrapped in a woolen blanket and scarf tied around his head. He was waving a paper. "I have a charter signed by Administrator Marlow himself giving us permission to camp here." He was weary and irritable, as if he'd had this discussion more than once already this night.

Without thinking, Henley manifested a sphere of mercus light over his shoulder so that he might read the charter. It was as the man said, signed by Marlow.

"Go back to your greathouse, sir," called a young woman. "Let us have the smallest bit of cheer this Winternight."

There was an accent in their voices that Henley knew well. "You're all from Tordain?" He remembered a discussion in the Citadel about refugees straggling into Starside through the Moriterran Pass. Tordain was in full civil war, the capital city itself in flames. And all because Coin Inlina had murdered the Autarch over possession of the Motherlight.

Henley returned the charter to the man. "I apologize for disturbing you. I'll go." And he did go, turning his back on the place that had been his home, leaving behind the childhood memories of Winternights past.

A hand caught his elbow, pulled him around. His mercus light illumined a young woman's face, gaunt and weary, smudged with soot on one cheek. It took him a moment to register the elongated nose and narrow jaw, and recollect the odd beauty the misproportioned features created.

"Terissa Viller?"

"Senny! I knew it was you. Did you know this used to be the Mast greathouse?" She stepped into him, curling an arm through his. She wore an oversized wool coat and a holey scarf. Her hands were bare, knuckles red and raw from living outdoors in winter.

It took him another moment to recall the false name he'd given her when she'd been a serving girl at The Wilde Moon inn in Tordain. She had been the most shameless—and most charming—flirt he'd ever met.

"My name is Henley," he said. "I'm Henley Mast, in fact."

She made a roll of her eyes. "I knew that. Yiqa told me. She never mentioned you were a Donse Master, though. That light is lovely."

"I'm not a Donse Master. Is Yiqa here?" The Alnassi killer had accompanied him to Tordain, had sneaked him into the dome of the Katteshan Throne. He'd returned to Starside with her and Coin Inlina, but she'd slipped away without a goodbye. Which had suited him just fine. The woman had not displayed the slightest friendliness, or even courtesy, during their time together.

Terissa led him through the perimeter of tents, past the irritable man with his charter, to the opposite side of the park, where his father's rose bushes had once encircled a reflecting pond. The roses had been ripped out, the pond drained. Now the trampled, muddy ground was covered with make-shift shelters. Terissa didn't let go of his arm as she ducked under a lean-to of limbs covered with a tarpaulin. Lying next to a small fire, amidst a pile of woolen blankets and tatty furs, was a slight, gray-haired woman. A veil covered her lower face, but Henley well knew the eyes. Gray, steely.

He untangled himself from Terissa's grasp and knelt by the Alnassi woman. She didn't acknowledge him, just stared back at him. Her lips were pale from sickness.

"She staggered into The Wilde Moon a ten-day after that strange mercus battle in the Katteshan Throne," Terissa said. She checked her next words and gave him a narrow glare. "Were you involved in that? I'll wager you were, seeing as you're a Donse Master. You never came back to the inn. We were surprised to find your horse in the stables outside the city. I was glad of it. Who'd want to ride behind Yiqa the whole way to Starside? Not me. You can count your skillets and add ten from my pocket if I'd do that willingly. Yiqa said your horse was called Sassy. Odd name for such a sweet beast, if you ask me. Yiqa had to be tied to her mount. No name for that horse. But who can understand half of what Yiqa says? She called it 'horssse' so that's his name now. She had to sell them both." Terissa looked fondly at the Alnassi woman and shook her head. "Poor thing. She sure can soak up pain. If I were in her skin, I'd have been screaming for a bowl of slymok smoke or somesuchthing to dull the pain. She just clamps her jaw and takes it, Ori bless the tough old crow."

Henley didn't know which shocking statement to react to first. Terissa filled his gape-jawed hesitation with a continuation of her narrative. "By the time Yiqa came back, the city was burning like Kil's kingdom. Battles in the street—children motherless—rapes galore—and so much looting! Even the looters were getting looted. She must have fought her way through it. One of her ankles was broken. An arm was shattered. She bled from several gashes. Mistress Sqinn and I did the best we could to mend her, but Yiqa did the most. She's masterful with brews and tinctures and whatnot. But there's only so much that even ferneater magic can do. She hasn't spoken much since she fell off of Horssse in the Moriterran Pass. She swallowed a pinch of herbs and went all glassy like you see her here. She's awake, but doesn't seem to see anyone—doesn't eat unless I put broth to her lips. Only twice has she come back into her own skull enough to say anything. 'Starside,' she said. And now we're here, thank Til and Ori and all the rest for it. Tordain's a right mess and I'm glad to be rid of it, truth be told. I thought I might see if my pa would acknowledge my existence. Maybe I could find a shack in Cheapsgate. But the monarch was nice and let us camp here. I hope she's got a thousand more lots like it. We're the first to get here from Tordain, not the last. We had horses, most are on foot."

"You said she came back a ten-day after the Katteshan Throne battle?" Yiqa had to have begun her return journey to

Tordain the very night he'd brought her back to Starside. "Why did she return?"

Terissa shrugged. "You know Yiqa. Not much for conversation. I tried to take her to the Baths of Ori when we got here, but the Watch won't let us through Dunne Medow Plaza. We're too shabbily dressed. Did you see the Cathedral? People say that Kila Sigh girl destroyed it."

"She damaged it," he said absently. "Yiqa needs out of the cold. I can take her to the Baths. She was loyal to the Voluptuary and used to stay there when she was in Starside."

"You think those tin-helmed men of the Watch will let us through? No offense, Henley Mast, but you are just a merchant, and by the looks of your greathouse, not one of much standing. Or does being a Donse Master give you privileges?" She nudged him. "You look clean and tidy, though. You must have a flat or room at some inn or another. Just take us there. Yiqa won't take up much room and I don't need my own bed." She said the last with a lift of her brows and a parting of her lips that suggested an endless supply of deep and unrelenting kisses.

"Er, you should recall I'm promised to someone—"

"Still? What a bother! But think on this," she said, flashing her eyes. "She doesn't have to know."

"You are impossible."

She leaned into him, hands curling around the back of his head and pulling his face toward hers. "I'm not only possible, my dear. I'm guaranteed." She kissed his cheek, but there was nothing sisterly in the lingering press of her lips. To his shame, he felt his heart-rate surge in respond to her touch.

He flared his mercus sphere so that she had to cover her eyes against the glare. He used this moment of separation to step away from her. "Terissa, please. Let's just get Yiqa to the Baths. You could benefit from a bit of a dunking yourself. I can get us past Dunne Medow Plaza quite simply."

"You can?"

He gingerly scooped Yiqa up. She had never been a large woman, and a long stretch of illness left her light as pillow. "Gather anything here you wish to take with you."

Terissa glanced around and discovered nothing of interest. "You're all I want in this city."

"Just hold onto my arm for a moment." When she hesitated, he sighed enormously. "Kil's eyes in a bucket. You wouldn't let go of me a moment ago. Just hold onto my arm."

The instant her fingers touched him, he dymensed to the entry of the Baths. Terissa let out a lusty sigh when they reappeared. Her head twisted all around. "Do that again! It's just"—she made a low groaning sound—"thrilling!"

Inside the Baths he found the serene Sensual Renna at the reception desk, flanked by a pair of novitiates. Renna recognized Yiqa instantly and flowed around the desk. She acknowledged Henley with a placid smile. But when her hand touched the Alnassi woman's forehead, her own creased in concern.

"Axli, come take this woman to the Pool of Lumne. She's dying." The young male novitiate took Yiqa from Henley's arms and solemnly carried her toward a steaming pool, one of three in the Dome of the Gentle Goddess. There were only four other patrons at the Baths, elderly folk whose afflictions were so great that they preferred the solace of the Baths to Winternight revelries.

Axli walked down steps into the pool, unconcerned with getting his filmy novitiate's robes soaked. Yiqa's body sank beneath the cloudy white water. The novitiate supported the back of her head so that her face remained above the surface. Yiqa let out a sigh and said something softly. Sensual Renna glided into the pool and dismissed Axli. She began to gently remove Yiqa's soaked clothing, starting with her veil. Her motions were slow and deliberate. Henley was struck that this was a ritual, stripping away more than Yiqa's garments.

"What makes you so certain she's dying?" he asked. "You didn't even use the mercus. Maybe I should take her to Kila—"

Renna didn't look at him, but tugged away Yiqa's trousers and let them sink. None of the woman's nakedness rose above the milky surface. "No Alnassi lay-esh would thank you for interrupting a well-earned death with unwanted mercus healings. I'm surprised she's clung to life this long. I can feel her injuries."

Henley didn't know the customs of the Alnassi, much less one of the feared lay-esh killers. But he trusted Sensual Renna's judgment. "Terissa said Yiqa wanted to come to Starside."

Renna swept a neutral glance over Terissa's face. "You did well to bring her here. She was a favorite of Voluptuary Sinlop's, and loyal to her."

Yiqa blinked several times, as if suddenly waking. "Hennnley Massst," she said, voice clear and strong. "Comme."

When he didn't immediately jump in, Terissa shoved him. "Go. She's dying."

Renna nodded encouragement, and he shed his cloak and satchel before sloshing down the steps. The water was hot, soothing, and smelled faintly of apple blossoms.

"Take hold of her," Renna instructed, guiding one of his hands under Yiqa's head, and the other to the small of her back. Yiqa's skin was smooth, her muscles still proud. Her gray hair fanned out around her, pale face soft and absent of tension for the first time. Sens Renna waded out of the pool and ushered Terissa well away.

Henley stammered vague comforts to the woman, uneasy to be given the responsibility of this moment. He and Yiqa had not been friends. But she was looking at him with soft eyes, the gray irises somehow luminescent in the brazier light of the Dome. "I hat too burrry the Vollluptuuary'sss sssisster."

The Autarch had been Voluptuary Sinlop's sister. Yiqa had made the voyage back to Tordain to make sure the woman had a proper burial. "I would have dymensed you back. I could have protected you."

At this, Yiqa smiled. It was a lovely, feminine smile, almost girlish. "Nnnothing tooo prrotect. Mmy hearrt dite vith Volluptuary Sseenlop." Despite the smile, a tear traced from her eye. "Lettt mmmeee gooo." She shoved weakly at Henley's chest.

He looked to Renna for guidance. She merely nodded, her peaceful face creased only with solemnity. He pulled his hands away. Yiqa floated unsupported, her eyes open, clear. Her smile soft. And then she drifted down, vanishing into the depths of the pool like a bird gliding behind a low-hanging cloud.

"Come out," Renna said. "Lumne's pool will surface her body once it has purified her. Her time is done."

He came out of the pool, absently forming bolts to squeeze the water from his clothes. The novitiate lost his calm for a moment to behold such a feat. Henley took up his things, slung his satchel over his shoulder. The Motherlight felt suddenly very heavy for the cost paid to retrieve it from Tordain. Terissa slipped her arm through his, sniffling and wiping away tears with a grimy kerchief. "We can wait for her to surface, can't we?"

He knew he should return to the Citadel, tell Kila about Pennie. But there was so much roiling emotion coming over his bond with her that he thought better of it. He could tell her later, after she'd slept.

"Yes. We can wait."

10
_____

CANDLE IN THE DARKNESS

Kila stood motionless for a solid minute after arriving back in the parlor of her suite. The fire was burning fiercely now that she'd added a bit of mercus heat to it. She was cold from her damp clothes, but moreso from what she'd done to Dox Viller. Her eyes watched the flames without seeing them, for her thoughts were still in Cheapsgate. Her thumb absently rotated her garnet ring around her pinky. The ring of the Highest of Kil had always been just a bit too large.

Nax lounged atop the pile of letters, eyes half open.

Henley was out in the city, apparently gone looking for her just as she had returned here. Two dancers out of step with each other.

Lately they had avoided the silent message-way of sending across their bond. One could not conceal as much when opening that connection. She wanted to hide her worry from him, and he probably wanted to hide his frustration from her. Silly, since she well knew his thoughts. They were plain on his face, and she knew he could read her just as easily.

He was always guiding conversations back to her duty as a

powerful merculyn, as Highest of Kil, as Saiya's guardian. She didn't want to talk about such things. Her responsibility was over as far as she was concerned. Yioth was captured, hopefully executed by now. The Hargothe was dead. The nosg armies had retreated to the Haelshoks, taking their flights of wyvoks with them. Even the Dragons of Night had vanished. All that remained for her to do was to bring up Saiya to be good instead of evil.

Dox Viller's throaty laugh returned to her, along with a vision of his spit-flecked lips as he slumped in his throne-like chair.

What's the difference between a just killing and murder? she sent to Nax.

Did you eat the flesh you slew?

Ugh! No. What's wrong with you?

A twitchy feeling came over the bond. Nax squinted at her, then sent: *Killing is killing. It's a good way to get food. Sometimes it's interesting.*

I shouldn't have asked you. You play with your prey.

And you don't?

An indignant squawk came from her lips, but her denials were cut short by another scream. From Saiya's room.

Kila was moving before she truly understood what she was hearing. Saiya's distress pulled at a deeper part of her, an emotional bond little different from her bond with Nax.

She charged through the hall, throwing mercus light ahead. Three dark figures stood before Saiya's chamber door. One pounded on it and pulled at the latch handle. Kila had locked it with mercus wards to keep Saiya from sneaking off, which she had threatened to do when her Winternight fun had been cut short.

The other two men held silvery blades. They wore the

rough, tea-colored woolens of Iron Scholars from the Hack-watch. The men raised their swords to protect the third man, who hissed and ran filthy fingers along the door jamb, as if feeling out Kila's ward. To Kila's mercus-heightened senses the men were abjectly foul, stinking of unlimed latrines, hair flat and oily, cheeks pale, lips crusted white. But it was their eyes that told her of a greater danger. They were unnatural, dead, unblinking.

She drew Cayne, knowing that trying to attack with the mercus would draw her into the grip of the Revulsion.

Revulyn! Nax sent. *Reviled!* She stood next to Kila, back arched, fur bushy with anger.

Kila had never heard the term "revulyn" before, but she understood it intuitively. A thick sludge of the Revulsion filled the corridor, so dense she could smell the foulness of it.

Ell! Kila screamed in her mind. *Come quick!*

Sending to Ell was never assured. It had always required the monarch to be in view. But desperate needs seek desperate hopes. She moved forward, Cayne out, toes planting to coil up her strength. She had trained with the best fighters in Ennith. Jil Pokti, the shadline who despised her. Gian Delp, a man she might have loved, who had wrapped her in his arms as easily as scooping up a puppy. Yiqa, the Alnassi killer. And Aggy, the awkward shadline girl of fourteen, who brutally defeated Kila in every sparring match.

The first reviled swung as if to chop a tree in twain. The speed and strength of the attack astonished Kila, and only her thiefly reflexes preserved her neck. Dropping beneath the blade, she stabbed into the man's groin. Cayne bit deep, hissing like hot steel quenched in water. The reviled moaned, a guttural sound more akin to ecstasy than pain. Kila ripped her blade free, rolled, and sliced through the second man's hamstring.

Bounding to her feet, she managed to backpedal as two sword tips arrowed toward her belly. The man at Saiya's door whispered softly, yet the sibilance of his words cut through the rattle and clang of the fight.

It is too thick! Nax sent. *They are full of the Revulsion. Behind you!*

Three more Iron Scholars with crusty lips and dead eyes rushed in. They must have been waiting in the suite's antechamber in case anyone entered. They had come for Saiya, but surely they wanted Kila, too. The trap had closed.

The mercus glowed in her awareness, beckoning. If she could take hold of her natural power it would be nothing to burn these men to ashes. But Nax's presence in her mind was like a staying hand. The Revulsion would seize her should she make any attempt to strike with the mercus.

She ducked and stabbed, scrambling on toes and knuckles past the man at Saiya's door. She put her back to her own bedchamber door. She risked the Revulsion by opening it with mercus touch, an idea forming at the same moment. The Revulsion tickled at her, emboldened by the presence of so many allies. Diving through, she slammed the door behind her. Her pursuers crashed into the thick wood plank and began hacking. The door shuddered and shook in its frame.

Ell comes! Nax sent.

Kila braced herself and reached again for the mercus, gagging upon the vileness of the Revulsion. Seeking, grasping, eager and starved.

But she was ready for it, and Nax's presence loomed boldly, lending her enormous willpower. She drank in the sweetness of the mercusine and formed the bolts for dymension, fixing a spot in Saiya's room firmly in mind. Once there, she would dymense Saiya away and—

Her bolts frayed like dry rotted rope. The Revulsion slipped in to fill the gaps. Her heart slowed, panic withdrawing. She knew she could use the Revulsion to dymense, but she knew also that she would turn those bolts instead to destroy the interlopers.

NO! Nax bellowed in her mind.

The Revulsion fled, leaving her empty of all power. She looked down at Cayne, then to the door. It split. Slivers of timber tumbled to her feet. The wormy face of a reviled pressed to the crack. He didn't smile, didn't make a sound, but simply pressed and pressed, stupidly trying to squeeze through a space too narrow for a rat. Another blade smashed through, then another.

Kila lowered into her fighting stance, knowing that Cayne had not slowed these men, even having dealt what should have been mortal wounds.

The door finally succumbed, tearing away from its hinges even as it burst into broken pieces. Beyond the men, a brilliant blue light flared into existence. The reviled hissed and cowered. The light died, revealing Ell standing at the opposite end of the hallway. Arrayed in a Winternight gown of blue and white, she looked like an ice goddess. Her eyes were chipped frost. Her mercus blast had stunned the vile men, and it had another effect that Kila noticed a hair's second before Nax shouted it into her mind.

The Revulsion had retreated. It was a momentary effect, a withdrawing tide already turning and preparing to flood back into the hallway. The men staggered and swayed, dazed by the unexpected loss of their power.

Now! cried Nax. *The mercus is clear!*

Kila drew in her power, but did not risk an outright attack. Instead, she dove forward, wrapped her arms around the closest man, and dymensed to a place she knew well. The grip of absolute cold suddenly wrapped around her nearly as hard as she held to the reviled man. But she didn't need to hold him any longer. She released him, gave him a hard shove. His sword flew from his hands, and his legs and arms began to flail. For he was falling toward a rocky slope a thousand spans below.

Kila had dymensed them to the very edge of the eyrie overlooking Starside, where even now the dragon Harnzyne slept among unsettled dreams. Kila didn't wait for the falling man to die before dymensing back to the Citadel.

She had been gone less than five seconds.

Her reappearance didn't startle the reviled, for they had turned to face Ell. She hammered them with mercus feats, but none reached them. Three of the reviled were advancing on the monarch, not even wincing as her mercus flames blasted toward them. Another force was negating her feats as quickly as she could mount them. The revulyn, the one at Saiya's door. He had turned away from his task and was standing with his head bowed, hands out. Kila felt his Revulsion impulses like sloshes of oil upon her skin. She recoiled even as part of her sought to feel the sensation more deeply.

Shaking the momentary spell away, she grabbed another reviled, dymensed him into free fall from the eyrie, then returned for another. When she came back the third time, Ell had backed from the corridor and was fighting the reviled with her little shadline dirk. Two fell guardsmen lay dead behind her. Behind them stood Eckso—the dragnithan now promise-bound to serve Ell—desperately casting mercus feats at the attackers. These told, for the revulyn had turned his attention back to Saiya's door. Fingers fondling the wood, he pressed his ear to it. Then, with a gasp of insight, he formed a foul bolt and destroyed the door. It cracked along a million spiderweb fractures and fell apart.

Saiya screamed.

Kila followed the man into the child's room. A gray blur joined her. Nax let out a furious growl and leapt onto the man's back, sinking her claws and fangs into his neck. Huff crouched on the bed, an orange ball of ferocity. Fangs bared, he spat and growled, barring the revulyn from Saiya.

Kila threw herself upon the man, stabbing with greater anger than she had stabbed Dox. The blade did not sing in disapproval, but the blows had little effect. Suddenly she was tumbling backward, rolling onto the rug, shoved by a disgusting blast of air that made her stomach rebel. But in her mercusine heart, something took hold. An easy decision. She would die before she allowed this man to harm Saiya.

She collected herself and ran at him, blade raised. She would saw through his neck if she had to.

Her body smacked into an unseen barrier, sending her sprawling again onto her back. Nax had jumped from the man and joined Huff to guard Saiya. The girl pressed as far away as the wall next to her bed would allow, holding up a pillow as a shield.

Outside the room, the cries and clatter of battle rose to an enormous racket. A squad of fell guardsmen had joined the melee. They screamed as they delivered what should have been killing blows, others cursed as they received them. Kila recognized the calls of a Fell Guard captain as he ordered his men into disciplined attacks. A woman shrieked in agony, or horror, and then the stomp of boots came close and a reviled burst into the room. He ignored Kila and went to stand next to the revulyn. The latter was whispering to Saiya, slippery words that Kila's mind could not grasp. While the reviled had easily passed through the invisible barrier, it still held Kila out. The way Nax clawed and showed her fangs, Kila knew she must be hissing and spitting, but she couldn't hear any of it.

But the revulyn wasn't attacking the cats. In fact, he kept well back of their small range. There was obvious reluctance in his posture to advance. Fell guardsmen poured into the room, then they too smashed into the invisible Revulsion wall.

One of them looked to Kila. "Why do you stand there? Attack with your power!"

"I dare not," she said, anguished by her impotence.

The stand-off between Nax and the revulyn continued. The man began to pace, blank eyes locked on Saiya. One of the fell guardsmen was pressing with all his considerable strength against the revulsion wall. Vomit stained his front, for any contact with the Revulsion made the bellies of good men rebel. But duty compelled him forward. And the others saw this as a challenge to their own honor. Soon five of them were straining. Their captain stumbled into the room, face white. Blood poured from a black gash across his arm. The skin curled away in an ever-widening chasm, showing a blackness inside that wept blood. "Her Enlightened has fallen."

The fell guardsmen moaned and cursed. Tears stood out in their eyes. The captain screamed, "It shall not be for nothing. Upon my honor. For the honor of the Brotherhood of the Fell Guard!" The wounded man threw himself into the Revulsion barrier, adding his waning strength to the effort. And seeing his valor, seeing his absolute commitment to his duty, Kila too leaned into the invisible wall, swallowing her gags and retches, ignoring the interior struggle of the mercus against the Revulsion. Knowing only that whatever separated her from Saiya, it would not stand while she had a beating heart.

A battle cry arose from men's throats, full of anger and sorrow. The captain wept and screamed, every muscle and fiber of his body straining. His men matched his efforts, boots scraping through the rug to the stone beneath. And from them came a crystalline resonance, a soft white glow, and a powerful surge that had nothing to do with the mercus, but which tapped some power known only to their military cult.

And then the wall succumbed and the men tumbled forward under unexpected momentum. Kila kept to her feet and jumped upon the revulyn. Cayne drove into his neck, hissing and spitting with each strike. The man moaned, but with a simple feat threw Kila back into the kneeling captain.

Before she could get to her feet, the revulyn's mouth stretched wide. "Accursed felnithel!" He grasped his remaining man and dymensed, leaving behind an acrid cloud of black smoke.

The fell guardsmen leaned upon their spears, sucking in gulps of air. Others lay dead or dying, all from what should have been insignificant wounds. Kila rushed to Saiya, took her in her arms. Nax joined them, pulsing emotion through the bond. Nothing needed to be said.

"Kila Sigh, come quickly," Eckso called from the doorway. "It's Ellishan."

Untangling herself from the girl and cat, Kila ran to the drawing room. The chair she had shared with Henley lay overturned. The side table and decanter of apple-cinnon whisky was in glittering pieces. The smell of the spill recalled again the scene in Dox's room after she had killed him. And lying amidst this wreckage lay Ell, Winternight gown rent across the belly. Her smooth skin was despoiled by a black crevice. Blood pulsed out in beautiful crimson streams.

Kila didn't have to battle past much Revulsion, as the departure of the intruders had carried the terrible thickness of it away. Nax's presence guarded her against the rest. She dove into the monarch's vile wound, seeking to stanch the blood and knit the flesh. But as she reached for the frayed edges of the cut, she found an eager foulness. A Revulsion-tainted blade had left behind its corruption. Like an infestation of maggots, it ate flesh, multiplied, and spread.

Calling upon the crimson light of healing she had learned

from Flaumishtak, Kila swirled her cupped hand. This light she poured upon the wound. The Revulsion did not shrink away, but merely turned its efforts to consuming the healing before it could heal. The effect was only to pause the inevitable destruction of Ell's body. Kila continued to manifest and pour, a delaying tactic that she could not sustain for long. It did nothing to stop the blood from spilling out of the woman's body.

Ell awakened, saw the damage. Her lips were taut. She reached for Kila's hand, squeezed it. Her flesh was hot, her grip strong. Where the Fell Guard captain had succumbed to a wound on his arm, she sustained life while her belly lay open. Dragnithan strength. But Kila knew it would not be enough.

"You will need . . ." Ell's eyes closed and she swallowed hard against a wave of agony. "You will need Night, Sigh. You will need them all."

Nax nuzzled Ell's cheek. Kila's hand was released and the monarch gently stroked Nax's fur. "Beloved felnithel . . ." Ell whispered, eyes glistening with awe of the creature. "Beloved Nax. The world dims."

Nax pressed close, purring comfortingly. The emotions coming through the bond made Kila's heart ache. The monarch's eyes widened as Nax returned her gaze. "Is that so?" Ell asked, wonderment filling her voice. Her body relaxed. Her blazing eyes closed. Her chest rose and fell. Rose and fell. Rose once more. "Felnithel . . . the honor was mine."

Her chest rose no more; the flow of blood from her wound ceased. Nax pressed a white paw to the dead woman's cheek, then turned to curl into Kila's arms.

Ellishan is no more, Nax sent. *Her body must be burned, now, before the Revulsion takes hold fully.*

Behind Kila, Eckso gasped. "It is released!" Mercus feats blossomed and vanished, and only the stink of mercus green remained. Eckso was gone, her promise-binding broken at the moment of Ell's death.

Boots tromped past as the surviving fell guardsmen carried their fallen away. Two stopped before Ell's body. They had discarded their helms. Tears streaked down their cheeks. "She must be prepared."

Kila shook her head. "She has been corrupted. All who have fallen here must be burned. You understand."

The man to her left bowed his head in grief, but Kila sensed something deeper than that. Shame. The man to her right held her gaze. He had the palest blue eyes she had ever seen. His jaw was square, hair matted from his helm, which lay on the floor next to his spear. Finally he said, "Then let it be done now." He called to his comrades and they brought their captain and their brothers to the floor of Kila's drawing room. They lay their men next to the queen.

The blue-eyed man said: "An undeserved honor, to be committed to Til next to her."

The weeping man choked and said: "Honor? Nay, it is to their disgrace that they burn next to the one they failed to protect. But it is to us who live that the greatest dishonor falls, for we too failed, yet in failing survived. I do not deserve the mantle of fell guardsman." With jerky motions he unbuckled his armor and let it fall. Even his boots came off. His comrades did the same, then left. Kila was alone with Nax and Saiya and the dead.

You must do it quickly, Nax urged. *The Revulsion is hungry. Should it claim their minds, you will have to kill them again. If you can.*

Marlow burst into the room, followed by a squad of fell guardsmen who had not heard—or had not believed—the news of the monarch's death.

Kila's lips quivered. She dragged her sleeve across her nose, felt her will collapsing as tears blurred her vision. She reached for Marlow. "Nax says we must burn the dead. Corrupted by the Revulsion."

"Do as the Beloved One advises," he said, taking her hand and urging her to stand. "And be done with it quickly."

She reached for the mercus again, lightly brushing away a skim of Revulsion. It did not tempt her in the least. She recalled a terrible moment long ago in the thinnie cavern beneath Starside. There she had added heat to the iron in the blood of her enemies, so much heat that she had burned them alive. Men, women, children. In her terror for Nax's life, she had released vengeful fire. Since then, she had used it countless times, sometimes merely to light a candle, other times to kill.

A candle, she thought. Let this be a candle in the darkness.

"Come Saiya," she a said, beckoning to the frightened girl at the door. Saiya had not awakened to her own power yet, but all who could sense the mercus potential in others knew she would be the most formidable merculyn who ever lived, even outshining Kila. "I want you to know that these people died to protect you."

Saiya didn't say anything, but merely buried her face in Kila's chest. The bolts came easily, and in a blazing instant the bodies of dragnithan and man were engulfed in flame. Ell's fire tinged blue, the men's orange.

On instinct alone, Kila wove more bolts and brought forth a draft that carried the smoke up the chimney. The heat went with it, and all that remained of the dead were ashy outlines of their bodies on the singed floor.

Marlow wrung his hands and cursed soundlessly. The fell guardsmen were unbuckling their armor. Their faces were stoney, or stricken, or in a few cases twisted with shame. Within a minute, they were gone.

A page skidded to a halt outside the parlor. "Administrator

Marlow. I have a message for you." He handed the man a slip of paper. It looked like a corner torn from a larger sheet. The hasty scrawl had the unique curl and swoop of First Race writing, commonly used when pageboys were asked to carry urgent and therefore unsealed messages.

Marlow crumpled the missive and dismissed the boy. Then he came to sit on the hearth across from Kila. He looked a ten-year older than when Kila had met him the first time. "The dragnithan prisoner Klayne is gone. Escaped."

"Eckso is gone too. Her promise-binding died with Ell. She probably took him."

The man's nostrils flared as he drew in a long breath and let it go. "Kil-damned and cooked," he said. Realizing what he'd said, he threw an apologetic glance at Saiya. Kila was grateful the girl didn't know who—or what—she was yet.

"The Revulsion did this," Kila said, feeling the weight of responsibility once more thump across her shoulders. "Nax called them revulyn and reviled. The revulyn uses—"

"Yes, I understand. Bolts of the Revulsion. And the reviled?"

"Dead, pale, undeterred by grievous wounds. These were Iron Scholars, so not particularly skilled with their weapons. But their blades are tainted with the Revulsion. I could not heal Ell."

Marlow took this in with heavy acceptance, as if a secret fear had been confirmed. He tossed the slip of paper into the fireplace, where it blackened and lifted up the flue. "I'll send for Highest Quiv, perhaps he'll help us to understand it."

Kila doubted merely understanding the Revulsion and its minions would be of any use. But she didn't have a better idea. "Dox Viller is dead," she said. To her own ears the words were flat, devoid of emotion. "I killed him."

Instead of asking her why, Marlow got to his feet, put his arm around her and drew her into a warm embrace, even as she held to Saiya, and Saiya held onto Nax. Kila felt the warm press of his lips on the crown of her head. "All will be well," he said. The words were meant to be comforting, but they didn't fool her. Nothing was well, and nothing would be well.

She pulled free, kissed Marlow's cheek, and took Saiya and Nax to her bedroom. There they curled under the blankets and, as dawn began to lighten the windows, Kila drifted into uneasy dreams.

11

CAPABLE, BUT NOT ABLE

The fastness of Ceronhel did not impress Yples. The elnisian architecture appealed to what was left of the man in him, but the qiznithan cared only about its usefulness. Right now it looked useless. What was the point of a fortification? His forces would never need safety. They would march forward, crush walls and cities alike. In the end, even this stronghold would become less than dust.

The only nosg who knew what was going on here seemed to be an idiot called Noi-Ick-Noi. The creature was sitting next to an empty wooden throne in the great hall. Yples had not turned him yet, for his mind was knotted with curious mercus wards he did not understand. They seemed to be some sort of bond magic. This intrigued Yples. "Has Devin returned with the child?"

"He returned. No child."

Yples found Devin standing atop a watchtower, staring at nothing. Next to him was a reviled, frozen through, sword in hand. "Why do you stand here when your task is incomplete?"

"There were felnithel guarding the child. Kila Sigh killed three reviled and was about to kill me. I could not succeed."

"What excuse have you for fleeing? Certainly it is not fear."

"No. I long for the final release of Annihilation. I thought you would prefer to know why I had failed."

Yples was not the man he had been. All that remained of the old Yples were the body, the name, and the bits of knowledge and memory his possessor deemed useful. As a qiznithan he well knew of the so-called Beloved Ones. The felnithel saw with the cold eye but did not long for Annihilation. They allied with neither Day nor Night. Insubstantial beings were these spark spirits. Yples the man had seen them.

"In this world they are but cats," he said. "Vermin. No more deadly to a man than a sewer rat. Surely even your meager power could have destroyed them."

Devin did not blink. "Surely. Yet I did not. My desire to destroy them was great. My intention to destroy them was clear in my mind. Yet I did not destroy them. I was capable, but not able."

"You couldn't reach past them and simply dymense a child away?"

"I could, but I couldn't."

The idiot was not intending to speak in riddles, Yples realized. He was at the limit of his capacity to explain a phenomenon he simply could not understand. Which made him nearly useless. All the revulyns were like this. Aware but lacking imagination. It was time to create a different sort. "Come with me to Sorgan, Devin. I will give you one chance to redeem yourself."

12

JUST A THIEF GIRL

The urgent need of Kila's bladder pulled her from sleep. Gauging by the light, it was nearly midday. As she slipped to the needs closet, she noticed the fell guardsmen's armor and spears had been cleared away from the drawing room, the rug replaced with a fresh one. Everything broken or stained had been replaced.

Once relieved and washed she staggered into the drawing room where men were engaged in a serious debate. She discovered Henley sitting at table with a pretty young woman and Marlow. They were in the middle of a meal.

Henley scooted his chair back and came to her. "Huff told me what he could. Marlow sketched in the rest. I'm just gutted to hear about Her Enlightened."

And he was. She could see it on his face. The sorrow, the worry. But she didn't care about what he was feeling. "Where were you?" She looked past him, at the girl. She had a remarkable face, with large eyes, a longish nose, and narrow jaw. She stared back with lively interest, and Kila just knew the girl was weighing Kila's appearance against her own.

Marlow got up too, swiping a napkin across his mouth. "You look much better for the sleep. Come join us. There is food."

She didn't move. "Where were you, Henley?"

His face flushed, from throat to hairline. Even his ears went pink. "I went looking for you. But I ran into Terissa. You remember me telling you about her. From Tordain?"

"The hussy who tried to bed you?"

The girl barked a laugh, but swallowed her smile when Henley scowled at her. He simply nodded at Kila. "She was with some refugees from Tordain. It was happenstance that she found me last night. Yiqa was with her. She was very ill." He continued with a tale of the Baths and watching Yiqa die and some nonsense about waiting for her body to rise. Kila didn't hear much of it. Her pulse was roaring in her ears, gaze fixed on Terissa.

"This girl found you? Happenstance? Either you're a wool-headed moron, or I'm an atlen egg. You never should have gone to Ell's summons. You should have stayed with me. You should have been here to help me. Maybe she'd still be alive."

"Saiya is unhurt?" he asked, not trying to defend his absence. It was the same as always with him. The patience. The willingness to take whatever abuse she dealt him. She hated herself for doing it, but she resented him for being so forgiving. And for being right all along.

"Get out!" she shouted at the girl. "Marlow, please. Get her out of her before I dymense her to Slirya."

Terissa's face went tight, but she smiled. "I've always wanted to go to Slirya. Maybe I should—"

"Terissa, this is not the time," Henley said. It was a tone he would never have used with Kila, which made her resent the girl more. Not that she wanted him growling at her, but at least he wasn't being condescending to Terissa.

Marlow had the wits to usher the girl out of the room,

mumbling that he would find her a suitable room and send a girl to her with some more appropriate clothes.

Kila turned away from Henley, embarrassed at her outburst. But also furious that he'd brought that girl into her rooms.

"You still think like a thief," Henley said softly. "It's a bit selfish. You see Terissa and think the worst of me, but you ignore her need. You hear I gave Yiqa respect in her final hour and think I neglected you. I had no way of knowing what was happening here."

"Maybe she is a refugee. Doesn't mean I'm going to let her swish her skirts at you."

He chuckled. "She still doesn't know you are Kila Sigh."

"You didn't tell her? The one time being me has some advantage and you don't use it?"

"I don't want her to be afraid. That's not fair."

"Fair? She wants to take you from me. Make you some sort of innkeeper. I don't have to be fair."

"After what happened here with Ell and the revulyn, you have greater concerns than Terissa Viller."

"Viller?" The warmth of the moment drained away and Kila stiffened, skin crawling with gooseflesh. She dragged her fingers through her hair. "Tell me she isn't related to Dox."

"His unacknowledged daughter. Or so she claims. I don't know how she could prove it. She was going to go see him and find out if he'll give her a place to live. I told her it wouldn't be necessary."

"Not even possible, now. He's dead." She sat at the table and began to spoon Marlow's leftovers into her mouth.

"Lots of folk dying recently," he said. "What happened? His hounds turn on him?"

"I guess he got stabbed. I'm surprised it took this long. There are a lot of people around who hate him."

Henley pulled a chair close to hers and retrieved his plate. "These eggs are cold, how can you eat them?"

"Thief girl, remember?" She kicked him playfully, but she didn't feel playful. She was feeling heavy across the shoulders. "The revulyn and his dead-eyed Iron Scholars came for Saiya. If it weren't for the cats he would have dymensed with her. We need to keep a cat with her at all times until I can figure out something else."

"How can a little cat defend her against a revulyn? It doesn't make sense."

"You notice how even Klayne and Eckso respect them? Flaumishtak, too. And the cats love him much more than he deserves. It's something in their nature. Demayne love them." She stopped chewing and put her fork down. "Ell said something just before she died. She said, 'You will need Night. You will need them all.' She was talking about fighting the Revulsion. Do you think she meant the demayne of Night, like Klayne?"

He made a noncommittal humming sound. "What did her letter say?"

"What letter?"

"The one I left on that table," he pointed with his fork. "It had a blue ribbon and some sort of mercus ward on it. She said only you could open it."

She went to the silver tray in the foyer where all the correspondence got dumped. Sure enough the tightly rolled letter was there next to it. The mercus ward was lovely and delicate, a lacework of incredible mastery. She dragged a finger over the roll, feeling both urgency and care woven into the ward. It buzzed into her skin, then dissipated, as if recognizing her touch.

She tugged at the ribbon and unrolled the last message she would ever get from Ell LiMinluit.

· · ·

Kila Sigh,

Highest of Kil,

Unsworn Shadline, Bearer of Fate Breaker,

Today I asked Henley Mast to loan me the Motherlight. If you have received this message, he refused. I half hoped that he would, for I would have used it to remove Saiya from your tutelage, if not from your parentage. I do not trust your guardianship of her. But that problem is no longer mine. Since I first took the Raven Throne I have known I would die on a Winternight. It will be this Winternight.

The future is not mine to make, but yours.

Dem-Kisk has long perplexed me. Like you, I thought events with the Hargothe and Yiothizandra were a culmination, but clearly those challenges were but a beginning. The true enemy of life is, and always has been, the Revulsion. You surely see that. As I write this I do not know the specifics of what is going to occur tonight, only that I will die.

Moonside stirs, Kila. You awakened the Revulsion at the Hack-watch, but I sense it moves with intention everywhere now. So too has the force of destiny been moving, to position you where you are and, I hope, Saiya to where she is. Henley's faith in you gives me hope that this is so.

The war to come will be waged on every front. Pennie died to warn us that the Evernight dawns.

"Pennie died?"

"I went into the city to find you and tell you," Henley said. "I'm sorry. Ell said that scream we heard was Pennie warning us. Something about 'Evernight'."

The handwriting blurred and Kila wiped a sleeve across her eyes. "What does it mean?"

Henley lifted a shoulder. "What does any prophecy mean? Bad things are coming."

Sniffing and clearing her throat, Kila looked blankly at the letter. "Poor Pennie. She never had a real chance at a life. She would have been better off if I'd taken her down to the Baths. Maybe they could have awakened her."

She continued to read.

YOUR TASK now is to prepare for the war and to protect Saiya from the Revulsion. I hope that you now see why I mistrusted you to be her guardian. Your own struggle with the Revulsion is the greatest danger the realm of mankind faces. If you falter, it will claim you totally. Under its sway, you will give Saiya to it. The god we call Kil claims many ill qualities, but he has never sought the annihilation of all matter and life. Should a godblooded entity like him succumb to the Revulsion, should he see with the cold eye, then Annihilation for all is certain.

The force of destiny whispers softly to me now, even as my pen forms these words. Ah me, it is not as I thought it would be. The spinning coin is chiming as it tumbles in my mind. A terrifying notion has arisen into my thoughts. My shadline instincts are afire with alarm. As my hand moves to ink these words, I tremble with fear.

I am a shadline, a dragnithan, and a queen, yet at this moment, upon the verge of committing to this paper my terrible insight, I feel like a child. Alas! It must be so, for the coin in my mind has struck and the shadline certainty is upon me.

I name you, Kila Sigh, as my heir. Upon my death, you will ascend to the Raven Throne. Lean on Marlow, for he is brilliant. Council with Shad Einlin. Of the Radiants, trust only Peline, Hiolly, and Gilok. You must search out the demayne of Night, for you will need all the dragnithor, and all the dragnithan. Yes, I fear you will need even Yiothizandra before the end. The Revulsion will be searching for them, will seek to turn them. Do not allow it!

May the force of destiny guide you, Kila Sigh. My dear, dear child. Keep faith with the felnithel and perhaps all will be well.

—H.E.M. Ellishan LiMinluit

"KIL BE A MERRY MAIDEN," Kila whispered, crumpling the letter in her fist. "That woman was Lumne-touched and half-witted before she went."

"What did it say?" Henley asked. He had shoved his plate away and was looking at her with great concern. And no wonder; her face was cold and numb, yet the top of her head burned with fever. The shock of the letter made the room twirl. She swallowed hard and blinked away the dizziness.

"Nothing. Just more silliness about raising Saiya." She took the note to the fire. She threw it in. The balled up paper sat in the flames for a moment, then of its own power rolled from the flames and onto the hearthstone. There it slowly uncrumpled itself until not a crease remained. Kila stared at it like it was a satin-adder just popped out of its hole.

Henley scooped it up. Kila tried to snatch it away, but he held it out of reach. "You don't want me to read it, I won't. But if it won't burn, maybe there's a good reason for it."

"Just read it and you'll see. By the time you're done, you'll be throwing it in yourself."

His eyes scanned the letter, face registering each revelation. When he got to the end, his face also drained of color. "Kil's handle!" But he didn't put it in the fire like he should. He set it on the table, unnecessarily smoothed the sheet with his palm.

"She had this prepared when I went to meet her last night. That means she had time to make other arrangements."

"What other arrangements?"

The knock at the door startled them both. To Kila's astonishment, a fell guardsman stepped in. "Administrator Marlow and the Radiants of your small council are here to see you, Your Majesty."

"No," she mouthed. "No, no, no."

But it was too late. Marlow came in carrying a red leather-bound tome. Radiants Gilok, Hiolly, and Peline followed him in. Gilok's red nose was angled into the air, his face sour with disapproval at this duty, which was to carry upon a velvet pillow Ell's diamond and sapphire crown. Radiant Hiolly was an elderly woman with fluffy white hair and skin the pallor of a snowbank. She carried a scepter, studded all over its globe end with gems. Radiant Peline, Quinn's mother, and of the same startling beauty as her daughter, bore a black raven feather fitted with a gold nib. A pot of ink rested on the palm of her other hand.

"The investiture will take place tonight," Marlow said. "But you are the monarch of Starside now, with all authority and privileges reserved to the occupant of the Raven Throne."

"Throne?" Kila said softly, reaching for Henley. He took her hand and at the same time sent calm through their bond. Even with that, she could not block a recollection of Dox Viller's bloated body, lips spread as he chuckled at her new misfortune. These people were mad. How could they simply accept Ell's decision to put her on the throne? "The throne? I've never even *seen* the throne. I can't be queen of Starside. I'm just—I'm just —" But she couldn't say she was just a thief girl from Cheapsgate.

"Her legitimacy will be challenged," Radiant Gilok said to Marlow, already mincing his words so as to not directly challenge the new queen. "Not just by the other Radiants, but by the merchant class as well. I doubt any in Terriside will be keen to support her claim, given the destruction she once caused that quarter. And many are listening to the cunning whispers of that scoundrel Tarek PiTorro."

"PiTorro is a sniveling worm, Gilok," Radiant Hiolly said. "He's been all over Gristenside trying to rally us against Ell LiMinluit, as if our armsmen could have defeated a single squad of the Fell Guard. PiTorro has always been overly bold for a merchant. I don't care how rich he is."

Gilok waved his nose in a haughty display of false patience. "I merely state that objections to Highest Sigh's legitimacy will be raised. It is my duty to council our monarch on all threats that come to my attention. But it is as you say. Her Enlightened's instructions were unambiguous and legal, in my opinion. I'll readily show my letter from her on the matter to any who question it."

"As will I," Radiant Peline said. She didn't look happy about it. She blamed Kila for Quinn running off to be a shadline, which wasn't fair. Quinn had come into her blade without any help from Kila.

"As will I," said a new voice. Highest Quiv scurried in, sandy hair and shoulders damp with melting snowflakes. He too was burdened with a big book in his arms. "Apologies, Your Majesty." He bowed to her, then made quick dips of his head to the others. "Administrator, Radiants, Henley Mast. The Fell Guard seem to be in disarray this morning, and getting to the Citadel took much longer than usual as there were none present to open the gates."

Kila's head jerked around at the mention of the Fell Guard. "Give me a moment," she said. She left them and went through the foyer and opened the outer door. Two fell guardsmen stood watch. The senior man turned his head to look at her and upon recognizing her, lowered his spear and dipped his head. "Your

Majesty. It is the Brotherhood's honor to be your guard against all enemies. Our lives are yours." The other man immediately echoed the words. "Our lives are yours."

"I thought you had disbanded after last night," she said.

"Brother Commander Docit received a letter early this morning from Her Enlightened Majesty Ellishan LiMinluit with new orders. She reminded us that our vow is to the Raven Throne, not to her as a woman. Our failure to protect her is to our shame, but abandoning our posts was more shameful still. There will be severe penance undertaken by all who lost faith, no matter how briefly. And even greater penance should you command it." All of this was said in a clipped and urgent cadence.

"Do you think it's right?" she asked.

The man blinked several times, as if unable to understand the question. She tried again. "I'm asking you as a man, not as a brother of the Fell Guard. Is it right that I succeed Ell?"

"It was Her Enlightened Majesty's decision to make. My vow—"

"But what do you think? Am I a fit replacement for her?"

He was silent a long time, offering only his expressionless blue eyes and square jaw. The hesitation told her much. But she wanted to hear it. "I command you to tell me what you think of me."

"I think you are rash, selfish, and dangerous. You disrespected your predecessor by ignoring her commands and advice. I shall add fifty lashes to my penance for saying this."

"You'll do no such thing. Consider that the wish of the Raven Throne." She retreated into the suite, pulling the door shut with an extra bit of muscle. The Radiants and Marlow were waiting, each face composed into practiced indulgence. Well, they would just have to wait a bit longer. "Henley, come talk with me without all these other ears listening."

They went into Saiya's room since the girl was still sleeping in Kila's. She closed the door and warded it against eavesdroppers, barely noticing the cruft of Revulsion she had to brush aside. "I can't do this. I don't *want* to do this. I understand I need to protect Saiya and fight the Revulsion, but why do I have to become queen?"

Henley looked as perplexed as she was, but instead of retreating from the silliness of it, he began to muse aloud. "Who is Kila Sigh to the rest of the world? A face and name from that handbill that was circulating. The Girl Who Flies, and all that. To the rest of the world you are a rumor. A terrifying one. An immensely powerful merculyn who rides dragons and travels with nosg armies."

"I rode a wyvok. And I was a prisoner of the nosg."

"Rumor never cares about the facts. My point is that as Kila Sigh, Highest of Kil, you aren't any realm's ally. In fact, from Sorgan to Slirya, you must be viewed as an enormous threat. Anyone who can dymense into a city, throw mercus spheres around, and simply fly away has to be viewed with suspicion and fear. Your association with the name Kil doesn't help matters either. But Starside is an ally to all city states in the east, and does enormous trade with the others, from Wantin to Slirya. As Starside's queen, with an interest in preserving those ties, the other lords of the world may view you a bit more favorably. They can't trust a nationless merculyn rogue, but a monarch who serves the interests of her realm . . . That's different. And finally, there's Moonside."

"What does Moonside have to do with this?"

"'Moonside stirs'," he said, reciting the most confusing part of Ell's letter. "She didn't put that in merely to be poetic. Who is the only one with access to Moonside? The queen."

"That's as comforting as a spiked pillow, Henley."

"I love you. Which means I won't lie to assuage your fears."

He smiled and cupped her chin. "I believe in you. Ell could have chosen a more experienced woman for the throne, but she could not have chosen a fiercer one."

"But I don't know what to do. They're out there waiting for me to put on the crown and start issuing charters or somesuch."

"You spent a lot of time with Ell, didn't you?"

"She didn't give me much choice."

"My point is that you got to watch her. You just said you don't know what to do, and I say, do what Ell would do. Pretend you are her. Start right now with me. What would Ell say to me?"

Irritation bubbled to the surface of her mind, bringing words with it. In an arch tone, she said: "I appreciate your faith in me, Henley Mast. But don't presume that gives you the right to tell me what to do."

"Well done," he said, smiling. He kissed her nose. "You even sounded like her."

Kila released the ward on the door and strode back into the drawing room, holding desperately to the false superiority she had just put on like a cloak. Saiya now sat at the table, cheerfully dipping bread into a dish of runny atlen yolk, feet swinging beneath her chair. She shared a few licks with Nax and Huff before popping the rest into her mouth.

The councilors stood away from the table, silent. Among them, only Marlow and Quiv knew for certain what Saiya was. But the others watched her speculatively, for all had witnessed her speedy growth.

Kila took a position between the child and her small council. Before she could change her mind and dymense away, she said, "Right. Let's begin."

This snapped the others from their thoughts, and all began talking at once.

13

A CLEVER RELIC

The Bige Barzho sprawled atop a sparsely shrubbed hill. It was a palace of swirling white and gold marble, with gold domes held up on white columns. The desert sun flared from it, making it a beacon amidst the surrounding cattle ranges. Despite the lack of rain, the land was green in some areas. For like the silky verdant lawns that surrounded the Bige itself, the pastures were fed from ancient irrigation pipes which drew water from the Barzho spring.

Eckso Ezeel sat before a delicate teak folding table upon the south lawn, enjoying the shade of an open-sided pavilion. A glass of mellow tea sweated before her. Chips of ice brought down from the distant mountain glaciers floated in it, bringing the drink to a sublime coolness. Her companion, the lord of this estate, sat across from her. Klayne Itopolo's hair was once again oiled and swept back from his broad, handsome brow. New hoops hung from his earlobes. A fine, loose shirt and trousers hung from his much reduced frame. His captivity at the Citadel had taken an obvious toll, for his cheeks were sunken, eyes giving a wide, startled look. When he spoke his mouth formed a haunting grimace.

A serving woman in a vaporous translucent gown stood by with her pitcher of tea, ready to refill their cups at the slightest nod. Like all of Klayne's servants she was beautiful and young. The woman watched Klayne with the worshipful expectation of a neglected daughter. He felt no paternal reflex toward her at all, Eckso was sure. Not by the way he looked at her.

She sipped her tea, noting the slight sweetness. The day was fine and hot, but a breeze caressed the hilltop, keeping them cool without need for mercus interference. They had not spoken more than four words to each other since she had rescued him. Fine. Let him stew in silence. She knew he wasn't conflicted by gratitude and pride. Klayne was a demayne of Night; gratitude was anathema to him.

Four girls in filmy gowns came down from the Bige bearing platters. Eckso was mildly diverted to discover they all looked the same. Not similar. The same. Identical. "Where did you find these lovelies?" Eckso asked, unable to allow the novelty to go unmentioned despite her resolve not to speak first.

"Slirya. I bought them from an orphanage a year or two ago." His eyes scanned across their bodies. "Put the food down and go."

The girls—certainly no older than seventeen—did as they were told. Klayne tossed aside the plate covers and took up his dining *stilf,* a tapered utensil of silver with a blade on one edge and a spoon divot in the middle. He used it to swipe huge mouthfuls of rice, chicken, and onion into his mouth. His captors had refused him food in an attempt to weaken his will. Eckso was not planning to mention that had been on her advice to Ellishan.

The food was spicy, and of course perfectly made. Eckso had always enjoyed the food of the far west, but had never found a cook in Trine who could manage such dishes. She ate slowly, like the noblewoman she had pretended to be for the past thousand years.

"Do you recall how Ellishan was before we came to this world?" she asked lightly.

"Self-important, arch, and judgmental."

"Are you sure you're not describing my sister?" Yiothizandra had surely been Ellishan's match in self-importance. If anyone would know how arch Yioth could be, it was Eckso, who had suffered her older sister's scornful ways her entire life.

"I'm glad you mentioned her. Your sister, I mean." He downed his tea. The girl filled his cup. "She's alive. Still captive in Stallid. She is to be executed soon. Or so my chief of household tells me. What do you think of that?"

"I wonder why they've waited so long. I hope they do it and good riddance."

"Loyalty has never meant anything to you."

"Nor to you, Klayne. Surely you never meant to bring the Motherlight into Yioth's service. Had you secured it, you would have used it to defy her at every turn."

"Not if she possessed Kil reborn. Though I would certainly have tried to remove the child from her possession. She's no merculyn, so I don't know how she expected to protect the babe once he was born."

Eckso covered her mouth with a napkin to hide a smile. Klayne did not yet know that Kil was a girl. Nor did he know how swiftly the child had grown. In fact, he didn't know that Ellishan was dead. Nor that the Revulsion had awakened and now walked the earth in human hosts. He was ignorant of everything, and Eckso hoped to keep him that way for as long as she could. This was *her* moment, *her* opportunity. She wouldn't have him using her or her knowledge to advance his own schemes. For once she would be in command. He didn't know that either, but he was about to find out.

She merely needed to add one accessory to his wardrobe: a little more gold. And then he would be hers to use as she saw fit. The gods and Hel Lords knew that he would do the same to her. But not yet. He was weak, but he was alert. He needed lulling.

"I'm impressed how well you held up in captivity," she lied. "But you were lucky that Ellishan did not have you executed." She had also recommended that to her cousin, but Ell had refused, always saying vaguely that Klayne might be needed later. As if the man would voluntarily be of any assistance that didn't benefit him.

"I found captivity quite interesting," he said, shoving a rolled up piece of yann bread into his mouth. Around it he said, "I meditated and I planned. My minders were growing complacent. No doubt within a ten-day or so I would have escaped them myself."

He would have done no such thing. Eckso inspected their quelling bolts daily, and made sure the merculyns were rotated through to keep them fresh and alert. Klayne didn't—and never would—know this. But he looked enormously self-satisfied at the moment, here in his Losstran estate fifty leagues from Stallid. Surrounded by his tribe, the Barzho, and his girls, and his horses, and atlens, and irrigated lawns and fountain-filled courtyards. In truth, Klayne had always been slightly lazy. There was no reason he was not king of half of Ennith. Though Eckso had to admit that the same was true for her and Yioth.

They had all been monarchs of various realms in the distant past, but such achievements were full of monotony. Only Ell had retained her throne. Silly girl, Eckso thought. So serious, so devoted to these humans, whose lives flared and faded like the shooting sparks of a campfire. Yioth had not resigned herself to an endless existence here, though. She had never been content to take a false identity, capture a noble house, grow rich, appear to grow old, pretend to die, and then move elsewhere to do the whole thing again. For Eckso and Klayne, it had been a diverting game, and had allowed them long stretches of leisure.

Yiothizandra had only thought of one thing. Escaping this world altogether. And look where that had put her, in chains and about to be executed.

Sure, bearing forth Kil was a marvel. No one would deny that. And Yioth was correct that a god could release the demayne trapped in this world. With Kil's aid Eckso could return to the demaynic realms, finally, and without risk of punishment.

But she didn't really want to leave this world. Here, where she was nearly immortal, well satisfied in all manner of pleasures.

But...

She saw the main chance before her. Just as Yioth had seen it. A god of Kil's power could do more than free her. Kil could lift Eckso up from demayne to goddess. And then no Hel Lord could stand against her, and those who had considered her insignificant and disappointing would bow and scrape and beg to be spared. Klayne included.

"I'm glad of one thing," she said, pushing her plate away.

"What's that?" he asked, taking her unfinished food.

"That Yioth called us to Ceronhel when she did. We hadn't seen each other for so long. Too long." Now was the time to employ her unassailable skills. The forward tilt of her head, the gaze through her lashes. The half smile. Her dress was modest today, yet it enhanced the curves Klayne had once enjoyed long ago. Her lips were rosier today than she'd allowed him to see since their reunion. These wispy girls he surrounded himself with were lovely, but young and unskilled.

Klayne knew this.

He was also extraordinarily observant and had an excellent memory. "What's your game, Eckso? Why are you seducing me?"

"You're keeping my children safe here in your home, no? Don't you have a right to expect something of me?" He had no such right, especially since she had rescued him. But she was counting on her natural allure, and his notorious weakness to such charms.

"Since when have you ever paid for anything?" he said, but that rakish smile of his came out. Spoiled, of course, by his gaunt flesh. She reacted as if he were his old self, the irritatingly good-looking self. A flush of red into her cheeks and throat. Hand touching her hair, eyes scanning over his shoulders and chest.

And then she stood and walked away.

THAT NIGHT he came to her apartments. Poli and Trevi were asleep. Her bedroom was prepared, full of blossoms, moonlight cutting through the high open doors, bed fresh and covered over with pillows. She wore a nothing gown, filmier and more sheer than anything his house girls wore. His dark eyes filled with the moonlight.

And still he was wary. She went to him, undressed him. Drifted her fingers—and then lips—over his chest and the stark relief of his ribs. Like a starving hound, he was. There were many things he liked. She remembered from ages ago when they had last shared such intimacies. To her astonishment he was unable to rise to the occasion. No matter, for she knew mercus tricks to alleviate even that obstacle. And when the blood of his passion finally rose, he ravished her in the most delightful ways. She hated him, but she felt no shame in enjoying his considerable skills.

She knew he would resent her knowledge of his masculine failure. But before he could lash out, she would present him with a gift he could not return.

Dragnithans are not humans. Exhaustion in battle and in love does not come quickly. And so they enjoyed bout after bout of lovemaking, and did not need sleep in between, for rarely does a dragnithan need such deep rest. But there finally came a languorous time, when Klayne lay upon the bed, naked to the moonlight. He allowed his eyes to close and with a little urging of a mercus charm, did finally sleep.

Eckso rose and went to a drawer at the bottom of her wardrobe. The silk bag came out. She was thankful she had been present for Kil's birth. But perhaps even more thankful that she had been present when Ell removed Kila Sigh's *vaz'on.*

She pulled the relic out of the bag, admired it in the silvery light shining through the open garden doors. She carried it concealed behind her back as she returned to the bed. Klayne lay as he had been, a sheen of perspiration glistening on his forehead and neck. She knelt beside him and began to caress his hair, crooning to him soft songs of demaynic melodies.

He would feel her mercus rising, so she directed to his manhood a rousing feat, not too full of vigor and urgency, but gentle with deeper stirrings. At the same time she formed another bolt, one she knew would not stand long against his greater power. But weakened as he was, from captivity and greedy lust, she was certain he would not defeat her mind probe before she could fit the *vaz'on* to his head.

When she struck, she did not do so quickly. No lightning jabs into his mind for her. Subtlety was called for, while his attention was lower in his body. His eyes remained closed, but a soft sigh parted his lips.

And so she socketed in her feat, distracting him more than quelling him. The *vaz'on* slipped over his head and the first bolt was halfway in before he opened his eyes.

She already occupied his most sensitive body part with her gentle mercus teases. Now she clamped down, sending fiery pain through it. He kicked and howled, but she screwed the first bolt of the *vaz'on* home. The most important one, which blocked him from the mercus. She tapped his own power through it and shoved an imperious willshift into his mind, stilling his motions. The remaining screws were easy and she smiled down at his frozen face as she gently turned them.

She released the willshift. As expected, he leapt at her. Too slowly. For now she could access the Will Gem, which granted her total authority over his body. His attack faltered instantly and he fell onto his face.

"And now we will discuss the future," she said kindly, allowing him the freedom to stand. He gasped and cursed her, spittle running down his chin. She forced his hand to grasp the bedsheet and wipe it across his face. Fury reddened his cheeks, and his stark eyes bulged wider.

"You have too long been a conceited bully, Klayne. And I have too long been a lazy lamb." She found a robe and slipped it over her shoulders. Going to a decanter on the dresser, she poured herself a glass of wine. She sipped it, holding Klayne's mouth shut through the *vaz'on*. His forced silenced thrilled her. Having him at her mercy thrilled her more. Let him stew in it, his hatred, his fury. His humiliation. He hadn't seen it coming. Hadn't given a moment's thought that Eckso Ezeel would attempt something so bold. That was because he was contemptuous by nature, never believing anyone else as capable as he.

Eckso tossed back the wine and put the cup down. Klayne sat on the edge of the bed, breath laboring as he struggled against the implacable Will Gem. She went to her wardrobe and recovered her little shadline dagger, Loveheart. A rondel dagger ideal for wedging between bits of plate armor.

Threatening Klayne further wasn't necessary. With the *vaz'on* on his head, he was hers totally. So she didn't draw the weapon, but merely set it on her bedside table. He had seen it in her hands. That fear was enough for him to remember it. Remember what it could do. She grinned as she sank back into the bed, knowing how horrified he was right now. For should she shove that dagger into his heart, it would force upon his mind a captivating love for her. All his hate and fury would be transformed in the last instant of his life to adoration. And he would thank her—truly—for his death. That was perhaps the worse torture he could suffer.

"Yiothizandra wanted to destroy this world—oh, do lie down." She released the Will Gem. He jerked around, ready to grab her, but he caught himself. Slowly, with great inner tension he lowered himself onto the bed. He put his hands on his belly and stared at the canopy. Eckso continued, "As I was saying, my sister wanted to destroy this world to escape it. I think you would do something similar if you could control Kil. But what else can be expected of a demayne of Night? You would trade every star in the sky for your freedom and never think about it again. Others' lives have no meaning to you. But I am of Twilight, and we are the practical ones. I'm not saying we aren't self-serving. But we are capable of love. I love my children. I am fond of some members of my household in Trine. Truly, I rather like Kila Sigh, and I adore her felnithel Nax. I do not wish to see all humanity and nosg-kin swept away. Why destroy this world at all, is what I wonder. Where Yiothizandra saw only a barrier to be shattered, I see a dense thicket that—perhaps—can be breached. I don't wish to leave this world forever, merely to pass among the demaynic planes as I wish. It's the Hel Lords who imprison us here. But the Hel Lords can do nothing against me if Kil forbids it. Especially if I am Anointed."

At this, Klayne's gaze shot toward her. "Anointed? Are you daft? Kil will crush you beneath his heel, unnoticed, like an ant in the grass. Why would he lift you from demayne to goddess?"

There was no reason to answer and a good reason not to. For

the unanswered question would burn up his guts with speculation and fear.

"The *vaz'on* is a clever relic, isn't it?" she said lightly, changing the subject. "The elnisian cult that created it would have been great had they not destroyed themselves with it. I know of two of them, though no doubt more are scattered here and there across the far flung realms." She touched the blue gem, set above and between Klayne's eyes. "This is the Eye Gem." A flood of vision and memory shot into her, nearly overwhelming her mind. She saw Klayne's life, and *knew* aspects of it as if they were her own experiences. Wincing at his most recent suffering in Starside, she withdrew her attention. "The Will Gem," she said, touching the one over his right ear, feeling instantly her control over his body.

"Now, tell me you love me," she said, reaching to tap the red gem over his left ear. "No? Ah, but you know what the Truth Gem will do to you if you lie to me. That is well," she said, pouting and putting on a baby voice, "for I *so* hate to see you suffer."

She pushed on his head to turn it. "We have this amber gem at the back of your skull. I've always wondered what it must feel like to—" She threaded a bit of mercus into the rear left gem. His body bucked and shook, and a groan parted his lips. "Ah, the Ecstasy Gem." She lightened her mercus thread and he relaxed a bit, squirming and smiling as pleasure coursed through him. She cut it off. "If you behave, perhaps you will have something to look forward to. On occasion. Let's try the other one." She shifted her mercus into the rear right gem. Klayne's face went blank.

"How does that feel?"

"Like nothing. I feel nothing at all."

She pinched the skin over his ribs, hard, digging in her nails. He didn't flinch. "The Numb Gem. Interesting. And perhaps merciful should I require you to walk into a fire for some reason."

Finally she turned her attention to the two green gems at his temples. These, she well knew, worked together. She placed her attention on them now; easily done for they drew her mind like lodestones. All of Klayne's considerable mercus power flooded into her.

She had experienced this before when she had placed this same *vaz'on* on Kila Sigh's head. Nevertheless, a ripple of ecstasy caught her by surprise and she threw her head back and laughed. "Kila was much more powerful than you, but there is something more satisfying in this." She stroked his cheek and pressed her lips to his. Hating him was fun now. Reluctantly, she released the Tap Gems and relaxed.

"Were you a mere human, the *vaz'on* would be enough," she said. "But you are a dragnithan, crafty and possessed of a power that your new crown cannot prohibit. "So I must promise-bind you, I fear." Demayne of Night were oily at best under promise-bindings. If one did not have an inner core of honesty, a promise-binding would slip off very quickly. Ellishan had known that, and had crafted Eckso's binding masterfully. The solution had come to Eckso while she was burdened with Ell's promise-binding. And so she accessed the Eye Gem—not bothering to touch it this time—and plunged into his whirlwind mind. The feat she wrought inside compelled him to act only in her interests and protection. She furthermore made it impossible for him to manifest his wings without her permission.

When she was done, she got up and changed into traveling clothes. "You dress too, dearie. We have things to do."

14

GONE HALF-DARK

Rain washed against the city of Sorgan, borne upon the winds of a dying fellstorm rolling in from the southeast. Such squalls were usual in midwinter, and the ancient city had been built to carry the excess water from roof and street and deliver it to sewers that spilled great deluges from the high-perched city.

The lower city was not so well designed. This sprawl of stone and timber lay at the water's edge, at the bottom of the innumerable switchback stairs hewn into the side of the rocky promontory. And so while Upper Sorgan remained relatively dry, if wind torn, Lower Sorgan was awash in flood.

The elnisian-built quays gave good support to home and shop, but did not aid in drainage. And so ingenuity—and in no small part, desperation—had contrived floating structures, held fast to their positions by thick chains. As storm floods rose, so too did the homes. But not the stone ones. Those simply submerged, which was why ground floors were sparsely appointed and featured boat gates letting into the first story.

Even the long-abandoned Cathedral of Til had such a

feature. And though the roof had burned and collapsed three hundred years ago, the stone still stood.

A boat dipped and dove on the enormous waves, struggling to reach this entry into the cathedral. Three of the six occupants offered fervent prayers for their deliverance. The boat rammed into the stone wall, cracking and sending one of the oarsmen overboard. Nothing was done to recover him.

The dark figure at the prow was unmoved by the dangers of the water. He merely watched the boat gate and reached out with his powers to pull the boat through. Rain did not dampen his filthy robe, nor did the cold chill his bare feet.

Yples was neither patient nor impatient. Rain was sun as far as he was concerned. The three prisoners who lay panting and retching behind him were weak, but he'd brought them here to grant them a great gift. Their suffering would soon end.

The remaining oarsman guided the craft through the interior of the cathedral. The water was relatively still, though rain continued to pelt them from above. The massive columns that had once held up the roof thrust up from the water and arched overhead like the ribs of some great, dead beast. The narrow windows, pointed at the tops, gaped to the gray sky, and whistled as the storm played its frantic tune upon their empty frames.

The boat bumped into a balcony and the oarsman secured the lines to it. Yples stepped out and motioned to the prisoners. The oarsman was reviled and would simply wait. Or perhaps he would be washed away. Or perhaps Yples would forget him entirely and he would simply stand there until his flesh rotted off his bones.

"Come," Yples said to the prisoners and marched into a black corridor.

He had one of each. A Spinster of Pol, a Sensual of Ori, and a Donse Master of Til. All three had similar mercusine potentials; two were quite skilled in its use. The Donse Master was not, but he had a secret mastery of ferneater lore. That would serve, particularly for the task Yples had for him. All were barred from using the mercus at the moment, for mere proximity to Yples covered it with the Revulsion.

Sensual Con was a gray haired woman of sixty, lean and severe. She had held up the best of the three so far, though her stomach had rebelled during the water voyage. Spinster Soth was young, likely only recently raised to her medallion. Yples understood that she was pretty, but he no longer responded to such stimulus. She was weak-minded and had lost all composure when he had forced her to taste the Revulsion. She whimpered continuously now and begged for freedom. She would get freedom, though not in the way she wished. Dunne Sault was middle-aged, but physically strong. He had been raised among men who schemed as naturally as they breathed. He suspected this was a test of his loyalty, or that perhaps it was a ritual hazing before receiving an invitation to join one of Sorgan's innumerable secret societies.

The passageway ended in stairs, which Yples led them down until the steps disappeared into the water. He formed bolts of the Revulsion and the water swirled and began to drain, leaving a tube of air through which the stairs descended. He continued down, ignoring the whimpers and oaths of those behind him.

At the base of the stairs was a door. This he opened and passed through, waited for his whimpering followers to do likewise, then shut and warded it. Behind the door the water flowed back in and covered it over. There was no light here, which he didn't notice until the Spinster began to scream and claw at the door, lamenting that she couldn't see.

Dunne Sault slapped her face. "May we have light?" he asked Yples. His voice reverberated in the large chamber.

"Wake, shamans," Yples said.

Eyegems came to life, casting a weird violet light across the damp stone of what had once been the cathedral's reliquary, a vault to hold relics of the Way of Til. Those were all long gone, but the walls were lined with mouldering wooden shelves. The center of the space was occupied by a stone table, where Donse Masters had once studied the relics they didn't understand. Around this stood three nosg shamans, each holding a staff. The Blackshine swarmlight had corrupted the gems, which now emitted a wavering glow from red to violet to green.

At the sight of the nosg, the Spinster began screaming again. "Zir-Fir, take her first," Yples said. "These others must be locked away."

The nosg shaman muttered orders and two shamans came forward to collect the Sensual and Donse Master. There was a brief scuffle, but both soon succumbed to blows about the head and body. They were then dragged away and locked in cells.

Zir-Fir's skull gems phased from red to black to blue as he approached the Spinster. The woman collapsed to her knees and shrieked. Zir-Fir took hold of her hair and yanked her to her feet, then shoved her at the table. She stumbled, caught her midsection on the edge, which pushed the air from her lungs. The silence that followed pleased Yples. He could have silenced her with his power, but that would not have suited his purpose. Her terror would be useful in the rite to come.

Zir-Fir hefted her onto the table and another nosg took hold of her ankles. They pulled her in opposite ways until she was supine. With disinterested but vicious tears, the nosg clawed the woman's garments from her body. Her screams were renewed, and then were trebled when iron shackles locked over her ankles and wrists.

Yples approached her, smiling. "You are exhausted, overwrought, terrorized. You are desperate, alone, cold, wet, pained, hungry, thirsty. Naked."

Her screams cut off and she began to beg between sobs, then choke upon the phlegm of her misery.

"Be still, child," he said. He trailed a finger up her shin, over her knee, along her thigh. Ever upward, he traced her flesh, belly, breast, throat. He paused to press against her lips, feeling the heat of her breath and the trembling fear of her mouth. Then he continued, sliding his finger up the ridge of her nose and stopping at the spot between her eyes. "Here," he said. "Let us begin here."

Zir-Fir brought his skull staff down, the black gems glowing with eerie violet rays. The Spinster let out only a squeaking sound now, gaze transfixed by the skull. Zir-Fir pressed the skull's forehead to hers, the gems not an inch from her eyes.

"Good," Yples said, feeling the Blackshine swarmlight of the Revulsion building in the eyegems. He then pressed a hand to other places on the woman's quivering body, showing where the other shamans must apply their power. Her breast, her belly, her sex.

The Spinster fell silent save for her panting breaths. And then she began to gag.

"What you feel is the Revulsion. It is the Unanswered force, the Denied Truth. You have been lied to your entire life. What sickens you is in fact true purity. The stench you find foul is the true perfume. The sour taste is the true sweetness. We will unburden you from the lie and reveal to you the truth. Cease your struggling and embrace it. Be flooded by it. Allow it to penetrate you fully."

The first time he'd tried to turn a merculyn of her power he'd been dismayed to discover enormous resistance. But experimentation had revealed the path. To turn a merculyn required one hundredfold their power in the Revulsion, for one had to overcome not only her mercus, but also her faith.

Deprivation and fear halved that ratio. Blackshine shamans

using the swarmlight halved it again. This Spinster would turn, and quickly. But he wanted something more of her, more than a mere revulyn. Revulyn Devin's failure had been instructive.

The Unanswered guided him, infused his thoughts with notions of clever feats. And Yples's experience, too, showed him a few secrets. For had he not, as a mere man, made of himself a hell-formed giant to fight Kila Sigh? Had he not already imbibed a bit of the Unanswered even then? This Spinster and her companions would turn, and with a bit of reshaping of the landscape of their minds, arise more powerful, and infinitely more capable than Revulyn Devin.

He took hold of one of her hands. "I'm here, child. Hold my hand. Trust in me. I give you the greatest of all gifts: release." He threaded into her mind a probe of Revulsion. With the assault of the Blackshine swarmlight already occupying her will, he had easy access to the deepest parts of her. Such as her name. "Mabri Soth," he crooned, "Spinster of Pol. Your goddess smiles upon you, for I have chosen you to do a great thing."

Finding the well of her mercus power was as easy as looking for a lantern in the darkness. This bud of power was engorged to bursting, for she was actively pushing through the Revulsion to access it. She was swallowing the fetid to get to the clean, or so she thought. Exactly as he wished.

"Trust me. Surrender."

He thrust his bolt in deep, encompassing her mercus well and pinching it off. He replaced it with a bit of his own Revulsion, pumping it into her eager mind. When it had been flooded, and the false light of mercusine fully extinguished, he surged in further to impart a seed of his own demaynic essence. Like pulling off a bit of clay from one sculpture and kneading it into another.

Her back arched off the table and the shamans were thrust backward. Vomit poured out of her, black and bloody. Three more convulsions wracked her before she lay still. Her hair was now white as sun-blighted bone.

Yples felt at her throat. Her pulse was still. Her eyes were open, irises gone half-dark. "You see now don't you?" he asked gently, pleased with his new creation.

"I see. I see with the *cold eye*."

The shackles were removed and she stood, untrembling, her nakedness no longer a vulnerability. He brought her a fresh robe, for she would be returning to the world. She had to blend among the unawakened.

He gauged her power, deemed it to be roughly what she'd possessed as a merculyn. Perhaps a bit greater now. Sufficient. "Soth, I name you Revnithan of the Unanswered. You are second only to me. Attend now. Learn this." He showed her the bolts and she repeated them without effort. He again pressed a finger to her forehead. "Bring the Donse Master."

She walked away, was gone a while, then dymensed back, holding the Donse Master's collar. The man was screaming, for she was threading revulynic bolts of terror into his mind.

Yples smiled falsely at the man as he commanded his Black-shine wurgu. "Zir-Fir. Take him!"

And so Qiznithan Yples created two more: The Donse Master was named Revnithan Sault. The Sensual became Revnithan Con. He already knew from his initial inspection of the Sensual's mind that she contained vast stores of knowledge. But the turning had revealed one particular piece he had not suspected. There was a revulynic relic in this world. An elnisian weapon called the Entifal. Originally made to defeat the Revulsion, it had become blessed by it instead. This discovery signaled what he already knew: the Unanswered moved all things to their necessary conclusion.

"A dagger no less," he mused. Yples had read deeply of the histories, and daggers had been particularly significant to the elnisians. They invested their greatest feats of shadlinic power into such weapons.

To each revnithan he imparted knowledge of powerful revulynic feats. "You shall be my daggers, and there is much blood to draw." And he took up nosg-made blades and blessed them and gave them to his revnithans to carry.

"Revnithan Soth. You will return with Revulyn Devin to Starside. There you will search out and take the god-child Kil. Revnithan Con, you must search out the Entifal in Slirya. Be alert for the god-child wherever you go, for Kil may be hidden anywhere. Revnithan Sault, you will go Ceronhel to take charge of the reviled nosg and Blackshine shamans. Use your ferneater lore to awaken and control every nosg. Prepare them to march south, destroy Lockt, and cross the Neer Plain into the lands of men."

One by one his new thralls dymensed away. And now he, too, had a mission to complete. This one far to the west.

15

SHOES, YOUR MAJESTY

"Your title is in question," Marlow said to Kila's reflection in the glass. She sat in a low-backed chair in Ell's dressing room, while no fewer than four maids combed, laced, trimmed, and powdered her.

Quinn had taught her to stay clean and to wear shoes, and Kila had since developed a keen interest in her appearance. In her thieving days, looking like a grimy boy was an advantage. Baths had been an infrequent punishment, usually coming in the form of a bucket of water over her head. Wen had enjoyed her shrieks and sputters, but he had not liked her ripeness in the close quarters of their Warren den. But no amount of vanity would make this treatment by the maid corps worth the irritation.

"Radiant Gilok predicted my legitimacy would be challenged. Ow! Pull my hair that hard again, Posey, and you'll sleep in the eyrie tonight." The maid was supposedly the best at her profession in Starside, but she wielded her combs and pins like a dungeon inquisitor. She spluttered out apologies, eyes filling with tears of terror.

Marlow's mouth turned down and Kila knew she'd been

overly harsh with the girl. Posey was skilled, it seemed. Kila had never imagined her hair could be so lovely, drawn up and pinned to form a nest upon which a crown could be mounted. But that would come later.

"I wasn't talking about your legitimacy," Marlow said. "The Radiants are rightly questioning if you can take the title of Her Enlightened Majesty. The 'enlightened' being the issue."

"I never understood what that meant, anyway. Won't 'Her Majesty' or 'Highness' serve? Or how about 'Autarch'? I never knew what meant, either. Bunch of fancy words, you ask me."

The maids kept their faces expressionless at this, but Posey continued to sniff and pull tentatively at Kila's tresses. At this rate, she'd still be brushing and pinning when Kila turned fifty. "Go on, girl. I won't dymense you to the eyrie. I promise. Marlow as my witness. Consider it a decree." Testing the mercus and finding the Revulsion relatively faint, she formed a simple mind probe and lifted the girl's spirits. Perhaps too much, for the girl started to sing at the top of her lungs and was four bars into "Sailor's Girl" before she realized the impropriety of *"Your ship'll sway from side to side, when up your mast and down I slide."*

Marlow hid his laughter in a fit of coughing. The other maids went bright red, mouths agape in a mixture of horror and anticipation. Only when Kila's spluttering laughter broke the moment did they dare to join in. And for the next five minutes, it was all anyone could do to breathe. Except for poor Posey, who excused herself and rushed out of the room sobbing in humiliation.

It was Kila's mirth that faded first, and she finally wiped the tears from her eyes and noted that the powder and primping had not hidden her tiredness, nor the bleakness of her situation. "This is good enough. Please leave me, ladies. You've done well considering what you were given to work with."

After a bunch of chirping about her natural—if unusual—

loveliness and fine eyes, the women filed out, leaving Kila to stare at herself. "I do not compare with Ell. She was an extraordinary beauty. I look like a girl playing at dress up."

Marlow came to sit by her, face still flushed from his laughing fit. His eyes sparkled with energy. And something else. Something serious and heavy, but not sadness. It was the look a father might give his daughter upon the day of her marriage. "Then you do not see what I see," he said. "You are a striking young woman. Not in the usual pretty way, I'll grant you. But such is not important for you to be a powerful monarch. That comes from here." He pressed a hand to his stomach. "Fortitude is not something others grant to you. It is something you earn through the trials of life. You have suffered and triumphed, and it shows in your face. Did you know that?"

"No," she said, feeling suddenly weepy, which made her laugh in a sorrowful way. Fortitude indeed! The irony of her tears was not lost on Marlow either, for he snickered and wiped at the corner of his own eye.

"I'm proud of you, Kila."

She put a hand on his and squeezed. Ell had advised her to lean on him, but she felt she had to cling to him now, like one adrift at sea. "You are a good scoundrel, Marlow," she said affectionately. "I hope you've diverted plenty of coin to your own accounts."

"Of that, have no doubt. Now, allow me to earn some of it. We have a bit of time before we must go down to the Cathedral." He opened a portfolio and began to read down his list.

"Saiya's safety is, as we agreed during our first council meeting, the utmost priority. Highest Quiv is scouring his library to learn what he can about the Revulsion. I had never heard of it until you and Ell related to me what occurred at the Hackwatch and in Stallid. It's very odd that such a force could remain undetected by so many. Even my brother avoided it, if he knew of it."

"If Ell hadn't been with me to explain it, I would have thought the mercus itself was tainted. And even then, the idea that the Revulsion could be *used* was not at all obvious. But Ell knew more than she told me, and I'll wager Eckso and Klayne know it too. It *is* obvious why the awakened Revulsion would want Saiya, but any more of those revulyns who come to her room will be sorely surprised."

Both cats were staying with Saiya, and the suite was occupied by two very stern fell guardsmen. And then there was Henley, the Motherlight at his side.

"The only problem with our precautions is that they make Saiya a prisoner. She's an energetic child with more curiosity than there is knowledge in the world to fill it. And when she gets bored, nobody is happy."

"The investiture will take only twelve to fifteen hours, then you can remove her to wherever you are planning to take her. As long as you do it quickly." His tone prompted her to tell him where that would be, but the point of hiding Saiya was to keep her location secret from anyone who might be corrupted or tortured by a revulyn.

"Twelve to fifteen hours! I thought they were going to read a few verses from the Theb and then plop the hat on my head. What takes all these hours?"

"The procession to the Cathedral will take an hour all by itself."

"Procession? I thought I'd just dymense us down there."

Marlow waggled his brows and clicked his tongue. "If you want to be seen as Ell's legitimate heir, you mustn't behave like a usurper. You'll ride down in an open carriage, walk up the steps, and listen to the choirs, the readings, the speeches, and endure all the pomp involved. Only then, when the 'hat' is put on your head, can you start thinking about returning to the Citadel. At which point, the public reception will begin. Everyone in Starside has a right to come up here and be received by you as you sit upon the Raven Throne."

Kila sagged in her chair, caught herself pouting in the glass, and turned it into a smirk. "How many flickbow bolts are going to hiss past my head during all this ambling about in public?"

"Only the ones that don't strike your head," he said. "But fear not, for I've heard that you are a merculyn of considerable skill. I'm sure you can ward yourself against such attacks. Also, there will be one hundred fell guardsmen escorting you, not to mention the ones out of armor peppered through the throngs to apprehend ne'er-do-wells before they can loose their arrows at your pretty head."

She sank lower in the chair, propping her bare feet on the vanity top. "You said before that I wasn't pretty."

"I said you aren't pretty in the *usual* way, my dear," he said. "Mark me, you will soon have dozens of suitors comparing you to the stars. Now, can we agree that Saiya is as safe as we can make her?"

"For tonight, yes."

He turned back to his list, and she glared at herself the glass. Annoyance was tickling her brain, giving her the distinct sensation that she was forgetting something. Was there something she meant to do? The glass showed her brow furrowing, and she was struck by the memory of her father's brow doing the same thing when he was bothered. She forced it smooth.

"Eckso and Klayne are gone," Marlow said. "Eckso's children, Trevi and Poli are also gone. No surprise. Highest Quiv sent a Donse Master to Trine via the Derslin Wheel. An hour ago I received his couriered report. Eckso has not returned to her home there. She has not been seen there for well over a month. She surely knew that would be the first place we'd look. Another problem is Highest Quiv. Or rather that he's facing his own legitimacy crisis. He appropriated the role of Highest of

Highests in the aftermath of that Fley imbroglio on Garden Island."

"I remember it well. I was there."

"That's not how the Highest of Highests is chosen. It seems he was within his right to claim the title on an interim basis, but a conclave of Highests and Nares must meet to choose the permanent successor. This requires Way of Til delegates from every major city to travel to Garden Island, where a long process of intrigue, scheming, and skullduggery will begin."

"Til's Tower on Garden Island is a pile of rubble. They should meet in Starside. Quiv can teach them the Derslin Wheel or dymensing and be done with it in a ten-day."

"You are ahead of me. For such a conclave to happen in Starside, Highest Quiv requires your permission. Many of the delegates will be hostile to both Quiv and you. Most will be Highests in their own diocese. All will wish to take Quiv's vestments for themselves."

"This sounds like Quiv's problem, not mine. What's next on your list?"

She crinkled her nose and frowned at her reflection. Again the notion of forgetting. Like trying to recall a word and having the very taste of the syllables bouncing around in one's mouth.

"Half of your army is at the Sablefort," Marlow said. "Ell sent them in anticipation of a nosg assault from the north. Our treaties with the eastern and southern realms require them to send a proportionate force to join our men. Tordain would have accounted for twenty thousand. They will now send none."

"The nosg went home. Our men should return to theirs. And stop the enlistments and rationing. Hey! Make that my coronation decree. That'll win me some grins in Terriside, at least."

"Ell was not convinced the threat had passed."

The welcome distraction of a knock rattled the door. "Come," Kila called, interrupting whatever argument Marlow was about to make. A fell guardsman stepped in, allowing Radiant Gilok to enter. "Your Majesty," the Radiant said, sweeping a practiced bow. "It is time."

Kila hoisted herself from the chair. She wore one of Ell's gowns, swiftly altered by the Mistress of Wardrobe to accommodate Kila's narrower hips and flatter chest. Blue, sheer, with a high ruffled collar, it was probably worth more gold skillets than Kila and Wen had stolen in their entire careers.

"Shoes, Your Majesty," said the fell guardsman, though how he knew she didn't have any on was a mystery, for the hem of the skirt spilled all around her feet. Sighing, she stepped into a pair brought up from Gristenside specifically for today's events. They were blue satin with pearls and a lifted heel. Ridiculous, but more comfortable than she expected. She flashed her eyes at the guardsman. "Satisfied?"

"If you must run, I would have your feet protected. There could be broken glass."

To get to the front courtyard of the Citadel would be a foot-journey of twenty minutes, most of it going down winding stairs. The very same that Radiant Gilok had just ascended, which had likely taken him thirty minutes. "All of you, grab hold of me."

There was stammering and the fell guardsman blinked severely. "But my second must come, too."

"Call him in here."

It took two entire minutes, full of apologies to Her Majesty, to get Marlow, Gilok, and two fell guardsmen to hold onto her arms. She dymensed to the courtyard.

16

H.M.

A roar of surprise filled the air when they appeared out of empty space. The entire staff of the Citadel, along with throngs of ambassadors and other supernumeraries, were already assembled in the grand front courtyard. In the rain.

Kila formed a weather-cloak to keep herself dry, then thickened it into an armor-cloak in case of flying bottles or arrows. "Now what?" she asked.

"The carriage," Marlow said, releasing her.

The mercus green rolled away from them and made the front row of the crowd cough. She wouldn't apologize for it. In fact, she studiously looked above everyone's heads. If she made eye-contact, they'd surely see that she was a fraud. The carriage had been brought out of some deep storage hall, cleaned, polished, and hitched up to the most fantastic team of atlens Kila had ever seen.

Blues were the rarest breed, known for their stamina and speed, and also for their intelligence. That wasn't saying much. They were birds after all. But these six monsters eyed the crowd as suspiciously as the Fell Guard. Their feathers were a deep blue, almost black. They glimmered with iridescence in the mercus light of the rainy evening.

The Fell Guard marched her to the carriage. It was very tall, with enormous wheels and three rows of open seats. "The very back, Your Majesty," the senior guard said, and then the little door was swung shut. The driver clucked to the birds.

"Wait. I'm riding alone?" she called to Marlow.

He merely smiled and waved.

The carriage began to roll. Out of the courtyard, and through a series of gates. She twisted in her seat to see the Citadel behind her. The new perspective drove a watery chill through her insides.

It was hers. All of it.

At each gate, the fell guardsmen on duty dipped their spears and helms. The stone tunnels through each gate held enormous portcullises that rose between fortified towers at her approach.

The city has lost its mind, Nax, she sent.

Perhaps it is you who have lost yours, Nax replied, faintly. She wished the cat were with her. She could use the warmth and the comfort. But she'd rather Nax stay with Saiya, no matter how frightening the path ahead.

The road came down past Radiant Gilok's greathouse, a massive palace set in an enormous green park. She again twisted to see the procession of carriages behind her. Dozens and dozens of them rolled in even spacing. Many were festooned with white garlands, the flowers plucked from Radiants' hothouses. Many of the Radiant class were ahorse, dressed in their finest regalia, sabers at their sides.

As she descended through Gristenside, more carriages came from the long drives of other greathouses to join the procession, including no small number of wagons full of household staff who had been given permission to attend.

By the time she reached the Baths of Ori, the procession snaked all the way up the Street of the Diadem to the Citadel. Presumably, Marlow was back there somewhere. That angered her. She was supposed to lean on him. Well, she needed him now, to remind her what was about to happen, what she was supposed to say, and tell her how much more she had to endure whenever she wanted to ask.

Henley, can you hear me?

No response. He was too far away.

She spun again to look at the procession behind her. Then up at the Citadel. She felt like she'd left something behind. No idea what. Maybe something in her backpack. She could hardly go to her coronation with her battered old backpack on. She patted the bulge on her thigh. At least Cayne was with her.

The rain continued to slant down at the city, driven on a stiff southerly breeze. A balmy wind had kicked up, bringing warmer air in to melt the slush. The crowds did not care about the rain. They had turned out in the tens of thousands to cheer and jeer at their new monarch.

The Way of Ori apparently did not care about the procession, for not even one initiate showed a face outside the Baths. Kila had heard that the sour-faced Sensual Taht had risen to Voluptuary. Taht had never liked Kila, and the feeling was reciprocated in full.

The Street of the Diadem narrowed at the Trialti Arch, where three hundred men of the Watch kept the public to one side. Else it would have been packed with people and the blue atlens would have crushed them. There was no stopping the birds. They trotted, heads jerking forward and back in unison, proud plumes refusing to be defeated by the rain.

The Trialti was a short tunnel opening into Dunne Medow Plaza. It seemed the entire population of the city had squeezed in. At the sight of the carriage, every voice lifted. There were cheers, but just as many hollers of disapproval. Many faces were twisted with disgust, and the air suddenly filled with flying produce that struck her armor-cloak and splattered into the carriage. A few rocks arced toward her and these too bounced away. After the first two, she refused to flinch.

The Fell Guard were upon these missile throwers at once, and the onlookers who favored Kila joined them. The whole crowd was on the verge of riot, and her supporters were far outnumbered by her detractors.

This was no way to begin her reign. "Driver, stop the carriage."

The man looked back at her, eyes a bit wide with fear. "I was ordered not to, mum."

"Stop the carriage."

He gave her one last pleading look before yanking back on the reins and calling for his birds to stop. They did, immediately. The crowd shrieked as if they'd won a great victory.

Kila probed the mercus, cautious to not let her own fear lure the Revulsion toward her. It was certainly thicker here, and she had to fight down gags to slide her mind through it and pull the mercus in.

She didn't know exactly what she should do, but felt that some show of her power might cow the crowd enough to at least let her pass without breaking into civil war. She decided on light, a blazing bluish-white light that emanated from her body. A spectacle to draw attention. And it worked. The jeers and cries turned to yelps, then hushed awe. Those closest to her carriage shrank back. The fell guardsmen dragged the offenders they'd caught into the open lane behind the carriage. Most were boys, but also a few gray-hairs who should have known better, and one ragged young girl with no shoes.

Kila locked eyes with the girl, noting the crudely cropped

hair and shirt sewn from rags. Cheapsgate. "Bring her," she said to the fell guardsmen. "Release the men and boys."

The girl cursed and wriggled, but the fell guardsman simply hefted her by her collar until only her toes remained on the stones. He drew up to the carriage and waited. Kila remembered Henley's advice to pretend to be Ell. Instinct told Kila that Ell would be generous in the face of such anger, offer clemency rather than punishment. She might even have the girl fed and given a gold skillet.

That wasn't enough. Kila stood and opened the door. "Come up here with me," she said. "You will be my representative from Cheapsgate at the coronation."

The girl's fury was not lessened by this unexpected invitation. "I don't wanna see yer crownin', ya Sourwater pikefish!"

"Well, yer gonna see it, if I have ta bend a line to yer yardarms and hoist ya up the Cathedr'l steps m'self. Get in!"

The girl got in. The odor she exuded caught Kila by surprise and she twisted up a bolt of lilac scent to cover it. "Sit." The girl sat, right next to her. The contrast between Kila's gown and the girl's rags was nearly as breathtaking as the girl's stink. Her feet were absolutely black, the frayed ends of her trouser legs soaked and muddy.

"Driver, proceed."

He cracked his whip over the birds, and they strained forward. Kila kept up her show of radiant light, doing her best to form her mouth into a pleasant, placid smile for the benefit of the uneasy crowd. Gauging by their faces, she hadn't won them over so much as astonished them. But at least they weren't fighting each other or throwing things at her.

"How are things in Cheapsgate?" she asked the girl.

"It's a right stew of dung and piss, and ya know it yerself. If ya came from there like folk say."

"I did. I lived in the Warren. Do ya know ol' Parlo Odok?"

"Rat Face? Him an' his lumberin' clubman Jocko've been makin' bold moves now that ol' Viller's dead."

"Parlo Odok is makin' moves? What sort?"

The girl squinted at her. "Were ya truly a thief?"

"I was. And you?"

The girl shrugged and made a rude gesture at a face in the crowd. "That one tried ta get marital with me," she said. "Alley groper."

Kila snapped a finger at a trailing fell guardsman. "Arrest that one. Take him to the Westbunk." The command was followed, and the man discovered he was being carried quickly back through the crowd and through the Trialti Arch.

"What if I were lyin?" the girl said, awed by the swiftness of Kila's justice.

"Were you?"

"No."

The carriage pulled up to the steps of the cathedral. Enormous divots in the stone spoiled their even march up toward the new doors Highest Quiv had installed. The front face of the structure was plain stonework, all the statuary, arches, windows, and spindles having been destroyed during Kila's battle with the Hargothe.

A raven perched on the edge of the roof. Seeing it gave her a moment's pause. Its shape raised that elusive feeling again, of having forgotten something vital. Odd. There were raven images everywhere in the Citadel. She had them on her jacket sleeves when she wasn't primped up like a Radiant's daughter. But this one . . .

A fell guardsman opened her door, pulling her back into the present. The girl hopped out, her mood now having shifted from dislike and distrust to a sort of adoration, as if Kila were a big sister. The age difference wasn't that great, perhaps four years.

Kila came down from the carriage. The girl shifted from foot to foot. The stone was cold here. Highest Quiv waited at the top of the steps, flanked by the Nares. These men were Donse Masters of a higher rank, and as such were to be trusted even less. The fact that the coronation took place here, rather than at the Citadel, was just another reason she'd been so uneasy all day. The Way of Til had been her enemy for so long. With a few exceptions, it still was. It was a sign of the unsettled times that Highest Quiv was her ally while his underlings hated her.

She ascended the steps and awkwardly accepted the nodding bows of the men. "Highest Quiv, can you send someone to find a frock and shoes for this girl?"

"I don't wanna dress like a Kil-damned Donse Master!" the girl hissed.

"They are just clothes. And you need something dry. And clean."

Quiv whispered a command and an acolyte was soon sprinting away. Kila made her way into the cathedral and waited in the space that had once been a grand vestibule. Now it was simply a cordoned off area of damaged floor. Beyond stood the forest of columns that held up what remained of the ceiling. The damaged areas had been patched with tarpaulins and hastily erected wooden beams.

The nave was still impressive, and to Kila's eye, less oppressive than it had once been now that some light could get in. The acolyte returned with a bundle of clothes. The girl was skeptical, but Kila merely looked at her with expectation.

"I'm not gettin' nakid in front of all these peepers."

"The chapel of Mayla is over there," Kila said. "Change in there and come find me. I'll be up front."

This pulled a wicked laugh from the girl and she marched off, arms full of clean robes, stockings, and shoes. The acolyte rushed after her, promising to also fetch a basin and cake of soap.

Kila nodded to Quiv, who led her to the opposite side of the church and into the Chapel of Ori. The Way of Til recognized the other Ways, but did not consider them truly independent organizations. The policy of the Way of Til had been that Ori and Pol were subject to Til, and therefore their Ways were subject to the authority of the Way of Til.

The other Ways disagreed. The Way of Til proceeded to install chapels to Ori and Pol in their cathedrals and form scholarly brotherhoods devoted to the goddesses. Kila didn't care about religious politics. She only cared about the refreshments awaiting her in the chapel. The Nares were dismissed to find their seats behind the altar. Kila took a seat and drank a cup of tea as the Fell Guard filed into the cramped chapel and closed the wrought iron gate.

Highest Quiv pulled a vast curtain, blocking the chapel from view of the thousand privileged souls who would be admitted to witness the coronation in person. The rest would remain outside in the rain.

The noise in the nave grew steadily as carriage after carriage disgorged yet another Radiant or dignitary. The incense of the Cathedral gave way to perfumes, and the discussion rose in volume until Kila had to yell to make herself heard to Highest Quiv. "I want that girl near to the throne where I can see her."

"It isn't a throne. That's at the Citadel. You'll be seated on the High Seat of the Diadem."

"What's a diadem?"

The man blinked at her then leaned close to her ear. "It's a crown."

That explained the name of the Street of the Diadem. She'd always wondered about that.

Quiv occasionally parted the curtain to peer out, but when the cathedral's bell began to sound eight bells night, he squeezed through an interior door. He gave her one last look.

"When I strike my staff twelve times, come out, come up the aisle, and face me. I'll guide you through the rest."

"Make sure the girl is where I can see here."

He nodded and slipped away. There were a score of fell guardsmen in the chapel with her, but she felt absolutely alone.

Ell's last words to her came back: *"You will need Night. You will need them all."* And then Dox Viller cackled and strained forward in his chair, blood pouring from empty eye-sockets. *"Had I known it was a shadline blade back then, I would have had him killed sooner."* And then the Hargothe loomed over her, skinless hands reaching from the sleeves of his robe. A black fog poured from his rictus of a mouth, and hissed words stung her ears: *"I shall have thee, girl. Mark me. And when I have Kil chained at my feet, your power will be a mere flickering candle in the gale. I shall possess thee utterly and use thee for whatever purpose I wish."*

Trembling, she hiked up her skirt and the five underskirts she'd been wrapped in, until her stockinged leg was exposed to air. Cinched over her stockings was Cayne, her father's blade. All she had left of either him or Wen. She drew it, taking comfort in the soft leather grip. The feeling of it in her palm jolted her again to that disconcerting feeling of forgetting.

The fell guardsmen noticed the dagger but did nothing other than to scan for danger in a small enclosed space where none was to be found. The audience in the nave had gone quiet. A man's voice lifted. It wasn't Highest Quiv's, but she recognized it. It was Highest Binel, the Highest of Til in Starside. This was his diocese, so it made sense that he would get a chance to speak.

There were coughs and sneezes, then a long chant, and finally Quiv's voice. She didn't hear any of the invocation as she stared at her blade, focusing on its edge so that the unbidden voices of the dead would no longer haunt her. And they *were* silenced, but the visions—which she knew were nothing but memories—continued to play before her. Pennie, curly haired and mature beyond her years. Critt Sanglo with his tarred sailor's queue and wide grin. Yiqa, veiled and severe. Wen, coughing and gazing at her as if he didn't recognize her.

"I don't recognize myself," she said him, turning the blade to inspect her reflection on the flat. But Cayne did not reveal her image. It soaked it in, showing her only a glossy black surface.

What am I forgetting?

She lifted it to her ear and listened, but there was no bell tone coming from it now. Returning it to its sheath, she floofed down her skirts and stood. Sharp taps resounded through the cathedral. Highest Quiv drove his staff onto the marble floor, each strike pulling her a second closer to a dreaded, inevitable, doom.

The twelfth rap sounded and faded. The Fell Guard drew back the curtain and opened the gate. A thousand faces turned toward her, and then with a rustle and scrape, all rose.

In the choir loft, fifty voices lifted in song. She knew it was in First Race by the lilting hop and skip of the syllables. She couldn't concentrate on the words, or the melody, for she was too conscious of the eyes on her. Somehow she was striding forward, hands at her side, eyes fixed ahead.

Some smiles caught her attention. Radiant Hiolly. Marlow. Kinnon Swile, Mistress of Kitchens at the Citadel.

Frowns were more common. She passed a row of white-haired young men. Keels. Ragin wasn't among them. The elder Keel sat on the aisle. She met his gaze, found it extraordinarily haughty, and lifted her chin ever so slightly in acknowledgment of his disrespect.

It wasn't until she was halfway down the central aisle that she noticed the light reflecting from the gems in the women's hair. The light was coming from her. She had never released the feat from the carriage.

Four fell guardsmen walked with her. Two in front, two behind. Their boots clanked on the marble until the floor suddenly became wooden planks. Another quick repair. The booms of their footsteps filled the nave, then turned to sharp clicks as the marble returned.

Kila came to the front row, occupied by the highest ranking Radiancies. Gilok was the first among them. He bowed slightly to her. Next was Highest Binel, who waited at the base of the steps leading to the altar. He looked pale, uncertain. She knew a bit more about him than either of them wished. She had once hidden in his bed, while he and a woman were in it.

What would Ell do? she asked herself.

Kila winked at Binel, which made his face go hot. She proceeded up the steps and finally stopped before Highest Quiv. He had donned special vestments of white and gold for this ceremony. Behind him, upon the altar were the crown, the scepter, and the huge red tome with raven quill and ink next to it.

He smiled at her. "Turn and face your subjects."

She scanned the faces of these people, the richest and most powerful Starsidians. Her subjects. No doubt she had robbed several of those present. She scanned the front row for the Cheapsgate girl. She wished she'd gotten her name before they'd been separated. It took a second look to recognize the scrawny girl at the end of the front row. Her face had been scrubbed, her hair rinsed and combed. She appeared to be munching on a heel of bread. The girl returned her look with curiosity, chewing open-mouthed.

Behind Kila, two Donse Masters rolled out a gilded chair, arms and legs elaborately carved into animal claws, the seat and back covered in maroon velvet. They placed it behind her. Their lips were drawn down, as if they'd been chewing on green mingberries, such was their disgust at her ascension to the throne.

Highest Quiv was reading a First Race passage, and it went by too quickly for Kila to pick up what it was. Something from the Theb. Finally he switched to Ennish. He talked and talked, mostly about accepting the great wisdom of Her Enlightened Majesty, Ell LiMinluit, and that her choice of Kila Sigh was designed to surprise and perplex and even vex, but that she had extensive experience with Sigh and knew her to be of noble heart, courage, and loyalty.

Someone shouted, "She's a thief and she consorts with cats!"

A wave of murmurs rose and crashed against the dais, and some began to applaud the heckler. Kila felt heat rising in her throat even as ice chilled her guts. Again Dox Viller's bloated face rose in her mind, wet lips spreading as he laughed at her misery.

Highest Quiv ignored the interruption and continued, though he did pick up the pace of his speech. Finally he got round to the task at hand, bringing forward the sapphire and diamond crown. "The diadem of The Raven Throne. May the gods grant you wisdom, to rule justly." Kila felt him settle the crown upon her specially arranged hair, which poofed up through the hoop of the relic and held it fast. It wasn't as heavy as she'd feared. And since she couldn't see it, she only felt slightly more ridiculous than before.

A buzzing resonance upon the mercusine told her it possessed some power, though she had no idea what it was. In fact, it carried an outward-projecting quality. As soon as it was upon her head, the faces in the front row slackened and a few women pressed their hands to their chests. So, it lent her a glamour of some sort.

Next came the scepter. Kila had never seen Ell carrying it about, so she assumed it was ceremonial. But it too was infused with the mercus. The jewels were sapphires and diamonds. Quiv placed it into her right hand, saying: "May the gods provide you strength to defend our realm against all who seek to harm it, from within and without."

She lowered it into the crook of her arm as she'd been coached to do, feeling out the senses and emotions so intricately woven into the relic. It was soothing yet invigorating, the emotions subtle and more akin to bodily sensations than thoughts. She realized her breathing had slowed and her heart had calmed.

Finally, Highest Quiv brought forth the great tome, while Highest Binel carried the raven quill and the ink pot. "The Register of Acts of the Raven Throne," he said, opening the book to a spread near the middle. On the left was a column of neatly written statements, each signed in the same hand: *H.E.M. Ellishan LiMinluit.*

The very last signed entry read simply: *"We declare Kila Sigh to be Our Heir, to ascend to the Raven Throne upon Our death. Long may she reign."*

At the top of the right page was a single line: *"We claim the Raven Throne."*

Kila took the raven quill, dipped the nib into the pot, and was very thankful for the calming effect of the scepter, for when she made her signature next to the newest entry, her hand was steady. She was immediately embarrassed by the crudeness of her penmanship, for she had little practice in it. The lines and loops were jagged and misproportioned, the hand of a child.

"You must put 'H.E.M.' before your name," whispered Quiv.

Remembering Marlow's discussion about the word "enlightened," she instead put 'H.M.' and returned the quill to Highest Binel. "I may be queen, but I will not claim to be more than that."

Quiv held her gaze for a moment, considering her words and then finding something amusing in them. He nodded solicitously and returned the tome to the altar.

"Please stand," he instructed softly.

She did, and instantly everyone seated before her shot from their pews. Even the Cheapsgate girl got caught up in the moment. The sour faces remained, but the disgust had softened. Kila thought it must be the mercus effect woven into the crown.

His voice lifted so all could hear his next pronouncement: "Behold! Her Majesty Kila Sigh!"

A few coughs resonated in the chamber, but there was no applause, no cheers. Clearly not a Cheapsgate crowd, Kila thought.

"Will you address your subjects?" Quiv asked softly. This had been a point of great debate among her small council. Her opinion, which was that the less she said the less troubled she'd be in, had carried absolutely no weight. It was agreed that she must speak, and a short statement had been prepared for her. She had dutifully memorized it, but now that she was faced with this mostly hostile crowd, she found the words uninspiring.

"I—I . . . No. I will not. Make sure the girl gets into my carriage."

Rather than witness Quiv's disappointment or disapproval, she simply began to walk. She was joined instantly by her Fell Guard escort, leaving Highests Quiv and Binel racing to catch up. Soon the exit procession was assembled around her, a song rose from the choir, and she slowly made her way to the doors. At her approach, these were thrown open and the bells began to toll. The crowd screamed, partly with delight, but mostly with hate.

This she endured while she returned to her carriage; while she climbed in and situated her skirts; while the Cheapsgate girl clambered in and sat next to her; and while the regal blue atlen team pulled them through a path opened by the Watch.

She kept her eyes fixed ahead, unfocussed, as the carriage wove through the Trialti Arch and into Gristenside. There were throngs along the exclusive shop gallery below the Baths, but the crowds thinned as the carriage ascended the Street of the Diadem. She did not wave or even look at those who watched. The impulse to simply dymense back to the Citadel and to the quietude of her dressing room came over her very powerfully.

"Ya look differn't," the girl said. "Like a queen now."

"Is that a compliment?"

She shrugged.

"What's your name?"

"Mayrie."

"Parents live in Cheapsgate?"

"Dead. Gran-gran has a shack by the sewer outlet."

Kila smiled sadly and finally looked out at the homes set amid their vast green spaces. "I hid in that house for a ten-day," she said, pointing at the Hiolly greathouse. "I stole a sword off a man in the plaza. My brother and I took it there so the merchant would think Radiant Hiolly had stolen it. Wen was going to get the merchant to pay us to retrieve it. Since I already had it, I would just slip out a window with it and we'd collect the payment."

"Like a recov'ry agent?"

"Just like. But the merchant wouldn't pay."

"Didya keep the sword?"

"No. It was marked with the mercus, so I had to leave it there."

It was an odd sensation to be so distant from the relatively recent past. The future she'd dreamt of then was long behind her now. She was infinitely wealthy, extraordinarily powerful in mercus, military, and political might. She looked down at the scepter still cradled in her arms like a bejeweled doll and was suddenly overcome with tears.

The girl dug into a pocket and pulled out the last bit of her bread. She offered it to Kila.

Tearful and nose running, Kila laughed and pushed it away. "Thank you, but I'm not hungry."

The girl shrugged and took an enormous bite. She chewed and considered Kila for a few more moments. Then, around a mouthful of bread, she said, "That's yer problem right there, Maj'sty."

17

DEATH IS BORNE

A warm, moist breeze curled through Fallo's hair as he looked over the elnisian city of Cigil-Tine. The gold-flecked boulevards gave it a sheen of recent abandonment despite the crumbling domes and choking vines that shrouded the magnificent palaces. But it had been empty for over nine hundred years.

Mostly empty. The phantom ranks of the *zol-hidir* still resided here. Nosg spirits, imprisoned to serve as guardians against unworthy intruders.

The breeze felt so gentle, so lulling. But danger haunted those blank windows.

"Don't be fooled by all the beauty and balmy air," he said to Quinn. "Lop and I almost got killed a hundred times over down there."

Quinn took in the lovely panorama, breathing deeply of the fruity scent on the air. "It's more magnificent than I had imagined. You never mentioned the maiden."

The maiden was an enormous statue. A hundred feet tall, she stood at the west end of a wide boulevard. She held a spear, shaft angling down to disappear behind some buildings, the tip facing up and west. Birds circled her head, a living halo. Her fierce gaze was fixed on the sinking sun. Behind her rose the mist of the falls, which poured from a gaping maw in one of the mountains that enclosed the city in a protective bowl.

"Right out of a balladeer's song," she said. "I could be happy there, I think. Imagine living along that wide street, our children exploring the empty halls. Fruit from the trees there and lunches in that park. The whole city to ourselves. An endless palace, all graceful and spirited with the memory of the nameless elnisians who built it."

"Children?" Fallo said, voice cracking.

"Two, I think. Kila and a Little Fallo."

"The nosg ghosts would find them a tasty treat. I doubt Kila Sigh would thank you for feeding her namesake to them."

Quinn trilled a laugh.

"We should make camp here," Fallo said, suddenly uncomfortable with the conversation. They hadn't come here to plan a future. "We need to get settled and out of sight before the *zolhidir* come out."

Fallo wasn't sure if they'd attack him again. But he wasn't going to risk it. Not after coming this far. Besides, his shadline instincts were pulling him elsewhere. His eyes drifted up to the peculiar peak above the falls. A perfect match to the drawing Zirhine had showed him at a chance meeting in the Sagmarsh. It was to that mountain he had to go. To the supposed Tomb of Man. That was according to the vergent ink writing Shad Linas had discovered on the sketch. The writing was a riddle, and he didn't like riddles anymore. All he knew was that his instincts were pulling him there as surely as if a rope were tied around his neck and someone was cranking it around a capstan.

"There are plenty of nice mansions down there," Quinn said. "Maybe even a bed." She flashed an eyebrow at him.

"Tempting, Lady Peline. Kil's eyes, you have no idea how

tempting that is. But I choose to remain unmolested. Uh, by ghosts, that is."

Where's that chicken you promised me? Lop sent. The cat sat atop Tolky, Quinn's beloved donkey.

Fallo grinned at the fuzzy black cat. *I lied. I don't have a chicken.*

The cat sent a torrent of tail-twisting sensation through the bond. *I'll have the pork then.*

They set about clearing a spot for their camp. Quinn collected firewood while Fallo found a few tidbits for Lop. He kept the more tender pieces for Quinn.

He began unburdening the donkey, who looked back at him with dark and patient eyes. Tolky whickered and stamped with relief as the packs came off.

Fallo kept sneaking glances at Quinn as she bent to pick up fallen limbs. His life had been unfortunate in many ways. An ugly face, a father who had tried to have him murdered, an unasked-for career as a shadline bearing three mythical dragon-tooth blades. But Quinn . . . Never had he imagined someone so captivating could love him. Setting her beauty aside (a ridiculous thing to attempt, he had to admit), everything else about her appealed to him. Her humor, her feigned impatience with his jokes, her fierce devotion to the shadline way, her loyalty to Kila, her affection for Lop, her flawless memory for old songs, and her hunger for adventure . . . all of it made him love her more.

"I wish I could hold the sun right where it is," he said. "See how it spans the gap at the end of the valley? It's twice the size of a midday sun. It's really something, isn't it?"

He cleared his throat and recited:

> "The clever cannot witness
> A beauty without naming;

The wisdom of the witless
is seeing without claiming."

Quinn stopped what she was doing, looked at him. The golden light softened her features, stilled them like the waters of a glassy pond. Fallo knew she was wondering why he was talking this way. He wondered it himself.

But he kept on blabbing. "My tutor was Dunne Binel. That was long before he became Highest in Starside. He said the sun was an aspect of Til. He said that the sun grows larger as it approaches the horizon to remind us that Til watches our night-time transgressions with greater judgment than he does our midday charities. I don't think Binel actually believed it. I didn't. But now I wonder . . ."

Quinn blew a stray lock from her eyes. "You wonder if the sun is truly Til's fiery eye spying on us?"

"No. Not quite that. But I do wonder if he grants us a sight like this to force us to stop what we're doing, and see. To really see, before it's too late, the beauty granted to us." Chuckling sadly, he shook his head. "Ah me, my tongue gets overly sweet at times. It's just the fading of the light. See how it casts the city in gold? And how it warms the faces of those peaks?"

Another snatch of verse came to him, heard long ago in his father's dining hall.

> "From gray night to cheer morn,
> Such wild moods life foments;
> Each second death is borne,
> While beauty hides in moments."

A gust buffeted the tall grass between them, now bringing a cold caress, a reminder that it was winter even here. He turned away from the magnificent arc of fire sinking to the west. He faced Quinn, whose black eyes caught and sparkled with the flame of Til's parting gift. It softened her face more, and her lips parted in response to his own warming gaze. He was helpless not to kiss her, to hold this moment as long as he could.

When they parted, her eyes were shaded, her soft face obscured by his own shadow. "Turn around," she said softly. "You're missing the moment you were just going on about."

"*You* are the moment, Quinn. You have been so since I first saw you."

She kissed him hard, and he held her until the sun dropped its gaze from the world. His back cooled and the shadow of night settled in around them. Lop meowed, annoyed by Fallo's lack of progress on dinner. In the valley below, only a few spires still held the gold of the lost day. And as that vanished, the elnisian city ghosted into shadow.

Fallo's shadline instincts forced his attention from Quinn, away from her vision of a city house and the phantom children who might have explored the hollow mansions. His eyes lifted to the rising crescent moon and the faint sparkles of the Goblet constellation.

Between those two heavenly signs speared upward the dark, jagged peak.

Somewhere in there lay the Tomb of Man.

18

ENDS IN FIRE

Her Majesty Kila Sigh had less than half an hour between arriving back at the Citadel and the start of the Presentation to the City. During this time she checked on Saiya, introducing her to Mayrie and making sure she was dressed for the event. She wanted Henley with her for a while, which meant Saiya would have to come to the reception. Besides, the poor girl had been locked away too long.

As all this was going on, her squad of maids appeared, bearing a change of clothes. It seemed that one could not receive subjects in the same outfit one had just been seen in by those same subjects.

She plucked the crown from her head and tossed it into a vacant chair. The scepter joined it. The squinting of all these eyes reminded her that she was still glowing with mercus light. She quashed it and everyone sighed in relief. For the rest of it, all she had to do was stand and wait while approximately one hundred buttons were unfastened down her back, then be tugged this way and that until she was stripped to her small clothes.

No sooner had she enjoyed two unrestricted breaths when

another gown materialized and she was manhandled into it. This one was also blue, with silvery details and innumerable pearls affixed on the bodice. Fortunately, this one did not require more than a petticoat, crinoline, and whale bone frame underneath. "Who dreams up these indignities?" she asked them.

No one answered, so Kila resigned herself to another round of primping, which included the complete deconstruction of her coronation hair in order for it to be coaxed into loose curls with a scorching hot iron rod. The crown was reattached with specially made clips.

Henley, who had been banished for the dressing, sent to her: *We don't need another child living with us.*

Mayrie is not going to live with us.

So you're going to send her back to Cheapsgate? After all this?

Of course not. Her gran lives in a shack in Cheapsgate. I'll pay for them both to live in Terriside somewhere. Marlow will see to the details.

As if his name were a summons, the man appeared. His cheeks flushed above his salt and pepper beard, and his eyes had the harried look of a housemother who'd discovered her kitchen full of stray hounds. Marlow carried his portfolio already opened to a page of trouble.

The maid squadron gathered their things and swarmed out. Kila sat at her vanity. She had to admit the curls were rather fetching, and the powder girl had dusted her eyelids with a sooty material that made her eyes look much larger. The addition of the crown made her look like a queen. Marlow looked up from his list. His reaction to her transformation was to stammer, "You look as if you were born to the crown, Your Majesty."

She remembered the mercus charge in the crown, was astonished to see how strongly it affected her chief counselor. There was no removing it now that it was clipped in. "Is it time for me to face my citizens?" she said. She tried to color her question with a wry note, but Marlow didn't hear it.

"No, majesty. We have a few moments to discuss the Way of Kila."

"What's to discuss about a bunch of fools being foolish?"

"Fools or no, their numbers increase. Much of the city is against them."

She recalled the last time she spoke to her putative devotees. It was on the road to Tearling, where she passed an encampment of them. Her face had been recognized and she had had to endure their unthinking adoration. But she was appalled by the squalor of their camp, and their outright laziness. After admonishing them to clean up and get to work, she'd stalked off, promising only to return when they were ready. Which, she had thought at the time, would be never.

"They have merculyns," Marlow said. "Dunne Quiv said his Seeker counted at least a dozen in the Blasted Quarter. Some have left the other Ways, others are simply unawakened youths. Even if you do not take control of the Way, you will be blamed for its actions."

Kila didn't have a chance to say anything more on the subject, for a bell tolled ten times. The hour of the Presentation had come.

THE HALL of the Raven Throne lay at the very heart of the Citadel. Kila's subjects came into it via the Citadel's main entry, through an interior courtyard, then through one of four arched passageways that led into a black marble gallery as wide as a boulevard. Statues of the first humans to occupy Starside stood atop square plinths, eyes gazing into a lost past. The walls were draped with banners of the Radiancies. An enormous flag hung directly overhead emblazoned with the Raven-in-Flight.

Every visitor passed through a narrowing at the end of the gallery to be scrutinized by the Fell Guard before being allowed to walk single file up the broad marble steps to the open doors of the throne hall.

Two fell guardsmen stopped each family at the hall's entryway—for many had all their children in tow, dressed in the finest garments they owned—to give them one last warning look. With a nod, each family was permitted to continue into the hall. Twice the size of the gallery below, it was like the nave of a great Cathedral, marble floor polished to a high shine. Columns soared to an arched ceiling, every inch of which was covered by a painting. The scene was of Til, wrapped in a linen loincloth, floating in a ray of sunlight. Pol stood to one side, holding a crystal sphere in her left hand, the other hand poised to catch a spinning coin. To Til's right was Ori, kneeling next to an emaciated man, and spooning broth into his mouth.

Opposite Til, amidst a bank of roiling black clouds, peered two malevolent eyes and the suggestion of limbs emerging to the left and right. Black fists held a three-tailed whip in one hand and a black sword in the other. And all around these figures swarmed dragons and human-like creatures with bestial heads.

At the far end of the hall stood a pyramidal dais, the top cut off to form a platform to hold the throne. The back of the seat was carved into the form of black wings. The top curved forward into the head of a raven. Seated upon a blue cushion below this black-eyed bird, was a young woman wearing a sparkling crown and cradling a scepter. Light emanated from her, casting shadows of those who came to bow before her onto the blue strip of rug behind them.

Each family was given a moment—scarcely enough for two deep breaths—to bow and speak a short sentence. Those who tried to ask questions or deliver lectures were instantly confronted by enormous fell guardsmen who blocked their view.

Radiant Runiss was not excepted from this policy. A man of middling years, with doughy pale cheeks, he had come alone. His bow was perfunctory and belied by his furrowed brow. "Your Majesty, I demand you abdicate at once. There are several Radiancies with a better claim to the—"

Whatever he meant to say next was transformed into an indignant squawk when he was lifted by the arms and carried to the exit by two fell guardsmen.

The new monarch of Starside turned to speak to a fiery-haired young man standing to her right and slightly behind her. He smiled but said nothing. The two girls next to him snickered. The scrawny one cupped a hand to whisper something uncouth and supremely inappropriate to her new friend, who snorted and turned red in turn.

The procession of subjects went on and on, for even those who hated the new queen were determined not to miss a rare chance to enter the Citadel. Monarchs lived a long time in Starside. Coronations were rare. Those who had seen Kila Sigh up close had been telling others of her peculiar voice, her fierce eyes, and her compelling beauty. Everyone wanted to see for themselves.

For Kila, it was intensely uncomfortable—her bottom and legs were getting numb from sitting so long. And it was boring. Marlow had told her it would last through the night and well into the next day. She was expected to endure it all with only a few breaks.

During the third such break, while she ate large squares of sweetbake and washed them down with cow's milk, she waved down Marlow's chief assistant, a young man called Chark. "Why haven't I seen anyone from Cheapsgate? I told Marlow that none should be barred from entering Gristenside simply because they didn't have shoes."

Chark leaned toward her, brows up and eyes squinting, as if he couldn't see well. "Pardon? Did you say Cheapsgate?"

"I did. You may have heard that's where I'm from."

He nodded vaguely. "That is true..."

"Kil's eyes! I know it's true. Now run off and make sure the Watch isn't keeping my people from getting through. Cheapsgaters have to come the farthest, so they should be allowed to skip the line."

He stammered for a moment before fleeing. Kila doubted he would do as she ordered. The man had a spine of thread, and probably wouldn't be able to stand up to a frowning captain of the Watch.

But he did follow her orders, for when she returned to her throne, she found a ragged line of smeared Cheapsgaters, easily identifiable by their grubby clothes, rag footwraps, and fishy odor. The first to come before her was a man she knew well.

"Parlo Odok, am I behind on my rent?" she asked.

Bald and slightly bent, he looked older than his four decades. He didn't bow so much as stoop. "Yer a right chicken, Sigh, an' I hope yer reign is short 'n ends in fire."

"I see you're still charming as ever," she said, waving the fell guardsmen back. "Don't you like it that a Cheapsgater is queen?"

"Viller is dead by yer hand an' all Cheapgate suffers fer it. Villers Killers are claimin' whole sections fer their new kingdoms. Now there're fifty Dox Villers 'stead o' one." He made a spitting noise and loped away, cursing under his breath.

"I hear you been makin' moves too, Odok," she called after him. "Stakin' out acreage fer yer own little kingdom."

"Who tol' you such lies?"

"I did," Mayrie said. "From Sewerbruck to the Warren. Yer

hired men're clubbin' out grannies and stealin' every rag they own."

Kila tilted her head and gave Odok a long look. "You hired men? Actually paid coin to them?"

His bald head had gone red, and he began to braise in his own sweat. He rubbed his cheek and stammered. "I might've suggested to a coupla fellas . . . some rec'mpense fer services of some nature. An' I never drove out no grannies, 'less they wouldn't pay their rents."

"You own the Warren, Odok. That's all. Understand me?"

"But Viller's Killers'll just take those shacks. They've no qualms slicin' open anybody with their gutters, neither."

The idea that Parlo Odok was a more just landlord than any other villain in Cheapsgate was laughable. He would sic Jocko on a toothless codger without a second thought. And if Jocko drowned a few children in the Sourwater, Odok would ask why it took so long.

"I'll deal with you later, Odok. Move along."

The next Cheapsgater reported the same chaos in the slums. "Ya shoulda left ol' Viller alone."

And the next. And the one after that. And so it continued until the few Cheapsgaters who had bothered to come all the way to the Citadel were past. At her next break Marlow had risen from his nap. "What can be done about Cheapsgate?" Kila asked him. "Folk are telling me it's about to break into civil war."

"There's not enough men of the Watch to police Cheapsgate without leaving the Blasted Quarter vulnerable. Several merchants have sizable barracks of armsmen in their employ. My little mice tell me the Keels are forming a militia to go in and clear the Blasted Quarter out. I've kept Watch patrols high to discourage it."

"Why do the Keels care about it?"

"Many in Terriside support the Keels' efforts because they're losing sons and daughters to the Way of Kila."

"What about my army? Can't they go in and settle things in Cheapsgate?"

"Most of them are at the Sablefort. The rest are at the Seawatch near Charton and a few other garrisons surrounding your realm. It would take a ten-day to get them here. And they are not trained to serve as peacekeepers."

So there was no solution to the problem of Cheapsgate. Kila began to see why Ell had allowed Dox to live. His power had kept Cheapsgate stable.

She returned to her throne and tried to acknowledge every face that appeared before her. She fell asleep on the throne only once, and had to be awakened by Henley. He had taken the girls back to the Privileged Suite so they could rest. Apparently, he'd slept too, for he was able to send wakefulness through the bond. At the toll of three bells morning, the Watch closed access to Gristenside, disappointing a few hundred stragglers. The last to be admitted came to bow before her at nine bells morning.

She immediately dymensed to her dressing room and was ready to cut her dress off, but a squad of maids hustled in and began the process of stripping her to her skivvies. "I'm going to sleep until next Tilsday," she said to no one in particular, yawning hugely. Her eyes closed and she swayed as her limbs were tugged and manipulated until she became aware that yet another gown was being wrapped around her and laces were being pulled taught.

"No! I can't sleep in this. I have to breathe!"

"You have a meeting of the small council in a quarter of an hour, majesty," said the Mistress of Wardrobe. "Marlow issued us your schedule last night."

A cup was thrust into her hand, and the mistress said,

"Drink this. You only need to make it through the meeting and you can rest."

She drank the bitter brew, which reinvigorated her enough to stay upright. It did very little to improve her mood. The new dress was blue—no surprise there—but less ornate than her coronation or reception costumes. She dispensed with her mercus glow, the crown, and the scepter. Cayne she kept strapped to her thigh. The maids had said nothing about it after she told them it was a shadline blade that would flay them by itself if they touched it.

The maids eventually departed and Kila was left alone. Not knowing where she was supposed to go for the council meeting, she lay down on the floor to rest her eyes and wait for Marlow to come pester her.

When he found her there, sleeping like a child, mouth open and soft snores lifting with each breath, he took pity. He looked at the agenda in his portfolio, saw the long list of impossible and urgent problems, and decided that for now they would all have to hold.

19

THE HALLOWED STILLNESS

The *zol-hidir* found Fallo and Quinn well before dawn. They came pounding up the path, hooting and grunting. Fallo shot up from his blankets, Telt and Shinane in his fists before he was fully awake. "Quinn, run!"

Sleep vanished from her eyes as she drew Black and faded from their camp, silent as shadow. The *zol-hidir* only took solid form at night. They could be killed—he'd slain dozens last time —but his shadline instincts urged him away from direct confrontation now. He crept after Quinn, feeling her presence even though he could not see her. Black conferred total silence to Quinn, no matter how she tromped through dry leaves or screamed at the top of her lungs. More recently, they had noticed another power of the blade. If she was trying to stay hidden, enemies and friends alike simply overlooked her.

Fallo wound through low trees of gnarled limb and pungent blossom. The crescent of the rising moon offered little light to guide him. A momentary flash of a shaman's red swarmlight showed him the thorny vines he'd bogged down in. Plump berries and slender leaves turned to smoke as the shaman's beam sliced past him. No instinct had guided him to avoid the attack. The shaman's poor aim had been Pol's choice.

Cursing and shivering, Fallo dove downhill. The red light had briefly outlined an enormous boulder ahead. He rolled to get it between him and the nosg. Scraped and bruised, he popped to his feet and pressed his back to the cool stone. Unlike living nosg, the *zol-hidir* did not possess any notion of subtlety or tactics. They trammeled through the scrub, hollering and hooting.

"Quinn?" he whispered.

His instincts told him she was near, but he couldn't see her.

Purple, green, and blue beams slashed into the foliage next to him. The shamans were using heat. That was typical of the *zol-hidir* he'd faced before. He took the tiniest bit of comfort from that. If they weren't using their full range of swarmlight feats, he might have a chance at escape.

In past encounters his shadline reflexes had kept him a moment ahead of every attack. But here, now, he felt nothing. He edged to his right where the foliage was thicker. Flattening himself to the ground, he worked into a thicket of wire-scrub, doing his best to be quiet. His fancy Dragon Tooth blades were forced into service as picks to help pull him along.

The gr'hils were drifting a bit westward, likely where the ground offered easier going. Fallo continued to crawl and hope that he'd feel a bit of inspiration soon. "Hope, Fallo?" he mouthed to himself. "Hope is the strategy of fools. PiTorros *scheme!*" He went limp and lent all his attention to his hearing. Surely his shadline skills would offer some hint or other. Usually they were quite insistent.

All he felt now was the ceaseless pull to the Tomb of Man.

Thinking back to his training with the Cloak and Zirhine, he tried to recall what sorts of signs they interpreted as shadline instinct. The Cloak had used much subtler calls than those Fallo experienced. Often the Cloak asked what would be most uncomfortable and went in that direction. Fallo considered that. The most uncomfortable thing would be to stand up, drop his pants, and offer the gr'hils a good view of his bare backside. Oftentimes a flea's whisker separated foolishness from shadline instinct, but he wasn't about to do something like that.

Lop? Are you still in one piece?

I'm with Tolky.

Didn't the nosg eat him already?

No. He broke free of that worthless knot you tied and took us uphill. The nosg didn't follow.

Can you see the nosg from where you are?

I see all.

Show me!

Lop refused. The fuzzy lump of lard never liked to share the catsight the way Nax and Huff did with Kila and Henley. She said it was too intrusive.

Lop, I need your help. If you show me the catsight I can get out of this prickly patch. Maybe even find some more pork for you.

The catsight flooded Fallo's vision, showing him a view of the hillside from quite high up. Tolky was a strong beast and could be fast when he wanted to be, which was usually never. Apparently protecting his own hide had been enough to get him moving.

From Lop's perch atop the animal (the donkey's head and half-perked ears clearly visible in the catsight field of view) Fallo saw five gr'hils quartering the hillside. Lop's nighttime vision was much keener than Fallo's. He spotted their campsite, the boulder, and the patch of berry-scrub in which he currently lay.

The closest gr'hil was twenty paces to his left. He squirmed right and eased out from the scrub until he could crouch behind it, well hidden. That was the most he could do for several minutes because the catsight disoriented him so badly. Closing his eyes did not make it go away. He waved his hand and saw it happen from afar. A sickly, watery swell in his gut convinced him not to try that again.

He decided the only way forward was to assess the terrain ahead, estimate how many paces he needed to scamper, then shout the count in his head as he moved, doing his best to ignore the catsight. After his first attempt, he tripped on an exposed root, smacked his chin on the dirt, then rolled over to spew up his dinner. The sound of his retching did not draw the closest gr'hil's notice, for at the very moment of his sickness the shaman fell backward and his skull-topped staff exploded, taking out the rest of the gr'hil in a flash of red.

Quinn. That lovely, sneaky killer!

Let me go, Lop. I can make it from here.

The catsight vanished. Fallo sprinted away, dropping to a paved path that wound parallel to the city as it curved upslope. His shadline instincts flooded in with a feeling of absolute rightness. This was the way to the Tomb of Man.

He stopped and waited for Quinn.

Over the next hour, shaman after shaman succumbed to her stealth attacks. Each time a shaman fell, its skull staff exploded from the accumulated swarmlight in the eyegems. Invariably, the remainder of the gr'hil was destroyed in the blast. After the last staff exploded, Fallo whistled and called out. Within a quarter of an hour, Quinn, Lop, and Tolky were with him, climbing toward the notched peak where goblet and moon shone just as they had been drawn in Zirhine's fate's-piece sketch.

The path ended facing a circle cut into the face of the mountain. The tunnel opening was rimmed with exquisitely carved vines and blossoms. "A vergent pass," Fallo said.

"I thought this path was taking us up there." Quinn pointed

to the notch in the mountain, now positioned a thousand feet directly above them

"It is. I think." But Fallo balked as he peered into the tunnel. "Does it look rather dark to you?"

"It's vergent magic, what do you expect?"

"I expect horrific things to happen, as has been my repeated experience these past many months."

Quinn rewarded him with a sympathetic laugh. "As true as that?"

"As true as that."

Lop, what do you think of this?

It's a hole. We should go in it.

That settled it. Quinn held Tolky's lead and walked next to Fallo as they plunged into absolute blackness.

Fallo's limbs were instantly mired in goopy, warm air. He had to lean and push to take even one step. It let go suddenly, and he stumbled forward, arms wheeling. Tolky honked and snorted, hooves skidding on smooth stone.

Quinn came through with a bit more grace. Lop hissed and batted Tolky's head, as if the animal was at fault for disturbing her comfortable ride.

They hadn't merely gone into the tunnel, they'd come out of it, too. Only one step, but what a weird one it had been. Behind them now was a rock wall. No retreat. Vergent passes went only one way.

"This is it," Fallo said. They stood upon a perfectly flat section notched into the side of the mountain, still thousands of feet below the peak. The vergent pass had turned them around so that they had come out in the opposite direction they'd been traveling.

"I don't see any gates," Quinn said.

"Let's try those stairs over there."

They were wide, deep, and low, each rising only a few

inches. The staircase curved upward to another platform. The air was cool. Far below, the city was lost in fog. The roar of the waterfall was masked by the wind, but the rumble vibrated in the stone beneath their feet.

And there, set into the flat face of the mountain, stood a wrought iron gate ten feet high. Many like it could be found all over Terriside and Gristenside, but none of such fine craftsmanship. Fallo whistled in appreciation, letting his fingers bounce over the lovely filigree pattern of the work. "This must have taken years to fashion. Look at where these turns join. The welds are perfect. The blackening under the dust looks new."

He gave it a shake. The hinges were bolted into bedrock, and the latch fitted so tightly it did not move at all.

He dug in his coat pocket for the key he'd gotten in Stallid. He weighed it in his palm. Dread added heft to the blackened iron, and he wanted nothing more than to toss it over the cliff.

Quinn put an arm around him. "All is well, Fallo. We are here together." Her eyes gleamed with excitement. To her this was like a shadline story from her book. A grand adventure.

The key slipped into the slot. Fall tried to imagine how many ages had passed since some forgotten elnisian had used it to lock the gate. If Pol favored him, the lock would be rusted fast and that would be that. They could go home.

Losing patience with his own hesitation, Fallo gave the key a twist. It turned a tiny bit until it met resistance. He put more arm into it. Something in the mechanism moved, then clicked. The gate swung out slightly on a squeak. The key would not come out, so Fallo left it. He pulled the gate toward him.

The hinges let out a long, warbling creak.

Fallo closed his eyes at the sound, smiling sadly. Against reason he had hoped the key a fraud. He had hoped the gate a legend. But more than that, he had long ago convinced himself the prophecy of Dem-Kisk the ravings of a madman.

The sound of those hinges was like the cry of his hopes falling over the cliff.

"Why are you just standing there?" Quinn asked. "Did you get something in your eye?"

He blew out a long breath and pushed the gate the rest of the way open. The creak deepened and sang the last few syllables of its dire lamentation. Lop meowed sadly. Tolky stamped and huffed.

The passage beyond the gate was dark.

"'*You will know Dem-Kisk by the creaking gate,*'" Fallo quoted softly, knowing with shadline certainty that this was the sound that long-dead seer had heard and then committed to paper. The ravings of a madman indeed.

Quinn fetched the lantern from one of Tolky's panniers. Fallo tore a flashtaper and set the wick aflame.

There was a circular entry chamber beyond. Against one wall was a haybunk, piled over with fresh hay. The trough next to it was full of clear water. The floor was covered with fresh rushes. "It's as if someone is expecting us."

"And they know we have a donkey," Quinn said, guiding Tolky out of the wind. The space was large enough to house three horses, so the donkey had plenty of room. Lop hopped down from the beast and nosed into a dark passageway opposite the gate.

Fallo and Quinn removed the packs from Tolky so he could rest easier should they be gone long. "I'll leave the gate open, I suppose," Fallo said. "Just in case."

"In case of what?" Quinn asked.

In case we don't come back, he thought. "Maybe Tolky will want to take a walk," he said weakly.

But Quinn understood. She rubbed the beast's nose and kissed him between the ears. "Don't listen to Fallo," she whispered to him. Tolky snorted as if such advice were obvious.

With the lantern held forward, Fallo went into the passage-way. The floor descended steeply, the walls narrow, square of corner, and cut with incredible precision. The stone was polished and black. As they walked, they were flanked by their own reflections, and the reflections of their reflections into a disconcerting infinity.

The atmosphere of a tomb came over Fallo instantly. The hard floor should have made their boot heels clomp loudly, but the air sucked the sharpness from their footsteps. Even their whispers vanished too quickly, as if the walls refused to release echoes that might disturb the hallowed stillness.

Lop vanished ahead, fearless and undisturbed by the eerie quiet.

Get back here! Fallo sent. He might as well have thrown an entire roast turkey ahead of him. The cat was gone.

Quinn managed to keep Black sheathed, though her hand rested on the hilt. Fallo kept his daggers stowed too. This was a tomb, after all. Everything in it should be dead.

20
———

THIEVING AND JUSTICE

Saiya and Henley had moved their things from the Privileged Suite to the Interior Palace at the base of the grand spire. Guarded by four fell guardsmen at the first entryway, and by three more squads of four at checkpoints leading to the second entry, the monarch's private residence was the safest place in all of Starside. The only other access into the residence was through the exterior doors which Kila had just opened.

"Kil be a merry maiden," she said, "look at that."

Before her lay a wedge shaped courtyard, narrowing a hundred paces out where it joined with the top of the Divide. There were low curbs on each side of the Divide, which itself spanned twenty paces across. If she chose, she could walk straight to Sea Bastion One five miles out to sea.

The day was fine and cold, with a sharp wind cutting across her private plaza from the north. Far below, to the left of the Divide, lay the green lawns of Gristenside. As grand as the greathouses of Gristenside were, they were tiny and insignificant from this perch. None who lived in them could doubt the supremacy of the one who lived high above them in the Citadel.

Kila pulled her thick cloak around her and strode a few steps onto the Divide. Behind her came Henley and Saiya. Two fell guardsmen had stopped at the doors, for they were not permitted on the Divide without invitation.

A lifelong curiosity about Moonside pulled Kila to the southern edge of the Divide. She felt Henley come up beside her. Saiya was singing softly to herself and looking back at the Citadel spires, which soared overhead. Nax and Huff slunk along the edge of the wall, using the curb as their preferred pathway.

"Moonside stirs," Henley said, echoing the warning in Ell's letter.

And it was true. A thick boil of cloud obscured the entirety of Moonside, all the way to the sheer cliffs that backed it to the west. The cliffs curled around to the south until reaching the sea. Another wall, a perpendicular extension of the Divide, closed off Moonside at the shoreline. "It's a bowl of fog," Kila said.

But it was more than mere fog, for the inky clouds moved in rolling waves, exposing depths of blackness interspersed with occasional red flashes. Behind Kila, gulls drifted upon the breeze, keeping watch over Starside's streets for stray tidbits. Not a single bird flew over Moonside.

"What made those clouds?" Saiya asked, coming to stand on Kila's other side. She had grown an inch in the past two days.

Kila exhaled and felt for the mercusine. The Revulsion spoiled it, though it was not particularly thick here. Henley was better at this sort of thing, but she wanted to feel it herself. The mercus was not only deep, it was dispersed across the world. One skilled in Seeking could feel the potential surrounding distant individuals. It was how the Hargothe had found her.

Stretching her awareness out, she felt the strong buzz of mercus around Henley, including the beacon of the Motherlight in his satchel. Saiya, too, was humming with it, though she had not yet awakened to her power.

Ahead of her, in the storm of cloud concealing Moonside, the mercus did not seem to exist at all. For covering the entirety of the sequestered city was the Revulsion. But it was muted, as if blocked off by an unseen barrier. "The wards in the Divide are powerful indeed," she said. "They mask the horror that resides so near. The Revulsion made those clouds. Can you feel it, Henley?"

His face was deep in the hood of his overcloak, but she saw his body shiver. "I haven't truly felt the Revulsion yet, but I can sense it's wrongness just by looking at it. We've lived so close to this all our lives, never suspecting."

"Ell knew."

And she had done nothing. Kila knew it wasn't fair to blame the dead queen. There wasn't anything to be done about the Revulsion. Building the Divide to sequester Moonside had been the best the elnisians could come up with, after all.

Ell's other warning came to her. *You will need Night, Sigh. You will need them all.*

She turned away from Moonside and looked over the city of the living. No dark clouds there, but plenty of trouble stirring in the streets. In every quarter. "That looks like scaffolding in the Blasted Quarter," she said, pointing.

"Yes. The Way of Kila is industrious," Henley said.

"Bloody morons. And Lower Terriside is being overrun with refugees. Marlow says Watch Commander LiTishke has the Westbunk stuffed full, for vagrancy. That idiot."

"LiTishke used to sleep comfortably in Dox Viller's purse," Henley said. "I wonder who owns his loyalty now."

"I do. Or, I will soon. I told Marlow to replace the man with someone competent. Do know what his reply was? He said, 'If you want someone competent for the post, you'll have to look outside the ranks of the Watch itself.'"

"The Fell Guard?"

All she could do was snort. "Brother Commander Docit declined, saying the Fell Guard's oaths were to the Raven Throne, not to the city. He suggested reassigning an officer from my army. But all the best ones are at the Sablefort. Just when we need order the most. The Watch has lost a quarter of its number to Ell's enlistments for the army. Guess who General LiMillar preferred to take?"

"The good ones?"

She nodded and smirked. "Governing is a scam. They give you a crown and a title and then conspire to make it so everyone hates your decisions. Right when we're forced to ration, I've got bakers refusing to bake bread. They've organized. Even Axehead Shine is refusing. Can you believe that?"

"What, is he running out of sawdust?"

Kila laughed and shifted her gaze further out. "Cheapsgate is my greatest catastrophe."

"They say you killed Viller," Henley said softly.

She changed the subject. "I saw one of Hackworth Keel's sons on Winternight. He was very much in his cups. I considered robbing him. I considered doing more, for burning down your home."

They were silent for a while, taking in this unique view of the city. Henley put an arm around her and she nestled close. Saiya had wandered back into the Citadel with the cats to get out of the cold.

"We all have our grudges," Henley said. "Justified by injustices done to us. Fallo swore to me, back when we lived in the atlen barn, that he was going to kill his father. I thought I would kill Hackworth Keel someday. Dreams of revenge warmed us both on many cold nights."

"Why don't you kill him now?" she asked, half wishing he would do it. Because then she wouldn't suffer alone from the heavy heart of revenge. "You can do it without any risk of reprisal, from the Keels or the Crown."

"Look at your city," he said. "How many are fed because the Keels have begun to import grain and beef on their ships?"

"At indecent prices!"

"And yet the food comes in. For now. Hackworth is a bully and a criminal. His sons emulate him, but they are not strong like him. If Hackworth died, they would fight each other rather than watch closely over the business. And Lower Terriside in particular would starve."

"Perhaps I should confiscate his ships, put someone of my choosing in charge of them. Lower prices at the same time."

"You can't even find someone to manage the city Watch. Even Administrator Marlow skims coin from the treasury. And he's the honest one."

Her skin went suddenly hot and prickly. She shrugged Henley's arm off her and ambled farther out onto the Divide. He had the sense to let her go.

A new understanding came to her rather abruptly as she stood there, perched between Moonside and Starside. Being queen wasn't about justice, it was about stability. And as far as she could discern, you could only achieve that by propping one injustice against another.

"These people need to wake up," she said. "We're not so far from Moonside as we would like to think."

Especially not with her as queen. No wonder Ell had been astonished by her shadline instinct to name Kila her heir. For she knew all that Kila was swiftly discovering. Moreover, she knew that Kila herself was perched between the Revulsion and the mercusine, between thieving and justice, between day and night.

"You will need them all, Sigh," she said to herself. Not just the demayne, but the men and women. The Dox Villers and the Sensual Rennas. The Hackworth Keels and the Henley Masts. The Critt Sanglos and the Parlo Odoks. Even the Ways served useful purposes beyond enriching the corrupted among them.

Dox and Critt were dead already. She didn't dare lose more. LiTishke would stay as commander of the Watch, for now. Axehead Shine would get his price increase. The Way of Kila would continue repairing the Blasted Quarter even as they undermined the families of Upper Terriside. Refugees like Terissa Viller would come in and receive bread while Cheapsgaters starved or froze or were stabbed. Kila would have to watch the suffering with a cold eye, even as she turned her fury against the Revulsion.

When she turned back, she discovered Henley had also gone into the Citadel. She returned along the Divide, her back to both cities.

Facing the enormous fortress—*her* fortress—she felt smaller than ever before.

21

WHITEFLAME

Their faces were placid, heads high as they invaded. Like a squad of elite soldiers, they barged into Kila's apartments. To Kila's mercus-heightened senses, their footfalls were like the stomps of plow horses. She shot up from her bed, Cayne flying from under her pillow and into her hand upon mercus touch.

A wash of light burst into her eyes, forcing her to blot it out with her hand. Squinting and cursing, she waved her blade to keep the attackers at bay.

"Pardon, mum," said the Mistress of Wardrobe. "Morning has come. Her Enlightened Majesty always required a hot bath upon rising. It is prepared in your bathing chamber. The Mistress of Kitchens has sent up your preferred breakfast. Administrator Marlow is waiting for you."

Kila carried Cayne with her as she was guided from her bedchamber, through a wide blue-carpeted corridor, cutting right, into a sun-washed tiled room occupied by an enormous beaten-copper tub. Steam rose from the water, smelling faintly of lavender. Kila was stripped to her skin by two mild-faced women and assisted into the water.

Still holding Cayne, she blinked at the brightness of the room and the heat of the water, and the suddenness of her awakening. "Where's Nax?"

"Still in your bed, mum," said one of her bathing attendants, who brought forth a cake of soap, a long brush, and two crisp white towels. "Will you require our assistance bathing?"

Kila took the soap and began to work herself over. "Ell did this every morning?"

"She did, indeed."

JUST AS THE Mistress of Wardrobe had threatened, Marlow was waiting for her in her "breakfast room," which was nestled on a balcony level above the study. The windows here overlooked the Divide courtyard.

"I was never allowed in here when Ell reigned," Marlow said after she had swallowed two entire bites of her breakfast in peace.

Kila lowered her third forkful of scrambled atlen egg. "Then what are you doing here now?"

The man did not look the slightest bit ashamed of his presumption. "Because you are a novice at ruling and the needs of your realm are dire. There's no time for niceties such as privacy and loitering about."

"Then why didn't you come to me while I was bathing?" She shoved the eggs into her mouth and followed them with toasted bread.

"Henley has the Motherlight," Marlow said. "I may not care much for propriety, but I do care considerably for my own skin. Now, let us begin." He opened his portfolio and sighed heavily. "Should I start with Cheapsgate?"

"No. The Revulsion."

"There has been no sign of the revulyn who dymensed away from Saiya's room. The Watch has not received any reports of such a person, but they are severely overwhelmed with other problems."

"I think he dymensed away from Starside."

"How can you be sure?"

She didn't know, so she took a sip of tea and poked at her eggs. Nax wandered to the table and jumped into her lap.

Want some egg? She sent.

No. I had cream and chicken. Tell them not to use so much salt next time.

Kila's appetite retreated in the face of the problem of the missing revulyn. "How did an Iron Scholar become a revulyn? I had never heard that term before Nax said it. Had you?"

"No. But no doubt there are books in the abbey's library that could illuminate the issue for us. They would be in the forbidden section of Wrong texts. Quiv will find any mention of it if such exists."

"The Hackwatch was thick with the Revulsion. If any place could sicken a man's mind, that place would. But to truly taste it you have to be awakened to the mercus. The intruder was an Iron Scholar; he lived there. And trust me, nobody sensitive to the mercus would choose to remain within those walls for a second longer than necessary."

Marlow raised an eyebrow, questioning why that was an important distinction.

Henley, are you still asleep?

Just woke up.

I'm upstairs having breakfast with Marlow.

I need to find something for Huff to eat.

Look outside your bedchamber. Cream and chicken.

Kila pushed her plate away and met Marlow's persistent gaze. "What I'm trying to say is that the Iron Scholar didn't drink in the Revulsion on purpose. He couldn't have known it was there except as something true merculyns whispered about. Something—or someone—else must have forced it on him."

"Who?"

"I don't know, but I know who might know." Her eggs and toast soured in her stomach, but Nax flowed excitement through the bond as she picked upon Kila's intentions.

"Clear out the staff," she said to Marlow. "Everyone out of the residence."

His eyes flashed with curiosity and he hastened to obey. It took less than two minutes before the squadron of maids and footmen were all on the other side of her entry foyer door.

"Flaumishtak, you smoke-haired scoundrel, come here!" she called to the air.

Nax slunk onto the table and meowed enthusiastically.

The demayne did not materialize.

"Flaumishtak, I know you can hear me. After your schemes with Yiothizandra, I don't blame you for being scared to face me."

A bloom of mercus green fountained before her and drifted away in spinning smoke rings, revealing the enormous demayne. He wore thick robes that tented around his bulk. His monstrous face loomed high enough that she had to crane her neck to look at him. His hair was swept back, fading into coils of ever renewing smoke.

The creamy nuisance that was Oly perched on his shoulder. The cat spat at Kila before leaping onto the table to nuzzle Nax. "I missed you, too, Oly," she said.

Flaumishtak's voice rumbled in the room like distant thunder. He swept a mocking bow. "Your Majesty, it was not fear that caused my delay in answering your ill-timed summons."

"Then what caused it? Never mind. I don't care. Tell me why an Iron Scholar revulyn came here to kidnap Saiya?"

"Saiya? Oh, you mean Kil. Well, that's rather obvious, isn't it? The better question is *who* sent him. I can tell you with absolute certainty that it was not me."

"I didn't suspect you. Who was it?"

Flaumishtak's hair smoke tightened into a single wisp and rose toward the ceiling as he contemplated this question. "This is a guess, but I suspect it was the qiznithan that recently came into this world."

Marlow dropped his teacup. "You lie!"

"I wish it were a lie. Alas, a qiznithan is among us."

Something in his manner made Kila's mouth go dry. It was his lack of humor, for Flaumishtak usually reveled in chaos.

He continued: "Of the demaynic realms, only that of the qiznithan is barred to me. For theirs is a realm of madness and suffering such that it imprisons any who enter it. Perhaps the felnithel could pass through it, but why would they want to? In any case, the qiz rarely communicate with the rest of us. The Hel Lords keep watch on them somehow, and I happened to know they were recently in council discussing what they simply called an 'absence' in the realm of the qiz."

Marlow daubed a napkin onto his tea-stained garments. "And you suspect that absence means a qiznithan has come here?"

The beast sighed hugely. His fiery eyes flared even as they narrowed. One clawed hand came up to scratch his hairy chin. "Indeed. Yet I am puzzled by how such a terrible passage could occur. Not even the most devoted of your demayncors would wish to summon a qiznithan intentionally. Few dare to summon a yoznithan like me, though in truth no others are *truly* like me."

He preened a bit and a fanged smile split his grotesque face for a moment. But whatever organ passed for a heart in him wasn't invested in the joke, for his shoulders slumped and he resumed scratching his chin. "Much is disturbed in the demaynic realms and none truly understand it. The Kil-notion coming to this world may account for it, I suppose."

"So a qiznithan is walking around out there?" Kila asked, pointing to the window. "And it sent a revulyn for Saiya. But why didn't it come for her itself?"

"A qiznithan could not manifest in any meaningful form in this world, for its home realm is not material like the others. It would require a host, some wretched human supplied for it to occupy while it remained here. The demayncors must have used a sacrificial merculyn during the summoning rite."

"So the qiznithan is a revulyn too? Then maybe it was the Iron Scholar who came here."

Flaumishtak grimaced and considered the question. Finally, he snorted. "If you were able to defeat the one who came here, I am certain he was not the qiznithan. He must have found an Iron Scholar with an unawakened mercus spark and turned him. He probably feared coming here himself, not knowing how powerful Saiya is."

"Why haven't you searched out this qiznithan? Surely you could if you applied your talents."

"I am impressively powerful, it is true. But I am not a fool. I wouldn't go near such a creature."

They sat in silence for a while, each deep in their thoughts. Flaumishtak's speculations were interesting but didn't help Kila know what to do. Except that the obvious course was to find the qiznithan and kill him.

"The revulyn who attacked here was powerful enough to dymense and to manifest an invisible wall that took a complete squad of fell guardsmen to overcome," Kila said. "And yet, he would not attack Nax and Huff. They were all that stood between him and Saiya."

Flaumishtak looked fondly at Oly and Nax and clicked his tongue at them. They swarmed off the table and into his arms. "I am not surprised by the felnithels' powers, but I'll be a dragon's lunch if I know the how or the why of it. Not a demayne of Day or Night would wish to harm a Beloved One. But the Revulsion surely wishes them destruction. It would be better if one of them remains with Kil—er, Saiya—at all times. Who guards her now?"

"Huff and Henley. Here they come."

The trio entered the balcony and joined them. Huff remained close to Saiya, which Kila knew had to be a struggle, for the cat loved Flaumishtak. Henley eyed the demayne with skepticism. "What's he doing here?"

"Speculating about revulyns," Flaumishtak said. "Well met, Henley Mast, bearer of the Motherlight."

"Ah." Henley took a seat and served himself some breakfast. The Motherlight's mercus hum drew Flaumishtak's eye to his satchel. But only for a moment before he turned the fire of his gaze back to Saiya.

The girl showed no fear of the beast towering over her. Flaumishtak knelt before her, then bent forward to place his forehead on the floor. Saiya's head pulled back and her brows furrowed. "Are you sleepy?" she asked him.

It was the demayne's turn to be confused. He straightened and cast a questioning gaze at Kila.

She doesn't know what she is, Kila sent at him.

Ah, he sent back. *That is probably well.*

"Flaumishtak is a demayne," Kila said. "They have a peculiar manner of greeting. He is visiting because he knows about the men who came into your room the other night."

Saiya noticed Oly and rushed to pet him. He allowed this with unusual patience.

"They will be back," Flaumishtak said. "You must know that."

"I had hoped to find them first, but I have been distracted by other troubles in the realm. Ell foresaw her own death but failed to tell me. She left me holding the crown and a city in disarray. She also warned that Moonside stirs. Do you know what that means?"

"It isn't good, especially in light of the revulyn attack here. The elnisians were the first to awaken the Revulsion, you know. They lost Moonside to it and erected the Divide to contain it. If Ellishan said she sensed something stirring within . . ." He seemed to come to a decision then, for his manner grew curt and his huge hands curled into fists. "You must take Saiya out of Starside. Get her far from here, somewhere the Revulsion is especially thin, a place one cannot even dymense to. And then you must go into Moonside and strengthen the trap."

Henley choked on his toast. "She's not going into Moonside. It's rife with the Revulsion. Do you know what would happen to her? She can barely resist it out here."

"So I've heard," Flaumishtak said, mouth twisting down in distaste. He glowered at her. "The Revulsion should repel you, girl. That's why it's called *the Revulsion*."

"It does repel me. I only used it out of desperation. Only twice."

Three times, Dox's raspy voice shouted from deep in her memory.

"I can resist it," she added faintly.

Through all of this, Marlow watched, salt and pepper beard hiding most of his expression. He closed his portfolio and set it softly on the table. "Flaumishtak, you were talking about strengthening a trap in Moonside. Start by telling us what the trap is, if you please."

The demayne collected himself, but his smokey hair stood up in several thin tendrils. "When the elnisians first awakened the Revulsion, it corrupted scores of merculyns in what is now the Blasted Quarter. The rest of the city's merculyns fought them there, which is how it came to be so weakened. The elnisian king noted how the revulyns sought out and attacked the strongest merculyns, especially those who possessed powerful mercus relics. He retrieved his most cherished relic, a sword called Whiteflame. It is nearly equal in power to the Motherlight. This he took to what is now called Moonside, declaring he would make his last stand at a temple of Ori. The streets of Starside were cleared to allow the revulyns to pursue him there.

"He then brought forth the power of Whiteflame and the revulyns swarmed to him. None know exactly what feat he produced, but the revulyns could not get close enough to him to consume the fountain of mercus power he established. They began to circle the temple as they strove against his power, which he increased to his utmost limit. With the subjects of the realm removed from that side of the city, the swarming revulyns had no more merculyns to turn. And so a balance was struck. The king's power so enthralled them that they did not return to Starside.

"The survivors in Starside circled and called upon other relics and brought forth the Divide by way of feats I cannot even conceive of. I've heard theories that the whole wall was dymensed into place from some other plane. Wherever it came from, the wall was then infused with wards to prevent the Revulsion smearing back into the city. Even so, the survivors in what came to be called Starside could not bear to remain so close to the vileness. A hundred years later they abandoned the city. Not long after that the last elnisians left Ennith entirely."

"But the Divide remains. It's huge, it's warded," Kila said. "Does it matter if Whiteflame fails?"

Flaumishtak's hair flattened before releasing a billowing plume to the ceiling. "I didn't say Whiteflame was failing. But with the Revulsion awakened, Whiteflame's power may not command all of its attention. Ell received the foresight on occasion. If she said Moonside *stirs*, what she truly meant is *that has wakened*. Whiteflame needs more power to quell this awakening and keep the Revulsion enthralled. Else . . ."

His silence was meant to convey something he didn't want to say. Kila didn't know what it was, but Henley did. He pointed out the window to the top of the Divide. "That thing could fall?"

Flaumishtak shrugged hugely. "I've heard part of Stallid's Indomitable Wall recently vanished into thin air." He looked right at Kila, nostrils of his flat nose flaring as he sucked in a breath. "Perhaps it wouldn't be as simple as that, though."

"Simple? You call that simple?" Kila said.

"Vanishing a wall with a mere thought is an act of the godblooded. Unless there's a godblooded in Moonside, it will have to use other means to escape. A breach, somewhere along the Divide's length. I recommend you do as I suggest. Find Whiteflame and increase the power of its enthralling feat. Even awakened, the Revulsion will be sorely tempted by such a bright source of the mercus. Make it irresistible."

Kila pushed back from the table. "Very well. I'll go into Moonside, find Whiteflame, and . . . do what? Flow more power through it?"

"Not you," Henley said. "You take Saiya away from here. I'll go into Moonside."

"You must find this qiznithan, Flaumishtak," Kila said. "Kill it."

"The qiz will be crafty and quiet until it possesses enough power to overwhelm all opposition. He will turn more revulyns and more reviled. He'll be difficult to find. But even if I find him I could not kill him."

Marlow was scribbling notes in his portfolio. "You think it's turning merculyns right now? That is not the sort of thing to go unnoticed for long, since most merculyns belong to one of the

Ways. Their absences will be noted. If we can prevail upon Highest Quiv to ask his Highests to report on truancy rates, perhaps we can learn how widely this sickness has spread."

"See to it, Marlow," Kila said. "But ask the Way of Pol to begin the same inquiry. They have the coin code and should be able to report in hours what may take days for Quiv to discover." Kila dismissed Marlow with a shooing motion. "Everything else can wait until I return."

"Where are you going?" Henley asked.

"Taking Saiya someplace safe."

Nax and Huff dismounted from Flaumishtak's arms. Oly remained. Saiya waved goodbye to the demayne and then he was gone. "Oly is funny," she said, grinning mischievously.

"What? Did he say something to you?" Kila demanded.

"Nothing important. So where are you taking me so I can be safe?" For a child who had nearly been kidnapped, and who had witnessed bloody battle, she was facing danger with eerie calm.

Henley leaned forward, brows lifted, eager to hear Kila's answer. She had an idea, but it was so speculative, and so unappealing, she didn't want to give voice to it.

"Don't go into Moonside until I return," she said to him, pushing away from the table. "Saiya, fetch whatever things you wish to take with you. Plan on being away from here for a good long while. Have the Mistress of Wardrobe supply you with clothing sized for a tall adult woman. If you don't grow into them fully, you can cuff the sleeves and pant legs. I'll fetch food supplies. Meet me downstairs in an hour. Henley, would you and Huff please go with her now in case the revulyn decides to return while she packs?"

He remained seated, still looking at her with the central question in his eyes. But she wouldn't answer it. For one thing, she didn't want him trying to talk her out of it; for another, she was mildly embarrassed about the imposition she was about to make on someone she barely knew. But above all, she was worried that he might succumb to the Revulsion in Moonside. If that happened, then everything he knew, *it* would know. He seemed to come to this realization on his own, though his face betrayed hurt.

She reached for him. "Please don't go into Moonside until I return."

He nodded and took Saiya away, leaving Kila alone with Nax. She petted the cat in long strokes from nose to tail. She had a request for Nax, too. This one she did not voice because she didn't want to do it, for her own selfish reasons.

But Nax sensed it already. *If I stay with Saiya I will not be able to protect you from the Revulsion. And if you are foolish enough to follow Henley into Moonside . . .*

Who else can stay with her? I don't know where Lop is and Oly won't leave Flaumishtak.

Perhaps we could find Startle.

Hope fountained in Kila's heart. Of course! Startle was the fifth of Nax's littermates. *But you said Startle's gone, that you can't sense his presence anymore.*

Flaumishtak took him somewhere.

Kila set the problem aside. She wanted Flaumishtak busy finding the qiznithan. Once Saiya was truly safe, perhaps then she would search out Startle.

22

THESE INSECTILE HUMANS

Yples sniffed deeply of the Revulsion fog he kept in a flask, drawing in the fumes to revivify himself here where it had thinned. Stallid should have been thick with it in the wake of Sigh's feats, but the Revulsion was inconsistent. Like foam, it was densely concentrated in some places and vanishingly faint in others. He could feel a deeper concentration ahead, and that was not simply because of the mild torture being applied.

No, the Revulsion gathered because of impending violence. A dragnithan demayne was just through this arching gateway. A demayne of grave darkness. The Revulsion danced and licked around her feet, drawn by the power of her hateful passion and of the painful fate awaiting her at dawn. Yples touched one of the gate guards, instantly reviling him. "Open the gate."

The man's eyes went gray as slate, his movements became stiff. He did as instructed, drawing concerned looks from his mate. When challenged, the newly turned reviled simply ran his partner through. Yples felt the man's life waft out of the body, like a puff of breeze through a window. Then it was gone, dissipated into nothing. As all things would soon be dissipated.

The courtyard beyond lay mostly in shadow, save for two braziers at the corners of an execution scaffold. Two more guards stood there, along with two chanting almen who sat with heads bowed in meditative prayer.

It was the almen in the city who thinned the Revulsion. Men and women whose deep faith obscured the truth of the cold eye. Yples felt an unawakened mercus spark in one of them. It was vanishingly faint. He bade his reviled guard to slay them all.

The prisoner appeared to be asleep. She was bound to a thick, upright post. Her arms were pulled away from her body, kept taut by chains locked to iron rings in the platform deck. Though Yples could assess physical beauty, the woman's appearance stirred no desire in him. Flesh was stone and stone was vapor, and all of it destined for Annihilation. He lifted her chin and thumbed one of her eyelids up. The dragnithan fire in her iris was banked to a low ember. "Look, woman," he said softly. "Look and see with the cold eye." He pressed a reviling feat into her mind.

Yiothizandra responded with a sharp inhalation. Yples formed the negation of her breath-fire without even thinking, mere reflex. Her attack was weak. It may have seared a human man, but it likely wouldn't have killed. Her captors had been starving her. A dragnithan like this one would require meat.

Even so, she resisted his reviling easily. Yples was unconcerned. This was expected.

"They have misunderstood you, haven't they, Mother of Kil," he said. "You came to conquer, to prepare a realm for your child, but these insectile humans resisted. They do not understand their purpose, do they?"

"Who are you?" she rasped.

"I am Yples. If you will allow me, I will release you."

"I couldn't stop you if I wanted to." She closed her eyes, and leaned her head back onto the post.

"I have sent others to recover your child. Soon you will be reunited with Kil."

Her eyes slit open a bit, the forge of her rage heating with an inflow of hope. Her high, arching brows knit, and she emitted a sorrowful laugh. "Gian Delp sent you to toy with me, didn't he? I'm no fool. Execute me or go."

Yples concentrated a moment, forming revulsion bolts to sever the chains holding her arms and legs. The collar came free from the post, but he decided to leave it around her neck. Now unsupported, Yiothizandra tilted forward and fell toward him. He side-stepped and she thumped onto the deck.

"Easy, child. Easy." Scooping her up, he motioned with his head at the newly turned reviled. "You are released." The man put the pommel of his sword on the ground and fell upon the blade, impaling himself.

"And now, my darling dragnithan, we will return to your holdfast Ceronhel."

"Why are you aiding me?"

"Shush. You well know I am using you. But take heart. The end of all suffering is near."

He formed a feat and they dymensed in Revulsion black.

THE COASTAL CITY of Slirya was awash in sharp rain, the skies a dull slate that would persist until spring. Where the eastern cities celebrated Winternight with a night of revelry, Slirya went into seclusion for a ten-day. Markets opened only once during the Solitude, and few other trades conducted business at all. Today was not market day. The streets were quiet, and that suited Revnithan Con. She stood on a hillside street, oilcloak shedding water away from her body to join the energetic runnels coursing into grated scuppers at the sides of the street.

Any who saw her there, frozen in the middle of the street, would wonder why she had paused so long where an atlen-drawn hack might crush her. But she was not concerned. There were few such carriages out and she would hear one coming long before it crested the hill and threatened her.

Elevated areas were best, she had learned, for feeling out the power of the Revulsion and the sweet pain of the mercus. It was odd being dead yet alive, but Con rather enjoyed it. It was a faint sort of enjoyment, dispassionate. An emotion felt from a distance.

A prick of mercus chimed in her awareness somewhere off to her right. An unawakened mortal with modest mercus potential. It attracted her, but not enough to bother seeking it out. What she was looking for should spark much more darkly. Lord Yples wanted the Entifal, and he would have it. But she was beginning to suspect the dagger had been cleverly masked. If so she might never find it. Unthinkable. A prickle of terror wiggled in her gut.

She remembered keenly how frightened she'd been when he'd taken her on that boat to the Cathedral of Til, had subjected her to the nosg shamans, had tortured her upon the turning slab. And how content she'd been once she'd seen the truth through the cold eye.

But whatever Yples had done to her, to make her Revnithan Con, it allowed a portion of her old human mind to leak back in, to feel. To regain the cold eye, she sometimes had to pause and sink deeply into the Unanswered.

She still did not feel anything powerful enough to be the Entifal. A quick visual scan of the city showed another high point several miles south. She would go there and try again.

THE MAN STROKED his fingers through his whiskers and turned his face side to side to inspect himself in the mirror. There was no rot in evidence. Not yet, anyway. That was well. His heart was silent. Breathing wasn't necessary except to speak. Eating was not required. Sleeping never occurred to him. He was dead by any usual definition. Dead, but apparently not decaying.

"Evil? I don't think so," he said to his reflection. The Revulsion was harsh. Its self-despising nature was anathema to life. He wouldn't argue about that. But its purpose was simple, the cessation of all suffering. How could that be evil?

He splashed icy water from the basin onto his face. It was a sensation, but it didn't make him shiver or gasp. Didn't make him more alert, either. A mooncrafter had taught him long ago to keep his skin clean. An old habit, now almost a ritual. A cleansing of the body to symbolize renewal.

Early on, right after he'd taken control of Ceronhel, Revnithan Sault had recognized the difference between himself and the reviled nosg. It wasn't the difference in race that stood out, but the difference in thinking. The reviled were dull-witted. Even the shamans, many of whom had been quite savvy leaders before their awakening, did not have any strategic notions at all. When given a task, they took the most direct action. If stymied, they were often left paralyzed, unable to proceed. The shamans were a bit more alert than the warriors and common-folk, but not by much.

He returned to his workbench, where dishes of mooncrafter ingredients were carefully arranged. He'd retrieved everything from his Sorgan workshop hidden in a cellar of a noble for whom he'd been House Donse Master. Clay pots of dried gerani root, bovine gelatin, oak gall, dandelion fuzz, pikenaught leaves, filishader of three varieties, and three hundred fourteen other containers. Then there were the mortars and pestles, the candles, the decanters, the alcohol, the pure water, glass tubes and flasks. The nosg shamans had provided numerous speci-mens of mimak, which he had quickly classified according to potency (often closely tied to toxicity), duration of effect, and rarity. So many varieties he'd never seen before. Truly a wonder.

He dipped a fingertip into his latest concoction, a concentra-tion of powdered Blackshine blended with two mind-exploding varieties of vergent's-cap mushroom. He licked his finger and took up the skull staff he'd fashioned: a bear skull fitted with demayne skullgems he'd bought at an Iopsean market a decade ago.

His mimak powder had no effect on the tongue. Frustrating, since his command of the Revulsion was rather weak. But his swarmlight had no limits. He sniffed a bit of the powder, hoping the nasal cavities would deliver the potency to him. This worked very well, and soon his green-black eyegems were aglow.

Now it was time to inspect his Blackshine shamans and see if Razk-Ka had been captured yet. The nosg wurgu had led a large force of his army away from Sault's reviled horde, seeking escape to the east. Yples would not be best pleased if Razk-Ka escaped. Sault had set his entire army in pursuit.

He had used his knowledge of dymension to experiment with the Blackshine swarmlight. A rather elegant trick, he thought. And so he gathered the inky vision into the skull staff and swirled away from Ceronhel.

23

HEART IS MIDNIGHT BLACK

At the edge of the courtyard, in a black shadow beneath a shade awning, Eckso moved through the picketed horses. They whickered softly in the cool desert night. "Come, Klayne," she whispered. He followed, hunched and thin. And obedient. His gold *vaz'on* caught glimmers of the brazier light from the scaffold.

The bodies of the almen and guards lay like mounds of clothing, indistinct in the dimness. "That was more than a revulyn," she said. "I'm glad I kept us masked."

"Revulyn? What makes you say that was a revulyn?" Klayne said, creeping up the steps. He picked up the end of one of Yiothizandra's severed chains, inspected the clean cut. "A merculyn, obviously." He looked down to where Eckso still stood. "Why would you say it was a revulyn? What happened in the Citadel? Tell me."

Eckso had not told him anything of Kil or the awakened Revulsion yet. She cursed her tongue for betraying this much. She dropped her mercus mask, reached for his Will Gem and clamped his mouth shut.

She inspected the reviled guard who had fallen on his sword.

His eyes were open, alert. Yet he did not move, as if he'd convinced himself he was dead. A terrifying thing to behold. In great enough number such men would rush into battle—or into an unprotected city—and wreak death without regard to their own survival. She put a finger to his throat, felt for the pulse. There was none. The eyes flicked up at her, a hand reached.

Her feat of fire took him, reduced him to ash. The sword clanged onto the courtyard stones. She knew better than to touch it.

She joined Klayne on the scaffold, ears perked for the sound of any patrol or nighttime visitors. She dipped into the mercus, feeling the sheen of Revulsion upon it. It was thicker here than elsewhere in Stallid.

Klayne was eyeing her, stark eyes full of speculation. She cursed herself again for talking about revulyns in front of him. Now he knew. But perhaps that wasn't such a bad thing. His opinion of her was very low, and since he was at her mercy, he was surely worried that she would have him confront a revulyn while helpless beneath the *vaz'on*.

"It *was* a revulyn," she admitted, releasing the Will Gem. "I felt it in him because I was searching for it. I'm surprised you didn't notice his feat wasn't mercusine. You can still feel the mercus can you not?"

He nodded vaguely, again looking at the severed chains. "What does he want with Yioth?"

"To turn her, obviously." She wouldn't likely succumb easily.

"Is this awakening of the Revulsion something she did?" he asked. "Is she so mad to escape this world that she would resort to such evil? I can't credit it. Even one as self-loving as she would not risk the destruction of *all* things."

"Listen to you declaring something else evil," she said with mocking pride in his newfound nobility. "You, whose heart is midnight black. But no, Yioth had nothing to do with it." She ran her fingers down the post to which Yioth had recently been bound. It was still warm. "You don't suppose . . ." The terrifying idea made her mouth go dry. She tried again. "Could the qiznithan who granted the Hargothe his oracular powers find a way into this world?"

"Not without aid. But those fools in the Shudderlins might have invited it by mistake." He caught himself a moment, brows furrowing as he picked up on the idea Eckso had been trying to push out of her own mind. "We know it seeded the Kil-notion in the Hargothe specifically to cause a rebirth here. I had thought that mere mischievousness. Delightful and interesting, but merely a grand bit of skylarking. But with the Revulsion awakened . . ." In the firelight his complexion was ruddy, but even so his face paled and sagged. "Kil provides a path to Annihilation. Do the Hel Lords know?"

"What does it matter? They can do nothing here."

"Take this thing off me. Eckso, I beg you to release me. I have to get Yioth away from that thing. If she turns, what chance will Kil have? A god he may be, but Kil's nature leans too close to the cold eye already."

"Yioth doesn't have Kil."

He mopped his forehead with a sleeve. "Then where is he?"

"Sigh has Kil. That was the qiz's intent all along, actually. The qiznithan gave the Hargothe more than the Kil seed. He hollowed him out in other ways, giving him an insatiable need to consume the mercus of others. The qiz made him a great Seeker, one who would inevitably sniff out the godblooded girl, born of Semūin, who would one day run the roofways of Starside. The Hargothe would capture her to devour her mercus, but would also possess her body and get upon her the unholy child. It was the Hargothe who was to raise the child, near to Moonside, and somehow lead him to total corruption. Yioth must have discovered part of this plan. She's devious enough, and indeed self-loving enough, to believe she could turn a qiznithan's scheme to her own ends. So she forced herself upon the Hargothe, conceived the child, and thereby stole Kil. Brilliant."

"And daft!" Klayne said. "She should have killed the Hargothe and put an end to it."

That was true. But it wasn't what had happened, so there was no purpose in fretting over it. "I had hoped to rescue Yioth tonight," she said. "I'm certain that she could find Kil no matter where he is. You recall how the unborn babe protected her, don't you?"

"I would rather not remember. But obviously the effect no longer persists or Yioth wouldn't have been restrained here long. Why do we need her if Sigh has the child? Sigh is easy to find and she'd be a fool not to keep the child close to her. We should just go fetch him."

"We?" Eckso said imperiously. "*I* will take Kil."

"And then what?"

She wasn't about to tell him. "Let's come down from this scaffold. I think I hear the guards' relief men coming. This city is about to be awakened by much shouting and consternation."

She collected Klayne's power and dymensed with him back to the Bige Barzho, well away from the city. They reappeared in his bedroom. She bade him sit on the bed while she paced and considered her choices.

Rescue Yioth? Dangerous if that qiz-infested revulyn was anywhere near. Even with Klayne's power at her command, she'd already seen how difficult it was to battle a revulyn of much less power. But she needed Yioth to find Saiya.

Unless she relied on Sigh to show her the way.

Return to Starside? Sigh would be suspicious of her, especially for stealing Klayne out of his imprisonment. Eckso doubted she'd keep the child close by, no matter what Klayne thought. And Sigh would never reveal where the child was stowed. Not to Eckso, not to anyone. Sigh was temperamental and fidgety. And much too powerful to toy with.

Eckso doubted Saiya was in Starside, much less the Citadel. Probably hidden away at the Baths of Ori in some realm or other. Maybe on Garden Island.

The child had considerable mercus potential, but Eckso was no Seeker. She'd have to be quite close to feel her. The prospect of wandering from city to city in hopes of sniffing out the child did not appeal at all. Besides, there wasn't that much time to squander. The qiznithan had Yioth and he would break her eventually.

That made her decision simple. She'd heard the revulyn mention Ceronhel, so to Ceronhel they would go. "Let's fetch Yioth," she said.

24

___

ITS WICKED FINGERS

I n anticipation of coming to the Tomb of Man, Fallo had allowed his imagination to erect enormous hidden temples, excavate dank twisty dungeons, and dig up dark catacombs. In fact, he'd envisioned every sort of funerary structure described in heroic tale and minstrel epic. Which was why the sight of the sunlit waterway pulled a string of astonished curses from his lips.

The eerie descending passageway had turned corner after corner, unchanging in width or material. No other corridors branched off of it, no sconces hung upon the smooth walls, and not a speck of dust marred the shiny floor.

And then a light had appeared ahead and the passage opened onto a broad, curved overlook of mossy stone. Below rushed a frothy river, curling in glistening waves to the mouth of a gaping daylit opening. There it spilled into the falls, foaming and misting and sparking rainbows that hung across the mouth of the cavern. Beyond the rainbows, Fallo could just make out the speartip of the warrior maiden statue.

The cavern was an enormous hollow of water-hewn rock. Huge dripping fangs of stone hung from the roof, except where a great opening at the rear allowed in a broad ray of sun. The sheer scale of the expanse stole speech from Fallo's tongue.

An elongated and narrow island split the rushing water near the mouth. Deeper inside, the river emerged from a low arched opening in the bedrock. The air smelled of damp stone and soil. The river's power rumbled in the ground beneath Fallo's feet and roared in the mist-filled air all around.

The regions of the floor blessed by the rays of sun were green with grassy knolls. A few solitary pines thrust up from them to greet the light. But one tree stood many times taller than all these. It was of a different sort. An oak, bole as thick as a house, limbs rising and spreading into a magnificent crown of reddish-purple leaves. It occupied the center of a breathtaking garden set upon the island.

"I see pillars beneath that tree," Quinn said. "And look, a bridge."

Fallo had to peer straight down from the overlook to trace the winding path that led to a white stone bridge. It arched high over the closest split of the waterway. Lop was already crossing it.

"Hear that?" Quinn said, head titled, eyes narrowing in concentration.

"All I hear is the river."

"It sounds like a hammer striking stone." She scanned the whole cavern. "I can't tell where it's coming from."

"The island, most like," Fallo said. "Come on. We'd better catch up with Lop before somebody hammers her skull."

The bridge was damp but not slick. On closer inspection it appeared to be carved naturally from the bedrock. There were no railings, and though it was wide enough for five men abreast, Fallo's vision swam a bit as his eyes were drawn to the rapids below it. His fertile mind could not help but sprout notions of falling into the water and plummeting down the falls.

So when he reached the island he sighed and drew a hand back through his hair. Quinn had not shown the slightest nervousness, of course. She had her hand to her ear. "You hear it?"

He listened. Heard nothing.

Lop, where did you go?

In.

Watch out for somebody with a hammer.

You mean Xilo? He has roast pigeon.

What? Who's—? Never mind. "Come on, Quinn. Lop's already found food."

A stone-paved path wound through a lovely landscape of shrubbery and mossy stone. Bunches of ferns and dark-blossomed flowers were nestled around little ponds fed by tiny streams. It was designed to look natural, but every vantage gave a lovely view. The whole garden was composed and peaceful despite the noise all around.

They came under the massive tree, the lowest limbs so high Fallo thought the spires of the Cathedral of Til would not have touched them. His mind instantly riffled through his mental catalog of verse and story. "'*From Otil's mouth a sprout did spring and grew into The Tree . . .*' You don't think this is *that* tree, do you?"

"Not unless Otil is buried beneath this island," Quinn said doubtfully. "The hammering is coming from behind that hedge."

He trailed after her, still gawping at the tree towering overhead. He finished the verse. "'*His blood suffuses every leaf; the source of mercusine.*'" His shadline instincts began to clang upon this last word. Not in alarm, but in certainty. All of the incessant noise and pull of the force of destiny had suddenly crashed over him like a curling wave against a shore. The moment left him breathless and he had to pause and put his hands on his knees.

"I've been here before," he said. To no one, it turned out. Quinn had gone through a gap in the hedge. He heard the hammering now. The sharp report of metal striking stone. *Tap-TAP. Tap-TAP.* He straightened and looked around. That flash of familiarity had vanished as quickly as it had come over him. Of course he hadn't been here. How would he have forgotten that? Ridiculous.

Tap-TAP. Tap-TAP.

Tap-TAP.

He followed after Quinn and came into what looked like a little burial yard, with low stone pillars thrusting up from moss-covered soil. Four pillars, each a span high. One of them had a little figure standing before it, wielding a hammer and chisel. *Tap-TAP. Tap-TAP.* He was carving something into the face of the pillar. Lop rested comfortably on the top of it, tail drooping down and flicking slowly.

I thought you were eating pigeon, Fallo sent.

I'm obviously not.

Quinn was scanning the carvings on the other pillars as she moved around to look at the little person. Not a child, though no taller than a common eight-year-old. His hair was long and fair, pulled back into a tail. His ears came to points, nose long.

Tap-TAP. Tap-TAP.

Tap-TAP. Tap-TAP- TAP-TAP.

"Well now I have seen everything," Fallo said. "It's a vergent."

Tap-TAP. Tap—

The creature paused in his hammering a moment, turned his head to look at his visitors, nodded a greeting, then continued hammering. *Tap-TAP. Tap-TAP.* He then spoke in a piping little voice that was somehow youthful and ancient at the same time. "I worried you would be late, and you are," he said. *Tap-TAP.* "I see you have the blades. Leastways you got *that* much right." *Tap-TAP.*

"So this is the Tomb of Man? Birthplace of Kil?" Fallo asked.

Tap-TAP. Tap-TAP. Tap-TAP-TAP-TAP. "Sure. It can be that if that's what you need." *Tap-TAP. Tap-TAP. Tap-TAP.*

Fallo shrugged off his pack and dug out Zirhine's fate's-piece, a small sketch of the mountain with Goblet constellation on the left and horned moon on the right. "This has vergent writing on it. It says in Elnisian, *'Mati il waun Kil. Entir il umak.'* Birthplace of Kil. Tomb of Man."

Xilo stepped back from the stone and studied his work, tilting his head this way and that. "I think that'll do. Not too bad, if I do say so myself. And I do." He chuckled and slipped the haft of his hammer into a loop on his belt. His shirt looked like a pillowcase with holes cut out for his arms and head. It came to bare knobby knees, shins, and feet. He turned his eyes back to Fallo, gaped a moment and offered a little bow. "If I'd known you were kin I would have prepared a meal. This Spark Spirit ate the last of my leftovers."

You said you hadn't eaten, Fallo sent.

No, I said I wasn't eating.

"What do you mean kin?" Quinn asked, kneeling to come eye level with Xilo. Her face was lit with awe and a bit of trepidation. Every child had heard vergent stories. All knew that such creatures could bestow blessings and curses on a whim, often granting both in the same breath.

"This hideous lad there has vergent blood in him." Xilo squinted and peered into Fallo's eyes. "And elnisian and human and . . . nosg. Ah, but that's because you've got those Dragon Tooth blades. You used Telt and Skye together, didn't you? Draws the victim's essence straight into you." He rubbed his chin and pooched out his lips. "That would be interesting . . . for someone with nothing to do. But I must be busy. Why are you both still here? Get going! Don't you know how little time you have? Idle hands tie ragged knots!"

He darted away, skipping down a narrow path that led toward the trunk of the tree. Quinn and Fallo went after him, exchanging confused glances. Fallo still held the sketch in his fingers.

They didn't have to go far. They found Xilo digging a hole next to a clump of berry canes. His little shovel scooped and settled black dirt next to his feet where an uprooted bundle of canes now lay. "You lot sure waste time," he said, jabbing in his spade and hopping upon it to drive it deeper. "That will never do if you're to get your tasks completed. Didn't you see? I just finished Til's marker. You've got no time to squander. Others hunt while you loiter." He tossed a clump of soil and looked back at them. "You're *still* here?"

"You haven't told us anything," Fallo complained, waving the sketch at him. "Is this sketch right?"

Huffing in irritation, the vergent left his spade stuck in the turf and snatched the sketch. He mumbled to himself as he held it up to the light. "This is a child's drawing!"

"There's writing on it, visible only in the light of a farlin-bright candle."

"Stay here!" The vergent dashed off, plunging into the thicket of berry canes.

Just when Fallo thought he had forgotten them, the little vergent returned, carrying a white candle flecked with gold. He held the scrap of paper before the dim greenish flame. "Hmmm. It is as you say. I *did* write this."

"You? Then answer me. The not-so-subtle call of the force of destiny pulled me here, to this place at this time. I'm here. What does it mean?"

The vergent began to pace, brows furrowed. "Birthplace of Kil. Birthplace of Kil . . ." He slapped his head. "Oh! I remember now." He crumpled the paper and tossed it over his shoulder. Reclaiming his spade, he returned to his digging.

Fallo was close to hefting the little man by his collar and dunking him in the river. "What does it signify, Xilo?"

"Don't get cross with me! You two simpletons have tarried here long enough. You've got work to do."

"The sketch, Xilo. Explain it." Fallo's hand was resting on Telt, and an unfamiliar heat was searing his throat. "Now!"

The vergent flinched and dropped the farlinbright. He held up his shovel in defense. "It doesn't signify! Not anymore. It did when I wrote it. That fool Illizshian called it prophecy, plucked the note from my hand and ran off with it." His eyes narrowed and he looked left and right, as if there might be eavesdroppers in the garden. "Those dim-witted elnisians drank prophecy like wine, got drunk upon it. 'Oh! Dire prophecy. It's dire and ominous! It must be *significant*! Oh, let us dwell upon it, direly, and be *moved* and believe that what'll transpire in the future is important and dire.' Prophecy!" he spat. "You want prophecy, ask the wind. What is to come will come. Bah. You and your friend have the wits of fish. Of course you took on board my little prophecy. But you think of it wrongly. Did I not just tell you that I finished Til's stone today? You *saw* me do it! Why are you still here, you dung-chewing turkey herders!"

"What does Til's stone signify?" Quinn asked, gripping Fallo's arm to keep him from throttling the vergent.

"Birth. Death. And everything in between. Death. Birth. And everything in between. Best get to work, you two. The Foulness isn't lazing about. Oh no, it's already on the hunt." He turned back to his work. Lop strolled past Fallo and went to peer into the hole. Then she got in it and curled up.

"What!" Xilo cried. "I can't do anything with you in there. Scoot!"

Lop did not comply, acknowledging the vergent with only a squint of disdain.

"Feed you more?" Xilo said. "I gave you an entire pigeon wing!"

"Xilo, what is our task?" Fallo asked. *Stay in that hole,* he sent to Lop.

"By Fo and her brood! What do you mean? I *told* you. Fetch the godlings. Keep them safe. I *just* finished Til's marker! Don't you know what that means?"

"No."

The vergent slapped his head and shook his whole body with fury. "Did I not say the Foulness wasn't lazy? What more do you need to know?" He stomped toward Fallo, came toe to toe with him. He looked up, face red, brows furrowed like a bull hound's. "Perhaps you aren't kin after all, for how could one of vergent blood be so daft? But no. I see it there in your eyes, behind the gray elnisian and the charcoal nosg. By Fo and her fecund loins! We've been *over* this already." He counted off on tiny fingers: "Ori, reborn. Finished that pillar right on time. Kil, reborn. Just as expected. Tappity-tap, all carved, right on time. Pol. Reborn. Pillar done. And now, Til, that laggard, has come too. Do I need to say more, you worm-riddled apple? Go fetch them. The Foulness won't sit around with fingers jammed up its nostrils like you two. The Foulness moves! Scrounging around in Sliryan cellars, it is. Oh it's looking all right, it's seeking with its wicked fingers."

He marched off with his shovel over his shoulder. "Spark Spirit, you can have that hole," he called to Lop. "You mischievous little wonder!"

Fallo was already starting after the vergent when Quinn spun him around. "I don't think we need more information from him."

"But I want to wring his neck. Just a little."

"Doubt that would serve any good purpose, assuming you could lay hands on him."

She was right. He tamped down his own anger at being treated like a simpleton by a fey-blooded pipsqueak who spoke as if they'd already had a lengthy conversation. When they most definitely *had not*. "I suppose we should have anticipated this." He sighed heavily.

"The vergent's madness?"

"No. I mean the other gods. It seems rather obvious now that we know that Kil isn't the only one of them to be reborn. I still don't see how this is the Tomb of Man. Or the Birthplace of Kil."

"You dolt!" cried Xilo from beyond a berm covered with ferns. "How many times do I have to tell you? But go ask those crack-skulled elnisians if you want to waste more time. I can't get them to leave!"

"Where are they?" Fallo called.

"You giant thorn in my arse! They're where they've been these last thousand years! At the prow!"

Quinn had to get in front of him this time, push him back. Relenting, he turned toward the narrowest point of the island, where the two sides of the river rejoined before plunging over the cliff. A high stone platform rose well above the splash of the water here. Upon it lay three dead elnisians and one not quite dead one. The bodies were fresh, as if they had simply slumped over and gone to sleep. Fallo nudged the breathing one, a regal-looking man of perhaps fifty years. His hair was red, redder than Henley's. Face pale, with high cheekbones and thin lips. He wore a black tunic over loose fawn colored pants. A gold collar —or perhaps necklace—lay over his shoulders. It appeared to be of fine woven wire, a band as wide as Fallo's hand circling around the elnisian's chest and back in equal measure.

The eyes opened, but not very far. Gray irises scanned Fallo's face. The man strained to press a hand to his breast. *"Il'et vuan e wom ci. En so, en so. Sha!"*

Fallo could read Elnisian writing, but his Donse Master tutor hadn't pronounced it like this. He looked to Quinn. She shrugged.

Lop moseyed up to the platform, nudged the dying elnisian with a paw. His eyes widened at the sight of her. *"Felnithel!"* She allowed him to stroke her fur. *"Il'et vaun e wom ci. Sha, felnithel. Pren err dulicat ci? Sha!"*

"I think that last word—*sha*—means 'alas'," Fallo mused. "*Il'et vaun* . . . Oh! Eel'ect van! I think I understand. 'He was to be born in me.' Or something like that. Are two of those women?"

Quinn studied faces. "This one here is male. Throat apple. These others do appear to be women. Why?"

The living elnisian had fallen unconscious, his breath was slow and shallow. Fallo searched for pockets. Found nothing. The necklace was not the same as those on the other three. He studied the gold weave. It was just a large circle around the man's neck. If he took it off and laid it flat it would be a golden circle. Like the sun. Like Til's judgmental eye.

"This one was to be Til," he said, then moved to the next one. Her necklace was tucked inside the throat of her shirt. He pulled it out and was astonished to see a medallion similar to those worn by Spinsters of Pol. It was larger, the relief of Pol's smiling face on one side and her frowning visage on the other was sharper and more elegant than on any Spinster's medallion.

"That makes her Pol." He stepped over the body and knelt next to the other male. A man of great age with black hair. His pendant was a golden circlet with three tines sticking up, each the shape of an upright spear. "Kil. So that one over there is Ori."

Xilo's voice came to them over the rush of the river: "Those doom-singers have been sitting there since I don't know when!" Fallo turned to find him, but he was hidden behind a shrub where a flurry of pruned off twigs arced into the air. "I'm glad they finally croaked," Xilo shouted. "I never thought they had much sense. And I was right!" His head popped into view. "Are you *still* here?"

"How do we get out? The vergent path to the gate only goes one way."

"Stroke my beard! Do you think me powerless? I'm Xilo, Tender of the Growing. Begone and take that donkey, too. Eating my hay and drinking my water, is he? Felnithel, never you mind my words. I address only the hapless fools WHO ARE STILL HERE while the Foulness capers about unhindered. Laziness earns ill sleep! Mark my words."

Throwing up his hands, Fallo turned away from the vergent. "Let's get out of here before I let Skeye carve him a couple new orifices."

Quinn stooped before each elnisian to relieve them of their splendid jewelry. At Fallo's scandalized stare, she arched her brows. "Shadline instincts. These are fate's-pieces." She stuffed them into her pack.

Come on, Lop. We've got to go.

Where?

He considered the question a moment, for it was a very good one. "Xilo, where can we find Til, Pol, and Ori?"

"Bend over and look up your arse, you craven-hearted self-fondling owl pellet!"

Quinn's face went blank, but a hot flush surged up her neck and into her cheeks. Her eyes watered and her lips quivered. And when she could contain it no longer, she spluttered out a whooping laugh and bent double.

So that was the extent of her loyalty. Fallo stalked off, leaving Lop and Quinn to either come after him or—preferably—fling themselves over the falls.

He did not get to the bridge before Xilo was calling to him again. "Not that way, you walking nosg hide!" Quinn appeared behind and waved him to follow, still covering her mouth with her good hand. And so Xilo led them the other way, along a winding path past flowerbeds and tidy rows of cabbages and through little groves of olive trees and over a tiny stream that pooled here and there along its mysterious course.

At the far end of the island they came to another bridge, this one leading to a black archway in the rock. Fallo pushed onward, eager to be done with the insulting vergent. But Quinn had stopped, and so he too stopped.

Xilo held her hand as she again squatted to meet his eyes. "You want to be a legend, dearie, don't you?" Xilo said, rather gently. "You wish to be a hero of the age. But you've been cast into the shadow of that disagreeable young man there. Your yearning will taint your love. But perhaps love isn't so important to you as fame. The force of destiny brought you Black, borne by Smoke in Shadows in one age, called Silent Sable in another. History does not remember the unseen, unheard hero. Until you can hold this blade and make yourself heard, you will remain smoke in shadow." His demeanor transformed abruptly and he cast away her hand. "Ah me! Why do I bother? You're as thick-skulled as your pumpkin-faced friend. Don't you have work to do? I do!" He stormed off, hurling curses behind him.

Quinn looked stricken as they walked toward the impenetrable blackness of the passageway arch. It led downward, deeper into the mountain. Lop trailed behind them, moving with no urgency whatsoever.

A somber silence arose between them as they passed beneath the arch. Fallo held up the lantern, which illuminated only a circle on the floor. A soft breeze tickled through his hair. He moved right, seeking a wall. There was none. None to the left.

"A Derslin Wheel," he said. "Looks like we have to go back anyway."

"Why?" Quinn asked, face dark and turned inward.

"Tolky."

"He's ahead."

"What? How? How do you know?"

"Shadline instincts." She was quiet again for a long time as they walked. But then she patted her cheeks and gave herself a shake. Her head came up, and her innate confidence again bolstered her posture. "It's odd to truly feel the pull. It has been so rare, so quiet for me all this time."

Tolky stood in the middle of the circle of columns. All his unloaded cargo was arranged around him on the floor. A little manger held fresh hay and a channel of water flowed nearby. Lop lunged onto the donkey's back while Quinn rubbed its nose and whispered friendly greetings.

Fallo turned slowly to study the columns and the mystifying symbols carved into each. "Too bad we don't have a merculyn with us."

"We were brought here," Quinn said. "An answer will come." A strange calm had come over her. As if she'd made some sort of decision. She fetched a book from her pack and sat on the stone floor, her back to one of the columns.

Fallo closed his eyes and listened. But there was nothing to hear. For him, the whispers of the force of destiny had fallen silent.

25
____

A HUMAN NOTION

The primary rule of dymensing was that one must have been to the destination in order to dymense there. Fixing an image of the destination in the mind, while not necessary, was thought to be helpful. The most important aspect of setting a destination was feeling it. Difficult to explain, simple to do once the skill was experienced.

Dymensing to a place one had never visited was terrifically dangerous. Release those mercus bolts and hope for the best. Rematerializing inside a mountain, or at the bottom of a lake, or half embedded in a tree would be a most unfortunate end.

Kila knew all of this, and it weighed heavily on her as she considered how to get to where she needed to take Saiya. If she chose not to risk dymension, she had three terrible options. The first was to ride a horse the entire way. Too long and too scary for someone who had little experience mounted. The second option was to use the Derslin Wheel, but there was no column available in the wheel for the place she had in mind. She might get close, but she'd still end up on foot or ahorse. She wasn't sure which was worse. Same problem with the final option, which was to use vergent passes and hope to get close. This might work, but it would require her to know where her destination was, which she didn't. Not exactly, anyway. All very frustrating.

Saiya held her hand, bulging pack on her back. Nax was nestled on Kila's shoulder, waiting patiently for the inevitable.

Thing was, Kila *had* been to this destination before, she just couldn't remember much about it. Perhaps the wisest course was not to attempt to get there all in one jump. Get close and walk the rest of the way. Closing her eyes, she sank into the mercusine web. The Revulsion bubbled in her awareness, drawn to her frustration and fear.

"I managed it on Garden Island," she said, more to herself than to Saiya. She'd had great need to escape Dunne Yples at the time, who had been trying to kill her, screaming "Dem-Kisk" at the top of his lungs the whole time.

"Kil's tears," she whispered as she gathered the mercus to her and formed the bolts. Her need was great now, and she wove that into her bolts. Inside, she grasped for half-forgotten scents and visions of her childhood. Not yet, not yet, she cautioned. Not yet.

She searched for the feeling of the place, waited for the sense of rightness. When it came, it registered as a moment of no thought at all. Just a sudden quietude in her mind. Releasing the bolts, she passed into the icy bath of dymension.

When the world returned, she looked up and let out a stunned, "Oh!"

A weird sense of familiarity struck her, leaving her dazed. "I've been here before." It was one thing to know she'd been here as a child, but quite another to recognize a place long shrouded from memory by time and mercus occlusion.

The occlusion had been removed by Annisforl, the last Highest of Kil. He had remained alive in Kil's Keep solely to remove her occlusion. Prior to his intervention, merely thinking of her mother had made Kila's head split with agony. Now such thoughts merely irritated her.

A snow-covered beach gave way to ice. Kila walked out onto it, listening for telltale pops and snaps that it was about to break, but the freeze was deep here. The only opening was an irregular circle around the base of the falls. Saiya came with her, craning her neck to look up at the cascade pouring down a column of ice.

Kila tested the mercus. *Do you feel the Revulsion here at all?* she sent to Nax.

Very faintly. This place is . . . Nax didn't finish the thought, but uneasiness trickled over the bond. *There is something under the ice.*

Kila knew what it was. Her heart began to slam in her chest. "Mother, I'm here."

A violet sphere appeared in the depths. It bloomed and brightened as a gush of bubbles reached the surface. And then a beautiful, youthful woman emerged, wet black hair curtaining down onto pale bare shoulders. Meeting those eyes, luminous, deep, and full of fierce emotion, sent a juddering sensation through Kila's head. It was like looking in a warped bit of polished steel and seeing a distorted reflection of herself.

"Hello, Mother. I'm Kila. My father was Wenton Sigh." She pulled Cayne from its sheath and showed it to the water spirit. "You gave him this blade."

Saiya cocked her head to one side and looked from Semūin to Kila and back. "Your mother is young, too."

Semūin continued to stare, saying nothing. She flicked her eyes at Saiya, lingered a moment, then looked back to Kila. Nax jumped down and eased close to the water's edge, nose quivering.

Semūin gasped at the sight of the cat. She covered her mouth with a delicate, dripping hand. "Beloved One. I did not recognize you in that form. It has been ages and yet it has been but a day since we last communed."

You know her? Kila sent.

Of course I do.

Why didn't you mention it?

Cats didn't shrug, but a feline equivalent crossed the bond—a surge of bored disinterest combined with a peculiar drooping ear feeling. Semūin did not dip her head to the cat as demayne did, but she smiled broadly at the animal before turning a much different gaze on Kila. Her lower lip protruded a bit and her brows dipped. "Why didn't you come sooner, my dear? I've been lonely."

"I didn't know you were my mother until very recently. I scarcely believe it now."

"Who is this?" Semūin said, tilting her wet head at Saiya.

"She's my daughter. There are those in the outside world who would harm her. I need you to watch over her for a while. Keep her hidden here where none can find her."

The water spirit pulled herself up to sit on the ice, hair so long it formed a sort of gown that covered her nakedness. The cold did not affect her at all. "Why are you being so formal, daughter? Come to me. Let me greet you as a mother should greet her child." Semūin extended her arms.

Semūin was offering an embrace, which made Kila uneasy. The memories she had of Semūin were sun-dappled and blurry. They were like stories she'd heard about other people. She searched her heart and found no love, no fondness for Semūin at all. If anything, there was bitterness, for this demigoddess had treated her father very poorly.

But it was the Cheapsgate custom to pay a price, be it coin, goods, or flesh, for large favors. She put Cayne away, knelt onto the ice, and accepted the embrace. Her mother's slim body pulled her tightly in, then tipped forward and took her plunging deep into the icy lake.

Her weather-cloak ward shattered. Freezing cold pushed from all sides, squeezing her breath out in gurgling bubbles. She flailed to escape her mother's embrace, but Semūin held her fast. A warbling voice came close to her ear. "Breathe."

Every instinct in Kila's body told her that to breathe in water was to die. Mercus rushed into her, but this time her desperation could not form any bolts of use.

Her eyes opened to discover violet light all around her. Semūin's gurgled words again interrupted her panic. "You are off me. Breathe."

But Semūin still held her, and was taking her deeper and deeper. The stabbing ache of pinpoint needles pierced into her ears.

"You are off me. Breathe."

It didn't make sense. Kila clamped her lips together as her lungs strained to draw in anything that would relieve the desperate need for air.

Semūin's lips pressed to hers, warm, soft. Her eyes glowed an eldritch purple fire. She suddenly blew hard into Kila's sealed lips, forcing in water. Convulsing, Kila could do nothing to resist. Her mouth opened wide and she sucked in the icy water.

And suddenly she was warm and renewed. Gasping in the water, she looked all around, marveling that the pain was gone and that she was still alive. Or was she? There was nothing to see here except for Semūin, floating amidst a void of blackness. Her violet glow underlit her drift of black hair. Her limbs moved in fluid strokes to hold her position.

Semūin motioned for Kila to follow her and swam away.

Kila kicked and swept her arms and found enough speed to keep the violet light in view. And then she emerged from the water in a little cave behind the waterfall. The pool here was still, and a shelf of dry stone rimmed it. She pulled herself onto the ledge, water spilling from her mouth. She breathed air now.

Semūin floated in front of her, smiling warmly. "See? You are of me. Now you can believe I am your mother without any doubt."

Reestablishing her weather-cloak and forcing her clothes dry with the mercus, Kila tamped down her reasonable anger. "You could have told me before you tried to drown me."

"I didn't try to drown you." Semūin splashed playfully at Kila. The water streamed from Kila's clothes without wetting them. Noting this, Semūin wrinkled her nose. "A merculyn? Why do you waste your power on such tricks? It's very human of you."

Kila had not given much thought to what meeting her mother would be like, but she had not imagined this. Semūin was childish. Yet she was so old that she had known Nax in a previous incarnation. It truly struck Kila then that she was seeing the legendary man-killer Semūin with her own eyes. This childhood story figure—one she had not believed in—actually existed.

"Tell me the truth," Semūin said, "who is that girl? I feel something in her that frightens me. She is kin to us both, but she is not your daughter. There are dangerous currents of madness beyond the peaceful shore of her mind."

"She is Kil reborn. She is not the daughter of my womb. Her father was a corrupt merculyn and her mother the dragnithan Yiothizandra. But she bonded to me, heart to heart, while she was still inside Yiothizandra. I cut her free with Cayne. I loved her instantly. She is mine. But she is also Kil reborn, and the Revulsion wishes to corrupt her."

Semūin, who was immune to the cold, shivered. "The Revulsion? What is that? I don't like the dribbles the word makes in my mind."

"The Beloved Ones say it is everywhere, a vileness that covers the mercusine. I feel it everywhere now, too, save here. Your vale is hidden from mortals, perhaps your power keeps the Revulsion away."

"Ah, I know of this serpent you call Revulsion. But by another name. The Unanswered. The power no god would claim. But surely it lies senseless as stone."

"It has awakened." Kila would never admit to wielding it. Not to her mother. "A qiznithan has come into this world. He uses the Revulsion to corrupt others. A revulyn came to Starside to steal Saiya. So you see why I must hide her away while I find a way to defeat it."

"Defeat it? Not even Til can destroy destruction. What hope has a half-mortal girl? Stay hidden with me here. Kil reborn and the Beloved One will strengthen the godwards that conceal my vale." She again splashed at Kila. "I have long wished to be free of this place, and of this world. But now I am grateful to be safe. The Unanswered terrifies even the gods."

Safe for now, Kila thought.

"I had thought the elnisians had learned their lesson," Semūin said, growing more agitated as she spoke. "Why would they awaken the Unanswered again?"

"The elnisians are gone. I have never seen one. All that remains of their kin are the nosg."

Semūin's fear of the Revulsion had drifted from her mind. She laughed at the mention of the nosg. "I adore the nosg. They are funny. I haven't lured one here in three ages. They no longer pass near enough. Only men come close, though I do love them too. La! I'm happy you have come, no matter the reason. But I am most vexed your memories of me were occluded. A daughter should remember her mother. It is only natural and right. I know nothing of this Yiothizandra, but even a demayne would be heartsore to be parted from her babe. But I feel danger in that child. Kil, you say she is? I wonder if it could be so. He always frightened me. Ah, but I see that you love her. And I love you. So I shall endeavor to love this dire child. Will she swim with me?"

"Saiya will swim, though I recommend you not pull her in as you did to me."

Semūin did not promise. "Will you stay a year or two? I wish to hear all about your life. Your mercus is loud! Why squander it so?"

"Squander? How else would I use it?"

"You are my daughter, surely you don't need to use feats and other such nonsense to exert your power. Just be what you are. Wenton was a lovely man. I truly loved him for the moments I loved him. Feelings flow down river, you know, replenished instantly by new ones. It all passes and flows. But I have loved you without cessation these hundreds of years."

"What are you talking about? I'm but seventeen."

"Age is a human notion. Best to dispense with that entirely. Why was Kil reborn in mortal flesh?"

The contrast between Semūin's keen intelligence and her distractibility reminded Kila of Saiya in her most difficult moments. "The force of destiny, I'm told," Kila said. "In truth, I don't care much about why things are as they are. Learning the why of a problem has rarely helped me to solve one, though everyone thinks it will. I am determined to bring Saiya up to be good and fair, not to be a god of hate and greed and everything base and awful."

Semūin giggled and splashed and did a quick spin in the water, hair fanning out and sending droplets in all directions. "This will be fun! I am beginning to love the girl already. You must stay a year at least."

"I'm sorry, Mother. The Revulsion spreads its corruption quicker and quicker. If I am to defeat it, I must go now. But I will return for Saiya when it is safe. I promise I'll stay longer with you then."

The water spirit did not seem satisfied with this, but neither did she object. Instead she dove and vanished into the depths. Kila plunged in after her and was able to breathe the water just as before. The violet light was faint, so she kicked toward it with all her strength and finally came up in the circle of open water beneath the falls.

Semūin was motioning for Saiya to come to her. "Bring your things. You will be able to breathe the water. Trust me, granddaughter. Beloved One, will you stay?"

Will I? Nax asked. *If the Revulsion can penetrate this place, I do not believe I alone will be strong enough to protect both Saiya and Semūin.*

Kila had not considered the risk of Semūin being turned by the Revulsion. A demigoddess could be a terrible force should she escape her vale, though Kila had little notion of what Semūin could do besides breathe water and glow.

Like the rest of her unsolvable troubles, Kila decided to let it lie. *Return with me. We'll find Startle later if need be.*

"Nax will go with me," she said. "She protects me from the Revulsion." Kila hugged Saiya, wishing she could tie a little bond into the girl's mind so that she could feel her presence even when parted from her. But Saiya's mind was too dangerous for that. She stroked the girl's hair back and cupped her cheek. "You'll be safe here with Semūin. Do not leave the vale, understand?"

"I understand." Saiya did not look afraid, or even particularly upset. If anything she was impatient. "Can I go in the water now?"

"Yes. Go."

Saiya dragged her heavy pack along the ice, then pushed it into the open water. Without a backward glance she dove in headfirst. Semūin waved a smiling farewell to Kila and disappeared.

Standing there upon the ice, amidst the splashy laughter of the nearly frozen waterfall, Kila stared at the churning surface of the water. "Goodbye, sweetlight."

26

HER STORE OF BREATH

The trouble with the reviled was their inability to show convincing emotion on their faces. For Revnithan Soth, this posed a challenge. A newly turned reviled stood before her in Devin's room, a garret he rented from a widow in Lower Terriside. Standing was most of what a reviled did. Unblinking, dark of eye, pale of lip, immobile. Any living human would note the oddness in him.

"Reviled Fweed, smile," she commanded.

The lips pulled back exposing yellow teeth.

"You must crinkle the eyes," she said.

Fweed squinted. If this was all he could manage for a smile, she doubted his other expressions would fool anyone. Not that it mattered, for the reviled saw only with an indiscriminating cold eye, untempered by the higher cause. In that, she envied him. Catching herself in envy, she willed herself to recenter in the cold eye. Lord Yples had done her no favors by making her a Revnithan, though she understood his reasons for it. Mindlessness would not serve during this time of building. The Revulsion needed focus, strategy.

Fweed could not pretend to feel. Nor could he understand emotions or their undercurrents in others. Already he had terrified the chamber girl who occasionally came up to clean Devin's room. Fortunately the girl was given to flights of terror about ghosts in the attic, so the widow ignored her ravings about the dead man upstairs.

Devin, for all his weakness in the Revulsion, had become better skilled at imitating the unawakened humans. He regularly passed among them now, even going to into common rooms to imbibe drinks and listen to the locals talk. He had been searching for employment at the Citadel. But to get such, one required a referral from someone already working there. Fweed was a footman to the Minister of Treasury. Soth had hoped he would get Devin a job. But the reviled Fweed was as useless as a hunk of rock.

He *was* a hunk of rock. "Dispose of him tonight," she ordered.

"It will be as you say," Devin said. A revulyn was fully turned in a way Soth had not been. Contempt and envy warred for supremacy in her mind. She turned her attention back to the problem at hand, the sooner completed, the sooner her ultimate release.

She would have to make a bolder move than merely getting Devin a position at the Citadel. It would not be unheard of for a Spinster to appear there. She would invent some pretense or other to gain admission herself.

"Describe for me again where the god-child has been moved."

Devin tilted his head and looked at the ceiling. "It is at the end of a hallway beyond the kitchens. . . ."

SOTH FOUND the kitchens easily enough, entering from a back courtyard through a door held open with an andiron. The cold winter air was welcome to those who toiled before great spit fires and ovens inside. Soth noticed neither cold nor heat.

A footman bearing a silver tray brushed past her, carrying off someone's tea. Another took a great platter covered with a silver lid. A vast table served as a pass where cooks delivered their dishes for the maids and footmen to carry off to various destinations within the Citadel.

Soth passed among them, ignoring the strange looks coming from a scullery girl and a lady tossing leeks into a bubbling pot. Enormous fires blazed under three arched cookways, smoke flowing up the towering chimneys. Pigs and atlen and lambs glistened on spits turned by serious, shirtless boys.

She passed by the iron cooktops and bakery ovens, all manned by the aproned corps of cooks and assistants. Past the office of the Mistress of Kitchens, who sat inside inking a ledger.

The hallway beyond was as Devin had described. Fweed had told of the girl recently moved there, the mysterious ward of Kila Sigh. It was foolish to leave her unguarded, relying merely on deception to keep her safe.

But what was 'safe?' Soth mused. To the cold eye there was no such thing. There was only suffering or not suffering. The god Kil was the one closest to the Revulsion, greedy, full of wrath, and expectant of blood, war, avarice, rape, and slaughter. His domain was that of lust, hostility, and delusion. Indeed, he was blind to his own suffering, so set was he upon wreaking it on others.

Yes, Kil suffered more than the others. Perhaps not in this reborn form, not yet. Soth remembered her own life of mortal toil—of the senseless longings, for food, for love, for pleasure, for status, for correcting the wrongs of others. All of it a form of madness. She saw that clearly now because she saw with the cold eye. The Unanswered power was the Revulsion. It was the negating force that revealed the lie of life and light, and the truth of Annihilation.

Here was the door.

Soth paused and listened with Revulsion-heightened senses. Heard the breathing inside. Felt the warmth. The door was not locked. Such fools!

She stepped in. A dim red glow came from banked embers in the hearth. Loaves of bread lined the floor along one wall. Soth knew that was odd, but she did not care about the purpose of the hoard. She stepped to the bed where a small, slim figure lay. The long hair was braided, the boney shoulders covered over with woolen blankets.

The head turned, drawn by the rustle of Soth's robes. The girl's eyes opened. "Kil kissin' thief!" she rasped. She sucked in a great breath, preparing to scream.

Soth felt nothing of power in the child. Not a thimble of mercusine. This was a mortal child. Her nosg-made dagger came free of its sheath and sliced in the same motion, parting the girl's throat so deeply that her store of breath bubbled out with the gush of blood. She fell back and writhed, then died.

Soth dymensed into Devin's garret. She was alone for a long while before Devin dymensed in. He blinked once at Soth and waited.

"The girl was not the god Kil," Soth said. "I must retire to my own room and think. Did you dispose of Fweed?"

"I had him walk into the Sourwater. He will not be seen again."

Back in her little room beneath Pol's Well, Soth reclined upon her cot and sank into the Revulsion. Lord Yples would be displeased. But she was more certain than ever that Kil reborn was not in the Citadel.

Soth decided not to return to Sorgan empty handed. She would bide her time a while longer in hopes Kil returned. Starside was astir with happenings. All was unsettled. The Revulsion hummed with building expectation.

The cold eye was patient.

27

THE WINTER SOLITUDE

Across the mountains and plains, swamps and forests, past the chasm of The Boil and over the desert, beyond woodlands and mountains, upon the western-most spit of the land men called Ennith, lay Slirya, city of a million souls.

Revnithan Con, who had once been a Sensual of Ori, stood upon a little rain-drenched lane in Seaside, a borough of fisher-wives, netters, and sailmakers. She had been born here seventy-eight years ago. Right in that little salmon-colored house with the white trim. She felt a scurrying unease as she turned away from it. The cold eye illuminated all emotion as a lie, but her human memories had a momentum of their own. Visions of her childhood continued to interrupt her search for the revulynic dagger called Entifal.

If only she could simply cease to exist. "Bah!" she muttered, annoyed by her longing for the ultimate release. Even that desire was a lie. This was the very suffering Lord Yples had spoken of. Even awakened as she was to the truth, existence harried her, weighed upon her, tortured her.

She'd been a scholar as a Sensual, an expert on mercus relics and a cataloger of animals, plants, and rocks. Even Donse Masters sought her out to confer about her system of describing, comparing, and categorizing insects. Looking back on her career, her life's work had been making order of a chaotic world.

Perhaps that was why she could not stop thinking about the contradictions inherent in the Revulsion. It wished for itself to not exist. But what did existence mean? And how could the world become nothing without leaving component pieces still lying about in some sort of unformed universe of potentiality?

And then there was what she considered the Big Problem. The Revulsion could be manifested into feats.

"That speaks to a generative property," she mused aloud as she moved along the lane. The Revulsion could negate mercus feats rather easily. But it could also *make*. Light? Yes, it could make light. Heat? Certainly. "Hmm."

She caught herself. "Stop thinking, you old bat!" She headed out of the empty lane and continued to listen for the distinctive hum of the mercus. Lord Yples had not told her where in Slirya she might find this Revulsion relic. He'd discovered its existence in her mind, after all. And there was nobody around to ask, were she foolish enough to do so.

She wasn't truly searching, merely walking and thinking. She had always done her best thinking when walking. Being awakened to the truth had not changed that. She kept her awareness alive in case she happened to pass near enough to the Entifal to notice it.

Lord Yples had discovered its existence in her mind because she had once read a scrap of a note during a visit to the Hackwatch. She'd been young then, barely forty. The Revulsion had revealed itself to her there with gut-clenching horror. She'd nearly fled. But she'd gone there with a purpose: to scour the Iron Scholars' library for any mention of mercusine relics to include in her catalog project.

The words of that note appeared in her vision now, overlaid on the misty street ahead of her:

"The Entifal was an elnisian failure. Crafted to allow mercus feats where the Revulsion is thickest, it soon accumulated so much foulness it became impossible to wield. The elnisians feared to destroy it lest its corruption be released. It is hidden in Slirya among those who know not to touch it or allow it to be touched. It emanates pure aversion and so has remained unclaimed. Praise be to Pol."

Any moron might read that and believe the mystery of the Entifal's hiding place not so great. The clue, a moron would say, was the final sentence praising Pol. That would seem to point to the reliquary of the Way of Pol. Con thought it obvious misdirection. But since she hadn't found it by wandering, she had to be sure.

Problem. How to get in? The Ways kept their vaults secret. She would need to gain entry to Pol's offices, poke her nose into every room and cellar, and face the innumerable questions about what in Kil's name she was doing there. This quandary she had not solved. Sneaking had never been part of her life as a scholar.

So she wandered and thought and thought and wandered. Pol smiled upon her (though she immediately saw the lie in any reference to Pol's grace), for Wintertide Solitude would extend for several more days here. Which meant the citizenry were isolated in their homes. The militia patrols were scanty, but she'd already been confronted by two of them. A show of her old token of Ori had satisfied them. It was usual for folk to host Sensuals for dinners during the Wintertide Solitude.

The cold did not bother her. A nice benefit of being heart-dead, she supposed. It had made her absent-minded about appearances, unfortunately. One shouldn't walk about in the rain without the customary oilcloak. Winter was a damp season in Slirya. A militia squad had stopped her and had nearly escorted her to a Temple of Ori in East Turn when they found her walking along soaked to the skin. She'd used Yples's clever distraction feat on them and slipped away, forgotten. Appropriating an oilcloak had been simple enough. Folk didn't lock their doors in the better quarters of the city.

Sneaking! Who would have thought old Sensual Con would do such a thing at her age. Or at any age.

Rain pattered onto the thick fabric of her cloak, beaded up and rolled away. The hood brim dripped a continuous curtain before her eyes. She supposed remaining dry would stave off the inevitable rot that would come over her flesh in the days to come. Already her aged skin had begun to shrivel a bit.

There were no mercus relics nearby, she decided. Not even a person with an unawakened spark. No surprise; Slirya screened all citizens for the spark as a matter of law. Every summer solstice, children of five through fifteen came to Seeker Square beneath the palace to be inspected by representatives of the three Ways.

She had served for three decades as Sensual Advocate at the Triumvirate Chapel in the palace here in Slirya, before being reassigned to Sorgan. She would have no difficulty getting into the Triumvirate Chapel and Offices.

"It's all very circular," she complained. "Wherever I am, I think I should be someplace else." That was another human quality that had not been overwhelmed by her awakening. She knew she was brilliant. She never forgot anything she read, and had a mind for reasoning unlike anyone she'd encountered. But she couldn't think of how to get into Pol's area of the Offices.

Unless she went in hard. Flinging Revulsion feats around

and killing indiscriminately. It wouldn't be difficult to do, especially against merculyns who did not expect it. Most had never tasted the Revulsion, wouldn't even understand what was happening. More than that, the merculyns in Slirya held fast to the strictures of the Synod of the New Pantheon, which prohibited using emotions in mercus feats. That limited their power greatly.

Ah, but going in hard would draw so much attention. That went counter to Revulyn Con's way. She had never liked being noticed. Being noticed was dangerous.

"Ha!" she barked to herself. "You worry about danger, you old bat? Wouldn't it be lovely to be discovered and killed." Lovely, yes. But only if she were truly destroyed. The thought of being beheaded but not killed disrupted the contentment of the cold eye. For then she would be aware *and* immobile. Imagine all the thinking she would get done then! "For someone longing for release, I have an odd concern about self-preservation. I'm a riddle!"

Lord Yples wouldn't want her to waste so many merculyns. How many resided in the Offices of Ori? Perhaps seventy. Maybe more. And when the time came to turn Kil, every last one of them would be needed. That worried her, for she didn't truly understand how a god could be born as a human. Furthermore, how could a god be turned? Wasn't a god's very godhoodedness an essential aspect of his being?

A stray dog wandered across the street ahead of her, ears flat, tail down. It was a ribby, scrawny beast. Con had always feared dogs. It saw her and came loping at her, tongue lolling. "Get!" she said, shying away from it. It changed course to intercept her.

Fear was also a lie. But knowing that fact did nothing to alleviate it. And so when the beast began to run at her faster, eyes wild with the hopes she might feed it, she reacted. The reviling feat formed and released as reflexively as brushing a spider off her sleeve. The dog howled and scurried away. It was dead before it got very far. Then it stopped and stood like a statue. And it would do so until its skin fell off. Maybe even after that. What a sight that would make when folk came out of Wintertide Solitude!

"Hmmm," Revulyn Con said to the street. It wouldn't do to leave a reviled dog standing around for the militia to find. She clicked her tongue at it and threaded a probe into its nearly empty mind. The animal came about as sharply as if she'd yanked on a leash. It padded next to her, dead-eyed and grinning. She still feared it, but she controlled it now. "You're my reviled familiar is what you are. Ha ha."

Thankfully, it did not reply.

"Trouble is, I don't want you." It was a rather large dog. Better for her if it walked itself away and curled into some trash heap to rot. But then a notion seeped into her awareness, a recollection of something she'd read about cats. After all that scurrilous gossip about Kila Sigh and her cat familiar, Con had done some reading on the subject. The elnisians worshipped cats. They could sometimes see through the animals' eyes, sending them to spy on friends and enemies alike. Con didn't like cats either. Sneaky creatures.

"Let me see your sight," she said to the dog. She felt around in its feeble brain. Had it been alive, it might have resisted these incursions, but now it stood there as inert as a pithed frog. The dog's vision came over her abruptly—the street as seen from a crouch. Interesting. A little willshift got the dog moving. She made it do a circle and suddenly she was looking at herself. A disconcerting effect indeed.

She withdrew and blinked a few times, fending off a wave of dizziness. "Success," she announced. She still didn't want the dog, as useful as the trick might be. She looked about for a trash heap, but didn't see one. She willshifted the dog under a hedge and released it. It would lie there until it decayed or until some other hound found it and ate it.

But now she had an excellent plan. The notion of its excellence pleased her, a feeling she knew to be a lie. The cold eye was very nice when she could hold onto it. In truth, it wasn't all that different from when she'd lost hours of her days deep in her work. No emotion at all, just a sense of rightness. Making things orderly. What could be more orderly than annihilation? Nothing left to catalog, no worries that a variety of tree or toad had been overlooked.

She brushed her hands and continued with renewed purpose. She needed to be alert now, for she was searching for a very specific sort of insect. "They like it on boletwist trees," she said. That sent her to Delif Park over in East Palace. A place she knew very well. Her gran had taken her there on sunny mornings when she was a child. "A bit early for greenmaks but it's uncommon warm this Wintertide. They do like it damp."

The park was a perfect square, manicured and lush. The boletwists formed a little grove near the pond. She walked among the ordered lanes of trees, slender trunks woven like the braidloaf her mother had made. Two distinct types of tree, with different root systems, different leaf patterns. Individually they were sometimes (incorrectly) called the silfbole and the dryabole. But they never grew separately, for they sprang from the same seedpod. In their fiftieth year, the trunks merged and shared arteries of sap. The crowns then burst forth with a blend of reds and greens.

The greenmak beetle lived in the crease between the merged trunks. Big as a mouse, and shiny as polished jade. Easy to spot too, which was well. Con's vision had not improved with the cold eye. She plucked the first one up and rested it on her palm. It bit her. She didn't feel pain anymore. Just a little tugging. But as she had done with the dog, she formed and released a feat on reflex.

Not a reviling. But a burst of dark blue flame. The beetle charred black and fell apart.

"Whoops!"

Her fellow Sensuals had always accused her of being irritable. But when deep in study who wouldn't snap at being interrupted? Nobody wanted to be bitten, either. She was more careful with the next greenmak, holding it by its carapace and watching its hairy legs flail. Its wings tried to flutter, but she held them down with her palm.

Most people thought insects mindless, no more than mobile plants or extraordinarily stupid rodents. Revnithan Con knew better. The reviling was instant. The mind probe quicker than with the dog because now she knew what she was looking for. But the beetle's vision, when it came, dropped her onto her backside. Her mind struggled to interpret the odd, fractaled world that came to her. She was about to give it up as a bad idea when her mind began to piece together the vision.

It would do. And truly, the greenmak was the only insect she'd dare to try such a thing with. Children could train them to do tricks, little leaps and flip-flops. Only jackroaches were smarter, but they were much too big for the task ahead.

"Ha!" she said, imagining a jackroach traipsing into Pol's Offices.

Carrying her six-legged familiar on her palm (a reviled greenmak wouldn't bite her), she went out of East Palace, heading uphill on Watermest Street. The homes were a bit smaller here. Bookkeepers and readers and scribes and all manner of palace-workers. Folk who carried eagle tokens. But even as privileged as they were, none were on the street during Wintertide Solitude. The turrets of the Grand Falchion Inn loomed in the mist ahead. She passed it and turned east onto Palace Street, which carried into the borough of West Palace and from there to the palace itself. Such a trek would have exhausted her before her awakening. Now moving was just moving. It required little effort and no breath at all. Another militia squad came tromping down the street at her. She flashed her token and passed them by. The captain spared a look at the beetle in her fingers but said nothing.

Lord Yples didn't want her turning common folk reviled. He had said it would alert the merculyns, who would then become harder to capture and submit to the turning chambers. She doubted any such operation had been established in Slirya yet. She'd feel the Revulsion bubbling if it had. Soon, she imagined. Very soon.

As a Sensual, gaining access to the Constellation Palace grounds would be easy. The Imperial Guard would respect her token. Patterned after Starside's elite Fell Guard, the Imperials—or "Queen's Imps"—as Con had learned to call them as a child, wore impressive helms and carried big spears. The grand gate to the walled-off city-within-a-city was closed for Wintertide. She bypassed it and found the Triumvirate Gate, which serviced religious folk like her. The Imps guarded this one, too. She flashed her token. "Voluptuary Quto is expecting me."

"The bug?" the man asked. His mustachios were as droopy and wet as the dog's tail had been. His eyes were dark and piercing.

"It is the subject of my visit. The Voluptuary is investigating new ways of healing. This specimen will be subject to experimentation." She droned on about various herbal salves and the way in which mercusine feats could be combined with such. To his credit, the man listened intently. Then he let her pass.

The Constellation Palace was lovely, or so she'd thought when loveliness hadn't yet been revealed to be a lie. From this entrance she saw the rear of the residential wing over the rooftops of the Triumvirate Offices and Chapel. The only such organization of the three Ways in all of Ennith. It made for very close communication among sects that did not like each other. The Donse Masters in particular chafed under the rules here, forced into a space not a single square span larger than that allocated to the others.

All the pale buildings were surrounded by gardens. Endless, perfectly kept gardens. She knew every race of plant, shrew, and fungus to be found within the walls. In fact, she had compiled a comprehensive catalog of them.

The Triumvirate Offices consisted of three long buildings joined at a central hub called the Triumvirate Chapel. The Offices of Ori faced south so that the Rose Hall could take the rising and setting sun. Pol faced northwest; Til northeast. Revnithan Con walked along Pol's colonnade to the very end where it turned toward the entrance. She sat upon a dry bench under the overhang and again went into her greenmak's little mind. The vision came over her and she released her familiar to fly. Willshift was easy and soon she had the bug doing loops and hovers. It was rather exhilarating, which was a lie.

The door into Pol's Office was closed, but there was a sizable gap at the bottom. The greenmak crawled right in. Night fell and nobody noticed the elderly woman sitting upon the bench, eyes closed. Had they noticed, they would have certainly thought her dead. She did not move. Did not breathe. Did not take notice when a nightskirl landed on her knee, loosed its bowels, then took flight.

Con's entire attention was upon her journey deep into Pol's Offices. Within two hours she had mapped the upper level. A waste of time, she knew. The vault would be below ground. But she had never gone into a building she had not explored and mapped in her mind. How else would one know where everything was? The stairs and doors and halls unwound to her explorations with ease. She stopped once to allow the greenmak to eat a spider's clutch of eggs. Not necessary, since it was reviled.

But she had been curious to see how the mandibles cut and tore, and how the forelegs operated to stuff bits of spider baby in. Curiosity was not in keeping with the cold eye. But alas. What was she to do?

Pol's reliquary turned out to be rather small, just a closet in the Coin's office. Con had expected as much. She alighted on a little shelf and studied the room, fixed it in her mind. Then she withdrew from the insect's mind and dymensed into the office. The beetle flew into her pocket.

The reliquary door was warded, of course. Revnithan Con leaned against it, lured by the lovely mercus emanating from it. The wards were mere locks. There were no traps in them. Not very skillfully done. She could negate them without fear of her body being engulfed in flame or her arms being dymensed to Ittiti.

There were physical locks as well. She understood the mechanisms well enough that a few minutes of probing with revulynic touch had them unlatched. The door swung open. The reliquary wasn't even a closet. More of a cabinet. Four shelves. The mercus relics delighted Con. Her fingers drifted over a glass orb, a class of bane eye. A book. Interesting. Few books were mercus relics. She picked up a statue of an atlen no bigger than her palm. The mercus was intense in it. "I've seen one like you before," she said to it. It would grant the bearer great speed afoot if one knew how to activate it. Useless to her now.

She took them all.

"I was right, greenmak," she said.

The Entifal was not there.

28

MAR THE INFINITE BLUE

Revnithan Sault had never been a submissive man. Even as a House Donse Master he'd tried to command everything and everyone around him. The hapless Sorgani lord who hosted him had wanted political connections to Starside. Sault had delivered them. In return, Sault had accumulated wealth, mistresses, and properties of his own. But he considered it modest recompense for the dream he'd been denied. His true calling, to join the Brotherhood of the Fell Guard, had been barred to him when he was a boy. Entering the Way of Til had offered new goals for his ambition. Those had also been denied him. He should have been made Highest of Highests by now, but he'd never even been considered for Nare. It was because his competence threatened those in power. That had always been the case.

Now that he was awakened to the Unanswered, he understood that those ambitions should no longer matter to him. Yples had chosen him, finally, for true greatness. Yet he couldn't thank Yples for leaving him this half-made state. Something between revulyn and mortal. Being a revnithan left him with his wits intact, unlike the fully turned revulyns and reviled. The cold eye had come to him, showed him the emotionless glory of true understanding. But it hadn't held long.

Then to be put in charge of the nosg . . . A supreme waste of his talents.

Yet Yples was undeniably powerful. More powerful than he, though perhaps not by much. Still, Sault was smarter than most and knew to bide his time until he was sure of his next move.

And so he clasped his hands and bowed his head in greeting to his supposed master. Yples stood over a woman slumped on the barren stone floor of Ceronhel's great hall. She had likely been beautiful once, but her matted hair and wan features made her look even more dead than a reviled. Yples claimed she was a dragnithan, a notion Sault found ridiculous. If such a creature existed, it could not possibly have been reduced to this state. Everyone knew of the extraordinary powers of demayne.

"She resists awakening," Yples said, looking down at her. His tone was of scholarly musing. "Dragnithan will."

"As you say, Lord Yples." Sault had found such phrases to be extraordinarily beneficial. It sounded like agreement.

"I will take her to less comfortable ground and set some shamans to the task," Yples said. "That too may fail. Consider your ferneater lore, Revnithan Sault. Perhaps you can devise some brew or tincture to reduce her will."

"I will do as you command." Sault already had something that might work. His little bash sticks. His continuing experiments with the Blackshine mimak had led him through some stunning mental ordeals. The hallucinations alone had nearly driven him mad. Only the cold eye had aided him, clearing away all the falseness brought on by the medicine. He'd prepared a number of the paper-wrapped bash sticks, which exploded to make clouds of Blackshine dust that befuddled any who inhaled it. Sault had no doubt a healthy dose would aid in awakening this woman.

He put a hand in his pocket, felt for a bash stick, ready to give it to Yples at that very moment. But he reconsidered. It would be better for Yples to think it a product of his recent command, else he might worry that Sault was working to undermine his power by enhancing his own. Yes. Even an unsubmissive man like Sault had to be subtle sometimes.

Yples put a foot on the woman's leg and dymensed away with her. Sault inhaled deeply of the Revulsion black the man left behind. The Unanswered cooled his teeming mind, allowed him to again return to the clarity of the cold eye. He saw instantly that Yples was needlessly distracted by turning Yiothizandra. The woman wasn't essential to their great endeavor, even if she were a demayne. Perhaps Yples himself was not fully in possession of the cold eye. There was hubris in him, a self-regard that had no purpose.

The cold eye loosened its momentary visitation. There needn't be any rush to bring on the moment of Annihilation. In fact it suited Sault to be lord of Ceronhel for a while longer. And when *his* force of reviled nosg had subjugated the cities of men entirely, he could—if he chose—reign for a thousand years over a new empire.

He retrieved his bear-skull staff and gathered the swarmlight. Dymensing with the swarmlight was a bit odd, and he'd not yet been able to explain the feat to any of his shamans. But it worked just the same, delivering him to the back ranks of his horde. Far ahead, many miles in fact, a battle raged between Razk-Ka's rear guard and the mindless reviled. It was incredible to Sault that so few nosg could hold back so many. But Razk-Ka was wily. He understood the value of choosing his ground. A small force could hold off a large one when the ground of battle was very narrow, naturally protecting its flanks. Even so, Razk-Ka's rearguard would soon be overrun. The reviled did not pause for rest nor meal. The living required both.

The commander of the horde was a shaman called Truj-Truj, formerly the wurgu of G'galas Truj. She was large for a shaman, thickly built and viciously competent with her long handled war spike. As a man with soldierly longings himself, Revnithan Sault respected those who had trained in the martial skills. His own prowess with his staff would have been of great interest to the warriors here had they not lost the capacity to be interested in anything at all.

Truj-Truj would be at the front of course. Sault had not been there, so he couldn't dymense to it. He called to a backrank elgin. Upon seeing its lord and commander, the elgin straightened to its full eleven foot height and bugled out an incomprehensible call. More elgins came loping back to gather up his barge.

To see over the heads of his innumerable reviled warriors he had ordered the construction of a huge platform, like a boat deck carried upon thick timber poles. Four shamans rushed onto it, taking position at the corners. A dozen elgins hoisted the poles onto their shoulders and began to carry the barge to the front. His shamans ordered the ranks to make way.

Sault needed no rest, but he'd installed a throne-like chair near the prow. The deck rocked and tilted slightly with each coordinated step. The wind was hard out of the north, ruffling his hair and crisping his beard. But there was not a single cloud to mar the infinite blue overhead.

The burden of existence still weighed upon him. But such could be endured with small amenities like the barge added to life. He noted the approaching battle din and the haze that overhung the fighting. "Bring Truj-Truj," he commanded.

A shaman kicked a rope ladder over the side and slid out of view. He was gone a quarter of an hour before returning. Truj-Truj's pike came into view before her head did. Like all nosg, she was hideous. Her pike was an unusual addition to the usual shamanic dress. To compensate for the weight of it, she forewent the skull staff, and instead wore the begemmed skull atop her head. This glowed with swarmlight.

He had denied her the Blackshine mimak, kept her unawakened, for one reason. To command the battlefront. Mind probes had kept her compliant and focused upon her purpose.

"Razk-Ka nears defeat?" he asked.

"No, Lord Revnithan. The rearguard fight with mad frenzy. They are surely drinking chyknok. They move too swiftly."

Chyknok was not new to Sault. A root that when pulverized and mixed with hot water provided intense surges of energy and keen concentration. The effects lasted several hours. It also often ended in death as the heart gave out under the stress.

A suicide stand. Razk-Ka was growing desperate. Excellent. All of these nosg would be turned and added to Sault's horde. "I don't understand why you cannot overwhelm them more quickly."

"They command a high position. The approach has poor footing. The reviled gr'hils often can't see the enemy behind their bulwarks and lose concentration."

Razk-Ka exploited the revileds' weakness of mind. Frustrating, but it didn't matter. Razk-Ka was exchanging his warriors' lives for time, a finite transaction. And when the battlefield progressed to open ground, nothing would slow the reviled horde.

Moved by his proximity to live battle, Sault began to pace and twirl his staff. He longed to push to the front and test himself against his enemies. But to fight against any who had drunk the chyknok would be stupid. He would welcome Annihilation on the day it came, but there was no reason to rush straight into it.

As had become his habit, he bade a shaman to call up a girnt from one of the nearby gr'hils. "You may return to battle, Truj-Truj. I expect victory here within the day."

The summoned girnt came up the rope ladder. Sault performed some knee bends and body twists. Unnecessary for his body, which had become as limber as a youth's since his awakening. But it got him into the mindset for sparring.

The girnt took his instructions without expression. He was reviled. He would do what he was told and never care that it would lead to his destruction.

The bear skull made a circle as Sault spun his staff. It had taken some experimentation to get the butt of the staff properly fitted with a lead counterweight. He moved through a few forms then began his attack. The girnt was strong but slow. Sault played with him for a while, tripping him onto his face, knocking him from the platform a few times, then finally staving in his snout with the lead weight. Being reviled, the nosg continued to climb to its feet and fight, but it could no longer see. Summoning the swarmlight, Sault lashed out with a black-beam, turning the girnt into a melty mess, like a statue molded from hot tar.

The fight had not been very satisfying, but it proved to Sault that he was still masterful with the staff. Perhaps someday he would test his skill against a worthier foe. Until then, he would have to content himself with killing reviled nosg.

29

A JERKY QUALITY

Avoiding Marlow and the other members of her small council was harder than evading the Watch in the Westbunk. Every time Kila turned a corner, there was Marlow with his portfolio of horrors. Or Radiant Gilok, red nose in the air and ready to accost her about taxes, rationing, and trade. She'd escaped that encounter only to run into Radiant Hiolly, sad of face and full of questions about what Her Majesty was going to do about the Way of Kila and the unrest in Cheapsgate.

It didn't help that two fell guardsmen were duty-bound to follow her everywhere she went. There was no sneaking about with those heavy boots trailing her. And the staff of the Citadel were a gossipy lot, always telling folk where they'd last seen her. She tried dymensing here and there to avoid such eyes, but Brother Commander Docit cornered her with a stern lecture about how she had shamed the Fell Guard by denying them the opportunity of protecting her.

"My predecessor was always going around without you," Kila countered.

"We had an understanding."

"How about we have an understanding?"

"Let's discuss it in thirty years."

"I hope your men enjoy dymensing, because I'm going to be moving around a lot."

His response was accompanied by the gray-eyed steel of fearlessness. "There will always be one hundred men ready to go within five minutes' notice. Twenty within one. Keep two with you at all times against emergencies that require instant movement. All will die to spare you harm. You do not yet comprehend us. In time you will. What supports our feet in the mud? What fills our bellies without bread? What sustains our spear arms even as the last of our blood soaks the soil? Duty."

Just what she needed. More lives in her hands. But there was something more than self-sacrifice in the man's tone, and it was in the face of every fell guardsman. She lacked a word for it, so she called it "doubtlessness." It differed from certainty, in that certainty had to overcome doubt. Certainty required faith. Doubtlessness did not. For it was an absolute state, requiring no other reference. It admitted no possibility at all of deficiency or failure. The Fell Guard knew their capabilities, knew their duty, and staked their whole notion of themselves upon fulfilling it.

Which was why, she supposed, they had momentarily lost faith when Ell had been slain.

So be it. If they wanted to die in her service, she would give them plenty of opportunities.

At the moment she was accompanied by Brother Nils and Brother Eyvin, both two and a half spans tall, with limbs as strong as anchor chain and thick as tree trunks. They braced her left and right and kept half a step behind, spears hard against their right shoulders, swords sheathed upon their hips. They smelled faintly of oil and polish. Two silent men who thought her a woolheaded child with a crown too big for her skull. They weren't far off the mark, in her own estimation.

"Marlow advises against bringing the army home from the Sablefort," she said as they walked through a wide hallway furnished with elegant side tables, tapestries, and polished marble floors. Liveried servants stood like guards at each doorway, ready to open a door, fetch tea, or scramble to fulfill any request she could concoct.

Her fell guardsmen said nothing.

"Do you agree?" she asked Eyvin, who was the senior man on duty.

"My opinion is uniformed, for I am not privy to the many facts required to make such a determination."

"Marlow says returning the army to the Moriterran Gate will strain their food supplies. He says traveling armies consume more than those at rest."

"Won't they be training at the Sablefort?" Nils said. "Your Majesty's army must never remain at rest, even when there is peace. Else you should sack your general and try him for treason. An ill-trained army is an ill-prepared army. Such would be a betrayal to Your Majesty and to the throne."

"So I should have them come home?"

"Are they needed here?"

Kila didn't know.

This section of the Citadel was part of the residential palace but doubled as a general reception and council space for the constant flow of dignitaries who had business with the Crown. It was a maze of corridors and galleries, and room upon room full of paintings, libraries, elegant divans and armchairs, ponderous wooden tables, and every sort of vase, statuette, and tea service one could imagine.

"Will any of your brothers be assigned to protect Henley?" she asked as she cut through the Grand Fleet Room, which was themed with nautical relics, tapestries, and one enormous painting of a squadron of triangular-sailed ships crashing through rough seas. *Her* fleet, though she didn't know much about it.

"If Lord Mast becomes your consort, and therefore a member of the royal family. Or if you assert your privilege and declare his safety vital to the realm."

Consort? That had a rather bawdy connotation. Her cheeks flushed and she made a study of her feet to hide her embarrassment. "He is about to enter Moonside on a mission of utmost importance. I would have him accompanied by two fell guardsmen."

Without breaking step, Eyvin rapped a fist onto his breastplate. Kila thought it a sort of salute, a recognition of her orders. But it was instead a signal, for a third fell guardsman caught up with them within four strides.

"Brother Eyvin?" the new man said.

"Where did he come from?" Kila asked.

"There are always several of my Brothers about," Eyvin said.

Eyvin gave Kila's orders to the man and he banged his breastplate and was gone, rather quietly Kila noted, despite his heavy boots.

She made the final turn and descended a dim stairway to come out into the stable yard. As monarch, she now owned a barn full of prized atlens, another barn stuffed with horses, and a third bursting with hounds. The third was a riot of barking, as it was mealtime. She was glad Nax had chosen to snooze in her chambers, for the slightest sniff of a cat would send the hounds into joyous rage. She had always liked dogs, but she didn't see any purpose to housing so many cooped up. "I should gift those poor creatures to folk who would love them," she said.

The fell guardsmen did not respond.

Between the atlen and horse barns stood an enormous stone building simply called The Crafters, with a sign above the enormous double doors depicting a hammer, needle and thread, and carriage wheel.

Inside she was met by a row of senior craftsmen and women, all bending a knee and dipping their chins to their breastbones. A chorus of "welcome, mum" followed. Somehow they'd all known she was coming, though she hadn't told anyone her destination.

Kila was learning to accept these shows of respect as an inevitable time waster. She fixed a placid smile onto her lips—as Ell would do—and thanked them for the greeting. "I'm looking for Henley Mast. I was told he was here."

A man in a leather apron spotted with scorch marks came forward. "This way, mum."

The other folk returned to their shops, each occupying large rooms equipped with every imaginable hand tool, material, furnace, loom, saw, or anvil a craftsmen might need. Some made special cloth for royal banners, some repaired chairs, or carriages, others forged weapons and armor.

Henley was in a storehouse at the back, where rack upon rack held armor, satchels, and barrels of who knew what. He stood at a table, his own sphere of mercus light shining down on the array of supplies before him. These he was carefully situating in a large canvas pack.

He was not alone. Terissa Viller sat on the edge of the table, tossing an apple from hand to hand. And talking.

Kila stopped short and listened.

" . . . mother went there as a child, or so she claims. Do you think I'd do well?"

He didn't look at her. "I doubt it. They require silence at times."

A lovely, evil smile crossed Terissa's face. "But those robes! Scandalous thin. *I* think so anyway. Wouldn't you like to see me all dressed up like a novitiate? I daresay I won't be cold though.

The things they say about the Way of Ori! Such wicked carry-ings on and all that. I suppose you've seen 'em howling at the moon and cavorting naked with their goat masks on. No? Don't tell me that's all made up! That's why I want to go. I want to be free!" She spread her arms wide, catching one hand on his cheek where it lingered.

He pulled away. "Terissa, you really ought to be ashamed of yourself."

"I really ought to be. But I'm not! What a girl I've turned out to be. Do you know of any Radiant boys who might need a wife? I'd do well in one of those greathouses. Imagine me stalking from room to room and finding dust over the doors and windows. I've learned from Mistress Sqinn where to find work for others to do. I'd be *brilliant* at it. My husband would rise in the ranks. I know the schemes those rich folk get up to. I wager I'd have three of the Radiancies bound all together in a ten-year and me the mistress of them all. La! Can you imagine me all puffed up and doughy with idleness, scribbling notes hither and thither to spark up some intrigue or another? Ah me, what a vision!"

Kila coughed and swept into the spill of Henley's mercus light. "Terissa. I thought you were going to find work downslope."

"Oh. I forgot I said that. I was just telling Henley—"

"'Your Majesty,'" Kila barked.

"Huh? I'm not 'your majesty'. Oh! Ha ha. Begging your pardon, Your Majesty. I forget sometimes who I'm talking to." She elbowed Henley. "Why didn't you tell me you were promised to royalty? I've wasted too much time trying to hook you."

Promised? Kila noted the flush rising up Henley's neck and into his hair.

"You may go," she said to the silly young woman.

"Oh! I see." Terissa patted Henley's cheek. "I want to hear all about your secret adventures when you return, lovie." She slunk away, but not before casting a lingering look at both Eyvin and Nils.

Kila waited for Terissa to leave the warehouse, then said: "Entering Moonside today?"

"I promised I'd wait. And now you're back." He barely looked over his shoulder at her. No smile. He returned to his packing. "Saiya is safe?"

"I hope so." She had been asking herself that very question since returning. Semūin was her mother, but that didn't mean she was a good caretaker for a child. "You didn't answer my question."

"Yes. I'm going in today."

"Two fell guardsmen will be going with you."

He turned his head. "Not necessary. I'd just have to protect them as well as Huff."

She lowered her voice and imitated Ell. "They are going."

He froze for a moment, then nodded and stuffed a cloth-wrapped loaf of bread into the bag. "They will have to bring their own supplies."

Kila looked a question to Eyvin, who simply said, "Master Henley need not concern himself at all with the welfare of the Fell Guard. They are spears to be wielded in service of the Raven Throne."

"Were you going to say goodbye before you left?" she asked.

There was a stiffness in his posture, a jerky quality to his movements now. Kila moved around the table to face him.

He flicked a quick look at her. "You could have searched for me when you returned."

"I did search you out. That's why I'm here and not in another boring session with Marlow."

She sent to him: *And you could have found me very easily*

simply by sending to me across the bond. Or you could have asked Huff to ask Nax. Or asked any servant you passed. Everyone knows where I am.

He kept his face down, but stopped packing. He leaned heavily on the table, fingers drumming the coarse wood of the top. "I'm sorry. I thought . . . I feel like I need to be on Marlow's list to get your attention."

If he wanted to sting her, he could not have chosen sharper words. "So you settled for Terissa's company instead."

He resumed packing with greater energy, stuffing in extra socks, a length of rope, a tin kit with flint, steel, and tinder. Kila saw the thought that had gone into assembling these supplies. Things a merculyn would not usually need—unless he couldn't rely on the mercus where he was going.

She instantly regretted her tone. "I'm sorry, Henley. Truly. I dymensed back to my suite thinking it would be empty. Marlow anticipated me. He was lying in wait, already telling me bad news before the mercus green had dissipated. And all these problems are so pressing. So many people affected, and each decision feels . . ." She didn't know the right ten-skillet word, so she made balancing motion with her hands. "Like a guess."

He tightened the last strap on his pack and slung it over his shoulder. "I know. I'm sorry, too." His face softened a little, but not completely.

She had hurt him. She schooled her face into a smile, masking a resurgent unease, the same she'd felt when Saiya dove from sight. Moonside held unknown dangers. And Henley had to face them with only two fell guardsmen and a cat. He would soon taste the Revulsion.

Remember, the Revulsion will sicken you, she sent. *So don't go far into Moonside until you're certain you can cope with it. It will tempt you. Huff will warn you.*

Head bowing, he let out a sigh. "Will you walk with me to the gate?"

"Of course."

He shifted his pack and headed out. She followed, watching his overstuffed bag bounce with every step.

"Is something amiss?" Eyvin asked.

Kila discovered she had stopped walking. "No. I just . . . I keep having this feeling I'm forgetting something." Whatever it was, it would return to her if it was important. And it *had* to be important or it wouldn't keep nagging her. She wondered if this was what shadline instincts felt like.

She caught up to Henley, kept pace with him. Her mind was overfull, that was all. She was determined that she would no longer be distracted. Not when Henley was about to go into danger. And yet the feeling persisted. There was something there just beyond the reach of her awareness. Something crucial, nagging her for attention.

30

THAT SKUNK PELT

"Presumably Kila has Kil in her possession," Fallo said into the dim silence of the Derslin Wheel cavern. Lop was asleep on top of Tolky, who was also asleep. Quinn still leaned against one of the columns, legs crossed, lantern at her side. She was hunched over her favorite book, stolen from a library on Garden Island.

Fallo was walking the circle. Again. He let his fingers drift over each symbol as he passed, not trying to remember any of them. Even so, he was sure he'd touched the slanting line with the two dots to either side twice in five columns. A strange place, this. He returned to his musing. "Ori, Pol, and Til. What are the chances all three were born in the same litter?"

Not a chuckle from Quinn, nor even a snort of disgust at the crudeness of the question. She was usually game for the off-color joke, but since coming to this dead end, she had been absorbed in her book. He continued: "The Way of Pol is very strong in Sorgan, I hear. If we could get out of this place and down to Cigil-Tine, I know of a vergent pass that will take us a good bit of the way." He rounded the final curve of the circle of columns and came to a stop in front of her. "Any ideas, Lady Peline?"

"Huh?" She didn't look up. "Listen. I always wondered why Black was never mentioned in the tales of the Shadline. But listen to this. In one of the Tales of Sephie, she says:

> 'O where is that Silent Sable?
> Her with the unheard blade;
> Would that I were Smoke in Shadow;
> For her this task was made!'

She looked up, eyes filled with wonder. "The 'unheard blade' is *my* blade, Black. Those names—Smoke in Shadow and Silent Sable—those are the exact ones Xilo used." She handed the book up to Fallo to read. "That passage right there."

He skimmed over it, already well familiar with the legend of the fabled archer Sephie and her bow, Dark Smiter. "This is interesting." He did not echo Xilo's full commentary. *For someone with nothing else to do.* "What are you hearing?"

Quinn lifted a shoulder and took the book back. She leaned her head onto the column and patted the floor next to her. "I don't know what will come, but our need will not go unanswered."

He sat next to her, his shoulder touching hers. Silence joined them now instead of dividing them. "I never wanted to be a hero," he said, stretching out his legs. "I always thought it would be too hard and too dangerous. I was right about that. But I had no idea how boring it could be."

"And yet it was just handed to you. *Three* blades." She set the book aside and drew Black. The steel absorbed the light. Her lips moved, but she was silent. He nudged her. She set the blade on the floor and restarted. "I was saying, I have *always* wanted to be a hero. I want my life to matter. And you are so nonchalant about it, so dismissive. It was just given to you, a place in history. It annoys me, though I love you anyway."

"Given it?" he said, stiffening. "Listen to yourself, *Lady* Peline. Look at yourself! You were born into a Radiancy. You were born beautiful. My father may have been rich—I won't dispute that—but to live with *this* face, to bear constant insults since I could understand speech, it has not been a gentle life. All I wanted was a snug home with a passel of kids, a few hounds, and a warm wife."

The vision of sharing such a dream with Quinn crossed through his mind, then dissolved into nothing. Their future held only discomfort and toil, following a thin trail of shadline guesses. None of it leading to rest and family joys.

"I love your face," she said gently. "Because it's yours. The way you talk about my beauty makes me wonder if you've ever seen past it. Ever truly seen me."

He comes! Lop sent. The bond sizzled with eagerness.

The column they leaned against began to vibrate, sending Fallo and Quinn scurrying. And just in time, for a fire-edged portal opened where the column had been. A familiar figure stepped through. "Interrupting an argument, am I?" Flaumishtak said. Oly chirped disapproval at Fallo, then dismounted from the demayne to greet Lop. "So, the Tender of Living Things allowed you to pass. What did he tell you?"

"I would never tell you," Fallo said. "Vile demayne, begone!"

The beast chuckled and moved deeper into the circle of the Wheel. "I see you are not aware of my amiable relationship with your friends Kila Sigh and Henley Mast."

"Lies!" Fallo circled, weapons forward. Quinn was holding Black and had already sneaked behind the beast.

"This is wearisome," Flaumishtak said. He looked at Oly, who hissed and chirped and meowed. Finally Lop sent, *Oly wants me to tell you that Flaumishtak is our ally.*

Do you believe him?

Of course! Flaumishtak is my *friend, anyway.* Lop jumped into Flaumishtak's arms and received a bit of raw meat pulled from a hidden pocket.

"Why are you here?" Fallo demanded. "Why the Wheel and not dymensing?"

"Excellent questions. You tell me why you are here and I'll reciprocate."

"You go first."

Flaumishtak sighed and looked about for a few moments. His slash of a mouth narrowed and the flames in his eyes flared. "Very well. You have the smell of a particularly stubborn man. Like your poor father. And Lady Peline, I know you're here somewhere. I do hope you don't plan to stick me with that sneaky dagger of yours."

Quinn was in fact directly behind him, dagger raised in an overhand grip. But she was frozen there, face twisted as she battled with indecision. And then she lowered her arm and sheathed the blade. "You're lucky, demayne. The force of destiny doesn't want you dead."

Flaumishtak jumped up and spun in midair, smokey hair billowing. Lop meowed in irritation and batted at his chest. "Forgive me, Beloved One," he said. "This girl startled me."

"We should listen to him," Quinn said to Fallo. His own instincts were telling him nothing except to fear this creature.

"What was that about my poor father?" Fallo asked.

Flaumishtak chuckled as he smoothed his robes. "Ah. He's one of Yiothizandra's spies. Not particularly skilled, I'm afraid. The dym-bonding does things to the mind." He made a flourish of claws near his ear. "What's your excuse?"

Fallo ignored the gibe. Xilo had gotten his hair up, but it wasn't going to happen again. "Why are you here? And why through the Wheel?"

Flaumishtak settled his mass onto the floor and cradled both cats in one arm. "*You* try to dymense near to a vergent's garden. I'm no fool. The elnisians learned that lesson in the most dramatic way you can imagine. I did not expect you to be here. But perhaps you can be of use. Do you know where the revulyn qiznithan is?"

"The what?"

The explanation that followed soured Fallo's mood more by the moment. By the time he understood that an awakened Revulsion occupied human hosts, and that it was led by a demayne from a realm even Flaumishtak wouldn't dare to visit, his gut felt like he'd drunk a flagon of turned milk. "And Kila did this Revulsion thing in Stallid?"

"Yes. And she then stole Yioth's infant god-child, who she now keeps as her own. Saiya, she calls her. A lovely girl. Quite precocious."

Quinn was pacing now, but she stopped to wrinkle her nose and point toward the entrance of the cavern. "Xilo kept saying the Foulness wasn't lazy. He must have meant the Revulsion. And our task—" She cut off and turned away from Flaumishtak.

But the beast was not to be put off by her clamped lips. "Come now. I've told you why I came. Tell me what that rude little villain told you. Perhaps I can help you."

They did need a merculyn to get them out of this place. Fallo figured the demayne would have attacked them by now if he planned do to it. Besides, Lop would not approve of Flaumishtak hurting his bonded human. At least, Fallo didn't think so. "Kil is not the only god reborn. It seems Ori, Pol, and Til have also been reborn. Til just today, if Xilo is to be believed."

Flaumishtak shot up from his seat, clamping cats to his side. "By the Hel Lords and the Bright Lords and all the nymphs in the sea!" But then he caught himself and turned away, just as Quinn had done. This wasn't to censor his thoughts, Fallo decided. For the beast began to pace, face down in thought. "Sensible," he mumbled. "But how would they know? Such timing! Yes, but there is precedent. And all this nonsense about Dem-Kisk. Those Shudderlin fools! But here we are. Yes. Here we are. Is this any different than expected? Not truly."

"What are you going on about?" Fallo demanded, putting himself in the demayne's path. A poor decision, for Flaumishtak strode into him and sent him bounding onto his backside. Flaumishtak didn't seem to notice, for he continued to walk back and forth, claws stroking through his facial fur.

"You must find these children. That much is clear." Flaumishtak stopped to scan the columns. "Where do you suppose they are? Not born to a single mother. And gender? Perhaps all mixed up. Til might be a girl. How will you know them? Ah, but they grow freakish quick. Saiya likely looks like a girl of twelve or thirteen today. In three days perhaps a year older. But what will you do? You're no merculyn seeker."

"These questions of yours," Fallo said as he got to his feet, "very insightful. But not at all helpful. Also, they've already been asked. By us. While we've been stuck in this bloody Derslin Wheel this past eternity waiting for something to happen. So if you don't mind, please open the portal to Sorgan and we'll be on our way."

"Sorgan! But you mustn't go there. The qiznithan has turned the whole city."

"If you know where the qiznithan is, why are you looking here?"

Flaumishtak's hair flattened, and the smoke tendrils shot back. "He's not there anymore. And just wandering here and there hoping to find him would waste time. I came to ask Xilo. Which would be obvious if you had a brain underneath that skunk pelt you call hair."

Quinn appeared between Fallo and the demayne. "Stop it. If

we're to be allies, the least we can do is be courteous to each other. We had thought to go to Sorgan because the Way of Pol is strong there. We reasoned that Pol might be reborn there. That's all. Do you have a better idea, Flaumishtak?"

The enormous beast shrugged and waggled his flat nose for a moment. "You're the shadline, girl. Just pick a column and go see what's on the other side."

To Fallo the comment was both insulting and irritating. Which meant it sounded exactly like something Cloak Einlin would say. "Quinn, do you feel any pull to a particular column?"

"No."

"Walk the circle." He added quickly, "Please."

She began at the closest column, and touched each one as she passed. The circle had a strange habit of being different sizes depending on where one was looking. So as he followed progress, he was astonished to see her suddenly grow very small in the distance. He blinked and just as suddenly she was twenty paces away, coming toward him. Her hand touched the next column and she jerked it away. She shook her hand as if her fingers had been stung. "Not that one," she said.

"Why not?" he asked as she came back to him.

"It hurt. It frightened me. I didn't like it."

The Cloak's teaching seemed to come out of his mouth. "Did your instinct tell you to avoid it or did you merely feel fear or pain?"

"Merely?" she asked, arching a brow.

"You wanted to be a shadline. This is what it's like. The call can be loud and insistent, or it can be subtle. Discomfort can steer one to avoid certain paths that must be walked. Kil's eyes in a flask, I do sound like Einlin!" He rubbed his face. "Return to that column. Please."

She had to make another complete circuit of the columns because the one in question had moved. Flaumishtak watched all of this with impatience, repeatedly huffing and mumbling and fidgeting. But when Quinn again jerked her hand back and sucked her teeth, they both went to join her.

Flaumishtak studied the symbol on the column. A slash with two dots. "Hmm. Slirya. You'll come out beneath a museum owned and funded by the Queen. It will be well guarded, with patrols inside and out. None of them mercusine, alas." He summoned his power and a portal tore into the air where the column had been. Quinn gathered up Tolky's lead while Fallo loaded the packs onto the beast's back. Lop meowed a farewell to Oly and Flaumishtak and resumed her post atop the cargo.

"If you see Kila, let her know what we've discovered," Fallo said. "Make sure the Kil child is well hidden."

"I will, Fallo PiTorro." Flaumishtak dipped his head. "Lady Quinn." He turned and strode away. Fallo followed Quinn and Tolky through the portal, which fizzled to nothing behind them.

31

MURDER WAS A MESSAGE

There was one gate into Moonside and it stood at the base of the Citadel far below the kitchens. As the city was bisected by the Divide, so too was the Citadel. The gate had been known to the Fell Guard for hundreds of years. Presumably, Ell had known about it much longer.

The first door was small and narrow, barely wide enough for a broom closet. It was made of steel plates. There was no handle, only hinges. It stood in a small chamber which itself was closed off by an iron-bound door with no latch.

For a merculyn of little skill, merely opening the door would have been impossible. Kila traced a finger over the steel door, feeling the embroidery of the mercus wards. It was shot through with deadly traps. But it was Henley, practiced with hair-thin mind probes, who saw how to unlock it without undoing it entirely.

He applied such small power that Kila could barely sense the bolts required. The elnisians knew that anyone going in must be suspect. So they required a bolt of pure intention to unlock it. For such a bolt could not be manifested by an ill-intentioned mind. No one, not even one as powerful as Kila, could unlock the ward if she sought to release the Revulsion.

Henley applied the feat and the door released.

It swung on silent hinges, a tunnel through the Divide. Twenty paces to another door. This too he opened. A haze of gray hung in the space beyond, illuminated by his sphere of mercus light. Thunder rumbled in the distance.

The Revulsion felt the Motherlight, felt Kila, and began to congeal into a smokey form before them. Henley quenched his mercus light and held up a lantern. "Quickly, men."

His fell guardsmen marched in; Henley followed with Huff on his shoulder. *Goodbye, thief girl,* he sent.

He pushed the door closed and the Revulsion subsided to its usual mild skim upon the mercusine.

When she tried to send a goodbye to Henley, she couldn't find him. Couldn't feel him through the bond at all. There was nothing but a vacancy. The same elnisian wards that masked Moonside's corruption had muted their bond.

She again traced her fingers over the door, oblivious now to the mercusine woven into it, only wishing she had said more—done more—to affirm her affection and less to reveal her jealousy.

Shamed at her own selfishness, she spun away from the hateful door. What would Ell do? Well, she certainly wouldn't cry in front of the Fell Guard. Not even in front of herself as queen. Such emotional spills must be reserved for her own private chamber, when she was just Kila.

So even as the fellstorm gales of loneliness and worry crashed against her resolve, which felt as shaky as a Cheapsgate shack in a storm, she willed herself to remain upright, face stoical, chin proud.

Clattering steps sounded behind her. A page, panting, brow

damp with sweat, came to stand before her. "Pardon, mum, but Administrator Marlow needs you. He sends his apologies, but says it's urgent."

The only urgent thing she felt was a need to open this door and run after Henley. It was Brother Commander Docit's lecture that buttressed her against the implacable storm inside her. *"What supports our feet in the mud, fills our bellies without bread, sustains our spears even as the last of our blood soaks the soil? Duty."*

And so she would carry out her own duties. "Where is Marlow?"

"His office. He begs your pardon for asking you to come to him."

Two fell guardsmen took position at the Moonside door, faces going stoney, eyes looking straight ahead. She didn't dare to attempt a reversal of Henley's unlocking feat, so she applied simple locking feats of her own.

"You may go," she said to the page. "Brother Nils, Brother Eyvin, take hold of my arms." It was forbidden for the Fell Guard to touch her without invitation or unless in the act of protecting her. But even with her command they hesitated.

"If you always delay this long, what use will dymensing be to me when the first half of a heartbeat could determine my life or death?"

Their enormous hands clamped over her elbows and she dymensed.

Two fell guardsmen stood in Marlow's office, backs to Kila as she reappeared. As usual the place was a disaster of papers, platters of last week's dinner dishes, and enormous, precarious stacks of books. None of this was why his summons had been so urgent. It was the body of a girl, laid across his hastily cleared desk. Her throat had been cut, staining her clothes a crusty brown. It was the Cheapsgate girl from Kila's coronation. Mayrie.

Marlow stood over the child, lips pursed, eyes ablaze.

"Who did this?" Kila demanded, voice distant and cold to her own ears.

Be careful, Nax sent. *You are at your most vulnerable when you are angry.*

I am right to be angry!

"Please feel her wound with the mercus, majesty," Marlow said.

It required barely a sniff of her attention. The edges of the wound were despoiled by the Revulsion. "Murdered by a reviled blade. Where?"

"Her room, near the kitchens." Marlow's hands were shaking. Kila noticed that his own fine clothes were stained with the girl's blood. His lips were white.

She reached for her bond with Nax. The cat was already on the way. "Show me."

Without a word, the fell guardsmen who had delivered the body turned and marched from the office. Kila followed, Eyvin and Nils at her side, closer now. Their spears were out from their shoulders. Their eyes scanned every possible place an attacker might hide.

Marlow shuffled along behind them. "A maid found her when she failed to rise for breakfast. Mayrie never missed a meal, so the maid thought it odd. We were fortunate that a fell guardsman answered the woman's scream. I took the liberty of muddling her memory. She believes it all a bad dream. I told her Mayrie had returned to Cheapsgate."

Hiding the murder would not have occurred to Kila. But it was well that Marlow had done so. The last thing she needed was a panic among the staff.

The girl had been given a small room intended for attendants of visiting dignitaries. Set at the end of a long, narrow corridor, it was set apart from other rooms by the entry to a descending servants' stair.

Nax caught up to Kila and was perched on her shoulder by the time she stepped into the room. The stink of old blood and soiled bedsheets was thick in the air. The deeper stench of the Revulsion was stronger here as well. A dresser, basin, and mirror sat in the corner. Stacked against one wall was loaf after loaf of bread. Even here, where Mayrie could eat whenever she hungered, her Cheapsgate instinct had been to hoard.

"Why would they kill her?" Kila asked.

"My guess is they mistook her for someone else," Marlow said. "When the reviled realized Mayrie was not its target, it slew her. No struggle. She was likely asleep when it came."

The devil had thought Mayrie was Saiya. Perhaps it had caught rumors about a new girl and had assumed Saiya had been moved away from Kila. But why kill her and reveal it had come into the Citadel? "It could have slipped out and Mayrie would never have known."

"She must have awakened enough to see it. Perhaps she had drawn breath to scream. So it struck."

Kila closed her eyes and sank into the mercusine, feeling out the contours of the Revulsion. It bubbled eagerly in answer to her anger.

Careful, Nax admonished.

I need to feel it.

The mercus existed upon its own plane, but that plane over-laid the world of matter and life. Eyes closed, she followed a trail of greater concentration of the Revulsion. "Majesty?" Marlow asked. "Where are you going?"

"Shhh. It went this way." She opened her eyes. She stood at the top of the servants' stair.

Marlow spoke softly to the fell guardsmen who had brought

the body. They moved in front of Kila. Eyvin and Nils followed. Marlow trailed.

Nax, can you feel that? Like tracks in the snow.

I'm no hound, came the reply, along with an indignant lift of her hackles.

I didn't ask if you could smell it. You can feel it, can't you?

She took the cat's refusal to answer as a yes. She continued along the corridor, gliding inwardly over the Revulsion, noting how it subtly left a trail of foulness.

At the bottom of the stairs she entered a long hallway that lead to the kitchens. The advancing two fell guardsmen seemed to occupy the entire length of it with their presence. Servants pushed tight against the walls to make way and watch the strange procession approaching.

"Remain where you are," commanded the senior fell guardsman when a few tried to slip into their rooms. Kila continued, no longer needing to keep her eyes closed to feel the trail. The first servant she came to bowed and muttered the appropriate greeting. No Revulsion in him. The same with the next and the next. None of those in the corridor were corrupted, and the trail did not turn into any of the rooms or branchways leading to other parts of the Citadel.

The kitchens were hot, full of clang and scrape and barked orders as cooks bossed around undercooks, who in turn berated cutters, stirrers, and spit turners.

"Your Majesty," said Kinnon Swile, the Mistress of Kitchens. She was a slim woman of no more than thirty. Pretty, with hair piled atop her head and pinned. She was respected for being the most organized, calmest Mistress in the Citadel's employ. "It is an honor to welcome you to your kitchens. Is there ought I can prepare for you?"

"I'm not hungry. Did a man in the garb of an Iron Scholar come through here last night?"

"What do they wear?"

"Filthy drab clothes. They smell like garlic and rotting pumpkins. This man would have carried a weapon. A sword or axe. He would not have been amiable in the slightest."

Swile passed the word and the question went through the kitchens like hot gossip. The answers returned with equal swiftness. "No one saw a man as you describe," said Swile. "A few personal staff of our visitors came in. There was nothing unusual about them."

A scullery girl about Kila's age with an enormous spot on the side of her nose seemed to be dancing with nerves behind the ranks of aproned cooks. "What's wrong with her?" Kila demanded.

Her superior told her to settle down, but the girl couldn't keep her mouth shut. "There was the Spinster last night. That weren't usual in the slightest."

Swile beckoned the girl forward. "Aimee, what Spinster?"

"Don't know her name, beggin' Her Majesty's pardon. Awful tight face on that one. Didn't ask fer bread nor tea. Juss went on stridin' through like she was Her Enlightened—Oh! Pardon, majesty!"

"Did she have a blade?" Kila demanded.

"Not that I saw, but I think Spinsters are spooky as Kil's own sisters, beggin' Your Majesty's pardon for saying so. I try not to look 'em up and down. Any one of 'em might toss a coin an' hex your loins, beggin' Your Majesty's pardon again."

A Spinster could surely be a revulyn. But why leave Mayrie's body after killing her? Why not dymense away with her?

The answer was as chilling as it was obvious. The murder was a message. The revulyn wasn't concerned about keeping her presence secret. She wanted it known. A tickle went up the back of her neck. Could they be watching her right now, waiting for her to lead them to Saiya? The temptation to dymense to Semūin's vale and check on her was indeed very strong.

She scanned the faces before her. None possessed the dead-eyed look of the reviled she'd already faced. And the Revulsion wasn't throbbing in any of them.

"I've been following her trail the wrong direction," Kila said to Marlow, now fitting the scullery girl's story into the scene in her mind. "The Spinster came in this way and dymensed from Mayrie's room."

The cook staff didn't know what she was talking about, and their faces were dragged down by confusion and worry that they were disappointing their queen.

"You have done well, Aimee. Kinnon Swile, I have a task for you. Shall we move into your office a moment?" After giving her orders to watch for a certain blank and black-eyed expression, Kila continued to follow the trail, but it faded at the kitchen entrance from the back courtyard. That didn't mean the revulyn hadn't been elsewhere in Starside. Or in the Citadel. Kila rubbed her elbows and looked over her shoulder for an unseen watcher.

She dropped her hands and stiffened. Ell would never betray such fear. "The Fell Guard is to be commended," she said to the men who had discovered the body. "You two may return to your posts."

Marlow was looking at her oddly, as if she had a smudge on her face he didn't want to point out lest he embarrass her.

"Out with it, Marlow."

"It's about the unpleasantness in my office. You gave me to understand that those slain by a reviled must be burned. My point is, well, do you wish to ... ?"

Mayrie was dead. The anger that had propelled Kila through the investigation suddenly gave way to a great welling up of guilt. She had plucked the girl from the crowd, had brought her here to feed and shelter her. To give her a few days of pleasure.

And she had helped neither the girl nor anyone else in Cheapsgate. The anger returned, redoubled, this time focused on herself.

"I brought her here, I will see to it. Fell guardsmen, take hold for dymension."

32

IT HUNTS

Judging by their strides, the fell guardsmen accompanying Henley felt no trepidation at all. Their eyes, however . . . Perhaps it wasn't fear that widened them so, perhaps it was merely a greater vigilance amidst so much shadow. Henley's lantern cast an orange glow into the odd, living haze that filled every room. The shadows were black beyond blackness, growing and stretching with Henley's progress. But even where light reached wall and floor, it weakened such that he could see only hints of the surfaces.

Thunder continuously rumbled outside, trembled in the floors. The trio's footsteps resounded in the hollow emptiness, coming back to them from unexpected directions. Henley stopped frequently, startled by these echoes, certain that something stirred in the ink beyond his light.

After the fifth such pause, he shook himself to be rid of his gooseflesh. If anything was going to leap out at them, he reasoned it would have done it by now. What he needed was a distraction. "What have you two heard about the Revulsion?"

The senior man, Brother Ryde, said: "It's an evil force akin to the mercus."

Henley told them a much abbreviated version of the history of the Revulsion in Starside. "So we are going to find White-flame and increase the power of the trap. Somehow."

"We will see you through to this objective or die in pursuit of it," said Ryde.

Do you feel the Revulsion here? he sent to Huff.

Yes, thick.

He had not followed Kila's advice to seek the mercus right away, to confront the sickness he would inevitably encounter. Perhaps it was foolish, but he feared his courage would not survive the experience if he had an easy escape nearby. Kila needed him to succeed, the world needed him to succeed, and he would never succeed if he fled.

"The air is close in here," he said, narrating his feelings to the fell guardsmen in hopes that they would agree. Or say anything at all. He'd feel much better if he knew they were as anxious as he was. But it was not in a fell guardsman's character to voice opinions or fears. They would warn him of danger, they would answer direct inquiries. Nothing else. The junior man, Brother Hannik, looked at him for a moment, then returned to his vigilant scanning all around.

It was more than stuffy in the sequestered Citadel. It stank. He imagined it smelled the same as the inside of a long-sealed, waterlogged casket. Rotten and suffocating.

These halls had been empty of life for so long the furnishings had crumbled into piles of dust. Only a chair leg here and a blackened picture frame there. Every surface was coated with a skim of sooty filth. Huff refused to walk on it, and so clung to Henley's shoulder with quite a bit more claw than usual.

"The air is greasy," he said.

The smokey haze coated the back of his throat, soured on his tongue. And it was always in motion. In rooms where there could be no drafts, it moved, swirling and curling in the light of his lantern. He had masked himself and the Motherlight before passing into Moonside, but the fog seemed to be searching for the mercus spark it had lost track of at the door.

Henley relied on the fell guardsmen to lead him from the basements to the main level. Brother Ryde said the layout was similar to Starside's. When originally built, both sides of the Citadel were part of one enormous fortress. There had been a grand central entry from the city, now blocked off by the Divide. But there had to be another exit.

The occasional thunder came louder now. The haze thickened, obscuring everything higher than the tips of the men's spears. They found an exterior wall and skirted along it until it vanished, floor littered with the iron bindings of a destroyed door. This one had not merely rotted, it had been torn from its hinges during the last days of the battle with the Revulsion.

The transition from inside to outside was barely noticeable. Only a gradual lightening from black to gray above as sunlight struggled to penetrate the low cloud cover.

The haze over the ground was thinner here, revealing distant shapes of roofs. Veils of black cloud drifted on swift currents, dangling capes of vapor. Henley realized that he was far upslope of the main city, just as if he had exited to overlook Starside. But instead of a descending boulevard bordered by huge statuary, the way down was a series of broad stairways, flanked by flat ramps. Lower down he saw a suggestion of tiers in the haze, vast open stretches of barren ground that would have been enormous grassy parks had any plant life been able to grow.

These parks were Moonside's corollary to Gristenside, except no greathouses had ever existed here. Those had been the creation of men, not the elnisians. In a flash he envisioned the whole ancient city of Stermūin as it had been. A wondrous citadel separated from the city below by a vast stretch of parks and forest, where citizens could roam and rest and be renewed. "It must have been grand," he said softly.

Brother Ryde and Brother Hannik waited like statues. Henley couldn't help but wonder what was going through their minds. In fact, he was tempted to probe inside those helmed heads and discover if they had any fear or wonderment at all. He didn't, for doing such was the way of the Hargothe, not the way of Henley Mast. Besides, he was masked and desperately wished to remain so.

And that was a problem.

"I must test the mercus here," he said. "I may become ill due to the Revulsion. Hopefully it'll be brief."

No use waiting. He dropped his mask.

The revulynic fog swarmed toward him. Thunder rumbled and bolts of red lightning arced in the deepening black overhead.

Ryde and Hannik looked up but did not flinch.

Henley reached for the mercus. His nose and mouth filled with the stench and slime of sewage. His stomach rebelled, forcing him to his knees. He retched and gagged. The mercus lay buried beneath a thick, black coating of corruption. It prompted visions of vomit and blood and rotting guts.

He drew back from the mercus, spitting and gasping. Icy sweat pearled on his forehead, and he shivered from hot chills. "Kil's eyes!" he gasped. How had Kila ever penetrated that vileness, much less used it?

It comes, Huff said.

Looking up, Henley scanned the thickening fog. It curled all around, centering him within the eye of a little fellstorm. Thick bulges emerged from the wall of whipping clouds, reaching toward him. They elongated, growing tentacle tips that wiggled, searched, and yearned.

The fell guardsmen lowered their spears, the meter-long steel tips ready to pierce anything that came within reach.

It comes, Huff said again.

I see the fog.

Not the fog. It comes.

What is it? Henley did not truly want the answer.

Huff sent fear through the bond, which did not help at all. Then came a vision of a black cloud shaped like a beastly head, pierced by flashing red eyes. It had a maw of utter blackness. A blackness darker than lightlessness. It was the absolute void of...

Huff hissed in his mind: *Annihilation!*

Thunder crashed in the distance. Vibrations shuddered through the stone foundations beneath him. To even mask his mercus required that he access the mercus. *I should have done as Kila told me, Huff. I can't get to the mercus.*

Red lightning flickered over the domes of the city, followed by a series of reports that glanced against the Citadel and returned to rattle in Henley's chest.

The Motherlight was blaring the mercus. The whirl of Revulsion fog tightened, perhaps emboldened by his weakness, or perhaps by its need to quench the Motherlight.

"Do you mark that sound, Brother Hannik?" said Brother Ryde.

Henley tried to get to his feet. He listened but heard only more thunder and wind.

"Voices," Hannik said. "Moaning."

Were there people—elnisians—still living here? Impossible. They'd been dead over a thousand years. It was inconceivable that anyone could live out a day here, much less survive for generations.

The spinning fog contracted around him, reaching with its

malformed arms. There was no retreating into the Citadel, no dymensing without grasping the mercus.

The only answer *was* the mercus. The Motherlight continued to shine at him and draw the Revulsion closer.

It's coming, Huff warned. *We must go!*

Henley sent to Kila, *How did you do it? It's so—*

But Kila wasn't there. The bond was silent. Blank.

"I have to do it. Til protect me." He had to drink from the chamber pot, suck down the entrails raw, bathe in the sewage. As his father used to say, "When the storm comes to the ship, somebody must climb the mast to reef the sails."

He pulled the Motherlight from his satchel and hugged it close to him. Dropping onto his knees, he lay over it, forearms on the ground. He closed his eyes and sought the mercus.

Though the Motherlight shone so brightly, he could not tap its power without first dipping into his own well. He could scarcely feel it beneath the surging sea of filth. The Revulsion gurgled like the blood-choked breath of the dying. Diving into it hadn't worked. He had to use caution. Stealth. He was adept at forming hair-fine threads of mercus that he could press into human minds. He would use that same skill here.

Like dipping a pen nib into ink, he tested the roiling rot. Instant nausea crushed his stomach in a giant's fist. Groaning and choking he squeezed his eyes against tears, against the axe-edged pain that clove his brain. He probed in harder, deeper. *Kil and his sisters!*

He did not relent. Sickness may turn his stomach inside out, pain may shatter his mind, disgust would shiver his skin with the legs of infinite spiders, but he would not die here cowering. He would not allow Ryde and Hannik to be so pointlessly sacrificed, or Huff to be consumed, nor to fail Kila and the realm simply because he was too weak of will to endure the vileness.

It's so deep! Endlessly thick.

Yes! Come down and let us in!

Jolted by this message—which came not in words but in eager intention—Henley ceased his striving. *Who is that?*

Huff's clear voice broke across the bond. *The Revulsion! Do not be tempted!*

How could anyone be tempted by this?

The fell guardsmen were talking. No, they were shouting. The world outside of Henley's ears was raging with wind and thunder. Even bent over as he was, eyes squeezed as tightly as they could go, red flashed through his eyelids in juddering beats.

Help me, Huff!

I'm here.

Holding to the bond he probed deeper. His stomach was a knot of illness, his brain full of chains and nails shaking and scraping against the inside of his skull.

It comes! Huff sent, lending urgency to Henley's endless dive.

A spark blossomed, then flared. Freedom! He plunged into the mercusine web. The Revulsion split away from his awareness. Drawing in a breath of relief, he straightened, cradling the Motherlight.

Motherlight, fill me!

The relic's power stormed into him. He stood, manifesting light. Pure white light that coursed into his flesh and through his bones. He sent it out to encompass the fell guardsmen, then pushed it hard against the whipping walls of the twirling fog-wind.

The Revulsion surged against his outward pressing power. He added more energy to his feat, holding the Motherlight over his head. A scream of rage tore out of his bile-burned throat. "Back! Stay back, vileness!"

Ryde and Hannik had become mere white shapes, arms shielding their eyes against Henley's light. Elongated shadows of their bodies and spears stretched behind them, then rose onto the wall of the pressing fog.

The Revulsion squeezed in, enlivened by the explosion of mercus. Henley tapped deeper of the Motherlight, filling himself and blasting forth even greater light. An answering darkness built up around them, a dome of twisting black cloud. Remembering Flaumishtak's tale of the elnisian king and Whiteflame, Henley realized this battle would never end until his feat equaled the totality of Revulsion in Moonside. He was drawing all of the formless Revulsion in the entire sequestered city to him.

Huff screamed in his mind: *It's here! It sees you!*

Whatever it was, Henley couldn't see it. Everywhere he looked there was a roiling wall of cloud sprouting forth tentacles to probe inward. He targeted these with bolts of fire. They absorbed each feat and grew fatter. He tried ice, tried to produce a countervailing wind of his own. The Revulsion tentacles delighted in these feats, fed upon them, and grew.

When the ship is taking on water and the rigging is frayed and the sails have shredded, the sailor's last refuge is prayer. But to whom could he pray, here in this forsaken place?

The garnet-red lightning sparked in constant flashes now, directly in front of him. The forks of energy twirled and congealed into concentrations of ever flashing light, and then became eyes. They were set wide apart, suggesting a head larger than a dragon's.

But there was nothing besides the lightning eyes to distinguish the awakened entity's form, for all around it was the boiling charcoal and blackness of the Revulsion storm.

Moonside stirs. This was what Ell must have felt. A creature seemingly formed of the Revulsion, embodying all of its insatiable hunger.

He was already pressed to his limits. The only answer was retreat.

Henley released his feat of light and quickly paired negations of sight, sound, smell, touch, and taste to mask his and the Motherlight's power. In that instant, the power vanished from him and a wave of Revulsion washed over the mercus.

Foulness engulfed him. Eager hunger prodded his mind. *It is easy! Only surrender and let us in.*

A deeper, more resonant voice interrupted the chorusing taunts. *I WILL SHOW YOU HOW TO SEE WITH THE COLD EYE!* It resonated like the voice of a god.

No! screamed Huff.

Henley pulled his mind up through the Revulsion, like crawling out of a mire of stinking, sucking muck. And then he was free of it.

And yet it was still there in his awareness, soiling his mouth, befouling his skin. The Revulsion was alive, and it was everywhere. Now that he'd tasted it, he would never be free of it. Something like despair threatened to take him to his knees. But he knew if he gave in to it he would never stand again. He would die and be consumed. And so too would the fell guardsmen and Huff.

He forced himself to focus on Whiteflame.

He had to find it, and it lay deeper in the city. The only light they had was the whale oil lantern. Its pathetic glow struggled to show them the ground at their feet. The whirlwind of cloud still flowed around them, though it warbled and moved, searching for the delicious power that had suddenly vanished. The red lightning eyes lost cohesion.

It hunts. It is hungry, Huff sent.

"All right, men," Henley said, squaring his shoulders. "We go down into the city."

The whirlwind that had squeezed in on them spun apart

now that it had no source of power to draw its attention. But the fog was more active than before.

Brother Ryde said, "Our spears did not tell against those vapor tentacles." It was not a statement of fear or confusion, but a simple statement of fact.

What was that thing? Henley asked Huff. *It had lightning eyes.*

Fear came over the bond. Huff's sending was so strong, Henley looked for a nearby hole or niche in which to hide. But hiding wasn't going to get him closer to Whiteflame.

Huff? What was it?

The chilling reply came: *Qiznithor!*

33

THE ENEMY OF ALL THINGS

Standing upon the Divide overlooking the boiling clouds of Moonside, Kila and Nax communed in silence. The bond with Henley remained muted. Nor could Nax feel Huff. They shared their worries only as feelings, taking what comfort they could in the knowledge that the bonds still existed.

The shrouded form of Mayrie lay upon the Divide next to her. Kila hadn't yet mustered the will to remove the covering, to behold again the face she had condemned to death with her generosity.

It is dangerous to know me, she sent.

It has ever been so, Nax agreed.

Kila stooped and tugged the shroud away, sent it fluttering over the edge and into the clouds of Moonside. The white face of death stared at her, eyes open, mouth slack. A look of disgust, it seemed. The wound across the throat had been deep, the blood a torrent. It had turned the girl's nightgown crimson down the front. The girl's hands were caked with dried blood.

Nax held back from the body, tail flicking.

Kila knelt and brushed the girl's hair from her face. Pulled the lids down. "Sleep, Mayrie. Sorry I pulled ya outta the crowd."

A lump under the gown drew her fingers. She dug under the hem and discovered a heel of bread pressed against the girl's gaunt belly.

"I'm not hungry."

"That's yer problem right there, Maj'sty."

And now Kila had to make the girl disappear, flesh into smoke. Smoke into wind, wind into the past. Invisible, forgotten. As if she'd never lived at all. Wen had been given to the wind, too. She'd cast his ashes from the Bath's bell tower. "Ah me, Naxie. Perhaps the lucky ones are already in the wind."

She put the heel of bread back on the girl's belly. Closing her eyes, Kila gave into the welling of grief that could no longer be denied. Nax pressed close to her, then squirmed into her arms. Kila clung to her, dampening her fur with tears.

Then she remembered Pennie, barely grieved. Had she been properly cremated? Kila didn't even know.

A cold hand gripped her wrist. Kila flopped backward, spilling Nax. Mayrie pulled on her, icy hand squeezing with iron strength. The eyes were open again, gone black. Mayrie's lips pulled back, teeth snapping. The gash across her throat spread, gibbering in an obscene mockery of a mouth.

The mercus retreated from Kila's seeking mind, bubbled over with Revulsion which eagerly sought to take hold of her. Nax's presence beat it back. Kila could do nothing but kick at the lunging child. A heel to the face, another to the chest. She wrested free of the small fingers, then heaved out a grunt and pushed with both feet. Mayrie tumbled back, scrambling to right herself. But then she vanished.

Panting, Kila got to her feet. She saw fingers on the lip of the Divide. Mayrie was straining to pull herself up.

Sobs blurring her vision, Kila drew Cayne, knelt and severed the fingers one by one. Mayrie fell away into black clouds, fingers tumbling after. A great stroke of red lighting blinded Kila, sending her reeling again.

She lay there, holding Nax for a long time. When her tears dried, she felt numb. Her failure with Mayrie had been total.

The cloud cover over Moonside rolled in huge waves now. Red lightning flickered continuously, wandering here and there, occasionally arcing in clear air over top the clouds. She turned her back on it and walked back to the Citadel.

The only thing now was to heed Ell's advice as best she could. "I'm going to dymense again," she said to Eyvin and Nils. Their hands closed over her shoulders. She released the bolts.

The wind blasted them as they rematerialized upon the ledge of the eyrie overlooking Starside. The fell guardsmen did not react except to urge Kila away from the edge. Nax leapt from her shoulder and darted deeper into the black cavern, seeking out its sleeping inhabitant.

Kila brought forth a brilliant sphere of light and sent it soaring toward the arched ceiling, spreading light throughout the space. It lit the enormous cavern and sparkled from the scales of the dragon curled upon the floor, nose to tail like a sleeping hound. Nax stood atop the dragon's snout. Enormous eyes squinted open and watched the approaching humans.

"Harnzyne," Kila said. "I share your sadness over Ell's death."

You do not mourn her, sent the dragon. *You mourn the death of your freedom.*

You don't know what's in my heart. Did you know what was in Ell's?

The dragon huffed out a great smokey breath through its nostrils. Nax clambered up between its eyes to perch atop its horned head.

Ell spoke to me before she died, Kila sent. *She said I would need*

Night to fight the Revulsion. Eckso and Klayne have fled. Do you know where they are?

No. And I don't care. They have always annoyed me.

What of Bazron and the other dragons of Night?

Probably asleep and dreaming of killing.

I need you to find him. The others will follow him.

He will kill me. He nearly did so the last time I approached the eyrie over Ceronhel.

Harnzyne had indeed been injured there, when Ell and Eckso had attempted to rescue her and Ragin.

What did Ell mean when she said I would need the demayne of Night?

I don't know. The dragon pointedly looked away from her. He was as surly as a wet cat. Nax balanced deftly atop the moving skull, tail flicking in annoyance that her warm resting place wasn't staying put.

Kila sent to Nax, *Harnzyne is being difficult.*

Harnzyne is a dragon. This matter of fact response seemed to be all the answer Nax thought needed. She curled up and snuggled on top of the dragon's head.

Where are the other dragons of Day? she asked Harnzyne.

Asleep and dreaming of killing.

But where *are they?* Kila realized she didn't even know their names. Fallo had mentioned one who had befriended the ferneater shadline Zirhine. Ulagatin. Zirhine might know where to find him. If Kila could find Zirhine.

Harnzyne wasn't answering.

Nax, what is wrong with this dragon?

He grieves for Ell. Such observances take a long time for a dragon, I think.

The Revulsion stirs in Moonside, she sent to the dragon. *It came to the Citadel to kidnap Saiya. It inhabits the minds of merculyns and they form feats of magic from it.*

Just as you have done, Harnzyne sent. *I saw you in Stallid, Kila Sigh. You used the Revulsion to part stone and flesh as if it were nothing. Ellishan was a fool to trust you, and now she is dead.*

I didn't kill her. A reviled did. I did all I could to save her.

You failed. Perhaps you did not do all you could, Your Majesty. The emphasis on her title was unmistakable.

Can you hear this, Nax?

No. What is he saying?

That I withheld my healing so that Ell would die. So that I would become queen.

Nax jumped down from the dragon's head and stalked around to put her nose to his. And then she let out a plaintive meow and swatted his snout. Her claws scraped against scales, not even leaving marks. But the dragon reacted as if Nax had thrust a flaming brand up one of his nostrils. He drew his head back and shook it, wings unfolding and flapping so that Kila was nearly blown over by the backdraft.

The fell guardsmen scrambled out of the way as the dragon turned to the entry and threw himself off the ledge. He plummeted a moment, then caught the wind under his wings and lifted over the city. He let out shrieks and roars, and spat flame into the sky.

What's he doing? she asked Nax.

A tantrum. I think he is shamed.

What did you say to him?

That is between me and the dragnithor.

Harnzyne continued to rage, circling the Citadel spire a few times then swooping down to alight on the eyrie's ledge. With heavy staggers, he crawled in to face Kila. Lowering his head, he submitted to her.

The felnithel has corrected my thinking. I was grief-blinded, though that is no excuse. I apologize.

I accept, noble dragnithor. And I hold no grudge. Your love for

Ellishan does you credit. Let us both honor her by seeking to fulfill her wishes. I need to parlay with the demayne of Night. That includes Bazron and his flight of dragons. But I also need Klayne. And Eckso.

Bazron will kill you on sight, or attempt to.

But you can speak to him from afar, as we do here. Speak before claw and tooth are bared in violence. Tell them what Ellishan said. Warn them of the Revulsion and its desires. Night wished to raise Saiya in its likeness, but surely it does not wish her to be corrupted by the Revulsion.

Smoke rings wafted on a skeptical snort. *You put more faith in Night's wisdom than I do. And you failed to mention a name you will certainly need should Ell's warning be true. She said you would need them all, no?*

She did.

Then you will need Yiothizandra. Pray she is not already destroyed.

Allying herself with Yioth was impossible. They hated each other. Kila had stolen the dragnithan's child; Yiothizandra could not be trusted. Better for everyone if she was dead.

Harnzyne, awaken the dragons of Day. Explain to them our need. The same with Night. We must meet on open ground where there can be no traps.

The great dragon bowed once again. *I will do as you command. Day will be ready to face the Enemy of All Things. As for Night? Dark hearts seek dark ends. But I will speak to them.* Once more the dragon leapt from the eyrie. This time he did not rage, but simply beat skyward and disappeared behind the mountains.

And what will you do? Nax asked.

Blowing out her cheeks she admitted to herself what she'd been trying to refuse. *I must free Yiothizandra, though all of Stallid will damn me for it. I hope it isn't too late.*

34

A FIERCE PRESENCE

The air grew markedly colder as Henley, Huff, and the two fell guardsmen descended from the tiered parks to the city of Moonside. Henley told his companions about his battle with the Revulsion and how he had been forced to mask the Motherlight and release his hold on the mercus. If they appreciated knowing this information, they did not show it.

Henley didn't care. He preferred to talk than to walk in silence.

The fog did not react to the noises of their passage. They were flesh and blood, warm with life, but the Revulsion did not take notice. Henley packed that observation into his mind to consider later.

The final tier behind them, they stood upon a broad plaza that Henley recognized. It was paved with the same stone as Dunne Medow Plaza. The central plaza of old Stermūin must have been vast indeed.

A powdery black dust lay over the plaza. It was littered with bits of black stone. Something odd about it made him crouch and turn a shard over in his hand. He lifted his eyes to the Divide, just a looming presence beyond the haze.

"Impossible," he said. He crossed the open space, boots crunching the bits of black rock or slipping on the powdery dust.

He came to the Divide, a smooth obstruction disappearing into the low cloud cover. He slid his hand over the smooth black surface. His palm came away feeling oily. He wiped his hand on his cloak and shivered. In Starside a lower wall ran parallel to the Divide. You couldn't get to the Divide, couldn't touch it. The city Watch patrolled the ramparts there occasionally. A canal flowed between the Starside Wall and the Divide. The elnisians had thought it important to layer protection upon protection, apparently. And having felt the Revulsion, Henley understood why.

But on this side it was just the Divide. He moved along it, dragging his fingers across the oily surface. He knew what he would find, but he desperately wanted to be wrong.

His fingers slid into open air. A great gouge had been smashed into the Divide here. All the powder and black rock in the plaza was ejecta from unimaginable blows that something had delivered to the wall. He paced the gap, counting forty strides. The damage went deep, fifteen paces. From his visit to the top of the Divide, he knew the width to be twenty.

The fell guardsmen did not study the damage. They took position facing away from the wall, spears out and ready.

"Do you mark any tracks in the dust?" Henley called to them from within the cavernous gouge.

"No, Lord Mast!" Brother Ryde said.

"No, Lord Mast!" Brother Hannik said.

Could the qiznithor do this? he asked Huff.

Nothing else could.

Masked to the mercus, he couldn't sense the wards in the Divide. But he remembered them. That an entity of the Revulsion could attack and damage the wall terrified him. How powerful must it be to endure the pain of the ward? Every blow would sting. *No wonder Ell said Moonside stirs,* he sent.

Leaving the Divide, Henley bore south and came across a dry fountain similar to the one in Dunne Medow Plaza. In this one, a half-clothed Ori pulled on a thick rope tied to the prow of a sinking ship. At the bottom of the empty pool was a ribcage and skull. Presumably of an elnisian. The cranium had a hole in the top, as if a spike had been driven in.

It was the first sign that anyone had been here when the Revulsion had swarmed in. Perhaps this poor fellow had been a foolish merculyn who had ventured in before the Divide had been erected. Or perhaps he was part of a rearguard for the king as he pressed deeper into the city with Whiteflame.

Assuming the king would have sought to lure the Revulsion as far away from Starside as possible, he continued directly away from the Divide. The plaza was enclosed by a gallery of very familiar buildings, all the same architecture as in Starside. The doors and windows were vacant where timber frames had long ago dissolved. He held up the lantern and peered inside an arched doorway. No telling what the space had been used for, residence or shop. It was empty save for mounds of dust.

He found an exit from the plaza, a smaller street flanked by ranks of homes. He didn't bother to look into any of them. The turret of a corner mansion had broken off, and the stone lay in the intersection. He skirted the debris, skin thrilling with the deepening cold and a sensation of eyes peering from the grief-stricken windows. A bucket sat in the street ahead. Inside was a skull, a spike hole in the very crown, the inside hollow as a conch shell.

He wondered if the merculyns had thought such a wound would stop a revulyn somehow. Or perhaps the revulyns had fed upon the brain matter of their victims.

He continued down the street, raising a hand to touch Huff's head. Offering and drawing comfort. The cat trembled on his shoulder perch.

It is too thick, Huff sent.

The scrape and squeal of an iron gate-hinge pierced the air, so at odds with the constant thunder rumble that Henley first thought it was the cry of a sea bird. The fell guardsmen were not fooled. They jogged ahead of Henley and lowered their spears, heads scanning the darkness. The weak rays of the whale oil lantern only showed them their shadows.

Henley gauged the wind. Not strong. Certainly not enough to move an iron gate. Thunder rolled overhead. Henley held the lantern as high as he could. The report of a rock striking stone—or perhaps the butt of a staff hitting the street—echoed weirdly from the buildings. It could have come from behind or ahead. The fell guardsmen continued their scan, spears traversing a wide arc, ready to lurch forward and skewer anything that appeared from the fog.

"Continue forward," Henley said. He wanted nothing more than to fill himself with the mercus. Instead he pulled his knife from his belt and crept ahead, staying behind Ryde and Hannik as they pushed south.

Can anything be living here? he sent to Huff.

Living? I doubt it. But something moves out there. The cat lifted his head, nose wriggling. His tail flicked side to side.

Another cracking sound bounced down the street, followed by the tumble of small stones. The fog grew thicker until the houses were lost in it.

Hannik stopped, knelt, then stood. He side stepped so Henley could see the skull he'd found. Hole in the top. The lower jaw was missing entirely. The eyes stared vacantly at Henley and he felt suddenly transparent, as if the skull looked at something behind him. He spun, knife up, lantern swinging and throwing wavy shadows.

Huff's claws dug for deeper purchase in Henley's flesh.

What is it? Henley sent. *You feel something?*

It's hunting us.

Where is it?

Everywhere.

Why can't it see us?

Huff didn't know.

Now backing down the street, lantern high, Henley mimicked the vigilance of the fell guardsmen, swinging his gaze in a wide arc, knife at the ready. He knew the futility of stabbing the fog, but he could not bring himself to put the knife back in his belt.

"Henley Mast," said Brother Ryde. "Left or right?"

They had come to a junction, this one descending steeply to the left, ascending to the right. Henley had no idea how far they'd moved south, but surely there was much more city in that direction. If he could sink into the mercusine web, he knew he could feel out Whiteflame if there was any remaining power in it. He dared not unmask himself.

He tried to remember what Moonside had looked like from atop the Divide. A bowl of fog. West had been the Honor mountains, north was the Divide. Far to the south the clouds had surged up against a leg of the mountains that thrust out to the ocean. He had sailed that region, knew the steep, granite cliffs. And east, where there had likely once been docks, an off-shoot of the Divide closed off the city from the sea.

Henley still believed the elnisian king had gone as far from Starside as possible. Unless there was something about Ori's temple that protected him or enhanced his power, the specific structure where he'd made his stand was likely arbitrary. At most it was symbolic, for Ori was the goddess of love, kindness, and healing.

He chose to go downslope, assuming fewer elnisian citizens

had lived on the lower slopes where the structures in Starside were more warehouses than residences. At the first opportunity, he bore south again, ever away from the Divide. Away from Starside. Deeper into the chill black shroud that covered the abandoned and grief-haunted city.

"The cold is wearing after a while," he said. "And the gloom. It's heavy as a sack of grain on my back."

The squeal of rusty iron hinges again arose, just like a screaming gull. It was followed with a metallic clang that echoed all around. Thunder answered from above. Henley's lantern glowed dimly in the haze. "Did you mark the direction of that sound?"

Brother Ryde turned to answer, then was gone as a thick cape of fog curled around him. Boot scrapes on the stone, rattle of armor, the clatter of a spear on the street. The zinging song of sword slipping from sheath.

Hannik twirled his spear over his head, then braced it at his side, bracer on his off-hand forearm forward like shield. With skipping steps he probed into the fog bank, calling to Ryde.

A grunt. More sliding boots. Hannik backpedaled, nearly knocking Henley over. Brother Ryde staggered into the weak circle of lantern light, spearless, sword in hand. He sucked huge breaths in through his mouth. "It's gone."

"What's gone?" Henley demanded. "What did you see?"

"A man. Or . . . something shaped like a man. This infernal fog masked him. He had the best of me for a moment, but I fought free."

"Are you wounded?" Henley rushed forward, lantern swinging and making Ryde's shadow dance wildly behind him. "Turn."

The man turned. There was no wound.

"Your plume is gone," Hannik said, pointing his spear tip at Ryde's helmet. Sure enough the atlen feathers were missing. A deep dent showed where something had slammed into his head.

"I think I got a slice of him." Ryde held up his sword then sheathed it. He cast about until he spotted his spear. With it back in his possession, he returned to his vigilant scans as if nothing had happened.

The helmet dent bothered Henley. "It was trying to poke a hole in your skull."

Neither man responded.

It hunts with all its senses now, Huff sent. And then the cat leapt from Henley's shoulder and darted ahead of the fell guardsmen. They whipped their spears to face the trail of the orange blur, but Huff had vanished into the fog.

Where are you going? he sent. *Come back!*

Huff didn't answer. He was moving quickly ahead, the bond thinning with every second. "Let's move, men." Henley walked as swiftly as he could while keeping the lantern reasonably stable. The fell guardsmen easily matched his pace, knees and bodies bent in attack posture.

The air grew colder still as they progressed. The sky had turned a deep charcoal, with only hints of red lightning penetrating now. A junction widened in front of them. Another fountain occupied the center, dry and full of mounded dirt and ash.

Bits of sleet stung his face and the wind picked up to buffet his chest. He'd come into Moonside before midday, but it felt like the day was failing already. Had they been here that long? He decided it didn't matter. He wasn't about to stop and make camp. He would find the temple and Whiteflame. There would be no sleep until the task was complete.

Huff? Where are you?

Looking.

Ryde and Hannik reacted to something Henley didn't see or hear. Suddenly their spears were in motion, their bodies sweeping through fighting forms so deeply ingrained they didn't have to think. Hannik deflected a long pike weapon that emerged from the fog. It looked like a whipaxe that the city Watch carried. The cruel beak-like blade chunked into the street. Hannik twirled and delivered an impaling strike, then yanked his spear back to shove the butt into the face of a second attacker.

They were tall, cloaked in greasy black, hoods concealing their eyes. All Henley could see of their flesh was wobbly lantern light highlights on nose, chin and cheekbone, severe and stretched tight.

A third attacker took a sword blade through the arm. The severed limb flopped onto the street along with its weapon. Ryde followed with a swipe that parted the gut, spilling forth black entrails.

Even disemboweled the man-creature wasn't finished. He crawled forward, reaching with his remaining hand. Hannik severed it, too, then the head. Only then did the body fall still.

These strokes of blade and spear were brief moments in a blur of violence. The fell guardsmen moved with such speed and precision that Henley barely registered one death before two followed. Ryde planted the butt of his spear, launching himself into the air. Boot met chin, crunching into a jaw. A dagger appeared in Hannik's fist, carving in a blur to sever tendon and artery of a throat. Black blood oozed out in thick globs.

Falling flat to the street, Ryde evaded another beak-pike, then swept his spear to trip the attacker. Hannik impaled the villain as he tried to scramble to his feet.

More came. They moved on silent feet, eerily skimming across the street as if they did not take any steps at all. The only warning Henley had was a thrill on the back of his neck. He ducked low and jabbed backward with his knife. It met flesh, a leg.

The spike of a beak-pike grazed his hair. He spun, staying low, slashing blindly. The edge of his knife scraped metal and bounced away. He'd struck Hannik's armor. The fell guardsman pulled Henley away by the collar, simultaneously cutting upward with his sword to kill the attacker.

Henley found himself between Ryde and Hannik as they circled to defend him against the phantom-like assailants. Bodies sprawled in every direction. Weapons clanged and scraped as more succumbed to the passionless violence of the Fell Guard.

Huff! We're being attacked.

I know. It presses you to unmask yourself.

The fell guardsmen were tireless, businesslike, and ruthless. Henley had not made a study of their training nor their fine weaponry. In fact, he had never seen them fight so much as a drunkard. He now understood why they prized their duty to the monarch so highly. Each man must have sacrificed his entire lifetime and every dream of family to train to this level of skill.

But as powerful as they were, the number of attackers was too great for them hold off forever.

Huff, I have to do something. They are going to die.

Then you will die. It knows where its claws are. I can sense the Revulsion thickening over you.

Its claws? Oh! These man-things were like the qiznithor's claws. And the claws had found them.

He did not want to confront the Revulsion again, to battle through the disgusting slime of it. But he couldn't allow these men to die so futility.

I found refuge! Huff sent. *Come quickly.*

Henley didn't question it. "Ryde, Hannik! We break through and run. Can you separate us from this throng?"

"Aye, Henley Mast," said Ryde, simultaneously spearing and sword-stabbing two separate foes. "Brother Hannik?"

Hannik speared a hooded face. "When my strength fails, when my blood fails, when the last of my spirit fails, even then shall I persist. Until the very last I shall fulfill my duty."

"Mast, come!" said Ryde. He spun and jabbed in a blurring succession of strikes that sent the front ranks of attackers reeling backward. The movement was so fast Henley would have sworn the man had performed some mercus feat to accomplish it. Ryde pushed Henley's shoulder and crowded behind him, using his own bulk to shield Henley as he ushered him down the street.

Hannik stayed where he was, dealing death in every direction. Henley strained to look back. A subtle light had formed around the man. His spear told with every motion of his arm, his sword deflecting and then severing. Arms, heads, legs fell all around him.

The garnet lightning congealed high above. The light in the eyes grew brighter and brighter then released all at once. Jagged rays arced down to explode into Hannik, throwing back dozens of attackers surrounding him.

"Run!" Ryde shoved Henley hard.

Instinct guided Henley as he sprinted down a narrow lane, feeling Huff drawing closer with every step. He stormed through a park where tree stumps still thrust up from the barren ground like tombstones. He leapt a wrought iron fence, sprinted down a narrow lane strewn with the crumbles of a fallen building.

Hollow shrieks sounded from behind.

"Faster, Lord Mast!" Ryde shouted.

A structure ahead rose out of the gloom. Columns supported a round, domed roof. The columns were great statues of women. They were all of Ori in her various aspects. Huff had found the temple.

A horde of cloaked figures swept in from their flanks,

racing to cut them off. Brother Ryde's spear felled four in as many seconds. Then he lifted Henley and threw him up a course of shallow steps and into the temple. Landing awkwardly, Henley stumbled, dropping the lantern. It shattered, spreading its remaining fuel over the marble floor. It burst alight and he scrambled away from its spreading dance of flame.

Huff was deeper inside the temple, sitting primly at the center. Just behind him was a brilliant white glow, apparently emanating from the floor. The relative stillness of the dome brought Henley's raging pulse to his ears. Bent double, he dragged in breath after ragged breath.

Brother Ryde emerged from the whipping fog just outside the temple. His armor was stained black, scraped and dented. He skirted the dying oil spill flames and scrutinized Henley for injuries. Once satisfied, he knelt on the ground and closed his eyes. He drew three breaths before again standing and beginning a patrol around the perimeter of the temple.

"Did any of their blades cut your skin?" Henley called. He knew the taint of reviled weapons could not be healed. Not by any feat Kila had tried, anyway.

"Several," Ryde answered. "It is of no concern. When I die, you will burn my body as was done to Her Enlightened Majesty and my brothers."

When Henley tried to stop the man so he could inspect the wounds, Ryde thrust him away. "Tending my wounds is not your objective. See to the task at hand."

Henley did not see any deep wounds on the man's exposed skin. But there were innumerable scratches. Perhaps they would take longer to progress. He hoped so, for he was not content to allow this man to die.

The temple entrance had gone black as the Revulsion fog pressed in. An occasional hooded figure lurched forward only to be repulsed by some unseen force. Masked as he was, Henley could not study the wards in place.

He went to Huff, who jumped into his arms. He took a moment to draw warmth and strength from the cat. *You fool*, he sent fondly. *You could've gotten cut to pieces by those things.*

They don't want me. Not yet.

How did you find this place?

While it was hunting you, I noticed it avoiding something ahead of us.

Wise felnithel, Henley sent, stroking the cat's head, letting the soft ears filter between his fingers. *What would I do without you?*

Probably die very quickly. And unless you get on with that sword over there, you'll die only a bit slower.

The light coming from the floor was impossible to look at directly. Henley saw no sword. He put Huff down and crouched before the light. Sliding one palm across the smooth, cool marble, he felt for its source. When his fingers touched the blade, a calming warmth spread into his hand and up his arm.

Eyes squeezed shut against the intolerable glare, he probed until he found the hilt. He lifted the sword, found it quite heavy.

"Are you well, Henley Mast?" called Brother Ryde. "I cannot see you."

"I'm well. It is Whiteflame." He lifted the sword as high as he could, but the light was still unbearable. Strength flowed into him and the blade began to feel lighter than before.

Thunder clashed over the dome.

It's here, Huff said.

There was enough power coming from the relic to keep the Revulsion outside of the temple. This would give him space and time to drop his mask and embrace the mercus. Maybe the Revulsion wouldn't be so thick here.

Dropping the mask was easy and instantaneous. His hope was dashed as the oily blackness flooded immediately into his awareness, souring his mouth and gripping his belly. But he did not concede to the foulness, for he was bolstered by Whiteflame. Plunging into the seemingly endless sea of horror, he strove for the mercus, shrugging away the oily tendrils that sought to clamp onto him.

Huff was there, too, a fierce presence that shielded him from the more vicious hooks and barbs with which the annihilating power sought to snag him. And then he broke free of it and was submerged in the pure light of the mercusine.

He drank deeply of it, relief easing his fear so that his breath came deep and relaxed. He didn't need to open his eyes to feel the mercus wards and feats in the air all around him. In fact, the entire temple from floor to dome was infused with the mercus. Whoever had thrown up these wards must have been a master surpassing any mortal's comprehension.

Whiteflame provided a constant flow of mercus to keep the wards alive. Turning his attention to the relic, he drifted his awareness across all the senses it deployed. It was not merely a reservoir of mercus power like the Motherlight. The sword itself was opposing the Revulsion.

And then it claimed him. Violently.

35

REALM OF BOUNDLESS SUFFERING

The snowblasted field lay between sheer cliffs deep in the Haelshok mountains. There was no way to walk out of this merciless place save a narrowing at the throat of the valley.

The exposure here was good, Yples thought. Under the blazing sun, upon a field of snow, isolated from any outside interference. He believed the desolate hopelessness of the place would weigh upon Yiothizandra's mind. Her resistance was considerable, so he would use every lever available to pry her open and fill her with the Revulsion.

He'd been disappointed to discover how impenetrable her skin was. Not a single blade had been able to cut her. It was a unique characteristic of dragnithans that they could either turn their mercus toward outward feats of magic or to manifest the physical invulnerability of dragnithors. They chose one of these paths very young and accepted the lifelong consequences. He wished very much to have Kila Sigh's blade, to bless it with the Revulsion and then merely scratch a mark on Yioth's cheek. The Revulsion would spread, slowly perhaps, but it would turn her as inevitably as a rising tide covers the land.

But that course was barred to him until Revnithan Con recovered the Entifal. The Blackshine mimak had merely provoked screams of terror. When the effect faded she had been as she always was, unawakened and willful.

So he would have to break her. She knelt in the snow before him, head bowed. To keep her from manifesting her wings, he had his nosg wrap chains about her body, pinning her arms tight to her side. Rusty, thick, *iron* chains. No dragnithan would break such easily, and certainly not without rest and feeding.

It was hunger that weakened her the most, he suspected. This dragnithan had devoted her mercus nature to her dragon aspect. Like dragnithors, such beings required meat.

A haunch of deer lay just behind him. The smell of it barely registered in his mind. It may as well have been a rock or a pile of dung for all it interested him. To the Revulsion all things were one, a state of unanswered suffering.

Suffering was his lever to split open the adamantine will of this dragnithan woman. "Surrender, child," he crooned to her. "It is simple. A feather upon your brow. And then you may eat. Eat all the meat you wish. Regain your strength. For your daughter."

Yiothizandra's head snapped up, eyes flaming. "My what?"

He smiled. He made it as compassionate as he could, though the feeling was absent in him. "You didn't know? Ah, that vile girl Kila Sigh. She took your babe from you, cut it from your womb, and didn't mention it was a girl?"

"You lie. All of you are liars and betrayers." She included the twenty-odd Blackshine Shamans he had brought to this place. Despite their number he did not expect this to go quickly.

"Would you like to see her?" he asked. "Or are you content to let Kila Sigh raise her?"

She screamed at him, straining against her chains. Tendons

stood out on her neck, and her teeth flashed in a wide grimace. "Release me!"

He stepped close and cupped her chin, unafraid of her inner fire. She hadn't the strength now to muster so much as a puff of smoke. "That is what I'm offering, child. Release."

"What *are* you?"

He bent close and whispered into her ear. "My name cannot be uttered, for no language can contain it. I am come from a realm of boundless suffering, where gods and demayne fear to pass. The Unanswered power is my ally and salvation, and soon it will be yours."

She shrank away from him, for the first time showing a flicker of fear. "Qiznithan!"

He waved his shamans in. They formed a tight circle around the woman as he stood back to observe. Their eyegems had gone black upon their awakening, but now they began to glow as they gathered the Blackshine swarmlight. Even under the unblocked sun, which glared from the surrounding snow, the eyegems shone with violets and greens, the rays smeared over with black swirls.

The circled shamans flooded her body with tortures big and small. Itching and freezing, rashes, and prickles. Two slender beams probed into her ears, driving in spike-pains. The woman strained against her chains, muscles standing out in sharp relief. Her starved cheeks drew in, bones of brow and jaw standing proud under taught skin.

"You are a demayne of Night," he shouted over her screams. "You too long for the Evernight. But you never knew its deepest meaning. Day has never been your true enemy. The enemy of both Night and Day is suffering, the intolerable consequence of existence. Submit now. Open your eyes and see the truth. Your daughter can still serve your purpose, to release you from this world. She can release all of us, from all worlds. And then the true Evernight will rise and will never know the evil of dawn."

He slipped a Revulsion thread into her. Even for him, this was dangerous. For she was full of violent rage, which clouded the depths of her mind.

Her screams and curses continued, and she did not relax a fiber of muscle. The shamans increased their tortures, ignoring her threats against them. Yples continued to probe and press, waiting for the moment of despair.

"Klayne!" she screamed. "Eckso! Where are you?"

Yples did not know those names.

"Flaumishtak! Help me!" Her eyes lifted to a spot beyond the circle. "Why won't you help me? Flaumishtak! YOU COWARD!"

That name Yples did know. He turned to scan the plain. But it was empty. The idea of turning a yoznithan was intriguing. It would be harder to do than turning a dragnithan, of course. But such power!

"Flaumishtak," he called. "Are you there? Your name resounds in the qiznathic realm. Amidst the agony of being, we hear of your doings. You have an appetite for killing. We are allies!"

But there was no answer. And clearly the yoznithan was not much of an ally of Yiothizandra's, else he would have interceded. Perhaps he feared facing so many Blackshine shamans. That was good. Very good.

But such musings were a distraction at the moment. Yples shoved his probe deeper into Yiothizandra's mind, fingering for her will. It roared up at him, a shrieking whirlwind of hatred and panic. Too wild to track and quite dangerous should he not meet it with an equal power of the Revulsion. But to snuff that will might kill her before he could turn her. He withdrew his Revulsion probe and decided to let the shamans soften her more.

He dipped his chin and sank into the Revulsion, drifting deeply to sense the ripples that passed through the thick veins that permeated the world. His revnithans popped into his awareness. Revnithan Sault was close, over that mountain in Ceronhel. Con was very far west and south in Slirya. Soth was in Starside.

His attention was pulled to a grumbling disturbance in the Revulsion. He lifted his head and looked southeast. The Hackwatch? But no, this was more easterly. There were other pockets of Revulsion, but this one was enormous and full of violent agitation. Yples the man had made maps, knew the lay of mountain, lake, and city. Starside was there, in that direction. Had Kila Sigh succumbed finally to the Revulsion? Or had Revnithan Soth somehow awakened Kil?

He would soon know. But first he had to address Yiothizandra. Perhaps this Klayne and Eckso she had cried out to were other dragnithans. She had expected to be heard, and no mere human would have answered such a call.

He sliced off a bloody hunk of deer haunch and carried it through the ring of shamans. He held it out so that Yiothizandra might smell it. Perhaps she would not be so resolute in protecting Klayne and Eckso as she was in defying the will of the Revulsion.

The woman's fiery eyes locked onto the meat, her nose flaring at the scent of it. Yples pinched off a small bit and allowed her to taste it. Her eyes dimmed, then closed as she swayed, savoring the relief this small morsel gave her. The moment passed as swiftly as a cloud shadow. She looked again at the meat in his hand. "More."

"Tell me of Klayne and Eckso," he said, motioning his Blackshine shamans to withdraw their tortures for a moment.

When she did not instantly answer, he dropped the meat into the snow, visible to her but just out of reach. The shamans renewed their assault. Her suffering doubled because it was contrasted against the pleasure of food.

She resisted an hour, but her will could not totally over-master her hunger. Even beset as she was by swarmlight pains and discomforts, her mind and focus returned again and again to the divot in the snow in which the meat now rested.

Yples merely waited, watching her with an impassive black stare, hands folded together. By and by she began to speak of two dragnithans. One her sister, the other a fellow demayne of Night. When he had learned what he needed, he again tore off a bit of meat and allowed her to eat. He bade the shamans to relent for a moment.

She groaned and panted, but she glared defiance at him.

"I will return in a day, maybe two," he said. "You know what is in store for you. You will surrender and be awakened fully. It is your decision how much you will endure before gaining your ultimate release. Should you wish it, ask a shaman and they will conduct you the last inch to freedom. Until then, you will remain as you are, in this place, learning agony in fine detail."

The shamans' staves flared once again.

36

PAIN AHEAD IS FEAR

"I've never been down here before," Eckso said, peeping around a corner. The narrow corridor was empty of both life and light. She floated a sphere of mercus light ahead of her, ready to wink it out of existence at the slightest noise, be it rat or nosg.

They hadn't seen either in the past hour, which she hoped meant that she and Klayne had delved deep enough below Ceronhel to avoid rediscovery. She hadn't realized how ill-prepared she was for fighting agents of the Revulsion.

Klayne was happy to remind her at every opportunity. As if he could have done better. He was panting, hand pressed to one wall, head down. With her light glimmering from the gems of the *vaz'on* he looked like an emaciated and exhausted king.

"I think we're safe for the moment," she said, allowing herself to lean into the wall. The stone, grimed with age, was cold and smooth against her cheek. The tiles of the floor were obscured by a thick layer of dust, only their footprints revealing the colorful mosaic underneath. Unlit mercus sconces were mounted on the arched ceiling at regular intervals, each shaped into a hawk of some sort. The nearest one had a gem in its beak.

The one behind wore a crown, gems also dark. The one ahead had a gem in its talons. All these gems needed was a font of power and the hallways would be well lit.

But these subterranean levels had been long abandoned and nothing but Eckso and Klayne's footprints gave evidence of living trespass in an age. She put her back to the wall to let her heart and mind calm a bit, finally feeling safe after a long, harrowing flight from those horrid Blackshine shamans. Each individual was relatively weak, but with their powers combined...

"You know something, Eckso?" Klayne said. "We could dymense away from here and be done with this madness." His cowardice surprised her, for he had always been a capable warrior. But since he could not defend himself with the mercus, he was at her mercy. Eckso knew that combat feats were not her strength in the best of situations. Against the Blackshine Shamans they did almost nothing. Those befanged villains negated every bolt before it could tell. There were simply too many of them. When she'd aided Ellishan against the reviled in Starside, a few of her attacks had gotten through. The reviled had not been particularly slowed by them, but at least they had been wounded.

She shivered, imagining a horde of these reviled shamans and gr'hils of warriors storming south to destroy the realms of humankind. She doubted there were enough merculyns in all of Ennith to withstand such an invasion.

All the more reason to free Yioth and secure Saiya. "We're not leaving her, Klayne. We just have to find a way out of the fortress."

"And what makes you think there is a way out from here?"

"A rumor I heard once," she said, thinking back to the days when elnisians had inhabited Ceronhel. What wonderful intrigues had played out in the ballrooms, bedrooms, and hidden niches of this fortress. Her time on this world had over-lapped with that of the elnisians by only a few decades. That elegant race was already in decline by then, warring among themselves and against the nosg. Men were arriving from the sea, and the elnisians wanted no part in more war. The Revulsion awakening in Starside had altered them, weakened their spirit. Once a great realm had covered Ennith, one of prosperity and peace. And within a few hundred years it was gone. They had vanished and were never heard of again.

"And what was that rumor?" Klayne asked into her long silence.

"That the lower halls connect with natural caves that give passage to the neighboring canyons. This valley they are keeping Yioth in must be close or Noy wouldn't be able to go back and forth."

It had been Yioth's nosg factotum, Noi-Ick-Noi, who'd told her where Yioth was being kept prisoner. Then the shamans had swarmed in. Noy had led her to a secret passage but had slipped away in the darkness, leaving her and Klayne to race through gallery and corridor, taking every downward stairwell they could find while being continuously harried by swarmlight attacks.

Klayne wiped a sleeve across his brow, face pained as the gesture aggravated the unhealed *vaz'on* bolt penetrations in his skin. "Without a map we'll be forced to wander. We're more likely to get lost than find our way out. I have a better idea."

She knew he wanted her to ask what his idea was. But she was finished letting him manipulated her. Weary and hungry and exasperated by his own desperate state, he finally blurted: "We should dymense to the eyrie above the fortress. Then you can simply fly over the area. You should be able to spot Yioth's valley easily enough."

Not a bad idea. Except that the eyrie was Bazron's lair. She didn't relish the idea of confronting the Blackdread and his flight of vile lizards. He would remember that she had recently invaded this area riding upon Harnzyne, a dragon of Day, to steal away her children. Forgiveness wasn't in Night's catalog of graces.

Even so, wandering in caves and tunnels might lead them nowhere and take more time than she had to spare. Klayne was right, though it burned her guts to admit it. The shamans had negated her dymension attempts before. But none had come to the beacon of her mercus light since they'd finally escaped.

She took hold of Klayne's elbow and dymensed to the eyrie above Ceronhel.

The arched opening showed a blue sky beyond and the snowy peaks of the Haelshoks in the distance. Something very large huffed behind her, and she spun throwing up a shield of mercus to negate Bazron's green fire.

But it wasn't Bazron standing tall in the center of the enormous eyrie hall.

"Harnzyne?" Klayne said, shuffling backward. "What in Kil's name is he doing here?"

Eckso bowed to the dragon, whose furious eyes glowed with inner fire. "Well met, honored dragnithor."

Enough with the false niceties! The voice exploded in her head and she couldn't help but cover ears in reflex. *I have been searching for you.*

Did you truly expect to find me here of all places?

I did not. And I am not pleased to discover you here now. Are you in league with the Revulsion?

She stamped her foot. *Of course not! I came to rescue Yiothizandra.*

The dragon let out a puff of smoke and settled his bulk on the floor. *Why did you aid that fool over there?*

Klayne? Well, uh, I—I—

You're up to mischief, Eckso Ezeel. As was always your way. What want you of your sister? She would do nothing to help you were the positions reversed.

True enough. But surely you see that she must not be made a creature of the Revulsion. For all of our sakes.

It is as you say, he admitted. Rather grudgingly, Eckso thought. Harnzyne had always been puffed up and self-righteous. Rather like Ellishan in that regard.

She recovered her composure and arched an eyebrow. *And if you have been searching for me but didn't expect to find me here, why are* you *here?*

I seek Bazron as well. I seek all demayne of Day, Night, and in between. Kila Sigh wishes to form an alliance of us all to stand against the Revulsion.

You? Ally with the dragons of Night? The Blackdread would eat his own tail before siding with you.

He need ally himself only to her. Ellishan spoke sooth before she died. She said Sigh would need us all. To defeat the Foulness, all disputes must be set aside. I have not found Bazron yet, but I will.

Eckso hugged her arms close to her as she considered this strange alliance. If one did not know of the enmity between Day and Night one would think an alliance reasonable. But Sigh would have more success roping the sun to the moon than establishing a truce between timeless enemies of the demaynic realms.

But Harnzyne was naive enough to believe anything was possible, especially if Ellishan had said it. The ridiculous lizard had doted on Ell as if she were his own little hatchling. Well, there might be advantage for her in indulging this fantasy.

If Ell said Kila Sigh would need us all, then that would include Yiothizandra, no?

It would. But your sister is beset by those black-souled nosg. I dared not to intervene whilst they surrounded her, else I may perish before achieving the task Sigh set for me.

She sensed no trepidation in the dragon. He merely spoke truth. And no doubt, once Bazron had been found, Harnzyne would swoop in and fight the Blackshine shamans. And probably fall in the effort. Eckso wouldn't mourn him long if he merely died in the attempt. But if Yiothizandra would be a horrific reviled, a dragnithor would be worse.

I will see to Yiothizandra, she sent. *All I need to do is reach her and dymense away. You should flee this place, for surely the Blackshine shamans have noted your arrival. They will be mounting an attack. Do not underestimate their combined power.*

Do not presume to tell me what to do. The dragon snorted and swished his tail. She had never seen a dragon of Day so agitated before. Harnzyne again stood, wings folding tightly to his body. His scales glimmered eerily, each a depthless pool. *It is well that you will rescue Yioth. Perhaps she can call to Bazron. Sigh wishes us to converse.*

Surely Yioth has called to him for aid already.

And he has certainly ignored her pleas. But the Blackdread is cunning. Perhaps he will see the necessity of an alliance, if only to scheme some advantage once the Revulsion is defeated.

More likely he will scheme to attack your lesser flight and kill you all at Sigh's meeting.

He does not know Sigh's power. With that he leapt from the eyrie and flew away.

Wait! Where is Yioth?

East!

"All right, Klayne," she said. "The moment you've been dreading is upon us. How long has it been since you last manifested your wings?"

His face paled and he again drew a sleeve across his forehead. "Five hundred years. Perhaps more. But surely you cannot expect me to do it before I've eaten and rested."

"Would you prefer I do it for you?" she asked, placing her mind upon the Eye Gem.

"No! No! Just give me a moment."

Eckso wasn't particularly eager to manifest her own wings. Unless one did it regularly, it hurt like Kil's own teeth ripping open your flesh. She moved to the ledge. She had never feared heights. But the drop to Ceronhel—looking like a toy fortress below her—was so enormous her vision swam. Klayne came to stand next to her. "I did it recently," she said, mouth dry. "It does hurt. But pain ahead is fear, pain behind is strength."

When he still did not comply, she mentally took hold of his Will Gem and forced him to jump. She released the willshift and jumped after him.

He was screaming so loudly that he couldn't hear her call out her permission for him to bring forth his wings. She didn't like sending to him, for it forced upon her a discomfiting intimacy. But she couldn't afford to let him die.

Do it, Klayne.

Her own wings seemed to rip from the flesh of her back, then strained as they caught the wind of her fall and lifted her to horizontal flight. Below her Klayne's wings finally tore free, beautiful golden wings of an eagle. His agonized scream reached her, high pitched and full of cursing.

He circled in his dive, then finally bent his course upward. She dove to join him. He shook his fist at her, face purple with rage. She ignored him and motioned east. For a moment she thought he was going to try to defy her, but at the last he simply looked ahead and began to flap his wings.

37

THE REIGN OF FOOLS

A wagon rumbled past, wheels sending up a splash that swept over Fallo's lower legs and boots. No matter, they were already soaked through. They needed a good rubbing with oil to reseal the leather. In truth, they needed to be thrown in the rubbish heap, which was exactly what he meant to do as soon as he and Quinn could find Regnal Boulevard.

"You'd think they'd put more covered walkways in a rainy city," Quinn said, shrugging deeper into her cloak. The fine weave was keeping the rain off her skin, but that wouldn't last long in this incessant drizzle.

"I hadn't heard that Slirya was especially rainy," Fallo said. "I'd only heard about the beautiful women." Of which he had seen none so far due to Wintertide Solitude. Not counting the one he'd brought with him. But even with the rain, the fabled city certainly had charm, if one could see through the gray gloom.

Slirya was the western-most city of Ennith, on the coast of the Kithe Ocean. Beyond the shore, the world supposedly continued forever, covered with water. The city had been an elnisian outpost, now overbuilt by the greatest craftsmen of humankind. The architecture showed how delicate and composed a human city could be. Block after block of five-story apartments of cream brick and filigreed facades. Warm, light-filled windows, and an abundance of corner parks. It was a city of artists and philosophers, and a culture particularly devoted to Ori. But if memory served, the Way of Ori was not well regarded here. None of the Ways were.

If Fallo survived life as a shadline, he hoped to return here one day. Return and idle for a few weeks at the corner eateries, sipping charlok and eating thickly buttered longbread. Maybe he and Quinn would bring their children. The fantasy of that warm future melted out of his mind as the cold, damp reality of the present moment seeped through his socks. "I'm afraid to take off my boots. My feet must look like parch-grapes."

They hustled down the street, shoulders hunched and heads down. Not heroic at all in Fallo's opinion. The stories never reported the blisters, the chills, the rashes or the road grime that was the everyday trial of a shadline.

They descended a hill and came under the bridge of a crossing street. It provided shelter from the direct rain. But the drainage in the low spot was dammed up by debris, creating a knee high pool of black water they would have to ford.

"Are you sure this is the way?" Fallo asked.

"I am not sure of anything. I'm just following the directions that skinny-necked scoundrel back there gave us." They had come out of the Derslin Wheel in the promised museum. Exiting that place had been its own silly adventure, requiring Quinn to sneak around in silence to create diversions to lead the patrolmen away from the donkey, whose hoof steps resounded like hammer blows in the empty galleries. They had come out into rain and had been in it ever since. Quinn's shad-line instincts had gone as quiet as Fallo's. Following the Cloak's "discomfort is the way" wisdom had produced good results. Good results meaning it made them irritable, uncomfortable, and tired. And *that* had sparked from Quinn a truly excellent idea.

"We should find the shadline cache."

The momentary enthusiasm this idea provoked was quickly squashed by the fact they had no idea where it was. But Quinn said she felt a pull, which they followed for a miserable hour, until they encountered a man with a very slender neck and a scraggly beard. He looked about as untrustworthy as one could imagine if one tried to draw the most unsavory, sneak-eyed villain in history. His attempt at robbing them had quickly reversed on him when confronted by three shadline blades.

"Shadlines, eh? Apologies." He made to dash away, but Quinn put him on the ground, Black to his neck. Her lips moved in a spurt of snarling questions. Fallo interpreted. "She wants to know where the shadlines might gather in this city."

"You mean the cache? That's over on Regnal Boulevard. Or so I've heard." He rattled off a long series of streets and turns, which Fallo did his best to memorize, and then scrambled away. And now here they were, sodden and doubtful that the man who had tried to rob them had given good directions.

The few wagon and carriage drivers they saw refused to stop or even deign to answer shouted inquiries. Quinn thought it was something to do with the tradition of Winternight Solitude. They hadn't seen a soul on the streets for an hour.

Fallo took the moment of shelter to shake out his cloak and squeeze water from his pant legs. Lop was dry and warm inside one of Tolky's packs. The sodden donkey's ears drooped and his head hung low. The poor beast looked as forlorn as a lost puppy. "Let's try again," he said to Quinn, then proceeded to describe how Zirhine had taught him to listen for the shadline call. "We listen for the slightest push or pull. It can be an inner desire to go in a direction. Even better, a desire to go away from something."

Fallo heard nothing. Except . . . ah, strange. There was nothing external guiding him now, merely an inner knowing that it was Quinn's turn to guide them. And as that notion crossed his mind, the absolute certainty of it settled over him. He drew comfort from it. Now all he had to do was coax Quinn into hearing the call without making her too angry.

He let her stand there, eyes closed, dripping, nostrils flaring as she listened in deep concentration. He could see the muscles of her jaw bulge out, the press of her lips as she tried to force herself to detect something, anything.

"You can't do it by hearing harder," he said softly. "Relax."

Her eyes flashed open, fixed him with a dagger glare. She didn't want to be told what to do. Fallo couldn't fault her for that. He'd wandered all over eastern Ennith with the Cloak and he hadn't wanted to be told what to do either. Looking back on that training now, he was rather disgusted to see how effective it had been.

"Turn your mind away from what you want. The shadline cache may not be our destination. Try not to think any thought at all. The pull of it can be soft as down upon your palm." Kil's eyes! He really was starting to sound like the Cloak. He distracted himself from this disturbing thought by watching Quinn's face. Not a hardship in the slightest. She had pulled her hood back once they'd come out of the rain. Her raven hair was plaited into a loose rope that rested over one shoulder. Her brow was high and smooth, regal. Eyelids soft, with dark lashes. Despite her irritation with his guidance, she seemed to be trying to follow it. And now her lips were parted, exposing the edges of white teeth. She was loveliness itself in Fallo's opinion, smudge marks on her cheeks and all. She held Black in her hand, the stumped wrist of the other tucked close to her breast. Her lips were moving. Talking to herself. She was silent, of course. She had relaxed, was no longer trying to force herself to hear something that could only come to a quiet mind.

An atlen squawked down the street and soon the rattle of wheels carried toward them. Quinn was standing in the middle of the street. Fallo saw the atlens coming, tall, soaked, gray. It was a hack for hire. Unexpected during the Solitude. A storm lantern swayed on a pole next to the driver, who was hunched under a huge oilcloak.

The gray of morning had begun to lighten the sky, but only enough to show the black bands of heavier rain threatening from the west. The birds were moving swiftly, heads low, legs driving. They saw Quinn and began to screech at her. But Quinn stood fast.

Fallo tried to guide her from her spot. "You're going to be flattened if you don't move."

"It will stop," she mouthed.

"But not until your skull is smashed open."

She pushed him away and held out her stump to forestall any further attempt at moving her bodily from the spot of her imminent death. Fallo waved his arms at the driver. But the man appeared to be asleep, whip across his knees and face down.

The birds were trained to avoid obstacles that might destroy a carriage, so they began to swerve away from Tolky. This brought them more directly on course to overrun the love of Fallo's life. The carriage was on the downhill roll now. Even if the birds slowed, the momentum of the carriage would force it into their backsides and push them along.

Tolky bleated and shuffled out of the way. The birds altered course again, sweeping themselves and the carriage through the space the donkey had occupied. A bird shouldered into Quinn, knocking her aside. And then the carriage was through, plowing through the standing water and sending waves to either side.

Fallo and Quinn were once again drenched. But this time the spray overtopped their heads and they stood spluttering, faces and hair soaked through. The driver came to his senses enough to pull the birds to a halt. "What are ya meaning ta do, ya dim-skulls?"

Quinn waded through the unsettled pool and knocked on the hack carriage's door, ignoring the driver altogether. The door cracked open and a woman's face peered out. Quinn raised her dagger, not in a threat, but merely to display it. There was a moment's pause before the woman pushed the door wider. "Come in."

A man slipped out from the other door and came to gather up Tolky's lead. "Get in, shadline," he said to Fallo. "I'll see the donkey gets to the stable. He'll be rubbed down, fed, and watered. I assure you. Please. Get in."

Fallo considered fetching Lop from her cozy pack, but decided the cat didn't deserve any particular consideration. He extended a hand to clasp forearms with the man. A sword hung from the man's hip, and his eyes held that knowing confidence particular to shadlines. "Well met. I'm Fallo PiTorro."

"I know. I saw you at the Armory with Shad Einlin."

"Ah. I apologize for not recognizing you. I didn't get much chance to make acquaintances there. Nosg invasions and all."

"Please, get in. A warm fire, hot food, and cool beer await."

Inside, Quinn had already shed her cloak, which lay in a squishy pile on the floor. She had stowed Black and was rubbing her hand for warmth. Her knuckles were red and raw, finger-nails ragged and blackened with grit. Fallo joined her on the forward facing bench. A woman sat across from them, a bare short sword across her knees. There was no threat in the display, merely a show of proof that she was a shadline too. Or so Fallo thought.

"Hold out your hands," the woman said. She was at least

sixty years old, weatherbeaten and coarse. Her hair was wiry and thick, pulled back from her head and bundled into a snood. Her cloak was black, cinched at the throat by a silver brooch. She was a Cloak.

Fallo held out his hand. Quinn extended her stump, its metal-capped bluntness provoking a raised brow. "It must cut skin," the woman said, taking up her sword.

Quinn pulled back her sleeve. "I don't have a hand to spare, so you'll understand if I wish to preserve the one I've got."

The woman nodded. Then with speed Fallo could scarcely credit, she lashed the tip of her blade across Quinn's forearm and the top of Fallo's hand. A movement of whiplike suddenness. The sting of Fallo's wound didn't register for several seconds. Then a line of fire tore across his hand and he sucked on the cut. But there was little blood. The Cloak woman had barely scraped the skin.

"You are not corrupted," she declared. She reversed her grip and rapped the pommel onto the roof. The carriage began to roll. "I'm Cloak Szill. I listen and obey. This morning I felt a calling to the streets, to search out who or what I could not say. I am certain it was you two. Well met, shadlines. The force of destiny leads us all to unknowable ends."

As the son of a prominent merchant, Fallo had been tutored in courtly manners. Such skills were expected during the course of business relationships. His penchant for informality had been a reaction to that training, his own reflexive instinct to contradict every quality he saw in his father. But Cloak Szill's bearing, her manner of speaking, the very stillness she created in the air around her, brought forth his better behavior. He nodded, half acknowledgement of her status, half show of agreement to the sentiments of her greeting. "Listen and obey."

Quinn echoed him, though a bit more perfunctorily. "Listen

and obey. I'm soaked and cold and am desperate for a needs closet."

This brought a smile to Cloak Szill's lips. "It won't be long now, though the way will be bumpy. Steel yourself."

And the way *was* bumpy, causing the carriage to jerk and sway more violently than a ship in a storm. When it abruptly stopped at their destination on Regnal Street, Quinn pushed out and dashed through the closest doorway. It turned out to be the entrance to a small, tidy inn called The Reign of Fools, indicated by a small sign next to the door. On it was a sketch of three men in plate armor, capering about with brooms for weapons. All three wore crowns. Inside was a warm common room, with aged plank floors worn smooth and dark by centuries of feet, spills, and moppings.

"This way," Cloak Szill said, leading him past a smiling innkeeper with an apron over his waistcoat and trousers. The cellar was packed with hogsheads of drink, baskets of root vegetables, and barrels of preserved meats. It opened at the back into another small pub, where a barman waited with a serving of hot tea for each of them. "And something stronger if you wish it," he said before retreating to take position on a stool behind the bar. "Jaynie will be down with dry clothes in a moment."

They took their tea to one of the three circular tables under the low ceiling. The space was warm and dry and smelled of herbs. "I'm Fallo," he said as he peeled off his cloak. "Thank you for finding us. We were desperate to locate the cache."

"Tell me," Cloak Szill said.

Quinn joined them while he was in the middle of his narra-tive recounting events since leaving the Armory at the Hack-watch. She had already changed into dry clothes, though her face was still smudged. Jaynie came in with a bundle for Fallo. He excused himself to change and returned feeling warm and dry, which rapidly began to weigh on his eyelids.

"What do you hear now?" Szill asked of them both an hour later. Empty dishes were scattered across the table, their contents now inside Fallo and Quinn's bellies. Lop lay sprawled atop the bar, ignoring Fallo as conspicuously as possible. The cat was angry for being abandoned in a sack, which is how she described being allowed to ride atop a donkey protected from all weather and harm inside a capacious pack. Apparently one of the stable hands had been less than gentle when unloading the Tolky's cargo.

The barman had provided Lop with choice giblets and cream, which ingratiated him greatly with her. *This is how one should treat a felnithel,* Lop sent. *Not like a spare sock!*

I love my socks, Fallo had responded. *I keep them dry and safe if at all possible.*

Lop stared at Fallo, and anytime he looked her way, she made a great show of looking away from him and flicking the tip of her tail.

"Shadline, I asked you a question," Cloak Szill said. Fallo pulled his chin off his chest. He'd almost been asleep.

"I hear that we must sleep."

"I hear we must search. Now." Quinn's eyes were heavy, too, but there was grave determination in them. "Urgently."

"Listen and obey." That was all a Cloak would ever advise, of course. "I must go."

And so she went, leaving them alone with the barman. Quinn pushed her chair back and stretched. "Back into the rain."

"Do you truly hear such a call?" Fallo asked.

"I don't know. What would it feel like? All I know is this Revulsion evil Flaumishtak spoke of wishes to corrupt us and the gods alike. I know that while we rest, it continues to scour the world for them. That seems a sufficient call to me. Or do you think a good long sleep will improve our chances of success?"

"If I fall face down in a puddle will you at least turn me over so I don't drown?"

"You won't fall," Quinn said. She pulled a little red bottle from a pocket. "Zirhine gave me this, remember? After I woke from the tresh. It kept me awake for the road. I didn't use it all then, against her warning that it would eventually demand more sleep."

"I remember," he said, wrinkling his nose. He didn't relish the idea of ingesting any ferneater concoction. In fact, he still had the maknek leaf and fillishader Zirhine had given him, untouched. Rather stupid of him, he knew. But old fears were fears nonetheless.

Quinn pulled the cork from the bottle. A little glass wand protruded from it, allowing one to dose out a single drop at a time. She put one under her tongue, then passed it to Fallo. He dipped it, sniffed it. His eyes watered at the strong odor. Not foul or bitter, but cutting and spicy. He put a drop under his tongue and corked the bottle, bracing himself for some violent moment of enlivenment. But the effect was subtler than that, coming over him as strength and deeper, more refreshing breaths. He popped up from his chair and stretched. He did feel better, his vision sharper. Even his mood was lighter. *Come on, Floppy Loppy, we have gods to kidnap from their loving homes.*

There was a moment's hesitation when Lop pretended to not hear him. But some core decency existed within the greedy cat, forcing her to hop down from the bar and slip ahead to the stairs.

They came out of The Reign of Fools into a downpour. Lop discovered true forgiveness in her heart instantly, and was quickly ensconced inside of Fallo's pack. He pulled the hood of his cloak over his mop of hair and trailed after Quinn, who was striding up the street. When he caught up to her, he nudged her elbow. "Anything yet?"

"No. You?"

"No. So we wander. And have faith."

She kissed him and smiled. "I have an idea. It's not an instinct thing, though." She led him under an overhang and produced her little book of shadline legends. "Remember how Xilo spoke of Silent Sable and Smoke in Shadows? I thought Xilo was talking about me. And maybe he was. But now I think he was also giving me a hint." She flipped to a dogeared page. "What was Sephie doing when she was wishing for the Silent Sable's help? It wasn't anything to do with her later heroics against the nosg. She was here during this story, here in Slirya." She licked her finger and flicked through pages. "Here it is. Sephie was trying to sneak a young girl out of an orphans' home. But she was caught and had to pay the housemother for her silence, and for the child. The girl's true identity was revealed later to be the niece of the dying king. She ended up becoming the Queen of Slirya."

"Why was she in an orphans' home?"

"To hide her. There were plots and schemes, and all manner of intrigues. Murders, kidnappings, beheadings, and every other sort of happening one finds in good tales. But none of that matters. Only one detail does. You see it, don't you?"

He did indeed. "Orphans' homes."

38

IT RAGES

Henley's eyes popped open, but he did not see the blazing light of Whiteflame. Instead his vision was filled with a black sky full of stars. A surge of shivering energy shot from the base of his spine, up his back, and out the top of his head. His throat tore with an involuntary cry as every muscle contracted.

Brother Ryde's calls of concern went unheard, Huff's perplexed sendings unnoticed. For at the center of Henley's mind there exploded a sphere of stillness where time itself did not exist.

A new voice spoke inside him.

Whiteflame!

The blade released him, and he smacked onto the marble, breath whooshing out. Huff sniffed at his cheek. *You were floating.*

Ryde was standing over him. The glow of Whiteflame had subsided enough that Henley could see the blade still clutched in his right hand. A slender sword of white steel with a gleaming silver hilt. He got to his feet using the sword as a crutch.

Looking up at the dome, he was awed to see the mercus

wards aglow. A breathtaking pattern of such intricacy that he knew one man could not have done it alone. It must have taken ten elnisians, perhaps a hundred, all working in concert to establish it. It repulsed the Revulsion by sending out tiny bolts of mercus. They were intentioned with noble ideals, gratitude, love, honor. The Revulsion did not devour or negate these bolts but simply repelled them back into the ward.

It was ingenious because Whiteflame provided the power to keep the wards alive, and was at the same time the lure to keep the Revulsion concentrated around the temple. Problem was, Moonside's recent awakening had disrupted the balance. Now some of these tiny bolts *were* being consumed.

"This is a shadline blade," he said, limbs still abuzz with the bonding.

Ryde turned away from him and took position near the entryway. This was Henley's problem to solve after all. Henley probed deeper into the relic, sensing its power, feeling for something, anything to suggest what he needed to do next.

Whiteflame, can you hear me?

No answer. Which, in truth, was a relief. He liked having Huff and Kila in his mind, but that was enough of such voices.

You are standing and doing nothing, Huff observed.

I'm thinking. That's not nothing.

He received the equivalent of a skeptical grunt through the bond.

Brother Ryde had moved closer to the wall of Revulsion whipping past the entryway. With a sudden hooking jab of his spear, he scuttered back into the dome. A hooded reviled was impaled on the spear, arms flailing. With swift efficiency, Ryde drew his sword and severed its neck.

"Lord Mast, come see what has been assailing you." Henley noted a hitch in the man's voice.

Ryde pushed the fabric of the reviled's hood away from the

detached head with the tip of his sword. They were all like this, Henley knew. Angular faces, thin noses. He was looking at an elnisian. It had been dead a long time, but the flesh sustained through the powers of its animating evil.

"Huff called these things 'its claws,'" he said to Ryde. "I don't think they are truly alive."

"They can be killed," Ryde countered, pointing at the now still body. Black ooze glooped out of its belly wound. A black jelly squeezed from the severed neck.

"Don't let any of that touch your skin," Henley warned.

Huff did not come near the body. His fur stuck out and he spat at the head in disgust.

"Can you bring in another one without killing it?" Henley asked.

Ryde took this as a command and returned to the entryway, as calm as a man walking to a pier to cast a line. He did not require such a man's patience, however, for within minutes he had another reviled on his spear. This he had caught in the shoulder. He dragged it in and thrust it to the floor, speartip pinning it. The thing's legs thrashed, and it beat a dull sword against the haft of Ryde's spear.

Gritting his teeth, Henley drove Whiteflame into its neck. The struggle stopped instantly. A jolt was transmitted through the sword and into Henley's arm.

The creature wasn't simply dead. It was gone. All that remained were the greasy, torn clothes. And glistening inside the empty fabric of the hood, a faceted black gem. It sparkled dully in Whiteflame's glow.

"The holes in the skulls," Henley said. "I think they harvested unspoiled gems from fallen elnisians in the last battle." Ryde prodded the dent in the top of his helmet, shrugged, and returned to his post at the door.

Whiteflame can kill them, he sent to Huff.

So did Ryde's sword when he cut off its head.

Henley went back to the severed head. He prodded the pale, sunken cheek with the tip of Whiteflame. The blank eyes turned to look at him, the mouth gaped in a silent shriek. "It's not dead. Yet." He clove the head in two, again feeling a jolt through his arm as the sword flared. The head vanished.

Henley realized the sword was needed outside of Moonside. Perhaps with study he could figure out how it destroyed the reviled. Perhaps more such weapons could be made. Trouble was, it still powered the wards that kept the temple secure, and more importantly lured the Revulsion. If that were lost, he doubted the Divide could long contain it. Especially with that qiznithor out there. It was already resisting the trap and had been battering through the Divide.

He moved back to the center of the dome where the sword had been. Now that its light had dimmed, Henley saw the gems. There were five of them. Four in a square, one in the center.

So here was the elnisian king, and four others who had died with him. He plucked them up. Sapphire, garnet, topaz, emerald, and diamond. They were the size of chicken eggs and weighty. He put them in his pockets, thinking vaguely to inter them properly when he returned to Starside.

There was nothing else to be recovered from the temple. But he was surprised to see that Ori's pools still held water. He flashed to his final moments with Yiqa as she sank beneath the milky surface. That had been Lumne's pool, the pool of death. But there were two others. One in which mothers bore children. And another, from which convalescents drew strength. "Ryde, come here. Go into that pool."

The man did not question the order. He simply strode down the steps until he was standing in it. The water came to his waist.

"Submerge yourself. Put the spear aside for a moment. The Revulsion cannot get in here while I possess this relic."

Ryde did as he was told. He stayed under so long that Henley thought he was going to have to dive in and order the man to come out to breath. He had just moved to the steps when Ryde stood, dripping in his armor, water flowing from his helm and over his face. He didn't so much as splutter or spit or even blink the water from his eyes.

Henley cast his mercus attention into the man's scrapes. They were healed. The Revulsion corruption was gone. Ryde strode out of the pool with the same strength as ever, but his breathing was easier.

"You feel it?" Henley asked.

"I do. It will be an honor to continue in Her Majesty's service for longer than I had previously thought likely."

Henley scanned the dome and the floor, making sure that he hadn't missed any other telltales of the elnisians, or any other relics.

Satisfied, he unlimbered his pack and dug through all the supplies he'd brought, laughing at the rope and fire making kit. The Motherlight came out, looking like an egg in its shell of red dragon scales. He set it on the floor and gently pulled at one of the scales. It came free and white light shot from the opening. He removed the others, nesting them together like dishes, then returning them to his pack.

The awesome power of the Motherlight again had him working with his eyes closed. But his work was with the mercus, so he did not need to see. The Motherlight was a well of power, willing to offer it to anyone who claimed it. It would provide more power to the temple's wards than the sword. All he needed to do was make the switch.

It was easier than hoped. For as soon as he established the Motherlight's tap to the wards, the temple glowed brilliantly with excess power. Furious thunder crashed outside, and in the lingering rumble Henley thought he heard frustration.

It retreats, Huff sent.

"I see clear ground," Ryde called. "Fifty paces, no haze." He crept out and looked up. "It's nighttime. A clear sky."

Henley smiled at Huff. *We did it.*

Of course we did. Why else did we come here?

A concussion from across the city drew Ryde around.

"What was that?" Henley asked.

Another concussion sounded. The ground trembled. It was coming from the north.

It rages! Huff sent.

Another explosion blasted through Moonside. From the north.

"From the Divide," Henley said. "It's back to ramming through. I thought the trap was going to distract it."

It's not mindless like the reviled, Huff sent.

No. It certainly wasn't. If it could endure the jolts and stings of the Divide's wards, it clearly had the wherewithal to ignore the lure of the mercus trap of the temple.

"Our mission is complete," Ryde said. "I must return you safely to Starside."

With Whiteflame in hand, Henley felt a stirring in his gut. Confidence filled his breast. He had come here to strengthen the trap. But it hadn't quelled the stirring Ell had warned of.

"You saw the breach in the Divide," Henley said. "We can't let the qiznithor continue that project."

"What is the new mission?"

Whiteflame sent a surge of determination and aggression through his limbs. "We hunt."

39

AXE COULD CHOP

The first thing Kila noticed when arriving in Stallid was the heat. Winter in the Destig Desert was dry and warm under the unobscured sun. Ahead of her lay the city. She had never truly seen it in its glory prior to the nosg siege. But the remains hinted at the bright miracle it must have seemed to the thirsty traveler desperate for shade and water.

A few towers still stood in the city proper, bright stone glaring as if lit from within. Pale yellow tiles rose upon the rooftops. For a roof runner like Kila, the city would have been easy to traverse without ever touching the ground.

No longer. For every tower that still stood, dozens were broken off, leaving jagged tops exposed to the sky. Entire lanes of homes and shops lay in rubble, charred beams poking out like splintered ribs. Streets once wide and open were now cluttered with debris and the ragged, filthy camps of the homeless.

Kila had been all over the city during the battle, and countless terrified eyes had surely memorized her face. Many would blame her for the destruction.

The Indomitable Wall surrounded only three sides of the

city now. She had unmade one entire stretch while possessed of the Revulsion. Seeing the gap now, which exposed the entire city to her, she could not help but shiver. For the wall had not been a single thing, but instead three concentric walls, each forty paces thick. She had simply vanished it all from existence with a thought.

A soft jangle next to her brought her out of her uneasy musings. Eyvin and Nils did not have their spears, for a fell guardsman would draw all manner of notice. Both men were dressed as merchants, with only daggers on their belts for weapons. Beneath their shirts, however, was light chain armor, the source of the jangling.

Kila wore the airy white wraps of a desert local. A broad hat kept the sun from baking her brain, the front brim drooping to shade her eyes and hide her features. Head down, she made for the makeshift entry gate the Stallidian's had thrown up since the battle. Stretching to either side of the new structure was a picket of ropes, patrolmen, and low towers of stacked rubble. Carts converged on the gate as outlying folk brought their meager wares and produce to the famous Stallid market.

Kila could have dymensed into the city. But appearing in front of folk out of vacant air would also draw the wrong sort of attention. She wished to find Yioth with as little interaction with the locals as she could manage.

Are you too hot? she sent to Nax, who rode concealed in her backpack.

No. Your mercus trick is working.

She had fashioned a weather-cloak around Nax, but had not done so for herself. Her wards and self-sustaining feats were never as subtle as Henley's. In truth, she rather enjoyed the heat after the damp chill of Starside.

Have you ever felt like you've forgotten something? Kila sent.

If I forgot something why would I feel anything about it?

The annoying sensation had subsided during Henley's awkward departure and the horror of Mayrie's murder. But as soon as she was preparing to come to Stallid it had risen again. Hard.

The gate guards were relaxed, dusty of face, and disinterested in the cart men. Mostly they were customs agents, directing each entrant to the appropriate tax post, where an assessment of their goods would be made and a tax bill issued.

When Kila's turn came, the guard eyed her up and down. "Alone, miss?"

"No. These are my brothers. We came to speak with an almen. Our father is ill with a fever."

"What's in the pack?" He didn't sound interested, merely a man asking a scripted question.

"Water, food, a bit of coin in case I can find a room."

"Good luck with that. Hope that pack doubles for a pillow, because you'll be sleeping under the stars tonight. Go through to the right." He handed her a square of wood with a line across it. "Give this to tax assessor ten." He eyed Eyvin and Nils. "Best keep those daggers in their scabbards, boys."

The fell guardsmen nodded but said nothing.

The great open plaza that hosted the market was not as Kila remembered it. When last here, she had fought against shamans. And against Yiothizandra. Dragons and wyvoks had soared over head, blasting down with fire, or with shamans on their backs loosing rays of swarmlight magic into the Stallidian army.

Kila handed her square to assessor ten, who waved her through. Apparently the token signified that Kila's pack did not need any assessment at all, which suited her just fine. Cats were loved in Stallid, but they were rather rare. And it was well known that she kept one as a companion.

The stands of marketers stretched out beyond the tax men. What had been a ruined plaza, full of blasted-out divots and thousands of dead men, nosg, and wyvoks, had been filled in and cleared out. Except for one area, a circle where nobody intruded, around which stood a palisade made of salvaged timbers.

Kila approached it, remembering now what lay within. It was well that folk were kept away from it. For at the center was a sword, blade embedded in the stone, hilt up. It practically begged for someone to grip it, attempt to pull it free. Yiothizandra's hateful sword, Flayshui.

Kila left it behind and picked her way through the city ruins, trying not to look at the dispossessed citizenry. They reminded her too much of the refugees in Starside. She kept her focus on the still-standing elnisian core of the city, On'lin Keep. The legendary fortress where the shadline heroine Sephie had rallied the forces of men to push nosg invaders back to the Haelshok mountains.

Yiothizandra was in there somewhere. In some dungeon cell, most likely. Kila's thiefly instincts lured her toward the keep, a vague notion stirring in her mind that she might sneak inside and descend to the lower levels. But a different voice overruled her. It was Wen's. Where Kila had been impulsive and rash, he had been careful and deliberate. She needed his guidance now more than ever. How would Wen find out where Yioth was stashed?

He would listen to the rumors on the street.

She knew just who to ask. And it would turn her lie to the gate guard into something approximating the truth. The Losstran nation—of which Stallid was the center—was unique in its devotion to a catalog of innumerable gods. Kila had always heard derogatory talk about their faith, worshipping the so-called "small gods." The upholders of the faith were called almen. Unlike the Triumvirate of Til, Ori, and Pol, the small gods did not have temples. Most almen were plain folk with jobs other than merely proselytizing and collecting tithes.

She searched faces in the plaza fronting the gate of On'lin Keep. Her brief time as monarch of Starside had tutored her in the dress, posture, and gait of dignitaries and bookkeepers. It was the latter she sought. Bookkeepers tended to be intelligent, serious, and logical.

A woman with her hair tied back, ink-stained fingertips, and fresh but plain clothing crossed Kila's path. She was carrying a woven bag in one hand. Papers were bursting from the top. She was a scribe or a stock counter of some sort.

"Pardon, mum," Kila said, lightly touching the woman's elbow. "Can you point me to an almen?"

The woman stopped and looked at the sun, which Kila thought an odd response. "I'm an almen. I suppose I have a moment. What do you need, child?"

Kila swallowed her reflexive indignation at being called child. "My papa was killed in the battle here. I come as quick as I could. Did I miss the execution of the fire woman?"

The woman's lips pressed into a thin line for a moment, but her eyes softened with sympathy. "I know you wish for vengeance. Maybe you think it will be a salve upon your heart." She took Kila's hand and squeezed it. "I never approved of the sentence. No almen would, of course. The goddess of your soul and the goddess of all souls will weep, for they recognize no such thing as a just killing. Be at ease. I will pray that the god of your father and that the god of all fathers lifts him up and eases him. And I will pray that the god of grief cleanses you of hatred and sadness and leaves you with wisdom."

These almen do go on and on, Naxie. I've lost count of the gods and goddesses already.

I like her voice, Nax sent. *I think she is wise. But killing feeds me, so I'll ignore that part.*

"Begging your pardon, but did they kill her yet?" Kila said. "They say she can fly. I don't want her flying off. My papa died 'cause of her." Kila tried to sound like someone who had heard wild rumors and that she barely believed them herself.

"They *were* going to kill her. She was upon a scaffold one night, almen praying for her. In the morning she was gone. The almen and guards were dead."

Escaped, Nax! A wild fear jolted her and she couldn't help but look all around, as if Yioth might be watching her at that moment. "Ah me."

The almen woman took it as a phrase of regret, rather than the mix of relief and fear that it was. "I must go to my ledgers. I will pray for you now so that you may be more at ease. Things are as they are. Accept what is and be at ease. That is wisdom, for it is peaceful. Good things come to you when you are at peace." She began to mumble and beseech Kila's heart god and her soul goddess and then the goddess of her belly and many more. Kila fell into a sort of bored stupor as the prayer went on.

And then it was over and the woman was walking away. Kila had to wonder how long she'd been standing there, staring at her feet. Strange. And her belly was remarkably loose feeling, her breath flowing in and out with ease. Had her lungs and throat been so constricted before?

Shaking off the languor, Kila looked around again. Yioth was gone from here. That was both bad and good. If Ell truly meant that Kila would need all of the demayne of Night, then it was better that she had escaped than been killed. But it would make finding her harder.

Why is her sword still here? she sent to Nax. *If she escaped, that would be the first thing she'd collect.*

Nax didn't know and didn't offer any guesses.

Kila doubted Yioth would linger in the city. But she wasn't the sort to cower and simply do nothing. Not unless she was severely weakened. But who would shelter her? She could have no allies here. Perhaps she had gone back to Ceronhel, to her nosg army. That felt more likely. But the sword . . . *Something smells like a Sourwater slubfish, Naxie.*

Good thing Lop isn't here. She loves slubfish.

Kila decided to skim a few more rumors before dymensing home. She needed a different perspective. Almen were too passive. Turning away from the keep, she found a military post surrounding a half-demolished tower. Horses were picketed around the perimeter where huge awnings provided shade over their troughs. A few off-duty soldiers lounged at a table, heads down over square trays of what looked like gray mush.

"Don't look much appetizing," she called cheerfully. "Don't his kingship give his soldiers bread and cheese?"

"Bread yes," replied one man, grin showing more gaps than teeth. "Cheese? I can barely remember what cheese is."

Kila slowed and shook her head sadly. "Wish I had some to spare. But what I've got is for my brother."

"You got cheese?" The grin squeezed into a sly interest. "Maybe we can make a bargain."

"You don't got anything I want," Kila teased. She ducked under the awning, but was careful to keep her brim down. He could see her mouth, but not her eyes. Eyvin and Nils stood by, looking bored, but ready to spring into violence at any second.

"Maybe I do," the gap-smiled soldier said. "I got a few coppers to spare."

"Coppers won't fill my brother's stomach. Or slake his thirst."

"Thirsty is he? What if I told you King Delp makes sure we get our ration of beer? Maybe we can barter, cheese for suds."

"Maybe we can." Kila shrugged off her pack and felt inside

for the wedge of cheese she'd brought along for Nax. Pulling it out, she showed it to the soldier.

"That much!" the man said. He swiped a hand across his sweaty brow. She saw now the war in him, between his longing for something tasty to eat and his devotion to his daily ration of beer.

"Are those maggots in your gruel?" she asked. "I hear they taste like toasted squeezle nuts." She made to put the cheese away.

"Hold up, lassie," the man said. "Where'd you get that anyhow? That's no cow cheese. I can smell it from here. That's *goat* cheese." This distinction was apparently more important in Stallid than it was in Starside, for now a gleam of avarice tainted the man's eyes. It must be worth quite a bit more than his daily ration of beer. He was probably calculating several trades ahead.

"My brother wants it. Sorry, soldier. He was heart-sore when that fire woman got away. Wanted to see her head cut off." Her transition to Yioth was inelegant enough that she winced inwardly. But the soldier was so focused on getting the cheese from her, he barely noticed.

"If your brother is so sore, he ought to go to Starside and demand her returned to us."

"Starside? That's on the other side of the world! What do they have to do with the fire lady?"

"They're thick with merculyns and witches. One came and cut her out of her chains and turned into a cloud. Vanished." He snapped his fingers. "I could get your brother a nice sword. He can go kill her in Starside."

Kila sensed this rumor had a bit of truth in it. "Why would anyone in Starside want her?"

"The Highest of Kil might want her. Seeing as she stole the demon's babe. Cut it right out of her guts, I heard. Maybe she wants the mother for a wet nurse. Damn me if I know. How about it, a sword for that cheese?"

"Who saw her turn into a cloud and vanish?"

"Nobody. The guards are dead. The almen dead. But the chains were cut cleaner than any axe could chop."

That did stink of the mercus. Somebody might have strolled in, found her, released her, dymensed with her. Was it Klayne or Eckso? "When did she go missing?"

"Four, five nights ago."

Then it wasn't Klayne or Eckso. The former had been a prisoner in the Citadel then, and Eckso still promise-bound to Ell. Kila pulled the cheese back out and tossed it to the soldier. "My brother won't miss it."

The man let out a whoop. "Hold fast, girlie. I'll fetch him a fine blade."

Kila didn't wait for the man to return before slipping away and heading out of Stallid. Someone had come for Yioth. To rescue her, possibly. Klayne and Eckso might not be the only dragnithans of Night in the world. There were over a dozen dragnithors, after all.

She stopped only once, in the market, to buy a cool drink of spiced tea, with ice chunks floating in it. Apparently men brought down vast slabs of ice from the mountains for the purpose. Eyvin and Nils refused a drink. As she sipped it, she considered the cordoned-off circle where Yioth's blade was stuck.

Yioth wasn't rescued, Nax. The blade would be gone, too. The only other explanation was that someone had stolen her. Just as Saiya had almost been taken. A revulyn had taken Yiothizandra.

She went out of Stallid, down the dusty paved roadway to the north. The fell guardsmen kept closer to her, knowing that Yiothizandra was missing. She walked past the cart men still coming to market. She walked until there was no one visible on the horizon. And as she walked, she considered the terror of Yiothizandra in the grasp of a revulyn. Would the horrid woman even resist the corruption of the Revulsion? If not, what an awful new enemy she would be.

I have to find her, Nax. And soon.

40

A RECKONING

"There is no crime in Slirya," the patrolman said to Fallo. His belly hung over his belt, and his jowly neck loafed up from his tight collar. "That is because of our good citizens and the Crown's generous funding of orphan homes across the city."

Fallo smirked at the man's recitation of the often repeated, and more often derided, fantasy that there was no crime here. Perhaps there was very little, but that very morning he and Quinn had faced a robber in the street. "Do you know where any of those orphan homes are?" he asked.

To his credit, the man knew in detail where they were. Fallo suspected he had delivered many a delinquent to these places, whether or not they were orphans. With this list of names and places in mind, they began their search.

The first was a fine brick building with a sign over the door that read Regnal Home of Unclaimed Babes and Children. The mistress of the house allowed them in, showed them the children, and informed them that any could be had for a donation of two silver. There were three children. Cautious of eye but polite. Fallo and Quinn left without any of them, both certain that none was a reborn god.

"The shadline instinct is rather odd," Quinn said as they continued to the next orphan's home. "I just *knew* that they weren't the ones."

"Me too," he said. "I wish we could have spared more coin for the mistress of the home."

The next two homes followed the pattern, save the adoption price was lower for the older children. According to the house-mother, the older ones ate more and were less desirable than the babes. Fallo's gut burned at the unfairness of it. He knew what it was to be unwanted, but at least he'd had a home and freedom growing up.

The next was set in a little green park at the end of a residen-tial street. A wrought iron fence surrounded it, giving one the impression of prison rather than refuge. The gate was locked, but there was light in the windows.

Fallo hadn't made a study of picking locks, and he didn't have any picks anyway. But the mechanism did not look all that strong. He wedged Telt in a gap and levered it until he could get his fingers in. He yanked and rattled the gate. The bolt held. He stepped back and looked at the fence. It was twice his height and topped with spear-like finials on each iron bar.

"You're going to draw attention," Quinn complained, pulling him down the street. "Let's try the back."

The rear of the yard was contained by a stone fence, and the alleyway was full of household refuse. It appeared that all of the kitchen leavings were dumped behind the wall to compost for the kitchen garden. The fence was obviously intended to keep children in and no concern spared for keeping people out. The compost pile put the top in reach. Fallo boosted Quinn, who helped him over in turn. They dropped into the garden, boots squishing into the mud beneath a row of beet greens.

They traipsed through the crop, doing their best to avoid mashing the produce. At the rear of the home, which looked like a tottering old mansion, a kitchen door stood open. They went straight in as if invited.

I smell food! sent Lop.

Stay in the pack, Fallo commanded.

An old woman in an apron stopped short at the sight of them, letting out an atlen squawk. She pressed a flabby, spotted hand to her mounded bosom. "The light of grace spare me!" she gasped. "What are you two doing? Is Madam Garret expecting you?"

"We're looking for a child."

"For what purpose," the woman demanded, reaching for a large spoon sticking out of a bubbling pot. She brandished it, chin lifting. "I'll have none of you abusing these poor waifs. I'll have none of it, I say!"

"We wish to adopt one into our family," Quinn said, putting on her gentlest and most noble voice. The cook's gaze darted from Quinn's lovely visage to Fallo's hideous one. She found his ugliness to be a problem. "The gate's locked. Nobody scrambles over a fence if they're sincere."

"We're leaving Slirya today," Quinn said. "Time presses upon us. But we wish to choose and go quickly." She patted her cloak. "We have coin."

"These sweet dears are not for sale!" she squawked. "Get out! Get out or I'll beat you senseless." The spoon whipped back and forth and she danced forward in a passable imitation of a true bladesman. Until Quinn caught the spoon in her hand and wrested it away.

"You misunderstand, my good woman," Quinn said. "I did not mean to suggest I wished to *buy* a child. Merely that I have means to feed, clothe, and raise a child. My husband and I are Starsiders. I'm known there as Lady Peline." She returned the spoon. The cook snatched it back and clutched it to her belly.

"Lady, eh? What sort of lady goes about in trousers, and amidst the Winternight Solitude, no less!" She didn't look at all convinced. And Fallo's face was still a problem. It was something he would have to get used to, this comparison of Quinn's looks to his. At the moment he was delighting in the fact that Quinn had called him "husband."

"Her eyesight isn't the best," he confided to the woman. "She thinks I'm handsome."

"He is," Quinn said. "I don't know why others don't agree. But surely you cannot doubt my sincerity, good woman. Perhaps go fetch the mistress of the house. Let her decide if our claims are credible."

The cook scratched at her chin and chewed her tongue. Finally she decided the issue was above her pay. She gave Quinn the spoon. "Stir that pot so it don't boil over."

Madam Garret wore a black dress with a high collar of ruffles that blossomed around her neck. The sleeves covered her hands entirely, the skirts dragged the floor. Her face was snowy, brows entirely missing, eyelashes long dropped off her lids like last year's leaves. She had a few black teeth, lips a purplish color that spoke of very ill health. When she came into the kitchen, she bore herself with the rigid spine of a soldier.

"Lady Peline of Starside?" she asked. "I understand you wish to adopt a child. I wish you had corresponded with me prior to your visit. We have but six children under this roof. I am to retire soon, and we must be rid of them before I do. Perhaps you would prefer to have several at once?"

"May we see them?"

Garret sucked in a long breath, then resigned herself to having to do some work. She bade them follow her into a heavily draped parlor. She had chosen fabrics of maroon and gray to cover the windows, for pillows, and for rugs. Even the walls were swathed in pleated fabrics that smelled of dust and mildew and sucked the sound from the air. Garret shouted up a stairwell for the children to come down.

They did so quickly. The oldest was a boy of perhaps fifteen. The youngest a girl of five. There was a set of boy twins in the middle, perhaps ten years old. They had mean, speculative expressions on their faces. Fallo knew with shadline certainty that they would one day grow up to be partners in thievery and murder.

Quinn walked the line of children like a general inspecting her troops. After kneeling to speak quietly with the youngest, she stood and gave Fallo a sad shake of her head.

"How can you know for sure?" he asked.

"How can you?" she countered. "Look at them and see if you hear anything."

Garret pulled her head back at this comment, chin disappearing into her ruffles. "What an odd thing to say!"

Fallo confronted the oldest boy. "How long have you been here?"

"Fifteen years."

The story was the same for the rest. All had come as infants. He closed his eyes and listened, did his best to stay calm and disinterested. But the force of destiny didn't care about these particular children. And now he was faced with the sad act of rejecting them. The cruelty of it made him ill. He knew they'd suffered a lifetime of it. And he knew how it felt to be unwanted. Quinn moved him out of the room, out of earshot of the children and Madam Garret.

"We must move on." Her tone was gentle, but firm. They made their apologies to Mistress Garret and retreated through the front door. Down the damp little walkway to the gate. A latch unlocked it and they were onto the street beyond. The gate swung in.

Quinn stopped it from latching shut with her stump. Fallo followed her gaze back toward the house. Not to the front door, but to a small window beneath the gabled roof peak. A round face of a child, palms pressed to the uneven glazing, peered out. And then another face appeared for moment and the child was pulled back into darkness.

Feeling his hair lift away from his scalp, Fallo cursed. Quinn drew in a sharp breath. They exchanged a knowing look. Then they were back inside the home, dripping in the entry foyer, and staring down Madam Garret. The woman obviously knew what they'd seen, but she had her chin thrust high out of her ruffles now. Full of defiance and righteous indignation.

"Get out," she snapped. "Mrs. Dill was right to suspect you scoundrels."

"Let us see the child you withheld," Quinn said. "Then we'll go."

"What child? I showed you them all."

"The child in the attic. Do not lie to us." Quinn let her hand drop to her dagger.

"Attic? There is naught up there but a few sticks of furniture and a stack of old trunks."

"Then you won't mind if we go up." Quinn put herself very close to the woman, which caused the aged face to retreat once again and form pleats of fleshy chins down into her ruffles. "Mark me, madam. We are shadlines, and not patient ones."

But Garret was not to be intimidated. She straightened to her full height, face purpling with indignation. But when she opened her mouth, only a high pitched shriek came out. Her eyes were fixed on Fallo's shoulder, where there had suddenly appeared a black furry face.

"What—? What is *that*?"

"Oh this?" Fallo said, scritching Lop's chin. "Just a little demayne. A very hungry one!"

The woman's face went slack. "A demayne you say?" And then she fainted into Quinn's arms. Fallo collected her and moved her to a divan in the parlor. Lop jumped down and slunk toward the kitchen where another shriek resounded. He listened for sounds of fighting, but Lop didn't hiss and spit. A quick check showed the cook kneeling and tempting Lop with a morsel.

Fallo and Quinn went in search of the mysterious child. The children they'd seen before emerged from their rooms, watching the intruders come up the creaking stairs. They did not seem fearful. And Fallo was relieved to see that none had formed a hope that he had returned to collect one of them. But it was the sort of relief that came with bitterness, for he saw they had allowed themselves no expectations anymore. No hope.

The oldest boy showed them the door to the attic. "Be careful of her," he said. "She's feral."

A narrow door at the top opened into an attic space with slanting walls. Old bits of furniture and trunks were indeed here, though all had been pushed to one side. A holey rug defined a sort of bedroom area, with a little bed, side table, and candle. Chained to the headboard was a girl in a blue gown, bare feet, and mess of curly hair. A fat man sat upon a stool nearby, head down in a book.

At their entrance, he looked up. "Get out."

"Madam Garret sent us up," Quinn said, pushing the man aside. He stumbled over his stool and dropped his book. His curses and demands were ignored. Fallo leered at him and twirled Telt before his eyes. This caused the man to shut up and back away.

The girl was perhaps fourteen, with wild eyes that darted all around the room. The flesh beneath her wrist manacles was scraped raw. There was evidence of injury around her ankles. Shackles lay on the floor by the bed. She was filthy, hair a tangle, dress torn. The frock was two sizes too small.

"Flaumishtak said the other one grows freakishly fast," Fallo whispered.

"This is one of them," Quinn said softly. "But which?"

"When was she born?" he asked the girl's guard.

"Kil take me if I know."

Fallo eyed the man's boots, let his gaze drift up to take in the paunch, the unshaven neck, the small eyes. He moved to the man while Quinn went to the girl. His hair was still trying to stand on end, but this time it wasn't because they'd found a reborn god. The force of destiny was not subtle now. Telt and Shinane came into his hands and he backed the man into the slanting wall, forcing him to duck forward. The man gibbered and made excuses. "I just watch her. I just do what Madam Garret says."

The tips of the daggers went into the man's belly. Not deep. They didn't need to go in deep. The man screamed and grabbed at Fallo's hands. But the daggers held fast. Indeed, they wished to drive in deeper. Only Fallo's will held them back. His eyes were drawn to the man's, and in the moment their gazes locked —one furious, the other agonized—Fallo's vision went black.

And now he was standing before the girl's bed, seeing the man's memories play out as if they were his own actions. A horror of abuse torrented into Fallo's mind. And his daggers did slide in deeper, and deeper still with each new vision. When they finally stopped, Fallo blinked hard against tears, saw his daggers now before him in clean air. The man slumped onto the floor amidst an ever widening pool of blood.

"Search him for a key," Quinn said softly.

There was a key and a coin purse. He took them, handed the key to Quinn and promptly fled to a far corner to heave up his

last meal. When he returned to Quinn, she had the girl's manacles off and was crooning softly to comfort her. The sounds that
came from the girl's lips were inarticulate, slurred. It was toddler
language. Bits and pieces intelligible, like "go" and "lone", but
most of it gibberish.

"Get Garret," Quinn ordered.

Fallo was happy to leave the scene, to catch his breath in air
untainted by the horrors of the attic. He stormed down the steps,
feeling a new sort of rage growing in his belly. All that he'd
endured at the hands of his father and other bullies, every
insult, beating, and taunt was nothing next to what had
happened here. "There's no crime in Slirya," he muttered.
"There will certainly be a reckoning. Oh, there will be a
reckoning."

He found Garret sitting up on her couch, staring at Lop as if
she were a wolf about to rip her face off. Little did she know that
the true wolf had now entered the room. He grabbed her by the
elbow and pulled her to her feet.

"Get your hands off me! I bruise easily!"

"Bruises will be the least of your worries when this day is
done." He manhandled her up the stairs, and when she began to
lag, he picked her up and carried her. The children again stood
outside their doors, watching this strange happening. The
oldest boy allowed a smile to play across his lips, but the
younger ones were terrified. "Go into your rooms," Fallo said.
"You'll have nothing to fear from Garret or the man upstairs ever
again."

At the sight of Garret, the feral girl screamed and ran at her,
fingers curling to claws. Garret tried to fend her off, but was
soon scratched across the face with ragged fingernails. Wild
slaps cuffed her ears and body. Quinn lifted her from the
woman. "Stop it!"

It took Quinn several minutes to ease the girl's failing rage-terror. She pressed a hand to the girl's cheek and forced her to make eye contact. "You're safe. You're safe."

Fallo again stood Garret upright. The woman saw the dead man on the floor and fainted again. He caught her and eased her to the floor.

"Her name is Illy," said a voice behind Fallo. The oldest boy had come in. He pushed back his overlong hair and took in the odd scene. "That's her real name. Madam calls her Chandra." He went to stand at the edge of the blood pool. "This is Mr. Garret. I'm glad he's dead." With glistening eyes and quivering lips he looked at Fallo. He was obviously trying to be strong, be manly, contain his emotion. And he failed. "I wish I'd been the one to stick him."

Madam Garret was stirring again. Fallo knelt and patted her face. "Did you know what your husband was doing to Illy?"

She needed not say anything, for her face betrayed her knowledge. It went frog-belly white and her lips pinched in. "He's not my husband. He's my brother. And I only know he watches Chandra, makes sure she doesn't fling excrement all over. She's wild and evil."

She was wild, all right. But one look at the trembling girl, who even now panted like a panicked little squirrel, showed nothing of evil. Only ignorance, fear. She *was* an animal.

"Who brought her here?"

"My brother. He sometimes hears of easy ladies in a bad way. Takes the child from them, protects their reputation. To better the lives of both. We give them a home. He—he sometimes gets weak."

"You allow it."

"No! But look at me. What can I do? He's stronger and I need him. Especially with this one. She's evil. Grew from a babe to that so quick! Take her, if it pleases you. Take her for free! I'll thank you to take her and let me be done with her."

"Oh, we will. But how will *you* pay? Surely your brother has been weak before. How many others here have known of his weakness?"

"All of us," the boy said. "One time or another."

Madam Garret burst in to sobs and threw a black-sleeved arm over her eyes. Fallo's anger flashed from white hot to pure ice. The moment before him was not one of passion, but one of a job undone. He did not want to make it bloody or violent. He drew Shinane and flashed the tip across the back of Garret's hand, just as Cloak Szill had done to him and Quinn in the carriage.

The woman gasped and drew back from him. He stood and motioned for Quinn to bring the girl away. "Come, lad. Let's go downstairs and talk."

"What about her?" he said, dipping his chin at Garret.

"She's dead. Or will soon be."

They filed from the attic, Fallo softly closing the door on Garret's moans of increasing terror. Shinane's power was working through her now. First her hand went cold, started freezing as if it were carved from a block of ice. The chill slowly climbed her arm. From there it spread. Shinane was called Bone Chill for a reason. Fallo tromped down the steps behind the others, collected the children and urged them to the parlor.

The older ones were pensive, looking to the oldest boy for guidance. He merely nodded encouragement to them, lips clamped. At the sight of Lop, they nearly broke and retreated. But Fallo corralled them and bade them sit. Quinn took Illy away to a back room, presumably to wash her and get her into new clothes.

"Mrs. Dill," Fallo called. "Can you bring in tea and cakes?"

"What do you think this is, an inn?"

It took only a moment of soft whispers to bring her round. She set to in her kitchen with extraordinary gusto and brought in a tray covered with cakes, toasted bread, and tea at the same time Quinn returned with Illy. The girl wore a clean maroon dress with white lace collar. It looked odd on her, not only because it contrasted so with her wild face, but because it was much too large.

The other children looked at her with curiosity. She returned their scrutiny with defiant stares of her own that darted from one to another. And then she saw Lop and her features brightened.

Lop ambled over to her, jumped into her lap, and submitted to a bout of gentle petting. All of Illy's attention focused on the cat, as if the rest of the world did not exist. She mumbled gentle toddler noises and brushed her cheek against the fuzzy black fur of Lop's face.

"You are shadlines," the oldest boy said. "I saw your daggers before. I thought something was odd about you."

With Illy occupied, Quinn availed herself of a cake and a cup of tea. Her eyes were bright over the brim as she inspected the children again. "I'm sorry we can't take any of you," she said. "It's Illy we sought. There are others would harm her."

This was met with silence.

"Do any of you know who her mother is?"

Silence. But Fallo's instincts were alert, and he sensed this quiet was not due to ignorance, but of reluctance. "Boy, what's your name?"

"Milfor."

"Do you know her mother?"

"I don't." A fleeting glance guided Fallo to the girl next to him. She was Illy's apparent age. Tall and thin, with tamed curls pulled back into a bushy tail. Her eyes were flat, and of them all, the least interested in what was happening before her.

"What's your name?" Fallo asked her.

"Her name is Reille," Milfor said. "She don't talk. She's—" He clamped his lips shut and looked down.

"She's Illy's mother," Quinn said. At this Reille brought her shoulders to her ears and covered her face. Her shame was impossible to witness, and Fallo was moved to comfort her. But when he approached, she flinched back from him. He drew away, wishing he had granted Garret an even slower, more painful death.

"Mr. Garret?" he asked Milfor.

All he got was a nod. And that was all he needed.

He went back to the kitchen and told Mrs. Dill that her employer was going away for a long journey. And that she would be in charge of the home from now on. He gave her the coin purse he'd lifted from Mr. Garret, added half of his own to the amount. "I can arrange for more. Simply send a note to Fallo PiTorro at the Reign of Fools with a request for what you need. You will get it. Milfor can help with heavy chores in the meantime." As an afterthought he said, "And don't go in the attic. Someone will be by to clean up the mess I made up there."

The next hour passed quietly as Quinn spoke to each of the children, spending the most time with Reille. The poor thing could not understand how her baby had grown so swiftly. She spoke few words, and gave the impression of a boarded up, abandoned house. There was no question of taking her with them.

There was no satisfactory answer to the problem of the orphan home. Fallo left the house feeling insufficient to the task ahead. He didn't know anything about taking care of a girl. And though Quinn had succeeded in calming Illy, she had the stark look of one ill-prepared for the future, too. Pol smiled on them in one way, he mused: Lop. If not for the cat, he doubted the girl would have come with them without being bound hand and foot. But she carried Lop in her arms, fur pressed to her face.

Something like a smile rested on her lips, and she did not resist their instructions to stay out of the middle of the street.

Which one is she, Lop? Fallo asked.

Which what?

Which god? Is she Ori or Pol? Til?

Ori.

How do you know?

How do you know your hand is your hand?

Because it's always been there, attached to my arm.

Just so. Are we going back to that shadline place? I like those giblets.

41

A WILLFUL ONE

Til's reliquary was much larger than Pol's, Revnithan Con noted. She stood in the doorway, drifting a reddish sphere of revulynic light ahead. The vault's heavy door had opened easily. The hinges were well oiled, and her strength as a revnithan was magnitudes greater than her living muscles had ever possessed.

She didn't have much time, however. The wards protecting the vault had been clever, set to alert the Highest of even the slightest touch on the steel door.

Objects glimmered under her ruddy light, fascinating her with their number and variety. "Greedy villains," she said, including all Donse Masters in her judgment. She had no way to carry so many, so she only swiped the most intriguing ones. A small jade bird on a chain. A shiny metal sphere. And a set of bronze earrings shaped like fillishader leaves. They throbbed with mercusine. So much so she was a bit dazzled, and only the sound of shouts and boots gave her the presence of mind to pull the door shut behind her.

The Entifal wasn't there.

"Bloody guts!" she said, vaguely shamed by uttering such a

vulgarity. If her mother heard her utter such a thing, why, Con's backside would have glowed for a ten-day. Several wands stood on little wooden stands. She left them. They were rather ordinary relics, capable of making light or finding lost keys or healing minor scratches. The Donse Masters probably didn't even know what they did.

She dymensed.

Now her pockets were heavy with a jumble of mercus relics. She would like nothing more than to investigate them in detail, but the mercus wasn't available to her. If she poked at them with the Revulsion, she would likely destroy them and possibly herself in the process. She paused in the street and collected what she could of the calm of the cold eye. "I'm back where I started," she said, noticing that she'd returned to Seaside, next to the pink house with the white trim. She began to walk, going the direction she'd been facing when she came out of dymension. No reason. Just movement. She needed to think.

She had expected to find the Entifal in one of the Ways' reliquaries. She knew that Ori didn't have it, for she had curated their little collection back when she'd lived in Slirya. Any new ones to come to Ori since then would have been communicated to her in Sorgan. Besides, if the Entifal was as foul as reported, no Sensual would have borne to keep it within the offices.

"That means the Entifal has been where it is right now for a long time," she said to the greenmak. She liked carrying the beetle on her shoulder now. Sometimes she would jam into its brain and look through its eyes. She did so now, sending it flying high up so she could see the lie of the land. This stunt no longer made her dizzy. The Constellation Palace stood above everything, sprawling and magnificent. Closer by, rooftops of curved tile spread all over the green slopes, all glistening with rain. Windows were alight and inviting. The moisture was making the greenmak's wings heavy. She brought it back to her shoulder.

"The Entifal is hidden '*among* those who would know not to touch it or allow it to be touched.' What does that mean, 'among?'"

The greenmak didn't know. She wondered if Her Highness the Constellation had a secret horde of mercus relics. The woman wasn't a merculyn. But her council had several merculyns on it. If something as powerful as the Entifal existed, wouldn't they have noticed? But not if it was weakly mercusine and highly revulynic. In that case they would have an aversion to it and possibly not even realize it.

She was about to dymense back to the Triumvirate Offices when a new thought occurred to her. "Among those who would know not to touch it.' Doesn't that sound like the people around it *know* it exists? It sure does, little greenmak."

Con knew the sort of folk who orbited the empress. Fools all. If they knew something wasn't to be touched, they'd touch it just to show each other how brave they were.

"I don't think it's in the palace." Even so, she was resigning herself to a thorough search of it. Best to rule it out even though mapping it would take days. Might even take a new greenmak. But there were plenty of those. A false ache made her throat clench up. The cold eye didn't feel attachments. So her regard for her beetle was a lie. She knew that. Again she stopped and sought the reassuring emptiness of the cold eye.

She came out of it an hour later. "Where am I?"

On a street in the rain. And a remarkable merculyn was somewhere out there. Had he been there the whole time? The individual's potential was rather stunning. "Where have you been hiding?" Con said. And then she twisted up her lips. "Now here is quandary, and no mistake. I must find the Entifal. But I must also find that merculyn."

To what end finding the merculyn, though? She couldn't turn one of even modest ability. And then she knew what to do.

She let fly her Revulsion awareness and quickly found the idle hound under his hedge. He sprang up to her command. He had enough mind remaining to sniff out the merculyn. She guided his paws through alleys and lanes and through holes in fences. And when there were no holes, she sprang him over. His reviled haunches were really something.

She set him to tracking the merculyn. It didn't take long for him to find a trio of dark cloaked people walking swiftly along the street. Con went fully into the dog. With his speed she caught up to them easily. Ah, she could feel the mercus coming from them through the dog. That was a fine trick indeed!

The girl. It was *the* girl. Lord Yples had told her to keep watch for a god-child. This was she. Nothing Con could do at the moment unless she wanted to willshift the adults. She was capable of it. But what would she do with the child if she had her? And that much mercus would be dangerous. If the child was awake to her power, she might burn Con just as easily has Con had torched the greenmak that had bitten her.

A solution came to her easily. The hound could track them, tirelessly. And she could track the hound if she put a little marking feat into him. And so she did. The dog got closer and closer to his quarry. The man looked back at him. His face was hideous! But a subtle gleam of mercus came off him. And from the woman too. Not the potential to use it, but as from a relic. Con knew that gleam so well that she knew instantly what it meant.

"They're shadlines, greenmak. What a notion!" And that ugly man was not the girl's father. The girl did not have any of his coloring and nothing of his weird looks. Shadlines didn't marry, as a rule. Revnithan Con had gotten along well enough with the few she'd met, though they were all cagey when it came to their weapons. Only one had allowed her to study his weapon, a club that made him enormously strong but which wasted away his muscles. He was always eating huge platters of food to keep up with the club's demands for energy.

And then suddenly she knew what that ancient scribe had been referring to. "Shadlines would know not to touch the Entifal," she said. "Listen and obey. Ha! And do you know what, greenmak? They have little caches in every city. Sure! There's one right here in Slirya. That's where the Entifal is."

She knew where the cache was. "The Reign of Fools. Ah yes. I should have thought of it first, but I didn't."

Shadlines were dangerous. And even if she weren't a dead-looking Sensual, one does not simply walk into a shadline cache. But she had her little familiar, and the Unanswered moved all things toward necessary ends. Surely Pol would smile upon her. Pol was a lie of course, but something had to stand for luck.

WHEN HER FINGERS closed over the hilt of the Entifal three hours later, it laid claim to her in violent fashion. But the cold eye sustained her through the tribulations of the body. When a shadline woman holding a longsword confronted her, she flashed out with blue fire. The shadline turned to ash and her weapon clanged onto the floor. The ceiling beams above caught fire, and soon the whole building was billowing blue flame and white smoke into the misty night.

She dymensed away to the outskirts of the city, to a little townlet called Burns Bend where she'd lived for three years after her father had drowned. Wintertide Solitude enveloped her. "Look at this, greenmak," she said. "A reviled shadline dagger." It boiled in her mind. Revulsion of enormous magnitude lay within it, yearning to be released. Like one of those fire mountains in the Shudderlins.

"A willful one, aren't you?" she said to it. "I'll have none of that nonsense. You do what I say."

It was a long knife and lacked a scabbard. It had a single edge, shiny and sharp. The spine rather thick. The hilt was a gold disc with a little loop for a knuckle guard. Of all the things in the world to organize into a catalog, weaponry had not attracted her in the slightest. She didn't know if it should be called dagger, dirk, or knife. Surely she could find a book on such things. But that would have to wait. She felt her dog familiar in the far distance, trailing the god-child. Lord Yples would like to know of this. He'd like it better if she came to him with the child in hand.

With the power of the Entifal on her side, Revnithan Con thought the two shadlines rather minor concerns after all. "I shall abduct that child and please Lord Yples, greenmak. Perhaps he will allow me to make a catalog of blade types before Annihilation brings peace to all things."

With this happy thought, she set off after the hound.

42

ANSWERED WITH SWARMLIGHT

ighest Quiv was in Marlow's office when Kila entered. He shot to his feet and bowed at her. Marlow did the same, though more slowly. The papers that had been swiped aside when Mayrie's body had been brought to his desk were still in their random piles on the floor.

"Clean this up," Kila said to him. "It's a disgrace."

Marlow paled and cleared his throat. "I can barely keep your government running as it is, majesty. I have not slept more than an hour in three days. Tidying up is a luxury—"

"Would you prefer I send my Mistress of Wardrobe to do it? She will have this sorted within an hour."

Quiv allowed a tremulous smile to interrupt his usually serious expression. "One in Marlow's station usually has a staff to assist with such tasks. Perhaps if one were less generous with curses, one could keep such people in one's employ."

"One would think so," Kila said. "What happened to Chark?"

Marlow made an irritated face and flipped his hand dismissively. "He was incompetent."

"Eyvin and Nils, please wait outside."

The men obeyed and Marlow's door clicked closed. "I didn't come here to scold you, Marlow. So don't give me that look. I have ill news. Highest Quiv, I hope you are here to report that none of your Way have mysteriously gone missing."

"I wish that were the case. I was just telling Administrator Marlow that several Donse Masters in Sorgan have vanished. Worse, the Way of Ori reports similar attrition in their ranks. The Way of Pol does not respond to my queries. That order is in total disarray following Coin Inlina's death."

Marlow wrinkled his nose. "Ill news all around. And what was your ill news, majesty?"

"Yiothizandra has been abducted from Stallid."

He put a hand over his eyes and sighed. "Another revulyn?"

"I think so. Her sword was still in Stallid. It's an evil blade. Powerful. I doubt she'd abandon it if she had a choice. Her chains were severed cleanly."

"Ill news indeed," Highest Quiv said. "Marlow told me what happened to the girl Mayrie. Do you think the same corrupt Sensual who slew her also took Yiothizandra?"

Kila shrugged. "Did Kinnon Swile search you out, Marlow?"

Marlow blinked a few times. He looked like a man who had just fallen asleep with his eyes open. "Who?"

"Never mind. I order you to go to bed and sleep until you awaken naturally. Then clean this mess up."

"But—"

"I command you as queen to do it." She turned and walked out. Her fell guardsmen moved with her as if part of her own body. Highest Quiv raced to catch up.

"Majesty. One moment if you please. Did you ever think upon the history I discovered? Of Illizshian and her scepter?"

"Henley mentioned it to me. You think she used the swarmlight like the nosg shamans."

"Just so. Do you see why I thought it important?"

"Not particularly. The elnisians and the nosg are cousins of sorts, no? Why shouldn't they both use the swarmlight?"

"It's just—how do I put this? You have also used the swarmlight. You reported that you could use it even with the *vaz'on* blocking you from the mercus. Do you not see the import of this?"

Kila kept walking, heading toward the kitchens. She would stop in on Kinnon and then continue down to the Moonside door. "Obviously. The swarmlight was essential for my escape from Ahl-Mish-Lah. I'm grateful that it worked, else I would be dead and Yioth would have Saiya and the Revulsion would have them both right now."

Quiv performed a shuffling sidestep as he attempted to face her and walk straight at the same time. "But you see, that means the swarmlight did not draw mercus power through you. I dare say it does not use the mercus at all. Not as we understand it."

"Why don't you fetch a skull staff and eat some mushrooms? You'll find out it is very much the mercus. It just comes from elsewhere is all."

"What? What do you mean it comes from 'elsewhere'?"

"Just that. The mercus lies beneath a skim of Revulsion. One must plunge through that to draw the power in. But the swarmlight comes from somewhere else. It's hard to explain. I never thought about it before. But why are we discussing all this? The swarmlight or the mercus, who cares if Illizshian used one or the other an age ago?"

Then she heard herself and simply said, "Oh." Maybe she could use the swarmlight without having to fight through the Revulsion. But that would require two things she didn't have. The first was a skull staff, though her garnet ring had mustered a bit of swarmlight on occasion. The real problem was not having any mimak.

Quiv nodded vigorously as the dawn of understanding lit up her face. "As I tried to explain to Henley, Illizshian had a scepter with six jewels, each pulled from the head of a warden. And before you ask, I don't truly know what a warden is. Likely some sort of guard. But the text I showed Henley was clear. Illizshian's scepter 'answered with swarmlight.'"

"I have a scepter." In fact, she wished she held it now for the calming effect it provided.

"Not the same one, I'm afraid," Quiv said. "I'm quite sure the one in question could be found if we knew where Illizshian was when she died."

Kila did know. She knew from Fallo, who had been in the elnisian queen's private room in Cigil-Tine at the time of her death. She told Quiv this.

"Then you must go there, find the scepter and summon the swarmlight. Perhaps this 'elsewhere' mercus can fend off the Revulsion."

Kila considered it, recalling that she had felt the blackness rising when she'd killed Ahl-Mish-Lah with the swarmlight. She had resisted it though, even with Nax far away at the time. But merely possessing the scepter wouldn't help her if she didn't have the mimak. Her eyes narrowed and she studied Quiv. "You already have a sack of mimak, don't you?"

He blinked a few times. "I know where one might find a few specimens. They are merely mushrooms. Such lore is not solely the secret of the nosg."

She was glad Marlow wasn't there to hear the conversation or he'd be scribbling another item onto his list: *"Find Illizshian's scepter."*

So many things needed finding. She was waiting for Flau-mishtak to find the qiznithan, for Harnzyne to find the dragons of Night. Waiting for Henley to find Whiteflame. And she mustn't forget that she was trying to find Yiothizandra. And Klayne. And Eckso.

Going to Cigil-Tine would be time-consuming in the extreme, even if she used Derslin Wheel portals and vergent passes. Finding Yioth was more urgent, she decided.

"You said Donse Masters were missing in Sorgan, Highest Quiv. I thought the Way of Til had lost its presence there. The cathedral's in ruins, I've heard."

The change in subject perplexed him enough that he stopped walking. Kila kept going, so he had to shuffle to catch up. "The cathedral there is in need of some repair, it's true. A bit of flooding. But there is no place where the Way of Til is not present. The wealthy value our counsel. Many noble houses in Upper Sorgan have House Donse Masters in their employ."

If the qiznithan was abducting and turning merculyns in Sorgan, then perhaps Yioth had been taken there for the same purpose. "Highest, have you ever been to Sorgan?"

"I have."

"Excellent, then you can dymense me there."

"I—I have not yet dymensed anywhere of my own power, Your Majesty. I believe I have the bolts correct, but I've been too fearful of reappearing with my feet embedded in stone. Or worse."

That's how Quinn had lost her hand, thanks to Kila. And Quiv had seen it. "Reasonable fears. Still, we are going."

"But if the Revulsion is strong there, perhaps having the swarmlight at your disposal would be advantageous. If Cigil-Tine is—"

She turned to Eyvin. "Put away your armor and spears. Common swords and daggers only, dress like merchants. We leave for Sorgan in a quarter of an hour from the Interior Palace."

Quiv's usual calm face had gone white. "How long will we be gone? I have people coming to Starside soon to confirm me as Highest of Highests."

"You can dymense back instantly if you wish. Just get me there."

43

KILL IT

Whiteflame poured strength into Henley's arm, into his whole body in fact. He had never felt so powerful, so ready for combat. So it was easy to ignore the new worry jangling in his mind. He knew the blade to be shadline, for the binding had been unmistakable, as had the explosion of its name into his mind.

That made him a shadline, he supposed. Did that mean he could hear the subtle call of the force of destiny? If so, he had no idea what it was saying. The little tone of worry didn't dissuade him from hunting the qiznithor. That thing had to be destroyed.

The fog was pressing toward the temple, pulled by the extraordinary brilliance of the Motherlight. Only the haze that swept past him noticed his enormous power. It slowed and spun in curls around him and Ryde, but it did not keep pace with him as he distanced himself from the temple.

The ground trembled from distant concussions. The qiznithor was back to smashing the Divide.

Why doesn't the Motherlight draw it?

Huff didn't have an answer for this.

Another, more disturbing concern now worked its way into his mind. How had the qiznithor come here in the first place? Flaumishtak hadn't mentioned anything about it. Unless perhaps it was a revenant from the elnisian age, just like the elnisian reviled. *"Moonside stirs,* Ell had written. Maybe the qiznithan's arrival in the outside world had stirred this qiznithor from its slumber. Or maybe Kila's use of the Revulsion had done so.

Moonside still stirred. The entire mass of cloud cover had begun to spin, centered around the temple. Sleet started again, ticking sharply on Brother Ryde's breastplate. The wind cut across their path, but the fog moved without regard to it, often directly counter to it. This made for a disconcerting effect that gave Henley bouts of vertigo.

Since leaving the temple, the concussions from the Divide had grown more frequent. Louder.

He and Ryde worked their way north. Occasional blurs at the edges of their vision made them turn and ready their weapons. They were met with swirling fog, but no attacks. It was full night, and even with the glow of Whiteflame the inky fog remained too thick to show much beyond ten paces. The garnet-red lightning arced very high up.

The street was wide, bordered by homes and shops of familiar design, though these did not have the human touch. The fascia of the buildings might have been pleasing in other circumstances, proportioned as they were for beauty as much as practicality. But the hollow doors and windows gave them a stricken, skeletal aspect. Henley could not shake the feeling of thousands of eyes peering at him from within those black openings.

Fallo would say something funny right about now, Huff.

Like what?

He'd sing a song or something. His mind rifled through his memory, searching for an appropriate verse. The only thing he could think of was a sailor's shanty called "Wild Winds."

> "We sail upon the merry seas,
> With dolphins as our guides
> Wild winds, wild winds,
> Lumne lift the tides.
> An island full o' merry girls,
> Appears when day goes down
> Wild winds, wild winds,
> Ori lift your gown."

Whiteflame continued to bolster his determination, but the anxious bell in his mind clashed with the tune. He could muster no jollity at all. Brother Ryde did not respond to the verses with smile or frown.

You don't understand Fallo's humor, Huff sent. *You need a song that relates closely to our situation but which is also inappropriate. Yours was only inappropriate, which made it offensive rather than diverting.*

"It's gone quiet," Brother Ryde said.

"Even the thunder has stopped," Henley said.

It was a heavy quiet.

It hunts you, Huff sent.

Good. Then we can get this over with.

They passed a statue of Til so tall that Henley was surprised its head hadn't poked above the clouds when viewed from the Divide. The legs to the knees were visible from the ground, the rest was lost in fog. Only the First Race lettering around the dais told him who the statue depicted.

And here was another temple. This one occupied a circle in the middle of the street, which made a full circuit around before continuing downslope. Henley sent a sphere of mercus light inside. A placard at the base of the central dais read 'Kil.'

He stopped and considered what he was seeing. "An actual temple of Kil." Odder still was the watery sensation inside of him, the realization that he had not only met Kil, he had held the god in his arms. Curious, he went inside, studied the god's feet and knees, then came out again. He sat on the steps and dug in his pack for some well-earned food. "Sit, Brother Ryde. You're making me antsy. Eat something."

"My duty is to guard you."

"You must eat and sleep at some point."

"You do not understand the Fell Guard, Henley Mast. What fills my belly when I have no bread? Duty."

"But you do have bread. It's right here." Henley offered half his loaf. The man eyed it. "I won't tell Brother Commander Docit that you ate some bread."

"But I would know. Besides, I do not need it. Duty sustains me. You will see." There was nothing plaintive or even argumentative in the man's voice. He was stating facts. Nothing more.

"I saw Brother Hannik before he was overwhelmed," Henley said. "He was all aglow. I wasn't open to the mercus so I couldn't feel the feat. I didn't know any of you were merculyns."

"We are not. Our merculyn brothers do not enter the Fell Guard."

"Then what happened to Hannik?"

"Some secrets are for the brotherhood alone." And that was all he was going to say on the topic, Henley discovered, for he ceased to respond to any questions related to Hannik's demise.

"Are your weapons shadline?"

"No. But they are not mundane. Our merculyn brothers see to that."

Henley had not inspected their spears and swords, hadn't noticed any mercusine hum that usually came from such relics.

He sent his awareness into the man's spear, listening and feeling for wards or imbued qualities. But such were either cleverly hidden or did not require sustaining bolts of mercus to persist.

"I did not appreciate the Fell Guard enough," Henley said. "I had thought I would be burdened by you, but you both saved me from death many times over. I am grateful."

"Do you wish to shame me?" Ryde asked.

"The opposite. I wish to thank you!" Kil's eyes in a cup, these men were thick-skulled sometimes. Henley munched on his bread and gave Huff some cheese. The nasty grime that coated every surface here no longer disgusted him, though he did his best to keep it off the food. In truth, he thought he could lie here and nap if that tiny, dissonant worry would just be still.

"Jingle jangle jingle jangle," he complained. "I have never felt stronger. So why do my breastbone and skull feel so abuzz with warnings?"

Brother Ryde turned his head slightly. "You said it was a shadline blade, no?"

Henley's head came up.

Shadline . . .

A pestering notion that something was amiss . . .

He hoisted himself to his feet, ventured away from the temple a few paces, holding the blade up like a torch and looking all around. What was it? It nagged at him, like when his father had sent him to the market and he'd failed to write down a list. There was always the one item he'd forget. Apples, or maybe an atlen egg. Maybe a book his father wanted from Dellis Quia over on merchant row.

He looked at Whiteflame, glow attenuated but still brilliant. Looked back to the temple of Kil where Huff sat. To Ryde who had accompanied him to this spot, and who stood ready to deal death in any direction.

Closing his eyes, he listened. Heard the waft and rustle of

wind in his ears, the flap of his cloak. Heard the rumble of thunder from above and felt the trembles it caused in the street.

It came to him as a thin, reedy cry. A human voice, full of pain and fear. A child's voice. North. "This way." He moved quickly. Whiteflame pulsed strength into his arms and legs. Ryde kept up with him. Huff trailed.

A long cry. Had there been a word in it? Help, perhaps. Help me.

Help me. Yes. A child was calling.

But there could be no child in Moonside.

"Do you hear that?" he asked Ryde.

"A girl calling for help. I mistrust it. This place is full of deceit."

True enough. But it was only right that he aid someone in need. Someone who could not be there. The contradiction blurred his thoughts.

"Help!" Ragged and full of agony.

"There!" Ryde said, pointing his spear. A small figure lay upon the street, hand outstretched.

Reviled! Huff warned.

Maybe so, but not a danger. It was a child, one arm and one leg bent at impossible angles, jagged bone protruding from shin, thigh, and forearm. Half the head was stove in, an eye dangling from its socket. The girl's face lifted, a half grin stretching the undamaged side. The other half of her face, jaw and lips smashed into a mass of shattered flesh and bone.

He recognized her. "Mayrie?"

She gripped the cobblestone with her good hand and dragged her broken body toward him. Her neck was sliced open at the front, a black gaping maw from which dangles of glistening black tendrils oozed.

"Kila pulled her from the crowd in Dunne Medow Plaza," Henley said.

"I was there," Ryde answered. "How did she come to be here?"

Even Whiteflame's bold certainty could not tamp down Henley's alarm. The girl had been in the Citadel when Henley left. He didn't know where she was being housed, only that she had been moved out of the Privileged Suites at Henley's insistence. "She hoarded bread and taught Saiya how to curse."

It is reviled. Kill it. Huff's insistence brought Henley out of his dark thoughts enough that he brought Whiteflame down to slash Mayrie's head from her shoulders. The body vanished in a drift of ash.

"Something is very wrong in Starside," Henley said. "If Mayrie is reviled and she is here . . ." But he couldn't finish the thought. He didn't know what it meant, except that it wasn't good. Kila's bond still remained, though he couldn't feel more of her than that. Surely it would vanish if she had been turned.

He recalled how proud Kila had been to have pulled the girl from the crowd. How she'd glowed at the prospect of bringing this early incarnation of herself out of a life of poverty and thieving. He'd refrained from pointing out that money and food alone would not retrain the girl's habits. Nor that lifting one soul out of Cheapsgate did nothing for those who remained.

He couldn't imagine this would have happened had Mayrie remained in Cheapsgate. Kila's generosity had killed her. He ached to be with Kila now.

He looked at the sword, glowing and filling him with strength. Three miles south, the throb of the Motherlight shone forth, luring the Revulsion close even as it repelled it.

"But not all of it," he said, realization now sending dozens of thoughts tumbling through his head at once. "I came to strengthen a trap," he said. "And instead I stepped into one." The emboldening power of Whiteflame had blinded him to the obvious. He'd been so intent on hunting down the qiznithor, he'd never considered the ground of the eventual battle.

Shadline instincts had been warning him, but he hadn't understood. "A reviled doesn't call for help."

Knowing one was in a trap and seeing the jaws closing were two different things. And for Henley, it made no more difference than it would for a fox; the click of the springlock leaves no time to leap away.

The ground trembled beneath his feet. Not resonating from thunder, but shaking of its own volition. Dust lifted up, obscuring the road. Huff raced to join him. The fell guardsman danced to remain ready for attack, keeping his balance upon the rolling ground.

The road dropped from beneath their feet. Henley fell, stomach lifting to his throat. Huff howled.

And then there was darkness straight above, pierced by two enormous eyes of garnet lightning.

44

A BUNCH OF MEEK MAIDENS

The darkness of a Derslin Wheel cavern no longer spooked the remaining thirty members of the *kilenishza*. These hardened merculyns marched in two columns behind Spinster Moirina Fiolt, circling their power and offering their combined mercus entirely to her.

She was a proud woman, prouder still to have survived this long. From Wheel to Wheel they'd traveled, occasionally opening a portal upon unfamiliar ground. But always searching, knowing that one day they would come out into Starside.

This was that day. Her scout circle had returned with confirmation just an hour ago. "And the Sigh girl?" she asked former Voluptuary Tritto, a much thinner man than he'd been a month ago.

"I felt her, I think. Far upslope. Gristenside. Perhaps the Citadel itself. A powerful merculyn just as you described." He paused a moment, worry crossing his face in the light of her mercus sphere. "But the city is troubled. We did not linger to ask questions, but I feel a great dissatisfaction in the air."

And why wouldn't the citizens of this great city be dissatisfied? Their so-called Enlightened ruler allowing Sigh to fling dark mercus powers here and there, rather than yoking her to a promise-binding. That had been the mission of Voluptuary Minn. But that woman was dead, killed in a nosg attack in the Derslin Wheel of Sorgan.

Moirina had led the *kilenishza* since then, the survivors of that first battle now fit in body and mind, trained in the killing feats required by war. In their wanderings they had found other encampments of nosg in Wheel caverns. All dead now. Moirina's fighting force of merculyns was a third its original number, but ten times as deadly. She did not fear an uneasy city, nor a delinquent monarch, and she certainly did not fear the girl-child merculyn Kila Sigh. Highest of Kil? Pah! The very notion made her want to spit.

They came out of the cavern into the abandoned cellar of an old jewelry shop in Upper Terriside. A clean and comfortable part of the city just below Dunne Medow Plaza. They would leave in groups of four, making sure that no one saw them exiting the shop. "Meet at Pol's Well," she instructed them. "North of the plaza two miles."

Upon her arrival at the austere center of the Way of Pol in Starside, she was displeased to discover the local Coin to be a dull-eyed woman of eighty years, bent from innumerable hours hunched over books. The Way of Pol should be training for battle, not reading useless prophecies. "And where is Coin Inlina?" she asked the woman. "She knew my mission. She will want a report."

"Inlina's dead," the woman said. "Isn't that right Spin Fria?" she asked the young woman who attended her.

"It is, Coin. She died on Winternight."

Inlina dead! For the first time in a month, Moirina was struck wordless. The Medallion herself, dead. Stubborn old crow, Moirina thought, how could she die? But apparently she'd been ill.

Perhaps it was for the best. Moirina wasn't content to subject herself to anyone's authority now. Her *kilenishza* was not of any Way, not truly. Its members were devoted only to defeating evil, wherever it was found.

"What have you done to apprehend the Sigh girl?" she asked the Coin.

The woman merely blinked at her and shrugged. "What can be done? She's the monarch now."

"What? Impossible." Moirina's fingers went to her medallion. She clenched it in her fist for comfort, muscles rippling under the silver cuffs encircling her upper arms. "She overthrew Ell LiMinluit and you just stood by?"

"I never said anything about overthrowing. Sigh was named heir." The Coin fetched a letter from her desk and thrust it at Moirina. "The Radiancies supported her, though many grumbled under their breath to do so."

"The situation is more dire than I had imagined."

"I doubt that. For Sigh has the child Kil in her possession. Treats it as her own, though I hear the babe has grown freakishly in the time she's been in the Citadel. Coin Inlina implored Sigh to kill the babe, but she was ignored."

"Of course she was. But I ask again, what are you *doing* about it?"

"I have spun hundreds of times. Pol does not guide me. We should discuss the merculyns you brought with you. I understand that many are Sensuals. They will have to go across town to the Baths. You understand."

"They will do no such thing. Who has risen to Medallion now that Inlina is gone?"

At this the old Coin sighed and flapped a spotted hand, annoyed by the question as much as the answer. "No consensus. Too many seek the position for themselves and all claim unambiguous spins in their favor. But we cannot have a dozen Medallions can we? Inlina's grip on the Way was strong, but now the fissures she held fast with her will have widened. In fact, they have reached our foundation and I fear the Way will split. Perhaps into a dozen factions."

"Did it ever occur to you to ally with Voluptuary Sinlop and join your merculyns? My *kilenishza* is mighty. With your combined forces, you could storm the Citadel and willshift the Sigh girl into shackles. Kill the child god and be done with it."

The Coin simply looked at her, a vacant expression in her face as if she hadn't understood a word. "Voluptuary Sinlop is dead. A Sensual called Taht has been raised, though I suspect she seized the title. That lot are a bunch of meek maidens."

Moirina didn't know Sensual Taht, but she respected a bold move. It was time to make one of her own. "You don't look well, Coin. Terribly pale. Perhaps you should lie down."

"I feel fine. You'll be lucky to feel as spry as I am when you're my age. And I don't like your tone. You have no call to question my leadership. None at all."

"Are you sure you're well? Should I get you a drink of water? Spin Fria. Fetch the Coin some water. I do not think she's well at all."

The Spinster dashed from the room.

The Coin frowned at Morina. "What's all this? I told you I'm fine. What are you playing at?"

The old woman didn't get any farther than that. Moirina was always source-tapped to a circle within her *kilenishza*, her power tripled by Voluptuary Minn's gold choker. Several of her more powerful merculyns also wore relics of their own, and thus the mercus available to her was considerable indeed. The willshift she crafted was not subtle. It didn't need to be. But it was fast.

She took over the woman's body entirely. And then she employed a technique perfected against the nosg. She stopped the Coin's heart from beating. "Coin? What ails you? Oh dear! Spin Fria, come quickly! I'm not schooled in healing."

The Spinster swept in, saw the white-faced Coin tipping in her chair. Dropping the cup of water she'd fetched, she lunged to catch the aged Coin as she flopped over. Moirina's willshift was already released. Fria apparently hadn't noticed it. And no wonder. She was very weak in the mercus, hardly worth adding to the *kilenishza*. But into the *kilenishza* she would go. And she would serve up what little power she could.

Every merculyn in Pol's Well would serve the will of High Medallion Moirina Fiolt.

45

RESCUED OR KIDNAPPED?

They pretended to be a family. Illy looked too old to pass for their child, so she had become Quinn's niece. And so it was that Fallo and Quinn *PiTorro* took a room in The Wine Cask, a massive stone inn dominating the central square of a modest Trayean town called Vanish's Gold. Illy was nearly of an age with Fallo now. She kept her head hooded as they climbed the winding steps to the third floor.

Fallo kept looking over his shoulder, convinced that too many eyes had marked them as they'd crossed the common room. Perhaps it was a shadline whisper, but more probably just part of his never ceasing worry. They had been dropping too much coin of late, enough that people might talk. But camping out in the open with Illy had proven too dangerous.

Once ensconced in their warm and comfortable quarters, Illy flopped onto her bed and cuddled with Lop. The two had become inseparable, to the point that Fallo had grown envious. Whether it was Illy's godblooded nature or her liberal generosity with her meals that bonded the pair, Fallo couldn't say.

Quinn shed her pack and splashed her face with water from

the basin. She had dark bags under her eyes. She touched her hair. "Gray? I think I see a gray hair. I'm too young!"

She was, in fact, a bit young to be going gray. But the times were what they were. The Graying Times, Fallo mused. That would be a good title for a tale or song about this strange age. "The housemother is sending up dinner soon," he said. "Don't give the maid so much as a copper plug. I've already paid for it and a little extra for the girl. I'm going out."

"Where?" Illy asked in a bored tone. "Can I go?"

Her speech had improved with extraordinary speed during their time together. She seemed to have gained the vocabulary of one tutored in the classics, and the argumentative reasoning of a law-speaker. Fallo had no intention of getting swallowed into one of her circular debates. "You may not go. Don't ask why."

He slipped out before she could start in. What was he going to tell her, anyway? That she was Ori reborn and that a force called the Revulsion wanted to corrupt her and use her power? Fallo didn't even understand it, having never felt the Revulsion. Not directly, anyway. But he'd never forget the dead-eyed men who had burst into their camp three nights ago.

There had been five of them, dressed as citymen, their cloaks and trousers muddy and torn. Lop had felt them coming, had warned Fallo awake. Telt had done little against them. Skeye delivered a good shock, which dropped them quickly. Only, Fallo had to endure a shock of his own each time. Shinane, good ol' Bone Chill, had told well enough, freezing them into immobility. It took a bit too long, though.

Quinn had stabbed and stabbed with Black, seemingly with impunity, for these reviled walkers did not notice her at all. But Black had not slowed them until she had taken out their eyes. They'd left one alive, if such horrors could be said to be alive at all. They circled it as it twisted and lashed about with its dagger.

Quinn disarmed it, and they bound it up in rope. But even under threat of fire, it would not respond. It struggled, face slack, emotionless. Its gouged out eye sockets turned this way and that, seeking, until finally stopping to point at Illy. And then in a reedy voice it did speak: *"I see you. I see you with the cold eye!"*

And then there was the hound. It had followed them from Slirya. Fallo thought it had given up after they came through the vergent pass. But a few days later it returned, keeping pace but staying far enough back that they couldn't catch it. It was Lop who warned that it was reviled. Fallo had always liked dogs, so he pitied the creature as much as he hated it. During the reviled attack it had come into the fray, bit Illy's hem and tried to drag her away. He still regretted having to kill it.

Down in the common room the evening crowd was growing. Not many folks on the roads during winter, so most had to be locals from Vanish's Gold. They huddled over their drinks and platters, casting suspicious glances at him. Talk was all about the bands of mad killers roving along the road up from Traye. The sickness. Everyone feared the sickness that turned father against son and wife against babe. Just a wound from a knife or sword or pitchfork would do it. Fallo kept his face down and headed outside, trying to let his mind relax enough to feel any tickles courtesy of the force of destiny.

The road was dirt, rutted and bleak. Stone houses bordered it, with a few shops and taverns sprinkled in. A broad, empty commons stood to the south, bordered by the Vanish-Let river which tumbled out of the Shanala Mountains to the west.

The city of Traye lay far to the southeast, where the Vanish-Let emptied into the Iopsean Sea. Fallo had never been to Traye, and from rumors he'd been hearing had no desire to go. He went onto the green, enjoying the bracing wind. The river was clearly at a low mark, the bed wide and rocky, with only a shallow stream tracing the bottom.

For the hundredth time in ten days he cleared his mind, closed his eyes, and listened. The wind raised a low roar in his ears. "We found one of them," he said. "Now show me were to find Pol or Til."

He wondered if keeping Illy's true identity secret from Cloak Szill had been a mistake. She was a fate's-piece after all. And shadlines were oathbound to share such things with every shadline they crossed paths with.

But no. Telling her would have increased the risk of discovery. There were bad shadlines, after all. Varl Akton, for instance, the Starsider who had treshed Quinn. And then there was Mack'Ti and Cinnon, two shadline morons in the pocket of a Stallidian called Klayne Itopolo. Surely there were more such scoundrels.

He shivered, recalling a reviled man's horrid eyes. Kil's tears, those men had been strange. *I see you! I see you with the cold eye!* Fallo made fists and knocked his knuckles together. You're supposed to be quieting your mind, he told himself, not riling it up. He tried again, standing in the wind for a long spell, noticing every thought, every breath, waiting for that little push or pull that would tell him what to do. Nothing.

He returned to the inn and found Illy and Quinn eating their dinner. Lop was tucking into Fallo's plate, and upon seeing him come in, ran off with a chicken leg. Fallo sat down to a half-eaten plate of peas, potatoes, and chicken bones. "Was there a sauce on this? Lop, did you lick off all the sauce?"

Illy giggled.

You devil! Fallo sent. *I was hungry!*

So was I.

Fallo had instituted Cloak Einlin's travel rules for Lop, meaning the cat had to hunt for her dinner while they were on the road. Somehow Lop had remained plump as ever and had never brought prey back to camp. Fallo eyed Illy, suspecting she'd been sneaking food to her at every opportunity.

"Hear anything?" Quinn asked.

"No. You?"

"No."

They had not come to Vanish's Gold by choice. The vergent pass they'd taken on the outskirts of Slirya had delivered them half-way between Traye and this town, near a ruined monastery of Til. It had been full of the reviled.

"They will find us here," Quinn said. "If not tonight, then in the morning. The town will be wiped out. Or turned."

"We'll leave at middlenight. Sneak out."

"And go where? There's only—"

The door rattled. Fallo had locked it.

A soft knock. A whisper. Then louder, "Shadlines, please."

Quinn sent Illy into the closet, then drew Black and faded into the shadows. Fallo cracked the door, Telt in one hand. A man in brown robes stood before him, hands crossed inside his cuffs.

"Go away, Donse Master. I don't have coin to spare for your collection."

"I'm not a Donse Master. Please. I can help you."

"We don't need help."

"You will if the reviled find you here. Truth be."

Alarm lifted Fallo's hackles. "Who are you?"

"Just let me in. The merculyn girl needs my help." When Fallo refused to open the door, the man sighed heavily. "Surely you understand how powerful she is. Any merculyn worth the name will feel her potential. You cannot hide her unless she is well masked. I can help."

"You said you weren't a Donse Master."

"Not every merculyn is a Kil-damned Donse Master!"

Fallo liked him a bit better for the cursing, but his sense of danger did not lessen. He grabbed a fistful of robes and yanked the man in. With a final scan of the corridor he closed and locked the door.

The man reminded Fallo a bit of Dunne Marlow: middle years, paunchy, with salt and pepper whiskers. He was bald, but wore an odd round hat with a stem protruding from the top. It reminded Fallo of an acorn cap. The robes were fine, but the hem was marred with road filth. His keen eyes took in the room before locking onto the closet door. "Come out, child. I won't hurt you."

When Quinn suddenly appeared before him, he gripped his chest. "Til protect me! Where did you come from?"

He was forced to conduct the interview again as Quinn peppered him with questions. These he handled with poorly hidden impatience, as one unaccustomed to explaining himself. "My name is Nefler Ernist. I am a merculyn and scholar. I am also a former member of the Counsel of Authority in Traye. Surely you've heard of that."

"Yes," Quinn said. "It makes you a politician. Either you were an incompetent one, and so lost your position, or you were so wearied by the job you chose to give it up. Which means you're weak. So which is it, are you weak or incompetent?"

"I served for twenty years," he said. "And I did so with honor. But my hard-earned wisdom—which I am not shy of saying I possess—was no longer welcomed among the younger counselors. I chose to retire to my country home and write of what I've learned for the benefit of those who come after me. Truth be, they won't bother to read it. Every man believes every other man a fool. Now, may I please see the girl?"

He needn't have asked, for Illy emerged from the closet on her own. Lop trailed out after her, which startled the man into once again clutching his chest. Fallo fetched a chair for him, which he accepted gratefully. "Til's light undimmed! I had not thought to ever see a cat again. Gone they are from Traye, truth be. Every last one, captured, caged, and sent off to Starside for some wickedness by the Way of Til."

That had been the Hargothe's policy, Fallo knew. The vile old seer had wished to bond with a felnithel to enhance his powers. The Way of Til must be powerful in Traye. And that presented a problem. "How were you allowed to study the mercus without being made a Tilsboy?"

"I *was* one. And then I got out. Bought my way out, truth be." He bent forward to look at Illy, who returned the stare with equal intensity. "Well aren't you a remarkable young lady," he said, more to himself than to her. "Such power. Stunned am I. Stunned, truth be. Child, do you feel the mercusine?"

It was not something Fallo and Quinn wanted brought up. Illy was easy to travel with, but they didn't want her awakening to her power when neither of them could offer the slightest guidance in its use.

Illy tilted her head, as if listening. "I don't think so. What is it?"

Nefler caught Quinn violently shaking her head. "Ah, it's just nothing. Come closer." He extended his thumb and pressed it to her forehead. Closing his eyes, he muttered under his breath. Quinn made to grab him, but Fallo motioned her back. Lop was sitting near Illy's feet, watching with curiosity but without alarm. Cats knew when someone meant them harm. And he doubted Lop would let harm come to Illy, either.

Illy's eyes widened momentarily, then rolled up to show only the whites. She slumped backward into Quinn's grasp. "What did you do to her?" she demanded, easing her to the floor.

"I masked her mercus and created a sustaining feat drawing from her own power. Her faint is merely a reaction to the sudden absence. She needs sleep and food." He licked his lips and studied her, thoughts churning. "Truth be, she is odd. I have known many merculyns, have studied the workings of their minds. Hers is . . . fascinating. Were she older I might think she is this Kila Sigh I keep hearing of."

Fallo moved to the window overlooking the street. It was starting to grow dark. It troubled him that this man had tracked them without notice. *Lop, did you know he was following us?*

No. Lop had snuggled next to Illy, who was muttering in confusion as she began to wake. He noticed Quinn's focus on the girl, the gentleness with which she stroked her hair. Perhaps they'd both been too distracted by her. This was Ori, after all. Reborn goddess of love and healing and compassion, among other things. Grief, too, was her domain. It shouldn't have been a surprise that she attracted a merculyn, he supposed.

Nefler Ernist was looking at him, calculating. Fallo knew what he was noticing. Had noticed from the start, and which had likely intrigued him more. Two young shadlines with a girl who was much too old to be their daughter, but who lacked enough resemblance to be a sibling. And the man had noticed they were pursued by reviled.

"My guess is that she's an heiress. From a wealthy family, perhaps. Royalty possibly," the man mused softly. "Rescued or kidnapped? But I know the shadline order to be mostly noble, though truth be any of you will do what is necessary if you deem it so." He was watching Fallo's face as he spoke, looking for a reaction. Fallo gave him none. And he wasn't about to spill Illy's secret to a stranger.

Masking Illy from the mercus would help hide her from the reviled, he hoped. But if she was to fulfill her destiny, she'd eventually have to embrace her power. There were lots of merculyns in the world. He trusted very few of them. Since Nefler Ernist had installed the mask, he must be kept close to take it down if the need arose.

The decision settled over him easily. Now he needed to discuss it with Quinn. He took her aside.

"What do you feel of this man?" he asked.

"I don't like the looks of him."

"That doesn't mean he is untrustworthy. Look at me, for instance. I wouldn't leave a puppy alone with me if I didn't know me."

She gave a short, humorless laugh. She sighed and shrugged. "We can't let him leave her masked forever."

"We'll take him with us?" He nodded slowly, seeking her agreement. She gave it, reluctantly.

"You wish to join us, Nefler Ernist?" he asked.

"I do."

"We leave at middlenight. Be ready."

46

THE WELL IS ANGRY

The reliquary of Til in Sorgan was crowded with shamans and revulyns. Yples stood at the turning table, now smeared with human excretions and blood. Three merculyns had resisted so long they had died before turning. A fourth had cut her wrists so deeply upon the shackles that she'd bled to death.

"This is the last?" he asked Revulyn Riley, eyeing an elderly revulyn just turned. She stood naked before him, upright and clear of eye.

"Yes, Lord Yples."

"So few? I had expected at least fifty more."

"A great many Sensuals and Spinsters left Sorgan prior to your efforts here. Led away by the Voluptuary of Garden Island. She was amassing a great force of merculyns to pursue Kila Sigh."

"To kill her?"

"Nay. To promise-bind her. Limit her mercus to healing feats. Furthermore to make her a puppet of the Voluptuary who wished to guide her through Dem-Kisk."

The urgent echoes of this last word resounded in Yples's

brain. Ah yes, the prophesied calamity. The qiznithan held it in total disdain. The nonsense ramblings of some forgotten elnisian drunkard. Dem-Kisk. "Red grass" in the lumbering language of men. It meant nothing.

"They were going to Wantin next," Revulyn Zhoe said from the back ranks of the assemblage. "They were going to all of the Baths and Wells to conscript merculyns into their army."

"Where is Revnithan Soth? Has she returned with the child?"

"No, Lord Yples," Riley said. "Neither has revulyn Devin returned."

"Starside," Yples said, feeling again the disturbance of Revulsion from that direction. Perhaps it was due to this army of merculyns. "Turn all who live in Sorgan, Revulyn Riley. Make every man, woman, and child reviled. I go to Starside to see what hinders Revnithan Soth."

He dymensed to Starside, coming out in the Blasted Quarter, which he had thought was abandoned. But his appearance amongst a throng of people in the midst of a midday market didn't startle him as much as it did a woman he had nearly destroyed by rematerializing inside her. That would have drawn all manner of wrong attention. As it was, she squawked and staggered away, gripping her child by the hand.

He glowered at her, putting on what he hoped was a look of indignation. "Do watch where you're walking, ma'am." He felt nothing save annoyance at Yples's incomplete knowledge of Starside. The Blasted Quarter wasn't abandoned at all. It buzzed with activity. This spot had once been a square amidst forlorn and empty buildings. Now it was part of a wide street, with newly constructed homes marching a half mile due west. The folk were dressed cleanly, with bright faces.

The woman muttered apologies and scurried off with her crying whelp in tow. "May we be ready soon," she said. Some sort of formal parting, he supposed. He hadn't come here to study those who would soon be reviled. He had come here to find Soth and investigate for himself the source of the Revulsion's rumblings. But he stopped midstride at the sight of an enormous flag flying over a stubby tower. It depicted a crown with three prongs thrusting up. Each prong a spear. It was the ancient insignia of the Way of Kil. But this flag had a new detail, for to each side of this crown spread raven's wings.

He stopped a man passing by. "What do the raven wings signify?" he asked, pointing to the banner.

"You must be from away," he said. "She has taken the Raven Throne, friend. May we be ready soon." He marched off, whistling.

Yples called after him: "Who is she?"

"Our stern mother, of course. Kila Sigh. May we be ready soon."

So Kila Sigh had taken Starside. Nothing Yples knew about the girl spoke to whether this was expected or not. Clearly she had caught hold of these people. He sensed a strong number of merculyns around him. No one in sight wore the traditional garb of the Ways. Except that man coming out of the tower. He wore a tan tunic over trousers and a black cloak belted in tight around his midsection. His staff was a spear.

No wonder the Voluptuary of Garden Island had sought to yoke the girl with a promise-binding. She was building both a Way *and* a territorial empire. Perhaps Yples had underestimated her.

He turned away from this scene. It was irrelevant. All would succumb, all would be awakened, and all would be released to the Unanswered.

Now, where was Revnithan Soth? He slipped to an untraveled byway of the quarter and sank into the Revulsion. The storm of activity he'd noticed when far to the north was a riot in his head here. But something obstructed it, muted it, even this close. Like standing at the edge of a conflagration, smelling smoke, but unable to see the flames.

Perhaps it came more loudly from the south. He wandered that direction until he came into Upper Terriside. The Revulsion storm was the same here, loud yet muted. Again he sank into the Revulsion. Forming subtle bolts he spoke: "Soth."

He felt her. To the west. Yples's face was known in Starside, so he pulled his hood up to shadow his features. Following this feeling of Soth he came to a tower that Yples knew as Pol's Well, the center of the Way of Pol in Starside. The Well's door was open to all, a rather unusual circumstance in Yples's experience. As he probed deeper into the tower, he noted the extraordinarily large number of merculyns present. They stood in small groups here and there, some meditating around the pit of the well itself. His search continued. A question here, a bit of eavesdropping there, and he soon discovered that the army of merculyns collected by the Voluptuary had recently come here. With so many new to this place, he did not draw any notice at all. His lack of mercus made him beneath their concerns anyway.

For that very reason, neither was Spinster Soth considered to be important. Nobody cared where she was or what she was doing, as long as she wasn't in the way of the so-called *kilenishza*. He found her secluded in a deep level of the sub basements. An area where newly inducted devotees were housed.

She sat in apparent meditation, gripping her medallion and seated on the edge of a cot. Her eyes opened at his entrance.

"You have failed, Revnithan Soth."

"I thought I had the child in my grasp, but I was misled. A decoy."

"Where is Devin?"

"He is hidden in the Citadel awaiting her return."

"Devin is too weak to feel her unless she is under his foot. And his face will be known to Kila Sigh."

"She has gone from Starside."

"Did she take the child with her?"

"I believe it to be so, Lord Yples. I was loathe to abandon the search, for I know turning Kil to be your great objective."

Yples turned away from her to face in the direction of the riot upon the Revulsion. "What is that? It is a tumult, yet I cannot place it."

"I feel it too. I think—"

Yples looked back at her. Soth's face betrayed nothing. Yet she hesitated. "Speak, Soth."

"I think it is in Moonside."

The qiznithan considered this, drawing upon all that Yples had known of the lost city beyond the Divide. But Yples hadn't known more than folk tales and drunkards' speculations. He'd believed some great sin had despoiled Moonside, causing the elnisians to wall it off. But his thoughts and memories were so burdened with the Way of Til's ludicrous rhetoric about sin and evil that they were useless. "There is no way into Moonside," he said.

Soth stood. "There was a moment, very briefly, when I thought I felt a surge of the mercusine in the Citadel. This is not unusual, for Kila Sigh and her consort are both powerful merculyns. They commit feats every day. But this was different, for the Revulsion seemed to answer it. Just for a scant moment. It was like a door opening upon a busy street, letting in the noise of the city. Just as quickly it was shut off, and there was quiet. Shortly after, the Revulsion began to stir up great waves. It pulls at me still, Lord Yples. Even Devin feels it. Moonside stirs."

Whatever had disturbed Moonside had also awakened an unsuspected revulynic strength there. Such would be invaluable in the war to come. Even the Divide, warded as it was, could not stand against a fully awakened and thinking Revulsion. If Yples could break through it . . .

But Yples's first task was to find the god-child. To Kil, in the fullness of her powers, the Divide would be like a tower of sand before ocean waves. Soth could serve two purposes. But not here in this hive of unturned merculyns.

"Revnithan Soth. What you compared to a door opening and swiftly closing in the Citadel may indeed have been a door into Moonside. While you lie in wait against Kil's return, you will search for such a door. I will show you how to divert a mind in case your presence sparks comment or alarm. But be wary, such feats will not serve well against merculyns of much power."

"It will be as you command," she said. He pressed a hand to her forehead and slammed knowledge of the new feat into her mind. She stood and dymensed.

Yples inhaled deeply of the Revulsion black she left behind. His mind thusly refreshed, he turned once again to the problem of finding the god-child. He couldn't simply wait for Kil to return to the Citadel. If he could come close enough to the child, he would feel her power. In fact, he believed he would feel it even from here were she still in Starside.

He worked his way up through the basements and through the bustling corridors of Pol's Well. He must soon begin turning merculyns here. It wasn't good to have so many congregated and apparently practicing feats of destruction. This warlike aspect was strange. He paused in shadow to listen to a whispered discussion.

"It is folly to do the spinning, old man," the woman said to her companion. "None of us is receiving from Pol more than random spinnings these days. She is going silent. The Well is angry. The new Medallion is usurping the old one's place, and all she is speaking is war, war, war. Her *'kilenishza,'* she is calling us now. Fah! Pol is favoring you when she is denying you the spark, for you are not benefitting the Medallion and so she is ignoring you."

News of Pol's silence was intriguing to Yples. He didn't know what it signified. Yples left Pol's Well and hurried into a quiet alley. He needed to expand the search for Kil beyond Starside. The bolts of dymension formed and he came again into the reliquary in Sorgan. He summoned the most powerful revulyns, assigning each a city-realm. "You will establish more turning grounds, well hidden. But should you discover a particularly powerful child, do not attempt a turning. It may be Kil reborn. Hide the child and wait for me to come."

His head came up, drawn by an incredible flare of the mercus nearby. In the direction of Upper Sorgan. The Revulsion throbbed in answer to this sudden appearance of power. A merculyn of remarkable capacity had just come into the city.

"Perhaps the god has come to me," he mused, then went silently from the ancient reliquary to search out this new beacon of power.

47

WITH SHARDED GLASS

Yiothizandra understood the pleasures created by suffering their opposites: hunger enhanced the joy of feeding, abstinence heightened the delights of copulation, intolerable insult inflamed the final glory of vengeance.

And what pleasure would she enjoy when she flamed down vengeance upon these shamans! These rot worms, these bestial half-witted mushroom hounds, these deplorable motherless and befanged rats. They would learn of tortures never dreamed. Prolonged sufferings upon unkilling spits, turning for days over the cookfires, repeatedly to be revived and sustained in order to prolong their agonies. And that was but the first of a thousand trials she imagined. Tooth by tooth, hair by hair, claw by claw, inch by inch they would be denuded of their bodies until their quivering muscles shone in clear air while their lungs and hearts yet pumped. These shamans would lose every part of them, until all that remained were the exposed raw nerves, which Yiothizandra herself would scrape with sharded glass. No orifice upon their body would remain unstabbed, no mother or son unmurdered before their eyes. If it took a ten-year upon this Kil-forsaken world, she would exact every bead of blood, every possible groan, every cry for mercy their breath could voice, until the last shaman was utterly exhausted. Only then would she feed them to her sword Flayshui, where a thousand more years of torture awaited their maddened minds.

The fire of these thoughts was an invigorating bath, into which she had retreated to soak since the man Yples had vanished. Her body, that shell of flesh, still endured the ceaseless pricks and itches and freezes, all of them barely noticed. She was a dragnithan of Night. Did these idiots think her weak? Did they think mere agony could break her?

The smell of meat trailed past her nose. Her belly answered by grinding and twisting. The deer meat Yples had fed her had been raw. She'd welcomed it then, but she was not a dragnithor. She did not relish bloody flesh, but instead loved to roast it beneath her own fiery breath.

A nosg was cooking meat somewhere. Not one of her torturers. Those villains were tireless, never stopping for food or drink or piss.

The Unanswered. Yples had wanted her to submit to something she didn't understand. She also didn't understand how he'd brought so many shamans into his cult. She'd always been able to feel the tickle of mercus feats being formed near her. But not this man's. Nor had she ever seen shamans wield such weird and startling swarmlight.

The Unanswered, Yples had called it.

As far as Yiothizandra was concerned, the only unanswered force in the universe right now was her wrath. He would suffer tenfold the worst she meted out to the shamans. His lie about Kil, saying her son was a daughter, earned him a second eternity on the rack of her mind. The needle of truth he'd jabbed her with—that Kila Sigh was raising Kil as her own—*that* had been his cruelest stroke against her. *That* had remained when mere agony had drifted to the periphery of her awareness.

He was powerful. That much was clear. If she allied with him, got Kil back into her arms, nothing would prevent her from betraying him a moment later. The Unanswered would be answered by Kil, for a god could end these worms—these *hounds*—with a single word. *"Die!"*

The smell of cooking meat again made her belly complain. She opened her eyes, allowing in light and the sight of twenty pairs of hateful eyegems. This brought the agonies back to the center of her attention. She retreated again into her thoughts. There had been no cookfires visible, only an easterly wind.

Cooking meat. Cooking meat.

A scream echoed in the canyon. She knew the call of a wyvok well. The shamans did not notice or did not care, for they maintained their assault. She shrugged in her chains, noting how the iron had rubbed her flesh raw. If she could but eat enough, she could call upon her own dragon aspect, covering over with scales and summoning twice her strength. And her flaming breath would sear the fur from these shamans—these *rats!*

Time did not pass in even pulses. Once she awakened from a long reverie of vengeful fantasies and the sun had not moved an inch. Another time she awoke with a start to discover the shamans had stopped their tortures, likely seeing it pointless to assault one who was not present to suffer. As soon as her eyes opened, they renewed their attacks.

This time she did not care, for beyond these shamans, upon the sunblasted plain of snow, something moved. A low wall approached. An army.

The shamans did not stop, even when gr'hils surrounded them and shamans with unblackened eyegems began to blast into them. Yioth did not order these attacks to stop, though she lamented the lost chance for personal vengeance upon her torturers. In moments it was done.

A nosg wurgu shambled forth, barking orders to the strongest warriors. These came to her, released her chains. The wurgu prostrated himself.

"Bring me meat, Prime," she said to Razk-Ka. "Bring me much meat."

He stood and studied her, but he did not obey. Of all the nosg she'd known, he possessed the brightest mind. That wasn't saying much. When he spoke, his words were lumbering, obstructed by too many teeth and a tongue as thick as a boot sole. "No, my queen." He motioned to the warriors. They picked Yioth up. She found that her arms wouldn't raise, nor her waist unfold. She had been chained too long on her knees, and starved in Stallid for thirty days prior.

Razk-Ka's army poured into the valley and began to set up camp. Yioth was placed in a sauk hide tent, given a small pot of stew from the hands of her stupid assistant, Noi-Ick-Noi. She demanded more stew. Noy answered with a grunt. "The army must eat, queen. The wyvoks must eat."

"Slaughter a wyvok," she said.

"The rest of them would abandon us, as did the Blackdread and all the other Dragons. Only meat keeps the wyvoks loyal."

"Bring me meat!"

"There is none to spare, great fire queen," he said. "It is good to see you have escaped Stallid."

"Sit, speak." She eyed his arms and legs, considering how much muscle lay beneath the fur. Not much. She could barely lift her empty stew pot, how could she strangle even this weak nosg? "Why is Razk-Ka here with my army?"

"It is all that remains of it. Thirty thousand nosg. The rest are all plagued, their eyes gone black. The shamans blast weird rays from black eyegems. Shish-Jek smiled upon you, for a wyvok outrider discovered you here in this sheltered valley. It is here that we will all die."

The canyon had no exit save for a narrow pass to the west. Even now Razk-Ka was ordering his warriors to narrow it further with piles of stone. The pursuing horde of plagued nosg were close now.

"We will stand against them as long as we can." He wagged his head, shoulders sagging. "Shish-Jek punishes us for attacking Stallid. She is so displeased, she will see us annihilated. Woe to us. I hate even the memory of the evil day when the Hargothe filled my mind with impossibilities. If not for him I would be in my den now, with my female, warm, my belly bursting with meat and drink."

"What say my spies?" Yioth demanded. Flaumishtak had dym-bonded several to Noy. Surely they had reported to him while she was gone.

"PiTorro says Starside boils. Kila Sigh has ascended to the Raven Throne. She coddles a young girl, who she claims is her daughter. Tordain burns amidst a civil war. My Sorgani spy has not touched my mind for a ten-day. She was fearful of dark stirrings in the city, which she never named. Now she is gone. Slirya hears awful rumors of Stallid. The Constellation fears Kila Sigh. The people are glad to be so far from Starside. Trist executed four shadlines who were accused of spying and supporting a faction to overthrow the king. Something stirs again in The Boil. A hundred warriors went in, none returned. Traye assembles an army, for they mistrust Jilin who musters its armsmen. Jilin sees the chaos of the world as opportunity to reconquer Traye and finally mend their Broken Empire. Lockt remains vigilant, ready for war against us, for they know of our army. Yet they mistrust a buildup of forces at the Sablefort to their south, where Starside has garrisoned much of their army. The whole expanse of Ennith simmers, my great queen. Perhaps *aggalamas-alamas* will pass us by and the realms of men will destroy each other."

"Sigh coddles a girl, you say?"

"Tarek PiTorro says so. He claims she grows freakish quick. Since Sigh's coronation, he has been expelled from the Citadel and all of Gristenside. He has returned to his greathouse in Terriside lest he be arrested by the Fell Guard."

"A girl." Yiothizandra recalled the hated memory of Kil's birth. Had Kila Sigh not been there with her accursed knife, Yioth would be dead. Kil was not going to be born of her loins, but of an explosion of her entire body, like a dragon hatchling bursting from its shell. But Sigh stole the child, as Ellishan had looked on, smirking. Ah, that mien of superiority still maddened Yiothizandra. "Ellishan is dead, then. Killed by Kila Sigh, no less."

"PiTorro says no one knows how she died, but many believe it is as you say."

Yioth had not thought Kila Sigh impressive in the least. The girl had once been her pet, crowned with a *vaz'on* and kept on a chain. That hideous Ahl-Mish-Lah had used her power to good effect, but had lost control of her early in the attack on Stallid. Sigh was more ambitious than Yioth had suspected. She knew Kil to be her step up to full godhood.

"A young girl?" she repeated. How odd. Yples had not lied about that. Kil could be anything he wished, she supposed. But she had carried him in her belly. Surely she would have felt the difference within her. "I do not know what this signifies."

As for the rest of Noy's tale, she did not know what any of that meant either. In the end, the chaos was good if it kept Sigh distracted.

"Kil is my daughter," she mused, liking the idea more. And the more she liked the notion of having a daughter, the greater became her longing to be reunited with the child. "She grows quickly, you say?"

"Shoes fit today, but not tomorrow, PiTorro said."

The babe had grown within her quickly too. But this was

incredibly frustrating! Intolerable! Kil should be next to her here, receiving her guidance and love. No torture at the hands of those horrid shamans had pained her as much as the idea that Kil called Sigh "mother".

Her yearning for her daughter pulled at her chest. Not merely a maternal instinct, she realized. Her head lifted, nose testing the air. She turned this way and that, but the pull was coming from the south and west. Yioth could *feel* her daughter.

"There is much killing ahead of me," she said, clamping down her longing and stoking her anger. "That is good. Find me meat so that I might be strengthened. I will burn these plagued nosg where they stand."

Noy bowed and promised he would try. But he did not return that night.

48

ALREADY DEAD

The reviled dog looked rather poorly when Revnithan Con found it alongside the road. It lay among several reviled men, head nearly detached from body, eyes roving. She regarded the living corpses and considered the phenomenon deeply. "They're dead, greenmak," she said. "No need for the heart to conduct blood throughout the brain, for the Unanswered somehow continues to sustain vision and thought." Not that there was much thought buzzing through the dog's mind, nor even the reviled humans'.

The dog had done its bit. Maggots and carrion eaters had already taken some of its muzzle flesh. Pity was a lie, but she washed the dog's flesh with blue flame until it was a smear of black char on the road. She left the rest of the carnage behind, unconcerned.

As she walked in pursuit of the shadlines and their godchild, she wondered how long a decapitated reviled's awareness would endure. Did oblivion require a certain proportion of brain matter to be destroyed? Did the brain figure into it at all? She didn't know, but she didn't like to think about it.

The cold eye came a bit easier to her now, for she had cultivated it as she had run along the roads. At some point the shadlines had shot far ahead, and it had confused her until she found her dog standing before the mouth of a vergent pass. The pass had stepped her untold leagues east in moments, to the edges of the Shanala Mountains. An uncomfortable little jump, that. The vergent pass had tried to keep her out. She'd been forced to pick up the hound and carry it through. It howled as if on fire. But once on the other side, it returned to its cold ways and continued its pursuit.

The shadlines would stay on this road. There was no choice, for the terrain to either side went steeply up or steeply down. The air was very cold, though Revnithan Con barely noticed. But the shadlines would wish to find an inn or house in which to shelter for the night. She came to a town with a sizable inn on the square. The Wine Cask.

She felt nothing of the god-child's mercus as she approached. That was odd indeed. "Where did she go, greenmak?"

The girl's mercus potential had shone across Slirya. If she were in this town, surely Revnithan Con would feel it. There was nothing for it except to ask. She found the stables and summoned a boy to answer her questions. She considered reviling him, but thought better of it. She didn't want to draw attention or alarm. The lad reported that two shadlines in company of a young lady and cat had indeed taken a room in the inn.

Con left the boy and returned to the square. She looked up at the inn's facade, scanning the windows. "Is she masked, greenmak?" She sent the beetle flying up to peer into the rooms. But the glazings were warped, and hazy with frost. The beetle returned to her shoulder.

"Hmmmm."

She didn't like the notion that the god-child had masked

herself. That spoke to an awakened power. A very dangerous power indeed. Con passed out of the town, thinking to lay some sort of ambush down the road for when they continued. But the Unanswered soon provided her with an alternative. A company of Trayean soldiers, the so-called Valiant Blades, was patrolling the road. They stopped her and demanded to see her eyes. Her revnithan eyes were still a living green, so they relaxed. They reported some interesting goings on in Traye. A sickness was spreading there. Well, she knew what that was. These men had been torn between escaping the growing numbers of reviled and their duty to protect the realm.

She solved this quandary for them by reviling them all.

Turning an isolated individual was easy, but they'd notice pretty quickly what she was up to if she did one with so many bunched around her. Thing was, she'd studied her lovely revulynic dagger as she'd traveled. The Entifal was a real gem of a find. The store of Revulsion in it was available for her to use. And so she sucked in a great load of it, formed it into a feat broad enough to encompass the company, and reviled the lot of them in less than a minute. All save one.

She bade her new reviled to hold the final man down. He cursed and spat and struggled, but his strength was nothing against the cold hands that gripped him. His rage quickly turned to terror, and this fear magnified twofold when she approached holding the Entifal.

As powerful as the blade was in providing Revulsion for her use, she doubted Lord Yples had wanted it for such a mundane purpose. After all, he could circle and tap revulyns to give him more power if he wished it.

An experiment was in order. She bent over the captured man. "What'll it do, little greenmak?" she said. "I think I know!"

She drew the edge of the blade across the top of his forearm. Not deeply, just enough to draw a thin line of blood. To her astonishment and delight, he convulsed and gasped. Within three heartbeats his eyes had turned to black coals. The Entifal was like a reviled's weapon, blessed with the power to turn. But it did so with incredible rapidity. It was this property, she suspected, that Lord Yples would find most valuable. The Blackshine shamans were effective, but rather slow in turning merculyns. This blade would do it right quick.

Another exciting thought struck her and she let out a little gasp. "Goodness me, little greenmak!" She forced herself to seek again the cold eye. But it eluded her, for a surge of wonder made her mind all abuzz. Might a little cut from this blade also turn the god-child? What a fascinating experiment that would be!

She decided to send her reviled into Vanish's Gold that very night. The shadlines would either be cornered by them or they'd be forced to come out and fight. While they were engaged in that, she would find the child and dymense her away. Oh, Qiznithan Yples would be pleased. Very pleased. *Doubly* pleased, because she also had the Entifal.

She stopped right there in her thoughts, delighted by an even more astonishing idea.

"Why didn't I think of it instantly, greenmak?" she said. "I will have both the girl and the dagger. Why deliver them to Lord Yples for him to use?"

She would cut the child with the Entifal and that would be it. Perhaps she could convince the god-child to annihilate her in that very moment. Ah, that would be sweet indeed.

But as Con followed her men toward the village, she reconsidered. She still itched to catalog the various types of weapons. And the Shanala Mountains had interested her deeply, for she had seen no fewer than seventeen types of tree and animal she had not previously recorded. So she would ask the reviled god to hold off a bit so she could complete her catalogs.

"And we're already dead, greenie!" she said, delighted. "Cold makes no difference to us, does it? No it does not. Nor weariness. We don't even need sleep. Think of how much work we can do."

The lights of town showed in the distance. The reviled soldiers stalked ahead in a wide picket. She'd had to command them to spread out. They truly were idiots once turned. And that got her to thinking about how they might be improved. As Lord Yples had created her to be something more than a mere revulyn, perhaps she could make something more than a mere reviled. More thinking, less dead. As she walked, she found again the cold eye and considered how to form feats to revile a man and keep him sharper of mind. Fortunately, there were plenty of subjects to experiment on in the houses ahead.

49

THE FINAL RELEASE

They came out in a sparsely traveled lane next to a stableyard. Quiv sucked in a huge breath and let it go. "I did it."

"Dymensing isn't difficult once you get used to it," Kila said, furtively checking her limbs. Everything was in order. Nax was perched on her shoulder. Brother Nils and Brother Eyvin stood left and right of her.

She probed the mercus. The Revulsion was thicker here than in the Citadel. So too was the stink of manure. An odd place for Quiv to have brought them. But then she recalled Quiv's nature as spy. He was likely more comfortable in dank back alleys than he was upon cathedral daises. "Will you return to Starside?" she asked him.

"Yes, Your Majesty. The conclave of Nares will cast their votes soon. I must be present."

Leaving him to recover his nerve for the return dymension, Kila turned off the lane onto a broad street bordered by shops, inns, and taverns. The buildings were of thick beams upon heavy stone foundations. The roofs were pitched low and tiled with slate. A blustery wind cut across the street, full of sea smells and moisture. Gray clouds scudded low overhead, the fringes of a recent storm.

Nax, if you were revulyn, where would you take merculyns you meant to corrupt?

I am not a revulyn. A irritable tail flicking sensation came with the sending.

Kila again turned her attention to the Revulsion, looking for any variation in the general skim of nastiness. She continued walking, going toward the towers in the distance. That would be the Anvil Palace, where Emperor Iodune and his wives lived. His "empire" consisted of one city, though every Sorgani harbored dreams of recapturing the whole peninsula one day.

There was no indication of Revulsion trails like the one she'd followed from Mayrie's room. Marlow had told her only the Way of Pol had a temple here in Upper Sorgan. Since that was the closest concentration of merculyns, she sought it out.

She found it on the eastern edge of the city, where a waist-high wall protected citizens from accidentally plunging two hundred spans into the ocean below. The tower stood alone on a bump-out in the cliff line. Pol's Wells were never particularly tall, but this one was typical in its massive breadth. Pol's way did not shy away from militaristic functionality the way Ori's did. The top of the tower was crowned with thick crenellations, and arrow slits perforated the stone walls at regular intervals.

The main gate was closed, with a heavy portcullis clamped down in front of it. Kila watched the sally port for a while, sitting on a bench fronting a small orchard park. Nobody went in and nobody came out. And there were no people on the streets.

"I've never been as good as Henley at feeling other merculyns," she said to her fell guardsmen. "But if there's a single merculyn in that whole tower, I'm a Sourwater pikefish."

Brothers Eyvin and Nils scanned their surroundings. They

wore fine merchant cloaks, but nothing could hide their military bearing, nor their exceptionally thick chests and arms.

"Please blink or nod or grunt, at least," she complained. "Acknowledge that you heard me speaking."

Both men nodded sharply, eyes never straying from their suspicious vigilance. Not that there was much to see. The streets of the city were vacant. There should have been wagons and carts, carriages and hacks about.

"Haven't seen a patrol of the city watch," Eyvin said.

"I noted that, too," Nils said.

Kila hadn't. "Is that surprising? Nobody's out causing trouble."

"The citizenry are afraid of something," Nils said. "The lord of the city should increase watch patrols to reassure them."

The Cheapsgater in Kila said, "Maybe they're afraid of the watch."

But the more likely cause of the city's emptiness was the Revulsion. If merculyns were being turned into revulyns here, then perhaps others had been corrupted. A reviled was in some ways more terrifying to see. The Revulsion was strong when they were near, she remembered. Again she glided her mind over the mercusine, noting the thickness of the Revulsion that lay between her and it.

"It is thicker here," she said.

Nils grunted.

She got off the bench and moved toward the tower. A moment's hesitation at the narrow wooden door, then she banged on it with her fist.

The Revulsion was just as thick here as it was near the park. Hard to say it was worse, though. She felt Nax's presence very strongly, for the cat was also vigilant for the Revulsion. This allowed her to sink through the vileness and into the mercusine web. There was not the slightest haze of mercus potential to be felt in the tower. No one answered her knock.

"Let's go down to Lower Sorgan," she said, starting away from the tower. The Baths of Ori were at the bottom of the Leeside Stair.

They passed no one on their descent to the lower city. "Where is everyone?" Kila asked.

A steady rain had swept in from the sea, making the carved stairs slick. Strange currents of breeze whirled around them. These winds had little power, but they changed direction constantly, pushing them toward the edge of the stairs in one moment and toward the cliff face the next. Without warning, a gust would waft up the stairs, billowing out their cloaks and pushing back their hoods.

The lower city glistened under the rain, slate rooftops sheeting runoff into wide scuppers and pouring it into paved ditches. But part of the city was submerged, including the ruins of the Cathedral of Kil.

Kila's thigh muscles were burning as she came down the last flight of steps. A broad curved walkway sloped down to the first homes and shops. Beyond those lay the docks where fishing boats were moored. The streets were empty.

The Baths of Ori enjoyed the highest ground in Lower Sorgan at the very tip of the peninsula. It was a small compound built on an out-thrusting stone platform. Elnisian work. The Dome of the Gentle Goddess was identical to the one on Garden Island, an open air structure supported by columns in the likeness of Ori in all her aspects. There were no merculyns in the blocky residence hall, nor any in the Rose Hall or library.

The Revulsion was thicker down here, but again Kila could not read any variations in its concentration. "It's as if the merculyns are all masked," she said absently.

They walked along the quays and studied the inns and

shops. The doors were all closed, the windows blank. They moved through the main square at the front of the docks. A statue of some forgotten Sorgani king stood upon a circular plinth, eyes shaded as he gazed south over the sea.

She went to an enormous inn on the south side of the square. The Whaleman's Skiff occupied nearly an entire block. A sign posted at the door showed room rates and daily menu. Kila tried the door. It was locked. She knocked.

No answer.

"Something just moved there," Brother Eyvin said, pointing down the street. Kila didn't see anything. She had a sudden urge to climb onto the roofs. She felt too exposed on the streets.

"Show me," she said.

Eyvin led the way. Despite the wind and the rise and fall of the sea against the cliff base, the city held a tense silence. The windows looked at them as the trio held to the center of the street. Kila probed through the Revulsion and established her armor-cloak, widening it to encompass her companions. The rain rolled off the invisible barrier an inch from their heads.

"It was here," Eyvin said. "A blur went across the street, from that alley to that one."

Kila studied the Revulsion. "Ugh, it's like a slimy coating of soot here. I can't sense any texture to it." Kila stopped at every inn and tavern to knock and call out. No response.

The city sloped into the water here and the homes and shops beyond swayed atop enormous wooden floats, huge chains at the corners holding them to anchors somewhere under the surface. They were surrounded by little row boats, tied close by so that inhabitants could make it to dry land.

"Behind you," Nils said.

She whirled. A hooded man stood in the center of the street. Flanking him were a dozen Sensuals and Spinsters. Kila felt no mercusine in them. Nor Revulsion.

Then the truth struck her. "Kil's eyes," she whispered. "They're masking their Revulsion."

But could they feel her? Did they know she was a merculyn? Her entire body knew the answer in the same way it would know it was falling from a great height. Her belly hiked up under her ribs and a thrill of fear buzzed in her limbs. She gathered up her mercusine, still flowing because she was actively sustaining her armor-cloak. Praise be to all the gods that she'd done so, for the Revulsion instantly surged to assault her mind.

Kila's backpack wobbled as Nax struggled to escape it. Then the cat was on the street, standing between her and the revulyns, fur sticking straight out.

That one! Nax sent, delicate face aimed at the central figure. *Qiznithan!*

Kila didn't need to know more than that. Her first instinct was to blast them all with fire, but experience had taught her she couldn't attack without the Revulsion tempting her.

A shield. She needed a shield.

She was already shielded by her armor-cloak feat, but it would only aid her against sword and arrow. No time to come up with something else. It was a start.

Recalling her feat of light during her coronation, she infused her armor-cloak with scintillating white light and leavened it with determination, love, and the sweet scent of tuber rose, lilac, and apple blossom. She poured every good feeling she could think of into the shield, making it as much an opposite to the Revulsion as she could.

Eyvin and Nils held their swords forward, one foot back, posture perfectly balanced. The revulyns did not move at all, save for the flapping of their robes in the wind.

The qiznithan watched her. And then he lifted his hands and pulled back his hood. An aged face, drawn and bony, confronted her. It sent a thrill of terror through her, for she knew that face.

"Yples!" she said. "What have you done?"

Kila poured more power into her shield, extending it outward. The curve of her barrier moved toward the revulyns. Nax stalked with it, body low and full of predatory intensity, as if she weren't merely a tiny cat, but instead an enormous dragon.

Don't get too close, Kila warned.

I hate it!

You can't kill him alone.

Frustration and spitting anger came over the bond. But Nax stopped.

Yples held his arms out, palms forward. "There is no reason for conflict between us," he said. His voice was deep and cadenced to be soothing. But the artifice in it grated in Kila's ears. It was a tone she had heard countless times from would-be alley-gropers in Cheapsgate, whose honeyed words were meant to lull a mark so she would lower her guard. Yples's words were too loud, enhanced upon Revulsion bolts.

Kila spared a thread of mercus to magnify her answer. "You sent a revulyn to steal my daughter, Yples. There will *only* be conflict until you are annihilated."

His mouth widened, showing teeth in an approximated smile. "Ah, that is all we ever wanted. But alas, you cannot grant Annihilation. Only the Unanswered can bless us with such relief." He moved forward in slow steps, arms still out in a pose of unthreatening vulnerability. "You are sickened by it only because you were born in filth. The Unanswered is pure. You know it. I feel it in you. You have seen with the *cold eye!*"

The assault came instantly, a ray of void-dark blackness originating between Yples's eyes. It met Kila's shield. An inverse explosion dimmed Kila's vision, as if a black cloud had obliterated the sun. She felt her shield weaken as its energy was pulled in by the qiznithan's feat.

He wasn't trying to blast through the shield. He was draining it, hungrily suckling from it. The remaining revulyns formed tap circles and lent their power to the qiznithan. The blackness emanating from his brow widened. It looked like part of the world had ceased to exist, like a painting with an enormous wedge cut out of it.

Kila flashed back to Dox Viller's bedroom and the perfectly vanished stretch of rug in front of his chair. This was the same feat she had unleashed, a great undoing of whatever it touched. Including the mercus.

In that moment she understood. The Revulsion would negate anything of weaker power. To even establish a stand-off between them would require her to match the revulyns' combined power.

Power was not something she lacked. Releasing herself fully into the mercusine, she allowed it to flow through her, intensifying and intensifying more. It seared her mind, made her limbs buzz with its numbing excess. Her abdomen and chest muscles began to cramp and quiver.

Her shield of light pressed forward, foot by foot. Yples poured all his own power and the combined power of every revulyn behind him at the shield. But he was forced to step backwards as Kila's wall progressed ever outward. A growl of anger came from him and he called to his companions to double their efforts.

Anger. Kila noted it. That was not an expression of the cold eye. "Dunne Yples! Can you hear me?"

The man's face went slack, as if the qiznithan too had noticed the emotional slip.

There was more mercus welling inside Kila, but she did not think she could release it lest she be blown apart from within.

Eyvin and Nils spread farther ahead, as if their bodies alone could secure the stretch of street Kila had claimed.

Nax stood halfway between Kila and the qiznithan, low to the ground in her stalker's crouch, tail flicking, ears pinned.

Kila had extended her barrier as much as she could. Now she walked forward, grimacing as her calves and thighs trembled. Her toes curled down as the bottoms of her feet were seized with cramps. The mercus was too much. She could not add more. She staggered forward again, her shield drifting ahead with her, again forcing the revulyns back.

But they did not relent. Yples shouted something Kila didn't understand. Those hateful black eyes were on Nax now. And then the words broke through into Kila's understanding. "Accursed felnithel. Phase Lord! Do you not see the truth? You who sees all with the cold eye? Why do you rebuke the Unanswered? It is all the same to you."

If Nax responded, Kila wasn't privy to it. But the qiznithan snarled, again showing anger. His Revulsion attack abruptly cut off and Kila fell onto her knees. She hadn't realized how hard she'd been pushing against him. The mercus continued to sear through her, but she did not let it wane. She knew Yples would renew his assault at the slightest sign of weakness.

"Kila Sigh, you are deceived by this creature," the qiznithan said. "I was once Yples, and I know all he knew. *He* saw the evil in the felnithel. *He* saw how close you came to the Unanswered in the thinnie cavern and then again on Garden Island. You think you protect those you love. You think your anger is justified. But you are ignorant. Every foe you fight is but your own reflection. You are afflicted, child. Afflicted by suffering. I can give you the final release. Surely you remember what it was to see with the *cold eye*. As you did at the Hackwatch, and in Stallid. The Unanswered did not pain you as the hateful mercusine does. It is easy, it is right. Come up from the filthy water of your ignorance, child. Come up and breathe the pure air. Existence is pain. The Unanswered is painless."

Every syllable he uttered sparked greater rage inside Kila. The blatant lies, deceits, and distortions warred in her mind. "Begone!" she screamed.

Yples bowed his head and then was enveloped in black smoke. When it dissipated, he was gone and the revulyns were popping into dymension one after the other. When the Revulsion black finally cleared, people began to emerge from their homes and shops.

They bore swords, and axes, and shovels, and lengths of lumber. Many held iron pans, or broken off furniture legs. They streamed toward Kila and her companions. At first they shuffled, and then they ran. She saw their black, dead-eyed expressions and knew what she had feared was true. Sorgan belonged to the reviled.

"Come to me," she called to her fell guardsmen. "Take hold of me."

Nax was slow to return, for she kept turning to hiss and spit at the charging throng of reviled. The first ranks struck Kila's shield wall, causing flares of sparks inside it and bursts of black outside. What remained of these vanguard attackers was merely a cloud of fine soot that drifted on the wind.

"Look!" Nils said, pointing his sword toward the stair from Upper Sorgan. Thousands raced down the Leeside Stair, those behind pushing at those ahead. Hundreds plunged over the edge. From high up, the reviled threw themselves over the city's cliff to get to her faster.

Nax climbed up her leg and clawed onto her shoulder. Eyvin and Nils gripped her arms. She dropped the shield and formed the bolts of dymension.

50

BURN FOR AN HOUR

*W*hat is *that thing?* Henley sent.

Huff trembled on his shoulder, claws sunk into his skin. Soaked fur pressed against Henley's ear. The weak gray light reaching them seemed to collect and gain brilliance in the cat's eyes. *As a dragnithor is to a dragnithan, so too is a qiznithor to a qiznithan. It is a beast of endless appetite. It destroys.*

It destroys what?

Whatever isn't it.

They were hiding deep in a partially flooded sewer tunnel, well away from the collapsed portion that had sent them tumbling. The water was icy and Henley's legs and feet had long ago gone numb. He wished to use the mercus to dry himself and his companions, but he'd masked both himself and Whiteflame during a desperate scramble to escape the smokey claws of their enemy.

The beast stomped directly overhead, seeking to break through the street and reach them. The trap, with Mayrie as bait, evinced more intelligence than Henley had suspected in the Revulsion.

Brother Ryde stood in front of Henley, spear at the ready. He was dripping but didn't show any sign of discomfort. "Lord Mast, I suggest we retreat further. Perhaps these sewers connect with those in Starside."

"I can't leave while that thing—"

"Our task was to renew the Revulsion trap at the temple. You did so, no?"

"I did. But—"

"And this sword tells against the reviled. Surely it must be brought out from here so it can serve against Revulsion foes still free to harm Her Majesty and Her Majesty's ward."

"But if I leave this beast to—"

"You cannot defeat it alone." Ryde touched his arm, squeezed it firmly. Gray eyes met Henley's. "Perhaps it would be satisfied to keep you in Moonside. That sword is very powerful, but you have not thought clearly since you took it up."

The sword? Oh yes, Whiteflame. He still held it. Masking its power had extinguished its light. But its touch still made him strong.

Did it truly? Or was that the shadline blade's subtle influence on his mind? He had heard such weapons could change a person's character. "You take it," he said, laying it over his forearm and presenting the hilt.

Ryde refused it. "I dare not. Take my scabbard and stow your relic in it."

It took a minute of rattling and jingling, but soon Ryde had his belt and scabbard tightened around Henley's hips. Whiteflame slid in and released its hold on him the instant he released his hold on it. He fell straight down into the water. Huff leapt onto Ryde's shoulder at the last instant. Ryde grabbed Henley's collar, yanked him upright. Henley's legs wouldn't hold him.

"Whiteflame has drained your strength," Ryde said.

The ceiling of the tunnel boomed. Dust and small rocks

pelted down onto their heads, pinging from Ryde's helmet and splashing into the swift moving current. Ryde picked Henley up and carried him deeper into darkness.

"I'm sorry Huff jumped on you," Henley said. Kil's eyes he was sleepy. "But he can't swim against this current."

"I am honored to be his raft," Ryde said. "Her Enlightened Majesty loved the felnithel above all beings."

"I had better hold the sword again," Henley said. "Then I'll be able to walk. But I don't think we can go far. I'll have to dymense us out of Moonside."

The ceiling behind them collapsed, sending a wave of water against Ryde and submerging them. Blackness engulfed Henley and terrified sensations seared across the bond as Huff strained to find the surface. Henley instinctively reached for the mercus. The Revulsion surged at him, stronger than ever. Even as his mouth filled with filthy water, so too was his mind defiled by a sickening blackness.

The water subsided and he was again pulled clear by Brother Ryde. He spat and coughed to rid his mouth of vileness. Inside he strained to break through the horrific thickness of the Revulsion.

But it was too much and he was too tired. Huff lent what help he could, but he was soaked and panicky from his dunking. The cat had kept his place on Ryde's shoulder.

"I can't dymense us," Henley said. "I can't get to the mercus."

The fell guardsman didn't answer. Instead he bore Henley forward, wading against an increasing current. Henley didn't know how the man could see anything at all, but Ryde did not slow. He chose a branching tunnel where the water was a bit shallower.

The resounding booms of the qiznithor continued to slam into the street. But these concussions grew more distant and finally stopped after a quarter of an hour. Henley slept until Ryde stopped and set him down.

"Where are we?" Henley asked. There was no light at all.

A flashtaper flared in Ryde's fingers and he lit a short wax candle. Compared to the darkness it was like the sun. Its rich yellow light warmed Henley despite the aching cold of his soaked clothes.

Ryde entrusted the candle to Henley. "It will burn for an hour. No longer."

"I may have some things to burn in my pack."

"You don't have your pack."

Ah, so it was. Henley couldn't bring himself to care. His mind was full of the surrounding darkness. Not the Revulsion, but simply weariness.

Huff, are you well?

I am wet and cold.

Ryde carried Henley west, taking them upslope. The water was much shallower here, just covering the man's ankles. His pace increased and he took every north passage they encountered. Toward the Divide. Toward the small chance they might find passage under it and into Starside.

They found the Divide less than ten minutes later. A seamless black barrier blocking the passageway. A dead end. But at least a dry one.

"Put me down," Henley said. "I want to try the mercus again."

Henley unbuckled the sword belt and set it aside. Then he slumped down with his back to the Divide. Huff circled into his lap, soggy and irritable. But as Henley sat there, gazing at the flame of the little candle, his eyelids succumbed to his exhaustion. He didn't notice when Ryde gently took the candle from him, blew it out to conserve it, and turned to face down the tunnel, spear ready to impale anything that came his way.

51

TURNED IN AN INSTANT

The reviled came at middlenight, just as Fallo and his companions were emerging from the stableyard, Tolky in tow. Black figures under scant moonlight drifted along the street. More of them filtered among the buildings. If they saw Fallo, they did not react. Something to be grateful for, he supposed. They did not seem to feel Illy or Nefler Ernist, thanks to his masking trick.

Fallo headed away from the reviled, taking the road west out of Vanish's Gold. The road was frozen dirt, with worn rounded stones protruding here and there. Tolky's hooves clopped too loudly. Illy hustled alongside Quinn. Nefler moved smoothly enough. But Fallo worried he would become an anchor when the time came to run.

"Don't suppose you know how to dymense?" he asked the man.

"Hmm. Interesting to hear you use that word. What do you know of dymensing?"

"I know that it would get us well away from the reviled." But the man's refusal to answer was answer enough. The reviled were a good way behind them, still proceeding through town.

They didn't move quickly during their searches, but they never stopped to rest. He tried to imagine what Illy's masking had felt like to them. All at once this bright beacon had been extinguished. They would think she was hiding in the town. Once they came to the end of it, they would turn around and begin a house-to-house search.

All the townspeople would be turned as corrupted swords and daggers drove into the bellies of mother and child alike. And within an hour, Vanish's Gold would be empty of life and full of a living death.

He handed Tolky's lead to Nefler Ernist. "I'm doubling back to thin the herd. Quinn?"

Her eyes glimmered in the silver moonlight. But her face was torn between eagerness and doubt. She didn't want to leave Illy alone with Nefler. Fallo didn't either. The man seemed to understand their quandary. "You must decide, shadlines. Can you risk trusting me while you return to save the town? I wish I could grant you certainty. But if it helps, I give you my word that I will protect this girl with my life. Truth be, I may not be able to dymense, but I am not powerless."

Lop, can we trust this man?

He hasn't fed me. But he might in the future.

That was as close to an endorsement as Lop would ever offer. Fallo's instincts were pulling him back to the town now. Not only to save it, but to take advantage of the rare opportunity the situation afforded. When Illy was unmasked, the reviled thronged toward her. But now they were dispersed, making them easier to take down.

He drew Skeye from her spot in his boot. The blade's eagerness charged through him. He patted Nefler's shoulder. "Your mercus will not save you should you betray us."

He didn't wait to witness the man's response before darting down the road with Quinn. At some point she veered from the road and into the trees. With Black in her hands she became smoke in shadow. Fallo left the road and circled along the river, crossing the commons to come around from the east. "All right, Skeye. Only you for now. Don't want to suck any of the reviled into my blood or memories today."

The first man he encountered was a soldier. Sword in hand, mail shirt. He'd lost his helm at some point. He walked woodenly, jingling with every step. The nearest other reviled was ten paces to the right, equally oblivious to Fallo.

The sensation of stabbing flesh and striking bone was familiar to Fallo now. And as Skeye went in, he felt the additional jolt as the blade took hold of his hand, refusing to let him release it as it imparted a shocking force into its victim. The hilt protruded from the exposed neck, tip wedged between vertebrae. The man jerked like a puppet, bouncing on his heels. The sword dropped from his hand and his jaw clattered. Fallo grimaced and took his own shock, the price of a guaranteed kill against these monsters.

With a grunt he yanked the greedy blade free, for it would not willingly be pulled out while drinking of its victim's blood. But the reviled did not give her any, which infuriated her. Skeye was stupid and rather immature. Rather than learn there was no nourishment to be had, she merely strove deeper.

I'm your master, he sent at the blade. He was never sure if it could hear him, but asserting his authority seemed to ease his own pain from using the dagger. And then he was off to the next reviled. Stab, judder, yank, clunk. These sounds did not draw any notice from nearby reviled. They were single-minded in their search, themselves as hungry for Illy's mercus power as Skeye was for blood.

And so he proceeded, leaving nine reviled men inert behind him. But as he moved to approach an isolated little house surrounded by a low garden fence, he noticed Skeye's energy change. She no longer encouraged him to kill. She was pressing him to stick himself. She wanted blood at any cost.

Nasty blade, he admonished.

He didn't need more convincing. He put Skeye away and drew Shinane. A killer as well, but slower.

The reviled were reaching the end of town now; some were turning back to begin entering homes. Two were at the little house's front door. They kicked the door, causing splintering bangs to resound in the still night. Dogs began to bark.

A voice called out from inside the house.

More bangs sounded across the town as more doors were stove in. More cries. A girl's scream. A man's warbling death shriek. Fallo raced toward the house, leapt the fence, and threw himself at the reviled as they entered the house. Shinane slashed the unprotected tendons at the back of knees, stabbed into a neck. The bone chill began its inexorable spread, but not quickly enough to keep swords and daggers from stabbing back.

Fallo's instincts were alight once again, guiding him to duck and parry, stab and slice with a dancer's grace. Eye sockets were best in cases like this. Stupid to try for in battle, but guided as his blows were, he delivered two simultaneously on two separate reviled.

That was the first time he noticed he was wielding Telt as well. Kil-damned shadline fighting skills!

The two reviled clumped onto the house's floor. A man in nightshirt and cap came out, holding up a candle, face drawn in terror. "If you have a weapon, get it," Fallo said. "The town is under attack!"

"Til's chestnuts!" the man cried. His face transformed from fear to fury. "If it's those damnable villains from Jilin, I'll show them the edge of my sword!"

Fallo had the vaguest notion of a past war between the states of Jilin and Traye. But whatever rage this man needed, deluded or not, would serve just as well. "Get your sword, man. For Traye!"

"For Traye!"

Fallo left the house and raced to the next. A reviled fell swiftly to Shinane's exploration of his brain.

Something stirred next to him, boots in the grass. He spun, lashing blindly with both fists. Two blades went into a reviled gut.

"Ah me," he said, just before the hilts gripped him back. His eyes sought his victim's and his vision went black. It returned with him holding down a living man. Three other reviled were helping him keep the man still. The man thrashed and shook his head side to side until his helm flew off. Blond hair scattered across the road. Fallo recognized him, the chain shirt, the sword. He'd already killed this one.

It was the reviled's memory. And yet it felt like it was happening to Fallo in the moment. A woman stalked forth, pale haired and saggy of face. She bent over the man, holding up a dagger. "What'll it do, little greenmak?" she said. "I think I know!"

She sliced across the man's forearm. The struggles stopped instantly and the man's eyes went dark. Turned in an instant.

Fallo's vision returned to the real moment, daggers coming out of the reviled guts. The body tilted back and fell away. Shaking off the memory, Fallo sheathed Telt.

He entered the next house and found a horrific scene in the bedroom. The haggard woman from the vision was here, hands clasped over a man's temples. A woman beat at her body with a broom. "Get off him, you handle-suckin' hag!"

The hag must have sensed Fallo, for she threw the man aside and turned to face him. An odd smile twisted one side of her pale lips. She raised one hand, fingers clawed, and reached out.

"Look, greenmak. It's one of the shadlines. Where are you hiding the god-child?"

A shiny green beetle lifted from her shoulder and buzzed around his head. Fallo's feet began to move, though he wished for them not to. But his will was not his own, and no matter how he fought, he continued to shuffle forward. His hand was forced to open. Shinane fell to the floor, stuck point first between the wide oak planks. The young wife had gone to her husband, who was struggling to stand.

He noticed her cries then, and with dead eyes, grabbed her head and thrust her down, nose smashing into the corner of a bedside table. She screamed and held her shattered face. He curled his fist in her hair and again smashed her face into the table. Her cries cut off and she crumpled.

The revulyn hag looked at the killed woman and then the man. "My experiment failed, greenmak. He was too weak-willed for the bolts. But this ugly shadline might stand up to it. Just think what a delight that would be!"

Lop! Fallo sent. *I'm about to get turned.*

Don't do that!

What excellent advice, he thought. *Why didn't I think of that?*

In my experience you're stupid.

Fallo sensed Lop on the move, coming very swiftly. But it wouldn't matter. The revulyn was looking at him with what might have been curiosity if her eyes hadn't been so mad. Even in the midst of horror, he couldn't help but note that her eyes were green.

The corrupted husband had come to stand beside her.

The willshift was clamping down on Fallo's body. His chest was tightening as the revulyn sought to forbid him even to breath. He took another unwilling step.

Don't! Lop cried. A surge of emotion came across the bond. Fallo couldn't tell what it was, but it warmed his limbs. And in that warmth came a modicum of control. He stopped his approach. The revulyn stood just a pace away. She held a dagger now and was muttering under her breath. Why she refused to come to him Fallo didn't understand.

"Remove his other daggers," the revulyn ordered her new reviled. "I will make a study of them, too. Just imagine! A catalog of shadline weapons!" The man came to Fallo, bent to draw Skeye from his boot. On contact the man jerked upright and thrust the blade into his own belly. Fallo would have laughed, but his lips were still not responding to his wishes. Good ol' Skeye.

Fallo's arm had a bit more freedom now. He strained, pulling it back, drawing his fingers across Telt. He gripped, pulled.

The second the blade came free, the willshift vanished. Fallo stumbled, surprised at the return of his bodily control. The blade came up, pointed at the revulyn. "Ol' Rusty!" Fallo cried triumphantly. With shadline dexterity, he impaled the beetle right out of the air.

The revulyn's face went dark with fury. A wash of blue fire came from her hand, blasting over Fallo, singeing his face, his clothes, the backs of his hands. A mental scream blew apart his thoughts, Lop's anguish flooding through the bond like a lake breaking through a dam. Fallo ended up on his back, seeing nothing but blue flame. It was coming from him now, from his cloak, his flesh. He smelled the burning meat of his own immolation.

An audible growl caught his attention, only for a moment. Lop, in her rage, had come into the house. She spat, hissed. And then Fallo's awareness of his own agonies faded out of existence. Blessed oblivion pulled him down.

52

LIKE A LIVING THING

Kila had always thought the small council chamber atop the spire an extraordinarily impractical place to hold meetings. Especially when some attendees were incapable of dymensing. Those pour souls were left to climb the winding staircase, which left even hardy folk winded and weak of knee by the time they reached the door.

But standing here now she understood the advantages of such inconvenience.

For one thing, it gave her time to collect her thoughts and compose her emotions before receiving her counselors. For another, the room and its position reinforced in everyone's mind that she was the queen. And it wasn't necessarily bad that some attendees arrived tired and out of breath. That put them on the back foot.

And then there was the window.

Ell had always kept it slightly cracked, as if the cold air were a tonic. Or perhaps she had merely been too warm, dragnithan that she was. Kila remembered how Yiothizandra had relished the frigid mountain air in Ceronhel.

But that hadn't been the only reason Ell was often found

standing before the window. For now Kila was standing in her predecessor's footsteps, her back to the empty room. The window gave a clear view toward the opening of the eyrie, and with a turn of her head, a magnificent view of the city. From Gristenside to Cheapsgate.

The glazing of the window was merely translucent, so to see anything the window had to be open. Kila had fashioned a weather-cloak to keep herself warm. No fire in the hearth would greet Marlow or Highest Quiv when they arrived. Just as Ell would do.

Harnzyne had not returned from his mission to find the dragons of Night. And if he had discovered Klayne and Eckso, neither had sought her out yet. She turned again to look at her city. The rooftops pulled at her, and she wished she were free of responsibility, free to run and chase whatever whim arose. How long had it been since she'd last enjoyed a bowl of Josef's chowder? An age, it seemed.

She felt the arrival of a merculyn outside her door. A fell guardsman let him in. She had dismissed Eyvin and Nils so they could rest and eat. They had insisted they did not need any food or sleep, but she sent them away anyway. "At least go bathe," she said, wrinkling her nose. "You smell like a thinnie's boot in an atlen barn."

"We shall do penance for offending your highness," Eyvin had said, and then they were off before she could order them not to.

Marlow came in, followed by Highest Quiv. Neither were out of breath, but Quiv was vaguely pale.

"You dymensed again, Quiv? Well done." She motioned to the chairs before the cold fireplace. "And Marlow, did you get some sleep?"

He claimed he had, but the dark half-moons under his eyes still looked like bruises. He hugged his portfolio and waited.

"Sorgan belongs to the Revulsion," she said. "I was confronted by the qiznithan. He inhabits Dunne Yples's body. So that's one mystery we no longer have to worry about. Every soul in the city has been reviled. Yiothizandra wasn't there."

"How do you know?"

In truth she didn't know with absolute certainty. But reason told her she was correct. "She wasn't part of those who welcomed me to the city. Nor did I feel any particular activity upon the Revulsion. Not the sort of exertion I'd expect if Yioth were being turned."

"So where is she?" Marlow asked.

Kila shrugged and returned to the window. "Did Kinnon Swile come to you?"

"What? Oh, yes. But she wouldn't tell me anything." He opened his portfolio and withdrew a letter. "She bade me give you this."

"What does it say?" Kila asked, not moving from her spot.

"It's sealed, Your Majesty."

Kila laughed and waved for him to hand it over. Surprisingly, the Mistress of Kitchen's seal was intact. She had expected Marlow to read everything that came to her before she received it, sealed or not. She broke the wax and read the message.

ALL IS PREPARED as you requested. Breakfast, tea, lunch, supper all delivered daily. Various cooks and maids have overheard what you wished for them to overhear. The Fell Guard reports no visitors yet. Is Aimee in danger?

KILA HADN'T CONSIDERED whether Aimee was in danger or not, but obviously she was. She rubbed her arms and swallowed against a dry throat. When had it become so easy to put a life at risk like that? "You've both heard rumors about Saiya's new hiding place, yes?"

Both men gave her ridiculously false looks of total innocence.

"Come now, tell me."

Marlow reddened under her stare and looked down as his portfolio. "Well, one of my trusted observers did mention a bit of gossip about a new resident in the Fell Guard's barracks."

Quiv's brow quirked. "Oh, I had heard something of that."

"Oh please, do you men think me an idiot? I know you know Saiya is hidden there." Kila returned to the chair of the monarch and plopped down into it. "Of course, she's *not* there."

Now true emotion lit up their faces. Mostly relief. Kila threw the crumpled note at Marlow, hitting him square between the eyes. "You *do* think me an idiot. Have some faith in me. Saiya will not be found by anyone, revulyn, nosg, or demayne. And certainly not by you two."

Highest Quiv made a sort of half nod, half bow of respect to her. "So you've contrived for a rumor to go out in order to lure in a revulyn. I approve."

"As do I," Marlow said. He scooped up the note and tossed it into the cold fireplace. "May I?"

"Of course."

His mercus flared and immediately the message burned up. But the logs also caught fire, which had certainly been his intention. They watched the flames in silence for a while, until she noticed Quiv's knees bouncing. She had never known him to be impatient, but she supposed he was still awaiting the decision of the Nares.

"There were Donse Masters among the revulyns in Sorgan," she said. "But mostly Spinsters and Sensuals. Does the Coin here know of Pol's losses in Sorgan?"

"I have not spoken to her," Marlow said. "But you should

know that there is a new Coin. Not the one recently invested, but another new one. I think you knew her. Her name is Moirina Fiolt, from Garden Island. She is claiming to be 'High Medallion.'"

"I know Moirina. She was Coin Inlina's little dagger, and Pol's ambassador to me at Kil's Tower. How did she get such a post? Even Inlina didn't call herself High Medallion."

"She took it," Highest Quiv said. "She arrived here with at least two dozen merculyns. I haven't been able to learn much else, but there was one concerning aspect that came to my attention. One of my, er, observers"—he smirked at Marlow's knowing smile—"overheard an accent from Wantin. More than two speakers with such a manner of speech. Several others spoke differently as well. Slirya. Sorgan. Jallisea."

"What of it?" Kila asked.

"I think Moirina has brought the force of merculyns being collected by Voluptuary Harrisan Minn. But Minn herself has not come to Starside."

"I thought Minn had a hundred or more. Do you think Moirina a revulyn?"

"No," Quiv said, pausing. "But either she broke with Minn and pulled away some followers, or Minn and scores more were killed somewhere in their journeys and these are the survivors. Do you know the Elnisian word *kilenishza?*" Taking her blank stare as a no, he continued: "It means Kil's Swords. They were an order of warrior merculyns, a sort of cult as I understand it. Medallion Moirina is calling her band of merculyns her *kilenishza.*"

"She came here for me," Kila said, checking with Marlow who instantly nodded agreement.

"Oh certainly," he said. "But it isn't as if you have other concerns to address." As if his words were an invocation, the door to her chamber opened. A fell guardsman stepped in and bowed. "Your Majesty! Cheapsgate burns."

Kila was to the window in seconds, head thrust out over the dizzying height, weather-cloak protecting her from the icy wind. Cheapsgate was miles away, but billowing black clouds rose beyond the ring wall. A ruddy glow illuminated the bottoms of the smoke clouds.

"I did this," she said. "I'm Kil damned and cooked if I didn't."

Dox Viller's wheezing laughs resounded in her mind, and visions of his spittle flecked lips gawped before her eyes. She pulled her head in, furious at herself. Now she understood why Ell had allowed him to live. As usual her understanding came too bloody late.

"I'm going to sort out Cheapsgate," she said.

She held out her arms for the fell guardsman to grasp. He did so and she dymensed. They came out in the Interior Palace. *Nax, get in the pack.*

Her battered old backpack hung on a hook near the door. She shrugged it on and crouched for Nax to climb up and slip under the flap. She was about to wield enormous mercus feats. She would need Nax more than ever to keep the Revulsion at bay.

As the weight settled on her shoulders that ridiculous sense of forgetting something returned. She pushed it away. "Take hold, men."

They flashed to the courtyard of the Fell Guard barracks, where a series of perfectly maintained wooden halls opened on a training yard. The senior man who'd come with her bellowed for his brothers to assemble. A dozen were already sprinting toward them, with more bursting from the barracks, fitting gloves and helms as they ran. Shouts resounded inside the halls, with more men emerging every second.

Brother Commander Docit rushed up to her and stood at attention. "We are ready."

"Cheapsgate burns. I must address both the fire and save as many people as can be saved. I will dymense squads to the Cheaps. Your men will wait there until I have brought all who are able to go."

"We must keep a reserve force here, Your Majesty. At least ten men, though they will be loathe to remain behind."

"They will do their duty," Kila said.

The remark struck the commander like a physical blow. He blinked hard and then bowed. "I will do penance, Your Majesty. For it is as you say. How many can you dymense at once?"

"They must all touch me."

"Then they must carry you." He nodded to the squads behind him. Ten men rushed forward and Kila was suddenly lofted into the air, with hands gripping her arms, back, legs, and feet. "We are ready," said a squadron captain.

Kila dymensed. A crowd of gawkers had begun to gather near the Cheaps. They screamed and dashed away at the sudden arrival of Kila and the Fell Guard. It was fortunate that none were standing in the particular spot Kila had chosen.

The guards set her on her feet. "Keep this circle clear," she said, then dymensed back to the barracks courtyard. She hadn't taken a breath before she was again lifted, face to the sky.

What is happening? Nax complained.

Kila realized a fell guardsman was pressing against her pack and squashing the cat. She dymensed. Once on her feet again, she reversed the pack to rest against her chest. She lost count of the times she dymensed, but she spent no more than a few seconds on either side.

Brother Commander Docit was part of the last group, and when they came out of dymension he instantly began shouting orders. The fell guardsmen had pushed back the gawkers and formed into squads of five.

The guards of the Watch who manned the Cheaps twisted their necks back and forth from the fire to the impressive presence of the Fell Guard.

Kila found the Watch captain, a plump man with his pot helmet tipped far back on his head. "Open the gate," she ordered.

"But *they'll* come through!" he said, pointing to the desperate Cheapsgaters pressing against the other side of the gate.

Before Kila could say a word, Brother Commander Docit shouted: "You are speaking to your queen, man! Do as she commands!"

The Watch captain scratched at his lank forelock and gazed up at the impossibly tall commander. "This little thing is the queen?" He jerked a thumb at Kila.

Docit dismissed the man from his attention and sent his own men in to crank up the portcullis. Cheapsgaters flattened themselves to crawl under it, then those behind began to trample the ones on the ground.

With gold on her voice, Kila commanded them to wait. She didn't know how she did it, for it did not use the mercusine. But the result was instant and awful to behold. The poor ragged folk froze, jaws going slack.

"Have an officer herd these poor folks in orderly, commander," Kila said. "Make sure they move up the street to make room for those behind. But make them go swiftly."

Docit detached ten men to see to it. Then Kila took hold of him and dymensed to the top of the ring wall. Men of the Watch stood upon the battlements marveling at the fire that tore through the shacks and shanties beyond.

It had started in the center. Right in the heart of Dox Viller's hive. Like a living thing, the fire now pushed outward, lurching across narrow alleys, collapsing patchwork roofs, and cooking inhabitants alive. Faint screams broke through the incredible grumbling roar of the inferno. The searing heat of it brought sweat from the faces of the men who watched. Kila bolstered her weather-cloak to keep the heat at bay.

A crowd of a hundred people were pressing through the Cheaps, with stragglers stumbling toward it in ones and twos. To the south, the docks were crowded with desperate Cheapsgaters, with more clambering onto the ships moored there.

The smoke rising from the core of the blaze twisted as it billowed skyward, lifting orange sparks like terrified souls racing for safety in the heavens. The fire would soon reach the dock-side warehouses, then it would burn the docks and everyone on them.

Several ships had cut free of their moorings and were trying to beat out of the bay. Small figures were flung overboard; Cheapsgaters who had sought refuge aboard now found themselves flailing to swim in a winter ocean.

Inside her head again came Dox Viller's rasping laugh, gleeful at the destruction she had wrought.

"Commander Docit, once the Cheaps is clear, get those folk off the docks. I will put out the fire, then you will go in and rescue survivors and establish order. The Watch is yours to command. Understood?"

"I understand. Where will you be?"

"Right here. Send two men up if you wish."

She didn't notice when he darted away, for she had already sunk into the mercusine. What this called for was negation, massive negation. And so she summoned the sensation of cold, formed the bolts, and sent them forth.

53

GONG AND SMASH

The woman who had once been a girl named Mabri Soth, who had grown to become a Spinster of Pol, and who had finally been awakened from the Great Lie by Lord Yples, stood back in the shadows of a deep cellar beneath the Citadel.

Her revulynic power was masked with the clever feat Yples had taught her, but that meant she couldn't readily use her other new skill, the distraction feat, to divert the overly curious from taking too much notice of her presence. Especially when she probed deep into places she had no business being.

Seeing with the cold eye did not make her a fool. In fact, she had never been so calculating. Relying only on feats to avoid notice would be pure foolishness. Especially since Kila Sigh had recently returned to Starside.

But now Sigh was off in Cheapsgate with her felnithel, as planned. It was time to strike.

Soth had appropriated clothing from chambers inhabited by an ambassador's wife. The woman apparently bought new dresses every day, for she had an entire bedroom set aside for storing her garments. Soth had traded her Spinster's garb for an expensive sheath of deep crimson. She found a feather hat with a strange half veil that did well to cover her eyes and nose. And so she went through the halls of the Citadel, drawing the occasional curtsy from the maids.

She had learned two interesting things during her rovings. First was that Henley Mast had gone missing, along with his felnithel. He had been seen by servants descending into the basements accompanied by Kila Sigh and some fell guardsmen. Soth found that intriguing because it made no sense. Unless there was a passage to Moonside down there.

But the other thing, the more important thing Soth had gleaned, was that a girl had been placed among the Fell Guard. Aside from Kila Sigh, Soth had not felt any exceptionally powerful source of the mercus in the Citadel. Kil should be magnificently powerful. She hadn't felt such a presence.

Soth had an explanation for this. Kil might also be masked. And if a child had been placed in the Fell Guard barracks, then surely that must be the masked Kil.

The challenge now was to get in there, take the child, and get away before being impaled by a dozen spears. She decided to take Devin along, for the Fell Guard would perceive a man with a sword as a greater threat and therefore ignore her.

She found him where he had been standing, totally still, for several days. The Privileged Quarters were the last known location of the god-child. Devin had found an attic and taken up his watch there. For Soth, now dressed as she was, her entrance to the palatial complex drew no especial notice. That she carried a travel bag in one hand merely suggested she was a new arrival, ready to take up tenancy in one of the vacant apartments.

"Kil is near," she said to Devin when she found him in the attic. "You must change your clothes." She opened the bag and drew out the footman's garb she'd stolen. Devin donned it. She smoothed his hair as best she could. It was overlong for a footman, and his scraggle of beard would surely draw the wrong sort of attention.

"Meet me outside of the kitchens in a quarter of an hour."

He met her at the appointed time, taking no note of her own change in clothes. Changing from lady to servant was easy, for Yples's feat of distraction worked miracles against the flighty mind of a maid called Avril. And so it was footman Devin who bore the tray from the kitchens, across the bailey yard, and to the door of Fell Guard barracks Number Five. Maid Soth carried a basket of bread.

The Fell Guard barracks occupied a section of the bailey north of the main fortress. In her life as a Spinster, Soth had never given a thought to military matters. But even to an untrained eye, the precision and strength of these men was obvious. "They will all be awakened," she said to Devin. "As reviled, their power will be doubled."

The gossipy Avril had told Soth all she needed to know. Trays were to be taken from the kitchens to the barracks five times a day. It required only a few questions to find out to which building. One knock at the door was answered by a fell guardsman. He was shirtless. A flicker of memory crossed Soth's mind at the sight, but there was no response to his array of muscles beyond that. He eyed her and the footman, then the tray and basket. "Why two of you?"

"The tray is heavy and I am weak."

Perhaps no other response would have worked, but to a fell guardsman admissions of weakness were so shameful they had to be true. There was one more man in the hall of bunks. He was also in the processes of donning his gear. She strode down the rows, head level. Devin was keeping his eyes down at her instruction.

The very back of the barracks had been rearranged, with two temporary walls thrown up to form a little room. Inside, huddled under blankets, was a girl. Soth had heard how fast the child was growing, so she was not surprised to see her larger than last reported. This looked to be a girl of sixteen, not twelve. Her head was covered with a bonnet. That was odd, but of no import.

She gave off no mercus potential. Masked, indeed.

The heavy boot of a fell guardsman scuffed the floor behind her as she led Devin into the room. She pointed to a little serving table. "Put the tray there." She went to the bed where the girl lay. "Your midday is here, miss. Are you hungry?"

"Are you feeling well, Avril?" the girl asked. "I've never known you to be on time for—" She turned over in bed and stopped short. "You're not Avril."

"She fell ill."

The fell guardsman was coming into the room.

Devin uncovered the tray and removed his sword from it. With no emotion in his face, he slashed it across the man's exposed chest. Soth grabbed the girl. A great struggle erupted behind her. Soth formed the bolts of dymension, but the girl fought like a cornered weasel, flailing her arms and kicking her legs. She caught Soth's belly with her heel and shoved her backward, dislodging the tray from the table. It fell to the floor with a gong and smash of porcelain.

The other guard shouted a question outside the room. Soth saw Devin swing his sword, saw the injured, shirtless fell guardsman deflect the blade with his hand, losing a thumb in the effort. The other guardsman pushed through, bearing his sword. A flick of his arm separated Devin from his head.

Soth lunged at the girl, throwing herself bodily onto her.

"I'm not Saiya! I'm not Saiya!"

The girl was sobbing and gibbering.

Soth pulled back, astonishment shattering the equanimity of the cold eye.

Another decoy! This one nestled inside a trap. Sigh was clever.

Soth produced a little knife from her waistband, drew its edge across the pale, quivering throat. The girl grabbed her gushing throat, eyes wide.

Soth was yanked backward by the collar of her maid's uniform, held up so that her toes barely touched the floor. The fell guardsman brought his helmed face close to hers. "Who are you?"

She released the bolts of dymension, bending them to take only his hand with her. When the world returned, she was still off her toes. Her weight returned, driving her down, unbalanced. The hollow attic above the Privileged Suites resounded with the thump of her body impacting the dusty floor.

She slammed her mask into place and slowly got to her feet. She kicked aside the fell guardsman's hand like a clod of cow dung. Now she knew the truth. The god was not at the Citadel. The trap had almost closed around her.

It was time to change back into the garb of a lady. The cool rationality of the cold eye slowly returned. By the time she'd affixed her hat and veil, she had decided on her next course of action. Kil was not in Starside. So now she would turn her search for that passage to Moonside.

54

DOES IT PLEASE YOU?

Cheapsgate smoldered.

Kila walked over simmering ash, stepping over the white crusted timbers of half-burned ship's hull ribs that had once been the roof of Critt Sanglo's tavern.

Only the shacks on the very periphery of the slums had survived. Nothing the fire had touched was worth salvaging. Even cookpots had turned to slag. None of the dead near the center would need a funeral pyre. The rest of the remains would be committed to the Sourwater. Hundreds of severely burned corpses littered the perimeter, where the Fell Guard stood in ranks to keep the curious out of the ash and looters away from the still standing homes.

Eyvin and Nils had joined her at some point. They had been scrubbed and spotless at the time. Now they were again stained and stinky from walking with her through the ruins, hefting beams, and carrying out dying Cheapsgaters.

The Warren was destroyed, the top floor having collapsed and slid into the Sourwater. Kila found Parlo Odok sitting on a charred chair amidst the ash of his lost kingdom. He looked at her and said nothing.

"Where's Jocko?" she asked.

"He burnt, then dove inta the Sourwater. Never came up. Ya shoulda let ol' Viller alone, girl. Ya shoulda stayed outta affairs ya don't unnerstand."

She nodded to Nils. He urged Parlo up and got him walking toward the refugee line. She was moving all survivors into Starside, sending the most grievously wounded to the Baths.

Brother Commander Docit stalked here and there while yelling at his men and at the cold, filthy citizens. She knew her personal guard could not police them forever. But the Watch was barely competent to keep the inner city orderly these days.

I'm worn out, Nax.

The mercus isn't food. You must eat.

"As true as that?" she said. A wave of loneliness struck her when there was no one to answer. She longed for Henley's warmth and wisdom. She missed Fallo. He'd say something inappropriate to cheer her up.

Bringing these people into the city was going to be a problem. Half the city already hated her, and those inside the walls generally despised those who lived outside them. They would not welcome these interlopers into their inns, and certainly not into their homes.

An idea flowered in that moment, brightening her spirits. Perhaps she could twist two problems into one. "I'm going to dymense."

Eyvin and Nils touched her and she let the bolts fly. She came back to the world and swayed on her feet. She really did need to eat.

The street before her was pristine, clear of slush or snow, the buildings to either side freshly constructed and painted. Folk had gathered in open areas and rooftops to watch the smoke over Cheapsgate, but now that it was dissipating they were returning to their homes.

Until they spotted Kila braced by two fell guardsmen.

Come onto my shoulder, Nax.

Gladly. The cat scrambled from the pack and took up her favorite perch. At the sight of her, the faces on the street lit up. They had suspected who Kila was, but now they knew. In a wave the subjects of the Blasted Quarter dropped to their knees, bent forward, and offered their palms in supplication. Kila walked among them, keeping her expression blank.

People began to pour from homes and shops and inns. Furtive whispers brought these newcomers to their knees as well. Kila had heard of a new-built tower for the Way of Kila. It was easy to find. A silk banner now flew over it, pearly white emblazoned with the black Crown of Kil backed by raven's wings. She made her way amongst the silent worshippers and came to the front entry.

"Who claims to be Highest of Kila in this place?" she asked, adding power to her voice with mercusine bolts. "Come forth and speak with me."

A man of thirty years emerged from the tower, hands pressed together at his chest. With every step he made a little bow to her. He was bearded and kindly of face, with long brown hair lying over his shoulders.

"You?" Kila said, astonished. This was the man she'd scolded on the road to Tearling. He'd assembled a squalid encampment of Way of Kila followers near the river.

"Is this the day?" he asked. "Do you deem us ready?"

She turned to study the crowd. Clean, well fed folk. Industrious by all accounts. Where the Way of Kila had once been the detritus of humanity, now their revitalized Blasted Quarter was beginning to outshine Upper Terriside. It lacked only the stately manors of rich merchants.

"That depends," she said, finally answering him.

"What must we do?" He kept his eyes down, palms pressed together, fingers tented toward his chin.

"Cheapsgate is no more. The survivors have no place to live. Will you welcome them?"

"None who follow the Way of Kila will be refused."

"And if they don't follow your Way?"

Conflict drew his mouth down. His jaw muscles bulged.

Seizing on his hesitation, Kila struck. Not with the mercus, but with judgment. "You are not ready." She turned away from him and scanned the crowd. "Will you offer no shelter, no food to your brothers and sisters from Cheapsgate?"

At once a roar of protestations arose. They would give everything to the Cheapsgaters, they would give over their homes. Then the stripping began. First an elderly man pulled off his tunic and shucked off his trousers. "I give even my own clothes!" he cried.

Dresses and robes and shirts and pants began to come off. Pale skin and brown skin met the cold air, and on every shoulder and back arose gooseflesh. Women waved their skirts overhead to show Kila how generous they could be.

Soon apples and carrots and potatoes were lofted toward her, as worshippers offered food. And behind her came their bearded leader, lean and muscular, bearing an armful of robes, his own included. "Does it please you?"

"No," she said softly. "I do not ask you to give up all you own, but merely to share a portion. Share a hearth and a loaf and cup. If you surrender all of this, the Cheapsgaters will take it and few will thank you. Their suffering is pitiable, but it does not necessarily make them noble. Trust me, I'm one of them. Do not seek to appease me through good acts, but act out of goodness and I shall be pleased."

He looked stricken. And very cold in his nakedness. Kila again powered her voice with the mercus so that all in the

Blasted Quarter could hear. "Your willingness to sacrifice warms me. Now put on your clothes, gather up your food. Return to your homes. Welcome those who will accept your hospitality. Be strong so that you can lend strength to the weak. Do not become weak yourselves or you will be overrun."

She looked to the Highest. "What's your name?"

"Mill. Highest Mill."

"Come closer."

When he came within reach, she pressed her hand to his forehead and shoved in a mind probe. She possessed no subtlety with such feats, but she knew what to look for. She rifled through his thoughts and memories, seeking his deepest intentions. Nothing as clear as a dream came through to her, and most of it was a muddle. But there was no Revulsion in him, nor any spark of the mercus. What she sensed was an earnest loyalty to her. He had been lost his whole life, feeling an inexplicable lack. She had filled that emptiness. Or at least the idea he had formed of her had filled it.

"You are indeed a Highest of Kila," she announced. "But do not forget that this quarter is not a city unto itself, and you are not its king. I can see the entire city from the Citadel. I shall know what you do and whether you honor or disgrace my name."

She withdrew her mind probes and flushed herself with imperious allure, another class of mercus feat she wielded more as a hammer than an embroidery needle. "Expect a summons from Administrator Marlow soon."

55

BURNT ONE

"**H**e was fortunate. That's all I can say."

"Fortunate? How can you say this is fortunate?" That was Quinn's voice. Strange how Fallo had never noticed how lovely it was before. Deep, a bit breathy. That Gristensider accent sharp and confident.

"She might have turned him," the man said.

Then, quiet.

Except for Lop's purring. That was the warm weight on Fallo's chest, he supposed. That was nice. Fallo felt warm, peaceful. Like waking up on the morning after Winternight, lazy and with the whole day free. At times like that, one's whole body would be numb, almost as if it didn't exist.

Lop chirped.

"Is he awake?" That was a man's voice. Oh, that's right. The merculyn man. What was his name? Nefler Ernist.

"I'm awake," Fallo said. It came out a croak, separating the dry leaves of his tongue and palate most painfully. The tearing sensation spread, like a layer of skin being peeled away all the way down his throat. And also across his face, and hands, and chest.

"Quickly, lass, the salve."

"There's not much left. Zirhine didn't anticipate this."

Zirhine? "Where is she?" Fallo moaned. "Ah me. My skin is on fire."

A cold goo swiped across his forehead and cheeks, instantly relieving the pain there. But it did nothing against the flaying feeling on his limbs and torso. A scream was about to come out. He didn't want to scream. Not in front of Quinn. She didn't need to know his weakness.

Wetness on his lips. Liquid poured through. He spluttered and choked. Why couldn't he see? His hands tried to reach his face. Something was on his face. But his wrists were bound. "Let me up!"

Again the wetness. "Drink, lad. Drink." He didn't have much choice. But what was it? Water? Tea? He couldn't taste it, but it was thick and lumpy.

Swallow it, Lop ordered.

Quinn was close to him, her breath on his ear felt like dragon fire. "I'm here. Let the trezz do its work. It has some of Zirhine's salve in it. I hope it will help."

In fact it was working. The pain was growing distant now. It was there, but not concerning.

"He's breathing easier," Nefler Ernist said. "That is well. I do not know much of mooncrafter lore, but this is impressive."

"Until he wakes again. We must find more. Surely there's a ferneater somewhere nearby."

"Around Traye? Not likely. Perhaps Trist. I do wish I had learned healing feats. Such require more than the five senses, you know."

Fallo heard no more of their conversation as the spreading numbness again pulled him in to Lumne's realm. If he dreamed, his memory wanted no part of it. And when he next began to wake, Lop meowed and the trezz concoction was again forced into his mouth.

The next time he woke, sunlight beamed through an arched window and spilled across his face. His body felt like he'd been beaten with hammers and left in the sun to be scalded head to foot. He blinked against a hard crust covering his eyes. Little granules of something flakey made his eyes sting, and no matter how hard he blinked he couldn't focus. That enormous, furry black face looking at him had to be Lop's.

You are too fat, Lop. I can hardly breath with you standing on me.

Nonsense. Wake up. You must eat.

I'm awake. I'm not hungry.

You will be.

A door closed. It sounded like it came from another room. He lifted his head, realized he had no idea where he was. A white bedroom with lots of frilly pillows, lace curtains, and what appeared to be wooden dolls on one shelf. The door opened and Quinn came in bearing a platter. The smell of tea, toast, and bacon tickled his nose. His stomach suddenly teetered between nausea and starvation.

Quinn smiled at him as she set the platter on the table. She shook a finger at Lop. "Leave that plate alone. It's Fallo's breakfast."

Then she was helping Fallo sit up. The muscles of his abdomen trembled with the effort, and he could barely lift his arms. "I feel like a dragon chewed me up and plopped me out."

"Nothing so bad as that," she said lightly. "A revulyn set you on fire, is all."

"Oh, well. Then I have nothing to worry about." He did have a memory of a revulyn in a house. And of a man smashing a young woman's face into a table. And of his legs being will-shifted. As each new memory rose, his nausea grew.

The fire. The blue flames. He tilted far enough to vomit onto the floor. Not much came up, but he felt instantly better.

His hands were wrapped in bandages. And so was much of his head and face. That was why his jaw and mouth felt so constricted. "How bad is it?"

Quinn came to sit on the side of the bed, holding the plate. She balanced it on her knees so she could use her good hand to feed him. First, she offered him a sip of tea. He drank it all. Then came a bite of toast. Her eyes were luminous, warm. Brows knit with worry, or compassion, or sorrow. Her face was clean, and she wore a new shirt. A loose, lace-throated blouse with puffy shoulders and tight sleeves. A cropped vest in burgundy, with smart brass buttons. Jodhpurs and knee-high boots.

"Answer me," he said around a mouthful of bacon.

"You were burned badly. You've been mostly asleep for a few days."

The bacon turned to ash in his mouth. Days? That was an eternity given the task they were to complete. "Illy?"

"Safe. Without her you certainly would have died. She's with Nefler Ernist."

He swallowed the bacon, then used his teeth to begin unwrapping his right hand. Quinn tried to stop him. "Leave it, Fallo. Please. Nothing good will come of it. We must keep your skin clean."

He jerked his hand away and continued to unwrap the bandages with his teeth, an awkward task at best, until Quinn resigned herself to doing it for him. When the last of the white fabric fell away he saw the back of his hand. Red, angry skin, all webbed over in white. Not smooth at all, but rising and falling in ridges and hollows. He tried to close his fist, but the skin was too tight, and it complained with rips of agony that cost him his breath.

"Kil's eyes." He forced a grin, felt the skin of his face resist.

He could only imagine how awful his grimace looked. He didn't have to, for Quinn pulled back from him. Not far before catching herself. But enough to tell him all he needed to know. Appetite gone, he closed his eyes and rolled onto his side, away from her. He felt her take up his arm, clamp it to her side so her remaining hand could rewrap his hideous burnt one.

Hideous Burnt One. That's me.

Lop picked her way down the bed, over his legs, and around to the other side. He heard her snuffling at the uneaten bits of his breakfast.

"Lop saved your life," Quinn said. "Stood right between you and the revulyn."

"Is she burned?" Terror made him turn over, seek out the cat who was eating his eggs. But she was perfectly intact, fluffy as ever. Rotund as a harvest festival pumpkin.

"The revulyn stopped instantly, backed away from Lop. It was the strangest thing I have ever seen. And the most incredible. She defied her like a dragon. I got a good stab in before she dymensed away. Doesn't make much difference on that sort, though."

He snorted. A worm of ingratitude curled around his brain. Perhaps Lop had done him no favors by saving him, Burnt One that he was.

"Where are we?" he asked. "Someplace with a seamstress nearby? I need a cowl fashioned that will cover my face. Something with eye and mouth holes."

"Oh hush. But since you asked, we are in Middlesbrit, just outside of Traye. We are the guests of Nefler Ernist's sister. And we will be leaving soon. The reviled are everywhere and rumors coming from inside the city are concerning."

"Where will we go? *How* will we go?"

"There's a vergent pass nearby." She put a hand on his shoulder, brought her face very close to his. Her eyes were alight. "The task Xilo set for us remains, shadline. We will see it through."

"Leave me here, then. I'll just slow you down."

"Don't tell me what to do." She kissed his forehead, a tenderness blunted by the fabric of his bandages. "I will lead us. Trust me."

"You hear something?" he asked, seeking hope in her eyes.

He found more than hope there. Certainty. "I know where another of the reborn gods is," she said.

"Where? And how do you know?"

She tugged her earlobe. "I met a shadline here. We exchanged fate's-pieces. I recognized the import of his instantly. Rest now. He will come to see you soon and tell you the whole story."

56

ELL'S GIFT

There were three bodies. The first was Aimee, the scullery girl who had posed as Saiya, covered with a woolen blanket. The second was the Iron Scholar, headless. The eyes still moved, following Kila as she moved around it.

And one fell guardsmen, slain by a slash of a reviled blade.

Three other fell guardsmen stood like statues nearby, faces grim in their failure to protect the girl. They hadn't been present, but they took blame as if they had been. Even Eyvin and Nils wore that look, of stupid men preparing to declare penance for a failure in which they had no part.

Kila studied the shrouded lump of the girl. The bait.

Brother Commander Docit was also there, an enormous wall of muscle and steel, jaw bulging. He was also waiting for Kila's judgment, waiting for her to announce her total displeasure. And she *was* displeased. But not with the Fell Guard.

What penance should *she* face? she wondered. And on the heels of that query, she wondered what good it would do. Aimee would not thank her for it. Flogging herself with the Fell Guard's three-tailed whip would not undo death.

"The fire in Cheapsgate pulled us away from here," she said into the heavy silence. "Perhaps this revulyn set it, or perhaps he merely saw the opportunity it provided. In either case, we caught him. Were there others with him?"

"A maid, Your Majesty. She dymensed with Brother Flinot's hand."

The revulyn woman who had killed Mayrie.

"This one isn't dead," she said, bending over the head, locking eyes with it. "Did you search its pockets?"

A fell guardsman dropped to one knee next to the body and did just that. He produced a knife, three copper plugs, a key, and small book. Kila took the book, noted the skim of Revulsion covering it. It was inscribed, part of the Hackwatch library. *A Short Treatise on Succession, Inheritance and the Rights of Income for Superfluous Sons.* She put the book aside and took up the key. Iron, simple. It could open any of a million doors in Starside or across the world.

She called forth a sphere of mercus light and tilted the key. The barrel was etched. *Mdm. Glivey's - Rm. 9.* A boarding house key. She gave it to Docit and told him to have the home searched top to bottom. The order was given and men ran. She doubted they would find anything of use to her.

"The Fell Guard will see to its own penance," she said. "Find a box for that head and have it brought to Highest Quiv. He will wish to study it. Burn the bodies immediately."

She left the barracks on foot. Dymensing would be more exhausting than walking. In fact, she had never felt so overfull of the mercus and wished to be rid of it for a while. And so she formed the final feat of the day—she hoped—and masked herself.

Food, she sent to Nax.

Indeed!

But it was more than a meal that drew her to the kitchens

and finally into Kinnon Swile's tidy little office. She closed the door and waved the bowing Mistress of Kitchens back to her seat. Kila hooked a foot on the leg of a chair and slid it away from the wall. With a huge sigh she plopped down on it. "I asked one of the cooks to make me that cheesy noodle dish."

"It's your kitchen to command."

"Aimee is dead. I'm sorry. A fell guardsmen was killed defending her. One of the attackers was injured and captured." She could hardly say beheaded but not killed.

The usually unflappable woman bowed her head and cursed, then wept softly. Kila waited for it to pass, and it did. With red-rimmed eyes and red-tipped nose the woman lifted her chin, a hint of defiance in her face. "Was it worth it?"

"The assailant hasn't been questioned yet. But I remain hopeful we will learn something vital from him. There was a fire in Cheapsgate and I took away the Fell Guard. Certainly a diversion."

Kinnon accepted this with a nod and dabbed her eyes. "Aimee was not on a path toward promotion here. She had likely risen to her highest post. Scrubbing pots. But she was earnest, worked hard, and didn't complain much. She loved knowing she was working so close to Her Enlightened. Pardon, majesty."

"I understand. And I know you don't think me worthy of Ell's crown. Neither do I. She was wise and strong."

"I never said you weren't worthy." It was a statement of truth, though Kila noted it wasn't actually a denial.

A rap at the door. A cook's assistant brought in Kila's tray and a dish of fried chicken giblets for Nax. Kila and Nax tucked into their dinners as Kinnon Swile watched. The noodles caused a flush of warmth to flow through Kila's neck and arms. "I was starving," she said around a mouthful.

"How well do you know Terissa Viller?" Swile asked.

Kila stopped chewing. "Huh?"

"The young woman Henley Mast brought here. She was in Tordain as I understand it. Before it fell apart."

"Why do you ask?"

"She wants a post here. In the Citadel."

"She was an innkeeper's maid. And a shameless—" She swallowed her bite and washed it down with a bit of watered trezz. "—uh, rather a flirt as I understand it."

"A young woman a flirt?" Kinnon mockingly exclaimed, dabbing her eyes again. "I've never heard of such a thing. But can she be trusted to work inside the Citadel?"

"You going to give her Aimee's job?" Kila ducked her head to hide the flush of shame that burned through her face. "I'm sorry. That was ill said. I didn't mean . . . What post?"

"She's asking to serve in the Interior Palace."

It was absurd. Did the fool girl think Kila a copper plug moron? Why would she bring that tart into her home just to have her making eyes at Henley day and night? "Isn't that sort of post reserved for senior maids and footmen? Why would an outsider from Tordain be brought into such a trusted position?"

Swile unfolded a note and gave it to her. "Henley Mast wrote this recommendation. The staff are uncertain what authority he has in such matters. It's making people uncomfortable. It would be well if you declared it unambiguously, Your Majesty."

Henley's handwriting was crisp and orderly, an "educated hand" as her father would have said. His words, plain and honest, spoke only to Terissa's abilities. Nevertheless, Kila felt a hot urge to tear it to shreds. An unbidden vision came to mind again. The white-faced corpse of Dox Viller; Terissa's father. She returned the note to Swile. "Henley is a fine judge of character. In matters of the household consider his requests my requests."

There wasn't much work for Terissa to do in the residence anyway. Kila was rarely there. And Henley . . . No. She would not dwell on his absence. She would know if he were dead, for the bond would vanish totally. At the moment it was simply silent, impenetrable. But it was there.

"I'm going to bed," she said. She scooped up the cat and walked through the corridors of the Citadel to the Interior Palace. She shooed the maid corps away, and ordered the Mistress of Wardrobe to wait until she called before intruding in the morning.

The bed was soft, the blankets sumptuous. Nax settled in next to her. And she lay awake, eyes open, feeling as hollow as a burnt out ruin. Time oozed along, taking her no closer to sleep. Even Nax's drowsy dreams seeping across the bond in purrful breaths did nothing to lull her. Instead, her mind filled with images of Yples and of the fire and of poor Aimee. They emerged from the bleakness of her mind, to play before her as if happening again and again. Failure, failure, failure.

Agitated, she threw off her covers and paced from the bedroom, through the hall to the library, down the curling stairs to the dimly lit reception hall with its stuffed chairs and tablescapes of statues and relics. She pressed through the doors and out onto the wedge-shaped prow of the Citadel, welcoming the cold air as it filtered through the sheer fabric of her night-clothes.

Bare of foot, hair flying loose, she breathed in the breeze, which had shifted westerly, bringing with it hints of ocean, ash, and dead fish. She walked onto the Divide and put her toes to the curb and looked down into Moonside. The night was clear, and a partial moon stood directly overhead, limning the Revulsion clouds in silver.

"Flaumishtak," she whispered. "Please come."

And he did, somehow knowing to dymense twenty paces away so that his mercus green would not disturb her. She felt his presence but didn't look. "The qiznithan is in Sorgan," she said. "It has taken over Dunne Yples. How come you didn't tell me?"

"I didn't know," came the soft, rumbling reply. "You forget that the Revulsion is appalling to me. It is no simple thing for me to sniff it out and track it like a hound." There was something petulant in his words, reminding her of Nax's similar objections.

"All of Sorgan has been turned," she said. "I don't think Yiothizandra was there."

"She isn't. She's in the mountains just east of Ceronhel."

"And you didn't bring her to me." She couldn't muster the anger this revelation merited. In fact, she couldn't bring up any emotion. Unless weariness itself was an emotion.

A heavy hand rested on her shoulder, clawed thumb draping down the outside of her upper arm. He forced her to turn and face him. She had to crane her neck to see the glowing, slitted eyes and slash of mouth. Oly stared down from the beast's shoulder, for once not instantly hissing at the sight of her face. Flaumishtak's wide nose flared as he breathed, eyes banked to amber coals.

"I heard her call to me, and I went. But I dared not to go closer," he said. "The nosg shamans now wield a black swarmlight, corrupted somehow by the Revulsion. The qiznithan found some way to turn them, though I do not know how. Unless..."

"Unless what?"

"The elnisians of Starside who were first turned ate of a certain mimak mushroom. Blackshine."

A deflating disappointment threatened to pull Kila down. She had not forgotten Quiv's hope that she could wield the swarmlight when the mercus itself was too dangerous to attempt. But if the nosg magic was corruptible, even that course might be barred to her. "You fear shamans that much?" she asked, hoping to taunt him.

"I do these. As should you. The qiznithan will turn them all, and he will send them south. Sorgan has fallen from within, and so too will many other city-realms. Traye is boiling over with a sickness, likely the Revulsion. Tordain is in civil war. Surely Yples will seize upon the chaos to begin turning there. There are more Donse Masters in Tordain than in all of the rest of the world. Whatever of humanity survives those incursions will be swept up by an unstoppable nosg invasion from the north. Sigh, I fear that flames have been lit on every edge of the page, and more burn holes from the center. Unless you can quench them —and soon—all will be ash."

"I can barely snuff out the fires I start," she said sadly. She wondered if Ell had ever faced such hopeless times. Wondered how the always calm and strong dragnithan woman would address these crises. She always seemed to know what to do, or at least who to ask. Very likely she would assemble a council meeting. But Kila was tired of talking. Tired of pretending to be strong and pretending to be collected. Tired of reacting. She had thought she was doing something good when she went after Dox Viller. But that had been more reaction.

Flaumishtak moved to stand next to her, to look out over the clouds of Moonside. The moon was a silver thumbnail overhead.

"I couldn't sleep tonight," she said stupidly. "Your ill news won't help."

"I could put you to sleep," he said. "A little mind probe and you will awaken in the morning fresh of limb and mind."

"Just tell me where Yiothizandra is. You once claimed that you can see all places. Explain where I can find her so that I can dymense there."

"What of the corruption in Sorgan? Are you simply ceding an entire city-realm to Yples while you rescue your worst enemy?"

"I cannot do it all at once!" she shouted, anger bubbling up out of her exhaustion. Oly chirped and turned to face the other way, showing her the underside of his tail.

She continued more calmly. "I've already faced Yples and his band of revulyns. I could not defeat them. Not alone. Ell said I would need all of the demayne. I don't *have* them all yet. I sent Harnzyne to find Bazron. I hope he's not been killed. Can you find him? Maybe together you can find Eckso and Klayne. I'll fetch Yiothizandra. And then all of us will meet to plan how we will face the Revulsion."

The response she got was not disdain, or outrage, nor even his typical rumbling laugh. In fact, there was no mockery in his tone at all. "I see now why she chose you, Sigh. You can speak with gold upon your voice. I am not your subject, but I am your ally. I will do as you ask. I cannot tell you where Yiothizandra is in such detail that you can dymense there. And you should not seek to do so anyway lest you come out amongst a band of Blackshine shamans. Go to Ceronhel. Find her nosg-kin facto-tum, Noi-Ick-Noi. He knows all of the secret ways in and out of the fortress. You know him from your time there. He can lead you to her. I will search out Harnzyne. The dragnithor may know better how to fight a qiznithan than I do."

Before dymensing he did something unprecedented. He bowed. Ever so slightly, but enough to make Oly cling harder for balance. The cat turned his head and spat, and then they were gone.

She had made her fell guardsmen wait inside the Citadel. She was alone.

All paths were open to her, she realized. Like standing upon the flat, empty plain of the Neer grasslands. She had never been there, but she could imagine the endless expanse of grass, waist high, uninterrupted by road or house for leagues on end. One could walk in any direction, unimpeded.

She could dymense to Semūin's Vale and collect Saiya. They

could track down Fallo and Quinn in Cigil-Tine. Or maybe venture into The Boil where none wished to go. Or perhaps board a ship, command its captain to sail east, from sea bastion to sea bastion until coming to some other land where nobody knew her. Perhaps she should simply step off the Divide, flutter into Moonside and find Henley.

"Perhaps you should drink in the Revulsion." Dox Viller's purple lips spread wide, moist and puffy. *"Be done with it."*

She shoved the thought away.

Starside lay behind her, alive, restless. Cheapsgaters sleeping in the streets. Way of Kila luring in Terriside's sons and daughters. Nares sitting in council to select the Highest of Highests. Unfriendly leaders in Pol's Well and the Baths of Ori. Radiancies scheming for her favor, scheming to undercut each other, scheming for power amidst the chaos. Reviled and revulyns walking the streets, more perhaps coming even now through the Moriterran Pass, posing as refugees from Tordain.

She had met all challenges, from the Hargothe to Yples to Yiothizandra. She'd beaten them all, but seemed never to defeat them. In victory she had hurt so many who had the misfortune of being in her way. "I'm tired, Wen," she said to the wind. A snatch of an old song came to her, pulling a humorless laugh through her nose. *"The queen of chaos wears a crown of lead."*

Indeed she does.

She recalled her scepter and its pleasant effect on her mind. It was the effort of a few seconds to retrieve it from where it still lay upon a chair in her dressing room. Dymensing back to the Divide, she sat cross legged, cradling the priceless relic in one elbow. Muscles in her neck and back loosened, her chest unlocked and breath came easier. Exhaustion was still heavy upon her, and soon the scepter's charms had her head drooping.

She slept, sitting in the wind.

A raven soared high overhead unseen by anyone. It was

black against blackness, and it flew very high. It did not need to flap its wings, for the westerly wind had stiffened. It kited there, above the sleeping woman, keeping watch.

A decision remained to be made, it knew. Had Cloak Einlin been present, he would have called Kila's lonely moment a fate-hand. But there was no council, no arguments, no listening for the call of the force of destiny. Merely a girl asleep. One who already knew the path she must walk.

Ell was gone. She could do nothing to invade Kila's dreams and seed her thoughts. Pennie had already voiced Roya Reth's last warning, expending her life to do so. The raven could squawk, but its cry would fly away on the wind tonight, never to reach an ear.

In Kila's dream she sat at Finta Sahng's time-polished table, drinking tea with Wen. The old woman, face of a million creases, joined them. Smiling, she spoke of small things, gossip of Lower Terriside, and of the healing properties of macwort and blood sedge. Cats were curled in laps. The fire danced cheerfully. The air was redolent of drying herbs and a stewpot on the simmer.

Outside the dream and inside the Citadel, beyond where the stolid fell guardsmen stood watching their queen sleeping, a backpack hung from a hook near the door. The top flap was open. A bluish light burst from it, painting the wall with faint and flickery splashes.

Kila's head snapped up, breath sucking through her teeth. She hadn't been breathing. Her heart slammed and she covered it with a hand. Groaning, she got to her feet and went inside. The sense of having forgotten something had fallen silent. She knew what it was.

Ell's gift.

Nax's incoherent dreams wafted through the bond, making

Kila's vision bleary despite the wash of wakefulness that filled her limbs. She had to look. Had to see. Right now.

The backpack came off the hook and went onto the nearest table, upsetting a vase. Her fell guardsmen moved into the room to watch over her. They kept well back.

Light spilled from the pack. She dug deep in, all the way to the bottom until her hand closed around a small handle. She pulled out the mirror Ell had given her so long ago and looked into the glass. The light emanating from the glass immediately began to haze over her reflection like frost upon a window. Her wide-eyed expression barely registered, nor did she note the circles under her eyes. The relic took hold of her and her vision filled with the glow until she had passed through the glass, like leaping through a window.

She flew over moonlit mountains, the snow-covered peaks' brightness making the valleys all the blacker. But far ahead that blackness was interrupted by pulses of light, sickly green and jaundiced yellows. As she swooped toward it, cliffs arose to her left and right, the boundaries of a valley.

The floor was a snowy plain, and in the center a circle of shamans blasted swarmlight rays at a kneeling figure. As Kila glided closer the head lifted and fire-filled eyes watched her pass. Recognizing Yiothizandra, Kila tried to turn and go back. But she didn't control her flight. It lifted again and carried her west, over a high ridge before again swooping low to bypass the stolid black face of Ceronhel's battlements.

She flew close to a broken tower, unrepaired yet by Yioth's work crews. The fortress passed beneath her and was then gone. She wished to look back at it, but the mirror showed only what lay ahead. The valley of the river Griln, a winding serpent of frost amidst snow-shrouded scraggle and grass.

Ahead, blackness. The snow should have reflected moonlight there. But it did not. Kila felt the wind whipping over her face as she sped along two spans over the ground. The wall of nothingness approached faster and faster, and then was revealed as she abruptly lifted and skimmed over a host of nosg on the march. Their axes and swords and spears glinted dimly.

Her flight stopped. She hovered, bodiless over the horde. All around her, eyes began to glow. She recognized the eyegems of shaman staves. They collected a violet light that warped and distorted the air. A thousand pairs of eyes, then more in the distance. Ten thousand. So many eyes. Looking at her. Looking *into* her.

Again she flew, coming at last to a great barge borne upon the shoulders of a dozen elgin. These giant nosg-kin lumbered ahead without strain. She hovered to keep pace, vision drawing closer and closer to a man standing upon the prow of the platform. He wore the robes of a Donse Master. At first she thought it was Qiznithan Yples, but upon drawing close enough to touch, she saw he was unknown to her. He had sharp cheekbones and a prominent chin. His eyes did not have the total vacancy of a reviled. They looked ahead. He held a skull staff, eyegems of dark green aglow.

Abruptly his head jerked around, he stared at her. His mouth opened in a strange grin. He laughed, a cackle of crazed glee. "So, you see me. Where is the child? Where?"

The mirror was wrenched from her hand. A fell guardsman stood before her, holding it. The light faded to nothing. "Majesty, are you well?"

Her hand was cramped from clutching the mirror. Nax had come, was standing at her feet looking up. "How long?"

"A few minutes, majesty," the man said. He offered the mirror to her, but she pointed to the pack. He put it in. "My apologies, but you were groaning and didn't seem able to breathe."

"You did well, thank you. Mercusine relics can be temperamental."

She took up the backpack and padded off to her bedchamber. Nax followed closely behind. "I'm going to bed," she said over her shoulder. "See that I'm not disturbed until I awaken on my own."

The fell guardsmen took their posts by her door. She closed it and quickly changed into fresh clothes. Black trousers with tight cuffs at the ankle. A tight-fitted undershirt and her plainest blouse. A looser jacket than usual, glossy ravens embroidered on the sleeves. The scepter went onto the bed. Too bulky to take with her, she decided. Nax would probably need room in the pack at some point.

She wished for a pair of good boots, but Ell's were all too small. She would have to settle for her canvas shoes and skillful weather-cloaking. She shrugged on a black cloak with a deep hood.

Where are we going? Nax sent.

Ceronhel.

She found herself looking around the room, casting about for anything else she might need. But she had no way of knowing what she would need. She was about to call for her fell guardsmen but cut it off. What could they do but slow her down and alert nosg to her arrival? A rush of hot shame burned her cheeks as she remembered ordering Henley to take two fell guardsmen with him.

But she was queen. She couldn't simply leave Starside wondering where she'd gone. She dymensed with Nax to Marlow's office. The man was asleep in his chair, teacup overturned in his lap. She found a blank scrap and scribbled a note, vaguely embarrassed by her childish scrawl. His desk was once again a disaster of papers and ledgers. He'd never notice one note amidst the debris. She upended his teacup and tented the note gingerly atop the base so he'd see it.

Let's go fetch Yioth, Naxie. If Pol smiles, we'll be back before anyone knows we were gone.

She knew just where in Ceronhel to dymense to. A place she wished she'd never seen, and which no nosg would wish to visit. She formed the bolts and released the feat.

High above the Divide, the raven cried out. Troubled dreams plagued the city's sleepers, and sudden chills crept over those still awake.

57

WITH RIGHTEOUS RAGE

If it could be said that Revnithan Soth feared anything, it was the blank stares of the Fell Guard. Soth had known of them by reputation prior to the debacle with the Kil imposter in their barracks. But that experience of them had increased her wariness. They were willing to block blades with their bare hands, fingers be damned. It was as if they could see with the cold eye. Soth banished the thought for the inanity that it was.

Still, she would have to be extra cautious around them. In fact, one had even stopped her to ask if she was lost, for she had passed him twice in the span of less than an hour when searching for a way into the cellars that did not pass through the kitchens.

Kil was not in the Citadel, and so as instructed she had begun searching for a doorway to Moonside. Though muted, the Revulsion still boiled over in there. An odd sensation, for it was both faint and powerful at the same time. She had hoped to feel that sensation of an opening door again, but it had not come.

She listened to conversations whenever possible, but the gossip was all about Cheapsgate burning and the demise of a man called Dox Viller. And if the hush-talk wasn't about that, it was about the Way of Kila and the wonderful contribution they were making by fixing up the Blasted Quarter. Alternative opinion was that the Way of Kila showed the terrible state of Starside, for if a cult could be allowed to infest the city, why not open it to all of Tordain's filthy refugees? And of course, every conversation eventually bent to a discussion of Kila Sigh. Those who served in close proximity to her adored her, those with less direct experience feared her.

Now she pressed back against damp stone, listening to the changing of the guard in the room beyond. She had been in this cellar for a full day. Not needing sleep or drink, the wait had not been a hardship. The Fell Guard had no reason to be down here. It had only been blind chance that she had seen two of them opening a heavy, disused door and begin descending to the basements. Knowing they could hear a mouse sleeping on wool, she had waited and waited. And then she had followed.

The guard changed every four hours. Two men with helms and spears marched past her, there were snapped exchanges about what had been seen by those on duty (nothing), and then the relieved men marched past going the other way. It was during one of these momentary conversations she had dared to lean out and peer at the door they guarded. It was a very narrow ironbound door with no latch. Heavy hinges. It looked similar to the vault doors she had seen deep beneath Pol's Well, where mercus relics were kept. But the lack of a latch or handle, and the presence of the fell guardsmen, told her all she needed to know. This was the door to Moonside.

So now she faced a quandary, and she'd been deep in consideration about what to do since the last changing of the guard. Kil might return yet to the Citadel. It was her responsibility to be ready. But if she could release whatever stirred in Moonside, perhaps the great power there could hasten the arrival of the glorious day of release. Kil would need to be turned, and surely the power in Moonside would aid in that task.

Decision made, she arranged her face into a look of confusion, as if she were indeed lost. Then she dropped her mask and dymensed fifty paces up the corridor so that she could make a convincing approach. This accomplished, she strode toward the fell guardsmen, head swiveling as if seeking some sign of where she was.

The two men watched her approach without moving an eyelash. Her feat of willshift was ready to release. Not yet. She needed them arranged just so.

The man to her left challenged her. "You must leave this place," he said.

"I took a wrong turn. I'm so daft. I thought I was going down to the kitchens."

"Go back the way you came."

"I tried, but I got turned around. I'm not sure how I got here."

"Turn around, go straight. Climb the ladder, go through the open grate, bear left and ascend the stairs. Madam, you surely knew you were going deep into disused basements."

Soth felt no alarm at being called out for her lies. This was a script, and she had foreseen all the lines. "You *dare* to speak to the wife of an *ambassador* in this manner? I'll speak to your captain. Now, one of you men must guide me out of this place."

"We will not leave our post. You will have to wait for the changing of the guard if you wish us to guide you."

"That is *un*acceptable! Do you know who I am?" She stomped a foot as she'd seen many an uppity climber do when confronted with someone they wished was beneath their station. "Why are you even here? This door has no latch. Where does it go?" She moved to touch it, and quickly discovered two spear tips an inch from her neck. "The *gall!* Threatening an ambassador's wife!" She pounded a fist on the door. "I demand you open this door at once."

A hand took hold of her arm and dragged her back. The fell guardsman was incredibly strong. But he was where she wanted him. Behind her. And his comrade had interposed himself between her and the door, spear tipped forward. She sent her feat into that man's head. His eyes went blank and he blinked several times. The tip of his spear lowered until it clunked onto the floor.

The Revulsion was pure glory inside Soth. She saw so clearly, saw how her feat wormed in deeper and deeper. The guardsman's thoughts were chaos now, but his will was straining to reclaim control. She pressed harder.

"Brother Siggil!" barked the man holding her. He had both hands on her shoulders and was pulling her into him. "Siggil! Stand straight!"

"He cannot," she said. "He knows it is wrong to mistreat an ambassador's wife." She shoved in the feat harder, seeking the moment. Just a brief break in his struggle. When it came, it came as a lull, like a man pausing for breath before again straining to lift a boulder. She did not give him that breath. The willshift feat struck, seeking only the slightest motion. His spear came up, tip driving into her chest, angling up through her back and under the breast plate of the man behind her. He gave a shudder when it pierced his heart.

She released the feat and fell slack upon the impaling shaft. "Ah me!" cried Siggil. "Brother Poilo!" He dropped his spear and she fell onto the floor, pressed down by the weight of the man behind her. Death was nothing, for her heart had stopped beating long ago. The impaled man bled enough for both of them.

She heard the rasp of sword drawing from sheath. "I have dishonored the brotherhood. I'm disgraced before Till!" What came next was the tap of a hilt on the stone floor followed by the drop of the idiot onto his sword. Soth felt no delight at this unexpected turn, no joy in a plan exceeding expectations—which it most certainly had. The Unanswered rolled with its own momentum now, turning events to her advantage. When the men's dying gasps finally went silent she burned through the haft of the spear and wrested herself free of it. Her gown was ruined with both a hole and blood. She cast feats into the fiber, expelling the blood and burning it into smoke.

The little distraction feat Yples had showed her gave her an idea. She sent a thread into the speared man. He was dead, his heart pierced through. She tested the other man, who slumped on his knees, balanced on the sword thrust through his gut and out his back. Life still burbled in the fading mind. "I will not allow you to be drawn into Lumne's embrace," she said, skimming through his unfighting mind. She gripped his head and pushed deep with her Revulsion. It took but a moment. His eyes opened, chin lifted.

"Stand, reviled," she ordered. He obeyed, sword still protruding from his belly, obscene and rigid. "Remove your sword."

The blade came out skimmed with crimson. The man held it before him and a wave of understanding came over him, for he blinked hard. "I see."

And then he surprised Soth by uttering the revulynic blessing over his blade: *"Rachizhach! Stilik noschk."* Red plasma arced over the weapon. The film of blood sizzled and smoked and the sword went black. He sheathed it, wrested his shortened spear from his fallen comrade and repeated the blessing. His belly wound stopped leaking. Looking into Soth's eyes, he declared: "I am Siggil. I see with the cold eye."

"You will do as I command, Siggil. We must go into Moonside and discover what stirs there."

For an answer he simply stared at her. That was well enough. She had nearly four hours before the next changing of the guard.

Her fingers caressed the steel of the door to feel the mercusine feats woven into it. The mercus always drew her, as a predator to prey. But such dangerous prey it could be! Soth's knowledge of the mercus was very useful now, for she could trace the contours of the wards. To her surprise they had been modified. The traps were disarmed, and only a simple locking ward put in place. It had to be Henley Mast's doing. He must not have wanted to contend with more dangerous wards on his return.

The Unanswered did indeed guide events toward the necessary ends. Soth might have smiled, but she did not feel any particular thrill. Perhaps the human aspect in her enjoyed a flush of certainty and rightness. But that was all. Negating the locking wards was easy. She pushed hard and the door swung in.

A short passage led to a second door. But as she went through, she discovered the way resisted her. Not by any physical barrier, but by a ward. She brushed her fingers along the wall, drew them sharply back. The wall *stung!* To one who had just recently been painlessly impaled upon a spear, the sensation was disconcerting. She saw now the black stone was flecked with gold. This was the Divide itself she was passing through. It was infused with mercus wards of its own.

She pushed harder, leaning into the thick air in front of her, seeking to feel how the wards were constructed. Whereas the doors were delicately embroidered with dangerous traps, the Divide's wards were undetectable. Only when she touched the stone had it loosed its moment of attack. As one who had wielded both the mercus and the Revulsion, she puzzled over how such was possible. For the Revulsion should negate all mercus feats, wards or otherwise.

Ah, but her skin wasn't of the Revulsion, though it was surely full of it. It was mortal flesh. The elnisians had built the Divide for one purpose, and that was to keep physical bodies from returning to Starside. Interesting. Also interesting was a self-masking trick embedded into the wards, making them very faint indeed. Even so, she could feel them now. It must not have been possible to mask them entirely and have them remain active.

The tunnel was obstructed with the web of this ward. It could not sting her if she didn't touch the wall. And yet, it acted upon her mind somehow. She pushed harder and waded through the thick air to the final door. She negated the locking ward. The door opened to her touch.

A glorious surge of the Revulsion welcomed her. It hung in the air, a fog of the Unanswered. She strode into it, arms spread. She breathed it in, relishing the infusion of power. The human aspect of her nature recognized a feeling of exhilaration now. It was a lie, but to indulge it for a moment would do no harm.

"Siggil, bring the body through. Drag it over there."

The reviled fell guardsman did as she bade him, painting blood along the floor of short passage between doors. That would never do. She cast her feats again, removing all sign of blood and gore. She took up the fallen man's spear and returned to Moonside, closing the doors behind her. There was no point leaving them open and alerting the next change of the guard. The unconscious haze of Revulsion would never have the will to penetrate the ward anyway.

When she returned to Moonside, Siggil was standing like a statue in the darkness, holding the fallen man's wrist and waiting for further instruction.

"Throw him away," she said.

With a casual flick of his arm, Siggil hurled the dead man into the shadows. The body struck with a clang of armor on stone. Soth regarded the spear she had collected. It was enormously long, the tip over a span above her head. Let it be my light staff, she thought. *"Rachizhach! Stilik noschk."* The blessing coursed over the weapon in arcs of red, burnishing the steel to a gleaming blackness. The steel blade took on a permanent red glow as she heated it with her power.

The lurid light spread through the fog, limning an arched ceiling and support columns with bloody highlights.

Now past the Divide, she felt the enormity of the Revulsion abiding within Moonside. It was overfull of it, a dammed up ocean. And it was not merely an eager fog. Something huge and supremely powerful was roaming about outside. The fury in it startled her, for the Unanswered should see with nothing but the emotionless cold eye.

She did not need her staff light, for the Revulsion drew her along. Eagerly. For it wished her to be united with its master. But she reveled in the sights and feeling of emptiness as she went up stairwells, through corridors, past galleries and halls and ballrooms. Finally she came out of the Citadel and into the wild winds of Moonside.

She felt that she stood upon the floor of a tempest-tossed ocean. For the world all around her was alive with powerful currents that made the fog dance. Her hair flew up and floated around her head, and she could not help but to spread her arms and bathe in it.

"Too human," she admonished herself, and she sought the centering rightness of the cold eye. The cause of the city's mighty rage screamed at Soth, *pulled* at her. A mercus beacon of unmatched brilliance lay down these steps somewhere to the south.

The ground trembled and red lightnings arced overhead. Soth's hair continued to swirl about her head, like a nest of serpents alive and eager for a feeding. The wind pressed against her back, encouraging her to descend. Moonside was alive.

Her spear staff clunked on the stone steps as she took them. Her attention snapped from the delicious mercus beacon to the hot rage of an entity she could only think of as the Mighty One. The beacon again lured her, as if she suffered a deep thirst. She settled on seeking it out first. She had gotten to the bottom of the seemingly endless stairs and was making her way through hallowed and haunted streets to find it when the Mighty One took notice.

You walk toward a trap from which you will never be free. Do as I bid you.

Who are you?

The name that returned was not comprehensible, for it contained an infinity of syllables in a language no tongue could pronounce. It was the name of madness and desperate suffering. A drumbeat cadence contained in a single boom, preceded by nothing and followed by nothing, yet eternal in its solitary rhythm. Her human mind could not grasp it, and she was rendered dazed and dumb by its resonances in her body. Her footsteps faltered and she fell, cheek mashing to the greasy cobblestone of the ancient street. Siggil stopped behind her, waiting.

You are possessed of the Unanswered, the mighty one said. *Do as I bid you.*

Yes. I see with the cold eye.

And who blessed you with such enlightenment?

A qiznithan called Yples. He will bring the longed-for day of Anni-hilation to this world and to all worlds. She got to her feet and searched the sky, for a great presence seemed to loom over her. *I came here to free Moonside. But I see there is great well of mercus here that must first be consumed and destroyed.*

That is a trap. You must ignore the lure lest you become enthralled. Do as I bid you.

You do not see with the cold eye.

The road next to Soth vanished beneath the vague form of an enormous claw, talons of swirling smoke puncturing stone as if it were paper. A smokey face took form high above, brow ridges and snout, gaping maw full of twisting spike teeth. Red lightning congealed into eyes that squinted at her. *I see with righteous rage! Interlopers sneaked in and emboldened the hateful mercus. To ensnare me! ME! Qiznithor!*

Soth again struggled to hold to the cold eye, for the Mighty One screamed into her thoughts. What remained of her human mind quailed to be scrutinized like an ant beneath that baleful glare. Yet it would be glorious to be crushed beneath that claw. Yes, her final release would be assured. Or would it? Did it not depend upon her doing what was necessary here? For that mercus trap would not run dry of its own. Nor would this fell entity roam free to aid in the battles to come unless she helped to release it.

Do as I bid you! Again the claw stomped down, shaking the street such that Soth stumbled into Siggil. *The interlopers hide below. Little rats, little spark spirit. Hateful, accursed felnithel! Otil's poison, it is. It obscures my sight. Do as I bid you and hunt them down, bring them to me.*

Soth felt her own anger rising, an infusion of emotion being thrust into her by the qiznithor. The cold eye held this time, for she now heard in the beast's ravings a tinge of madness. Perhaps that was a qiznithor's nature. Perhaps long imprisonment in Moonside had twisted its thoughts into a mortal tangle, blinding it to the ultimate lie of existence.

She also sensed true danger for herself, for if she defied the Mighty One, it might crush her. And then her mission would fail. If it did there was a true risk that the day of Annihilation might not come, that she might remain trapped here with the qiznithor for an age of ages, awash in suffering without even a body with which to writhe and strain. Surely madness, the greatest suffering of all, would claim her then. The cold eye would not survive it, and she would dissipate into suffering fog, nerves alive to the scrapes and scaldings of uninterrupted time.

Recalling again the incomprehensible name of the qiznithor and of the single beat cadence that had stricken her, she knew that to serve it now would lead to it serving Yples later.

I will become your snout and eye and claw in the sewers, she said. *Siggil and I will slay them and you can feast upon their mortal blood.*

NO! Capture them. I will devour the life and mercus in them! And then I will break free of this prison. GO!

The claw came down again, this time breaking through the surface of the street and rending a great opening into darkness. Soth peered into the blackness. A sewer tunnel.

"Come Siggil. We hunt." And she went down into the darkness, her speartip aglow with ruddy light to show the dank flow of water below.

58

A FAMILIAR

Regret was a lie. Revnithan Con knew this down deep because the cold eye showed her that all emotion was lie. Even so, Lord Yples had left enough of her humanity intact that she fell under emotion's sway on occasion.

Regret was not a good feeling. "I didn't do well, greenmak," she said. She wasn't speaking to the new beetle, but to the old one. The one that horrid shadline had impaled upon his dagger. The cold eye eluded her now, for she kept remembering her instant rage upon seeing her little friend so cruelly killed. And on the heels of rage had come violence. Blue fire to ash the man where he stood.

"But I burnt you up, too, didn't I?" she said to the memory.

Con hadn't much experience with failure. Her life had been quite a long series of successes. Purposefully so, for she'd confined her activities to those she was good at. Reading, learning, cataloging. Not fighting. She'd been a Sensual before Yples had enlightened her. What did she know about war?

She sat in the gardens of the Triumvirate Offices in Slirya, among the dormant winter apple trees. She'd found a greenmak beetle to replace her incinerated little friend. It just wasn't the same. This one was a little smaller, so its weight didn't feel right on her shoulder. "I'll get used to you, greenie," she said. She couldn't call this one greenmak. That didn't feel right, either.

She held the Entifal in one hand, absently waggling it and patting the flat on her thigh. Her feat of fire had been wild and destructive. But it had acted slowly upon the shadline, and the cat had stopped it altogether.

"No, that's not right, greenie. *I* stopped it. But that tubby cat *made* me stop. How could it do that? I'll tell you how. It was no mere cat."

It had looked like an Eastern Blackbrush Cat, a broad class of coastal cats that lived upon crabs and estuary fish. In truth, all cats were of the same body plan, same general habits. Their coats and skull shapes varied a little to suit their habitats. Con had always admired them for their ruthless efficiency. In cities where the Way of Til hadn't eradicated them, cats were deployed to good effect to keep the mouse and rat populations in check.

"Not just any sort of cat, greenie. You see that, don't you? Kila Sigh is reported to have such an animal. A *familiar*, make no mistake. Never heard of a shadline having such, but I saw it with my own eyes." That meant the Eastern Blackbrush Cat she'd seen was, in fact, a so-called Beloved One. Or, as the elnisians had called them, a felnithel.

She hadn't recognized it for what it was when she'd been trying to burn up that ugly shadline, but upon reflection, what else could it be? Its mere presence had made her stop burning the man up.

"I still mean to burn him up, greenie," she said. "Someday soon."

She'd wanted to stab the cat, too. The Entifal would've been happy to oblige. But she'd just stood there, wanting to stab and still not stabbing. Her newly turned reviled hadn't done anything either except try to twist the shadline's other blade into his own gut. Useless reviled!

"Where did that other shadline come from?" she asked. She'd mended the hole in her back where the sneaky woman had stabbed her. "As if she dymensed behind me." But that couldn't be. Revnithan Con would have felt the mercus in her. "I don't like sneaks."

The attack had so startled her she'd dymensed to safety. "I'm already dead," she complained. "What safety do I need, greenie?" It had been fear, that instant emotion outside the clarity of the cold eye, that had made her flee. No help for it now, she decided. The Unanswered was powerful, but she couldn't think of how it could bend time to let her fix her mistake.

The failure still rankled her. Now she would have to find Lord Yples and confess that she'd had the god-child close by but had lost track of her. The Entifal would please him, but she doubted it would appease him. She'd been back to Vanish's Gold. The shadlines were gone and nobody knew where to.

"He might grant me the final release out of anger," she said. She half craved it, half feared it. She didn't want to go just yet. Curiosity had taken root in her now. Not only did she wish to complete several more catalogs, but she just had to study the felnithel.

"It's much too risky to go to Lord Yples now, greenie. I have to find that ugly shadline and his sneaky friend. I have to have the god-child."

She reasoned that they would draw attention wherever they went. Her knowledge of maps was quite good. She closed her eyes and envisioned where Vanish's Gold lay, west of Traye. Traye was upon the eastern coast of the Iopsean Sea, which itself was a huge bay along the southern coast of Ennith.

They traveled by vergent passes sometimes, which would make her search more challenging. The only thing for it was to continue from Vanish's Gold, heading toward Traye and ask everyone she passed about a burned man and a beautiful shadline.

59

DIRELIGHT

"There is no way to pass under the Divide," Henley said, standing before yet another section of the wall. He and Brother Ryde had explored every north/south tunnel they could access, hoping to find a way deeper. But the sewers had been constructed ages before the Divide, and when the wall had been erected or dymensed into place, the elnisians had specifically wanted to bar any way out. The Divide plunged through every passageway, and Henley suspected miners would find that impenetrable stone even a thousand spans deeper.

They would have to leave the sewers and make a dash for the Citadel and hope to find their way back to the cellar door. But even then he would have to call upon the mercus to release the locking wards. And right now, he couldn't bear to even search for the mercus. The Revulsion was too thick, and he was too weak.

The snatches of sleep he'd collected gave him enough energy to walk, but not much else. Huff had taken to riding in Brother Ryde's satchel to spare Henley the weight. The fell guardsman was covered in filth, his face drawn, but his strength had not flagged. He had not slept since entering Moonside.

A distant boom trembled through the tunnel. Loose dust and pebbles shook from the ceiling and drifted onto their heads. The qiznithor was still hunting for them. It perplexed Henley that it had the wherewithal to ignore the lure of the Motherlight. Even with him and Whiteflame masked it continued to rage and hunt.

Killing it seemed fanciful to him now. Whiteflame would give him more strength if he dared to hold it again, but he feared its subversive power over his will would lead him to a confrontation he could not win.

"Are we agreed?" he asked Ryde.

The man blinked inside of his helm. "I will do as you command, Lord Mast."

"Take us to a grate ladder close to the Citadel."

"We will have to ascend the terraces in open air."

Henley knew that. Knew that he did not have the strength to make it up even one flight unaided. Yet that was what he would do. Gain the Citadel and hope the qiznithor didn't notice them, or lacked the power to break into the fortress. An awful lot depended on hope.

During their searches for a way through the Divide, they had ranged farther and farther east, away from the Citadel. Now they would have to backtrack, relying on Brother Ryde's reckoning. In the dark.

They moved forward slowly, Ryde's speartip feeling along the floor and wall. Each junction became a series of taps and splashes, then Ryde would return and report the layout. This verbal assessment wasn't strictly necessary, since Henley was completely lost. He left the navigation to Ryde. The man moved with confidence, as if he could see their destination.

Ryde was tapping out the dimensions and openings of just such a junction now, while Henley stood miserably in knee-deep water. He took some consolation in the fact that no living beings were using the sewers for less savory dumping than rainwater drainage.

Someone is near, Huff sent.

Henley clicked his tongue to get Ryde's attention. The spear tapping returned, and Henley held out a hand. "I'm here," he whispered, touching grimy breastplate. "Huff says someone is coming."

"The beast?"

The qiznithor, Huff?

No. A revulyn.

Henley's body wicked up the chill from the water, and it rose all the way up to the crown of his head. He checked the mask over Whiteflame. The revulyn couldn't know that he was here. But where had it come from?

He told Ryde what Huff had said. The man made no response. He was waiting for Henley to issue an order. But Henley had no idea what to do.

Where is it?

Coming closer.

From which way?

Huff couldn't tell him, and ensconced in Ryde's pack, there was no way for Huff to show him.

"How many openings in this junction?" he asked Ryde.

"Four, including the one we came through. The water is deeper from the north."

North and west was where the Citadel stood. And he was about to suggest fleeing in that direction, when he thought better of it. If a revulyn had come, it must surely have come through the Moonside door in the Citadel. Unless it had been here all along. But he didn't think that likely or they would have encountered it already.

What he could not figure out is why it would be in the sewers. Unless the qiznithor had told it to come down. The idea that the qiznithor could talk doubled his chill. He was certainly not going downslope. All the smashes and booms of the qiznithor came from that direction.

"South and west," he said with more confidence than he felt.

He took hold of the ragged remains of Ryde's cloak, like a child holding to his mother's skirts, and let the man guide him forward. They sloshed through the junction, blind. Ryde did not tap his spear now, but somehow led them true. The current swept past Henley's legs and then abated as they entered the new tunnel.

A brightening ahead told of a surface grate. The gray light penetrating the gloom was barely enough to show him the outlines of Ryde's helm and shoulders. They paused here while Ryde climbed the ancient iron ladder to the grate. Henley held the man's spear, which was considerably lighter than it looked. Ryde pushed at the grate, but time had sealed it to the stone.

He managed to descend with little sound other than the jingle of his armor. "I could see nothing other than the eaves of some houses. The fog is very thick." Henley held to the ladder, mind feeling like a trezz crate stuffed with sawdust to protect the glass of his consciousness. Very few thoughts rattled around inside. He could think of nothing to say.

Closer, Huff sent unhelpfully. *It's using it.*

What's using what?

The revulyn. The Revulsion.

"Lord Mast, look," urged Ryde. He guided Henley around by the shoulder, bade him look back the way they'd come. At first all Henley could see was the abject nothingness of the tunnel, the gradient of gray light that quickly failed into the void. But that wasn't all that dwelled there. A bloody light stained the walls of a distant junction. It grew in intensity with a seeping slowness.

The revulyn. Using the Revulsion. For light to see by. Henley stitched these thoughts together, but little else came to mind save an inborn certainty that death approached. The light brightened further, and then flared into a pinpoint of jeweled crimson. And there it stopped.

Ryde's keener eyes picked out far more than Henley's. "A fell guardsman accompanies her." He betrayed true emotion now. Outrage.

"We need to go. Quickly." Henley bent and sloshed fetid water onto his face. The bracing chill shocked him to alertness, though his head throbbed with the pain of exhaustion.

Henley looked up the ladder. It seemed terrifically tall, the grate very small and far away. "Can you open it?"

"It will not be quiet."

"Go."

The revulyn had not moved from the junction, was likely pausing there to seek for signs of life. Maybe his own whisper would be enough if she enjoyed the heightened senses of a merculyn.

Ryde seemed to be released like an atlen at a race. He bolted up the rungs, not slowing at the grate. His gauntleted fist smashed against the iron. The clanging impact resounded in the tunnel. The ruddy direlight of the revulyn rose.

Ryde smashed again. The epochs had sealed the grate shut.

"Hurry," Henley called to Ryde. "She comes!"

He plunged inward, searching for the mercus. But he might as well have sought it in the water at his feet. All was foul blackness, bitter and stinking.

The concussions of steel against iron resounded in the tunnel like a sinister bell. Ryde was slamming the pommel of his sword against the underlip of the grate. Even clinging to the ladder in an awkward position, Ryde delivered heroic blows. Dust and bits of rust flaked down, stinging Henley's eyes. He backed into the tunnel to escape the debris, leaning on Ryde's spear for support. The light was approaching quickly, so bright it concealed the one who bore it. Henley turned, thinking he must run. The darkness of the tunnel seemed to reach for him, seeking to draw him forever into the cold black. Above him, Ryde was a small silhouette against the gray beyond the grate. Hammering, hammering!

If there are heroes sung of after this, he sent, *let Ryde be among them.*

As long as you aren't the one singing, Huff said. *Is he almost done? The noise hurts my head.*

A tremendous concussion shook the tunnel. Ryde had to cling to the ladder as the world trembled. Another boom came soon after. They had drawn the qiznithor's notice. Henley urged Ryde on with his whole body, knuckles white around the spear, his teeth a vise, his heart a war drum. He released the ladder and gripped the spear in both hands.

The grate gave with striking suddenness, flipping out of its nook and disappearing into the street beyond. Ryde followed it. "I see nothing," he called down to Henley. "Come."

Henley started up, one hand, two feet. The spear was all wrong, too thick to allow him to hold both it and the rail of the ladder.

"Drop it!" Ryde shouted.

Henley instead tossed it as high as he could. Ryde caught the butt and pulled it up. Henley clambered up the rungs. The bloody light flooded along the bottom of the tunnel. Fear infused Henley with an unsuspected reserve of strength. He surged upward.

Ryde called encouragement. And as soon as Henley was within reach, he pulled him through the opening and set him onto the street. Henley fell over, lungs dragging in air that gave no sustenance. Weak daylight filtered through the Revulsion overcast. The rest of Moonside was hidden behind a pea soup fog.

Ryde slammed the grate over the opening. "The stairs are this way," he said, again lifting Henley and setting him on his feet. Huff meowed from somewhere in the distance.

You should be in Ryde's satchel, Henley sent.

You *should be in Ryde's satchel. Hurry now. It comes.*

And so it was. For the unmistakable booms of monstrous footsteps carried through the fog behind them. Henley looked back, looked ahead. He had no frame of reference, could see no rooftops, could not see the stairs. Ryde steered him along, half holding him, half pushing.

The grate clanged onto the road behind them. Red light blared from the opening, and then emerged a head and shoulders. The expressionless face of death looked at him—beautiful and feminine and at the same time terrible and demaynic.

Boom! Doom! Monstrous footsteps shook the world. The unseen foe sent thrills through Henley's hair. A glance skyward revealed no eyes.

Hurry! Huff sent. The cat was far ahead. Henley stumbled, regained his feet and staggered after. Ryde turned in the street and held his ground. Henley wanted to bid him follow. He almost ordered him to. But this would be the end of all of them if Ryde did not slow the revulyn and her fell guardsman.

Henley came to the stairs sooner than expected, a small grace. He knew the distance he must climb to gain the Citadel. It might as well have been twenty leagues for all the strength he possessed.

The stairs were shallow, which was good, but also they were deep. He could not take one with each stride without lunging. This made for a clumsy stutter-stepping gait that drained his strength faster than if the stairs had been steeper. At the top of the first flight, he fell to his knees. His breath was hot in his throat and phlegm clogged his lungs, making him cough and sputter.

"I cannot do it without Whiteflame," he said. "I cannot."

His arm felt devoid of power, muscles refusing to respond to his will. He had to swing his shoulders to flop his hand upon the pommel. He rolled onto his back, strained to get a second hand on the grip. By inches he drew it, gasping and cursing. And then it came free and his body seethed with lithe energy. Bounding to his feet, he turned and began to descend. Whiteflame was aloft, held high over his head, its blazing light casting the fog into sharp relief.

No! This way! Huff shouted. *Be master of the blade.*

Henley stopped, though his heart longed to join battle.

The clouds parted upon a gust of wind, shredding the clingy fog for a bare instant. Below, Brother Ryde twirled his spear, a white-gold aura blossoming around his body. And as he moved through these forms, he seemed to grow in stature. His spear blurred into a disc of white as he spun it. The red light of the revulyn approached swiftly, black-blue feats flying out at Ryde. These he deflected in scintillating white ricochets that flew off to impact with the surrounding buildings.

Sacrifice.

To wade into battle next to Ryde would be to squander his sacrifice. It would be to dishonor him.

I will not be ruled by a sword, he sent at it. Perhaps it heard him. Perhaps more importantly, he heard himself. The spell seemed to have passed. Henley turned again and ran toward the Citadel.

60

ALL SHALL CEASE

Nax stalked around the perimeter of the round chamber, avoiding the grisly stains at the center. Clerestory windows banded the top third of the wall, allowing in a sickly light. Kila was thankful for the dimness. She didn't wish to see more than necessary of this place. It was a torture room. A murder room. She didn't know what the elnisians had designed it for, but the nosg shaman Ahl-Mish-Lah had dragged her here many times. Kila's ankle ached with the memory of a shackle and chain that had rubbed her flesh raw.

The mercus green of dymension dissipated slowly as Kila stood very still, head tipped forward, focusing all of her attention on her hearing. This was Ceronhel. Full of nosg. Many would remember her as a shaman's pet. But they would all know of her escape from bondage in Stallid, and of her fierce turn against them.

Why didn't you bring your men? Nax asked.

I can't sneak around in the Citadel with the Fell Guard, how would I do it here?

Her mercus heightened senses detected no footsteps, no

wheezing breaths of nosg in the passage. She moved to the door and down the little hallway. A stairwell opened here, leading to the dungeons. Another corridor continued to a heavy door. That gave into the area of the fortress where the nosg lived and slept.

She went through. Nax slunk along, a wisp of gray. The corridor here was wider, lit with torches that gave off an acrid smoke. It was too hot with all the flame. Still no sign of nosg. She moved swiftly down the passage. A bit of breeze came from the left. She went toward it.

Boots scuffed ahead. A nosg warrior ambled toward her, club on his shoulder. A patrol. Not very attentive. He was making a clatter with his boots and decorative necklaces of bone and shriveled ears. She needed to be swift, decisive.

Nax, distract it.

The cat came out of shadow and went down the middle of the hall. The nosg snuffled and stopped short, looked at the cat.

Kila stole heat from the flames of the passage torches, then light, forming fast negations that sped down the corridor and quenching them all. Now in blackness she sprinted forward, Cayne drawn. The steel found flesh, the throat parted, the nosg fell spluttering. She continued on, Nax darting with her.

Releasing the feats, the torches flared to life, showing her the way. The nosg was climbing to its feet.

Reviled! she sent. *Why didn't you warn me?*

I thought you knew.

Rushing back to the nosg, she sliced leg muscles so it couldn't stand. It stood anyway. She leapt onto its back, drove Cayne into first one eye then the other. The creature flailed and rammed backward into the wall, crushing Kila against it.

One final twist of the blade severed something essential in the nosg's brain. It collapsed. She extricated herself from it and fought off a shiver of disgust.

"Where is that dining hall of Yioth's?" she asked the darkness. The air was growing colder, which meant she was nearing the outside. The great hall had always been open to the outside air when Yioth was there. She continued to follow the hint of breeze until she came to a short stair climbing to an opening. There was a large space beyond. The sound of movement, the rattle of plates and tankards on wooden tables. This was it.

Creeping on toes, staying as low as she could, she ascended the steps until she could peer into the hall beyond. A gallery of columns stood out from the doorway supporting a balcony that ringed the hall. She slipped out, ducked to the right, taking her closer to the exit. The doors stood wide open. The air was bracing. The nosg didn't seem to mind. The enormous hearths were all cold.

The shadows here were deep, but she felt terribly exposed. She formed a muffling feat, a bubble surrounding her that no sound would escape. She knelt behind a column and studied the scene. There was something odd going on. She had once been forced to sit upon that dais there, where Yioth's crude throne still stood. A figure sat on the throne now. She squinted. It was a human in Donse Master's robes. For a horrifying second she thought it was the Hargothe. But this man was younger, with a full head of hair. He had his eyes closed. There was no mercus in him. The Revulsion was very thick here.

That's a revulyn, isn't it? she asked Nax.

Of a sort . . .

There were several nosg merely standing along the sides of the room. They were motionless, weapons out. As if they were guarding the nosg at table. No. That wasn't quite it. They weren't protecting those eating. These looked like prison guards making sure nobody got out of hand. They all had the dead-eyed look of reviled.

Kil's handle, Naxie. Do you see?

I see. They are the standing dead.

That nosg over there is moving. A shaman.

The shaman was bent over as he walked, leaning upon a staff. He was making a slow circuit around the whole hall. The click of his staff on stone echoed above the noise of those eating. He crossed before the dais and turned to come in Kila's direction. She saw the skull atop its staff, the gems gone black. She shrank behind the column, pressed her body tight to the cold stone.

Click!

Clack!

She closed her eyes, holding fast to the mercus and hoping the corrupted shaman would not feel her mercus power.

Click! Clack!

Nax had hidden in the corner, gray coat blending into the shadow. Kila willed herself to flatness and needlessly held her breath.

Click! Clack!

The sound seemed to come from everywhere, even behind her. The Revulsion boiled in her awareness, drawn by her power and by the presence of so many reviled.

Click!

The shaman was just on the other side of the column now. It had to be her imagination, but she thought she could feel the chill of its body.

No clack sounded. She strained to hear any hint of its footsteps. She watched to see it emerge from behind the column and continue on its way. It didn't. The back of her skull chilled at the thought that it had sneaked around to strike her spine.

Nax! Is it behind me?

No. It's standing there, looking at the column.

It senses me.

Cayne was already clutched in her fist. The black steel looked eager to her.

Clack!

The shaman continued its patrol. Kila waited for it to pass the gaping exit, then peered from behind the column. The nosg were finishing up their dinner. It was odd they were eating anything at all, being dead.

She had to move now. She backed to the wall, edged around to where Nax was crouched in the corner. Together they inched into the open and toward the gaping door.

"Welcome, Kila Sigh," came a bold voice. Hearing her name made her shoulders creep up to her ears. "Welcome, felnithel."

She looked back to see all the nosg frozen, looking at her. The shaman, too, with its black-gemmed skull eyes. But it was the Donse Master who drew her attention. She knew he must be a revulyn, but he did not look like one. Not entirely. Even from this distance, his eyes were different. Not robbed of all life. His robes were clean. He stood and slowly swept from the dais and walked among the motionless nosg. He carried a skull staff of his own. A huge bear skull atop a thick staff. Its greenish eyegems were alight.

The man's voice boomed out: "I did not expect you, else I would have prepared a room. Please, come join the feast. All who eat of the Blackshine mimak are blessed."

"Where is Yples?"

"Seeing to necessary tasks, do doubt. Come. There is nothing to fear here. Fear is a lie, as you well know."

His voice was soothing, as one practiced in delivering Tilsday sermons. Nothing could have chilled her more than to hear good humor and manners from a man obviously corrupted by the Revulsion. Her mind hovered over the oily foulness, sensed a great coalescence of it around the man.

"Stay back, revulyn."

"I am no revulyn, Sigh. I am Revnithan Sault, anointed by Lord Yples as master of the nosg empire." His name jolted through her. She had never known a Dunne Sault, but the title of 'Revnithan' stirred in her blood.

"I was delighted to feel you arrive here," he said, still striding toward her. His free hand was out to his side, a show of welcome. "Your mercus is substantial. Very impressive. I had long doubted reports of your power, but I see now they understated your true potential."

Kila wanted to slap herself for not instantly masking upon arriving.

The mercus shield she'd used against Yples sprang out, a glowing barrier infused with all the goodness she could summon. The man stopped, frowned. She backed to the doorway, Nax at her feet. Sault stood in the center of the great hall. His frown melted away and he was again smiling.

"What are you?" she said.

"What is anything? All is suffering, as you well know. You, who has seen with the cold eye. Isn't it freeing? But I see that answer doesn't satisfy your question. Very well. I am an awakened man. More than a man. More than a revulyn. Why don't you come in? I won't harm you or your Beloved One. Let us talk."

"I care nothing about what you have to say, Donse Master."

"I'm a Donse Master no longer. Lord Yples showed me the truth and it is glorious. I ache for the day of release, when all shall cease to suffer."

"Then why don't you kill yourself? Get it over with."

His smile faltered. Kila wasn't sure if her question hit close to a question he'd been battling or if he merely tired of her resistance. She was very aware that he had not attacked, had not sicced his nosg on her either. That was more restraint than she'd suspected the Revulsion capable of. It spoke to his control over himself. And it revealed caution.

"Where is Yiothizandra?" she demanded.

The smile returned, accompanied by a deep laugh. "Ah, I see. You are bitter because your enemy escaped justice in Stallid. Come to see it through, have you? I'm afraid I cannot allow that. Yiothizandra will serve Lord Yples soon, just as you will. I truly wish you'd listen to me. The cold eye unmasks the lies that lead to misery. If you would but allow me to show you."

He struck with Revulsion feats and swarmlight at the same time. The shaman's skull eyes burst to life with Blackshine swarmlight. Their attacks blasted against her expanded armorcloak. Revnithan Sault basked in it. His blackbeams leeched onto her shield. They sucked in great pulses of the mercus, soiling it with the Revulsion. The shaman sought merely to bash through her defense, but his efforts were too weak to be of concern.

The Revnithan pulled something small from a pocket. A stylus or small stick. The stomp of boots echoed in the hall, distracting her from the motion. More shamans burst in, skulls throwing blackbeams at her.

"You need not be destroyed," the revnithan said, his arm flashed forward. No additional feat came forth, just a dark blur. It arced toward the ragged fringe of her defense, then popped, sending up a glittering blue cloud of smoke. It hazed through her defense, which had been designed to keep out attacks, not smoke or fog.

"You could be there at the final moment," he said. "You could be among the last to be dissipated and achieve the final ecstasy of Annihilation. You know Wenton would approve."

Father's face filled her vision. Kind eyes, strong weathered skin. "You must listen, sweetlight," he said. "Sault is a good man. He knows the truth."

Get out! Nax sent.

Kila gagged upon the smoke. The room swayed, columns stretching and compressing. She felt like she'd drunk a jar of trezz on an empty stomach. She backed from the hall and into the cold clean air of the bailey.

"Listen to Revnithan Sault," came her father's voice. Except it wasn't her father's. It was Dox Viller's. He laughed softly and said, "Perhaps I am your father. Did you ever think of that? I had hundreds of whelps. Wenton stole you from me. That's why he had to be killed. You're Terissa's sister. Terissa's sister. Terissa's sister."

Lies. She knew the truth, knew how Semūin had manipulated her father. It was not something to be doubted.

And yet she did.

It was the smoke. A ferneater trick.

She stumbled down the steps, bearing right and into an enormous open space where grass had likely grown in summers past. Now it was a mud-scape of gouges and dungpiles. For it was here that a flight of wyvoks had once been marshaled. Here where she had tamed Jathesh and saddled him so that she and Ahl-Mish-Lah could fly over Stallid and rain swarmlight upon the helpless citizens.

The memories made her heart race. A panicky confusion rose in her. *I don't know what I'm doing, Nax. I don't know where to go.*

"Wenton was an exceptional thief," Dox's voice said. As if speaking wetly into her ear. "Do you not think he could steal you from me?"

Nax thrust back into her awareness. *Standing in the open is bad. They're coming.*

True enough. Her vision was clearing a bit now that she'd gotten a few breaths of clean air.

"I expect more of Terissa's sister. Terissa's sister," Dox's voice said. "Try to be more like her." A raspy laugh seethed into the other ear.

I feeeeel you, Kila Sssssiiiigh.

The Hargothe's serpent-tongued voice spun her around. Sault's smoke made the bailey bend and sparkle. A long shadow stretched over the frozen mud, the elongated shape of the hooded Hargothe. *I seeeeee you.*

"Kil take ya! I ripped yer heart out."

Shaking her head, she edged hard against the outer wall of the great hall, racing behind the fortress proper to a section of the bailey she'd never seen. She found a stables, a smithy, and several long stone barracks lined against a sheer cliff that rose to dizzying peaks.

"Kila Sigh!" shouted the Revnithan from somewhere behind her. "The more you resist the more you suffer. Do you not see that simple truth? It is so obvious."

He was taunting her, daring her to attack. Surely the false voices of her father and Dox were meant to provoke her so that the Revulsion would claim her. She scanned the bailey for a hiding place. Her eyes lifted to the mountains.

A score of nosg shamans had come out after her. They stood behind the revnithan. The throng reminded her of her encounter with Yples and his revulyns in Sorgan. She knew how that had ended. Sault's Revulsion feat continued to suck at her shield. The shamans had formed a circle of some sort, and their attacks shuddered through her awareness. More shamans poured out of the Citadel.

Nothing for it but to flee.

61

DISCOMFORT IS THE WAY

S had Hannisar Lykea was the epitome of what Fallo thought a shadline should be. Tall, strong, wise, amiable, and handsome. Fallo had first met him at the Hackwatch, had been impressed with the Shadline Knight's innate nobility and sense of justice. Much of that came to him from his sword, Lightstorm. It was perhaps the most storied blade in all of shadline lore. And when the man entered Fallo's room it was this relic that drew his eyes.

Inset into the pommel was a sapphire of spectacular brilliance which sent its jewel-light sparkling against wall and floor. The man's road-worn boots made the floorboards creak.

"Shadline PiTorro, well met." He removed his sword belt and leaned the precious weapon against the wall. One side of his beard was braided, the other side full and combed. His mass of hair was swept back from a noble brow. He was every depiction of prince and king one had ever seen in storybook or mural.

He dragged a chair across the floor and took a seat next to Fallo's bed. He reached into an inside pocket and produced a small glistening item. A gold ring with a flat spot stamped on the top. An image of a dragon's head was embossed into it. "My fate's-piece."

Fallo had to use both hands, bandaged into blunt appendages, to cup the ring. He brought it close to his eyes. "Fine work. I don't hear anything." He pushed it back to Lykea. He was grateful the man had followed shadline custom of sharing fate's-pieces instead of asking him about his health. His bandaged head and hands told all that anyone need know. As for the rest—the war he was losing in his mind—nobody needed to share that burden. Someone as handsome as Shad Lykea wouldn't understand what it was to be disfigured anyway. He'd feel mostly fear, and then gratitude that it hadn't happened to him. But he couldn't comprehend how it felt to be made so useless one could not even grasp a teacup, much less the hilt of a dagger.

"My fate's-piece is somewhere else in this house," Fallo said. "Surely you've met Illy already."

"I have. Shadline Peline did not say anything about where the girl came from. She seemed to believe it was none of my concern. She also showed me some interesting pieces of jewelry, necklaces in the symbols of the four gods." He smiled, showing a wide row of even white teeth. "You have entangled yourself with a considerable power in that young woman. Pol smiled on you."

Fallo grunted. "Pol smiles, she frowns, she smiles, she frowns. Mostly she frowns. And at the end of my days, she will smile and I will die."

Lykea's amusement faded. "Be grateful for her smiles *and* frowns and you will have lived a life of gratitude."

There was no point in arguing with a man so privileged with grace of appearance and manner. The world despised ugliness as if it were catching.

"Tell me more about the young lady you found," Lykea said, breaking into Fallo's sour ruminations.

If there was anyone Fallo trusted with the truth, it was Shad Lykea. "The gods are being reborn. Illy is one of them. Quinn's necklaces were taken from four dead elnisians who believed they were to be possessed by the reborn. They were wrong about that."

The proper response to such a revelation was something like, "Your burns have reached your brains." Or "How much trezz has Quinn forced down your throat?" But Shad Lykea merely closed his eyes and took a long deep breath through his nose. On the out breath he bowed his head. "What you say comports with a vague unease that has plagued me these last ten years. The culmination we identified at the Hackwatch, what we thought was Dem-Kisk, is greater than the crisis of a dying age. It is the crisis of a threatened world. For how can the gods tread upon the world and not break it apart?"

That was very poetical, Fallo thought. Just what he needed: evidence that Lykea was not only wise and good looking, but also graced with the tongue of a bard. Even so, it was impossible to despise him. If anything, the comparisons Lykea forced upon Fallo, made Fallo despise himself all the more. His daggers were arranged on a chair across the room, put there with great care by Quinn. He wished he could drive them into his own throat.

"Which god is Illy?" Lykea asked.

"Ori. Quinn and I met with a rather impudent vergent who told us to also seek out Til and Pol. I've been waylaid here too long. There is another seeking them." He told Lykea about the qiznithan and the spread of the reviled.

"Aye, I have seen them," Lykea said. "They don't die easily, even separated from their heads. Quinn said a revulyn did this to you."

"And Lop saved me. I don't know how."

"Our lore about the felnithel is shallow, but the little we know speaks to their extraordinary power. I count myself fortunate to live in a time when their presence is known. That one of them is bonded to a shadline of such great ability, that is greater fortune still. It bodes well for—"

"Stop it!" Fallo snapped. "You cannot manipulate me into happiness, or hope, or whatever it is you wish to impart. Don't you see that I am nothing? I'm useless. I'm a scalded abomination." He threw up his hands. "These wraps are not to protect me. They are to protect you from seeing the horror of what I've become."

Shad Lykea didn't flinch in the face of Fallo's rage. He merely witnessed it with clear, ingenuous eyes. He got up, and Fallo thought he was going to leave. Fallo felt embarrassed at his tantrum, skin going prickly underneath his wrappings. But Lykea fetched his sword, unsheathed it. The blade was a matte silver, etched with black runes. The crossguard was a time-patinated steel, also decorated with etchings. Lykea brought the sword to Fallo's bed and again sat, resting the blade atop his knees. The sapphire sparkled boldly.

"Lightstorm came to me when I was about your age. The previous shadline to carry him was Shad Elineth, a swordmaster of unmatched grace. Or so I was told. I never met her. The force of destiny chooses who will bear Lightstorm, not the sword itself. I was overwhelmed by the call. It forced me from the sheep farm of my father and grandfathers and onto the road. I roved from Jilin to Slirya, sleeping only when my legs failed me, eating only what I could beg or steal. I was enslaved in Trist for three years. I escaped and crossed The Boil, found comfort in an almen's house in Stallid, and eventually came to the door of a shadline cache in Slirya."

"The Reign of Fools?"

"That very one. And in that cache I found Lightstorm, amidst a pile of common blades in a barrel. The smith who manages that store did not know how it came to be there. The moment I gripped the sword, I was claimed by it. And from that day forward it has led me through discomforts far greater than my first long journey to Slirya." His eyes gleamed. "And I am grateful."

He lifted the blade on the edges of his hands, thumbs curling over top. He presented the hilt to Fallo. "Take it. It won't reject you."

"I already have more than my share of shadline blades."

"You will not keep this one. Go on, take it."

Fallo pinched the hilt between his bandage-mittens. It was very light. And warm. Even through the wraps he could feel the heat of it. As morose as he felt, he couldn't tamp down a surge of boyish delight. This was Lightstorm. *The* Lightstorm. "Does it truly call down lightning bolts from the sky?"

"It does. Though I cannot command it to do so. The reviled I have killed have not demanded it. But a revulyn was blown apart by a particularly brilliant one." He shook out his sword arm, as if he could feel the jolt even now. "I lied, by the way."

"What about?" Fallo said absently, turning the blade this way and that to study the runes. They were very finely etched.

"About it not rejecting you."

"I'm holding it just fine."

"That's because it finds you worthy, Fallo. You noticed I left it against the wall over there when I came in. A shadline only parts from his weapon if he knows a thief cannot abscond with it. Do you have any notion what happens to people who try to steal it?"

"Um, lighting bolt?"

"Just so. I have killed men merely by letting them hold this blade. I listen and obey. And I knew you must hold it. Not to prove your worth to me, but to yourself. Your task is not complete. You told me so yourself. Get up, get going. I will take Illy to safety."

"There is no safety."

"The Dirth has summoned another Armory. The shadline call presses on us Knights to assemble for battle. I will take Illy with me to Rethnian. It is well hidden, defensible, and well stocked for a siege."

Rethnian. The invisible fortress on the Sagmarsh Wash. Fallo had found it the first time he had truly listened to the shadline call. That's where he'd found Shad Linas, one of the original Shadline Knights. And it was there that Linas had revealed the writing on Zirhine's sketch, which led back to Cigil-Tine and to his infuriating encounter with Xilo.

Fallo returned the sword to Lykea. "Help me stand."

What followed was awkward, for Fallo's legs wobbled and splayed like a newborn calf's. He had to rely on Lykea to unwrap his hands. Sight of the burned flesh did not disturb the Shadline Knight. His only comment was, "Be grateful you were not struck by Tosuin." That was Cloak Einlin's sword, which often immolated its victims. "No one who feels that fire survives."

"Yes. That's right," Fallo said flatly. "I'm so grateful."

The wraps around his torso peeled off, leaving a gooey green substance on his skin. It smelled like a kitchenyard middens. The flesh beneath was white in some areas, red in others. The burns were not as bad as on his hands, which had been bare when the flames had engulfed him. Amazingly, his legs had taken the least damage. There were even spots where hair still grew. His most private areas, while red and tender, were wholly intact. Standing there naked, his hideousness exposed to Lykea's sight, Fallo's humiliation collapsed under its own weight. Much of that was thanks to Lykea's lack of embarrassment on Fallo's behalf.

Water from the basin and patient dabbing and blotting removed the foulest residue of the healing salve. Then came Fallo's clothes. He had never seen these before. But they were very expensive and well suited for rough travel. Trousers and shirt scraped across his angry skin like a million little teeth. But once dressed and shod, a bit of strength returned to his limbs. He continued preparing, securing his blades on his person, then whipping a new cloak over his shoulders. His hand ripped with pain every time he had to take hold of something, but they didn't split, didn't get worse. It seemed the skin merely needed to relearn how to stretch.

"Your healing is remarkable," Lykea said. "The mooncrafter's salve Quinn used is powerful. I was able to provide her a bit more from my supply."

Fallo went to the glass over the basin, studied the ridiculous ball of wrappings enclosing his head and face. He found the loose end tucked under a fold and tugged it free. Lykea watched him in the mirror, not concerned. The binding came away in a long continuous strip. As the final turns peeled off, stretches of healing salve stretched like melted cheese. Fallo pulled these off, then dabbed the rest away, wincing at every touch of the cloth. He dared not to rub his skin, for it was cracked and fragile. He didn't want to wipe away his face and leave only bare muscle exposed.

When he had cleaned it the best he could he regarded his image. "And I thought I was a monster before . . ." He pulled up the hood of his cloak to shadow the damage. He would need some sort of mask or he would pelted with stones the first time he tried to enter a town.

His eyes teared from the slide of fabric over his skin when he came down the stairs and into the little drawing room where Quinn and Illy were waiting. He was stunned to see that the child had grown, and now looked like a girl of sixteen fully blossomed. Her face was placid, and she greeted Fallo with a grave look. Quinn stared daggers at Lykea, but the man took no notice. It was a testament to her regard for the Shadline Knight that she didn't reprimand him for bringing Fallo down. He sensed a lingering argument in the air here, and guessed it was about whether or not he was ready to dress and travel.

Well, he *wasn't* ready. And that fact did not matter in the least. "Dem-Kisk waits for no one," he said to the room. His tongue felt covered with fur. He searched out a pitcher of water and drank his fill, gasping over the rim of his mug. "Illy, you will go with Shad Lykea."

"I know," she said. "I feel your pain too keenly. I wish I could do something more for you." She had her eyes closed and was swaying a bit. He had thought her expression mere empathy, but he realized that she truly was feeling his pain.

"Where's Nefler Ernist?" he asked.

"He will return momentarily," Quinn said. "He wants to go with us."

"Does he know what we're up to?"

"He has suspicions. I think it's clear we will need him. Especially if we are to travel by Derslin Wheel. Which I fear we must. And when we find the next one, he or she will need masking."

"Do you hear something?"

"North. Lykea's fate's-piece resonates in my mind. It is a sigil ring of a Flyssn lord. My mother used to get correspondence sealed with a ring just like it."

"And what does it have to do with our task?"

"I don't know. I listen and obey." She took his hand, careful not to touch the burned back. He turned his head away, so that she would not see his face. But she brought her stump wrist to the side of his face and urged it back round. She peered at him, brows soft. "Are you ready?"

Fallo turned to Lykea, extended his hand. The man grasped his forearm. It burned like raw flame. "Listen and obey."

"Listen and obey," Lykea answered.

Fallo moved to escape the room, to be done with the parting

quickly, and to remove his agony from Illy's presence. The poor child had endured too much already, and if he had to guess, worse lay ahead of her, godling or no. But she intercepted him. Putting up her hands, she pushed on his chest, forcing him to stay.

"I lack something," she said. "I don't know what it is. But I lack something that would help you."

The mercusine, he thought. But that was good. She would attract the reviled if she were unmasked. And she had no training anyway. There was no reason to expect that she could—

He drew in a sharp breath as coolness washed over him, like a soothing dip in a summer lake. Illy screamed and jerked her hands away, then turned to sob into Quinn's breast.

Nefler Ernist came in then, bringing in a waft of freshness from outside. His cheeks were red and he rubbed his hands together for warmth. He nodded sharply to Fallo. "It is well that you are up. There are rumors of deathless riders scouring the countryside. The descriptions match what we saw in Vanish's Gold."

Illy glared at the man. "Unmask me. I can heal Fallo. I know I can."

"And risk your being discovered? No. You would sacrifice all Fallo has suffered."

"But you could mask me again. Or show me how to do it. I know I could learn it."

Fallo knew how it felt to be denied, to be controlled. No one at her age would relish the restrictions placed on her. But she didn't know what she was. He considered whether it would be better to tell her. Be done with it. But what a burden such knowledge would be. His instincts gave him no guidance. He decided it wasn't his job to tell her she was Ori reborn. His task was to find the others.

"You've eased my pain greatly, Illy," he said. "For that I am thankful. As for the rest . . . I am a shadline. Discomfort is the way. Farewell. Perhaps I will see you again at Rethnian, should the force of destiny will it. Nefler Ernist, we must go."

The man looked from Illy to Fallo and doffed his stemmed cap. His pate was smooth and spotted. "Do you truly know of a vergent pass? Of Derslin Wheels?"

"If you come with us, you may come to regret all the mysteries you will see."

And so they made their farewells and headed to the stables to collect Tolky. Lop was already atop the beast, as were their packs.

To Fallo's surprise a stablehand led three horses from the barn, all saddled and laden with packs and supplies for travel. It had been a long time since Fallo had ridden. He was given a gray mare with a white splotch on her left hindquarters. She snuffled at his hood as he patted her nose. "There's apples in this bag," the hand said. "Miltie'll do anything for someone feeds her apples."

Miltie took his weight with a whicker and sidestep. She answered to his heels readily. Ernist and Quinn mounted too. Ernist on an older roan called River, with plaited mane. Quinn sat upon a black gelding called Fleetheart. She looked like the hero she was. Fallo could only imagine what an awful figure he struck. Should he pull back his hood and show his face, no man could be blamed for thinking him a reviled. Or worse.

The horses' bodies steamed in the morning chill, but the sun warmed his shoulders. His face and hands didn't notice the cold at all. Whether that was because of Illy's healing or a permanent deadening of his skin he couldn't say.

Lykea stood at the door, watching. Presumably he would leave with Illy when his instincts told him to. Fallo waved and turned his horse north.

62

LIKE A WHIP

The eyrie above Ceronhel was an odd place to begin when one's destination was a Derslin Wheel deep in the guts of the fortress. But Kila had no wish to enter the great hall again and confront Revnithan Sault or that creepy shaman with his *clicky-clacky* skull staff. Besides, the whole place was now astir, with nosg probably already climbing up to catch her. The Revnithan could surely feel her mercusine, and he'd know it was high above him. It would not take a man of much intelligence to reason that she was in the eyrie.

But he hadn't immediately dymensed here. Two possible explanations. The first was that he couldn't dymense with enough shamans at once to aid him. The second, and simpler, reason was he'd never been in the eyrie. That had the feel of truth. Which meant she had time to catch her breath.

It is warm on this spot, Nax said. She had curled upon the floor, right in the middle of the great cavern. Unusual for a cat who preferred to find a cozy corner, shelf, or nook to occupy. Kila pressed a palm to the floor next to Nax. Sure enough, it was warm.

You think Bazron was here recently? Kila asked.

Some dragon or another.

Whichever one it was, it was gone now. She doubted any dragon would long remain near a festering hive of Revulsion. And just as well. The last thing she needed was a reviled dragon to contend with.

I didn't see Noy among those reviled, she sent to Nax.

Who?

He was Yioth's nosg helper, a sort of do-all. Flaumishtak said he'd know where Yioth was.

Not every reviled was in that hall.

No. But Kila remembered Noy as being a special sort of nosg. Obsequious, a bit dimwitted. But he was effective. If any nosg could escape the reviled, it would be Noy. But where would he be?

The only place in Ceronhel that she'd felt reasonably safe was that horrid torture room. Noy hadn't been there. But Flaumishtak had said Noy knew all the secret ways in and out of the fortress.

She went to the ledge and peered down at the fortress. The elnisian stronghold was formidable, even from this height.

And then she knew the perfect place for Noy to hide.

It meant going back into the fortress. But she didn't dare dymense back to the torture chamber. She again peered over the ledge.

Let's get on with it, Nax.

She hadn't told the cat what she planned to do. So when Nax climbed into her pack and she buckled it closed, she ignored Nax's alarmed wriggling.

Let me out!

Give me a moment. Kila grinned as she backed from the ledge. A running start wasn't strictly necessary, but if she was going to do this, it might as well be fun. *Don't worry.*

That's an alarming statement. What are you doing? It's something rash and ill-considered, isn't it?

Nax didn't have more time to fret about it, for Kila launched herself into open air. She spread her arms and molded her weather-cloak to block the wind from drying her eyes out. The sensation of falling lifted her gut high into her chest. A horrified meow erupted inside her backpack.

Sorry, friend, she sent.

All that came back through the bond was terror and anger. It occurred to Kila that she could have done this without Nax, established her familiarity with the interior of the tower below, then dymensed back to the eyrie to fetch her.

You were right, Naxie. This was ill-considered.

In the past, Kila had managed to fly using a feat of wind. Each time it had happened without her thinking about it. She'd been too furious. When her emotion was high, the mercus bolts came easily, instinctually.

Her fall continued, the rocks below fast approaching. Ceronhel had started the size of a doll house, but now it was expanding and the tower she wished to reach seemed a long, long way off. She closed her eyes, refusing to think about what senses and emotions she needed to bring to bear. Flaumishtak had taught her that the more one divided and divided again the component senses of a feat, the less control one had over it.

The mercus rushed into her mind's grasp. She did not focus on the feats, but upon the broken wall in that tower. The vertical gash of blackness beneath a conical roof. She yearned to go into it, to be lofted upon a cushion of wind, and set gently inside upon her feet. All her attention focused to that end. The mercus answered with all the necessary emotion.

She recalled the sensation of her old rag-quilt shirt being lifted by an upward gust when running a rooftop. Of pressure upon her feet as she deer-sprang across an alley, then landed with a dancer's grace on the other side. Of the hot thrill of pursuing a mark in the darkness, confident of every move. Feeling deeply the absolute necessity of taking the purse when Wen needed his medicine. Of staring down at the Hargothe, small and insignificant below, her mind imperious in her wrath.

And the wind rose up from below, icy and hard. It fountained like water, supporting her body now, letting her slide toward her objective. Her stomach returned to its proper place in her body, and she rotated upright.

The opening in the tower came at her fast. She adjusted her slide with mercus feats as quick and mindless as she did her balance when running on solid ground. And when she came through the opening and finally released her feat, weight returned to her toes. She rested a moment as the fading swirls lifted from the floor into a lazy devil that spent itself and finally vanished.

Let me out!

Kila let Nax out. Gray fur floofed like a bottle brush, and the white feet seemed to stomp upon the weathered planks of the tower garret. Kila had not often seen Nax's tail flick so hard. Like a whip. And so she thought better of saying anything at all. Instead she began an exploration of the ruined chamber for an exit.

She lifted a fallen beam aside with mercus touch and gently set it aside. It should have taken five strong men to heft it. For her it was like lifting a teacup. She caught herself mid-thought. This was no time to congratulate herself on her power. The thrill of her flight was still in her veins, and the feats it had required left residual emotions in her. That could be very dangerous. She would have to be careful about that when she flew again. In truth, it hadn't been actual flying. More like sliding upon a controlled upward wind. She doubted she could traverse over ground very quickly doing that. She checked outside and noted a cloud of dust and snow she'd kicked up with her feat. Not subtle in the slightest.

If the Revnithan hadn't felt her presence in the eyrie before, he surely felt it now.

A doorway led to a crumbled stairwell. Nax quickly slipped out of sight. When Kila came to the opening at the base of the stairs, the corridors were silent. Nax was already out of view.

She knew generally where the great hall was in relation to the tower, so she took the corridor leading in the opposite direction. Her suppositions proved to be accurate, for she now went through empty corridors where the floor dust had not been disturbed save for a dainty set of cat tracks. She added her own prints to those as she swept along, ignoring the various rooms and halls that opened from it. Nax knew what she was looking for. Kila simply followed the tracks to an opening at the top of another set of stairs. Down she went, sensing that Nax was already far below.

THE CAVERN of Ceronhel's Derslin Wheel was just like the others Kila had visited. A black expanse that gave the feeling of being outdoors at the same time as being in an enormous cave. She did not go quickly now, mostly because Nax was going slowly and she didn't want to leave her behind. Nax refused to get into her backpack.

She knew a mercus light would forewarn Noy if he were camped out among the columns, so she went in blackness. Her mercus senses were alive, and even now the flush of her glide from the eyrie continued to enliven her. When the sourceless light of the column circle finally appeared, she slowed her pace. It did not change the speed with which the circle approached. A little fire burned in the center, sending up a curl of smoke. The smell of roasting meat drifted in the air. A familiar figure was hunched over it, picking bits of crispy flesh from the roast and delicately giving it a test upon his lips.

"Noi-Ick-Noi," she said, entering the circle. "Where is your mistress?"

"Wah?" The nosg jumped up, grabbing the haft of a hatchet. "You?" His Ennish was slurred and thick, encumbered by fangs and a tongue suited to the lurkmire language of his kind. *"Kichet scinli!"* Whatever it meant, it wasn't kind. The nosg charged at her, hatchet raised over head. His little eyes squeezed tight and his lips pulled back in an animal snarl. Kila's willshift caught him hard, and he staggered sideways and fell over. The hatchet slid away. He lay there, still with one arm raised. Kila gave him his limbs so that he could get himself upright. She went to him, crouched.

"No need to attack me, Noy. I want to help Yiothizandra. You know where she is. Take me to her."

"Wah? No! You will kill her again!"

"I didn't kill her. I delivered her babe."

Noy blinked and looked away, saw Nax and tried to scurry away as the cat approached. Kila released the willshift completely. But when Noy made for the hatchet, she brought it to her own hand on mercus touch. Seeing this eerie movement of his hatchet, Noy croaked and covered his eyes.

"I'm not going to kill you," she said softly. "I need your help. Take me to Yiothizandra. She must join me to fight against the reviled. You must fight, too." She again lifted the hatchet upon her powers and floated it toward him, haft first. He peeked through his claws and cowered at the sight of it. She set it gently onto the floor next to him.

When he refused to uncover his eyes, or answer her questions, she went closer to him. Again she crouched, like one would do with a frightened child. "The Hargothe went into your mind. Don't make me go into your mind. Tell me where to find Yiothizandra."

"In the valley," he said, still covering his eyes.

"A valley in these mountains? How can I get there?"

"The goat path. Only way."

"Show me." When he still wouldn't budge, she said, "Or I'll let my cat climb onto your face."

"Nooo! I will show you!" The claws came away and waved at her and the cat, seeking to hold them back with his horror alone. He jumped up and went to his cooking meat. "I make a roast for the queen. She starves." He pulled the roast—which looked suspiciously like a large rat carcass—from its spit and put it into a burlap sack. This he slung over his shoulder. "Come. Don't let wee beast climb me."

63

THE SUFFERING PORTION

With Whiteflame in hand, Henley covered four steps in a stride. With Whiteflame in hand, his breath was no longer labored. With Whiteflame in hand, his head cleared as if from a good night's sleep. He stretched his arms up as he ran, rocked his head side to side, enjoying the pleasant pops of vertebra. He turned and again scanned the impenetrable fog, longing to see Ryde following after. But there was only the thick fog.

Boom! Doom!

So much closer. A sharp odor drifted past him, acrid smoke and the fetid vapors of a charnel house. From the distance came a red flash followed by a piercing white flare. A thunderous concussion followed a moment later and then went still.

The flight of stairs ended and he dashed across the barren parkland to the next stair. He searched overhead for the qiznithor. And then behind, still desperate to see Ryde chasing after him, victorious over the revulyn and her reviled.

Do not slow, Huff scolded. *It is close.* And with the words came an imperative feeling that set Henley in motion up the next flight of stairs.

Doom! Doom!

It has our scent, Henley called to Huff.

Yes. Run.

Without Whiteflame in hand, he would already be dead. He hoped the relic itself didn't kill him.

The last flight of stairs opened onto the Citadel plaza. Henley knew it only by the paving stones blurring beneath his feet. Huff was just ahead. The fortress loomed before him, a vague darkness beyond the haze.

Beware! Huff sent. *She is here.*

Impossible.

A jeweled red light sparked brightly in the fog ahead. Henley ran straight at it, as if running downhill. Whiteflame sensed an enemy and yearned to engage.

Something the size of a house crashed off to his left. *Boom!* Bits of rubble kicked out from the impact, stinging his cheek. More debris skittered across his path. The qiznithor had thrown part of a building at him. Mid-stride, Henley darted a glance back. The garnet lightning eyes hovered high up, the suggestion of an elongated snout formed in the clouds beneath it. His hair began to pull upward, drawn by a gathering force overhead. A strike was coming. He skidded, spun.

There was no point masking the blade any further. To unwind the ward did not require Henley to access the mercus directly, and he released it as easily as unknotting a bootlace.

The sword flared alight, sending white beams in all directions. Henley held it aloft, body throbbing with the weapon's power, with its eagerness for war.

The qiznithan released its strike. A bolt of lightning arced from its right eye, speared at Henley. Its plasmic light stained the surrounding fog and cloud bellies a gory crimson. Henley brought the sword around, taking the lightning on the flat of the blade.

Whiteflame countered with a burst of its own, a swell of outward pressing brilliance. Henley flew backward, sliding on his backside. Boots thundered behind him, the unmistakable weight of a fell guardsman's stride.

Ryde?

No. The reviled.

The man's spear arrowed at him, hurled with godlike might. Whiteflame swung round to deflect it. But the spear stopped in its flight as if striking an invisible barrier. Out of the haze stepped Brother Ryde, holding the spear freshly plucked from the air. He tossed it down, gave his own spear a twirl and stood between Henley and his reviled brother.

Hair lifting, Henley rolled and brought up Whiteflame. Garnet lightning flashed down, was again intercepted by the mercusine blade and thrown back in a blast of white.

Boom! Doom! Enormous claws struck ground. The world trembled.

Henley scrambled to his feet, smiling. A foe worthy of the fight.

Behind you! Huff screamed.

Henley turned to find the revulyn woman facing him, her spear aglow, hair swirling around her head. The pallid face watched him intently. But no revulsion feats blasted toward him.

Boom! Boom!

The furious qiznithor's eyes gathered the lightning. The snout and wriggling tentacle teeth were distinct now, as if the fog they were formed of had solidified into bone and flesh. And above all, stretching in vague shadows, the suggestion of wings.

A heaviness in the air warned Henley of approaching death. Not in the form of the beast itself, but of something material soaring at him. He shuffled to his left on instinct alone. A shiver animated his shoulders as he dove, ducked, and rolled.

Another partial building crashed into the courtyard, spilling rubble in all directions. Boulders bounced toward the revulyn, but were knocked away at the last moment by revulsion feats. She continued to watch.

She's been told not to kill me, he sent to Huff. *The qiznithor wants to do it.*

No one may kill you! I forbid it!

In the midst of chaos, Henley had not noticed Huff drawing near. But now he was at Henley's feet, crouched low, ears back.

Steel clashed upon steel behind them. Ryde and his reviled mirror image contended with swords now. The white glow had returned to Ryde's body. He was backing away from a furious blur of strikes. His reactions were a fraction slower than the attacks. Weariness was beginning to tell. The reviled's helm was missing, and his expressionless face struck terror into Henley's chest. The movements reminded him of a clockwork puppet he'd seen at market in his youth. Its head and arms had danced to music, frantic and jerky. An imitation of life, creepy and comical. But to see such motions in a man was nothing but terrifying.

Boom! Boom!

The carrion stench of the beast billowed down. Henley gagged, trapped in a miasma of evil. He held tightly to White-flame, raised it. But the blade was not content merely to defend against lightning bolts. It wanted to bite, to sever. It wanted to right the absolute wrongness of the qiznithor, and it strained to command Henley's will to that end.

The revulyn stood still, speartip glowing red, hair afloat. She barred the way into the Citadel. Ryde retreated slowly from the untiring assault of the reviled fell guardsman. The qiznithor gathered the lightning in its eyes. It towered over Henley now, a colossal monster of nightmare. Henley felt like a mouse beneath the gaze of a cat.

Two claws, each the length of a two-masted ship, struck in a great clapping motion. Huff thrust his feline reflexes into

Henley's body. Henley jumped, Whiteflame adding tenfold his usual strength into the leap. He flew backward as the claws slapped together. The concussion was followed by a blast of wind.

He tumbled like a stone. Dust filled his mouth and he choked and coughed. Grit stung his eyes. Again the sword granted strength and he thrust up onto his feet. Despite the sword's urgings, Henley backed away, awed by the towering beast.

Huff? Where are you?

Behind you. Come! Into the Citadel!

Lightning jagged at Henley. Whiteflame glanced them away, the counterforce spinning him around. Another flashed down. This time he was braced, and he angled the blade like a mirror catching sunlight. It deflected toward the revulyn. Not close enough. A divot blasted out of the face of the Citadel, and a section caved inward. No time to watch. Henley's skin came alive to imminent danger. He again leapt back, legs infused with Whiteflame's strength.

A claw raked through the courtyard, talons like plowshares curling stone into jumbled rows. He saw this from above. No human had ever jumped so high. Terrified, he scanned the trajectory of his flight. Below him a glowing Ryde contended with the unceasing flurry of the reviled. This melee drew closer and closer as Henley's flight bent downward.

If the reviled saw him, it did not mark the path that would land Henley behind him. Henley's feet struck. His knees bent to absorb the impact. His sword arced out, carving through the reviled's body, from flank to flank, severing flesh and spine like it was a strand of hair.

Reviled flesh turned to ash. Armor, sword and cloak spilled onto the courtyard like the bones of a skeleton. Brother Ryde, still aglow, still oversized in his sacrificial fury did not pause, but dashed straight for the revulyn.

Inside! Now! Huff sent. And again Huff's imperative overtook Henley's movements and he was running toward the gaping entry in the face of the fortress. The revulyn blasted out feats, Ryde met them with blurs of his spear. Each time, his aura flared. Each time it returned a bit dimmer than before.

The qiznithor blasted forth a hot cloud of charnel stink. It rolled over Henley, robbing the air of all nourishment and setting his throat into convulsions. Nausea wracked his belly. Ryde came closer and closer to the revulyn, and her outward feats grew more desperate. But his aura was fading fast. Whatever power he drew upon was failing him. He had shrunk to his usual height, the glow only faintly limning his body.

With a cry, the man threw his spear. It clattered onto empty ground obscured by Revulsion black. The woman had dymensed. Henley sprinted, swinging Whiteflame in wild arcs to deflect lightnings. The backthrust of each blow pushed him into a barely controllable stumble. He righted himself and caught Ryde in a wrestler's tackle, hoisted him and deadman carried him through the black opening in the Citadel.

Huff was somewhere within, a mental beacon that drew Henley on. Whiteflame wished to go the opposite way, to confront the evil it so despised.

"I am your master," he said to it.

The blade did not answer. Not with words. Henley felt a distinct surge of frustration as he entered the fortress and ran across the atrium.

The Citadel entry blew apart behind him as a snout smashed through. A serpentine tongue, covered in twisting spike tentacles, shot forward. It wrapped around a support column and pulled it from its base. The ceiling gave. The outer wall gave. A storm of stone rained down.

Henley carried Ryde onward, passing from the entry hall as columns tilted into each other, collapsing and releasing their burdens to fill the floor Henley had just traversed.

Ryde's glow had vanished. Blood wept from numerous wounds. A gaping hole in one shoulder leaked blood into Henley's cloak and warmed his skin.

Following Huff, Henley sprinted through gallery and hall and finally half-tumbled down stairs to the relative quiet of a corridor. He put Ryde down and coughed and spat out globs of dust-thickened phlegm.

Ryde fell against the wall. The hole in his shoulder told of a spear strike that should have rendered his sword arm immobile. He took two breaths, then struggled to his feet.

"Can you walk?" Henley asked.

"When my strength fails, duty sustains me." The man tottered a moment then tensed all his muscles, as if commanding their obedience. "We must retreat further. I cannot defeat that beast."

"Huff is this way. He will lead us true."

Ryde brought up the rear, turning and pausing every twenty paces to be the rear guard, to take the first blow, to buy Henley a fraction of a moment more of life. Huff, a smear of orange amid the haze, stood in a far doorway, mewling frantically.

Henley followed.

Something impacted above them. Whether it was the qiznithor or something it hurled, the noise was the same. The whole fortress rocked, and enormous slabs tipped from cracked walls and ceilings. Huff leapt and scrambled, relying on inexplicable instincts to know where the clear path would be.

Ryde cried out. Henley turned to see him pinned under the collapsed lintel of a doorway. Henley backtracked, thrust his sword under a gap and levered the stone up. Ryde pulled himself free, stood and nearly collapsed. His right leg was shattered, the boot encasing a slurry of bone, blood, and flesh. His helmet was stove in on one side and blood drained alongside his face.

"No!" Henley shouted. "It will not be!"

He put an arm around the man, heaved him up and dragged him along. Ryde managed to use his remaining leg to steady himself. "Leave me, Lord Mast. I can still fight. I have more to give than blood."

"You will give it in service beyond this place."

Ryde groaned, hand clamping painfully into Henley's shoulder. "I will not thank you for keeping me from my duty."

"I will not accept a pointless death as your duty." Henley's strength grew as he pulled Brother Ryde along. Whiteflame still wished to fight, but it seemed also to relish the honorable rescue of Ryde from certain death. Behind them came another enormous crash. A billow of wind and dust blew through the passage behind them.

Down they went, taking every stair Huff could find. The cat led them unerringly, and as they went deeper into the belly of the Citadel, the concussions behind them grew both more frequent and more distant.

Ryde did not complain any further. And it was only when they came into the final cellar, with its low arched ceilings that Henley realized the fell guardsman was unconscious. He was bearing the full weight of the enormous man.

The door to Starside was ahead. Huff faced it, fur standing straight out, tail high, ears back.

The revulyn woman stood before the door, barring the way. Her pale face was grimed with dust, her cloak tattered and filthy. She leaned on her spearstaff. The whole room was alive with the lurid glow of its revulynic light.

"If you will but listen, you will be free," she said. A cold voice, but human. The tone of a tutor reasoning with an unwilling pupil. As if there was something obvious that, once understood, would clear up Henley's simple ignorance.

"The Revulsion is not freedom, Spinster."

He didn't know why she hadn't attacked. The qiznithor was surely digging its way into the Citadel, but judging by the trembles it was not close. Surely it would allow her to use her vile feats to delay him, perhaps to turn him.

"You know nothing," she said, "for your view is as if obscured by stained glass. You are dazzled by colors, of illuminated shapes. You call them life or love or pleasure or duty. Could you but, for an instant, see with the *cold eye*, you would discover that all flesh and thought and pleasure is torture, all a lie. You would discover the truth, that all life—all existence—is suffering. Even the stone of this fortress suffers in its way. The very latticework that is matter itself is unnatural, untenable. Unacceptable." She took a step toward him, the butt of her spear staff clicking on the stone. The tip's ruddy light made her pallid face a bloody mask. Huff stood between them, fur out, tail flicking. Seeing him in her path, she hesitated. Stopped.

But she didn't stop her cold lecture. "The Unanswered underlies everything. The Revulsion, you call it. You think it evil. But the cold eye perceives it truly, as our refuge, our haven. Our salvation. It is woven through the stitchwork of lies you call life, a simple unfrayable thread. We need only to tug upon it to begin the great unraveling. The fabric of stone and bone are the same, and they throb with an anxious need. To be undone." Her eyes widened and took on the glow of her spearlight, flaring with jeweled crimson. "It cries out, Henley Mast. And it speaks the only sacred word. And that word is 'Annihilation.'"

She seeks to go into your mind, Huff warned.

He couldn't sense the mind probe she had threaded. No doubt it was poised very near to him. The speech was meant to be a distraction, and it had worked. But Huff's presence blocked her intrusion. She hissed and tilted the spear down, pushing the pin-sharp tip at Huff. But she didn't give the thrust any muscle. The spear wavered a foot from the cat's head. Vile and terrible as she was, her posture reminded Henley of a housemother warding off a snake with a broom handle.

The qiznithor's concussions and rumbles went suddenly quiet, leaving Henley in a silence disturbed only by his own ragged breathing. He kept his gaze fixed on the revulyn even as he plunged into the inner realm of the mercusine. The Revulsion surrounded him instantly, greedily.

"You feel it," the revulyn said. "It is repellent to you, for you mistake good for evil, freedom for imprisonment. In every opposite pairing you know, you have occupied the suffering portion."

Huff tried to silence her with an angry hiss.

The Revulsion pounded against Henley, clawed at him. It lay thickly upon the mercus, obscuring it. Depthless, more viscous than molasses, thick as hot tar. Into this Henley probed, stomach rebelling even as his spine twisted in disgust, even as his bones froze from the horror of it. He tightened his grip on Whiteflame, drawing strength from it.

THERE YOU ARE!

The qiznithor's voice pummeled him, a sledge inside his skull. He lost his breath, nearly lost his grip on the sword.

"There you are," the revulyn repeated softly.

I will not permit it, the cat sent.

THE FELNITHEL CANNOT PROTECT YOU! the qiznithor blasted into his mind.

"The felnithel cannot protect you," the revulyn echoed.

It comes, Henley! We must go.

"How long do you think the Divide will stand?" the revulyn crooned. "The qiznithor was long asleep, but now you've awakened it fully. The elnisians did not account for his mighty rage when they erected the Divide. Do you believe you've seen the

Mighty One's ultimate form? You have not. It hates you and will destroy you. But your suffering will not end in death. Better tortures await you, Henley Mast. For when you pass the threshold of his maw, you will enter the flaying agonies of the craw. The Mighty One will consume you, rend you, but you will be aware. Until the release of Annihilation, you will continue to perish in nerve-searing tribulation. Every second an eternity, your voiceless shrieks heard by no one, lamented by no one. If you could but see with the cold eye! Release stands before you. Submit and be free. Banish the felnithel and surrender to me. I will open your mind. Cast away that foul blade. The Mighty One squirms ever downward. Even now he approaches, him of the thousand writhing fangs. Dare you chance to be eaten? Dare you risk shackled agony when painless freedom is before you? I offer a boon. You sense it, don't you? You feel the blazing urgency of it as you worm your way through the Unanswered toward the glowing lie of the mercusine. Reverse your view. You burrow through nectar to reach a dungpile. You see it, I can feel it in you. The Unanswered force of the universe awaits. You need but grasp it. Pull the thread, unravel the illusion."

"STOP!" Henley shouted. "Hate-witch! Cease your yammering. You, whose heart beats not. Foul woman who is no woman at all. Soulless liar."

The Revulsion squeezed away from his mind as he plunged, seeking, swimming, holding back gags. Tears blurred the world as he forced himself ever deeper. He held to his bond with Huff, he clung to Whiteflame who steeled his legs and guts against the assaults of foulness.

A tooth-juddering grind arose beneath his feet, the grate of stone against stone. And inside Henley the Revulsion solidified. No longer liquid, no longer penetrable. He was encased in it like a fly in amber. Suffocating, he panicked, mind afloat now in a sightless realm. The horror of a bodiless existence in the void overtook him. His body answered his terror by writhing about, sword tip scraping against the floor. His eyes popped open but could not take in sight. His mind was wholly occupied by the trap.

It comes! Huff sent. *It burrows toward us now.*

I can't escape, Huff. I can't breathe!

"The felnithel cannot protect you," the revulyn said.

Huff's presence pressed more fully into Henley's awareness. He clung to it, tried to enfold it around him. *Help me,* Henley sent.

I cannot defeat it alone.

THE FELNITHEL WILL JOIN US ALL IN ANNIHILATION!

"The felnithel will join us all in Annihilation," the revulyn said. "Submit to me now or be tortured for an infinity of infinities. Inside the madness of the qiznithoric gut outer time moves not."

The burrowing, grinding, and ear-scorching scrape of the approaching beast increased. The sounds of the world registered as vibrations in Henley's chest, in the very bone of his skull. He strained against the Revulsion, sought to crack it by heaving his mind against it. The mercus was there, somewhere. If he could but glimpse it he would have it.

An ominous rumble thudded into his chest. That was not the sound of stones crashing or grinding into dust. It was guttural. The qiznithan was straining toward him. Again came a hot miasma of death. Rotting corpses and burning flesh.

Kila would do something. Kila would find a way.

Kila would use the Revulsion.

Even in this moment of hopelessness, the idea was repugnant beyond all thought. To embrace it would be worse than to be destroyed by it. There was no question of using it. Not for Henley Mast.

So be it. If he was to die let his defiance be his victory.

I see you, Henley sent at the beast and the revulyn. *I see you with a clear eye.*

YOU SEE NOTHING! BEHOLD!

"You see nothing!" the revulyn whispered. "Behold!"

Vision blasted into Henley's eyes, his attention released from the void of Revulsion to the grit-clouded air of the cellar. A great hole had opened in the arched ceiling, a perfect circle of blackness half the width of the room. Inside were two garnet eyes. Inky claws emerged to grip the sides of the opening, the span-long talons piercing the stone. It pulled, forcing its mass through the hole. Sliding like a serpent it squirmed into the cellar, coiling to bring its whole mass in behind it. It had condensed from its vast size outside of the Citadel, but now its form was solid. Its wings were folded tightly to its back, insectile and glimmering.

The features which had been indistinct among the Revulsion clouds outside now showed themselves. It was a dragon. No. It *looked* like a dragon, but there was no grace in its skull, no beauty in its spines. The scales were fluid, never holding shape long. All was black, but despoiled with foul greenish brown bruises that swirled and oozed with a life of their own. The maw stretched, wet with gooey strings of Revulsion. Teeth of curved spikes were arranged at random over the bottom and top of the mouth, spreading inward over tongue and throat. Teeth, all the way into a narrowing infinity. Above all this perverted chaos were the lightning eyes. Orbs of constant motion, arcing with red bolts and blossoms of red fire. They narrowed as they turned down to regard him, baleful and brimming with hate.

Huff crept away from the revulyn, trod over Ryde's body, and confronted the beast. The orange fur still stood out, but now the tail was low, the ears flat. The cat hissed and spat and grumbled deep in his body.

The qiznithor, the dragon-like manifestation of hatred, paused.

So this was death, Henley thought. Could it be this easy? Whiteflame assured him it was. He stood sideways to the qiznithor and the revulyn, ready to swing his sword in either direction. The woman lowered her head, regarded him with eyes of flaring red.

He did not fear the Revulsion anymore, though the solid wall of it barred him from the mercus as completely as did the Divide from Starside. He stepped over Ryde, drew Whiteflame over his head and rushed at the writhing maw of his enemy. Huff darted forward too. The qiznithor lunged, jaws gaping to embrace them.

Henley's sword came down, edge eager to split apart a hated foe. His heart leapt as he gave himself to Whiteflame's battle lust.

With a flare of brilliant light, the sword bit deep. A jolt stung his arm. The qiznithor's fangs lashed out like tentacles and ice penetrated Henley's flank. A soul-shattering squeal spiked his mind. Whiteflame and beast and felnithel clashed. Huff's claws scraped, tiny fangs penetrated. Blade blasted into darkness. Squirming tooth whipped from a mouth of foulness to impale human and felnithel alike.

The stench of a rotting battlefield belched over Henley's face. Whiteflame flared. Blindness from darkness and brightness competed, strove to obliterate all sensation from Henley's mind.

Huff's presence grew larger in his awareness. Agony came with it. Huff was hurt. Henley was pierced through. A tongue of thorns had wrapped itself around him, was drawing him into the maw of eternal pain. He struck again and again. Each blow pulled life through his arm and into the blade. It no longer gave him sustaining strength. It consumed it, used what little remained in him against this fell enemy—this implacable manifestation of timeless chill.

Huff!

No answer.

HUFF! He slashed with the sword, sawed the edge against tooth, against tongue. Everywhere the blade connected, the Revulsion flesh parted and withdrew, scurrying away like insects into shadow.

HUFF! Don't leave me.

Panic took him again. Not for his sake. He did not care about living. Huff did not deserve to be destroyed. The mere idea was intolerable to hold in his head. The rage of total vengeance overtook him, combined with his desperate need to find and hold his dearest friend, his loyal companion, the spark spirit who had been his greatest gift.

Hold, Huff! Do not leave me!

An explosion tossed Henley into the air. He landed on his off-hand shoulder. Whiteflame scraped into the floor, sending up brilliant sparks as it tore into the stone. Henley's head struck next, shaking his vision. When it cleared he beheld Brother Ryde, balanced on one foot. The man appeared to have grown to twice his height, his whole body aglow. He moved with pain-free fluidity, striking at the flinching face of the Revulsion-formed dragon. At his feet lay Huff, a lump of orange, fur blown to and fro by the breath of the beast.

Henley clawed toward the cat. Digging fingers into the gaps in the stone tiles, pushing with his toes. The battle between man and beast continued, the tongue of thorns again wrapping around human flesh. This time it was Ryde they pierced. This time it was three separate tentacles, each covered with thousands of spike-teeth. Ryde did not scream as he was pulled into the vast maw. His arm remained free, his spear told countless times. His aura increased as he did his duty, as the pure power of his honor exploded forth.

The revulyn struck, driving her spear into Henley's leg and pinning him. A Revulsion feat followed, boring into his mind.

"The felnithel cannot save you," she said.

A cold finger probed in his mind. It was so much like the Hargothe's intrusion that Henley wished to curl up and scream. But pain, mere suffering, mattered nothing to him against the need of the orange animal now curled in his arm.

"But I can save the felnithel," he rasped.

He pulled the limp form close to his face. The light of Brother Ryde was eclipsed by the qiznithor's closing mouth. The lightning eyes flared again, and Henley's hair again rose. He dragged White-flame around. Ah, it was so heavy. A sword of lead. His arm was lead. His body, his mind. All leaden. There was nothing remaining of him to receive the empowering might of the mercusine blade.

Lightning flashed out. Whiteflame took it, sent it glancing away. The sword whipped away, hilt nearly tearing from his grip. He caught the ball of the pommel in his fingertips.

Huff's presence began to thin out.

Stay with me!

AND NOW I SHALL GORGE UPON YOUR SOUL!

"And now I shall gorge upon your soul!" the revulyn said. The spear twisted in Henley's thigh and the Revulsion probed deeper into his mind, seeking the masked wellhead of his mercus power. She sought the very part of him he could not gain for himself.

I can save the felnithel. I can stand up. I can stand against evil.

When strength fails, duty sustains me.

The maw opened again, the spiked tongue thrust out for him.

There was hot, sticky dampness on Huff's fur. Was it Henley's blood or Huff's? In the end there was no difference. All was one between them. *Join with me,* Henley sent. *Surrender.*

As Huff had once saved Henley from suffering by holding within him Henley's whole existence, now Henley took in Huff's. A trembling, vague presence. A speck of ice in soup, reducing and reducing.

Stay with me!

He opened his eyes, saw that he was standing. That the revulyn's spear had been chopped in half by his own sword. He tugged the speartip from his flesh and threw it away. He lurched toward the woman even as tooth thorns wrapped around his calf. She backpedaled, throwing up her arms. She was afraid of him though he trembled like a newborn fawn.

"I contain the felnithel." He held Huff's limp, bloodstained body in the crook of one arm. The cat's delicate head dangled. But Huff, the spark spirit, was in him, joined.

The qiznithor's tongue retracted, yanking Henley from his feet. Whiteflame slipped from his hand. Huff's body spilled lifelessly, limbs splaying unnaturally on the floor. The revulyn appeared to retreat as he was dragged away from her and toward doom. Dragged slowly. Even now, Huff's essence made Henley an unappetizing meal for the qiznithor.

The revulyn trembled, hands out. A blur of black smeared in her hands as a feat of Revulsion formed. He could not negate it or deflect it.

The felnithel. Ah, the glorious spark spirit.

Huff, dearest friend. The honor was mine.

The little ember was fading in his mind. The joining could not be sustained if the body died.

The revulyn's feat built, but she did not release it. The qiznithor had him anyway. Dragged him back, away from the bloody lump of Huff's body. Away from the Starside door. Away from life.

Abruptly the revulyn's head tipped to one side, parted from her neck. It fell onto the floor and rolled to face him, eyes still awake and alive, mouth open in astonishment. Her body crumpled. Men rushed over her. Men in gleaming breastplate, with plumed helms. Spears and swords in their hands.

Boots leapt over Henley, fresh hems of crimson cloaks dragged across his face. Five fell guardsmen threw themselves at the beast. As one they seemed to grow and their bodies shone forth with that lovely aura. The din of their oaths and the chunk of their swords and spears came to Henley as if through a batting of wool. Everything around them dimmed, Whiteflame dimmed.

His leg went numb and the spikes withdrew.

Now a robe hem swept into view. Henley was lifted. He strained to reach for Huff's body, but the cat was lost in the fray. Henley was carried through the Divide and into Starside. A door slammed in the hollow distance behind him and the battle cries of the sacrificial fell guardsmen went silent.

His bond with Huff vanished.

64

HOW FAR IS FAR?

Noi-Ick-Noi was much faster than Kila had expected. Once out of the Derslin Wheel, he did not lead her up to the higher levels of the fortress, but instead took her deeper. The fine elnisian work of the corridors ended abruptly at a great oak door, bound in straps of riveted iron. The metalwork had been blackened with a thick coating to protect it from rust, but time had chipped it away in places, weakening the hinges in particular. The door stood ajar, canting forward dangerously. Noy squeezed through the gap and beckoned Kila to follow.

She sent her floating sphere of mercus light ahead of her, fearful that Noy was leading her into a trap. But the space beyond was open and without trip rope, falling boulders, or a pit of spears. She went through and gawped at the cave. Enormous fanglike formations hung from the roof. It recalled to her the size and shape of the dragon eyries. Kila sent her light upward, giving more power to it to better illuminate the cavern.

The walls sparkled with flakes of crystal, giving the impression of stars. The elnisians had discovered it, recognized the beauty of it, and had preserved it as it was. Noy was indifferent to it. He loped along, sack over his shoulder, darting the occasional glance back. Not to see if Kila was keeping up, but to make sure Nax wasn't getting too close. Nax, naturally, harried him, staying close to his heels.

Kila jogged to catch up. But even the urgency of her mission could not keep her from gazing up in awe. She wished she could have enjoyed all the wonders she'd seen during her adventures and been spared the horrors. But that was not how life worked.

With a last reluctant look back, she left the cavern behind and began to ascend through a tunnel that seemed rather hastily hewn. None of the elnisians' attention to detail and artistry was in evidence. A nosg tunnel, she thought.

An awareness brought her head around. Nax moaned at the same time.

Henley's back, Kila sent.

I can't feel Huff!

Is he . . .? She couldn't bring herself to ask, but bent and huddled close to the cat. Nax trembled.

He's gone!

Frantic, Kila searched her bond with Henley. He was so distant she couldn't sense any of his emotions. *It's like he's asleep,* she sent.

Nax mewled and pulsed anguish over the bond.

Noy came back and muttered something.

"Just wait!" she snapped.

Nax stiffened, then went abruptly quiet. Something cold passed through the bond, something steely. *We must continue,* she sent.

But what about—

We must continue.

Kila released Nax and they went on. Time went by, marked by untold twists and turns. Noy took tunnels branching to the left or right, none of them marked as far as Kila could see. The farther they went, the narrower they became. When she had to go on hands and knees to squeeze through one particular section, she noted the greasy residue that covered the floor. She sniffed it and gagged. It was like something she'd find growing along the floor of the Starside sewers. A brown-green slime, slick and gooey.

"How much farther?" Kila demanded as they came to yet another junction in the tunnels. This one was circular, with five exits, not including the one they'd come through. No signs, no scratches, no blob of paint to mark any of them. Noy unburdened a hide sack from his shoulder and took out a skin of some sort of liquor. The smell of it stung Kila's eyes. Noy offered the skin, which had what looked like tattoos on the side. She declined. Noy shrugged and put it away.

"I asked you a question, Noy."

"How far is far? It's a walk, and no less."

"Very helpful."

But as they continued, she pestered him with more questions. In time she extracted enough information to give her hope. Yioth had been saved from a band of Blackshine shamans who were trying to turn her to the Revulsion. The bad part was that she'd been saved by Razk-Ka and the remains of his army. Now this force was backed into a closed valley and fighting off a horde of reviled nosg. Noy didn't refer to them as "reviled," but instead as "dead." And that was accurate enough. When she pressed him for more about how the shamans had been corrupted, he simply waved a claw and shrugged. "Blackshine mimak."

They emerged from the tunnels through a cleft so narrow Kila had to push her pack out ahead of her and shimmy through. To Noy's credit, he didn't use her vulnerable position to attack her with his little hatchet. He seemed resigned to her command, and perhaps hopeful that she would be of some aid to his queen.

The opening gave onto a shallow slope of a mountainside where stubby shrubs reached with wispy twig arms toward the pale blue sky. Clumps of snow, smooth and droopy as half-melted butter, lay over everything else. A partially flattened game trail led away from the hole. And down they went. Noy's boots had little nails in the soles, giving him good purchase. Kila wore her stupid canvas shoes, which offered no grip and less protection against the snow. She infused her weather-cloak into her shoes after expelling the moisture. But she couldn't conceive of a way to use the mercus to keep her from slipping every few strides.

The trail went down very steeply, then curved along the inside of a sheer cliff, the ledge barely wide enough for her shoulders. Noy did not seem slightly concerned about the thousand-foot drop. Kila was confident she could fly, or at least glide, to safety if she fell, but she preferred to have the choice of falling be her own. Nax sent worried trembles through the bond, but she knew the cat's concern was with Huff rather than the dizzying track they followed.

A vista opened below them to the south, showing a deep valley churned to mud by a great host. Fires burned at the rear where a sprawling encampment had been hastily thrown up. Even from this perch, the mass of nosg at the throat of the valley was unmistakable. They surged forward in large bands, attacked something at the narrows, then retreated just as the next wave came up behind them. And in this manner, Razk-Ka's army alternated at the front of the battle. It showed much more tactical prowess than had been displayed during the assault on Stallid under Yioth's leadership.

"Are those wyvoks?" she asked, squinting and shading her eyes against the sun. Black flecks circled and dove over the battle. She counted at least a dozen. She was too far away to see if swarmlight magics were being hurled about. If those were wyvoks, she would have to give Razk-Ka far more credit than she had done thus far.

"This is going to be tricky," she said as they continued their descent. Unturned nosg were better than corrupted ones, but that hardly made them her friends. "Yioth is down there?"

Nosg pointed his hatchet at the encampment. "I bring her meat. She starves."

65

BRING OUT YOUR WINGS

"I would've paid ten thousand gold to witness a battle like this," Klayne was saying. "And here it is, free. And these seats!" He sat upon a north-facing ledge overlooking the valley, rubbing his shoulders and smiling. Eckso sat next to him, legs dangling over a five-hundred-foot drop. Her back ached, her neck was cramped, and even though she'd released her wings from existence she could still feel them.

Klayne was in a jolly mood despite the *vaz'on*, for she had allowed him a sip of trezz after they had found the valley. What they had not expected was to discover a pitched battle raging at the mouth of it. "You think Yioth is down there somewhere?" she asked, studying the battle formations. War was not her particular area of study. "I would have thought she would be aloft, blasting fire down upon the enemy. Or swinging that horrid sword of hers around." Eckso squeezed her elbows at the mere thought of Flayshui.

"Yioth won't be among that rabble," Klayne crowed. "If they got her away from the reviled, she's back in that camp, probably astride some poor girnt. Lust runs in your family, you know."

Eckso backhanded his shoulder, hard. "Are you drunk?" He

winced but grinned at her and winked.

She snatched the trezz bottle from him. It was nearly empty. Enough to knock a sailor into oblivion. She tossed it over the ledge and watched it tumble. "Should we go down and search, tent to tent? Do we dare?"

"I don't care what you do. Find Yioth. Don't find Yioth. It's all the same to me as long as I've got this thing on my head." He flicked a nail against the gold circlet, raising a sharp ping into the air.

Eckso wasn't the sort to go running about among nosg without knowing whether they would attack her or not. She could keep them at bay with the mercus, of course. Easily, now that she could tap Klayne's power. But throwing such feats about while those shamans drifted overhead on wyvoks made her cautious.

"You feel that?" Klayne asked, grin waning into sober concentration. "There's a merculyn across the way."

The *vaz'on* blocked him from using his mercus, but it didn't block his sensitivity to it. Nor would it muffle the heightened senses it granted. Eckso had never been much of a seeker of merculyns. She tried to concentrate and feel for mercus potential in the valley. But the chaos of battle overrode those attempts, just as it had apparently obliterated her repeated calls to her sister.

"Bring out your wings, Klayne. It's time to glide down."

"Bah! Stick your wings up your—"

The Will Gem was so handy. It required no effort to seal his lips and freeze his body. She gave him a shove and toppled him off his seat. She released the gem from her thoughts. A second later his agonized curse drifted up at her. His wings sprang into existence. Eckso was about to jump after him when she felt a searing pain grip her chest. A sob tore from her throat and the world went black with anguish.

66

I KNOW

Marlow was clean, haggard, and in very fine clothes. His hands were folded on his lap. A sad expression pulled at his mouth and eyes. The smell of smoke colored the air, which was very dim. The haze of a lacework bed canopy stretched overhead. To Henley's exhausted mind, the whole chamber felt like a warm cocoon. He could not feel his limbs. His lips were cracked, his tongue dry and rough as a grain sack.

"Huff?" He couldn't feel the cat's presence in his mind. No bond. Just emptiness.

Marlow simply shook his head, confirming what Henley already knew. "A fell guardsman retrieved him before the Moonside door was closed. Finta Sahng has his . . ." The words trailed off and dampness made Marlow's eyes glisten. Henley went inward, again searching for the bond. Grasping for the unreachable.

HIGH ABOVE THE city a guttural call sounded from the throat of the raven. All who lived below felt its anguish. Hearts ached, eyes welled up. Mothers dashed for their babes, and men paused to catch their breath amidst their labors.

In the Cathedral of Til, the Highest of Highests shivered beneath his vestments. The satisfaction of his confirmation as Highest of the Way vanished beneath a heavy wave of grief he couldn't understand.

In Lower Terriside the patrons of The Grunting Hog went silent and discovered they were weeping for no apparent reason. The barman wiped a towel across his eyes. Across the room a Cheapsgater started to sing "Sink Me in the Sourwater." Cracking voices lifted to join him.

In the Blasted Quarter, the Highest of Kila fell to his knees, overtaken with an inexplicable sadness. The twenty-odd Cheapsgaters bedding down in the Hall of Spears started to sob.

Hackworth Keel sat in his business office, scribbling in his ledgers. His quill-tip scraped a jagged line across his profit column, obliterating months of totals. He coughed and wiped at the corner of his eye, then stared at strange wetness that had come off on his hand.

A burned shadline on a gray mare held a trembling black cat, pouring tears into its fur. A raven-haired woman looked on, pained and helpless to do anything to ease his pain. Their merculyn companion bowed his head and muttered quiet prayers to Ori.

Ori did not hear these prayers. She rode behind a Shadline Knight. Her body was wracked with sobs. "I cannot bear it, Shad Lykea. The heart of the world breaks and I feel it *all.*"

In the unmapped north, far beyond the Haelshoks, where the world remains ice year-round, a yoznithan demayne held a creamy cat in his immense arms. He shushed and cooed to the moaning animal, willing in that moment to trade all his power could he but ease the felnithel's anguish. Alas, he could barely bear his own.

From Garden Island to Slirya, the heavy grief pressed upon mortal souls everywhere. In the Sagmarsh the shadline mooncrafter Zirhine tried to comfort the dragnithor Ulagatin. Billows of blue fire shot skyward from the soul-tortured beast, an insufficient tribute to the felnithel now lost.

And so it was with every dragon of Night and every dragon of Day.

At the base of a frozen waterfall, the god Kil emerged into open water. She scrabbled to grip the ice and climb free. Semūin grabbed her ankle and pulled her back. "You must not!"

The girl lashed out, half-heartedly. "But it must not *be!* I can undo it. And if I cannot undo it, I must—I must—" But she couldn't finish the thought, for she didn't know how to end it. Only that there was a great surge of wrath in her body, sizzling up her spine like molten iron.

"Come, child," Semūin said. "Let us weep together. But not for long, for the felnithel are eternal."

MARLOW WAS THERE when Henley woke from a cold, dreamless sleep. He looked at the man, looked at the room, looked at his blankets. Then he looked for the mercus. There it was, soiled by a skim of the Revulsion.

The revulyn woman's words returned to him.

"The Mighty One will consume you, rend you, but you will be aware. Until the release of Annihilation, you will continue to perish in nerve-searing tribulation. Every second an eternity, your voiceless shrieks heard by no one, lamented by no one. If you could but see with the cold eye!"

He had escaped and yet he had been consumed. For this life

—this existence without Huff *was* nerve-searing tribulation. His mind dipped in and out of the mercusine, each time sniffing at the foulness of the Revulsion.

The cold eye. How he craved to feel nothing at all.

But to embrace it would be to betray Huff.

Marlow cleared his throat. "Your ailment is perplexing. I would that Kila were here to use her powers. Alas." He waved to someone Henley could not see. A young woman came in and set down a tray. The smell of muffins and tea provoked a welling up of nausea. He rubbed a hand across his midsection, discovered his belly wrapped in bandages. And above them his ribs standing proud from his skin. He'd been bitten by the qiznithor. Maybe he would turn reviled.

"I want Huff."

"Finta has him. When you're ready. For now you must rest and heal."

Flashes of pain and visions of red light fluttered across Henley's vision. The revulyn's spear twisting in his leg, the qiznithor's vile tongue spikes penetrating his body. Huff's presence fading, thinning out, going silent.

"I want him. I want him. I want him."

"Easy, Henley," Marlow said. The man held his wrists. His bedclothes were half off him. "Let me help you."

Henley felt a pressing in his mind. It was heavy-handed. He allowed it. He would allow anything that eased his agony. "Ah me. I need Huff. I need Kila." His words slurred and the world dimmed.

MARLOW WAS THERE when he woke, dressed in fresh robes and looking as if he'd slept too. And then he blurred as tears flooded Henley's eyes. But there were no sobs to be given now, just an undammed flow of grief. The hollowed out place in his chest had no bottom. This was what his life was now.

"Your wounds are healing well," Marlow said. "Finta has remarkable skill."

"I should be reviled," he said, half-wishing he were. Wishing the choice could be removed from him. That way he wouldn't betray Huff. But at least he'd be released from the qiznithor's craw.

"Highest Quiv believes Whiteflame seared the corruption out of you somehow. Brother Ainlin nearly lost a hand trying to pick it up. Terissa, how about some food for this young man?"

"Of course." The woman came into view, a sad smile curling the side of her mouth. She scooped an arm under Henley's shoulders and eased him to a sitting position, his back against fluffy pillows. The smile broadened, sharp features pretty and friendly. She tousled his hair. "You do need food, Hen. You look like a stick after too much whittling. Almost as scrawny as that Sigh girl."

"Don't call me Hen."

She brought a tray to the bed. He nibbled at the muffin, but it felt like sawdust on his tongue. He set it aside. "I'm not hungry."

Marlow shared a momentary look with Terissa. Her mischievous gleam dimmed a moment, but returned with apparent effort. "You are probably just thirsty. Here, nurse this tea a while to awaken your belly."

The tea was bitter, but he welcomed the cup's warmth in his hands. He closed his eyes. Flashes of red. The revulyn woman's glowering face rushed at him. He woke with a start. Marlow was lifting the teacup away and blotting a spill seeping into Henley's blanket. "Do you feel strong enough to tell of what happened in Moonside?"

Henley's cheeks went cold and he slumped deeper into his

blankets. He didn't want to remember anything about Moonside. But he did. In particular he remembered Hannik and Ryde, men who had sacrificed themselves for him. At the last, more of their brothers had rushed through the Moonside door. "What happened to the fell guardsmen who rescued me?"

"They did their duty. Brother Ainlin is recovering from handling Whiteflame. I daresay it spared him by choice."

"Ori's grace upon them all."

They were silent a while longer. Marlow shifted uncomfortably. He placed a warm hand on Henley's arm. "Moonside. You must tell me what you discovered."

Terissa came and went twice over the next two hours, bringing food, bringing tea. Henley swallowed a few cups, but couldn't be compelled to eat anything solid. He suspected Finta had dripped some sneaky herb-oil into the teapot, for the brew left him warm and drowsy. His voice sounded distant to his own ears as he related all he could recall of Moonside: the temple, the qiznithor, the revulyn and reviled fell guardsman, the damage to the Divide. Of Brother Ryde's final sacrifice.

"And the sword?"

"I found it in the temple, powering the Revulsion trap. I replaced it with the Motherlight. I knew I had to bring it back. It destroys reviled, turns them to ash."

"It's not much fond of the living either. I told you about Brother Ainlin. But after tending to your wounds, Finta took hold of it. I've never seen anything like it. She did a little shuddering dance as a fit took her over, then she set it down and *scolded* it. After that it allowed her to move it." He twisted in his chair to look behind him. "It's on that table. Finta suggests you not take it up again until you are recovered."

"Where's Kila? She feels very distant." But the bond was there. He clung to it even as he resented it. Its mere existence made Huff's absence all the starker.

Marlow did not answer for a long time. Henley had the impression the man didn't know where to begin. "The Revulsion has grown and spread. We now know that it's being led by a qiznithan who is using revulyns and corrupted nosg shamans to turn more merculyns every hour. Kila confronted him in Sorgan but could not defeat him."

"Go on," Henley said, sensing even worse news.

"He inhabits the body of Dunne Yples."

"Where's Kila?"

"She is seeking out Yiothizandra and the other demayne of Night, as Ell instructed her to do."

"Yioth was in Stallid."

Marlow shook his head, lips pursed. "Kila went there first, but Yioth had already been rescued. Or I should say kidnapped. The qiznithan took her, no doubt. I pray she has not already been turned. Kila has gone to Ceronhel to search for her."

Henley pointed toward her. "She's that way."

Marlow again twisted. "North." He shrugged. "As I said. Ceronhel. Nothing to be done to aid her from here. You must turn your energies to your own healing. You have done her and the realm a great service. If that blade can destroy reviled you will be called upon again to fight. If the Divide falls, it may be sooner than—"

The door opened to admit Terissa again. She did not carry a platter this time, but instead a bucket of steaming water. She leaned hard to one side to bear the weight of it. She had a thick towel over her shoulder and a basket in the other hand. She set the bucket next to his bed and shooed Marlow away.

"Time for a bath, Hen," she said cheerfully. Her eyebrows waggled in mischievous glee.

"Don't call me Hen. I can manage on my own."

"I'm sure you can. But Finta gave me strict instructions. I'll need to see to your bandages."

Marlow patted Henley's hand and stood to leave. "I'll let you get cleaned up. I'll have my dinner brought here. We can finish our conversation then."

She pulled from her basket a cake of soap and a sea sponge. She folded down his covers and started to tug at his sleep shirt. He tried to fight her off, but was soon so winded he had no choice but to submit.

For once she was quiet, and she worked diligently and gently. He was too heartsore to be embarrassed. When she was done, he felt refreshed enough to move to Marlow's chair while she changed the bedclothes. Then she eased him back into his pillows and gathered her bucket and sponge.

"Terissa?" he said, reaching for her.

She set down her things and took his hand, a lopsided smile turning one side of her mouth up and other side down. She rubbed her thumb over his knuckles and sat on the edge of bed, ready to listen.

He felt himself failing, felt the anguish rising again. "I tried to save him. I tried!"

She bent and embraced him and crooned nothings to him. She stroked his hair and rocked him as he cried. "I know you did, Henley. I know. I know."

67

NOT MERELY KIL

As Kila and Noy came down the last leg of the goat trail, she lost sight of the battle. They had come out at the very back of the valley, where two opposing cliffs converged. The trail was so steep they had to scurry down, crab-like, on hands and feet. She'd shifted her pack onto her belly so it wouldn't drag. Nax was out and slinking downslope as easily as if it were flat ground.

A pulse of ache came through the bond and it was all Kila could do to continue forward. She marveled that Nax could move at all. The cat had only said one thing since Huff's passing. *The Revulsion does not rest.*

"As true as that," Kila said to herself. A rock-hard foulness had taken up residence in her belly. It weighed her down, making every step a chore. She wanted only one thing, to dymense back to Starside and hold Henley. Hold him forever.

But Nax was right. The Revulsion wouldn't stop to wait while they grieved. And so she swallowed her grief each time it threatened to blur the world and curl her into a ball.

A vile stench came up to them, born on an easterly wind. A latrine pile lay at the mouth of the trail. There had been no time to construct jacks trenches and those who needed to relieve themselves had simply come here. Kila tried to breathe through her sleeve and looked away from the mess. Noy didn't seem to notice it. She fell in behind him, full of the mercus and weaving feats to banish the stink.

"If any girnts or shamans come out here," she said. "You tell them I'm an ally."

Noy grunted and continued, weaving among the tents. There were very few nosg in them, and those who were, were busy. Some were preparing food, slicing huge sides of meat with cleavers, or dicing up foraged root vegetables, or stirring boiling cookpots. Others sharpened swords and axes. A crude smithy had been erected near the center, where fifteen enormously muscled nosg hammered repairs into weapon and armor alike. Stacks of damaged, bloodied supplies lay near each of them. The workers' creased foreheads were bent over their anvils, or dripping with sweat in front of their forge fires. An elgin, a giant more than twice the size of a common nosg, lay on its back, a vast gash across its belly. It held in its steaming guts as a team of hairy females attempted to sew him shut with bone needles and sinew. If he had been injured by reviled weaponry, Kila knew they wouldn't succeed.

"Noy, when that elgin dies, he must be burned."

"We know. See?" Beyond the tents was a smoldering pile of bodies. A pyre upon which the dead were hastily thrown. They must have learned early the insidious danger of reviled wounds. The image of Mayrie lurching toward her, hand outstretched flashed to mind. Shaking her head against the guilt, Kila pushed faster. Noy turned to pass between two tents and stopped before a guard. Upon seeing Kila, the guard charged. Noy offered several barked suggestions, but it was up to Kila to defend herself. Willshift dropped the nosg face down, sending his axe flipping into the tent behind her. An aggrieved howl exploded from inside and then fell silent.

Kila went into Yioth's tent. She had been prepared to confront a beautiful, tall, imposing woman. She had expected the fire-eyed glower of one born to high station, and to whom every mortal was beneath contempt. She expected long stretches of exposed leg and abdomen, a scene of languid repose.

She found nothing at all inside. She spun and grabbed Noy by a necklace of ears. "Where is she?"

Noy's lips pulled back. "Yiothizandra." He pointed past her head. Kila let him go and looked again at the pile of rags at the back of the tent. A face lay among them on one side, a mat of filthy hair balled against the skull. Sunken cheeks, sunken eyes. An ancient, desiccated corpse. What one might find in a crypt niche, with coins over the eyes.

But the shadowed eyes were uncovered, and open. Nax crept closer, tentative, nose alive and testing the smell of the person.

Is that her? Kila asked.

It's her.

A croak parted the cracked lips. "Felnithel. Ah me, has one of you truly left us?" Then the eyes lifted to take in Kila. The banked embers of her inner fire flared, but it could not sustain. "Where is my daughter?"

How did she find out about Saiya? Kila sent.

Nax didn't know, so said nothing. Kila went closer, carefully, bolts of fire negation ready. But Yioth did not stir at her approach. Kila knelt well out of reach and regarded her enemy. "Noy brought you meat. Can you eat?"

The eyelids fell closed and the head turned away. "Where is my daughter?"

"Safe." Kila motioned for Noy to come forward. She snatched

the sack of roast rat from him and peeled the bag away from the roast. Definitely rat, she decided. It had gone cold during the long trek here. She put heat into it with the mercus. "Eat this, Yioth. I need you strong." She pulled Cayne and sliced off a thick bit from the haunch. She flapped the meat over Yioth's nose.

The dragonmost part Yioth's nature got the better of her, as Kila had thought it might. She had witnessed Yioth's feeding sessions, sitting up on her throne, half a deer next to her. Had watched the woman flame roast it with her own breath and then eat it like a bear in the wild.

The cracked lips parted and the rat meat went in. Yioth swallowed it whole, like a sea bird slipping down a fish. And so Kila cut pieces from the rat and fed them to Yioth. When the meat was gone, Yioth ate the bones, and when the skull was gone she asked for more.

The nosg guard Kila had spilled to the ground was still under a heavy willshift. She bade him return to the tent. "Fetch meat for her," she ordered. When she released the willshift entirely he jumped at her. Again she felled him by freezing his legs and arms. "Fetch meat!"

"He's a slook. No Ennish," Noy said, looking down at the nosg with more haughtiness than one would imagine possible. Noy stood a full head shorter and was half as thick as the girnt. "He's . . ." He waved a claw in a swirling motion about the top of his own head. "Stupid."

"Tell him to fetch meat."

Noy gave the order, which was answered with anger. Noy tapped the nosg's head with the haft of his hatchet and barked something else. He nodded sharply to Kila. This time when Kila released the willshift, the guard scrambled off.

Yioth's eyelids had grown heavy, the feeding having drawn all her energy to her belly. "Sigh, I will flay you, burn you, and feed you to Flayshui."

Kila went closer and mockingly stroked the woman's forehead. "You're so kind. But perhaps you should spare your generosity for a while. You've seen what the Revulsion is. What it can do. Even *you* are not that stupid. The Revulsion hunts for Kil. I have hidden her away, safe."

Yioth's hand blurred, shooting from under her pile of furs. It clamped around Kila's throat, squeezing hard. Her iron-spike nails couldn't penetrate Kila's armor-cloak feat, but she held on. She snarled and yanked Kila down, nose-to-nose. Her breath was hot and stank of meat and sickness. "You will take me to her. Now!"

The Revulsion swarmed at Kila, begging her to take hold of it, use it. She didn't want to risk even pushing out her defensive shield, so she pressed Cayne to Yioth's throat. Not lightly, for the woman's skin was tough as leather. And so they were poised in a moment of mutual murder, Cayne biting a thin line across Yioth's throat.

Nax's gray body squeezed between them. White feet stood on Yioth's chest and the small gray face wedged in the narrow space between their noses.

Stop, Nax sent. *You fools!*

Yioth's eyes shifted, the flames in them faltered. The pressure on Kila's neck relaxed a little. Kila eased Cayne away, then pulled at Yioth's wrist. "Let me go. I'm trying to help you."

"I don't want your help. I want you dead."

Kila straightened and rubbed her neck. Yioth hadn't hurt her, but the suddenness and strength of the attack had surprised her. Whether Yioth's desire for Kil was out of motherly love or her innate greed for power was impossible to say. Kila doubted Yioth would know the difference.

"Ell is dead," Kila said. "Killed by a reviled blade in the Citadel. The reviled and a revulyn had come to steal Kil. You know why."

This news broke through the dragnithan's imperious anger. "You slew them. Tell me you slew them all."

"Some of them. They are difficult to kill."

Yioth sighed and turned her eyes from Kila. "If it were not for this Beloved One and her extraordinary anguish, I would expend my last breath, the last spark of my fire, trying to kill you here and now." Yioth was looking at Nax, who was sitting atop her breast. Nax was looking at her, watching her as she might watch a mouse hole. "But I have never been so graced by a felnithel as I am in this moment, and I would not go against her will." Yioth offered Nax her hand, which got a good sniffing over before the little gray head ducked under it and allowed herself to be petted. "Mark me, Kila Sigh, I am not your friend, felnithel or no. I wish I had killed you when I had you in the *vaz'on*." Her eyes closed and her hand fell away from Nax. She was asleep when the nosg guard returned, carrying half a goat.

And he wasn't alone. Kila felt a massive haze of mercus potential hovering outside the tent. Not a revulyn, not a shaman. "You out there, merculyn!" she called. "I cannot be bested in feats of the mercusine."

To Kila's shock, Eckso ducked in, followed by Klayne. The former smirked, the latter grinned. Klayne made a mocking bow; Eckso threw a willshift. Kila negated it and struck back with her own, freezing Eckso still. Kila noticed Klayne's crown of gold. "A *vaz'on*? Is that your only move, Eckso?" Kila shook her head as she walked toward Yioth's sister. "You think Klayne's power is enough to overpower mine?"

Klayne's body went stiff suddenly. He drew his dagger and lurched at Kila. Had he controlled his own muscles, he might have gotten in a strike. But Eckso was operating his body through the *vaz'on's* Will Gem, making his attack slow and jerky. Kila eluded him easily. Cayne came into service again, this time against Eckso's throat. "Release the Will Gem, sweetie. Let us all relax and have a discussion."

Klayne raised his weapon and threw it at her. Kila deflected the dagger with Cayne. The slook apparently approved, for he bounced and cheered, still holding the partially roasted goat. Noy collected Klayne's dagger from the dirt floor and inspected it.

"Keep it, Noy."

Kila backed from Eckso and pointed at a spot on the floor. "Sit. And put Klayne next to you. Noy, tea! And tell the guard to return to his post. Kil's eyes, have him leave the goat behind."

Eckso didn't have much choice but to obey. Klayne was clearly willing to do whatever he was told since he was as powerless as a toddler among the merculyns.

"I sent Harnzyne to find you and the other dragons," Kila said when they were all settled. "We need an alliance against the Revulsion."

Eckso's face went slack when she spotted Nax. Lips trembling, she bowed low. "Beloved One, I know not what to say." Nax must have responded, for her back went stiff and she said. "Ah. I see."

Klayne merely nodded to the cat and looked away. "What were you saying about an alliance, Sigh?"

Eckso's smirk reappeared, but it was forced. Her eyes were holding back tears, and she looked very pale. She crossed her arms across her ample bosom. "An alliance to do what? Die together?"

"Together or apart," Kila said, making a balance of her hands. "Ell thought we had a better chance together. She said—"

"I don't care what she said! She promise-bound me. Do you have any idea how humiliating that was?"

"I imagine it's almost as humiliating as having a *vaz'on* put on your head. Like you did to me at the Hackwatch. I see Klayne nodding in agreement. Maybe you should wear it next, Eckso. It is a lovely looking circlet, very regal. The tap gems'll really bring out the color of your eyes."

Klayne gave a sad chuckle. His face was loose, his cheeks and nose flushed. He appeared to be drunk. Kila couldn't blame him.

"What's your scheme, Eckso?" Kila demanded. "What were you hoping to achieve coming here?"

The dragnithan woman's gaze went to Nax, who was now curled atop Yiothizandra and regarding her with slitted green eyes. Eckso's throat and cheeks reddened and her mouth drew down. And then she looked away, refusing to answer.

Kila answered for her: "With Yioth weak as a starving fawn, you thought you'd have a go at becoming queen of the world."

"I would not disrupt my leisure to aim so low," Eckso said, putting on a bored air. She even pretended to yawn.

The pretense was so obviously false Kila couldn't help but laugh. She winked at Eckso and pointed Cayne at her. "Your problem is laziness. So perhaps what you say is true. But you didn't risk coming here just to save your sister. You hate her almost as much as I do. So what is it you want with her?"

Klayne belched. Eckso looked away from him in disgust. When she did, he winked at Kila and made a rocking motion with his arms, as if cradling an infant. So that was it.

"You want to take Saiya, do you?" Kila mused. "And you think Yioth can find her."

Passions run wild in dragnithan hearts. And in Eckso passion revealed itself in entertaining fashion. She whipped around and jabbed a finger at Klayne's face. "What did you say to her? Are you sending?"

He held his hands up, the epitome of innocence on his face. "I said nothing. And I can't send to her with this thing on my head. Bah! You're such a fool, Eckso Ezeel. Now you've confirmed Sigh's suspicions. Might as well confess. Listen to her offer of alliance. Maybe we can escape this catastrophe with our lives."

"I'll ally with her when you swear yourself to celibacy."

Klayne shrugged and said sadly, "Sorry, Sigh. Eckso will never, ever, ever ally herself with you. I was considering joining you, to tell you the truth. I like you, even if you are rather daft."

"We will not call it an alliance," came a voice from behind them. Yioth was stirring. "Give me that goat."

Kila lifted it upon mercus touch and delivered it to the sickly woman. The wet sounds of feeding came instantly afterward. This went on for a surprisingly short duration. The woman could bolt chunks down that would choke an atlen. Nax refused a share of the meat. She came to curl miserably in Kila's lap.

"I hate you Kila Sigh," Yioth said. "You stole my child, hid her away. For that there can never be forgiveness. But the Revulsion is here, and it will wipe us all away, even Kil, if we do not contain it. I cannot be allied with you. But for Kil's sake, I'll agree to a truce. A temporary truce."

"We can't merely contain it. We must destroy it," Kila said.

Klayne snorted and lay back to look at the tent ceiling.

"Destroy destruction?" Yioth asked. "Perhaps you would like to drown a river, or singe a fire while you are at it. The Revulsion is not something that can be annihilated. It *is* annihilation. Surely you who has wielded it so readily knows its nature. You, who has seen with the cold eye."

Klayne's jollity vanished in that instant, and he forced himself upright. "She *used* it?" He began to scoot backward to distance himself from her. "Then all is already lost."

"I'm no revulyn, you idiot," Kila said. "If I were, why would I be here trying to rescue Yioth?"

"If you wished to rescue her, why is she still here?" Eckso said archly. "I think you came here to kill her because you fear she will find Saiya and the girl will love her more than she does you."

"Who is Saiya?" Klayne asked. "I thought we were talking about—oh ho! So *that's* the reason Eckso has a twisty tongue when she speaks of Kil. Female, eh? Interesting. Did you know, Yiothizandra?"

"The qiznithan, Yples, told me. To taunt me with his better knowledge of my own child." She sat up and folded her legs under her. Already her cheeks were filling in, the haggard lines around her eyes and mouth fading. And the flames in her eyes were stoked high. She was growing more dangerous by the moment. Kila adjusted her armor-cloak, again preparing fire negations to protect against the dragnithan's breath. The woman was glaring at her. "You dared to name her Saiya? I do not like it. Sounds too much like Sigh."

"That's how she came up with it," Eckso said.

"Saiya's name makes no difference," Kila said. "Eckso seeks to create division between us. A ploy to provoke you to attack me." She glared at Eckso. "Yioth cannot kill me. And you cannot willshift me. So let's be done with this nonsense. You all behave like spoiled children. The Revulsion answers to Qiznithan Yples. He spreads it like a sickness through the city-realms across Ennith. Sorgan is already lost. A horde of reviled nosg seek to break into this valley. When they do, all of Razk-Ka's gr'hils will be turned and join their number. Yples will then bring them south. Lockt will fall. The Sablefort after that. The army of the Revulsion will grow as it conquers. And who will stand against it? Tordain fights itself. The other realms are being eaten away from the inside."

"Then it's hopeless," Eckso said. Gone was her indignation and her embarrassment. Now her eyes were pleading. "Unless you are willing to use Saiya."

"Yes," Yiothizandra said in a rare moment of accord with her sister. "Kil will soon awaken to her godhood. And if we serve her well and earn her favor, she will destroy the barrier that separates this realm from the demaynic. Those we favor will be allowed to escape before this world perishes. When we're safe, the Revulsion can claim it and corrupt it. Or it can annihilate it. But Kil can seal it off."

"As long as I can bring my children, I will follow that plan," Eckso said. "Who will you bring, Klayne? Assuming I allow you to bring anyone at all."

He didn't answer. He merely looked at Nax, who looked back with unblinking eyes. His face was somber now.

Kila said, "What you propose is what the elnisians tried with Moonside. But not all of the Revulsion was trapped there. Nax says it is everywhere, always present to some thin degree. Even if Kil could do as you suggest, the demaynic realms would not be free of its taint."

"But it would not be awakened and motivated by thinking minds," Eckso countered. "It would return to its quiet state, barely noticeable. And we would live quite comfortably."

"We can't abandon this world," Kila said. "Saiya would never allow it."

"You think the god of death would forbid death?" Yiothizandra said. "You do not understand her power, nor her intention. Or did you think you could teach her to be like Ellishan? My insufferable little cousin probably slipped that poisonous idea into your thoughts. She was always a slick-tongued schemer. Listen to me. Kil's nature is inviolable. It can't be steered or sculpted. Kil will destroy this world. That is forgone. All we can do is seek her favor so that we may be spared."

Such certainty. And if Kila didn't know Saiya, she might have taken Yioth's lecture on board. Might have lost hope along with Klayne and Eckso. But even so, she would never consign her world to destruction. She could see her father's face as it had been in Dox's painting. Noble, friendly, powerful. He had not taught her to be honest, nor charitable, nor even particularly compassionate. But he possessed all those qualities. Even as a thief. Then she considered Semūin, her mother. Selfish, bratty, pitiless. So what had their daughter, Kila, become? What force had shaped her nature? She was godblooded, but nothing about her had been "forgone." From situation to situation, with coin or without, she had served her own interest without murder, without seeking power over the masses. She was a child of Cheapsgate. Had she not been blessed with the mercusine, she would be like Mayrie. An urchin, filthy and light-fingered. But here she was, holding council with demayne, and she was no longer driven by a thief's selfish instincts. She would not simply slip out of this realm, close the door, and leave everyone else to die. And neither would Saiya.

She stroked Nax's slim body. "You forget, all of you, that Nax is here. And the other felnithel." Her voice broke and she warred to keep her lips from trembling. "None of you has witnessed the wonder of one of them facing down a revulyn. Had you, you would not be so confident of the Revulsion's invincibility. The felnithel know Saiya, they love her. Nax, do you believe she will simply allow the Revulsion to destroy this world?"

No. Saiya would die for this world.

The looks on the dragnithans' faces showed that Nax had sent her answer into all of their minds. Eckso wiped moisture from her eyes. No way of knowing if she was inspired by Nax's words or crushed by them. Klayne blew out his cheeks and seemed to become instantly sober. And Yiothizandra, who up to that moment had been a cauldron of boiling anger, simply gaped at the cat. "So certain, are you?" she asked. "How can you know this?"

How does one spirit know anything about another? One simply knows it, as I know the minds of my brothers and sisters. Saiya is not merely Kil, as you are not merely Yiothizandra. Surely you know this already. It is obvious.

Kila was astonished to hear this long sermon from Nax. She didn't fully understand it, but she didn't need to. Nax wasn't trying to convince her of anything. She was addressing the dragnithans, demayne of Night, whose only moral code was self-interest.

"Where is my daughter?" Yioth asked. Something seemed caught in her throat. She coughed and swallowed. "Where is she?"

"Safe," Kila said. "And don't bother asking for more. Should any of you fall to the Revulsion, you could not help but betray Saiya to it."

"And what if you fall to it?" Klayne asked. "You are closest to it, aren't you?"

"Nax guards me, keeps it from me." True, as far as it went. But this was not the time to confess how close she'd come to annihilation herself. "Now, we need to convene with the dragnithors. Harnzyne was searching for Bazron, but I have not heard anything from him."

"He still searches," Eckso said. "We met him in the eyrie above Ceronhel when we came here."

The nosg guard stumbled into the tent and began shouting. *"Stik muchg! Stik muchg!"*

Noy shot up. "Razk-Ka is hard pressed. The front is failing."

"If you truly wish to fight for this world," Klayne said, shaking his head at the silliness of it the idea, "you should save Razk-Ka's army from destruction. Get it south."

Yes. If Razk-Ka's force could be moved, it could be added to the defensive barrier at the Sablefort. "We have to push back the reviled nosg to give Razk-Ka space to retreat."

"Dragon flame would do well against them," Eckso mused. "Yioth, can you fly?"

The woman tried to stand. But even with a full rat and half a goat in her, she couldn't keep her feet for more than a moment. "Not now. I need rest. I need *meat!*"

"The Girl Who Flies will have to demonstrate her full power," Klayne said. He looked delighted at the prospect. He noticed her hesitation. "You *can* fly, can't you? Please tell me those handbills weren't mere fancy."

Those Kil-damned handbills. Kila leveled a glare at him. "They weren't mere fancy."

68

THE VOICE OF THE SUN

Kila had no illusions about herself as a military strategist. But it was obvious that she could do nothing to aid the living nosg until she had a closer look at the fighting. And thanks to Klayne's impertinent question about her ability to fly, Kila left the tent with both a clear idea of what to do and enough irritation built up to do it.

The bolts formed without thought. An upthrusting current of air carried her up over the camp. But her control over the wind was poor. Sauk hide tents pulled from their supports and took flight, stakes ripping from the ground as her fellstorm winds lifted her higher and higher. She came to a hover, sliding away from the encampment and toward the battle. Snow and debris from the camp fountained below her feet as she moved away. Tiny figures looked up at her, mouths agape. Some shook their claws in anger, others fled.

She went higher until she could see the whole valley. A large band of nosg warriors were running her way. To her relief, the pitched fight still raged at the mouth of the valley. But it had moved inward. Razk-Ka was losing ground with little remaining before the reviled horde could break left and right and pour into the valley. When that happened, the mass of reviled behind would flood in and all would be consumed.

Nax, tell Eckso and Klayne to get into the air. Eckso can push the reviled back with mercus spheres.

A shadow crossed over her. She ducked. A wyvok winged a circle around her. It banked sharply to come at her. The mouth parted, showing teeth. Kila let herself fall. Ten feet from death, she cushioned her descent and alighted with barely a jolt.

The wyvok folded its wings and dove straight at her. She ran, looking for any hollow she could flatten herself in. Wind washed over her, the sun went black. The wyvok skimmed so close she smelled its gamey odor.

But it didn't grab her in its jaws or claws. Instead it spread its wings, caught the air and came down with a thud. Its serpentine neck curled around and it hurled a cry at her. A wash of stinking breath blasted into her face. And then it laid its chin on the ground and settled its body.

Kila stared at it, astonished. "Jathesh!"

The beast squawked and crawled toward her, chin low. Even when she'd been with the wyvok every day it hadn't behaved so submissively. She touched the trembling snout and crooned soothing words to it. She had never had much success sending to it. Such beasts were very stupid. But she shouted in her mind for it to be calm.

Jathesh's saddle had long fallen off since Stallid. But she hoisted herself onto his back, clamping hard with her legs and holding fast to one of the spines. At her command the wyvok leapt skyward. She leaned with it, urging him toward the battle. The wyvoks she'd seen from the goat path had landed, the beasts taking much needed rest. And that was likely why the battle had turned. Without shamans aloft and sending swarm-light into the onrushing reviled, the swords and axes of the living nosg were not sufficient to stem the tide.

Jathesh glided over the battle, swooping in from the rear of Razk-Ka's force, then lifting at the mouth of the valley to sail over the massing reviled.

"Kil's eyes!"

The horde filled the wider valley that lay beyond. Just as in the vision from Ell's hand mirror. They were a solid mass of nosg-kin, with many of their taller elgin cousins towering over them here and there. Shamans with black-gemmed skull staves threw blackbeams at her, forcing Jathesh to swerve and twist so violently she was nearly thrown free.

The beast beat out of the range of the shamans. "Take me back," she shouted, pressing with her heel on the wyvok's flank.

She landed Jathesh near the resting wyvoks. She leapt off and ran straight at an outpost of tents where a little smoke tail drifted up. Shamans sat around the fire, sipping cups of steaming broth. One whiff told her it was a brew of mimak. The shamans looked weary, shoulders slumped. Some had set their staffs aside and simply looked into the fire with blank expressions.

"Who is wurgu here?" she demanded as she approached.

One looked up dully. He didn't seem surprised to see a human approaching him. "You address Wurgu Mac-Ook of G'galas Ryxok. You were Queen Yiothizandra's pet. Where is your crown?"

"You must fly and fight," she said.

"There is only death aloft."

"There is only death sitting here like a common slook! Get up. And give me a staff."

The other shamans looked at her, eyes dull with numb despair. She barged among them and looked in the pot. She snatched up a cup and dipped it, saw the red caps of prized mimak floating in a grayish brown slurry. The thick gunk burned as it went down her throat. She hoped she never learned what the broth was made of, but she thought she knew. It tasted just like the nosg smelled.

One shaman was struggling to breathe, he lay on his side gripping his staff. There was no swarmlight in the gems. It was safe to take, so she took it.

"Get off yer hairy arses and get into the air," she told the rest. A resonance tinted her words, made them seem to sparkle. The elusive gold of command had come again. She welcomed it, but even more its effect. For as one, the nosg shamans stood and found new strength. They took up their staves and dashed to their flying mounts. Kila returned to Jathesh, cast about for a moment before finding what she sought.

Her time away from the wyvok had not lessened her mastery of saddling him. The saddle went on, the bindings knotted and tightened just so. She mounted and bade Jathesh to fly. Never had Jathesh obeyed so readily. But where there had been fear in him before, a bold determination now radiated from his body. She felt a wonderful unity with him. She needed to only lean left or right, forward or back to signal her wishes. And in this way, Jathesh's wings became her wings.

She held up the skull staff she had taken. It was not topped with a nosg's skull, but with a wolf's. The exposed fangs snarled into the wind, the red eyegems asparkle with sunlight. As she waited for the mimak to take effect, she flew alongside Wurgu Mac-Ook. The other shamans drifted over the battle and began to loose rays of blue or red or violet down at the front wave of reviled. These feats of swarmlight told with huge upheavals of limbs and turf. Some areas blossomed with orange flame while others frosted over and crumbled apart.

Blackshine shamans answered with their vile blackbeams. These oozed out, slower than swarmlight, but of much longer duration. The shamans extended their beams of light-eating magic and swung them about, whiplike. The wyvoks knew the range of these attacks well, and were quick to beat skyward after their shaman had delivered his round of attacks. And so the wyvoks circled, dove, swarmlight blasted down, and then they climbed.

Not every wyvok had perfect timing. Directly ahead of Kila, a blackbeam seized on a wyvok. It latched onto flesh as if tipped with hooks. The wyvok screamed and beat back with its wings, desperate to pull free. The shaman on board loosed a ray of swarmlight, which was met with a negating blackbeam. So began the inexorable descent. More blackbeams latched onto the beast, and all at once the pitiable creature gave up, tucked wings and plowed nose first into the throng. Dust exploded from the impact, scores of nosg reviled were crushed. Twice their number closed in to hack and bash and slice the writhing wyvok. Of the riding shaman, nothing more was seen until his skull staff gave its final explosion of unreleased swarmlight. The reviled nosg were insensible to their own safety and a score more were immolated in the flash.

Jathesh followed Mac-Ook's mount on an attack glide. The wurgu's power was considerable, and his yellow beams tore through the front ranks of attackers. Kila kept Jathesh right behind.

The mimak stew sparked nothing in her. She still held the mercus, but could not see how to use it without inviting the Revulsion in. That was a battle she most definitely did not need to fight right now. They passed over the horde without diving. Razk-Ka's front line held firm but had not regained any of its lost ground. They fought valiantly, their weapons a blur of flashing metal all across their front. But a wound was nothing to a reviled unless it severed limb or clove skull. For the living, every wound was a death sentence. The corrupted fought with wooden, jerky movements and did nothing to shield themselves. It was this advantage that allowed Razk-Ka's force to hold as long as it had.

Kila circled again. She saw something flying to the south. No, two somethings. Too large to be birds. Ah, it was Eckso and Klayne. She realized she should have made Eckso release Klayne from the *vaz'on*. It would be dangerous, but they needed Klayne's skills right now. Eckso's strongest abilities with the mercus were allure feats, the sort of thing suited to parlors and bedrooms.

Get into the fight! she scream-sent at Eckso.

The dragnithan bent her course and came toward the battle. The sunlight was blinding behind her, sending sparkles of color from her wings. The sparkles suddenly grew and hatched sparkles of their own. Kila couldn't figure out what manner of feat was she attempting.

But it was no feat at all. Kila noticed the ground below her divide into triangles. These spread apart and seemed to melt. The cliffs drooped. It was the mimak finally taking effect.

Kila held onto the horn of her saddle and closed her eyes. Stomach roiling, she tried her best to keep the mimak stew down. Her brow flashed cold with sweat, and her palms grew slick on the skull staff. "Not the time to sick up yer lunch," she said to herself. Gritting her teeth, she guided Jathesh in a tight turn and gathered the swarmlight.

Her next run at the reviled front made her stomach clench, and hot acid burbled up her throat. She spat behind her and coughed. And then there was no more time to indulge in sickness, for the wave of reviled was below her.

To manifest fire from the swarmlight was to see fire through the eyegems. Her vision went red, and the nosg below her received a blast of flame. The reviled ignited.

It works, Naxie. The Revulsion isn't even whispering at me.

The cat's response came from far back in the camp. *I will stand guard for when it does.*

Keep an eye on Yioth. We need her.

She's feeding.

As Jathesh clawed his wings up in a steep climb, Kila looked behind. A dizzying view of the massing horde swarmed below her. It was a testament to Razk-Ka's leadership and the will of the living nosg that they had held on this long. The valley he'd chosen must have been known to him, for the narrowing below allowed only thirty nosg abreast. It had been fortified with hastily arranged rocks forming a slight wall and a low rise to give the defenders the higher ground.

The wounded nosg screamed in terror. Elgin collected them, twisted their heads to grant quick merciful deaths. All were thrown upon smoking pyres at the periphery of the battle to keep them from turning.

Razk-Ka's shamans had learned a defense against their enemy's swarmlight. Domes of glowing blue shielded the front lines. They sparked as blackbeams struck. A swarmlight test of strength ensued. When a dome dissolved, the vulnerable warriors behind it were instantly consumed with black fire.

Eckso swooped down from straight over the battle. A wise tactical move, for the enemy was distracted by the wyvoks gliding in. Kila felt a feat forming in the woman, charged with a considerable flow of mercus. Eckso drank heartily of Klayne's power. She released her feat, an iridescent sphere of mercus, the surface roiling blue with veins of black. It was the exact recipe Flaumishtak had taught Kila.

A Blackshine shaman saw it coming and desperately whipped his blackbeam toward the onrushing attack. Too late. The sphere struck amidst his gr'hil. Sparkles of blue lightning spidered out from the point of impact, taking a score of nosg in the face. Skulls exploded.

For a moment, the corpse-field turned liquid. A dozen more reviled were sucked under. Like a boulder tossed into a pond, the feat sent a rippling pressure wave through the ranks surrounding the point of impact. It hurled nosg boots over helms. Elgin flopped backward and flattened entire gr'hils. The wave continued, lessening in power as it spread, but still upending scores of reviled. When it subsided, a gooey, smoldering wound remained in the body of the horde.

As Jathesh turned back to the valley, Kila leaned far over to peer down. Like the Revulsion itself, the wound oozed closed as more reviled nosg flooded in. There was no concern for hauling away the injured. Flesh became turf. The liquified gore quickly cooled solid, giving footing to the relentless boots of the fearless dead.

Eckso and Klayne were climbing, preparing for another run. It would tell. But it would not be enough to give Razk-Ka's gr'hils more than two breaths of rest before the surge continued. The shamans on the wyvoks were adding their efforts. Together their attacks were just enough to pause the inevitable. With the wyvoks already exhausted, they would not manage more than a few more runs before simply gliding into the enemy to be hacked apart.

This won't work, Kila sent at Eckso.

The woman didn't answer.

It can't end like this, Kila told herself. But it *was* going to end like this. And if she was struck down during a futile attack run, what hope did anyone have? The best course was to return to Yioth, dymense her away. Perhaps Kila could return to the valley enough times to dymense a few hundred nosg away before the rest were overrun. If Eckso helped, maybe they could save a few hundred more. But most of Razk-Ka's thirty thousand were going to be turned.

A wyvok cry came off from her right. It was Mac-Ook's mount, flaring its wings to alight on the cliffside directly above the battle. The creature slumped the moment it landed, then made a quarter roll like a boat keeling over. Its sides worked like a bellows.

The shaman spilled from the saddle and went to his knees. Exhaustion had caught up to them both. The shaman crawled to the edge, teetered there. But he caught himself and used his staff to regain his feet.

He dipped into his mimak bag, stuffed his maw. Then with feet spread, he began to send swarmlight down into the attacking reviled. He was a bit too high up for his efforts to make much difference. The beams sizzled across heads, but did little true damage.

Kila steered Jathesh in an arc to keep eyes on the lone shaman's efforts. She had never suspected the creatures to possess even the slightest nobility. But this display revealed an unsuspected depth of character, a willingness to use oneself up entirely in the service of the many.

The cliffs of both sides of the narrows were sheer and high, made of solid rock. The shaman looked tiny, barely higher than the scraggles of shrub that pushed through the snow-blanketed ground behind him.

Straining her head all around, she searched out the other wyvoks. Ten still flew with her, though they were gliding high up and no longer making attack dives. Pulling out of her red-stained swarmlight perspective, she gathered up bolts of mercusine. The Revulsion seethed, threatening to gag her with its foulness. But she formed bolts to make her voice as loud as a god's. "Rally upon the cliff! Rally upon the cliff!"

The nearest shamans heard and bent their flights toward her. The others followed. She urged Jathesh down hard. The force of the wind against her became so great she felt like she was pushing through water. Jathesh flared, landed. Kila bounded from the saddle and raced to join Wurgu Mac-Ook. He leaned heavily upon his staff, the eyegems aglow but no longer forming attacks. He breathed hard, as if he'd been running for hours.

The other wyvoks were landing behind Jathesh, and not too gracefully. One appeared not to know it was approaching the ground and failed to flare its wings to land. It smashed into the snow, slid toward Kila. She pulled Mac-Ook aside just as wyvok and shaman slid over the edge and plummeted into the horde.

The other shamans straggled toward her. "Come. Quickly!" she called at them. When they gathered, they stared at her dully. "If you have mimak, eat it." When none moved to obey, she grabbed the bag from Mac-Ook's hip and began to parcel out doses to each of the shamans. "Eat!"

They ate, chewing slowly, nostrils flaring wide to suck in air. None said a thing.

"We have one chance to save Razk-Ka's army." She held up a finger. "One. Are you listening?" She glared at each of them in turn. They stared back, almost as blank-eyed as the reviled themselves. "Wurgu Mac-Ook, listen and convince these slooks to do as I say. We do not have the strength to defeat the corrupted nosg here. The front will not hold much longer. Not this way. We need time. I know how to get it."

Mac-Ook snuffled and sucked in his lips. Kila knew nosg mannerisms well enough to see uncertainty in the expression. She took hold of his elbow and led him back to the ledge. Pointing across the narrows, she said: "That cliff overhangs the narrows. We must break it loose." She stamped her foot. "We must break this side loose as well."

"Impossible!"

"True. If you shamans work alone," she said. "Your swarm-light will not cut through stone quickly enough, or deeply enough. You must circle and combine your power. Do you know how to do that?"

Mac-Ook tucked his chin in and spluttered his lips, as if offended by the very idea. "It isn't done."

"But you know how to do it?"

"Yes. It is not done. These shamans are not of G'galas Ryxok. You've seen their weak attacks. They bring shame to us all."

Kila grabbed a fistful of necklaces of colored stones, teeth, ears, shells, and dried out nosg fingers. "There is no G'galas Ryxok. There is but one g'galas. That of the living nosg. You must be wurgu to all nosg right now. I've seen your valor. Take these shamans in hand and show them what must be done!" She was shouting by the time finished, a spray of spittle flying into Mac-Ook's eyes. The gold upon her voice lingered in the air.

She had hammered through the set ways of his nosg mind and sent a shivering crack through an age of tradition. "Swarm-light *can* break stone," he admitted. Looking past her he cracked the butt of his staff into the slushy snow and called to the assembled shamans.

His words were in the lurkmire tongue, so Kila didn't know what was said. The shamans reacted like scandalized house-mothers, all gripping their necklaces and recoiling. But Mac-Ook strode to the nearest and whapped him in the backside with his staff. He reiterated his commands and slowly gained grunts and nods from the shamans.

Eckso! Where are you? I know you can hear me.

"No need to shout. You're giving me a headache." Eckso stood behind her, right on the lip of the fall.

"Where's Klayne?"

"He's circling."

"Can you use the tap gems with him that far away?"

"Of course. Are you ready to fetch Yioth and dymense away? Klayne has a lovely palace outside of Stallid. There's plenty of room there to—"

"We aren't abandoning thirty thousand warriors. We will

need them all. Look over there. We're going drop that cliff into the pass and block it up."

"Fantastic plan, Sigh. That will give Razk-Ka hours to rest up before being overrun entirely."

"There's a way out of the valley. Noy brought me down a goat trail. It's difficult terrain, but the living nosg will manage it easier than the reviled will." She recalled the scene in Sorgan, where reviled from the upper city had swarmed down the Leeside Stair, pushing each other off in their eagerness to get to Kila. "The wyvoks can haul out supplies once they've had some rest and meat."

Eckso didn't look at all convinced, arms crossed and lips clamped in a smirk. But she finally gave a shrug. "We're friends now, so I suppose I don't have any choice but to help. What sort of feat will shake the rocks loose?"

"Mac-Ook will undercut it with swarmlight, and we'll smash it from above until we drop off a huge chunk."

Kila told Mac-Ook the plan. He grunted, distracted by his own task. He seemed doubtful that he could wield so much swarmlight. "Gems strong. Maybe not strong enough." He gave his staff a little wiggle and looked into the skull's eyes. "Too much swarmlight not good."

She mounted Jathesh and took to the sky. Eckso joined Klayne. They circled high over the narrows like crows over a carcass. Below, Mac-Ook was shouting at the shamans. They had clumped close to him at the ledge, forming a tight half-circle. The swarmlight oozed from their staves, yellow, red, blue, violet, green. It converged on Mac-Ook, surrounding him with scintillating light. He stood with his head bowed, tight grip on the staff. Abruptly he looked up and held his staff aloft. Even from high above, Kila could see the intense flare of swarmlight in the eyegems. He released the power in an explosion of light.

Kila shielded her eyes against the intensity of white-yellow that flashed in a leg-thick beam. It looked like frozen lightning, a sizzling, quavering bolt of plasma. It struck the face of the cliff. Boulders flew out. Dust plumed. It bored into the stone and droops of melted slag oozed out below. He moved the beam with agonizing slowness, eating deep into rock, cutting a channel into the face of the cliff.

The ejected debris crushed reviled and living nosg alike. At first none of the combatants seemed to notice, but soon the back ranks on both sides had turned their attention upward. The living hooted and shook their weapons, urging Mac-Ook on, the intent of his feat obvious.

Kila did not know where Razk-Ka was, or if he even still lived. But someone down there saw the strategic moment for what it was. A fresh cohort of nosg surged forward to relieve those at the front. The remainder began a slow, measured retreat back from the narrows.

A reviled shaman released a blackbeam, whipping it to and fro trying to reach Mac-Ook. But the wurgu was out of range. This did not deter others from trying the same. Their beams struck the cliff well below him. Kila whooped, delighted. As long as Mac-Ook wasn't dropped before completing his work, she would tolerate the Blackshine shamans' distraction.

And then the reviled elgin began to climb.

Given their size, they were the last creatures Kila would have expected to attempt such insanity. Even with her own skills at climbing, she wouldn't have dared to scale a sheer face like this. But the elgin jabbed thick hands into crevices, found outcroppings for toes. And they were *fast.*

Pressing a knee to Jathesh's flank, Kila steered into a circling dive, bringing up her staff. The swarmlight answered, and she severed an elgin's fist from his arm, dropping him onto a mass of milling reviled. She got off another blast before Jathesh had to swerve away. A Blackshine shaman whipped a blackbeam at them. The air around it popped and sizzled.

Jathesh screamed and beat higher. Kila scanned his wings, his tail. She didn't see any wounds.

Eckso! Take out the climbers.

For once the dragnithan woman had taken the initiative, for she was already on an attack glide. She blurred past Kila. Her sphere was already forming in one hand. She threw it, leaving a gore-stained divot in the rock where an elgin had been. Kila went higher. Eckso was very fast on the wing compared to the wyvoks. The Blackshine shamans lashed at Eckso, whipping their beams after her. But the farthest extent of their beams moved too slowly and she gracefully curved out of their range.

Klayne followed Eckso on the next attack dive. Were he not such an annoying man, Kila would have thought him beautiful. His golden eagle wings shone brilliantly in the winter sun. The circlet of the *vaz'on* looked kingly upon his brow. Kila could not understand why a demayne of Night would risk himself among the blackbeams now seeking him out like the tentacles of a deep sea creature.

And then his purpose became clear. The attacking shamans had no concern for strategy at all. As Klayne skimmed parallel to the cliff wall, they dragged their blackbeams after, cutting through stone and elgin alike.

Eckso knocked two more elgin from the wall on her next pass. Kila cheered them on. Mac-Ook was still channeling his pulsating swarmlight through the opposite cliff. The molten slag now fell in long, gooey bulbs. Wherever they struck, flames sprouted, and reviled were destroyed.

Mac-Ook was more than half-way across his cut now. Putting Jathesh into a dive, Kila arrowed straight down. She popped a mimak, the taste making her lips retreat, her tongue draw in.

If she were using the mercus, she would bring forth a

mercus sphere like Eckso's. The swarmlight didn't answer in the same way. The god-fisted blow she wished to deliver to the top of the cliff had to be envisioned.

A fist. Yes. A fist as large as the overhanging rock itself. The essence of that giant fist gathered as swarmlight in the wolf skull's eyegems. The dammed-up power throbbed in the staff. Jathesh squawked a warning. He would have to pull up soon. She released the swarmlight, sending an outward expanding wave of brilliant red. Her fist struck the plateau, forcing snow and rock out in all directions. A roar washed back at her, the sound of the world's bones cracking. Coming with it, a backdraft of wind, hoisting Jathesh higher. Kila was thrust down in the saddle, head snapping forward.

"Again!" she shouted to her mount.

A quick glance showed Eckso hurling two spheres in quick succession. Klayne was lifting from another daring skim along the far wall. Mac-Ook was on his knees, his trembling beam of yellow plasma starting to falter.

Kila's next dive came and went, the impact shaking free a section of cliff that slowly tumbled into the reviled. An echoing boom washed up, resonating in Kila's chest. The reviled nosg at the edge of the impact were thrown up like a spray of mud.

Mac-Ook's swarmlight flickered. His skull suddenly flared. The beam vanished. The skull exploded. Sparks arced away from it in all directions. Flaming pieces of the wurgu tumbled away. The section of ledge he'd occupied blew out and smashed into reviled and living alike. Rask-Ka's army took this as the final signal of defeat. Horns blared from their midst, and the battling throng peeled away, some sprinting, many staggering, a few crawling. These last were soon consumed by the forward surge of the reviled.

Eckso joined Kila on her next dive. Eckso's mercus spheres smashed the cliff top, Kila's swarmlight fist slammed in fury. A thousand reviled squeezed through the gap as she climbed for another pass. The swarmlight already throbbed in her wolf skull's eyegems. Jathesh was tiring, no longer shrieking with battle lust, but squawking with every exertion of his wings. Eckso's spheres struck again and again. The cliff shed boulders and slabs. Kila's vision blurred red as she again brought to mind the god-fist.

The staff shook in her hands, sent painful vibrations into her bones. Cracks spread like spiderwebs over the wolf skull. Brow protrusions flaked away into dust. She reversed her grip, and this time did not release the swarmlight. As Jathesh began to pull from his dive, she hurled the staff like a spear. She did not see it strike, but she heard the concussion as the swarmlight finally blew the gems and skull apart. Searing red light limned the underside of Jathesh's wings.

She twisted to see past the wyvok's tail, thinking the cliff must have succumbed to the blow.

It had not. But the debris they'd shaken loose had narrowed the gap. The reviled were crushing each other in their frenzy to pass through. But blackbeams were already at work, turning rubble into slag.

The living shamans had retreated from the ledge. They lay on their backs, apparently knocked unconscious by the backlash of power from Mac-Ook's destruction. She considered swooping down to take one of their staffs.

There simply wasn't time. She worried Jathesh couldn't take flight again once he landed. She patted his neck and crooned to him. She sent comforting feelings at him. If he noticed, it made no difference.

This is it, Nax, she sent. *Be with me.*

I am. Always.

The mercus was there, a bright and seemingly infinite sea of energy. She hadn't released her hold on it for fear she'd wouldn't be able reach it. But even with it present in her mind, the slightest move toward it drew the Revulsion.

This is not an attack, she told it. *This is not an attack.* But her desperation, her fear, belied the mantra. The mercus was safe for her when dymensing, less safe when willshifting. The stronger the aggression, the more the Revulsion leapt with excitement. And so she was tentative when she opened her hand, palm up and brought a tiny sphere of mercus into existence.

Eckso glided next to her. "Look!"

Kila pulled her attention to where Eckso pointed. Beyond the throat of the valley the horde continued to build like a great flood. But now it was parting. A platform borne upon the shoulders of six elgin came forward. Upon it stood a man holding a shaman's staff.

She felt him upon the Revulsion, a concentration of blackness.

A feat of Revulsion swirled up at her but stopped short. His voice crossed the gap, as if spoken in her ear. "The Unanswered feels you, my darling girl. Why do you strain so to bar it entry?"

It was Revnithan Sault from Ceronhel.

"Come join me, daughter," he said. His tone was genuine and friendly. "I cannot harm you. Not truly. You have too much command of the mercus. You know that. Come. Let us talk. I'll have my army stop."

And upon the word, the reviled froze. Blackbeams cut off. The reviled who had broken through also stopped. Echoes faded from the valley and went still. Kila heard nothing but the wind of her flight.

"Keep bashing that cliff," she called to Eckso.

"Don't go down there!"

"I'm going to kill him."

"Surely you know it's a trap."

It probably was. Certainly was. "I'll keep my eyes open."

The hairs on the back of her neck thrilled as she guided Jathesh low over the horde. A powerful sense of been-here-before crowded her mind. This was the vision from the mirror.

She still had the tiny mercus sphere in her hand. She threaded more power into it. The Revulsion seethed. *Yes! Destroy!* The foul tentacles of rotten offal and chamber pot slime probed into her mind, slipping over top the mercus she drew in.

"You feel it, dearest," Sault said. "You think it foul, but you must reverse your perspective. All your life you have thought up was down, cold warmth, evil good. Come join me here. Let's talk. I will show you."

The Revulsion rose like a black surf sliding up a beach. The mimak and mercus and the man's voice swirled in her head. The odd silence of the motionless horde weighted the air. Kila's eyelids drooped.

"There is nothing to fear, sweetlight," the man said.

"Don't call me that." Her tongue felt thick and weak. Jathesh squawked plaintively and strained to look back at her.

Another voice wafted to her, a woman's. Eckso's. She didn't hear what was said. Kila leaned forward, guiding Jathesh lower. The reviled in front of the platform moved aside to make a clearing. Jathesh landed, panting heavily. Kila slid down, found herself looking up at an elgin giant. Its eyes were charcoal, staring at nothing.

A concussion far behind her made the ground tremble beneath her feet. Her syrupy thoughts could not latch onto the cause. She should know why that had happened. But she didn't. Didn't care either. The air was smokey here. It burned the back of her throat.

A rope ladder unfurled from the deck of the platform four spans up. It dangled in front of her, an invitation. The Revnithan stood just at the top. He smiled down, kindly, friendly.

"Come up, sweetlight."

"Don't call me that."

"But I've always called you sweetlight." His voice had changed. It was tender, the soft little words a father says to a girl of four. She looked up to see Dox Viller standing above, robe parted to show his pale belly. He smiled and beckoned her up. "Come, daughter. Let us talk."

She climbed the rope ladder. At the top he reached for her, pudgy hand offering to aid her the last step. She took it. With surprising strength he pulled her up. His purple lips spread wide over his smile, eyes crinkling. He didn't let go of her hand, but pulled her into an embrace. "Oh, my sweet girl. My dear, dear child. I've missed you so."

Against her ear came hot breath and a raspy laugh. The embrace tightened. She struggled to break free, pushed at the flabby chest. But where her hands touched skin, she felt fabric. The illusion shattered. Dox's skin sagged away and vanished, revealing again the lean face of the Revnithan. His eyes shone. Not black, not like the other revulyns she'd seen.

Her mercus sphere was long gone. She held to her power through a thin channel squeezing through the Revulsion. The mercus was the flickering wick about to be quenched by pooling wax. She thrust for it, catching it before it could be extinguished. Her armor-cloak suddenly pinched and tightened at her flank, responding to a strike.

Her elbow came up, took the man in the nose. He released his grip and stumbled back, more from shock than pain. That, too, was odd for a reviled man. "What are you?" she demanded, vaguely wondering why she'd come to him so readily. Her throat ached.

She drew Cayne even as she sought to widen and strengthen her mercusine protection. The man pulled an object from a pocket, flung it at her feet. It exploded with smoke. She kicked up a mercus wind blowing it away before she breathed any more of it. "No more ferneater tricks." She advanced now, dagger forward. He held one too, a small dirk no more than five inches long. He'd tried to stab her with it, she realized.

He frowned and considered her weapon. Four reviled shamans stepped forward, eyegems aglow with warbling violets and greens. "An interesting protective feat you've devised," he said, nodding appreciatively. "I doubted reports of your merculynic prowess. Now I've witnessed the full extent of your power. Even the swarmlight answers to you. Impressive. Most impressive."

"Where is your master, the qiznithan?"

"Lord Yples attends to many things. He anointed me his Revnithan, to marshal his nosg horde and to sweep away the cities of men."

Revnithan. Kila did not like the flavor of that word. She felt an enormous well of the Revulsion around him, but now that she was closer it was stronger from the staff than from him.

The staff was topped with a bear skull, very large, bound to the shaft with thick leather cordage. The gems, too, were enormous compared to what the shamans had. Bone around the eye sockets had been chipped away to fit them. Their light oozed from black to green.

Jathesh's head rose into view just off the edge of the platform. He cried out and fluttered his wings.

"Easy, Jathesh," she said. "It's just a reviled Donse Master. A weak revulyn, else he wouldn't have to rely on nosg magic."

The man's easy features tightened. "You will call me Revnithan Sault, you—" He caught himself, gave his head a little shake. "You seek to provoke me, daughter. But I wonder why. You claim to be the most powerful merculyn of the age. Yet you channel your power into mere defensive feats. Your blows against yon cliffside were of the swarmlight." His lips spread in a smile, self-satisfied and condescending. Kila blinked hard as Dox's face overlaid his, pale and bloated as a waterlogged corpse. She felt the rising hatred she'd felt in Dox's lair. The urge to drive her blade into the man's heart came over her.

She blinked hard and Dox's face vanished. This fool must have salted the air with his ferneater smoke before she'd gotten there.

"You've seen with the cold eye, haven't you, my dear?" he mused, nodding. "I had heard tales from the shamans about your impossible feats in Stallid. I hadn't credited them." He motioned with his staff and the shamans parted. Emboldened by his insight, he moved toward her again. He was tall, with boney shoulders. Yet his corded neck and hands spoke of physical strength. "Once you've held the Unanswered within you, why hold anything else? I had not thought you so close to the precipice, but I see now that you dare not attack with the mercus lest you be awakened completely."

He smiled broadly and looked out over his horde of unmoving reviled. "And that is why you did not flame these nosg to ash nor cause the ground to split and swallow them up. You did not bring down lightnings or ice balls or stinging clouds. Because you refuse to accept the gift."

He came forward another step. The butt of his staff clunked onto the deck. "You see now that you have no choice, don't you, daughter? To save the lie-masked world you love, you will have to embrace the Revulsion. With it, you can undo my very flesh. You can make this horde dissipate like a fog under a morning sun."

"And then turn my cold eye upon the living? Do Yples's work for him? Never." She lunged at him, thrusting Cayne at his belly. He danced back. Her blade met the side of his staff. Sparks flared at the impact. Her arm jounced back, repulsed.

"I did not achieve my first aim in life," he said, shaking his head in mock regret. "My father wished that I join the Brotherhood of the Fell Guard. I trained with the staff from the time I was four until the age of admission at ten. I was the best in my cohort. But on the eve of my journey to the brotherhood's hidden camp I awoke to the mercusine. I could not bear the idea of seeing my warrior brothers training while I was relegated to studying with their scholarly sect. So I went to the Way of Til."

He spun his staff. A bulbous lead weight affixed to the butt balanced the bear skull. "Come, Sigh. Let us fight. No feats of the Unanswered or mercus, no swarmlight. Just blade against staff. Skill against skill."

He didn't wait for her refusal. The bear's truncated snout flew at her. The blazing green gems filled her vision. It struck her square in the face. The armor-cloak absorbed the crushing force of the blow, sparing her nose. But her feat could not dissipate all the power of the strike. She flew backward off the edge of the platform. She flailed for the bolts of flight. No time. She curled into a ball, hoping her armor-cloak would soften her crash into the slushy mud.

The impact never came. An elgin under the platform caught her one-handed. It lifted her back onto the platform.

Revnithan Sault twirled his staff, moved to her left. She circled right, Cayne at the ready. But she had no illusions she could penetrate his defensive skill.

Jathesh, she sent. *Can you hear me?*

The wyvok screeched.

Help me kill this man.

A mournful groan was all Jathesh had to say about that. Kila didn't have time to press the issue, for Sault moved in. Her speed and agility spared her another fall from the platform, but she might as well have thrown Cayne away for all the opportunity she had to attack.

Sault delivered hard blurring strikes that seemed to come

from every direction. And every dodge put Kila in the path of another long arcing blow. The mercus pulsed in her mind, almost a taunt. Her heels suddenly overhung the edge. Jathesh squawked behind her. The elgins below held the platform like stone columns.

Sault blurred forward.

Catch me, she sent. She leaned back and thrust hard from the platform, face to the sky. She arced beyond the reach of the elgins. Jathesh's leathery wing caught her.

She clambered onto his back. "Fly!"

The beast leapt and flapped hard. The Revnithan called out, "Your resistance to the Unanswered makes you weak, daughter!" The skull eyes flared to life, shooting forth hot rays. Jathesh screeched in agony.

The reviled horde began to move. Shamans gathered the swarmlight into their staves. Kila inflated her armor-cloak to encompass the wyvok, turning Sault's power away. Blackbeams wormed from hundreds of staves and latched onto her feat. Mercus charged through her to feed these insatiable leeches.

"If all you can do is defend, you will surely be defeated!" Revnithan Sault cried.

Jathesh beat higher, fueled by terror and pain. The blackbeams stretched and thinned until they began to fail. Once clear of them, Kila eased her flow of mercus and drew in great breaths of clean air.

A huge cloud of debris again arose over the throat of the valley. Eckso had not stopped throwing spheres at it. Her efforts had told, for the overhang slanted hard over the drop.

Jathesh beat higher, sides straining.

Eckso threw two more spheres. The cliffside shook. It began to slide. Snow and shrub and stone vanished in a greater cloud of dust. The leading edge of the cliff slipped free of the debris-haze. Its fall increased in speed. Joy surged up Kila's spine, made her cheeks fill with buzzing excitement. She whooped. And suddenly the mercus arose in her through a wider channel than before. Testing this boon, she again formed her little sphere. The Revulsion lunged, but Kila's buoyed spirits kept it at bay as she fed more and more power into the feat. Soon a little blue world spun over her palm, swirling with green and violet.

The collapsing cliff obliterated the reviled in the narrows. Blackbeams vanished in an instant as the shamans became gore stains beneath tons of rock. More chunks continued to fall away from the cliff, a stream of boulders and rocks and pebbles so dense it looked like liquid.

Dust billowed up from the narrows, obscuring everything below.

Yet reviled continued to stream into the valley beyond. Kila kneed Jathesh around. She had to take advantage of the moment, and of the emotions Eckso's success provoked in her. It was so much easier to use spontaneous feelings than to manifest them from a cold heart. Joy was the hardest of all feelings to create. The Revulsion still sought her, but Nax was there, an imposing and dauntless presence. Tears of gratitude for Nax blurred Kila's vision. She drew a sleeve over her eyes as Jathesh bent for his final dive.

I need everything, she said to herself. I need it all.

Remembering Huff, she threaded sorrow into the feat.

Now her hands were in front of her, spread wide to contain a new rolling sphere of power. She filled it with joy and gratitude and sorrow, with the thrill of running the roofway and the fear of sparring with Yiqa. It glistened and shone. But it wasn't ready. What gave true destructive force to such feats was anger. And anger was what she dared not use.

Already back rank shamans were sending forth their horrid blackbeams, eating away at the new obstruction in their path.

And though the tide of invading reviled had been reduced, it had not been stopped.

Intolerable.

Anger was needed, so anger it was.

The instant she called upon it, the Revulsion slammed hard into her. Nax's presence wavered. Then it returned. Even so distant, Kila felt the magnitude of the cat's effort. Without it, Kila would have been lost long ago. Without it, she would be on the other side of this battle.

The horror of that possibility took her over, and she had to shake free of it with pure will. The cold eye was tempting. Beyond tempting. The Revulsion solved all problems. But it knew only one solution, leaving no room for life or love. No room even for her blessed felnithel.

"Get away from me!" she shouted at the Revulsion.

Anger could not be solely a domain of evil, else rage at injustice was evil. And that made no sense. Surely it was a woman's prerogative to feel anger without being corrupted by it. Surely a woman did not have to surrender a portion of her *power* to her enemy.

The Revulsion hammered at her. Jathesh dove, a plummeting spear of scale, flesh, and fury. The cliff ledge where Mac-Ook had so nobly made his final stand was raw and exposed, white as a protruding bone. Below it ran fissures the Blackshine shamans had so recklessly carved chasing Klayne's flybys.

Reviled nosg surged below. Behind them the valley was filled with many more, all bearing tainted weapons. Elgin towered among them. The black-gemmed staves of still more shamans waved side to side, stark-eyed and full of hunger as they marched forward.

"I will not surrender my fury!" she shouted at the Revulsion.

Anger was a necessary energy. It had assured her survival in Cheapsgate many times. Only when misdirected, as with Dox

Viller or as in the thinnie cavern, did it turn back against her. Anger was a dangerous blade in the hands of a novice.

"I am no beginner!" she said through gritted teeth.

She tried again to infuse her mercus sphere with the final bolts it needed, drawing thin strings of anger from her thoughts and into manifested existence.

The Revulsion was overjoyed. *Yes! Yes!*

It was right there, that untapped power that could vanish the horde—weapon, skull, and skin—as if it had never existed. She had done it before. She'd vanished the Indomitable Wall in Stallid and had pulled back, had retreated to stand upon the righteous side of the living. Why could she not do that again? Use their weapon against them. It would be over in seconds.

You must not! Nax screamed. *Do not betray me! DO NOT BETRAY HUFF!*

Jathesh shrieked and began to lift from his dive. His body curled in, tail tucking. It was taking all his strength of wing to keep them from smashing into the ground.

"No!" Kila shouted at the Revulsion, turning her anger toward it. "You are nothing! You seek to make everything nothing! Anger is not yours!"

She shot her sphere full of black swirls of rage, and it became a scintillating ball of blackness. Not like the hateful swarmlight of her enemies, but the deep blackness of a storm-head. Or of a raven in flight. There was no Revulsion in it. Only the pure emotion of her own heart formed into a righteous feat. Anger served life in desperate, hair-thin moments, when one instinct alone demanded everything. Survival.

She hurled the sphere, a guttural cry pulling from her chest. The sphere expanded and blurred as it went, leaving a sparkling trail behind.

Jathesh wheeled around, flapping with renewed energy. His animal instinct recognized the consequence of what Kila had done before she did. His fear infected Kila, for she did not truly know what she had released upon the world.

The impact did not come as a concussion as with Eckso's spheres. Instead a great gong tone resounded in the air, deep as the voice of the sun. It fell in pitch until the air became shaky and Kila's teeth clattered. She covered her ears. Her chest and spine throbbed with the resonances of the interminable tone.

She looked back, saw the air distort around an inflating sphere centered on the cliff top. It was full of dust and smoke and mercus. It rushed outward faster than Jathesh could fly. The concussion wave caught them. The blast bent the wyvok's wings forward.

The sky became noise. The incessant basso gong, the tick-tick-tick-tick of stone striking stone, the whoosh and roar of wind past her ears, the report of a crashing cliffside.

Her armor-cloak spared her and Jathesh some of the heat, but the fringes of her shield came aglow like a ruddy aurora all around her. Jathesh's scales began to smoke. Swirling currents rolled off the blast, making the air a chaotic cloud he could not keep under his wings. Kila's belly told her they were falling.

The mercus answered her need, thrusting a gust from below. It shot dust up past them, a reverse rain of dirt and pebbles. Even with her mercus protections in place, grit clogged her nose, choked her breathing. Jathesh broke free of his plummet, barely two spans above the ground. He squawked in surprise, pulling up his hind legs. Spear tips and battle axes of Razk-Ka's retreating army blurred beneath them. The wyvok kept aloft, speeding to the encampment. Half a dozen other wyvoks were already there, shamans leaning against their heaving flanks.

Camp followers stood in a loose row, staring skyward at the rising cloud caused by Kila's feat. Their faces were slack, painted with red light of the pluming flame. Jathesh's feet bit turf, plowing a furrow in the snow as he skidded. Kila was thrown forward hard, launching from the saddle to land in the mud. She lost her command of the mercus and it slipped away.

She peeled herself off the ground and stood on trembling legs. Nax jumped into her arms. She welcomed the cat with a warm nuzzle. Eckso alighted nearby, followed by Klayne. He was grinning. Eckso's face was flushed, her hair tangled. Tears traced clean lines through the grit on her cheeks. Her lips opened to say something. She either couldn't think of anything or didn't dare utter her thoughts.

"Where's Razk-Ka?" Kila shouted over the ringing in her ears.

A blacksmith aimed his hammer toward the onrushing nosg, now in full retreat, panicked by the enormous shaking in the earth and the billowing cloud behind them. Unless they'd seen her hurl the sphere, they wouldn't know that it wasn't a new attack from the reviled shamans.

Razk-Ka was not at the forefront of the runners, but at the back. As the warriors filtered through the tents, they slowed, and finally stopped to collapse onto their backs and gulp in air. Many looked at Kila with obvious fear. They had surely seen her on Jathesh, wielding swarmlight and mercus. Rumors about her had already spread through Razk-Ka's army when she was Ahl-Mish-Lah's pet. They all knew Ahl's power had been magnified many times courtesy of Kila's *vaz'on*.

They gave her a wide berth until she found herself inside an empty circle, surrounded by exhausted nosg. Their snouty noses gave out bursts of steam. Fang obstructed lips dripped with foaming saliva. Through this throng came a disruption as the nosg parted for Razk-Ka. Kila noted the grime and scratches on his armor and clothing. He marched forward, skull staff strong in his fist. "Kila Sigh, your actions were timely."

"The Blackshine shamans will not long be waylaid by the

blockage. Marshal your force into marching order. They will take the goat trail out of the valley."

He scratched his chin and peered doubtfully to where she pointed past the dung heap.

She said, "It is passable. Noi-Ick-Noi brought me here along it. The reviled will struggle, especially on the narrow parts."

It never became the argument Kila had feared it would. Razk-Ka was tired, but he had not lost his will to fight. For him, saving even a small force was better than succumbing entirely. But he was not satisfied. "You should fly back. Use that magic against them. Kill them all."

It was such a simple, obvious idea. But she did not have the strength to reclaim the mercus. Didn't want to. She felt scalded inside. That left the swarmlight. The mimak did not come without its own costs. And even if she ate all that the surviving shamans had, she could not destroy the entire horde. Eyegems could only hold so much swarmlight. Besides, Jathesh wasn't going to fly soon.

So a different argument arose between them than she expected, for Razk-Ka could not accept her weakness. To Kila's shock, it was Eckso who interrupted him. And not with a cutting remark, but with an elbow in his side. "Do not presume to tell Kila Sigh what her task is. She has provided you an escape. Stop wasting time. Go!" Tears welled in her eyes.

Razk-Ka could not argue with that, and he didn't try to. "I must take the queen in the vanguard."

"Leave her to me," Kila said.

Kila couldn't bring herself to be grateful to Eckso, who she suspected had not meant to defend her. The blockage was Eckso's accomplishment too, and she probably didn't want to see the moment squandered with bickering. Razk-Ka had remarkable command over his forces, and after a few minutes of bellowing at shamans and warriors, they began to organize. A scouting squadron was already ascending the goat path.

"I'm as hungry as Yioth," Kila said.

"Nobody is as hungry as Yioth," Klayne said. There was more in his statement than mere fact. His eyes glimmered with mirth until Eckso gave him a pinch-lipped glare. A glare through tears.

Kila looked back to the narrows. An enormous black cloud billowed high into the atmosphere. "One of you must fly over the blockage and gauge how much time we have."

"I'll go," Klayne said. "I'm rather keen to see the damage you've wrought. I did not imagine such a feat possible, not by a human anyway. It's a pity we are bound to lose in the end. You intrigue me."

"I don't suppose Yioth left me any of that goat," she asked Eckso.

Eckso drew a dirty palm across her cheek. She looked at the smear of tears and grime on her hand. It moved her for some inexplicable reason, and she closed her eyes and wept, shoulders shaking. Kila had never seen the woman like this. Not dirty. And certainly not crying.

"Are you injured?" Kila asked.

Eckso again made to say something, then clamped her lips shut. Her eyes welled with more tears. "No." She looked away, toward the mushrooming cloud. "I feel . . . I understand something I didn't before. After the felnithel died. And then what you did. No one can do that. I *felt* it, Sigh. I felt what you put into that feat. I felt it in here." She thumped her breast. "The joy, the gratitude, the sorrow, the anger. I didn't think this world had a chance. But now I wonder if maybe you can save it."

That was something anyway. Kila started for Yioth's tent, determined to eat something, even if it was the sauk hide of the tent itself. Her legs felt very wobbly.

"Wait." Eckso's voice caught her, pulled her back around. Tears flowed freely down the woman's cheeks. "Until I saw how fierce you were, I didn't know how fierce I could be." She rushed forward and embraced Kila, hooking her chin over the shoulder opposite where Nax was perched. "Thank you. Kil's eyes! Thank you for making me fight for this world."

Klayne stood back holding his elbows and pursing his lips. The *vaz'on* gems sparkled. He watched them with calculating eyes. When Kila caught his gaze he grinned and made a mocking bow.

She disentangled herself from the sobbing dragnithan. Kila did not for a second think Eckso's outburst of emotion a signal of lasting change. The woman would likely forget it once she'd had a bit of rest.

Kila again turned toward Yioth's tent. Her knees gave and she tipped face down into the mud. She did not feel Klayne's arms lifting her, nor hear Eckso's orders for furs to be fetched. She did not know how tenderly she was placed inside the tent, nor how Eckso pressed her ear to her chest to be sure of a heartbeat.

All Kila knew was the oblivion of exhausted sleep.

69

OF BEING HUNTED

A chanting shout brought Kila out of Lumne's realm and into the hell of the waking world. The interior of the sauk hide tent was warm, the filthy fur on top of her heavy and smelly. A burbling pot sat next to her, but there was no fire nearby.

"I found stew," came a voice. Yiothizandra. The dragnithan woman sat cross legged at the other side the tent. She was feeding Nax bits of meat and stroking her fur. Kila's head throbbed as she rolled up onto one elbow. Crust fell away from the side of her face. Mud. She rubbed her cheek and groaned. "Who hit me?"

"Eckso says you fell asleep on your feet. The ground hit you."

Kila peered into the bubbling pot. It smelled vaguely edible, though the dark bits and gray slurry looked suspiciously like sewage. "What's in this?"

"It's what I could demand from Razk-Ka's pavilion," Yioth said. "He was loathe to be parted with even that much."

Kila picked up the pot. "Eckso once warned me that you don't share food. Or anything else." The pot was of heavy fired clay, glazed over in a delicate green. Rather fine work for clumsy nosg claws. She sniffed the stew again. Vaguely edible indeed. But possibly poisoned. Her stomach complained.

Nax, is this safe? Are you sure Yioth didn't put some foulness in it to make me sick?

Yiothizandra will not hurt you while I'm present.

And so Kila had to trust the woman. She tipped back the pot and sucked in a mouthful of scalding mush. No chewing; it was too foul tasting to allow long on the tongue. She got it down. It stayed down. The first mouthful made her appetite surge, and she hastily ate the rest.

"How many has Razk-Ka gotten out of the valley?" she asked.

"Well more than half. The nosg are excellent climbers. Better adapted to the mountains than humans. But they will stretch out for miles upon miles the further they go. Do you know where that trail comes out? Somewhere on the Lockt Road, I suppose. It passes right through Lockt. Those men will never let a nosg army pass through their city. Then the reviled will come up behind Razk-Ka's army, where it will be pinned. Razk-Ka and Lockt will fall. Likely within hours of each other. Your generalship of this army may be the worst in all the ages of Ennith."

Kila hadn't thought about any of that. But the goat trail had to lead *somewhere*. Goats didn't just appear out of thin air and start walking down to the valley. Surely they went valley to valley. She hoped they did.

"You don't know where it goes, do you?" Yiothizandra tilted back her head and laughed. It was the lusty, throaty laugh of true amusement. "Perhaps the Hargothe was right about you. Your survival has been due to luck alone. It's the godblood in you, I suppose."

Seeing Kila's surprise, she laughed again. "What? You think I didn't know about your mother? I once knew Semūin very well, the bratty little trollop that she is. Such creatures are insufferable, neither fully gods nor demayne. Tell me, has she given you her special skill? No. I can see you are perplexed. I doubt the force of destiny could tolerate more than one of you. Semūin can swim through time as readily as she does water. It amuses her greatly, but locked away as she is, she has little chance to do much with it. No. All she gave you was the godblood, along with the mysteries it grants. The depth and breadth of your mercusine is surely attributable to that. Your pluck is merely your mother's nature rising in you."

"Interesting speculation," Kila said. She sat up, and rubbed her eyes. The headache lessened by the moment as the food spread strength through her. "Do you think your child will show aspects of your nature? For I have not seen any sign of them yet. Saiya never angers." She smiled, suddenly missing the girl. It probably wasn't wise to provoke Yioth like this, but she desperately wanted to steer the conversation away from Semūin.

Nax meowed and stretched, providing a needed distraction for them both. The glow of Yioth's eyes bled all over Nax's gray fur.

"We must get away from here," Kila said. "Has Klayne reported on the reviled efforts to remove the rubble?"

"He said it would be a few more days by his estimation. I might be able to manifest wings by then. It would do me good to burn a trail among them."

"You'd have to fly too low. The blackbeams would singe off your wings and you'd be lost."

"And you'd be joyed. Who are you to tell me not to fight them? You were the one who forced this alliance upon me."

Kila dragged a finger around the inside of the pot and licked off the last residue. She'd tasted worse in Cheapsgate on occasion. "Ell told me I would need you all. That's why I'm *asking* you not to fight. Not just yet. Not until we meet with the dragons. If we act in concert our efforts will tell more greatly against our enemy. If we act separately, we will fall one by one, and perhaps be turned to their service."

Not even Yioth could argue against her reasoning, though she didn't offer any noises of agreement. She simply assented with silence. Kila would take it, happily. She was tired of arguing. Rising, she discovered her legs were stiff and sore. Riding Jathesh had strained muscles unaccustomed to such work. She went out. Night had fallen. The valley was emptying quickly.

Eckso was sitting by a little fire, her wings gone. Klayne stirred a cookpot. His wings were still out, probably to avoid the agony of manifesting them if needed soon. Kila expected they would be.

"You should have seen Eckso mopping up the interlopers out there," Klayne said. "I never suspected her of such ferocity, though her lovemaking should have forewarned me. I must say, playing spectator to all this is rather more interesting than I had thought it would be." He frowned a little. "But she draws too deeply of my mercus. I'm tired. I hate being tired."

"You hate any discomfort at all," Eckso snapped. She too looked tired, but not pained. If anything, she had the aura of great contentment about her.

Kila went to check on Jathesh. All the wyvoks were asleep. One of the shamans stirred when she passed. "Have the wyvoks been fed?" she asked him. He growled something that sounded like a yes. "What did they eat?"

"Us."

She pushed down the thought that Yiothizandra's stew had probably been full of nosg meat. The more she tried not to think of it, the more certain she was she was right. It wasn't good for the wyvoks to eat the nosg. They might start eating them any time they felt a pang. But there was nothing for it. The beasts needed meat. She needed the beasts. The rest followed as naturally as a stream tumbled down a falls.

She went back to Yioth's tent and slept. When she next woke it was day and Yioth was on her feet. Though thin and shaky, she was tall, impressive. And the glow of health was beginning to return to her face. At some point she'd combed the tangles and matts from her hair, which now fell in red waves across her shoulders and breasts. Even with her torn and grimy clothes, she was imposing.

"I can dymense you part of the way along the goat trail," Kila said. "Noy knows the area well."

The woman's jaw bulged, her desire to contradict Kila pushing hard inside her. But she was still weak. If she couldn't fly, she'd have to walk. She didn't look that steady on her feet as it was.

"If you wish to take this tent," Kila said, "you should pack it up now."

The idea that she should perform any actual labor seemed to stun the woman. Kila left her to stew, knowing Yioth would press Noy into doing it.

Nax followed Kila out, nose and whiskers twitching. *You risked everything.* She was talking about Kila's feat of anger.

I need Razk-Ka's army.

The cat's emotions warbled across the bond. She clearly did not see Kila's logic. Kila wound through the few remaining tents, stepping over the hastily discarded items too heavy to ruck through the mountain trail. Weapons, bits of armor. The whole stack the smiths had been repairing now lay abandoned. A supply depot was still piled with casks, sacks, and crude wooden boxes. Wagons with thick pull rails were lined along the cliffs. Thick leather yokes lay in the mud between them. It appeared the elgin were sometimes put in harness as beasts of burden. All of it was useless for the escape route they were now embarking on. Yet all of it was as necessary as the nosg themselves if the army was to survive.

"I wish there was a Derslin Wheel here," she mused. "These supplies could be loaded and rolled through." For that matter, she could have let rank upon rank the nosg through as well. But there wasn't a Derslin Wheel and she could conceive of no way to use the mercus to create such a portal.

At the sight of her, Jathesh squawked and let out a long series of chirps. He accepted pats on the snout with enthusiastic and stinky huffs through his nostrils. She wondered what he'd endured since Stallid that he was so delighted to see her. Then she considered that perhaps she had simply misread his demeanor back then. As soon as her backside met the saddle, he launched into the air. Nax sat just in front of her, claws dug into the saddle leather.

They skimmed along the goat path, following the endless line of nosg toiling up the steep slopes. Jathesh glided between the peaks, casting a morning shadow on the sheer, exposed faces of rock. The shoulder-width ledge she and Noy had traversed on the way down was now clogged with nosg. They were generally wider than men, but they seemed more secure in that precarious place than she had been. Even the elgin managed it, side-stepping where it narrowed, face to the wall.

She kneed Jathesh into a long turn and flew back over the valley, across the long expanse now mostly empty save for the smoldering pyres of the dead.

Ahead, the blockage she and Eckso had made filled the narrows like a dam. A truly impressive mass of stone. Smoke lifted from behind it. Jathesh flew over, and Kila saw the Blackshine shamans pouring out blackbeams at the stone, eating away at it with single-minded determination. It was difficult to see how far through they had burrowed. The reviled behind them stood absolutely still while they waited. She leaned forward, urging Jathesh lower. Blackbeams shot up instantly. The wyvok flared up and out of reach.

They're just standing there. I could kill them all.

So do it, Nax sent.

Kila sought the mercus. The Revulsion constricted tightly around it, more solid than sludge. She strained to pull more, to bring into existence another terrible sphere. But what she manifested was something akin to Eckso's feats from the day before. Contemplating spilling bolts of anger into it made the Revulsion constrict more.

What's happening? Nax sent.

The Revulsion is stronger than yesterday. It's hardened somehow. I can't draw in much mercus.

You are weakened by what you did yesterday. A flash of visions and sensation crossed before her eyes. Pouring rain upon cobblestones, soaking her fur to her sides. The view of peering out from a hole in a barn wall. The feel of being hunted. Pain in the hips, licking wounds, tasting one's own hot blood. Hunger. Shivering. *You must rest and build your strength.*

But I feel strong.

Do you?

She was a bit sore, still very tired, and hungry again. The mercus was there. Just . . . less. A new fear sprang up. What if this were all she could do now? What if her mercus well was going dry?

Jathesh circled, now in command of his own course. Kila petted Nax and absently dropped her sphere down into the nosg reviled. It destroyed a dozen, knocked over twice that. But given the multitudes assembled she would have to do this all day long, every day, forever. Kil's eyes.

To the west the reviled were stirring. Strange. They were so far away they could not have been disturbed by her attack. She turned the wyvok that way, curious. The reviled did not stand in formations, but instead were packed forward like a crowd pressing to see an execution.

But in the middle they were splitting aside, creating space for some reason. She saw it then, two men with a child. Her throat clamped tight. Saiya? But surely that was impossible. Not daring to fly lower, she had to strain forward to pick out any detail of the figures. *It's that Revnithan. And the other is Yples.*

I feel them, Nax sent.

They have a child. Is it Saiya?

Nax did not answer immediately. But then came a cautious declaration. *Not Saiya. Someone like her.*

Who else could be like her? Kil is Kil.

Powerful. Dangerous. We should flee. Now.

She wasn't about to flee, not while qiznithan Yples still moved and schemed. *The child must be a merculyn,* she sent. *Maybe Yples plans to turn her and use her against the barrier. But she looks too small, too young, to have awakened to the mercus.*

We must flee. They are dangerous and you are weak.

But Yples is right there, Naxie.

You could not defeat him in Sorgan. You could not defeat the Revnithan here. Your mercus is weak. Your body is weak. You need rest. Do not be a fool this time.

Nax's strategic insight surprised her, and she found herself struck silent by it. Nax was right. She was in no shape to face Yples right now. She'd only get them killed. The wyvok seemed leery of the man and was quite eager to follow Nax's plan.

With a last look back at the parting nosg army, Kila urged Jathesh to return to the encampment. Yioth awaited her with Noy in attendance. The tent had been disassembled and rolled into a long bundle. The nosg factotum had also gathered some supplies next to it. He sat upon a cask and mopped his forehead with a rag even though the morning air was very chill.

"You will dymense me now," Yiothizandra said.

"I'm not your subject," Kila snapped. "I'm a queen."

"I heard. You usurped my little cousin's throne. Well done.

Now you are among the largest of the small." She held out a hand, as if Kila should kiss it. The intent was for Kila to dymense her. Kila looked at it, but didn't grasp it. It wasn't because of her mistrust, or even her resistance to being ordered about. It wasn't even the irritation provoked by Yioth *allowing* herself to be touched.

In truth, she worried she could not manage to dymense them both. She couldn't have Eckso do it, because Eckso hadn't been to the destination Kila had in mind. *I need you to help me,* she sent to Nax. *Help me widen the Revulsion.*

I can't do that. I'm not a merculyn. I keep the Revulsion at bay.

Kila closed her eyes, sank into the mercusine web. It felt thin, stretched out. A strange sensation, for she had always thought it to be an endless ocean. The Revulsion lay over it, a layer of stinking dung with just the slightest penetration where the pure, joyful light of mercusine flowed through. She placed her attention in that narrow space, squeezed in. Immediately, it began to contract, not only seeking to cut her off but to come into her. Nax's presence surged forward, a looming goodness that made the Revulsion pull away.

Not very much. But enough.

Kila moved swiftly, the bolts already forming. She plopped herself atop the tent bundle, a leg thrown over cask and sack. "Grab hold of me, both of you," she ordered. "Take hold of me or I swear I'll dymense without you."

They did. Noy out of startlement and Yioth sighing heavily for having to take three steps to comply. As soon as they touched her, Kila released the feat and they vanished into dymension.

70

A GOD REBORN

Emotion was nothing.

The qiznithan who called himself Yples moved through the standing throngs of reviled nosg easily. They sensed him coming and knew to step aside. And so a miles-long opening grew ahead of him. The ground was packed snow and frozen mud, churned up by the horde's boots. They were all still, no steam rising from brow or nostril, for none of them breathed. Yples noted the filth coating their hide clothing, their rough hammered armor. Noted the chips and broken bindings on blade edges and torn sinew attachments on haft of spear and axe. The nosg were a backward people, a population that had endured more than their share of suffering. The Yples part of him flailed from hating the nosg, to pitying them, to raging at their state in life, to absolute indifference.

He paused a moment to stare up at the empty sky. To where Sigh had been spying from atop her flying lizard pet.

Yples had sensed another force with her, the spark spirit of the felnithel. That had troubled him more than the girl's presence. Her power had felt thin to him, weak. She had obviously used enormous reserves to block the narrows.

"You had her within your grasp, Revnithan Sault," Yples said, not deigning to look at the man. "You had her and you allowed her to escape."

The man said nothing in his defense. There was no defense for failure.

Lowering his eyes from the sky, Yples continued along the path made for him. He chose to walk rather than to ride upon Sault's elgin-borne barge. Mostly to deny Sault the convenience of it. It was petty. It was emotion. And emotion was nothing. Yet he felt it.

For Qiznithan Yples, occupying a human mind had come at a severe price. His demaynic power was enormously reduced. And strange thoughts continued to play in his mind. Sometimes the thoughts infected the very tissue of his body. Even possessed of the Unanswered, he endured gnawing doubts in his belly one moment, hot surges of frustration up his spine the next. For a qiznithan the only reasonable emotions were rage and suffering. And truly, there was no difference between the two. The intolerable state of being was existence itself, and that was all that mattered.

He looked at the child he'd found outside of Trist. A boy of ten. Ever since he'd discovered the lad, the cold eye had warbled. He didn't know if it was because of the boy's tremendous power, or if it was because the boy's very existence had shaken his understanding of events.

Yples's human mind often overpowered his purer qiznithan perspective now. Such was not useful, for it made him act rashly. Even now, anger boiled in him. This horde had expended far too many fighting warriors and shamans in pursuit of the last bucketful of nosg to be turned. The living nosg were led by a savvy commander it seemed.

Revnithan Sault had been a poor choice for commander. He'd allowed himself to be lured to this ground, forced to breach a highly defensible narrows. All while possessing not a single wyvok of his own to harry the force on the other side.

He looked down at the boy. "Come along. It is time to awaken."

He was a reed thin lad. He staggered along, face drawn and filthy except where tears had cleaned tracks on his cheeks. Yples had found him in a small village east of Trist where horsemen rode range, circling up huge cow-like beasts called kilsoks. The boy was a prodigy. Born only a few ten-days earlier to one of the chieftain's women. The labor had been horrible, and the babe had finally torn through her belly and crawled out. And then to everyone's astonishment, he had stood upon chubby legs, returned to his mother, and laid tiny gore-smeared hand on her wound and sealed it up.

Yples had found the woman and turned her. The child had screamed as if experiencing the torture himself. Yples had delighted in this.

"Your sickness cannot be healed," the child had said to him. "You are foulness itself."

"You think so because you are blind."

That had been their last conversation. Until now. Yples jerked the boy forward. "There is an obstruction keeping the forces of Annihilation from pursuing its destiny. You must remove it."

The terrain sloped upward as he approached the barrier, for it was filled with disabled reviled and the destroyed flesh of the lucky who had been burned or blown apart. Yples's feet squished into the muddy gore. The child cried and tiptoed.

The Blackshine shamans ahead felt him coming and one by one ceased their efforts to blast through the rock. They had not concentrated their efforts onto one spot, for they were blinded by their drive to kill. Yples was not angry because of their stupidity, but because of the delay.

He shoved the boy forward. "Go in, use your power to remove this wall of rubble."

"I don't know how!" More crying, more sobbing, more snot running from the nose. Yples was disgusted by it. He was also annoyed. He shoved the boy Pol forward.

The boy scrambled ahead, weeping and shrieking each time he stepped on a reviled face, or had his foot squish into a rotting belly wound. At the rubble pile, he looked up at the biggest hole the Blackshine shamans had bored. With a backward glance he called out, "It's too high. I can't climb it."

It wasn't necessary for Yples to do more than search out the closest elgin and beckon it forward. "Put the child in the hole."

The boy screamed in terror as the elgin lumbered forward. A few nosg were trampled. The rest were aware enough of their purpose that they pressed to the side. The elgin grabbed the boy in both hands and lifted him up. The hole was still too high, so it tucked him under its arm and climbed. It put the boy into the hole.

The hollow sounds of crying came out. Yples shouted up. "Bore through, or explode it apart, or melt it, or make it vanish entirely. You will not come out until your task is complete." Yples turned away from the wall and began the trek back through the horde. "Come Revnithan Sault."

The man had been keeping his eyes down, but Yples discovered him now staring back. Brazenly. His ridiculous bear-headed staff was aglow with swarmlight. Behind him stood a number of nosg shamans, staves similarly ready.

"Do you truly think you can best me?" Yples said.

The swarmlight feats unleashed squirming blackbeams that smashed into Yples's face and chest. To him these feats were like channels of power, filling him with strength.

Seeing his mistake, Sault ceased his attack. Backing away he tossed a small object at Yples's feet. It exploded, filling the air with greenish blue smoke. This too added to Yples's surging energy.

"You misunderstand what I am, Revnithan Sault," Yples said. The cold eye became absolute again, perhaps for the first time since he'd found the boy. His anger and frustration vanished. His need for vengeance, quenched. Sault escaped destruction in that instant, which was unlucky for him.

"Come to me," Yples demanded.

The man came. He did not tremble, nor beg, nor offer profuse apologies. He simply obeyed. Yples took hold of his shoulder. "You sought to displace me. That is reasonable. You failed. The Unanswered cannot destroy me. You understand that now. Your ferneater trick is clever. It disperses into the air. What effect has it upon the unawakened?"

"I have only tried it upon Kila Sigh. It created confusion, but she is protected by the felnithel. Otherwise, I believe she would have succumbed. I had intended it for Yiothizandra, as you commanded."

"Ah. Well, she is lost for now. A pity. But I have found someone much more powerful."

"The boy? I sense much mercus in him."

"You should. For he is a god reborn."

"Kil?"

"No. He is Pol."

A god, but human. Just as Yples's qiznithan power was constrained by his mortal shell, there would be limits to what the boy could do. And unfortunately it was Pol. A god not noted for feats of power like Til or Kil. But Yples knew the lie of the gods. Their names and their domains were not essential aspects. Kil was no more god of death than Til was god of justice. No, the gods were all aspects of Otil, the Hated of all Hated. The one god from whom all existence sprang.

The boy Pol could do well more than move a pile of rock. He

merely needed to discover his strength. And Yples knew better than any mortal the power of suffering. Yples wove a ward at the front of the hole. The child would not be able to scale down the rock, nor even jump from it. More importantly, Sault would not be able to get in.

"Turn your horde around, Sault. Sigh will lead her nosg to Lockt. You will trap them there and turn them." He prepared to dymense.

"Then why leave the boy here?"

"To make him suffer, Revnithan Sault. And in suffering make him strong."

71

IN THE WIND

"We're losing the day," Quinn said from atop her mount. Fleetheart's shiny black coat rippled, and his front hoof stamped in impatience that mirrored her own. Fallo felt it too. They'd escaped three bands of reviled already. It seemed every village and town outside of Traye had been corrupted.

It was Nefler Ernist who caused the delay. He sat atop his horse, still looking north, muttering under his breath. At least they'd gotten him back on the beast. After the inexplicable fall he'd taken, Fallo wondered if some malady of the aged had overtaken him. But aside from his pale face and slack-jawed wonder, he seemed hale enough.

"Nefler! Are you even listening?" Quinn barked.

"What?" His head slowly swung around.

Fallo grunted and stroked Lop's head. The cat had stopped trembling, but hadn't budged from his arms since . . . Fallo gave himself a shake and forced a laugh. "I think that spill did something to Nefler's head."

The merculyn huffed and straightened his stemmed hat.

"My head is quite all right. I told you, a mercus feat of astounding power was unleashed to the north."

"Kila?" Quinn asked. She was looking at Fallo. Fallo shrugged. He couldn't feel anything beyond Lop's anguish.

The old merculyn gave a skeptical smirk. "I don't care how powerful she is, no mortal could wield so much power as that. It was so full of rage and—" He turned his gaze north again and fell silent.

"Rage and what?" Fallo asked, instincts zinging to life. He wasn't sure if he welcomed a reawakening of his shadline skills.

Nefler Ernist shrugged in his cloak and scratched his beard. "I can't say but that it felt like gratitude, truth be. I don't see how such would be possible. A merculyn must feel the emotion he means to form into bolts. Rage and gratitude cannot occupy the same mind at the same time."

Quinn had no response to this except to heel Fleetheart onward. Nefler's roan followed of its own accord.

Fallo considered Nefler's assertion as they continued north, following Quinn's instincts this time. But his were still alight. "Who says rage and gratitude cannot occupy a mind at once?"

Nefler waved an irritable hand. "Doubt me? Try it for yourself."

Fallo didn't bother. He wasn't a merculyn. But as he thought about Kila he had a flash of insight. "Had you been raised by Cheapsgate, perhaps you could."

The old man had no response for this. A light rain began, misting over the heath bordering the Iopsean Sea. Fallo bent his head down to keep it off his skin. He felt a sudden turn inward, searching his own feelings. It was roiling with contradictions. Pain, self-loathing, anger. But there was another feeling in there, something Lykea had seeded in his wounded heart. Purpose.

∽

THE FELL GUARD barracks were spotless, orderly beyond reason. Every bunk had the identical single woolen blanket over an oak-plank pallet. Deep blue, free of any lint or wrinkle or frayed edge. No pillows. No mattresses.

Henley hobbled down the aisle until he found Brother Commander Docit in the third bunk on the second aisle. Nothing distinguished it from any of the others. Officers of the Brotherhood did not receive special amenities. The man was bare chested. His shirt lay upon the bed, folded to square perfection. He stood to attention at Henley's approach. The rest of the men did the same. Henley knew better than to ask them to relax. "Brother Commander Docit."

The man met his gaze. "Lord Mast."

Henley let the unearned honorific pass. He wasn't here to reprimand or correct the Fell Guard. Quite the opposite. "It was my honor to be accompanied into Moonside by Brother Hannik and Brother Ryde. They both fulfilled their duty." He paused, considering carefully what to say next. "I live because they died. I will never forget them."

"As you say, they did their duty."

"I would know the names of the five others who rushed in to fulfill their duty on my behalf."

"Brother Flint, Brother Nyme, Brother Squlch, Brother Eyvin, Brother Nils."

"What?" Henley's face went cold. It had taken most of his strength to get here, and he sagged under the weight of those last two names. "But those last two were Kila's guardsmen."

"We are all Her Majesty's guardsmen, Lord Mast. It is true she preferred those two, for she was familiar with them. Alas, she left here without them. Without any of us. They were shamed. They volunteered to replace the two guardsmen slain at the Moonside door."

"You should have made them stand down until she returned! Do you know what this will do to her?"

Docit merely looked back at him, cold, blank. Henley noticed then the red tongue of welt showing atop one of the man's shoulders. A quick glance around showed many more of the same on the other men. The fresh marks of penance.

Reminding himself that he had come here to pay respect, he tamped down his rising anger. "Brother Hannik died fighting a swarm of the reviled. The others were killed by a qiznithor. Nothing about their deaths merits the penance of the living."

"We do not take penance for their deaths. But for the failure of Brothers Siggil and Poilo, who allowed a revulyn to open the Moonside door and to enter."

It was the first time Henley had heard those names, but he knew that one of them had been made reviled, had become the revulyn woman's dark warden. He weighed telling the man, knowing more penance would follow. But such was irrational, for Siggil and Poilo had not been too weak, or undutiful. They had merely been unlucky. So Henley spared their brothers the added pain. "The Fell Guard is to be commended."

Henley turned and strode down the aisle, feeling small and weak beneath the imposing presence of so many tall, strong men. But before he got to the door, Brother Commander Docit called out. "Lord Mast, if you wish us to do more penance for our failure to save the felnithel, please speak it and it will be done."

Henley stopped, looked at his feet.

"Commander Docit, Huff did his duty."

HENLEY FLED THE BARRACKS, fled the sound of weeping fell guardsmen. His heart slammed in his chest and the looming

Citadel seemed to sway and tilt before his eyes. His wounds ached with every step, but he started to run. The mercus boiled in his gut and he embraced and formed the feat he'd been putting off.

He dymensed into Lower Terriside, just outside Finta Sahng's little apothecary shop. His breath rasped in his throat as he knocked on the back door. When it swung open, he pushed past the little wrinkled woman and threw himself into a chair by the little time-worn table in her kitchen. "I can't breathe."

Her gnarled hands gripped his shoulders and squeezed. She pressed her lips to the crown of his head. "Be easy, child. Be easy." She bustled about her kitchen and soon set a cup of spicey tea before him. With trembling hands he lifted it and sipped. It was good, biting, mildly sweet.

She moved her chair to sit right beside him. She patted his hand with hers and gave him a long silence in which to grieve. He sniffed and coughed and swallowed and sipped. Finally his shoulders let go and he relaxed, feeling utterly spent. "I came to get him."

"I know, child. I know. Do you want me to fetch him now?"

He nodded.

She scraped back her chair and padded from the room. She returned a short while later with a wooden box. She slid it onto the table and set a little brass key atop it. "Will you put him in the wind?" she asked.

"Are these ashes?" he said, pushing the box with a finger.

"Not yet. I thought that best left up to you. But I can make arrangements if you want."

"No!" He sighed heavily. "I'm sorry, I didn't mean to snap. You've been very kind to me."

"For a Beloved One there is not enough kindness to be given," she said, then cackled softly. "Even ol' Oly merits love for what he is, if not *how* he is."

Henley snorted a little laugh, then he was gone for a while. When he returned, his cup had been filled and a little muffin placed next to it. He discovered he was hungry, so he ate it. "I wish Kila were here. I need her."

Finta again patted his hand. "We are in a war. And war tears folk apart who need to be together. War digs graves and leaves them unmarked. War puts whole cities into the wind. And it makes all of us warriors, whether we will it or no." She touched Huff's box. "Huff gave you strength. But it has not left you now that Huff is gone. The strength to bear this box to its pyre. The strength to face your enemies. The strength to do what is required. Even the strength to do it all without Kila Sigh at your side."

Henley soaked in her words. He doubted their wisdom, but he appreciated Finta's generosity and kindness. He kissed her cheek and left.

Dymensing to the top of the Divide, he looked first over Starside and then over Moonside. He set Huff's box down and sat cross-legged before it. The Divide vibrated for a moment, then stopped. It happened again. Then again.

The qiznithor.

He took the key up and put it into the lock, turned it. He wanted Huff in the wind, so that wherever he went he would feel Huff around him. He lifted the lid, pulled on the white linen towel Finta had wrapped his body in. It slipped free and then was sharply tugged from his fingers by a gust of wind. It disappeared into Moonside.

"Oh."

It was all he could say.

The box was empty save for a brilliant, faceted topaz stone.

Huff was in the wind already.

~

THE DAY WAS FAILING. And with it went the last strength of the living nosg. They had to rest. Already the road was littered with stragglers too exhausted to keep up with the main body of Razk-Ka's army. Some didn't move at all. A few had built little fires by which to warm themselves and a meal.

Kila saw this from above, carried along by Jathesh. Nax stood in front of her, claws dug into the saddle leather. Kila had managed a weather-cloak to protect them both from the chill wind of flight. The effort hurt.

The reviled horde had turned away from the blockage and were now winding westward. Toward the road. The moon was rising now, shedding its partial glow across the snowy peaks. The road below did not benefit from any of this light, so Kila could not see its path. She only knew to keep flying west.

Jathesh was again complaining of exhaustion. He would have to land soon, and when he did, he would need meat and a long sleep. But if the strange message she'd received from Flaumishtak was correct, Jathesh would have plenty of both soon.

Nax felt them first, the bond coming alive with excitement. *Oly and Flaumishtak are down there with the others.*

There were no lights to mark the space, but a sudden billow of green flame below showed Jathesh enough. He bent into a steep spiraling dive and alighted upon the bald dome of a hill overlooking the Griln River. They were not far from Ceronhel by Kila's vague reckoning.

She had enough claim on her mercus to manifest a light, and it shot brilliantly into the air, illuminating the gathering in whiteish blue. Nax bounded from the wyvok's back and shot to greet Flaumishtak, who stood at the center. Kila dismounted stiffly and bade Jathesh go. He squawked and scrambled downslope and into the forest.

Kila turned a slow circle taking in the great eyes, the snouts, the folded wings. "Hail, Bazron. Hail to you all, Dragons of Night."

The End of *Dagger of Deception*
Book Eight of the Starside Saga

AUTHOR'S NOTE

You might remember from my note at the end of the last book that *this* book would be the conclusion of the series. Well . . . as you might have noticed, it's not quite over.

The next book will be the last in this series. Whether it'll be the last in the Starside world remains to be seen. I do love writing those fun little exchanges between humans and their bonded cats. I'm always surprised (and amused) by what the cats have to say.

Do you want me to let you know when the final book comes out? Sign up for my newsletter.

ericedstrom.com/newsletter

I'm heading back to my writing desk now to see how this whole thing ends.

—Eric Kent Edstrom (Spring Prairie, Wisconsin)